Corpse Hunters

J.J.J.W

Published by J.J.J.W, 2024.

This is a work of fiction. Similarities to real people, places, or events are entirely coincidental.

CORPSE HUNTERS

First edition. November 1, 2024.

Copyright © 2024 J.J.J.W.

ISBN: 979-8227003096

Written by J.J.J.W.

Table of Contents

Corpse Hunters 1
1-Dragon 3
2-Hunting 11
3-Homeward 33
4-Big Apple 47
5-Grave 52
6-Faery 63
7-Pass Time 72
8-Shadow Sealing 82
9-Control 87
10-Challenge 92
11-Guile's Afternoon 105
12-Magnolia 108
13-Separated 118
14-Deadly Premonitions 124
15-Flower to Fruit 134
16-Cure for Shadows 142
17-What Matters 148
18-Reunions 159
19-Pure Spirit 171
20-Training 181
21-Teamwork 197
22-Testing 205
23-Magic Qualifiers 218
24-Selective Sight 225
25-Magic Tournament 234
26-Second Round 262
27-Chain Reaction 277
28-The Tale of Titania 291
29-All of the Truths 298
30-Bounty Hunter 303
31-Faerie's Retreat 309
32-Planning Phase 326
33-First Assault 338
34-Father, Son 345

35-Wargames 350
36-Castling 355
37-Capture 360
38-Archfield 367
39-Duet 380
40-Death, Glutton, and Lust 389
41-Wrath en Passant 403
42-Sloth and Envy 417
43-Greed 427
44-Pride 432
45-Black Soul 445
46-Of Magic and Legends 458
The Aftermath 474

Contents

1-Dragon
2-Hunting
3-Homeward
4-Big Apple
5-Grave
6-Faery
7-Pass Time
8-Shadow Sealing
9-Control
10-Challenge
11-Guile's Afternoon
12-Magnolia
13-Separated
14-Deadly Premonitions
15-Flower to Fruit
16-Cure for Shadows
17-What Matters
18-Reunions
19-Pure Spirit
20-Training
21-Teamwork
22-Testing
23-Magic Qualifiers
24-Selective Sight
25-Magic Tournament
26-Second Round
27-Chain Reaction
28-The Tale of Titania
29-All of the Truths
30-Bounty Hunter
31-Faerie's Retreat
32-Planning Phase
33-First Assault
34-Father, Son

35-Wargames
36-Castling
37-Capture
38-Archfield
39-Duet
40-Death, Glutton, and Lust
41-Wrath en Passant
42-Sloth and Envy
43-Greed
44-Pride
45-Black Soul
46-Of Magic and Legends
The Aftermath

  A Message From the Author

1-Dragon

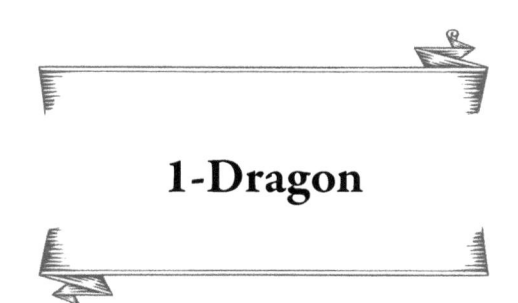

I stared into the abyss, waiting for it to stare back. Instead, the veil of darkness lifted, and I could see my ceiling clearly with what little light made it through the curtain cloaked over my window. Everything was oddly still and serene. Silence permeated every corner of the room and even my bed made no sound as I lifted my hand and put up three fingers. Three, two, one. As soon as I reached zero, a knock resounded at my door. Right on time.

"Who is it?" I asked.

"Me." The familiar voice needed no introduction.

Rolling over, I stood, reaching for a pair of pants to dress myself. I opened my room door to Doc on the other side. I couldn't see much detail as only his silhouette stood against the light as he towered over me like he does everyone else. The hallway light bothered my eyes a little, so I blinked as it flooded into my room.

"Were you asleep, Krow?"

"Yeah, but it doesn't really matter that much. I just woke up a few seconds before you knocked."

"In that case, get ready. We got a mission."

"Where?" I stretched and popped my joints before finding my way back to my bed and taking a seat.

"The Vatican." Doc was now leaning against the door frame.

"Huh, I thought they could take care of their own stuff."

"Looks like a special case. You're taking the lead."

"Me, really? Alright." I looked for a change of clothes in the dark instead of turning on the light. "Any special reason?"

"If I take the lead, the likelihood of them seeing my magic goes up."

"Oh, yeah. You're a demon to them. Who else is coming?"

"Just us. It's the Vatican, remember?"

"Oh, yeah." I stretched out my finger. "***Light ball.***" A small dull sphere of light blinked into existence at my fingertip. Its wide spread of low light was much preferred to the all-encompassing blindness the room light would have caused. "Speaking of it being the Vatican, how did they even contact us?"

"Through a mutual."

"Undead?"

"Do you really think they'd work with undead?"

"They work with vampires."

"Not since what happened to the Archfields."

Reaching into nearby dresser drawers, I began assembling an outfit. "Alright, I'll be up and moving in a bit."

"I'll leave the letter they sent." Doc tossed it on my bed and closed the door.

After finding what I needed, I gathered my clothes, went to the bathroom, and took a shower. On the way back to my room, I heard someone quarreling downstairs. Sara likely caught wind of the mission and wanted to come along, but it was the Vatican. Times may change, but they only ever worked with men except under special circumstances. That thought got me wondering if the reason we were going qualified as special enough despite the contents of the letter only asking for men specifically.

The conversation was still going by the time I got to the stairs leading down. I couldn't see either participant since they were in the living room away from the stairway and the hall was clear to the front door.

"I already told you what the letter said. Only Krow and I are going. This may be a special case, but for some reason, they're not making exceptions." Doc sounded calm as always, but he was obviously annoyed. Likely more about the letter than Sara.

"I still think it's stupid. If they're having that much trouble, shouldn't we all just go?" Sara was as persistent as always.

"I know, this is the third time you said that, but like I said, we're dealing with the Vatican and they're not making exceptions."

"Doc, I'm at the door," I called, opening the door to the enclosed porch, and quickly making my way outside through the next door.

"I'll be there," he called back.

I waited about a minute before Doc appeared in a red long-sleeve and black jeans. We dressed similarly. I had on a gray short-sleeve and black jeans.

"Sara still where you left her?" I was sure she wouldn't be able to hitch a ride on Doc so easily without him knowing, but it was still worth asking.

"Probably still where I left her." He looked ahead to the edge of the yard in the distance.

Wasting no time, we headed into the nearby forest and stepped in between the trees. The letter we held began to glow and tug away from us as it led us along a specific path. Less than a minute of travel later, the trees grew taller and more varied than the oak and pines that surrounded the house. Eventually, the dense forest we walked into was replaced with one of a much smaller scale and I could see ruins in the distance accompanied by the sounds of tourism.

"Looks like we're here," I said, taking a full turn around and taking in my new surroundings. Closing my eyes, I felt the natural energies swirl around me. It was both calming and volatile. Opening my eyes, I saw the city from above. There was nothing but partly cloudy sky in all directions as I faced downward, wind whipping by me. This was accompanied by a feeling of danger and euphoria as if I was at the cusp of death yet drowning in awe of my surroundings.

I felt a hand on my shoulder, and I was back on my feet in the forest. "Astral projecting again?" Doc smiled. He was the only one who could tell when it happened.

"Not really. That's not how it feels." I shrugged.

"But it's like you leave your body every time," he said like he does every time.

"Eh, probably." I started walking again, exiting the small garden-like forest. "So, when are we going to meet the client?" I asked.

"Before nightfall. That's when we get down to business." He reached into his pocket and pulled out a map of the city, littered with markers. "But first, where do you want to go? They have good yogurt here as well as shaved ice."

"I like ice."

We wandered around the city trying the local delicacies. Despite the wide variety of historical structures, we only visited the ruins. After all, the most interesting part of humanity is what's left behind.

An hour before sunset, we headed for the Vatican. There were swarms of tourists traveling around either with or without a guide in search of sights to behold. Doc and I went straight for the Apostolic Palace. We headed for a side entrance but a guard in blue stopped us.

"Excuse me, sirs, the main entrance is over there." He pointed over to where most of the crowds gathered.

"Oh, what a terrible night for a curse." I gave the phrase we were told in the letter while looking toward the sky.

"Right this way." The man led us between the buildings until we were in an impossibly placed parking lot near the Sistine Chapel. We entered through a gated door and down one of the many marble hallways before turning toward a blank wall. It vanished to reveal a gray stone spiral staircase lined with torch lamps.

As we descended, I noticed something peculiar about the lamps. They had a strong aura of magic and a bit of something else that I couldn't quite put my finger on emanating from them.

"What's up with these torch lamps?" I said, eyeing each one as we passed it.

"Those are holy lanterns. They are enchanted so that when exposed to holy energy the flames turn gold and when exposed to unholy energy, they turn blue." Doc and I looked at each other in recognition as we continued to descend.

The staircase didn't lead far, maybe around three stories down to a large, dark, stone room. There was barely any light, despite being lined with holy lanterns. They only showed as faint orange glimmers in the distance.

"This is as far as I go." The guard turned and headed back up the stairs.

We took a few cautious steps into the eerie blackness. One of the lights on the far side of the room turned a bright blue and began growing larger. I looked over at Doc, knowing that he wouldn't make a mistake, but he was no longer there.

I watched the light continue to grow as it rapidly approached and something struck me as odd. There was no heat despite it being a ball of fire. I concentrated on my eyes and cast 'sight'. The darkness lifted and the rest of the room came into view.

Like the stairs, this room was stone, but it wasn't half as big as I previously thought. The lamps made more than enough light to see the small crowd of old men in pale cloaks. They turned and went through different doorways in separate directions. All except one.

"This way." The cloaked man led us through a series of well-lit corridors to a large red oak door shaped like a cross. The man knocked twice, paused, and knocked once more. I could hear a faint voice from the other side of the door and then he opened it.

The inside of the room was completely different from the outside. Wooden shelves filled with scrolls, books, and religious trinkets lined the walls. There was some sort of a heating element as the temperature rose drastically when we entered. The few lamps dotting the walls shone with bright gold flames. A large, wooden desk stood on a crimson rug in the middle of the room. At the desk sat a heavily wrinkled, bearded man in white.

The door closed behind us as the man at the desk spoke. "I am Father Peter Nicolas, the highest advisor to the Pope in the realm of magic and legend. I trust you are the Corpse Hunters we sent for?"

Doc looked at me, and I spoke. "My name is Daniel Moore, and this is my brother, Docter Ganger. We're here because you stated in your letter that this was an emergency, but this is the Vatican. Surely, you have someone capable of solving your problem." My name was an alias, as most others in my line of work use them to protect themselves from those who would rather see us all perish. Doc, on the other hand, used no alias as his namesake made it nearly impossible to identify him. He can change his appearance at will.

"I'm afraid not. We were surprisingly ill-equipped for an event of this magnitude." Peter opened a drawer and pulled out a short stack of papers. "There are six demons that have been terrorizing this country over the past month." The man in the pale cloak received the papers and handed them to us.

Each document described the six 'demons' as follows: An Alghoul, a succubus, a specter, two fairies, and an adolescent dragon.

The demons weren't demons in the traditional sense. This was just the name given to any magical non-human threat capable of severe casualty or mass fear among the populace. This was, however, only according to the Vatican.

"You have a succubus on the loose yet, you sent for men specifically. Why was that?" My question was rhetorical.

"Getting permission for the exception of calling in outsiders came about by a long and arduous vote from the holy court. Any more voting would have cost more precious time. You will be considered a temporary part of our order as long as you work with us, but first, you must meet our requirements, or you wouldn't be here. As transcribed in the letter"

"Do you realize that we'd have a small army of more than capable hunters here if your order wasn't so narrow-minded?"

"I'd gladly waive that stipulation if it meant ridding this country of those demons all the faster at this point." He nodded. "But it's not just up to me, however, it doesn't matter who the men we hire work with."

"Oh, and another question. This one, I've been wondering about the most. Why call a company that is mainly female and ask for men?" As I asked, I realized he already answered. "Never mind."

"Most of the particularly malevolent activity happens after ten PM when the Apostolic Palace closes to tourists." He sat back in his chair. "And there is one more thing." He gave the cloaked man a look who then promptly left the room. "The dragon only flies on nights when there are meetings of importance among me and my colleagues."

"You think the dragon's not just a dragon?"

"I fear it may have replaced a member of the high court. If not, then a member of high standing." He reached into another drawer and pulled out a softball-sized white crystal. "We will hold a meeting tonight to discuss important matters unrelated to the demons, but you will be there with this." He held it out toward us.

"What is it?" I inspected the device in his hand. It looked like a white billiards ball, but with no distinguishing markings or features.

"This is a truth-seeking orb." He sat it on the table. "Its activation is tied to the phrase 'shine my light'. Once you utter the phrase with this in your grasp, a beam of light will follow your gaze and expose any truths you seek. It should help expose the imposter among us. Be warned, however, it only has one use and it shatters thereafter. I could only afford to create one, so you only have one chance."

"If that's the case, why can't you do it? I'm sure someone with as high a standing as you would have a practical version of that orb as a spell ready to use."

He sighed. "It's against our code to suspect each other without due reason and process. If I were to make a move on my own, it would only allow them the opportunity to escape and incite scrutiny upon myself."

"I see." I tugged on my collar, and the color of my shirt shifted from gray to black with slivers of red before lengthening out to a jacket closer to a trench coat. Doc did the same, except his was more like an all-black cloak. I picked up the orb and placed it in one of my many pockets.

Peter took a quick look at a small clock on his desk. "The meeting will begin soon." He stood and ushered us out of the office, down a few corridors, and into a large room.

The room was a half-circle. The flat wall to the right of the entrance was a chalkboard stretching all the way to a wide opening on the other side that seemed to lead into the unknown. It looked like it led into the catacombs.

There were rows of seats starting at the front and rising twenty rows upward into a multi-layered column. It narrowed toward the top until it reached the rounded far wall. The seats were being filled with cloaked men ravaged by old age.

Doc and I sat in the front row of younger men, still at least thirty years my senior. Peter traveled up the stair-like structure to a red oak chair at the top.

The meeting proceeded with a slew of topics that were uninteresting as far as it involved me. The whole time, I was concentrating on sensing the presence of those around me. Particularly the presence of any magical aura that felt at least the slightest bit familiar. After all, a dragon should be able to know another when they sense them.

I was so preoccupied with my endeavor that I didn't notice that I was being called to stand as a guest. It took Doc nudging me to realize what was happening.

I stood to short applause and said, "Good evening, gentlemen. My name is Daniel Moore. Your country's elder adviser called me here to help capture and relocate or destroy the six demons that have been terrorizing this town."

Peter, ever so high up, stood and sat back down in recognition. His smile masked his wrinkled age by at least fifteen years.

I pulled the truth-seeking orb from my pocket and held it above me. "He asked me to shine my light."

The orb levitated from my hand and as it did, all the flames on the chandelier above flickered and turned bright gold. I scanned the crowd with my eyes and a jet of light from the orb followed my gaze.

I stopped. I spotted a man who seemed pretty normal with a large coat, dark pants, and navy blue shoes. Who, for no reason, seemed oddly more suspicious than others that the light touched. Then, all at once, it happened.

His skin shredded off, showing a dragonoid body with long and slender scales and thin wings, black all over. He flew over the column of men and into the large opening.

I had jumped clear over the column toward the opening and into the chase. A few of them were behind me. A dim laser marked through the air in an irregular pattern. It was likely a wizard spell, but it missed completely. I continued to chase after the dragonoid.

On the chance that someone was working with the dragon, I summoned my sword within the folds of my jacket so they wouldn't see it appear out of thin air. A black katana marked with red. "Let's go," I said, sprinting toward my opponent. The blade sparked and glowed a faint red as I went. I turned the corner and stopped dead in my tracks.

There was a wall of water backed up from the base maybe six feet high, a foot or two from the top, and made of glass bricks. It looked like it led outside as sunlight was shining through.

I saw the dragonoid soar into the opening at the top. After that, the water swelled up and closed the opening. It didn't spill. It just closed the opening. It seemed like a river blocked by an invisible wall. Visibility also decreased on the target. It disappeared into the murky blue.

I ran toward the wall with a few people behind me. Holding my sword in a reverse grip, I pulled the top blocks out. As I pulled off the glass blocks, water poured down from the new openings. I stopped breathing on instinct as the water poured over me. I gave up after four or five blocks, then the water went back into the wall formation as before. I could breathe again.

Before I could take a breath and dive in, something moved inside the water, causing me to back off. A small ball shape sprang open into a creature and jumped out at me.

I caught it with the flat of my foot and kicked it to a far wall on the right. It jumped back at me. This time I pinned it to the hard stone floor. It squirmed and started stabbing the air with a large stinger.

Now I could clearly see that it had two claws or pincers about the same size as small twigs, about eight small legs, and the color was off. I couldn't tell if it was red or black. But then as I realized it was a scorpion, a man came to me and gesticulating and ranting about a poisonous freshwater scorpion.

Puzzled at his explanation, I looked down at just the right time to see it sting me.

5. 4. 3. 2. 1. Seconds.

I blacked out.

2-Hunting

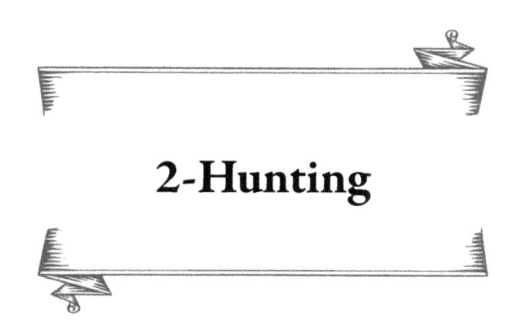

I awoke with a start, staring at a pearly white ceiling. I was in a hospital in Rome, just outside the Vatican.

"Hurt on the first day of this one, huh, Dan?" Doc was sitting next to my bed.

"Hey Doc," I said, casually. A nurse just tenderly wrapped my ankle before I woke, so when I moved my leg, it felt a little heavy.

"Bad luck," I said as I slowly sat up.

"Luck, of all things," said Doc sarcastically.

"Yeah, luck." I chuckled. "You said poison, right?"

"Yeah. The water scorpion's poison can kill a man within three hours," said Doc matter-of-factly.

I scoffed "How long was I out?"

"All night."

"Oh, really? That's a while."

"Don't worry. We got you the anti-venom in time."

"Well, it'd be pretty obvious if you didn't. Thanks. That scorpion was a hell of a surprise. I should have stomped it."

"Well, you'll be glad you didn't."

My eyebrow rose as I knew where this was going. "I'm guessing that scorpion was-"

"It was me," A childish female voice cut me off.

The voice came from the door; it cracked open.

"It was reflex. I was in scorpion form and... I panicked." The door sounded sort of anxious and very sorry. We waited a moment. Then she came in.

At a child's height and size. Her name was Scarlett, but everyone calls her Sara for short, and her codename was Jill. She had loose-fitting pink and gold pants with a matching shirt, and shoulder-length jet-black hair tied into a wavy ponytail with gold-colored bracelets that were just small enough to make it.

"Are you mad at me?" She had a solemn look on her small face.

"Nah. You're just lucky I didn't squish you. Besides, you know full well, that people tried more creative ways to kill me before. Still, why did you jump at me like that?"

"Well, I was on standby in the water watching you on your mission and something brushed past me and grabbed onto my back, so I jumped out and I guess I jumped straight at you."

I scoffed. "Of course."

"Yeah... Well, yeah." She sounded uneasy.

"Wait, you said that something jumped onto your back?" asked Dock.

"Yup, but it didn't stay. Nothing's there now. I jumped out of the water so fast I don't think it could have."

"We'll need to see if that thing left a mark-"

"Hey wait, Dan. You got anything to say about almost squishing me?"

"I would have been in the right to." My response was quick.

"No, you jackass. An apology or something?"

"Well, you almost killed me too, you know. Plus, you came at me first as a freaking scorpion. Besides, you butted in on my mission, kid."

I struck a nerve and she started fuming. "I'm older than you." She balled up her small fists like she was going to punch me.

"Three years ain't much. Besides, whining about it makes you look *so* immature." I tried not to grin and failed.

Sara folded her arms with a huff. "I'm way more mature than you."

We argued like this for a few minutes until Doc settled it with a proposition. Since neither of us *tried* to kill each other and none of us died, there should be no problem. We all agreed on this.

I took off my cast, and Doc explained to the nurse at the desk of my recovery. A few tests later, I was ready to go. After, we went to a run-of-the-mill motel that Doc saw on the way to the hospital. We all went to the front desk of a light-gray building shaped like a medieval castle and got a room to stay the night.

We recapped what happened thus far before heading back out. By we, I mean me and Doc. Sara opted to be a lookout and stayed in the hallway to watch the pedestrians pass by. We enchanted the walls already so no one could spy on us without us knowing but we had no idea what kind of magic the Vatican had at their disposal. The only person that would hear us was Sara.

The revelation that a dragon was walking among them put the clergymen in a tizzy. My absence the rest of the night put them more on edge. To make matters worse, the body of a woman was found mutilated next to the corpse of a man who'd been drained of his soul. The woman was also missing her blood while the man was simply dead with his pants down.

Either the succubus had taken her first female victim and the alghoul took advantage, or she was working with the alghoul. Regardless, things were getting worse.

"So, do you know how she got here?" I gestured to Sara outside.

The moment I said that, she burst in exclaiming, "Doc knew I was here the whole time," while folding her arms and turning her nose up at me.

"Oh, come on." I sighed.

"It was my idea for her to find somewhere to hide. I just didn't think she'd be that creative with the hiding spot," He confessed. "Of course, this was before we had the go-ahead for women to join us." He looked down in thought for a moment. "Now that I think about it, we got side-tracked earlier, but how *did* you get there?"

"Oh," said Sara, looking up in recollection. "While I was wandering around for a place to hide, I saw water coming up through some cracks in the ground. It looked like there was a light source down there, so I shrunk myself down and dove in."

I raised my brow. "Without a second thought?"

"Hey," she said defensively. "I felt your presence down there, so I figured it was safe.

"The presence of a dragon?"

She nodded. "Yeah, I guess. You got both a dragon and an angel in there and I figured you wouldn't want the Vatican of all people to know you had innate holy magic or something."

"Yeah, alright." I rolled my eyes. "Even I couldn't sense the dragon's presence and I was in the room with it. Let's take a look at that crack in the ground."

Sara started glowing bright gold and started shrinking before leaping onto Doc's shoulder as a small black scorpion. She guided us to an innocuous spot tucked away between some residential housing. There was a crack in the stone just wide enough to slip my hand into. There was water tensioning at the surface that appeared to be bubbling from below. The surrounding cracks were also saturated. There was, however, no light.

Sara spoke up. "This is it. The light's gone though."

I placed my hand on the ground. "Down we go, then. **Pull**." Slowly, I raised my hand and the cracked stone followed suit. Understandably, the water didn't follow. It seemed enchanted or magical in nature.

Just underneath the loose stone was a round hole a few feet wide filled with groundwater. I cast 'light' and held the resulting ball of light just below the surface, illuminating the darkness ever so far into the clear water. Sara cast 'water breathing' on us and we dove down. Even though we could breathe, doing so was difficult. The water was heavy with the stench of holy blessings. This was holy water.

"Jill," I said. "Did it smell like this last time?"

"More or less," she said. "is something wrong?"

"Doc, did it seem like holy water when I was drenched in it before?"

"No, but they could have been in the middle of blessing it. Could have been why it was glowing."

We continued downward until we met stone. It was smooth as if it was eroded, but it looked like it was newly chiseled. There were also traces of claw marks. Upon closer inspection, there were two different types. One was small and sharp and the other was larger and serrated. They were likely created by the same creature. Probably the dragon as it sank in the water while escaping. Even so, it could have been a tunnel built by a giant mole and repurposed by the Vatican. More likely, it was a connecting point between the catacombs and the Vatican tunnels. Something large probably came through that cleared the area or created the tunnel, to begin with. Aside from the water, the only feature of note was how large the hole really was once we started descending. It was more than wide enough for the dragon to soar through and big enough for a grown dragon to climb through.

To the right, was where I chased the dragon from. Going that way, we found the glass wall. The bricks I pulled down were back in place and more were placed to completely cover the opening. I touched it and the wall started glowing white before it split along the center. The seam between the bricks parted and the water followed suit, leaving us dry as both halves of the wall as well as the water phased through the surrounding walls.

Looking left and right, I said, "Secret passage? Deterrent? What do you think?"

Doc hummed in thought. "I doubt it was supposed to be a secret passage. It's too obvious. Given how relatively easy it was to find an alternate route in, I'd say it's not a deterrent. Maybe a trap?"

We waited a moment in silence in case Doc was right. When nothing happened, I spoke up. "Let's check the other direction. See where it leads." We turned around and went on our way. A few feet in, the wall closed and the water did the same. Since the water breathing spell was still active, we transitioned from walking to swimming seamlessly. A thought crossed my mind at that moment. "Where are the lights?"

Doc looked around for a moment before his gaze landed on the light ball in my hand. "Now that you mention it, if this was supposed to be a passage, there would be lights. Put out your light and let's see. Nobody needs any warning if we approach here anyway."

I dismissed my 'light ball' and cast 'darksight' to see in the dark. In a moment, the surrounding walls began emanating a golden glow. Not enough to see normally, but it was there. It was probably the enchantments used to create the environment we were swimming in, but we took no chances and since we already didn't touch the ground or walls while submerged, we continued not to. Following the passage, we found it had no offshoot paths and just went straight. Some parts of the walls seemed like they were filled in and there was still no sign of draconic energy. There was, however, an exit on the other side. There was no wall of glass, the water simply stopped.

We stepped out into the catacombs. The large and open room was lined with graves. It spread out into many separate passages. None of which showed signs of the claw marks from the water passage or draconic energy.

"What do you think?" said Doc.

I scanned our surroundings a couple of times and looked back at the water. "I think either this dragon is incredibly good at covering its tracks or someone's helping it. There's no point in following the tunnels. It'll take too long. We should deal with the rest of the problems first. I'll check the openings at the surface just in case, though."

After getting back to the surface we wandered around the city both as a group and as individuals until twilight approached. True to my word, I went around to each opening to the catacombs that I knew existed and found faint traces of magical residue as black powder smudges on the ground but no sign of a dragon. Doc went to the nearby ruins to search for signs of necromancy and Sara went faery hunting.

As soon as the sun was near the horizon, we reconvened at St. Peter's Square. While both Doc and I came up nearly empty-handed, Sara returned with shaved ice and two twinkling creatures the size of dragonflies by her side. They were bug-eyed and green with stick-like limbs and leaf-like appendages. They hovered with butterfly-like wings that fluttered much faster than butterflies.

"Whatcha got there?" I asked, eyeing the faeries.

Sara looked at the treat in her hand and responded with a shrug, "Shaved ice."

"Nice. So, what's up with the faeries?"

"This is Marigold." She motioned to the one with yellow leaves adorning it. "And this one's Sunsettia." The other one had soft pink leaves that turned yellow at the base. "They're the faeries we were looking for." They were pulling at her as if they wanted her to follow them.

"They don't seem to be cursed or anything," said Doc, examining them from a distance.

The one called Marigold spoke into Sara's ear, prompting a response. "They can see you, it's fine."

The faery hovered toward me and Doc cautiously. Once it came close enough, I lifted my hand and stretched a finger out. It sat on my finger and began making noises akin to the sound of bubbles underwater.

I smiled and said, "I can hear you, but I can't understand you."

It looked at Doc and he shook his head. Despite that, it continued to talk. Thankfully, Sara was there to translate, and it told us everything we needed to know about what was going on.

The dragon was indeed the start of the unrest, but it didn't start everything. It appeared in the city from the east nearly a month before and with it came dread. As if a blanket of negativity swallowed the city starting from the catacombs upward.

At the time, the faeries were companions of a wizard who they'd grown attached to. He traveled into the catacombs with them in search of the source of the growing unease only to be attacked by the dragon. The two faeries escaped, but the wizard didn't.

The alghoul would roam the roof and treetops in the dead of night. It would viciously attack and drain the blood of its victims. It appeared to be a man of short stature in a ceremonial red, yellow, and blue guard uniform. It was around before the dragon, buried in the depths of the catacombs along with many others numbering over a hundred. They were awakened when the dragon came, but the wizard was able to seal most of them. Around ten got away, but only one began actively feeding.

The succubus was a blue-skinned demonic woman. She would appear around morning when the night guard's shift was about to end and entice them. Shortly after, she'd drain them of their life in exchange for pleasure. Many thought her to be the one who summoned the alghoul, but was instead a coincidental occurrence, only adding to the turmoil.

The specter was working with the faeries to warn people of the danger and lead them away from the city where they would be safe. They had stumbled upon him while wandering about in distress and he encouraged them to help in his cause. He was a martyr who passed while helping citizens escape during the fall of Rome. Usually seen during twilight hours, he was an embodied spirit already known for kidnapping people and leading them to 'safety'. He wouldn't keep them for long until recently.

Everything she said checked out with the information we got from Peter and filled in many gaps left in the reports. In the middle of her story, the fading image of a man in a short tunic appeared in the distance. He seemed to just watch for a while before vanishing.

Our plan only needed slight adjustments with this new information. Once this was decided, the Faeries fluttered away with a parting and the presence of the ghost also faded.

Sara brushed off the faery glitter on her with a cloth barely the size of her hand and stuffed it into a small metal cylinder before hiding it away in a pocket.

Now that it was just us three, all that was left to do was wander around and wait.

Once the moon was high in the sky, an eerie feeling washed over us. We were being watched and it wasn't friendly. Looking at each other, I nodded to my companions before stopping as they continued on. The presence stayed with me.

I closed my eyes, focusing on the feeling as it closed the distance. I heard a raspy almost cough of a breath nearby and I turned to look at the top of the nearest building. I was looking into the blood-red eyes of a member of the undead. His uniform was barely recognizable in tatters, but his teeth were long and sharp. Despite presumably being dead for decades, he didn't seem to rot much. Even his stench wasn't as foul as I expected. He had been partially mummified.

We locked eyes for nearly a second before he lunged at me. I snapped my fingers and said, "***Burn***," casting the spell. The man burst into flame as I took a step to the side, and he flew past me.

Standing with a screech, the flames dissipated, and he lunged again.

Summoning my sword, I blocked a swipe of his claw and created a splash of sparks. I parried his other claw and plunged my blade deep into the middle of his chest.

There was a moment of silence as even he needed time to register what happened. I could feel the pressure of blood being dragged through his vampiric heart. There was no pulse, only an uninterrupted flow. His human heart had long since been silenced.

"***Pure flame***." I cast the spell through my sword and the man lit up once more except from the inside out and with white flames. This wasn't enough to kill him immediately, but he would die.

I removed my sword and he stared at me for a second before turning and hopping onto a nearby roof and sprinting across the rooftops.

Doc and Sara joined me as I followed the white beacon from the ground. His vampiric survival instincts were turned on and was now returning to his kin. Exactly what we wanted. The only thing we had to worry about was running into someone on the way, but the fact that he didn't go after Doc or Sara helped push the thought of what could happen in that situation away.

Eventually, we chased him into Italy and to a house at a river where he dove through an open space down below from the street.

"***Vital sight***." Doc cast the spell to determine the location of every living creature within the house. "There is nothing alive in that house. We'll stay out here."

"Got it," I said, slipping down into the space underground. The floor and walls were made of bare stone, lightly touched by age, and looked as if it might have once led to the catacombs farther below.

The dead man dying stood in the middle of the open space surrounded by others of his like. Around ten men, women, and children. All of them were motionless, staring straight with blood-red eyes, but very little decay. They had been fed just enough to stay content; dormant.

The man now kneeled with his hands on his knees facing toward me. I was shocked. What little intelligence he had from his past life allowed him to avoid a potential catastrophe. Now his job was done, he was ready for it to end.

"Thanks, you made my job easy." I raised my hand and cast a spell. "***Sacred flame: Inferno***." White flames sprouted from the ground and quickly reached the ceiling, incinerating everything around me in an instant. Using purifying magic made sure not even their ashes remained.

I climbed back up to street level. "It's done." I put my hands in my pockets and walked back into the Vatican with Doc and Sara.

Since it was now just past midnight, we still had some time before the succubus was likely to show up. I reached into my jacket and pulled out a small book from my left breast pocket. Its cover was hues of red. On it was a charred angel-winged cross with a small lizard crawling up it, charred as well. It sported a single wing vaguely resembling a feather. A dragon almost in name alone. Flipping through, I studied the pages. Each one had a picture, a description, and a collection of symbols only I understood. At least most of them. Some were indecipherable to me, but I'd attempt to read them every once in a while.

"Do you remember anything?" said Doc.

"Nope. I got nothing this whole time. Looks like my past has nothing to do with the Vatican."

Hours passed and Doc tapped me on my shoulder. I looked up to see him pointing at the sky where the moon was ready to fall on a clear night. Sara had already gone to play her part in the plan to catch the succubus still on the loose.

"How long has she been gone?" I asked, aloof.

"She's coming back already. Look sharp."

"Oh, alright."

I heard two sets of footsteps approaching from behind followed by Sara saying, "There you guys are, I was looking for you two."

Doc and I turned around to see her walking toward us with a woman in a long black dress and high heels. The feeling coming from her hit me like a brick and the smell of flowers wafted by on the wind. This strange pressure nearly held me in place as if with glue. I didn't take my eyes off her as her tan skin slowly shifted to deep blue and her eyes shifted from blue to bright gold. Small horns the size of pocketknives sprung up from her hairline and a thin forked tail sprang from under her dress.

Under her spell, I had become privy to her true form. If I was a weaker man, I'd have been drawn deeper, but there was a problem: Even a tired guard would be able to resist her. Every breath I took felt like it was through molasses, but I didn't break eye contact until she did so herself and since I resisted from the start, her spell broke instantly.

Sara looked between her and us and said, "Thank you for helping me find my brothers."

The woman crouched down and responded, "You were right, they're all dark and broody just like you said." She rubbed Sara's head. "But since I helped you find your brothers, can you do something for me?"

"Sure, what is it?" said Sara, bouncing left and right energetically.

"Die." She opened her palm with her claw-like nails as she swiped at Sara's throat.

"High five!" Acting fast, I put my hand in front of hers and they collided.

"How-" The look of surprise on her face shifted to abject horror as I clinched her hand in my fist to the sound of knuckles popping. She tried to rip her hand out of my grasp but was held steady. "Let go!"

"You're already caught, stop struggling." I raised my hand with hers, stretching her arm upward and forcing her to turn toward me.

"*Release me*-ow." Her voice was layered with magic, but I stopped the incantation by breaking her concentration with a flick to her forehead. The ease with which I did it helped me make up my mind about what was going on. She was far weaker than was let on.

"Just come peacefully, we only want to talk to you," said Doc.

The woman looked between us with her fangs bared and ever-present fear in her eyes. As if torn between fighting and surrendering, she hesitantly raised her other claw.

Sara firmly gripped her wrist. "Just stop already. We don't wanna put you down."

The woman took a breath and her features returned to how they were. "Ok, just don't hurt me anymore." She sounded dejected.

"That'll be the least of your worries." Sara handed me the girl's other wrist. "Best we can do is request something lighter than a death sentence, but they'll probably ignore us based on what you did."

"No, I didn't-!" She struggled, but I kept my grip on her.

"You *just* tried to kill someone."

"I-..." She sighed again and kept silent.

"*Bind*." I cast the spell and thin red threads of magic appeared around her wrists and held them together. "Let's go." We started walking toward an entrance to the underground part of the Vatican. "So, what's your name?"

"Anjelica."

"Okay Anjelica, how many people have you killed?"

"I... I- I don't know."

"What do you mean you don't know?"

"I... lost count."

"I don't believe you. A blue demonic succubus. However specific that is, you fit the bill, but I don't think you could have done all that."

Anjelica stayed silent.

"Ok, new question. Why are you here?"

More silence.

"There are places that would even welcome you. Even make money doing what you do... Or not."

The silence continued.

"Something drew you here, what was it?"

Still nothing

"Or did someone bring you here?"

The rest of the way was silent aside from the wind.

Once we arrived below ground, we found news of what we did spread and there was already a cell ready for the woman under our care. It was an empty cube with a metal door carved into the stone with magic. I walked her in and closed it from the inside. Doc stayed outside with the small group of men in gray cloaks that greeted us on the way down. Sara took the form of a scorpion and hid herself in Doc's cloak before we got there.

Anjelica sat in the farthest corner from the entrance while I stood against the wall next to her. She looked as if she was just waiting to be executed until she looked up and noticed me there. Surprise spread across her face before she looked back at the ground.

"Ready to talk again?" I snapped my fingers and dispelled the bindings around her wrists.

"You don't think I'll use my charm on you?" She planted her palms on the floor and leaned forward, clearly showing her cleavage.

"Right now, you're not even strong enough for it to work on one of those guards up there." I tilted my head toward the door.

"That's not true." She stood quickly. "If I wanted to..." She raised her palms facing me and a rush of energy flowed from her in all directions.

"'If you wanted to' nothing. Even if you were naturally strong, you're too inexperienced to get away with it for this long. I mean, who tries to murder someone in front of two other people like that? You should have been able to tell that we resisted your spell."

She opened her mouth and took a breath. I cast 'gust' and blew a sharp breath. The wind carried a green hue to the back of her throat and knocked her back.

"Ack-" The energy coming from her died down instantly as she fell to her bottom.

"Listen. If you don't cooperate, you're going down for quite literally stealing the virginities of more than a handful of Vatican guards and at least one murder, not to mention attempted murder. They don't consider you human here. If it was up to them, they would have probably killed you on sight and called it a night." I sighed. "I'm not a detective and I don't have the time to be one, but I want you to know that when I leave out that door, the next people to come in will probably be the last people you see if I don't go out there with something to clear your name."

She went into the fetal position and stayed silent.

I leaned away from the wall and went to the door. "Your choice. Whoever you're protecting won't come for you."

I reached for the door and heard something hit the floor. Looking back at Anjelica, I saw a silver band now on the floor next to her and she was in her true form. She was just staring at me, waiting for my departure.

"Ok, your funeral." I opened the door.

As I stepped out of the room, I felt the door accelerating against my hand. I pushed against it in case the door had fast hinges, but it didn't even slow down.

Turning back, I kicked in the door. "**Push**." I cast a spell just in case. The door swung open and wedged against the far wall as it raced toward me. I reached my hand out toward Anjelica. "**Pull**." She raced toward me through the air and landed in my arms as I turned back out of the room. She screamed the whole time.

In the end, a gust of wind followed us out while the door held the wall back, being made of a stronger material than stone.

Anjelica trembled in my arms. "I... I..." Tears were streaming down her face as she choked up on her words.

"Alright, what's the meaning of this?" I turned to the cloaked men.

One of the cloaked men muttered, "A captured demon need not be left alive."

"We were contracted to capture and relocate primarily. Killing's on a case-by-case basis for us." I shot them a look of disapproval. "We're not those kinds of monsters. Besides, you don't consider her human, right? Just as good as a wild animal? That means we can use her as bait for the other wild animal."

The men began to murmur amongst themselves.

"If you have a problem with it, let me know."

The cloaked men simply scattered, loitering off in different directions. Each of them rambling on to themselves.

Doc retrieved the silver band Anjelica wore and gave it back to her. We then returned to our temporary motel base. I carried Anjelica the whole time. She had quieted down by the time we left the underground and stayed silent the whole way. I dropped her on a bed and she laid there dead-eyed for a moment before sitting up with a sharp gasp. It looked like she was watching her life flash before her eyes.

With a shaky voice, she said, "Why did you..." She seemed hesitant to finish her sentence.

"Alright, little lamb," I said. "Tell us who your shepherd is before the wolves come and get you."

After a moment of hesitancy, she said, "You're not the wolves?"

"We can be. Just not right now."

"Am I really just bait for that dragon?"

"Oh, so you didn't go completely deaf after your near-death experience? If the dragon isn't long gone, we can find it ourselves. The real question is: how did you know the animal I was talking about was the dragon?"

She seemed to shut down for a second. "I..." She sighed. "I'll just tell you..." She took another shaky breath. "I'm not the succubus."

I folded my arms. "Well, that was obvious. Who is?"

"You said capturing was your priority, right?"

I shrugged. "We didn't kill *you*, did we?"

She looked me and Doc up and down then said, "It's my brother. I'm not actually a succubus, I'm just demonic. He's *actually* a succubus, well, incubus... I don't know anymore."

I sat down beside her. "Mind giving us more details?"

"Well, His name's Marco. like me, he's demonic, but unlike me, he doesn't look much like it. He has a tail, but that's it, really. Anyway, he needs psychic energy to live. Before you ask, no, food doesn't do anything for him. Those are his magic traits"

"Why is he in the Vatican?"

"He said he wanted to be a priest. Since he feeds on psychic energy, he said he could understand human nature. He wanted to be a psychiatrist, but I guess that changed when he was introduced to religion."

"So, why are you here?"

"He called me and told me a succubus was running loose and the Vatican was going to execute him if he couldn't find out who actually did it. He asked for my help."

"I get it. Lust is psychological in nature. He could feed on it. So why did you attack us in such a provocative outfit?"

"He said to look for you. He told me to hypnotize the boys and kill the girl. Said she was the succubus and you were helping her. Thought it'd be easier to catch you off guard if I looked like a hooker or something... I guess I was pretty stupid in hindsight."

"So, when we caught you, you must have figured it out and just played coy, right?"

"Well, yeah. I didn't want to think he'd set me up like that, but then I almost died..."

"Did he also tell you about the dragon?"

"Yeah, he said stay away from it. I never ran into it, though."

"Well, given how he set you up, we can conclude one thing. None of the stuff happening here is a coincidence. The question is how far the plan goes." I stood up. "Welp, we'll just have to find out as we go. Jan, stay on her."

The small scorpion leaped from Doc's cloak and nestled herself in the folds of Anjelica's dress. There wasn't much to hide in, so instead, she seated herself over the deep cut in her neckline and clasped the sides together. She looked like a decorative broach and Anjelica looked a little more modest.

I stood and looked out the window. The encroaching daylight reminded me that we were out all night. I made my way to the other bed where I plopped down. "We should get some rest before heading back out."

Sara hopped off Anjelica and transformed back to her normal form. "First, you're all 'Jan, stay with her'. Then, you're all 'We need to rest'. Make up your mind."

"Well, I forgot we worked all through the day. Even we need rest. We'll head out again at twilight."

Doc traipsed over and laid down next to me on the bed. "When you're right, you're right."

Sara sighed and plopped down next to Anjelica. "Whatever."

The day passed and I slept only a wink or two. The feeling that someone was attempting to peer through the veil of magic we placed around the room came and went until dusk.

As soon as the sky glowed orange on the horizon, we moved out. Sara stayed with Anjelica while Doc and I went off on our own. I went into the catacombs and Doc went above ground, just outside the Vatican.

Doc's role was to lay low. He'd snoop around for anything useful he could find with his transformation ability allowing him to blend in seamlessly. Sara's role was to just stay with Anjelica who was bait, like I said she was.

In the catacombs, I searched around for the dragon even though it had likely skipped town by then. With a ball of light guiding me, I found what looked like the remains of a man who got lost in the tunnels and a breadcrumb trail that ended some ways away. Since I had nothing better do to, for the time being, I investigated.

The man was dressed in streetwear but the grass marks on his pants made him look like he traveled through a forest recently. He had a mostly crumbled piece of bread on him and an empty backpack. The only thing in his backpack was an old underworld map.

After roaming around the area a bit, I realized it was impossible for the man to get lost to the extent he'd die. There wasn't much to the catacombs themselves. That was when I remembered the part I saw with Sara and Doc. Some parts were inaccessible to the public in one way or another. This man likely came through a secret passage unknowingly or ran into any number of supernatural events in the night.

I retraced my steps back to the body and found nothing but even fewer remnants of a breadcrumb trail. Someone was getting rid of evidence, and it didn't seem magical in nature. I would have left it alone, but I still had some time to kill, so I continued. Examining the ground, I found the difference between where the crumbs were gone and where they remained. Since the crumbs were spread across the ground instead of a straight line, some of them were within cracks and crevasses while the majority of what remained was in the groove between the floor and wall. With that in mind, I followed the trail.

After some time, I noticed a shadow dart through the darkness and reacted by reaching my hand out toward it. "*Pull.*"

The shadow flew through the air and landed a few feet away. It was an empty black cloak. It didn't seem magical but it could have easily been anti-magic. Albeit, anti-magic weaker than my magic or the spell would have been ineffective. With that in mind, I continued following the trail until I met a wall lined with graves like any other. I pushed my hand into it and found nothing. The illusion fell away and I stepped into a hidden part of the catacombs.

The air had become lighter as if it became easier to breathe and at the same time, my surroundings became darker. It was already pitch-black aside from the light ball I kept hovering over my hand, but now, I was in the underworld. What overworlders would consider a space between spaces had the overworld itself not been confirmed to be exactly that. Normally, I couldn't tell much of a difference but in a place with so much energy swirling around, the difference was great.

I picked up a heavy sense of misery and faint chanting down one of the many corridors. Following the sound, something gave way under my foot and nothing happened. I was sure I stepped on a pressure plate and was ready for a trap, but even sensing for an illusion, I found nothing.

Continuing onward, a few more non-traps sprang. One at least made a sound, but it was only stone grinding against itself and nothing more. Mildly disappointed but still alert, I continued toward the sound of chanting as it got closer. Turning one corner of many, I saw the orange glow of lamplight against the walls. Behind the orange, however, was gold. They were holy lanterns.

Creeping closer, I saw shadows across the ground, It looked like a group of people were praying. The chanting was echoing off the walls and resonating with the nearby lanterns which flickered in response.

Continuing toward the golden light, I saw a group of people praying around a stack of bones in a large chamber. Under the stack of bones was a deep blue light surrounded by a golden one that radiated outward. The lanterns around the room pulsed slightly, unlike the ones in the hall. They pulsed to the rhythm of the unintelligible chanting.

I watched silently for a moment until all of the lamps went out at the sound of a hushed breath. The chanting stopped abruptly as this happened. I still had my light ball so I could see my surroundings if something like this happened. The people praying were gone but the stack of bones remained.

A whispering voice echoed from nearby, just outside the range of my light. "Your unholy presence is unwelcome here."

I said, "Well, I was hired to be here. And here I am."

What felt like numerous eyes landed upon me from every direction despite there only being two directions in the hall. At the same time, the nearby lanterns shined with blue flames. Unlike last time, these gave off heat.

The voice returned. "Unholy one, leave or be executed."

I shrugged. "I was just looking for whatever killed that other guy I found in the overworld down here. The trail led me here and this doesn't seem like enough to execute someone over."

The lanterns further away started glowing faintly yellow despite there being no flames within them. "The executioner follows. It is too late. Death to the unholy."

"If that's how you want to play it." I summoned my sword to my hand. Its black surface reflected more light than the metallic spots within it. When I did, the torches surrounding me flickered gold for a split second. "You know what this means, right?"

Just then, the amount of eyes on me multiplied. I couldn't hide my grin as my mind landed on a few possibilities. At the same time, I felt something heavy approaching me from behind. However, I didn't feel any danger. A shining golden light engulfed me and then faded to nothing. The lanterns flickered gold as well. They stayed that way for a moment before turning blue again.

"I see." I dismissed my light ball and cast 'sacred light'. The space above my palm where the light ball was glowed bright white and expanded to cover the hall. All of the surrounding lanterns turned gold, but not just the flames, the housings, too. "Blue flames mean unholy energy. As you can see, in the presence of my magic, they can only be gold. So, you tell me; where is the unholy energy coming from?"

"You deceive." The voice wavered as if whoever was behind it was nervous.

I looked toward where I felt one of the many eyes looking at me from and the feeling vanished. I looked in another direction and it vanished from there as well. One more vanished as my eyes landed in that direction before all of the lanterns blew out again at the sound of a hushed breath. The lantern housings stayed gold, however.

"So," I said, "You gonna show yourself or am I gonna need to find you?" I closed my fist and the white light surrounding me was replaced with a raging fire coating my fist. "I'm good at hide and seek." At that moment, my phone chimed. It was the sound of a bell reverberating sharply for a split second. I extinguished my flame and replaced it with a 'light ball'. "On second thought, I think I'll go."

I turned around and dashed back the way I came. The chime came from Sara. She found trouble and sent out the signal through her phone, using all its remaining charge to send the signal, far enough, even far enough underground to reach me. I sensed something following me and I cut a groove in the ground below my feet with my sword, casting 'wall' as I dashed over it. The spell activated and sealed the space behind me with a translucent red wall of magic. There was an immediate thump from the other side but the wall held long enough for me to lose the presence and leave the catacombs.

Once I was out, I cast 'blast off' to launch myself into the air and 'levitate' to control where I was going. On the way up, my perspective changed. I was looking down at myself from above again. This lasted for less than a split second as my focus forced me back into my body. In that time, I saw that I was surrounded by a golden aura that was rapidly fading.

Taking out my phone, I saw a beacon on the screen from within Vatican City. It was pulsing rapidly. I turned toward it and cast 'push' to jettison myself toward it. After dodging around a nearby building, I had a clear line of sight from above.

In a spot where a collection of roads converged by the train station, there was a man cloaked in white firing bright yellow spells from something in his hand at Sara and Anjelica. Behind him were three more white-cloaked men. Sara was deflecting the incoming spells with her dagger while Anjelica cowered behind a golden barrier glittered with pink.

As soon as I was directly overhead, I cast 'fire drop'. Coated in flames, I dove down in a straight line, trailing red and yellow behind me. The ground cracked beneath my feet as I landed between Sara and the man. The man was thin with a pale complexion and a boyish face.

Looking the man in the eye, I said, "Do we have a problem here?"

"Thank god you're here," said the man. "The succubus has an accomplice."

"No, that's my partner." I gestured to Sara. "Anjelica. Is this him?"

She whimpered as she cowered on the ground for a moment. Eventually, she responded, "Yes."

"So, you're Marco," I said, waving to Sara to retreat. She transformed back into a scorpion and sat atop Anjelica's shoulder. "Still got your tail or did you cut it off to become a priest?"

"Don't listen to that enchantress," said Marco. "Open your eyes or we'll have to execute you, too."

I shrugged. "Is Marco your name or not?"

"My name is Elijah, and I am a servant of the lord. Be at ease that I am not who that harlot would lead you to believe."

"Oh yeah, you guys like to change your names, don't you? How about we check to see if you got a little nub on your butt? Maybe a scar on your lower back? Can't always get rid of a tail completely."

Marco raised a crucifix and fired a beam of bright yellow light at me.

I lifted my sword at an angle and deflected the spell. "Are your buddies gonna join in or are they just witnesses?"

"They're here in case I succumb to her charms like you." Marco fired another laser spell, but this one split into multiple lasers that homed in from different directions.

"***Flame veil***." I cast the spell and a thin red veil of magic surrounded the barrier around Sara and Angelica. I proceeded to deflect the few that went toward me with my sword. The ones that collided with the veil returned to sender surrounded by a red hue. The spell would hold for a moment if not broken.

Marco dodged to the side as his own attack crashed into the ground at his feet. Next, he cast two spells at once. One was a barrier around himself and the other was a yellow ball that grew at the end of his crucifix, aimed at me.

"Going on the defensive, huh? Guess I'll attack." I turned my wrist and held my sword in a reverse grip. Swiping it at Marco, I cast 'blade wave' and unleashed a red translucent wave of magic from the tip of my blade as it arced forward.

As my blade wave sailed toward its target, the orb in front of him burst forth in a blast of energy. The two collided and I turned, swiping another blade wave at the blast, and canceled out his attack with both of mine.

"Or maybe you just can't fight up close? Are you perhaps a wizard? Like the one casting spells from the back while I was chasing the dragon?"

"***Silence***!" The spell forced my throat to tighten up and my jaw to clench.

I took a breath and cast 'fierce roar', breaking his spell. "***No***!"

Marco's face became shrouded in fear as a result of my spell. He took a weary step back and held his crucifix in shaky hands.

"Too much for you?" As I said that, I heard what sounded like bubbles being blown nearby as well as the sound of a light hum.

I looked up to see the two faeries from earlier fluttering toward me. They were babbling on about something until they started swirling around my hand. They stopped and one said, slowly, almost humming the words, "*Basiel. Magic*."

I guided the faeries behind me with my hand. "Wait back there with them. I'll get back to you soon."

The faeries did what I said and Sara let them into the barrier. As they did so, Marco spoke.

"You really *have* been enchanted by them. Fine then, we'll have your head. Let's have at them, brothers. Kill them all at once."

"Or you can not and say you did." I pointed at Marco. "I'm only here for you right now."

One of the cloaked men reached out his hand "***Ogre***." A large sickly green humanoid creature with pronounced fangs and heavy armor wielding a mace appeared at his side. This man seemed to be a summoner.

Another man drew a series of golden crosses in the air with his fingers. They all vanished and reappeared in front of each man as well as the ogre. He drew a sword and took a stance as two crosses appeared, circling him. He was likely an enchanter.

The last one reached into his cloak and pulled out a collapsed spear. Extending it, he clasped it in his hands and spoke. "***Dear lord, use my form to smite your enemies.***" After his words of power, his eyes started glowing gold and he dashed at me. It didn't seem like he used magic so it was probably a magic trait. In the meantime, anyone not charging me spread out.

I funneled flames down my sword and took a stance. "Fun, it is." Pressing my hand against my chest, I cast 'strength'. A faint red glow coated my body as I readied myself. The spell would supplement my own strength so I wouldn't have to overexert myself physically.

The man with the glowing eyes got just outside his striking range and launched, not only his spear, but himself at me as he spiraled through the air.

Hopping to the side, I avoided the spear, but not him. I used the flat of my blade alongside the flames to absorb the impact and the sound of metal-on-metal told me he was wearing heavy armor as well.

I rolled against him off to the side only to see a mace flailing my way. The ogre was close behind.

Instead of ducking the mace, I pressed the edge of my sword against it and used the spikes as a guide to swipe my blade straight through its neck. The flames around my sword vanished on their own just before impact as if they hit something else.

The ogre's form dissipated. Its head didn't have time to hit the ground before it was gone.

At that time, I was surrounded by yellow beams of light from above. While this was happening, the ground became bathed in a golden glow in all directions.

The enchanter was kneeling with his hands on the ground. I dashed toward him. Letting him create a mana field was a bad idea. When I went, a series of lasers fell from the sky where I was standing. Glancing at Marco, I saw he was waving his crucifix above his head, casting another spell.

"***Angelo Santo, speak to me.***" The summoner clasped his hands, preparing to summon another creature.

With a flick of the wrist, I sent a blade wave his way.

In response, he didn't even flinch as my magic crashed into him. Only the cross hovering in front of him vanished. He pulled his hands away from each other as a circle of feathers around a childlike figure wreathed in gold appeared in front of him. He pointed at me and the figure hovered toward me in the blink of an eye. Before it reached me, it reached out with something else. It was amorphous, gold, and shimmery.

I didn't see what it was before I cast 'sacred flame', coated my blade in white flames, and parried the angel's strike.

The angel stopped as if surprised. It then spoke angelic as it backed off. "I have not the strength to harm my own." It then vanished.

Lesser angels sometimes refused to fight me as they saw it as fighting another angel. I was lucky this one refused as well.

The summoner froze in place, shocked at the angel's words. It looked like his faith had been shaken, even if only temporarily.

I continued toward the enchanter but this time, a blue circle appeared in the ground before me accompanied by Marco's voice. "**Sacred Geyser.**"

A torrent of water speckled with yellow blasted up from the ground within the circle.

I didn't have the time to defend as I entered the circle, so I didn't. Instead, I cast 'flicker'. In a whisp of flame, I teleported to my target, using the water as cover.

My body and everything on me turned into clear flames, carried by the heat of my spell until I reformed, whole at my destination.

Once I was behind the enchanter, I struck him with the back of my blade. I felt like I hit something, but it wasn't him. Both crosses hovering In front of him vanished as well as the flames on my blade.

Before I could strike again, the point of a spear entered my field of view. The spearman with glowing eyes would have been the only one to see me teleport and seeing his spear meant his attention was on me the whole time.

I wasn't able to dodge the spear completely and it put a hole in my sleeve as it grazed my shoulder.

"**Sacred burst.**"

I heard Marco's voice and had no time, if any, to react. I was already on the back foot and felt like I was in danger no matter which direction I went as long as I stayed close to the enchanter. Even so, I hooked my foot under his arm and pressed it against his chest before launching him into the air with a kick. Getting him off the ground was my goal. Severing his contact with it would stall his spell and give it time to unravel before he could complete it.

A bang resounded from around me as a blinding yellow light filled my field of view. It was as if the impact radiated from inside me and blasted outward. I didn't feel much more than the impact immediately, but I'd feel the rest later.

Wasting no time, I leaped after the enchanter before I could see again. He couldn't have gone far and they'd be looking for another teleport from me. I collided with something but it didn't feel like a person. It was likely a barrier, so I pushed against it and cast a spell. "**Fire vortex.**" The flames bellowing out from my spell encompassed us with an updraft, keeping whatever was in the spell in the air.

As soon as I could see, I scanned my surroundings. Through the flames, I saw Marco in the middle of casting another spell, the man with the glowing eyes was charging my way, extending another spear, the summoner was still standing in shock, and the enchanter was huddled in a bubble shield above me that was burning away.

Leaving the enchanter to be carried away by my spell, I cast 'push' to launch him slightly higher and myself to the ground to engage the spearman.

Instead of doing the same trick again, the spearman used his range to his advantage with a series of pokes. After the first one, he steadied his feet and slid toward me.

I attempted to parry the first one, but he pulled it back and his momentum changed as he slid.

His second strike was slower but had much more force behind it.

I tried to parry this one as well but the force of the strike pushed it past my sword. In response, I pushed it toward my already wounded shoulder to mitigate my losses while I closed the distance.

Instead of allowing his spear to land, he pulled it back as if that wasn't his intention to begin with and struck again.

I felt waves of danger from him, but something seemed off. Regardless, I wasn't backing off.

His third strike seemed more serious, but I was able to dodge that one completely by using my blade to force it off to the side.

When I came within striking range, I swung at his spear arm with the back of my blade.

He took the hit with his armor and grunted as his arm flailed to the side. He used his other arm to grab at me.

That's when I realized that getting in close was the danger. In a knee-jerk response, I headbutted his hand and used the momentum to go into a front flip, resulting in an axe kick. I was unsure where my foot made contact, but when I landed back on the ground, the man was facedown. It looked like headbutting his hand destroyed the protective enchantment on him and my kick did the rest. I wasn't expecting him to stay down but it didn't look like he was getting back up. His eyes weren't glowing anymore.

The ground was still glowing but it was slowly fading. The enchanter was still in my fire vortex, keeping his shield alive as it continued to burn away.

Marco was still waving his crucifix as if he was trying to find a signal, but now he looked scared. His spell was likely incomplete.

I took steps toward him. "Ready to come clean? Or are we gonna keep having a good time?" I noticed something running down my upper lip and wiped away the blood with my thumb. "We didn't kill *her*." I gestured in Anjelica's general direction. "And we won't kill *you*. *If* you cooperate."

Marco swallowed hard. "**Heavy water: sacred rain**." A bright yellow cloud appeared overhead and lit up the area. Yellowish rain down poured that hit like paintballs. The spell forced my fire vortex to dissipate, freeing the enchanter.

"And the good times roll. Sit tight, I'll get back to you." I turned toward the enchanter. "Do you want to keep fighting or do I get to do my job?"

"Do you think this is fun?" said the enchanter. He sounded winded. "We're fighting for our lives. Are you some kind of devil?"

"Well, it is kinda fun. I mean, you're fighting for your lives and I'm just not killing you."

He took a deep breath and composed himself. "And you think you can use your flames in a place flooded with holy water?" He drew a golden cross in the air with his fingers and it started rotating around him as a second appeared and did the same.

"I don't need to." I swiped my hand through the air, batting at the cloud above us. "***Wuthering***." A violent wind of a green hue came through and eviscerated the cloud, leaving us in the dark yet again. The enchantment causing the ground to glow was already long gone. "My wind's just as strong, unlike this guy's spells." I pointed at Marco. "They're not even gold. Only yellow. You think if he believed what he fought for, his 'holy' spells would only be yellow? I'm willing to bet his natural color is white. Maybe with a blue tinge."

The enchanter gave a heavy sigh. "Are we really to believe our brother in arms betrayed us?"

I shrugged. "I was hired for a reason. By your people, no less."

"Very well." He turned toward the summoner. "Brother George… Were the angel's words that profound?" Next, he made his way across to the unconscious man and struggled to move him.

Seeing him struggle, I said, "Low on mana?"

"Close. I'm just not very martially inclined." He pressed his hand on the man's back. "***Levitate***." He lifted the man as he glowed blue and carried him away.

I turned my attention back to Marco. He was slowly sneaking away as if I wouldn't notice. "So, you're done fighting too, huh, Marco?"

Instead of answering, he waved his crucifix near his legs and they started glowing white before he bolted away.

I reached toward him and cast a spell. "***Pull***."

Before he could turn a corner, he flew toward me as if he was flung with a rubber band. The back of his neck landed in my hand. As soon as I touched him, he spoke. "***Release me***."

I felt my eyes glaze over as his words washed over my mind. This was far more powerful magic than anything he used until then. I felt compelled to loosen my grip and back away. After a moment of consideration, I responded, "Alright." I took a step forward and slammed him into the ground. "*That's* the kind of hypnotic power I expect from a succubus." I let him go and kicked him to turn him over. He looked unconscious. "Well, you're brittle even for a wizard."

His eyes shot open. "Ah!" He gasped. "How'd you-" He winced.

"High resistance to mind control. Bordering on immunity, really."

He turned his crucifix toward me. "***Possession***." It started glowing white, bathing me in light.

I felt like my mind was being overridden as my thoughts started fading and something else tried to take root. The feeling faded as I slapped the crucifix away with the flat of my blade. "That was the fastest advanced spell casting you did this whole time. Is that the best you can do?"

Marco didn't respond. He just looked dejected.

I cast 'insight' and looked into Marco's eyes, I peered for what was far beyond the surface. It took a moment but I found it. "Any last words?"

As soon as I said that, I heard rapid footsteps approaching from far behind me. It was Anjelica. "You said you wouldn't kill him!" She sounded as frightened and panicked as I thought she would.

I reached toward her and cast 'bind', wrapping her arms and legs with magic. I heard her hit the ground immediately after.

"Please! Don't!" she pleaded. "You said you wouldn't!"

I smirked. "I lied."

The look in Marco's eyes shifted as if a dam had broken In his mind. A scream grating enough to daze me emanated from him. It sounded like a banshee. Probably a psychic scream.

A swift feeling of danger overtook me and I hopped back as a pale tail tipped with a bony blade stabbed at me.

Marco stood as his voice emanated from him without his mouth moving. "*You had one job. Kill her. I have not sinned. I just lived. It's not my time to be judged!*" His face became slightly malformed as his teeth became fangs. Bony bladed wings pierced the back of his cloak and he took flight. In the moonlight, he gained a blue tinge to his skin.

The enchanter, who was still nearby spoke. "The blue demon..."

I clapped my hands together with my sword in between them. "Alright. About time you showed your true colors. Now, come at me like you mean it."

Another voice came from the shadows. "You had your fun." Black tendrils reached from the ground and wound around Marco. He struggled to free himself but was surrounded by an orb of blackness. Doc stepped from the shadows on the ground like it was a staircase. "Our job is done."

3-Homeward

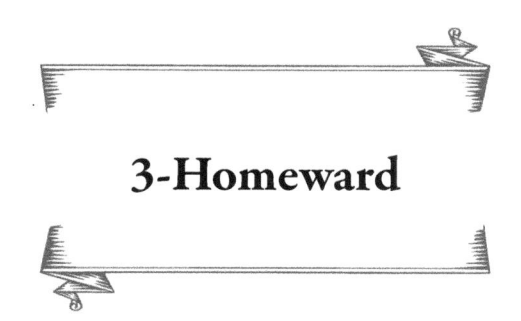

The faeries danced around my hand almost solemnly. They spoke enthusiastically and Sara translated. They sensed the magic of their beloved wizard on my hands. One just happened to have stronger traces than the other. Hearing this, I told them about the body I found underground as well as everything else that happened.

"Corruption never fails to run deep," said Doc. "It could have been any number of things, but I'd bet against a coincidence."

Sara spoke up from Anjelica's shoulder. "Looks like the only coincidence was the wizard showing up. Then again, maybe not. Who knows what could have led to him coming this way."

I finally dismissed my sword and popped my joints. "Whelp, not like any of that matters anymore. We did our job and I'm pretty sure that dragon is long gone. I doubt it'd stay around with people knowing it impersonated a Vatican member anyway."

Anjelica was staring at the black orb carrying her brother. "So, what are you gonna do with him?"

"Same as you," I said. "Getting away from here. We were hired to capture or kill. Didn't say we had to hand anyone over to them. We're just going to get paid now."

"What about the faeries?"

Sara answered, "They're going home when we leave. No use sticking around a place like this."

Soon, we were close to an entrance to the underground. We were in an alley between a few buildings when Doc stopped. The rest of us stopped as well. He looked at Anjelica. "You look like you still have questions. It's best to ask them now."

"Well, I heard all the stories about Corpse Hunters leaving all kinds of death and destruction in their wake. You guys don't seem all that bad, all things considered. Are you guys just different or something? You *are* Corpse Hunters, right?"

"Yep," I said. "But there's not much difference between us and a guild. The only difference is the label. Anyone with that label has a bounty on their head. And most that do, just so happen to be wielders. Like us."

"So, Corpse Hunters are just adventurers with bounties on their heads?"

"Wielders with bounties on their heads, although not all corpse hunters are wielders. I guess there's also a difference between us and a normal bounty target that happens to be a wielder."

"Can they really do that? I mean, would the Commissioner's guild really just allow that?"

"Most people don't know this, but both the price, and the label are from C.H.E.S.S. They're not an organization the Commissioner's guild can just say no to."

Anjelica began to look more and more bewildered. "That's like if the witch hunts were a universal thing. That's stupid. Is there even a reason?"

This time, Doc spoke. "C.H.E.S.S. was created during the latter half of the wielder's war as a haven for wielders, but they existed by a different name before that. They experimented on wielders before trafficking them out. I think they're just covering their bases in case someone wants revenge. Then again, they probably never stopped experimenting. They say corpse shadows were a result of those experiments, hence the name."

Anjelica frowned. "That's... Awful. It's like, you're Corpse Hunters, but you're the..." After those words, she fell completely silent.

Picking up where she left off, I said, "Hunted? Perhaps by a corpse of the past." I shrugged. "Idunno. Some people do things and everyone else suffers for it."

"Is that all you had on your mind?" said Doc.

Anjelica shifted around nervously. "Well, after all this, I can't just go back home..."

"If you want to join us, don't," I said. "As far as guilds go, being corpse hunters, we'd classify as an immortal's guild. Anyone not up to it just dies."

"N-n-n-no, no, I-I w-w-wouldn't..." She stammered heavily. "I mean, I live in Streghaven. Basically, at the Vatican's doorstep."

"Oh, that's what you meant. Streghaven's at odds with the Vatican, so they'll help *you*, but your brother's on his own. We didn't kill him but we can't just set him free."

"Oh, yeah... Him..."

Before she could finish, Doc said, "We can hand him over to the Vatican, if that's what you'd like."

"I... I mean..." She seemed lost in thought. "Where would you put him otherwise?"

"Gratamal, Streghaven's capital. He'll be relatively safe there. He still committed verifiable crimes but since laws are different everywhere, he might get a slap on the wrist if he's lucky. Knowing the Vatican, they'll advocate for execution. I doubt it'll go that far. Probably house arrest and counseling at best. At worst, a life of jail time. Either way, he won't be free for at least a couple decades."

She looked down with a solemn face. "Alright... I don't... want to leave him behind."

Doc continued down a set of steps into the underground. "Then it's decided." The rest of us followed.

As we passed holy lanterns, the flames of each one turned blue. After the third one, the rest ahead vanished. In their place was a portal to another part of the tunnels. It looked like the same type of cell Anjelica nearly died in.

I walked up to the portal. "We're taking the demons with us."

The portal closed and in its place was a pedestal. On it, was an envelope and a note. The note read, '*Do not return*'. In the envelope was our payment.

"I can live with that."

Back above ground, we made our way into Rome. As soon as were out of the Vatican, we all breathed a collective sigh of relief.

I asked the group, "So, what spot are we passing through at?"

"The Coliseum," said Doc.

With that, we walked to the coliseum. Under a shroud of invisibility, we let ourselves in through a spot not closed off by a fence or a gate. The small void inside the coliseum was directly linked to its counterpart in Gratamal, the capital of Streghaven. With our collective intent, we crossed the void into the underworld.

The coliseum in the underworld was almost completely intact. It got destroyed frequently so it was rebuilt often and there were no surrounding buildings. By the time it was out of use, it was already rebuilt one last time.

"Wait," said Anjelica. "Why did we come all the way to the coliseum to get to the underworld?"

"You don't know?" I said. "A lot of magical blood was spilt there, even if nothing magical lives there. It makes the boundary a little easier to cross with people that don't want to." I gestured toward Marco, still in the black bubble.

"No, I mean, couldn't we have done that in Vatican City? Like, anywhere in the city?"

"That place is so full of energy from both the overworld and underworld that they kinda mix. It's hard to pass the boundary on purpose there since everything's kinda all mixed into one. Even if we did cross the boundary, we could still get flung back to the overworld or separated after leaving. It's best to leave there in the same way you entered unless it's by foot. We came in through a guiding note from the Vatican, but you're not going where we came from so it's as good as a one-way trip. Not like anyone else could use it to go where we came from anyway."

"That's not why," said Doc. "It's because the Vatican's underworld is surrounded by a void so dense, it acts like a difficult barrier and not a portal."

Confused, I said, "Really?"

"The catacombs. It's why Vatican city is one of the few places that even has a direct underworld counterpart."

"Oh, yeah. Didn't think about that."

"I also just wanted to see the underworld coliseum."

"I came in through the underworld," said Anjelica. "I didn't notice anything like that on the way in."

Doc smirked. A rarity. "You would on the way out."

Anjelica paused and shuddered. "Well, at least we're out." She removed the silver band on her wrist and stretched out her arms and tail. She then paused and looked at the black orb holding her brother with a saddened expression.

From there, we made our way to the nearest precinct and explained the situation at the front desk. After a couple of rounds of questioning, we were able to fully explain the story to some detectives who made notes of everything. We also left them the guiding note, the documents we got from Father Peter Nicolas, and the note that was on the pedestal.

After all of that, Doc floated the black orb he was carrying into a secured prison cell and released Marco. Through the glass, we saw him emerge with a shriek that was barely audible through the layers of enchantments inside. His wings had vanished and his face was back to normal, but his tail was flailing about dangerously.

Anjelica stayed behind as we left. Before we left her behind, I reached into a pocket and gave her a deep red and green slip of paper.

"Use that in the case of an emergency."

She nodded and stared at it for a moment before putting it away.

From there, we traveled to the nearest park. Deep into the park, we checked the moss-covered undergrowth for a ley-line, faint traces of magic that led a trail between the trees. We followed it with the thought of home. As we went, the trees became gradually shorter and the leaves thicker until we exited the other side where we walked onto a wide, flat road in front of a small, gated mansion surrounded by forestry.

We were home.

From the street, we entered the gate and made our way up the stairs and to the door. Opening it, we stepped onto the enclosed porch. It was much darker than normal as the motion-sensing lights didn't turn on. Someone must have turned them off.

I snapped my fingers, and a small flame appeared over my thumb, illuminating the porch. While Doc took to unlocking the door, Sara sat on a nearby rocking chair. It slid back on the tiled floor before rocking back and forth.

The door opened, and we entered into more darkness. I expected most of them to be off doing their own thing, but I didn't expect there to be no sign of anyone.

"Hello!" Sara called out to no answer.

"I guess no one's home?" I extinguished my flame.

"Seems so," said Doc, flipping two light switches on the wall, one for the porch and one for the hall leading to the rest of the house.

"Fine by me. I just need to lie down. I don't want to be standing when I relax. It's all gonna hit me at once." Removing my jacket in a single motion, I hung it on the nearby coat rack. I examined my shoulder and saw a little hole poked through the skin. My arms were also starting to feel sore. I should have tried to defend a little more instead of just taking hits. My stomach grumbled. "I'm hungry, too." After a moment of considering whether to eat or nap first, I decided. "I'll eat later."

"I'll eat now," said Sara. "I'm starving." She went straight down the hall and made a right into the kitchen. On the way, her phone rang. "Hello?" she answered. "I'm in the kitchen." She looked at me and said, "Krow's right here. I'm putting you on speakerphone." Hearing this, I caught up with her and listened in.

"We've been trying to reach you guys for hours." Leuna's voice came through loud and clear, with the sound of birds chirping gleefully in the background. "We're all outside right now. There's something wrong with the void around the house."

"What do you mean?" I said, "We got here without incident and the void seems fine. Otherwise, Doc would have said something."

"It's not getting in that's the problem, it's getting out. If you go in the forest or down the street, you'll come back from the same direction going straight. Outgoing calls also don't seem to work."

"That's not good." I took the nearest chair at the kitchen table.

"What should we do?" said Sara, as she began pacing back and forth.

"Mom said 'stay in the house'. We'll be back soon."

"Ok." She took a seat as well.

"In that case, I'm gonna get Doc." I stood and left the kitchen toward the entrance. I took my jacket from the coat rack and made a 180 up the stairs. From there, I continued forward down the hall to the last door on the right. His room was across from mine.

I knocked, and he responded, "Enter."

I opened the door and explained to him what was going on. He was shuffling through drawers in his dresser for a change of clothes.

"Where's Sara?" he said.

"Still in the kitchen."

"We should stay together, then."

By the time we made it to the kitchen where Sara sat waiting, we could hear the front door unlocking and opening. In came Leuna, built like an athlete in shorts and a short-sleeve, who moved to the side and held the door open for the rest. Carona came in close after. A large woman, Carona gave birth to Sara and acts as both a mother and leader to all of us. Ariel was second in that regard, as she was the oldest among the girls. She was in a tank top and sweatpants, likely rushed out of the house considering the situation. Last was Caroline, Considered the 'middle' child, she always wore mostly blue, which is how she got the codename 'Blue'.

"So, what now?" I said, "Did you figure out what's wrong with the void?"

Carona responded, "It's looking like a structural issue. Something's probably spooked the fae in the forest. We won't know for sure until tomorrow."

With that in mind, we continued through the day. I Buried the remains of Anjelica in a space we reserved for similar incidents below the house and spent the rest of the day sprawled across my bed, dosing in and out of sleep. I was having a dream that would continue whenever my eyes closed until I drifted off completely.

I awoke sitting up on a stone-tiled floor. The walls were tiled similarly but I didn't or couldn't perceive the pattern. It was as if it was relegated to my peripherals. Looking around, I saw around four or five people resting on open sleeping bags. Some were against a wall and others were closer by on the floor like me. They were much bigger than me. Looking at my hands, I saw that I was a child.

There was an open hole in one of the walls that led to the open sky in every direction with wind whipping by from all directions. Strangely, the wind had no effect inside the room.

I stood and made my way to the open doorway in the same wall as the hole in the wall. It was there the whole time but I couldn't acknowledge it until I stepped toward it. It was to the left of the hole.

I took a weary step into the dark and my eyes adjusted a little. The room was big enough that the hole in the same wall should have led to the room but it didn't. The walls were metal and covered in thick tubes, wires, and electronics. There was a wall to the right that gave way to a railing after a few feet.

There was a switch that I could barely make out to the left of the doorway but no matter how many times I flicked it, the lights never turned on.

I began walking through this futuristic walkway. The cold seeped into my bones; a new addition to the slowly growing list of sensations. I could almost hear myself jittering from the chill. Fear seeped in equally, another new addition, but a far less welcome one.

I took a shaky step back but my foot went forward. I wanted to turn around and leave, but I felt like there was something I had to do and it was through the darkness. The farther I went, the more I felt I was being watched by someone or something.

Something zoomed past my narrow line of sight and I realized how right I was. The terror made me freeze in place. I tried to turn back and run, but I couldn't. The longer I stood, the more the pieces of what was experiencing came into place.

The creature I saw was a vampire. What little details I saw of it made me certain that it was among the deadliest of vampires; a Nelapsi. It could kill me with so much as a hostile glance.

When the full realization set in, I felt like I could move but my body refused to respond in kind. My vision fractured for a split second as if there was somehow a glitch in my experience. This was followed by an odd static effect that raced through my field of vision. Seeing this, I finally took a breath and instead of running back, I walked forward. I took a single step and used it to turn around and walk back.

Halfway, I turned at the sound of a moan. It was far too close to even consider getting away from it. I turned back around to see the creature coming my way faster than a bullet. It wasn't very close, but it was too late to run now.

And then darkness. No sound. No cold. Warmth.

"Hey! wake up! Wake up, Krow!" I heard a familiar voice echo through my consciousness.

"I know that voice. Is that Caroline?" I said, moaning and squinting my eyes open.

"Yes, wake up, come on, let's go!"

"I don't want to," I moaned.

"You have to, it's an emergency," she said, with urgency.

"What kind of emergency? Because if you gotta pee you can go by yourself, besides you are old enough," I joked.

"Now's no time for jokes, I had a vision."

"A vision?" Caroline's visions always came true, and they were always bad. I sat up in my bed. The room was dark and eerie, like that dream I had. I got up and quickly dressed myself in the dark. I stood next to Caroline and said, "When did you get so short? Maybe I just got taller? No, you're just gravitationally challenged."

"That's way off-topic." My sarcasm went unappreciated.

"Maybe we need to get Carona and ask her," I suggested, still functionally half-asleep.

"Yeah, we need to find Mom," she said with certainty.

"Yeah, I guess we do," I replied, "About your height. I'm towering over you," I put my hand on her shoulder "But you are the perfect height for me to do this," I put my elbow on her shoulder, replacing my hand. Her scarf made her stout shoulders comfortable to lean on. I turned on the light at the same time so I could see her next to me and removed my elbow while putting on my shoes. Afterward, I just stood there.

"Where is everybody else?" I asked, groggily blinking each eye in a sequence as they adjusted.

"Leuna, Sara, and Ariel are waiting for us at the basement door. That's where I saw an intruder."

"Worse than I thought," I said to myself.

"Mom's missing too," she continued nonchalantly.

"Carona's missing?" I sighed. "This may be even worse than I thought."

"I'm telling you, keep up." She snapped her fingers.

"Okay... I'll go find Carona. You should go downstairs with everyone else and see what's happening down there."

"Deal." She took off down the hall, down the stairs, and further.

"Alright, let's go." I Left my room and started looking for Carona. I searched her room, all the other rooms, the front and back porch, and even the attic, but there was no sign of her.

Being one not prone to panic, I took a moment to think. Carona's a problem solver. She'd be somewhere there was a problem to solve. What came to mind sent me toward the edge of the forest where I found the unbelievable.

Carona was sprawled out on the ground just within the forest edge with deep claw marks on her back next to a hole in the ground large enough for two people. Doc was next to her with his hands over her back. She was inside a translucent bubble of his making.

"What happened?" I asked.

"She was blind-sided. Whoever did this has an extremely potent poison. I can't completely remove it, so I put her in stasis. Where's everyone else?"

"Downstairs dealing with whoever did this."

"We better get down there. Anybody who can surprise Carona like this could threaten all of us." He stood. "Take her in the house and head down. I'll follow this tunnel. They probably have info on us, too. Be careful"

Doc gently laid Carona in my arms. I turned around and sprinted into the house with her. Gently, I sat her on the sofa in the living room and ran downstairs.

Down, down, down. The basement was bigger than the house as it went down five floors. I rushed down them. There was an explosion halfway down the stairs, so I went faster. By the time I got there and took my last step, I saw that whatever battle there was, was over.

The fifth floor was a large, gray room with a few smaller rooms stemming from it. Ariel was sitting unconscious next to a doorway with a gash across her calf and her lance at her feet. Leuna was leaning against a wall with cuts across her arm as she barely gripped her bow. Caroline barely stood, leaning on her half-moon blade for support. Sara was hanging in mid-air, dangling high off the ground. Her throat was in someone's hand.

The person was dressed in silver. He had on a silver fedora and what seemed to be an all-silver suit, with silver boots, gloves, and his jacket hanging off of his shoulders.

I called out, "Sara!" in fear for her life. I was unsure what I could do before the worst-case scenario could take place.

The man tightened his grip until she coughed up blood. Then he threw her at me by her neck.

She landed directly in my arms, and I dropped to a knee, ready to either jump or dodge, just in case. With blood on her lips, she could only say, "Krow... He's... Poisonous," before she passed out.

I sat her down gently. In a fit of rage, rushed directly at the man. He sidestepped my punch and kneed me in my stomach. I slid back on my feet into a wall. At the sound of a crunch, I could tell that the wall took more damage than I had.

He laughed and said, "What's wrong, Krow? Or should I say, Daniel? Or better yet, the Kid Phoenix."

Hunched forward, I picked myself up and said, "How do you know that name?... And what the hell's a Kid Phoenix?"

"I know all about you and your kin. They're pretty weak. How about I test you next?"

"No, **reach**!" I cast the spell and mana pooled into my right hand burst out into a large red talon, grabbed him, and pulled him toward me as It disappeared.

As he was coming at a high speed, I moved my feet into place then cast 'impact' and slammed my fist into his face while it still glowed red. The sound echoed through the halls and he slammed into the floor so hard he made a hole in the ground. He then flipped on his side and landed on his feet and one hand.

"Wow, you really are stronger than I thought," he said in mockery.

I sighed, having released my momentary rage, allowing myself to focus properly. "I'll ask you this once. Do you think you'll leave here alive?"

"I don't need to." The man vanished, leaving behind an afterimage. He likely teleported or became invisible, but I couldn't sense his presence to follow where he went.

Summoning my sword to my hand, I followed my instincts and swiped across the air in front of me. When I did, my blade clashed with something. The man reappeared with a three-bladed claw seated in his hand. There was some clear liquid dripping from the claw blades. He was mid-attack and I stopped it.

Raking his claw down, he cast a spell. "**Blade wave**." In that motion, he yanked my sword down and sent three razor-thin blades of metal from this claw that carried through the air barely a couple of feet away from my face.

I hopped back at the same time and swiped at the projectiles, shattering them.

The man smiled and said, "Call me Blade."

"**Burn**." I cast a spell and the space around Blade ignited in flames. If he was hoping to have a conversation, it wasn't happening.

The flame didn't seem to take hold as he vanished again.

Facing my palm to the ground, I cast 'shockwave' and the floor shook violently. At the same time, I gripped my forearm with my other hand and did a full rotation while casting 'blade wheel', creating a red circle of magic around myself that would cut anything that crossed its boundary. The first spell was meant to trip him up if he was on the ground and the second one was to prevent a conventional approach.

I heard something clash with my blade wheel and I dodged to the side as a block of stone flew my way. The walls and floor were unaffected so it had to have been a spell. Next, a feeling of danger made me hop back as another stone slab landed in front of me.

I turned my free hand upward. "***Skyfall***." At the sound of a nearby thump, I stabbed my blade into the ground.

Blade reappeared, rolling away from where I stabbed the ground. He stood as if nothing happened.

"***Silence***." I cast a spell I almost never did and Blade staggered backward a little. It seemed that I caught him off guard and whatever spell he was planning to cast got caught in his throat.

Realizing the position he was in, he opened his mouth and released a shout that both broke my spell on him and caused shards of metal to spring from beneath him outward in all directions.

Reacting quickly, I swiped at the shards flying at me. "***Inverse horizon***." Spreading out my arms. I cast the spell around the both of us and prevented the shards from going near the girls.

"***Meteor shrapnel***." Blade's claw shined silver before a flash of light followed by a burst of metallic shrapnel sprayed from it.

"***Shatter***!" I shouted the spell, casting it through my voice and blasting the shards away from me. They passed harmlessly through Blade, but my spell didn't, sending him hurling into my barrier where he bounced off and landed on his feet. I cast 'burning step' and 'whirlwind blade' as I charged forward with flames at my feet and a swirling vortex around my sword.

Blade stood ready as a coating of silver ran across his body. He placed his hand on his outstretched arm and pointed his claw at me as sparks of grey electricity ran up to his shoulder. "***Railgun***."

As the blinding light raced toward me, I remained steady, knowing I already had the momentum I needed. I just also needed a bit more power. I cast 'draco burn' to mingle the flames with the wind around my sword and creating a blazing whirlwind. In the end, the two spells combined into another spell. "***Infernal tempest***". I guided my blade, backed with wind and fire, through the light until I felt a slight resistance. It was the projectile fired by his spell. The flames at my feet gripped the air and I pivoted into another spell, turning in circles as I went. "***Dance of the fireflies***." This spell scattered red specks of magic from my blade around the space inside the barrier where they settled in the air, ready to be detonated.

Blade dodged to the side with the only casualty being the silver aura that was surrounding him being shattered. He reapplied it just as quickly.

Given that it took the brunt of my attack, it meant I had to hit him twice to end it. The edge of my peripherals briefly started fading to black. The implications made me smile. This seemed to unsettle Blade enough for his face to change. It was brief, but long enough for me to see it change to anything other than smugness.

Noticing this, I took a confident step forward and allowed my sword to change. The black blade flashed silver and the red marks along it turned black.

In an instant, Blade sank into the ground. He was trying to teleport away. He probably sensed the danger he was in.

"***Pull***." I cast the spell and yanked him out of the ground before he could vanish. "***Reach***." I cast another spell and grabbed him again with a red talon.

A slew or silver blades sprang from Blade's body and pierced the talon before running across his body and severing its grip on him. Even so, he was still flying toward me.

I created a flame in the palm of my hand and wrapped it in a condensed vortex of wind the size of a baseball. "***Palm explosion***."

The silver coating around Blade seemed to become thicker. He likely recast the protective spell on himself. Given that he didn't just stop his own momentum instead, proved that he couldn't.

My spell hit him and it expanded around him before exploding, shattering a layer of his armor. I would have moved back to avoid being caught in the blast, but I needed him in place, so I grabbed his collar and snapped my fingers. Before the dust could settle, the particles in the air expanded and filled the space with a blinding heat. While not much for me, it shattered the second layer of Blade's armor as well as my 'inverse horizon' spell.

The heat surrounding us vanished quickly, but not on its own. The heat split down the middle alongside the still expanding explosion around both me and Blade, diffusing both.

I looked up to see Doc with his weapon in hand; a black scythe with teeth along its entire edge. He was shrouded in a cloak of darkness and his eyes were glowing pure red.

With a second's delay, Blade's body flew into a sliver of color, All in different shades of silver. From shiny light silver to gray. His blood was the same color. As this happened, he split in half from the top of his head down.

"A clone," said Doc, seemingly unsurprised.

"What gave it away?" I said, sarcastically. "The silver ooze, or the audacity to come here alone?" I wiped off the silver that splattered onto me.

I heard footsteps rapidly descending the stairs in a matter of seconds. It was Carona. Whatever cuts she had were healed completely like they never happened. I was amazed but not surprised. Carona was fluent and efficient with healing magic. I was sure that whenever she regained consciousness, she would heal herself with no problem, and whatever injuries the rest of us might take would be healed thereafter. The problem was it would be difficult for her to heal her own back. Whatever damage there was seemed to reverse on its own.

"Is everyone ok?" she called out, looking around wildly like a frightened animal. It was very like her not to worry about her own condition.

"Was I down the whole time?" Said Ariel, getting up from the ground.

"Looks like it," I said, glancing over at Ariel.

"I think whatever poison that thing hit us with just wore off. Thanks for killing it." She was flexing her healed leg while Leuna stood away from the wall and Caroline found her balance.

"You're not dead yet, right?" said Doc, eyeing Blade. "Not decommissioned yet either, by the looks of it."

"What-t d-do y-you want-t withh m-me?" Blade's voice was fading due to the fact that he was cut perfectly in half.

"Who sent you, for starters," said Doc, casually.

"You-u allr-read-dy know the answer."

"So, it's safe to say you sent yourself? Were you just sent to taunt us, or was there more to it?"

The halves of Blade's face twisted into a smile before his form essentially melted into a puddle.

"Clocked out early," confirmed Doc as he observed the semi-gelatinous mass of silver that was left of Blade. It looked like a lump of bad CGI. "At least he didn't self-destruct."

"So now we know who sent him," I said.

"Assuming he sent himself," added Doc. "But not the reason behind why. Likely something he wanted us to know and questions he wanted us to ask."

"So, how do we find out?" asked Caroline.

"I got an idea," said Sara. She had just gotten her throat healed be Carona. "We'll have to go find a friend of mine. He lives pretty far, so it'll be a road trip."

"And where are we going?" asked Carona.

"New York."

Carona tilted her head toward the stairs. "Alright, let's head up. We need to get ready."

We had all accepted the chance of finding the real Blade were dwarfed by the chances of running headlong into a convoluted trap by leaving instead of staying. Even so, the odds were almost never in our favor, so we packed up and got ready to move.

Once we were packed, we all went outside on the street. Everyone just got out that far when, BOOM! I whipped around to see the whole house destroyed. Hundreds of metal spikes replaced the house, sticking up from what was the basement, shiny and metallic.

A feeling began creeping up on me, and I turned to see Doc. A black aura was wafting up from his feet, surrounding him, and disappearing over his head. He looked at me and said, "I think our little friend was set to evolve. So, I'm gonna break him and make sure he stays broken this time."

He held his hand out and in a flash that contained all the colors of darkness, his scythe was in his hand.

It started shimmering, then it started to transform. Like two people back-to-back, a second blade appeared behind the first, making a double-bladed scythe. A clean edge replaced the dog-like teeth.

He moved fast. I watched as he went right up to the spikes. A few jerked upward and flew toward him. He slashed at them, breaking them effortlessly. He jumped and landed directly on top of one of the higher spikes and ran forward until another spike spiraled downward and crashed into it. He jumped again, this time, clear into the air.

A few spikes shot at him and he effortlessly cross-slashed them. It was like an action shot. As he continued his descent, more spikes shot up at him. He slashed at them furiously as if one got past him it would be all over, but he still let one slip through right past his shoulder. He then twirled his scythe in his hand and then. DING! He stabbed his blade into the silvery center.

He made a large crack in the dome-shaped middle of broken spikes. The one spike left turned around and raced toward him.

An orb of darkness surrounded him, and he disappeared with it, teleporting.

The spike that was shooting toward Doc crashed into the crack and split it in two.

"CAAAAAAAAAK!" There was a deafening scream from the clone. *Blop blop.* it started bubbling up and expanding.

"A shield!" Carona called for someone to make one and before we knew it, there was a wall of street and sidewalk in front of us made by Ariel. BOOM! it exploded. The clone and its fragments turned to liquid that rained down. Ariel extended the wall to cover us.

The silvery slop that resulted from the explosion soon started moving back into a single mass, pulling whatever it touched with it. It pulled what was left of the house, grass, dirt, and the earth wall we had in front of us too. It condensed itself into a marble-sized stone, silvery and clear.

"It's a core stone," Doc said, hopping down into the hole and picking it up.

Core stones are solidified leftovers of a wielder's core. Like with any other magical being, a wielder's core holds the basis and energy from which to draw their powers. Like a witch's hair or a summoner's dominant eye.

"I'm gonna go scout the area," Doc teleported back out of the hole and walked toward the shade of a nearby tree, disappearing.

"Okay, how do we find your friend?" I asked Sara.

"We use this spell he taught me," she said, matter-of-factly.

"What kind?" said Doc as he was back from doing a thorough survey of the area to find nothing.

"The ability to teleport anywhere I want."

My eyebrow rose. "So, this guy might actually be worth looking into."

"See." she pointed a couple dozen feet from where she was standing. "I can teleport myself anywhere I've already been. Watch." Her body began to vibrate violently then she vanished.

"Oh," said Caroline in surprise. Sara had always been considered out of her element when it came to teleportation spells, and this one seemed particularly high-level. She reappeared where she was pointing a moment later. Again, shaking violently.

"With enough time, concentration, and a strong memory of where I've been, I can go almost anywhere." She smiled.

"Nice!" I said, giving her a thumbs up.

"Yep, I can do that now!" She smiled proudly. "Now grab hold of me."

Carona approached Sara with her hand out. "What do you mean by that?" she asked.

"You know, grab... my shirt or my hand or something so, when I go, you'll go too."

"By the way, what's your friend's name? We need to know who we're looking for."

"Oh, Graven."

"Does he go by anything else?"

"No, just that. He's not a hunter, so he doesn't need another name. He's more like a night watch."

I placed my hand on Sara's shoulder. "Given how America's not all that against hunters like us, I'm not surprised."

A moment or so later, we were holding onto her clothes, hands, and hair.

"Is everybody holding on?" asked Sara.

"Yep," I said, "With two hands for safety."

"Hey uh, Sara, have you done this before with this many people holding this much stuff?" asked Carona, nervously.

"Nope," she said matter-of-factly. Before any of us could let go, we teleported.

Everything, even the air began vibrating and then all our surroundings vanished.

4-Big Apple

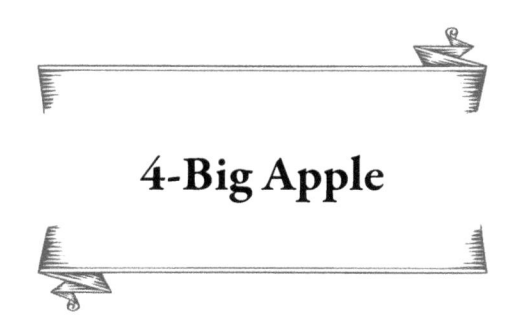

Scenery vibrated violently into view. We seemed to be in an alley or parking lot. There were a few cars here and there, and it seemed ancient. The buildings looked dark and desolate as if they were empty in the night.

"Is this where he stays?" Doc scanned our surroundings repeatedly to gain his bearings.

"Yep, he lives near Central Park because there's a crime group that operates near there. They like to summon stuff and cause chaos to distract the police from their other crimes. It's part of his job."

"Speaking of crimes and summons." Doc was looking toward what seemed to be Central Park in the distance. "I can sense something big that was just summoned. Probably a colossus class."

"How strong do you think it is?" I smiled, ready to jump.

"I put it at about four."

"You look for the summoner, I'll see what kind of summon it is. That okay with you, Doc?" I looked back at him, and he nodded in agreement.

I leaped into the air and summoned my sword. It burst into flames and I stood on it as it carried me further into the air. Hovering just past the buildings surrounding Central Park, I saw a huge creature standing in the middle of the park, it towered over trees and some buildings. It was dark, but I could see it had an alligator snout with oversized k9 teeth, beady red eyes, and long hair. It seemed greenish, the skin and the hair. I hovered over the creature's head. "Hey ugly!"

It looked up after what I said with a grunt when, with the sound of clashing metal, a purple orb of what seemed to be gravitational energy appeared around the monster's head. I felt tremendous pressure coming from it as if it was trying to pull me into it as one of its intended targets along with the surrounding air. The wind picked up as the gravitational field shrank and increased in pressure, pulling harder. My stubbornness kept me in the same position despite the danger of being dragged in. The orb imploded, swallowing the entire head of the beast then, came the body. The scaly, slimy, oozing body, followed into the resulting black hole where it vanished. I wasted some energy levitating myself away from the volatile reaction to stay at the same distance.

An upbeat male voice pierced the wind. "That makes fifteen."

"Fifteen?" I said without thinking.

"Yeah fifteen," he responded.

I looked up. He was sitting on a rather large wielder sword. It was the same size as me; about six feet from end to end, a foot from side to side. He was looking down at me in a purple half-mask and a form-fitting jumpsuit, purple as well. He looked like a ninja.

"That's a pretty hefty sword," I said through the wind.

"So, do you happen to know who summoned that giant, or are you just a thrill seeker with a death wish?"

"I'd say I have a death wish but you were just showing off, right?"

He folded his arms. "I don't need to show off."

"Alright, mister ninja." I scoffed. "Not showing off. If you weren't showing off, we wouldn't be having this conversation." I opened my palm with a fireball between my fingers before extinguishing it with a fist. "Unless you want to really show off."

"You know what? Maybe I'll take you up on that." He and his sword disappeared in a gust of wind. He did a good job hiding his presence and I could barely follow it.

"Here he comes." I crouched down and reached for the handle of my sword.

His presence stopped next to me and I swiped my blade from under my feet in that direction. Our blades collided with a shockwave as if we were both on the assault. His blade was flat against his back to absorb my strike as if he saw it coming. He turned and faced me while I slid back on my feet from the collision as a translucent purple surface materialized below us. It felt like gravity magic in how it pulled me down ever so slightly.

I leaned back and cast 'transit gale', melding with the wind. Following its flow, I teleported behind him and struck at him with my sword.

With a buzz, he was gone in a flash of light.

"Whoa," I said. He was so fast it was like he wasn't even there. I had ruled out the possibility of him using a light spell because it didn't feel like magic was all it was since there was no trail to follow.

I felt his presence again and our blades collided as I swiped mine upward in an arc, both attacking and defending. He appeared above me, falling with his blade pointed down.

The force of his fall made me slide back, fall, and roll on my back, landing on my feet. I needed to either predict his movements or keep him in place somehow. Given the ground we were moving on was made by him, keeping him in place was impossible.

"*Whirlwind.*" I cast the spell and the wind already swirling around us picked up speed as it gained a green hue.

The guy seemed like he was leaning into the wind to teleport, but he seemed to misunderstand that I wasn't just taking advantage of the wind's presence like he was. I was in my element.

"*Turbulence*." This second spell disrupted the airflow, creating an unstable environment. Where he was would have been hard to breathe, let alone move into the wind itself.

Instead of melding into the wind, it bounced him around, but he didn't lose his footing. The ground he made beneath our feet probably helped him keep his balance. He pivoted around with his sword and slashed at the turbulent winds surrounding him, splitting the green hue and allowing himself space.

In the meantime, I created a 'fireball' in my hand and tossed it at him. In response, he continued his turn and split my fireball sideways. It seemed like he was content of fighting defensively if he couldn't be elusive.

I readied myself to rush forward and close the distance, but he raised his sword. I felt like I could reach him before he brought it down, but I had a feeling that wasn't a good idea.

He slammed his sword down sideways and I dodged to the side. The air in a line in front of him seemed to vanish and the resulting rush of air to fill the space pulled me back in. It didn't seem like a vacuum, more like 'compression'. He tried to squish me.

Two could play that game. I cast 'air pressure' downward, keeping the air compressed beneath my feet and giving it a slight green hue. At the same time, the guy vanished into the darkness of the night.

I waited for a brief moment before a rush of energy came up from below me. It felt threatening, but I couldn't tell in what way immediately. The moment I moved my foot, I found it was stuck in place. Even so, I continued to wait. He was going to approach soon.

I felt something shifting behind me, so I crossed my legs and turned with my blade pointed downward. As soon as it made contact with something, I dropped my sword and grabbed his with both hands. I then pulled it closer, using the flat of my blade as a buffer between me and the sharp edge.

The guy tried to wrestle his sword back, but I leveraged the gravity keeping my feet in place to pull him to the front of me. Next, I let go of the sword and released my 'air pressure' spell.

The release caused a pressure wave out from the origin. While I was rooted in place, the guy wasn't. He was flung upward.

"*Transit gale*." I was whisked away by the wind and teleported so I was behind him. I knew he could tell I was there and he seemed to wait for my next move. In that case, I dismissed my sword and locked my arms around him before rotating downward head-first. "*Bomb cyclone*."

We were surrounded by a green vortex that sped up both our rotation and our descent until we met the translucent purple surface beneath us. I let go just before impact and landed on my feet.

Before I even touched down, the guy was gone. In his stead, was a cluster of black balls scattered around like mines. Like mines, they exploded in a display of light and sound.

To do something so quickly and expertly, the guy had to have been completely unphased by the impact. With that in mind, I decided to hit him harder myself. I dual-cast 'whirlwind' and 'turbulence' around myself to deflect any incoming attacks and alert me of anything that got close while I was blinded.

It wasn't long before the volatile vortex was disturbed. My instinct told me to dash straight in the opposite direction of the disturbance and I followed it unquestioningly.

I passed through the vortex with my eyes closed and leaned to the right, away from something that came to meet me. Assuming it was what it felt like, I summoned my sword and swiped it upward. I heard the sound of blades clashing as I launched something upward. Immediately after, I threw my foot forward. I felt my foot whiff, but I could sense the guy trying to disengage and put distance between us.

While my eyes were still adjusting, I raised my hand into the air and dual-cast 'light ball' and 'explosive ball'. I cast them both to be large enough to cover my subsequent approach. The ball of light was wrapped in the volatile orb of wind as they rotated in unison before I tossed them.

Casting 'tailwind', I launched myself forward behind it, but before I could reach the guy, he got blasted away by my spells.

It looked like he tried to cut it the same way he did the rest, but miscalculated, resulting in an unexpected reaction. Given the size of the ball and that I hadn't used any explosive spells before then, it made sense. He flew fast and the gravitational force that he was using to keep us in the air started fading.

"Uh oh." His spell unraveling told me the unexpected explosion knocked him out. Taking advantage of my boost in speed, I extended my dash forward to catch him. Even so, he was out of my reach. "***Transit gale***." I teleported over and caught him before his spell unraveled completely and we started falling. I cast 'levitate' to slow our descent and land safely.

At about twenty yards from the ground, a flutter of pink and gold colors swirled upward to meet us. After the colors engulfed us, they vanished with the guy.

Returning back to where I came, I found Doc waiting for me leaning against a concrete wall next to an open door with stairs that lead down. Nobody else was there.

I asked, "Everybody down there?"

"Yep." He leaned away from the wall. "Sara's pissed."

"So, was that who I thought?"

He scoffed, stifling a giggle. "Oh, how the tables turn."

"Yeah, whatever." I headed down followed by Doc.

Down below was a rather spacious underground apartment. The stone-colored walls would make an eerie backdrop in the dark and the one small light overhead barely made a dent in the darkness. The guy was lying on a steel spring mattress, but my attention was taken by Sara who was tending to him.

When she saw me, a pink aura surrounded her entire body. This only happened when she released an excess amount of energy or if provoked by high emotion. There was a sigil of a gold scorpion with pink butterfly wings on her chest that controlled her size, but anger was more than enough to override it. She would grow to her proper size but would soon revert unless she purposely transformed, and she would stay that way until she'd conceal her energy again. Her clothes were also enchanted to grow and shrink with her.

She looked me in the eye with balled fists and said, "Do you know who that was?"

"Would you hit me if I said, 'yes' or 'no'?"

"I'm gonna hit you regardless!" Mid-sentence, she threw a punch and it landed on my chest, close to my face. "That's Graven."

"Hey, don't be mad at me-"

"I'm mad at *both* of you. She stamped her foot."

"Oh, well, I kinda guessed who he was."

She sighed, exasperatedly. "And I'm sure he guessed who you were... Fighting for no reason."

I sighed and shrugged.

"Not going to apologize for blowing him up?"

"Can't apologize that he didn't stop himself from blowing up. A real fighter would just be annoyed."

Sara simply looked at me with a face of annoyance.

"So, you are mad," said Graven from under his covers.

"Disappointed." Sara hoped to his side. "Got yourself blown up. Now what?"

Graven sat up. "It's not every day I get a fight that's not to the death, you know? Better to get knocked out than killed."

"Was pretty fun, though, right?" I said, to a disappointed look from Sara.

She shook her head. "Shut up." She breathed the words so fast, it was as if she didn't speak, to begin with

I couldn't help but chuckle.

Graven popped his shoulder and stood beside the bed. "Well, you guys are here for something. If Sara's told me anything, it means there's a good reason. Anything I can help with?"

"We're looking for someone," said Doc. "But first, I'm more curious about how you two met. Now's a good time to tell us about it."

Off in a nearby chair, Carona nodded in agreement.

"Fair enough," said Graven. "I know a lot about you guys. I guess it's best you know a thing or two about me."

5-Grave

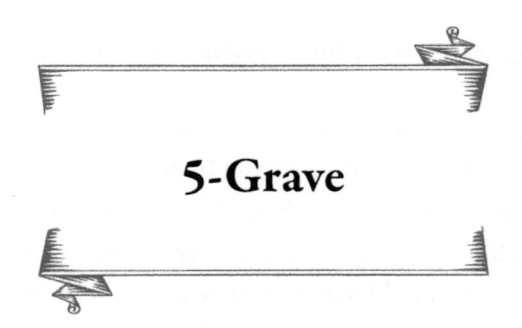

[Graven Lockhart]

It had been years since I had been back in my home country. You'd think that returning would give me a sense of nostalgia, but coming back held nothing for me but headaches. The first sign things weren't going to go so well was transport. None of the magical transportation routes to Japan worked correctly. The Yokai no Meiji government sent out a request to all of their affiliates for help in solving the matter. The Humanitarian Association of Magic was one such affiliate, and they sent me from our American branch in New York to the one housed in Tokyo to help.

Since a small boat through enchanted waters or a hike in an enchanted forest was out of the question, I came by plane from New York to California to Hawaii to Japan. The trip wasn't particularly exhausting, but I also couldn't hide away in the shadows like I usually did. This was the most usage my passport had ever seen.

After getting off the plane in Haneda, I wasted no time heading up the road on foot. A few minutes into my trek, a black van pulled up beside me. I continued walking as if nothing was happening and the van kept pace. I could feel someone glaring at me through the tinted windows as they continued alongside me.

This continued until I heard a muffled voice yelling, "Are you that dense? Stop walking!" I stopped when I heard the voice and the rear passenger door swung open aggressively. "Get in." Inside the car sat Kirara. Her face was scrunched up under the black bandanna she had wrapped around her head. She was displeased.

I said, "If you wanted me to get in, you could have rolled down the window, said something, or, I don't know... Not drive up like you're trying to kidnap me?"

She rolled her eyes and scooted over to make space. I got in and closed the door, then the car started moving again.

"So, how are you doing?" Kirara leaned onto my shoulder and turned slightly, shifting her cleavage into my line of sight. She had her bright red jacket zipped open just enough to entice, but not too loose to let anything slip.

"We're on official business, can you stop with the games?"

"Oh, foo... You're no fun." She sat back and zipped her jacket up.

"So, what's the situation?"

"The same as you've heard. The magical transport into the country is shot, and nobody knows why. Some think it's a natural phenomenon, others think it's an angry god, and some think sabotage."

"What angle are we coming from?"

"We find the problem and solve it, that's all."

"If that's the case, why am I here?"

"In case the problem turns out to be human."

"Then, why isn't Vincent here?"

"Because I asked for you personally." She giggled.

"And why is that?"

"I thought you might miss your home a bit."

"What gave you that idea?"

"You haven't been back in far too long. Don't you have family here?"

"No."

With a smile, she said, "You're a terrible liar, you know that? Especially when you don't have your mask on."

"It's not just a mask."

"It never was, was it?" Her smile died.

The rest of the ride was silent.

We arrived at a tall, gray apartment building and entered a service elevator down to the basement.

"Welcome back to the H.A.M Tokyo branch. Make yourself at home," said Kirara, leading me out of the elevator and down one of the gray hallways. "Everything is still in the same place as before so you shouldn't have any problem finding anything, but if you need any help, don't hesitate to call or find me."

We continued down two more halls before coming to a meeting room. The door was open and inside was a steel round table surrounded by chairs and a large monitor on two opposite walls. Five of the twelve seats were already filled with people I don't care to name. None of them were of any importance and were only there for formality.

I felt a new presence approach behind me, and I stepped into the room. I sat silently in the chair farthest from the door. The presence followed me and as soon as I was seated, a hand landed on my shoulder.

"Nice to see you again, Graven," said Mame, the man responsible for putting together the meeting and the head of the H.A.M Japanese branch. His labored voice fell on deaf ears. "Are you coming back for good this time?"

When I didn't respond, he removed his hand and sat down.

Once most of the seats were filled, the meeting began and proceeded. It turned out that the government also asked for help from independent contractors I'd have to look out for. If it was a human problem we were dealing with, any of them could be an enemy.

Including myself, the H.A.M. called for five people from other branches for assistance. Since the Japanese branch was considered a neutral party above all else, it fell to the rest of us to act without help if the problem we faced was human. They could only afford to fly out one person from each branch, and that's why there were so few of us.

When the meeting ended, I was the first to leave, but Kirara caught up with me before the elevator.

"Where do you think you're going?" I was just about to press the up button before she spoke.

"Anywhere but here." I pressed the button, and the doors opened.

"Not without me." She got into the elevator. "I'm in charge of making sure you don't cause any trouble."

"Suit yourself." I stepped in and it took us back up.

In no time, we were back on the streets. I turned toward the parking lot and began walking. Kirara followed. The streets were crawling with crowds of people, bikes, and cars as always.

"What do you plan on doing around the city?"

"Same as always, recon."

"That's just like you."

"This is a mission, not a vacation, and I'm going to act like it."

"So, what? You gonna canvass the entire country checking for anomalies?"

"Not exactly." I walked toward the car that was sitting and waiting. "I'm driving this time."

"That's my car."

"You don't know where we're going." I put my hand out for the key.

"Wherever we're going, I can drive just fine."

"Not from the back seat. It'll take more than a bit of magic and street smarts to get there."

"Sure, whatever." She pressed the button to unlock the car and tossed me the key.

We both got in and I started driving. We drove for just over an hour and through two tolls before arriving at the ruins of Hachioji Castle. What once stood as a great castle and stronghold over four hundred years ago was now nearly empty.

"Here we are," I parked the car and handed Kirara back her keys.

"I could've driven us here."

"You would've taken only back roads and we would've still been on our way."

She scoffed. "You know me too well."

"That, and the spirits don't like waiting." I led the way down the forested path, across the bridge, and up the stone steps into the clearing that once housed a castle. Stones that once stood as a foundation now marked the spot that bore witness to the deaths of many and a memorial to the past.

"A haunted ruin. Are we here to talk to the spirits?"

"Yes, but not the ones you think." I turned north once I reached the perfectly spaced stones on the ground and continued.

"I guess that means we're not visiting Goshudeno Falls." Kirara followed closely.

We penetrated the tree line and went a couple of yards in. There was a single stone with a hole drilled into it between two trees.

"Sesshomaru, I have come for you," I said, standing proudly with folded arms.

"Welcome." A voice came from the stone, and above it appeared the apparition of a masked man cloaked in green. He was slightly transparent and sat atop the stone. "Why is it you seek an audience with me?"

"There is a disturbance in the state of this country. The transportation ley-lines are disrupted. I wonder if you know anything that can be of help to us."

"Hm..." He closed his eyes in thought. "There have been sightings of unsavory folks encroaching upon local fae territory. Rumor has it, they sabotaged the ley-lines for some sort of nefarious purpose. What that may be, I know not."

"Thank you," I said, taking a brief bow.

He returned a bow and said, "So, who might that lady friend of yours be?"

"I'm Kirara, nice to meet you." She stepped from behind me and held her hand out.

"My name is Sesshomaru. The pleasure is mine." He bowed. "I would shake your hand, but I am a ghost, and I would rather conserve my ethereal form."

"I understand." Kirara bowed.

"Is there anything else you would like from me?" His lower body began fading to transparency.

"Do you know who those people are or where they came from?" I asked.

"Unfortunately, no. Any fae or spirit that got close to them was captured, killed, or exorcised. Whoever they are, they are powerful and want complete secrecy. They do, however, seem uniform, like pieces of a larger puzzle making moves on this nation."

"Thank you." I bowed again, and Kirara bowed as well. He bowed to both of us and faded completely.

"Who was that?" asked Kirara as we exited the woods.

"Sesshomaru. Besides what he's told me, I don't know much about him. He was apparently a shinobi from before they had a name. He was both feared and respected as the 'Oni'. Able to slip in and out without ever being noticed, he was the epitome of shinobi."

"If he was a ninja like you say he was, how was he feared? No one would know he was there, right?"

"Right, but unlike most shinobi, his job was in a high societal position as lord of his own domain. He hid in plain sight, and everyone knew his face. The problem arose when the first assassin sent by his enemies managed to slip past his guard."

"What happened?"

"The assassin died mysteriously before they could get close enough to assassinate him. This happened a few times, and he became known as Lord Oni as people believed he forfeited his humanity for such power."

"And in reality, he used magic."

"No. He says that every instance was coincidental, but that makes it even less believable." I stopped walking as we reached our next destination. A river eroded the ground into a rocky waterfall littered with outcroppings lined with cliffs on either side.

"Oh, we're at Goshudeno Falls." Kirara looked down into the base. "Are we going to talk to the spirits here?"

"No, according to Sesshomaru, this used to be a ley-line. There was never much of a magical presence here, and that kept it mostly hidden. This entire forest has a spiritual presence, but since what happened during the raid on Hachioji Castle, the activity has taken attention away from other parts. That made this area obsolete."

"He sure knows a lot."

"He was here as a ghost long before the castle. Before humans and yokai became nearly indistinguishable. When the stories of legend were current history." I jumped down the cliff to the rocky base of the waterfall.

"That far back?" Kirara jumped in as well.

"Before this river was a waterfall."

"If he's been a ghost that long, wouldn't he be something other than a ghost by now?"

"Normally, yeah. Most of the stories I've heard about this place confirm that he's been here since prehistory. There are too many mysteries surrounding him to shake a stick at, but he's not why we're here." Reaching a deeper spot where water had pooled in the side, I reached out both of my hands and said, "*I call for the passage of the living, dead, and beyond. The doorway of Eight Princes.*"

There was a pause as if time had stopped, followed by an unidentifiable pull toward the deeper part of the river. I was being drawn in by the spiritual presence of a now-open portal. There was no visible difference in our surroundings aside from faint rippling in the air over the water's surface.

"Is it working?" Kirara stepped closer to the portal. Having been born with magic, she never learned to sense spiritual energy, so it was understandable that she couldn't tell what was happening.

"There's a corresponding point in Mount Ibuki near Nagoya. Step in and see if it takes you there," I said, looking at her and the portal.

She looked around awkwardly, sighed, and said, "Alright, don't do anything stupid if this works."

"I won't," I said, gesturing toward the open portal.

"I'll be back," she said, as she stepped forward before disappearing into nothingness. I snapped my fingers eight times in succession, causing the portal to close.

"Now, I can get to business." I reached my hand to the top of my head and pulled down nothing. My mask appeared on my face as I summoned it. Next, I pulled the collar of my purple shirt, and it lengthened out as it shrank to fit my form while my pants did the same. I jumped back up the short cliff I came from.

There were three of them equally spaced apart and hiding invisibly between the trees. I could feel them. Despite being trained to hide their bloodlust; it was easy to notice.

"I'm going to give a verbal warning first. Show yourselves or I'll consider you hostile."

I waited a minute to no response.

"Alright, your choice." I picked up a nearby stone, threw it at a tree, and it bounced off before crashing behind another tree with a thud.

Soon after, a man appeared and fell from behind the tree. He wore an orange-collared uniform and a red tie. The rock hit him square in the head and knocked him out. Before he could hit the ground, another one started moving.

Their presence disappeared and reappeared behind me before a small explosion took place there. They teleported into a trap of explosive caltrops I set when I came back up. A woman screamed as it launched her off the cliff behind me. Her scream cut off as she landed far below.

The last person hurried to their fallen comrade, and the guy I rendered unconscious flashed bright blue. When this happened, their invisibility dropped and a small androgynous person in a blue uniform and red tie appeared crouched next to the man in orange. They had a badge of a silver queen on their right shoulder.

The man awoke before standing and as he stood, the badge on his chest of a silver rook became visible. He reached out his hand, and a chain of orange crystals linked to form a whip appeared in his hand, a wielder's weapon.

I took a step forward, and the guy flicked his whip at me. As the tip ripped through the air, the ground rose to meet it.

It reached me quickly, but before it could snap back, I caught it before giving a sharp yank.

He didn't budge, but now he was struggling to keep his weapon in his hand. He reached his other hand toward the ground, and I yanked the whip again, forcing him to re-grip the handle with both hands. The healer behind him seemed to have no idea what to do.

We stayed in this stalemate for nearly a minute before I heard the rushing of wind above me. I moved to the side, away from the stalagmites made by the whip in my hand. Less than a second later, a purple lance with a blade shaped like a curved diamond crashed into the ground next to me. The ground began melting and stone crumbled into the ravine.

This was the person I was waiting for. On missions, they would always split into four-man teams. Now, all of this team was present.

The woman on top of the lance didn't wear a uniform and instead wore a black half-jacket over a purple sports bra with matching sweatpants and fingerless gloves. She had a gold knight badge on her right glove. Her rank was much higher than the rest, she was the leader.

"*Pull*." I cast the spell and the man still holding his whip left the ground and spiraled toward us out of control. Once he came within reach, I released my grip on the whip and kicked him into the lance, knocking it off balance.

The woman leaned with her lance, swung it around at me, and I dodged. The action left her in mid-air, so I grabbed the pole of her weapon and swung her over the precipice before letting go. She didn't fall and instead flew toward me. I dodged her lance again, and this time landed a headbutt. Her eyes went blank as blood ran down her forehead and she fell back to join her teammate below.

The man in orange found his footing and tapped the ground with the tip of his whip. "*Crystal Forest*." The spell he cast made the ground shiver, and opaque crystal stalagmites sprung awkwardly from the ground surrounding me. He whipped his weapon at me again, and I caught it again. This time, I had no choice but to. "Dion!" The man called, and the person in blue put their hands together as if in prayer while glowing blue. In less than a second, they opened their hands and a blue ball of magic appeared between them before becoming a volatile blast of energy heading straight for me.

I yanked hard against the whip, and the man pulled back. When he did, I jumped, and he pulled me directly to him. I flew at him with my foot extended at his face in a kick. He dodged it but not the elbow, following closely behind it as I passed over his head.

He rocked backward and almost fell, but he caught himself. He turned around and attempted to strike me, but I ducked and jumped to headbutt his chin before hopping up and gripping both sides of his head while guiding my knee into his forehead. He staggered back until I gave a decisive kick to the head that knocked him over the edge.

Now, the only one left was the one in blue. They were panting hard on the ground. Apparently, the attack spell they cast took all of their energy. As I approached, they tried sheepishly to crawl away.

I crouched down next to them and said, "Mind telling me what you guys are doing here?"

"No... You're the enemy," they said, between bated breaths.

I looked back at the orange crystals they destroyed with the blast. "Children shouldn't be on a battlefield." I grabbed them by their collar, and they failed to struggle.

"Go ahead and kill me like you did everyone else." They stared daggers at me with sharp, yet teary eyes.

I hoisted them onto my shoulder and cast 'shadow binding'. Seven purple rings appeared around their body and tightened to immobilize them.

Turning back to the waterfall, I walked back to the ledge. Looking over the side, I was greeted with high-pitched screaming from over my shoulder. I hopped down, and the screaming reached a peak. I landed, and they went silent by passing out.

After checking each body, I walked up to the closed portal and re-opened it. Kirara fell through while yelling something about sea lions and penguins. It sounded threatening. Landing in the water, she splashed around a bit and stood.

Once she spotted me, she said, "What was that all abo-" She noticed the three bodies behind me and the one over my shoulder. "What happened here?"

"This is our 'human' problem," I said.

"Are they...?"

"They're from C.H.E.S.S. Got the badges to prove it." I turned the one on my shoulder to show the badge on their shoulder.

"Not that..." She looked at the heap of bodies and looked back at me. "Are they dead?"

I gestured to the woman in a red uniform and a silver pawn badge on her chest. "She doesn't have a pulse. If she does, I can't find it." Next, I gestured to the man in orange. "His neck is broken, but he might survive." Finally, I gestured to the woman in purple. "She won't walk this off so easily, but she's alive as well."

"Well, what about... " She inspected the one on my shoulder. "That... One?"

"They're just unconscious." I reached my hand out toward the three in the stream and they started glowing purple. Raising my hand, I lifted them up and back to where they all fell from. I looked back at Kirara and said, "Follow my lead." She quickly nodded despite the worried expression on her face.

I cast both 'silence' and 'invisibility' on the kid and called ambulances for the three near the waterfall. I sat in the backseat with the kid and Kirara drove us back to HQ.

The invisibility wore off as we entered the city. The kid was awake. They were looking down and not struggling. I dispelled the silence and their jaw dropped slightly before closing up again.

"Dion, right?" My words seemed to alarm them as they jumped slightly, then turned to face the window. "Dion, I'm going to ask you one question. Do you know what's happening here?"

They stayed silent.

I snapped my fingers, and the binds around Dion disappeared. They seemed to panic momentarily with a sharp gasp and a few darting eye movements before folding their arms and turning farther toward the window.

"You don't have to talk if you don't want to. We're taking you to a homeless youth center."

"I'm not a kid." The small person looked at me and spoke.

"What are you, like eleven, twelve?" I analyzed them.

"Whatever, I'm old enough," they mumbled, looking around, nervously.

"You're right, you are old enough," I said, "Anyone who enters the battlefield is an adult. It's all life-or-death so we're taking you where we take adults."

"Are you sure?" Kirara voiced her concern.

"Adults get interrogated." As the words left my mouth, I could see fear building on Dion's face before turning and looking back out the window.

It took around the same amount of time to get back as it did getting there. Dion didn't struggle or protest as we guided them into the building and down the elevator. It took a little over an hour to get the paperwork in order. The whole time, they confined Dion to a small room with two chairs and a table.

I entered the room alone and slammed a folder full of papers on the table before taking the only other seat.

Dion spoke. "I don't know anything. This was only my first mission... I was just told to be support."

"Ok." I stood and turned toward the door.

"Wait... That's it?"

"For now." I closed the door behind me.

"I see what you did," said Kirara. She was waiting outside the room. "What's in that folder?"

"The truth." I leaned against the door and we both remained silent.

Since it was an impromptu interrogation room, there was no two-way glass. Instead, I had to rely on my other senses to determine what was happening inside the room. Ten minutes passed, and I heard the soft rustling of paper from inside. They opened the folder. I waited around five more minutes and went back in.

They were staring at a piece of paper from near the middle of the pile. Tears were streaming down their face and their expression was undeniably sad.

"What is this...?" They held back a sniffle.

"That is the report on the incident that took your parents two years ago. The complete report. It's what C.H.E.S.S. never bothered to show you. You're smart, I'm sure you can figure out what really happened."

"How- how did... but this..." They stuttered.

"Your teammate used your real name instead of your codename and because of that, I was able to track down some information. That led me to what you're holding in your hand right now." I sat at the table.

"No, you- you faked this..." The look in their eyes said they didn't believe themselves.

"This is what they do to get vulnerable new recruits. Then they train them to do the same to others." I spoke from experience.

Dion wiped their eyes. "A- alright... I'll talk, I don't- I don't care anymore..." The way they spoke told me there was more evidence than what I showed them and they were already doubting the organization.

After a long conversation, the kid was taken to a shelter to be housed until everything calmed down.

Hours passed, and night approached rapidly. Since we identified the problem, all the affiliates that they called were scattered. They sent me to the city oceanfront where I'd sit and wait for the next phase to begin.

Night fell and soon I noticed something strange about the water. Something was odd about how the waves rippled. It was as if the natural mana was reacting to something. I followed the direction the ripples were going, and it didn't seem to lead anywhere until I detected a presence approaching rapidly. The sheer maliciousness nearly frightened me until I realized I'd felt this before.

Preparing myself for combat, I walked into a nearby park and waited for my would-be assailant to arrive. His presence disappeared and reappeared above me, so I hopped forward to avoid the attack from above. The sound of metal on concrete scared away a group of cats nearby. I turned around to face my opponent.

He looked to be the typical show-off type though, one would be wise to believe otherwise. Loose black pants, a pink and black striped scarf, and no shirt. Those are his trademarks. In his hands sat a broad sword. It was almost a meter wide, over two meters long, and jagged along the rounded tip and down the sides.

"Hey, Solo. Haven't seen you in a while," I said, summoning my sword and standing it next to me.

"Grave." He lifted his blade and pointed it squarely at me.

"Where's the rest of your team? After what happened last time, I thought they'd keep a better leash on you."

He huffed and charged as his sword began glowing pink. Despite him being a strong esper, he only ever used his psychic ability to enhance his body and increase the cutting power of his weapon. His magic also never had a defined element, but he never used it to his advantage.

I took a wide stance and pretended to swing my blade down as he came closer. Instead, I created an illusion and left an image of myself then, I cast 'shadow skip' and faded into the darkness.

Traveling through the shadows, I swerved behind him and launched a dagger from my position before retreating farther away.

He cut the illusion in half and barely dodged the attack as it soared by his face. I finished the spell and teleported away from him in the direction he came from.

I hopped out of the shadow of a fan on a building a few blocks away and continued traveling by rooftop. I traced a pattern on my chest and my clothes turned from purple to dark blue as I continued on my way.

Nearly a minute passed and then I felt Solo's presence again. He was approaching faster than before. I changed my color to match the gray of the apartment roof I was on and crouched down; staying calm to conceal my presence.

I was expecting him to look for someone cloaked in invisibility and panic when he couldn't find me and go back to his team, showing me the way. Instead, he landed on a roof near the end of the block.

"I know you, you're still here." I could hear him speak despite him being so far away through telepathy. "*Ethereal cell.*" It seemed that he was using his telepathy by accident as I heard him cast his spell. What looked like pink webs appeared in the sky and spread down to the ground in less than a second as if it was a giant cage.

At that moment, someone happened upon us, running at high speeds down the street. They entered the range of the spell as it was being cast and hit the other side as it came down. A small girl landed on her back and stood, dramatically transforming into a larger version of herself. She stood, cloaked in a dark turtleneck and matching pants with her hair pulled back in a long ponytail.

Both of our attention fell on her. Solo went invisible and I got a bad feeling.

6-Faery

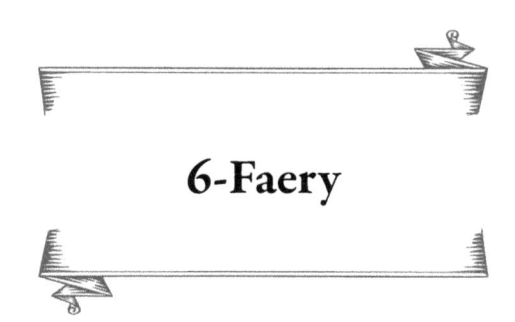

[Scarlett Hunt]

Leuna; codenamed 'Moon', Caroline; codenamed 'Blue', and I went off to Japan on a call from the Yokai no Meiji. They had been having trouble with their transportation into the country and resorted to calling corpse hunters to help solve the problem. Doc, Krow, and Ariel were on a mission when we got the call, and Carona, having been retired for years, stayed home.

Being corpse hunters, we had many private avenues open for transportation, but none were considered official, so we took a long route. We had to enter the enchanted forest behind our house, and we were transported to a waypoint in west China. We continued to another one on the outskirts of Wuhan then, one that took us to Seoul in Korea. The last one from there took us to Hallyeohaesang National Park in Geoje. This was as far as the teleport waypoints could take us.

We continued by casting 'flight' and maintaining the spell until we reached land. Doing so, we crept through the darkness of night east. We landed on Tsushima where we continued quickly to the other side of the island and sped back into the sky. It was tiring, but it made us stronger in the long run. It was also the cheapest way to get there. This continued until we reached the mainland. It took more than a night, so we rested during the day before continuing our journey. It was two nights of constant travel by air over water, and on the third night, we traveled on land by foot. Eventually, we came to our destination, Tokyo.

The city felt busy, even though not many people were around when we came. There was a shallow breeze coming off the sea nearby, and the sky saw few clouds. Vibrant lights and lively sounds escaped the distant center of the city.

"Now, we just have to get to our clients." Leuna was looking between the buildings and checking our location on her phone. "It should be straight ahead by Tokyo Tower."

"We should get going, then." I went ahead and my sisters followed.

With an unusually whimsical air about her, Caroline made an unusual suggestion. "In that case, let's make this a race." She was usually the one to take suggestions. This time, she was giving one.

"Just fine with me," said Leuna. She seemed happy to oblige.

"In that case, let's go!" I said, ready to run.

We split up and went separate ways. Caroline took a route near the water because she liked the feel of the watery mist on her skin and being engulfed in a serene-like manner. Leuna went high on the buildings because she liked the wind in her hair and the way it tunes out all sound. Despite my height, speed was my strength, so I took the sidewalk off the mostly empty street. I was sprinting along and avoiding random bystanders and cars. What I was doing was probably illegal, but it was fun.

I reached an oddly empty street lined with apartments when I bounced back and landed on my butt.

"Oww!" I ran into some sort of invisible wall, face first and hard. First, I was hurt, then I was angry. Within a second, I involuntarily transformed. It would take them a while to notice that I fell behind since I was too far away from them. "Damn it, what the hell?" I took a moment to look around and noticed a spider-web-like pattern in the air in front of me.

A wave of danger hit me as if someone was holding a knife to my throat. A mysterious man in a slim gray outfit and a mask grabbed me before jumping out of the way. There was an explosion where I was standing less than a second later.

On contact, I could feel his emotions rushing through me. Despite his calm, there was unease, panic, and fear.

I landed on top of him and rolled off quickly to stand. He stood as well, summoning his sword with fear building in his heart.

"Calm down, fear won't get you anywhere," I said, summoning my own sword. My blade was a short sword, and the sides of the hilt curved back in to make handguards. The blade had a gold, pink, and green hue from the back edge to the front.

"Fear?" He held his sword ready.

"It's a magic trait. I can feel people's emotions."

"Alright." As he spoke, the fear was subsiding, only to be replaced with worry.

"I'm guessing you didn't just try to blow me up?"

"He's nearby."

I pulled out my phone and ran magic through it while double-tapping the call button, sending a distress signal.

"Heads up." Said the man. "Your allies might not get that message." As he said that, what looked like a pink translucent hexagon surrounded by a ring of pink crystals appeared next to the man, a 'magic missile'. It almost made contact, but he noticed it in time and jumped away. Before I knew it, he had me under his arm as well.

"I can dodge on my own," I said, folding my arms.

"Sorry." He let me go, and I stood away from him.

Five more magic missiles appeared around us, and it became a minefield. The man pulled a dagger from between the folds of his clothes and tossed it barely a foot above his head. When he did, another magic missile appeared and they nearly collided. He looked at me and I nodded, preparing to act.

The man opened his palm, and purple energy gathered into an orb above his palm. At that moment, a jagged sword comparable in size to his appeared, and flew at the man. The man reacted, clashing with the blade using his own. His orb was forced to disperse.

He swiped the sword away, and another magic missile appeared before colliding with the blade, causing a chain reaction of explosions.

As soon as I saw it, I cast 'horizon', creating a translucent bubble around myself that changed from pink to gold from the base in a wave pattern. The explosion caused a nearby car to flip down the road and land upside down. My shield cracked and fell to shambles after the first few explosions, and I was bounced around by the rest.

I landed on the stairs of an apartment and had trouble standing. "So much for dodging," I said, struggling to my feet while casting 'alleviate' to recover any injuries I had yet to feel.

The man next to me was now using his sword as a crutch. He placed his hand on his chest, and he began glowing a dim purple before leaning off it.

"Graven, Graven, Graven." A shirtless man appeared on the roof of one of the buildings, holding the sword that caused the explosion. "You just don't like dying, do you?" He jumped from the building and landed a couple of yards in front of us. "You did a good job surviving too, girl." It sounded like he was commending my survival, but it felt like he was laughing at my existence.

"I don't die easy," said the man called Graven.

The shirtless man lifted his blade toward Graven's chest and tried to pierce him with it. Instead, he missed as his target ducked to the side and brought his own sword around. The shirtless man quickly turned in the opposite direction and swiped backward, causing the blades to clash.

Locating my target between the two, cast 'needle shot' and launched golden needles the size of daggers from my open my palm. Both the shirtless man and Graven moved away from my attack, which flew until it bounced off the barrier surrounding us.

Graven struck at the man and locked him in sword combat. Since both of their blades were so large, they moved kind of slowly aside for the spells they cast between. Whenever there was an opening, I would attack, and the man would either disengage to dodge or block it with either a spell or his sword. This put the fight in our favor but only slightly as Graven also dodged my attacks seemingly on instinct.

The battle dragged on and both of them fought tirelessly, but Graven began slowing down. His spells also seemed less potent. He backed off and his sword started glowing as the blade grew much wider, but only the edge, resulting in a guillotine shape. The ends of the guard also reached out to encompass the reach of the blade.

"Oh, now you decide to get serious," said the man. He held out his blade and it widened by about half a foot and became rectangular with just the far edge being jagged. All the while, he used the flat of his weapon to block my incoming projectiles.

They began clashing back and forth and I was barely any help at this time. Despite their blades getting bigger, they were moving too fast for me to get a clean shot in the noiseless street. Even if I was sure Graven would move out of the way, I couldn't guarantee it.

As they fought, I noticed the sky and our surroundings began to go dark. On top of that, there was a translucent purple floating platform that lifted them probably ten feet from the ground.

They were moving as if dancing. One twirl, two leaps, three flips. It was as if they were ballet dancers in deadly action; like they knew each other so well that they couldn't fight conventionally. Still trying to keep up, I was drawn in, to the point that I couldn't see that Graven began to lose his balance and fall behind in the battle. It seemed his wounds were reopening.

"Lady!" Graven called out to me.

His words sounded unnaturally clear. I snapped out of it, shook my head, stopped my distant stare, and looked closely.

Graven was sliding back on his feet. He then fell, still sliding. Casually, the man threw a pink ball of energy and it exploded; sending Graven yards away over buildings until he crashed into the barrier, breaking it.

I went for it. The man was watching Graven fly away as a pink explosion enveloped him. So, while he was distracted, I cast 'speed', allowing me to move twice as fast as normal. The magical floor beneath the man began to fade away and he was floating down but didn't seem to notice. He looked like he was busy planning his next move.

I took my chance to strike. As I got closer, I felt his aura hit me. It felt like I just hit the back of a sturdy dresser. That energy changed something in me, but I wasn't sure what.

As I closed the distance, the man took notice and moved his sword toward me sideways. Not only did he block my strike, but he also knocked me onto my butt again.

"Run away or I'll kill you," he said, threateningly.

"Let's see you try," I said, annoyed.

"Okay. You asked for it," He carried his sword into the air, giving me just enough time to almost get up before his sword came crashing down in a flash of light and energy. The power from the blow sent me flying into a street lamp. What I remember from there was a little fuzzy, but not too fuzzy to remember.

I got up slowly. I felt like it was a dream, but I knew it wasn't. The blade in my hand began to glow and change. It lengthened and curved, and the handle had a wider grip with greater length.

I slipped into a deeper unconsciousness, and it felt like I was watching a dream instead of being in one. Not only did my weapon change, but my body did too. I could feel it. My hair grew, my ears seemed to become pointed, and I could also feel my eyes change.

I moved, faster than I thought I normally could, even with a spell. I attacked over and over again. He seemed to keep up with my speed with his freakishly huge sword.

"That sword can block anything," I thought out loud. I jumped back, then ran forward before hopping into the air over him. Turning down to face him, I slashed a cross into the air, and cast "**Checkpoint**." Next, I swift-cast 'blast off' and accelerated down at the man.

My blade rang as it hit the pavement and I looked up to see that he jumped out of the way and that his sword was coming down. It hit the pavement and slashed a hole into the ground and what would have been me.

Reviving at the checkpoint and picking up speed, I continued my assault. He looked up and caught me in the same field of energy that I felt the first time I decided to attack him on my own. He held me there, scanning my mind.

"*Who are you?*" I heard him in the fuzziness. He was talking through telepathy. No matter how hard I tried to think straight, my thoughts still began to wander. I started thinking. About what I was planning to do, how I was planning to do it, and my strengths, as well as my weaknesses. At the very least, I was able to keep my true identity to myself. "*Your neck huh? Well, I'm surprised you leave it open like that.*" He reached out and grabbed something invisible in front of him and my neck tightened. He was choking me.

"No..." I struggled to draw a breath as I realized how little I was already breathing. My vision began to fade.

"**Oracle arrow**!" A bright green arrow raced from behind me. Afterward, more came from the same direction. They all surrounded him and went in at once. This all happened in a split second. "Direct hit!" The voice was familiar.

I fell to the ground and barely caught myself. "Moon." I crawled backward until I was on soft grass.

"Don't worry, we got you," said Caroline, coming to my aid. I could hear them coming toward me, but before they could get to me there was a flash of green, then pink light.

"Stay sharp," said Leuna.

"Yeah..." I coughed.

"**Blade wave**." The man swung his blade and a wave of pink energy ran from the edge and into the air. Caroline was only fast enough to block with her weapon. Leuna dodged upward and it missed her cleanly. Regardless, they both began glowing bright pink. Leuna fell to the ground and Caroline followed soon after being carried into the nearest building by the attack.

Forcing myself back to my feet, I brandished my blade, wavering ever so slightly. The man loomed over me taller than before with a ball of pink energy in his hand.

Trembling, I cast 'faerie star' and dropped my blade as it stabbed into the ground while glowing bright pink. It was followed closely by another light coming from the sky. It was like a shooting star except it raced straight for my target.

Noticing the light, he looked up and swiped at the small meteor as it came for him. I took the opportunity to grab my sword again and rush to strike him down.

Instead of bashing away the falling spell, he struck down at me. It took me by surprise and a hot pain raced down my body as I was flung into a patch of grass. At the same time, Graven came racing in from the side feet-first.

He dropkicked the man in the face from the side who flew down the street, leaving his sword behind. Next, Graven used the flat of his blade to redirect my spell at its intended target, causing the man to bounce into the air and land again from the impact. Graven looked back at me and said, "You alright?"

"Yeah, I jus-" The intense pain reached from my collar to my waist. I leaned on some nearby stairs. "A flesh wound." I pressed my hand onto my wound. "***Alleviate.***" I started glowing gold and the pain receded, but only a little.

Graven looked at the unconscious man. "You done now?"

A voice came from the ground. "Yeah, he's done." He appeared like a shadow from beneath the broken pavement. In a shroud of darkness, I could see a white visor with a black, smokey lens on his face. "Guile."

"What?" said Graven, pointing his blade in the shadow's direction.

"Guile Pain. That's what you wanted to know right?"

"What do you mean?"

"That's my name. I'm frankly surprised we haven't met until now. He always had a way of getting away from the team. This time, though, I had to meet you myself Karasu."

Graven flicked his wrist and released a blade wave from his sword. The full blast seemed to have been redirected without having been interacted with. It hit the fallen blade and knocked it into the air.

"Sorry about that." The shadow teleported a few yards right of the unconscious man, catching the sword. "I don't have time to fight you. I don't really want to, either."

Graven's poise sharpened as he pointed his blade with even more vigor. "Then, what *do* you want?"

"I want to get this one back to HQ before he causes more trouble." He held the shirtless man up by his scarf. "And to let you know that you have people you can trust on the inside." He went as he came. A literal shadow in the night. With his comrade in tow, he left.

Silently, Graven came back and examined my injuries. "Faery," he said, under his breath.

"Yeah..." I could barely get the word out through the pain. My healing spell wasn't doing much. My wound was deeper than I thought and I lost too much blood.

He sighed. "As I thought."

Despite trying my hardest to keep them open, my eyes fell closed.

"What the hell happened to you!?" A striking voice with an English accent stirred my unconscious mind. A gray-haired man was standing in a doorway wearing sunglasses, a long-sleeve black shirt with a blue waxing moon on it, and blue jeans. "We don't see you in a few days and this is how you come back? You're lucky Anna isn't here right now."

"Forget about me. Worry about them." Graven was holding both Caroline and Leuna in his arms while I was over his shoulder.

"Okay, get them inside." He quickly brought us inside the old, rusty apartment building.

"So, you cast 'jump' to get here... That was a dangerous move with your injuries." The Englishman followed close behind.

"Yeah, well, I was on my own. No help from the organization," said Graven, bringing us into an elevator.

From the elevator, we were brought into the closest room down a series of gray hallways. There was a row of beds of different types against a wall, and we were each laid down on one.

"Graven!" I heard a woman's voice enter the room shortly. "What happened? How bad is it?"

"Take care of them for me, will ya?" I could tell he meant me and my sisters.

"What about you? That's a lot of blood."

"It isn't mine."

I heard hurried footsteps come to my side. "She's so much worse off than the others, what happened?"

"C.H.E.S.S. happened."

"Poor thing. I could just wrap her up in a blanket and hug her forever."

The Englishman giggled. "You could just hug everyone forever."

I opened my eyes wider to better take in my surroundings. It felt like only a moment passed since I was laid down, but I was coated in bandages that looked like they were in place much longer.

"She's up!" said the woman, excitedly. She looked elven, with pale skin, pointed ears poking through her long brown hair. She wore flowery clothes and brandished a green guitar between her fingers.

"Where are we?" I asked.

"It's my place-," started Graven.

"Our place, thank you!" said the woman, ignorantly.

"No not that," I said. " This place doesn't feel like Tokyo. The energy's different."

The woman replied, "Tokyo huh? Well sorry, this is New York,"

"But how? We were on the other side of the world." For a second, my surprise outweighed my injuries.

Graven explained, "I cast a teleportation spell to get us here."

"By the way, my name's Hinata Schield." The lady reached out her hand. It was disproportionately large.

My gaze lingered on the hand, then I looked at Graven. "That spell... Can you teach me?"

"I can." His response was unexpectedly quick.

"Are you sure about this Graven?" asked Hinata. "She's only a child and worse than this can happen just trying it."

"Hey, I'm not a kid!" I limped to my feet. "If you notice I'm the first one of us to wake up from a fight like that. The other two are still knocked out and they only took one blow. If that doesn't solidify your decision, then what does?"

Graven folded his arms. "I only said I can. I didn't agree to."

"Good. I don't like teaching someone so cute something so potentially deadly," said Hinata.

"Then how about this," I concentrated my power on my chest and undid the seal that kept me small. I grew, but my power became much less stable. "Or do you want to see how cute I really am? I can handle it."

Graven asked, "You have Mediocris, don't you?"

"Yeah, so what? I'm not actually small or cute. -Oww!" Hinata jumped up and hugged me. It didn't hurt as much as I thought. It seemed like my wounds were being healed by just being in that room.

"You're even cuter!" she said. "Willing to stay in that small form to prevent your power from going unstable. Oooh, you're even more adorable now! There's no way I can let Graven teach you that now!" The way she spoke was almost baby talk.

"Schield." Hinata jumped at the level of seriousness in Graven's voice. When she backed off, he continued. "What's your name?"

"Sara."

"What's your attunement?"

"Poison and emotion."

"Are you a corpse hunter?"

His question made me pause for a moment. If he really wanted to know, he could just look me up in a wanted book. Then again, it'd take far longer than asking me. "Do you know what it means to be one?"

"I know claiming a bounty on one is worthless." I could still read his emotions and he didn't seem to be lying.

I nodded. "Yeah, I am. So are my sisters." I motioned to Caroline and Leuna.

He sighed. "Alright, I'll teach you."

Hinata started protesting. "But Graven, It's too dangerous-"

"Stop it," said Graven. "She's a corpse hunter. I'm sure she's survived worse than this."

"He's got a point there," said the Englishman, re-entering the room with ice bags. "Besides, once someone's taken his fancy, you can't argue with him."

It took a while, but I learned what Graven had to teach me. During that time, Leuna and Caroline stayed unconscious. In the end, we couldn't get rid of the pink glow surrounding them and I came home with his help.

The glow faded when we got home. Eventually, they awoke and thought nothing out of the ordinary happened. Being hunters, what happened wasn't out of the ordinary, so I had reason to think they lost their memory.

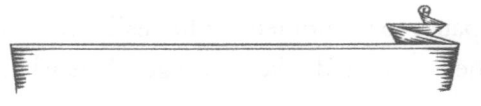

7-Pass Time

[Krow Hunt]

After listening to their story, the rest of us sat in silence for a bit.

"Anything else?" said Graven. "I have to go back out on patrol soon."

"We're here for a reason," said Carona. "Do you happen to know anything about someone named Blade? Code-named or otherwise."

"Can't say I do."

"Do you know anyone who does?"

"I might. At the top of the building is an ex-info-broker. She's someone you gotta be careful with, but she might know who you're looking for, depending on how recent the info you need."

"Fair enough. Can you take Krow to her? He knows the most about the guy we're looking for."

"I do?" I said.

"You fought him," she reminded me.

"Oh, yeah."

"Alright." Graven made for the door and I followed him. After a walk to the highest floor, we took a small staircase up and out. "Here we are." As we stepped onto the roof, he called out, "Hey, Naomi, you here?"

"Yes." The voice came from everywhere at once.

"Here you go." Graven stepped back down into the building and the door closed behind him.

"And you are?" said the voice.

"Here for information. I heard you had some."

"Name?"

"Daniel. You can call me Dan."

"No, *your* name."

"I told you my na-"

Everything went silent. The wind and the birds quieted in an instant. "Codenames are unnecessary here. They're a sign of distrust."

"Alright, my name's Krow."

The sounds of nature resumed. "It wasn't that hard, was it?"

"Can we get to business now, or is there more I need to do to earn your trust?"

"You're a Corpse Hunter, aren't you?"

"One of the best. Of course, there's limits to what kind of jobs I'll take, but if you need something in exchange for info, I'm all ears."

"So be it. What do you need to know?"

"Before that, how could you tell I'm a hunter? Also, where are you? Trust is a two-way street, you know. I can't trust who I can't see."

"I'm right here." The darkness receded, and she was standing in front of me. She wore a navy-blue long-sleeve shirt under a dark blue jean pocketed vest, black stockings under same color shorts, light blue flat shoes with white soles, and a blue and red polka-dot headband. Her hair was white and stringy, and it was flowing in the wind toward me. "You have a bloody aura and the scent of someone who's died before. Like every other Corpse Hunter."

I shrugged. "Well, even a scent can be misleading."

Nonchalantly, she said, "We'll see. So, what do you want to know?"

"Do you know of anyone named Blade? Code-name or otherwise."

She closed her eyes and took a deep breath. "Anything else you can tell me to help identify them?"

"As far as I can tell, he may be capable of manufacturing clones equal to the ones used in maximum training facilities and probably has the color of silver metal. I need as much information on him as possible."

She opened her eyes and seemingly scanned me with interest. "I'll need a day."

"A day? Alright." I crouched down and sat on the ground beside the door. "I guess I'll wait here."

"N-no... No need to do that." The woman who sounded so cold now sounded embarrassed.

I sat forward. "Why not?"

She looked around in all directions for a moment and then sighed. "You can stay, for now. Just so you know, I live up here. This is my home."

"Huh, this is New York. Don't you get cold?"

"I have ways to keep myself warm. Don't ask." She sat in the fetal position. "Oh, you can still see me." She vanished.

I smiled and mumbled, "Must get pretty lonely up here, huh?"

"It does." Her voice came from everywhere again. "Are you offering to keep me company?"

"For a little bit, if you want. I don't have much to do at the moment." After a moment of listening to the wind whipping by, I started feeling a little awkward. While I was planning to meet her on the roof again, I wasn't planning on staying up there all night. "So, your name's Naomi, right?"

"It is. Is this where we make small talk?"

"We can if you want. I was planning on heading back down and going to sleep after taking a walk around town. I thought I'd just sit for a bit and leave, then come back tomorrow and meet you here."

"You don't have to stay here if you don't want to."

"Well, it feels kind of like I'm sitting here by myself, and you're just kind of... *somewhere*."

"Well, thank you for not trying to see through my invisibility. You can go. Just make sure you return. If it turns out I did all this work for nothing, I'm going to get you." She sounded more playful than serious, but you can never tell with some people

I couldn't help but chuckle. "Alright, don't threaten me with a good time." I stood and headed through the door. "I'll see you later."

Traveling out of the building, I took a stroll down the street and observed the nightlife of the city. There were late-night bars swarming with people and theaters either closing for the night, flooding the street with people, or opening up for late viewings, lined with people. There were many more spaces filled with many more people, and even though I liked roaming between the crowds, I found myself at a small restaurant in a quiet part of town. Eventually, I crossed a busy street to a grouping of trees I spotted between the buildings. Looking around at the sparse ponds and architecture, I realized I found my way to Central Park. There were couples on a stroll and nocturnal animals prowling about. I wandered between walkways and foliage alike until I noticed the sunrise. At that point, I decided to head back. Checking my phone, I found a few messages telling me I was sharing a room with Doc. I went to the room and went to bed.

The next day, I went with my family to the nearest ley-line. It so happened to be in Central Park. That made sense, since it was the largest area covered in nature by far. Since Leuna was the fastest of us, she was sent through the ley-line back to the remnants of our home. If anything went wrong, she'd be able to react accordingly and either get back quickly or buy us time to pull her back by force.

Doc cast a spell that connected them with a black thread and off she went. After a few minutes, the string lit up bright green. As soon as it did, Doc yanked it. Leuna came flying as if pulled by her collar as she appeared.

"What happened?" asked Carona.

Leuna sat down on the grass. "Still can't leave or send a signal from there. Ran in every direction and still ended up back there."

"If that's how it is, we have no choice but to stay here. At least we packed well enough for an extended visit."

With that, we planned for a long-term stay. Since we already had somewhere to sleep, that's where we stayed. Otherwise, nothing about how we operated was going to change. Only our base of operations was different.

By the afternoon, I was watching TV with Doc and noticed the sky getting darker outside the window. At that moment, I remembered meeting Naomi on the roof. When I got there, she was sitting on a mass of shadows.

"You're late," she said.

"We didn't agree to meet at a specific time."

She closed her eyes and pointed her nose up at me. "Hm." She reached into the air and a piece of paper appeared in her hand. "This is everything I could get about this 'blade' of yours." The paper began emitting smoke that died down shortly. "Take it."

"Thanks." I took it from her and read it. There was a wealth of information written on both sides of the sheet. It was layered but readable across the page. His real name was Conrad, and he was a rank 3 gold Rook. He was part of a team called Stray and worked separately from them in the R&D division to develop weapons and tools. It turned out his code-name was never Blade, but Silver. Blade was a code-name for subjects of his that were intended for destruction. That was the least of the information.

Even though I worked with reliable info brokers before, I was a bit overwhelmed by how much someone could know about someone else and be ready to give it out. I walked over to the ledge and sat while reading. The wind blew my jacket back behind me the whole way.

"Anything else you want to know?

Naomi came and sat beside me. "Is there anything else you want to know?"

Her question gave me pause. If she could get this much info on one person despite no longer dealing in information, I wondered what other kind of information she could give me. Above all, I was more curious about her. "You know, curiosity killed the cat, but you know what? I'm curious about you."

"I'd tell you about myself but since you came late, you'll try again another time." I could see the shadow of a smile on her lips.

"Well, I guess that's it. I wasn't really expecting an answer anyway." I stood up, turned around, and started walking back. "Guess I'll try again later."

"And where are you going?" Naomi asked without looking.

"Back downstairs, why?" Looking back at her, I realized that an eerie air seemed to be whirling around her.

"The price for information isn't cheap." Again, she spoke without looking.

"Oh yeah... We never talked about that, did we?" I looked around, awkwardly. "So, do you need something done? Of course, nothing too extreme."

"The price this time will be..." She seemed to touch her fingertip to her lips. "Since this is your first time..." She tilted her head backward and looked at me. "A nickname and some information that only you can give."

"Sure, why not?" I said, unsure of what exactly I got myself into.

"I got it!" she said, now bending backward to face me. "It's a nickname you won't like, so I'm not telling you." A smile spread across her face.

"Why not?" I asked.

"I have my reasons." She got up, walked toward me, and went on her tiptoes to kiss my forehead. "Now, for that information."

I tensed up in surprise, not knowing what would happen next. Would she make another move? If she did, would I accept or decline her invitation? If I did, where would it go from there? We were alone on the roof. What could possibly happen? I was no stranger to seduction, magical or otherwise, but something about her told me that wasn't her goal. At that moment, I felt like I had fallen into a trap.

"Why so tense?" She grabbed my hand with hers. "You need to loosen up." The warmth from her hand gripped my soul. As her dark brown eyes stared me down. I was being drawn deeper into whatever she was doing.

"Stop it and just tell me what you want," I said, shaking my head, a little frustrated.

"So that's how you get around women."

Keeping my cool, I spoke. "No, that's not it. You're just-"

"Seducing you? So, it's working?" As she said this, she grabbed my face with her hands. Her hands felt nice. They were warm and gentle. She began as if she was going to kiss me again, but instead, she said. "You have a fragile heart that you guard stiffly yet... you're still quick to love. How peculiar."

"So, is that how you get information? Bending people to your will? Why don't you tell me *more* about yourself?"

"In due time." Her smile hardened to a grin. "Let me look into your mind." She touched her forehead to mine. "**Mental trace**."

"You can't just-" Her lips touched mine and I went silent. It was as if my entire nervous system shut down and all I could do was stand there.

"Thought that'll shut you up... Maggot."

My sight went black, and a volley of images began rushing through my mind. All of them were miscellaneous things that I learned over the years. Nothing particularly important was among the images and the only sound was the rushing wind.

"Information for information's sake," said Naomi "Don't worry, I won't pull anything that's blocked or too personal... This time." My mind went blank. As soon as that happened, she said,

"I'm done. I only took a small amount this time, but next time I'll take more. Got that?" She let me go and I fell to the ground. "If there is a next time."

"Yeah, I got it." I could hardly get up after she let me go.

"Don't get up. Just look up at the stars with me for a while." She laid down next to me.

I stopped trying and just looked up. "Looks like that's all I can do for now."

"You want to see the stars. I'm not making you."

I scoffed. "Trying to be commanding, now?"

"You're helpless as you are, right now. Just keep me company."

"I can do that."

The stars were somewhat difficult to see from the middle of the city and frequent clouds obscured the view. Regardless, they were there, twinkling in defiance of the city lights below. Once one of many clouds passed over, I found myself looking down from high up. I relaxed as the wind swirled around me and I watched the city lights as they twinkled in the night.

"Hey, Krow." Naomi grounded me with her voice.

"Yeah?"

"Where did you go just now?"

"Nowhere."

"Remember that 'trust' thing? That still applies."

"I didn't go anywhere. It's just a weird thing that happens sometimes."

She scoffed. "That explains it."

"What?"

"Nothing. There's just a lot of top-down images in that head of yours."

I yawned. "You think I can fall asleep up here?"

She stifled a giggle. "You want to sleep with me? I'm not a straight arrow, you know?"

"Sucks for you. Not what I meant, though."

"Yeah, you can sleep here. It's not like you can go anywhere else right now."

"Not unless I use magic."

"Now, why would you go spoiling the mood?"

I chuckled. "What mood? You're not interested in me."

"People make exceptions."

"So, I'm an exception?"

After a long moment of silence, she responded. "No. Not now, anyway."

I sighed. "Whatever. I'm going to sleep." The moment I let my eyes droop, I dreamt. I had a dream where I was floating in an endless expanse of water with the stars shining bright above me. I could hear the gentle waves pushing against me and feel the ebb and flow of the sea as I dragged across its surface. The milky way was visible near my feet and reflected across the water as I gazed upon it. At some point, the gentle rocking stopped, and I was still. The waves stopped rolling and there were only stars as far as the eye could see.

When I woke up, I noticed that there were no stars. it wasn't cold, and there was no wind on the roof. Artificial darkness couldn't do all of that alone. I sat up to see Naomi asleep, turned as if she was looking at me when her eyes closed.

"Cute," I said. "You fell asleep watching me sleep, huh?" I couldn't help but brush her hair back and kiss her forehead. A little payback for what she did.

"What are you doing?" She mumbled in her sleep.

"Talking in your sleep?"

"Get over here." She rolled over and head-butted my chest.

"Are you still asleep?" I asked.

She mumbled something and continued to sleep.

"Nice."

"Mmmnup-" She rolled off of me.

I still felt tired, so I fell back to sleep. I had the same dream again except the stars were fading out and being slowly replaced with a silhouette. I tried to reach out to it, but my arm was heavy, and I couldn't. Once the rocking stopped, the dream ended, and I was left in darkness.

"Hey, Krow." Naomi's voice cut through the darkness.

"Huh?" I opened my eyes as something hit my arm. The daylight hit my eyes, but it was dimmed by a dome of shadows over the roof. "What was that?"

"I'm trying to wake you up." Naomi was sitting next to me in a different outfit. It was a black tunic with a red belt. Her hair was in a ponytail in the middle of her head.

"Oh. Well, I'm up."

"Thanks for watching the stars with me." Naomi was staring up at the deep blue sky.

"Well, I have no idea how long it would have taken to get the kind of info we were looking for. Could have been months in comparison to how much you got so fast. So, thanks in kind."

"You're welcome," she smiled.

"Only problem now, is that we might have a target on our backs from C.H.E.S.S. That's a can of worms and a half, and we can't always keep a lookout."

"I guess we could try..." She looked deep in thought.

"What?"

"I'll tell you if you promise to come back and watch the sky with me. It's the perfect pass time."

I thought for a moment and decided to accept. "Sure, I can do that. The perfect pass time."

"Good. Go to Vincent and ask him about his creation magic. With your abilities, you might be able to come up with something that can help you. It might not, but it's always worth a shot."

"Alright, I'll do that," I stood and began walking toward the blue-green door that led downstairs.

"Oh, and Krow." An ominous feeling began emanating from Naomi.

"Yeah?" I said, weary of this change.

"If you ever mess with me in my sleep again, you will live *only* long enough to regret it. Got it?"

I chuckled, realizing she was awake. "Yeah, got it."

"Are you sure, because you seem to think it's cute."

"You know, I didn't think you'd get mad over it." I walked backward toward the door, keeping my eye on her. Something seemed familiar about the vibe she was giving off but I couldn't quite put my finger on it. "Just consider it payback."

"You're not taking me seriously."

I dropped the playful tone as I reached the door. "I am."

Her hand was on the door behind me in an instant. Her energy began to fluctuate and surge. I stared into her dark, saddened eyes for a moment. There was something just beyond the surface that was itching to come out.

I ducked under her arm and jumped off the roof determined to avoid escalation. Making my way back inside, I went to Graven's room He was talking with Doc about something but they stopped when I entered.

I folded my arms and stood against a wall. "Naomi's possessed by a corpse shadow, right?"

"She is," said Graven. "That's why you have to be careful with her."

"You didn't think to tell me that ahead of time?"

"I figured you'd sense it."

I sighed. "Well, I didn't. I think it's going out of control."

"If she chased you off, then that means she doesn't want you to see her fighting it. It happens once every few months. She'll regain control soon enough, but for now, it's best to stay away from the roof."

"She has to fight it that often?" said Doc

"Most types of seals don't work on her and the few that do, don't last long. She's got heavy resistance to sealing magic. That's why she lives on the roof."

"To think someone like that exists. Powerful enough to resist the kind of sealing necessary for a corpse shadow, but still host to one."

I headed for the door. "In that case, I'll leave you two with that. I'm gonna go find Vincent."

Vincent was in his room on the second floor. His door was open, and he was standing on his hands in the middle of the living room. He had on gray sweatpants and no shirt or shoes.

"Hey, you stuck?" I said, from the doorway.

"Mmmhm... Just fine... Trying to get down." His light brown hair was wavering.

"Good, because Naomi told me to talk to you."

"Aah!" There was a soft *bop* as he hit the floor. "Naomi? What for?" He sounded a bit frantic and a little nervous. "Did she break the roof again?"

"Nah. She said something about 'creation magic' and told me to come see you."

"I don't know about that..." He looked sheepishly around the room.

"Then what do you think she meant by that?"

"Never mind, I remembered." He glanced at the doorway behind me.

I looked behind me and saw nothing, but there was a small presence somewhere in the room that wasn't there before.

"This is what you mean, right?" He put his right hand over his left one. The sound of rushing steam followed by a faint blue light came from between his hands.

"Here you go." He held up a small dragonfly in his hand. It was all black. "Go on." It flew into the air and hovered for a second before dissipating.

"Magic by birthright?"

"Yep, that's my creation magic. I can make idle and moving objects from solid magic, among other things."

"Seems super useful."

"It would be if I could make it so they don't disappear after a couple of minutes."

"So, is it possible to make stuff out of other people's magic?"

"That's easier said than done, but so far, I can make small things like that dragonfly with only a little effort. Anything bigger takes a lot out of me."

"So that's why Naomi sent me to you. If we can find a way to make it last longer, you can even make artificial familiars, am I right?"

"I should be able to, but just getting a regular familiar should do the job well enough."

"Well, what about-"

"Wait. Sorry to interrupt you, but something's wrong. You were *just* talking to Naomi, right?" He seemed to get more serious.

"Yeah, what about her?" I shrugged.

"Were you in like a peaceful moment and then, she just chased you away?"

"Yeah, I just talked to Graven about it."

"Something's wrong, I can smell it. Is there a member of your group with a corpse shadow?" The look on his face was stone cold serious as he put on his shirt.

"There's one. Why?" I started focusing on Caroline's presence. I could feel that she was still near the building.

"Where are they now?" He got his shoes on and started for the door.

"I don't know, but she's close by."

"I think they're resonating." He basically launched himself out the door and I followed.

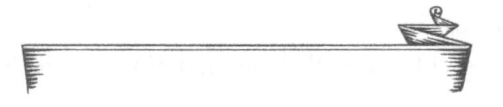

8-Shadow Sealing

[Docter Ganger]

My conversation with Graven leaves my mind the instant a feeling begins slowly creeping up on me. It's like a foreboding hum emanating from an unidentifiable source. We both go quiet as we try to identify its origin.

"Doc! Out back!" Krow's voice echoes from the hall outside the room. His tone tells me more than his words can.

Another voice calls soon after. "Graven! The roof!"

"Vincent?" Graven responds.

"They're resonating." Vincent's voice travels further away accompanied by the footsteps of the pair as they sprint by.

Graven and I exchange glances as we stand and simultaneously jog out of the room to our designated locations. The feeling becomes more distinct as I exit the back of the building. Caroline is standing in the middle of the lot, staring up blankly at Naomi who stares back the same despite the great distance between them. One of my greatest fears come to life.

"Caroline!" I call out to her.

"*What's happening*?" I see her silently mouth the words as she had already started floating a couple of feet off the ground.

"Krow!" I call for him.

"I'm here!" he says, appearing a few feet behind Caroline.

"We're going to do a 'compound restriction'. Where's Ariel?"

"I don't know."

"No time. We're going to have to use Sara."

I feel a rustling in my jacket and see a small black scorpion crawl onto my shoulder from inside my pocket and jump off. In a pink glow, it transforms into Sara as she lands on her feet.

"I'm here!" she exclaims.

"Good, let's do this." I summon my scythe into my hand then slam the edge into the asphalt, creating a groove where it rested while calling the name of my weapon, "***Black death***."

Krow summons his blade, stabs it into the ground, and calls its name as well. "***Black flame***."

Sara does the same. "*New dream*." We were each on a different side of her, making a triangle.

"*Heaven*." Krow starts the spell.

"*Hell*." I continue the spell.

"*Earth*." The echo in Sara's voice signifies the spell being set for casting.

"*Trifecta*," we say in sync, casting the spell.

A triangular prism forms over Caroline with each of us at a side. What we created is a spiritual barrier using the three main forms of spiritual energy. The pure red flame of Heaven on Krow's side, the dark desolation of Hell on my side, and the natural qualities of Earth on Sara's side.

Caroline belts a disturbing roar from inside the seal, straining her voice. Bright multi-color light flashes from her. The many seals keeping the corpse shadow suppressed break rapidly. She curls up, holding her arms, chest, head, and all as tears begin streaming down her face. She tiredly whines, her expression shifting to defeat as if she resigned herself to suffering. Soon enough, she seems to pass out, still floating.

Scanning my sight over Sara and Krow, I see each of them gritting their teeth. Sara likely has it worse, sensing all our emotions. She holds back her tears valiantly, but a couple still get through.

As long as the foreboding feeling emanates from Caroline, we have to hold the seal. It's the last line of defense if the corpse shadow takes over completely. Even if it doesn't, there's a chance Caroline can't keep it restrained with how many restrictions are broken already. As time passes, that seems more and more likely.

With a moan, Caroline straightens up, still floating with her eyes closed. Her hair turns blue, but briefly. It signifies her power rising to a point where she can no longer hold it without decaying or changing shape. Her entire body drains of color, her nails lengthen into short claws, and her floating continues closer to the ground. The feeling emanating from her becomes more intense. It seems like she's losing the fight within herself.

By this time, there is a small crowd outside watching and helpless to what's going on. No one approaches. They all watch with bated breath as the barrier holds.

Caroline opens her cold, blank eyes and smashes herself against the wall close to me. The energy pushing against the barrier from inside compounds against it as she does so, threatening to push me back. I hold my ground and don't budge as she begins thrashing around inside the seal. Krow still holds strong, but Sara begins to lose her balance.

A high-pitched scream escapes Sara as the last few blows are on her side where Caroline breaks through causing her to scream again, this time a deathly cry, cut off by an impact.

"Sara!" Krow and I call her name, alarmed at this development.

"*Push*!" I cast a spell and jettison Caroline off Sara.

"Sara!" calls Krow as he, Carona, Hinata, and Ariel rush to her side. The other three are late but arrive, nonetheless. A red puddle is rapidly forming below her.

"Leuna!" I shout.

At my command, Leuna fires her bow, already having it trained on Caroline just in case. "**Oracle arrow!**" One arrow turns into many as it closes in on the corpse shadow-taken Caroline whose clawed hand was bathed in blood. "**Whispering wind**, Burst." The green ivory bow transforms into a metal one with blades on the ends. Leuna begins pulling back on the string.

"Something's wrong," I say, feeling something strange. I have an odd sinking feeling.

"What is it now?" Still drawing her bow, Leuna looks around wryly, noticing the second disturbance as well.

"It's coming from the roof," says Hinata.

Looking up, we all see Naomi looking down from up high, her eyes dimly glowing red. The veins around her eyes are also visibly red even from so far away. We're surprised to see the one in control lose it and the sealed one escapes its chains. Both of them lost control.

"*You*," Her voice echoes from everywhere while pointing at Caroline. All the arrows dissipate as Naomi beckons her with her finger. Caroline, without getting up, turns and begins ascending upward toward her beckoner. Naomi then lifts from the roof and begins descending toward her where they meet in between.

Naomi says something short and unintelligible, followed by a similarly clear response from Caroline. They're in a trance, barely a nose-twitch away from each other. Their words seem to quicken with every other sound as if slowing down was a detriment. Although barely audible, their voices are everywhere and quickly meld together as they begin speaking intensely in unison before finally saying something in a tangible language.

"**Shadow**." Naomi calls the name of her weapon and summons her blade to her hand, two long dual-sided daggers.

"**Blue waves**." Caroline follows suit with a blade curved halfway around, with a long handle reaching between the sides and slightly longer than she was tall. Both weapons, solid black and blue, respectively.

"*Kill*," they say together.

Before we know it, they begin fighting. First by striking at each other, resulting in a clash that sends them both back, then by reaching out their hands and sending orbs of chaotic blue and black energy at each other.

"Nope." Krow jumps directly between them. In doing so, their energies combine and knock him back. "Ah, that stung," he says, just before crashing to the ground.

I say, "What else did you expect?"

He sighs. "Based on that blast, it looks like they're trying to kill each other."

"That's why we have to do something to stop this," I say.

Graven's voice echoes from the roof "Hinata!"

"Graven?" she calls back. "Where's Vincent?"

"He lost it... Blood. I need a vortex and Doc; I need a sheet of darkness. Advanced darkness, if you can."

"Sure," I say. Neither Naomi nor Caroline seems to notice anyone or anything other than each other.

"Let's go while they're still oblivious!" says Graven, diving from above. "Guillotine." His Blade transforms into its second form.

"*Air gear.*" Hinata removes the guitar from her back, and metallic wings sprout from the larger part of it as it glows green. Her weapon is fused with her guitar.

Still after cancelling each other's magic attacks, the girls back off and rush at each other with their weapons. Both of their blades clash with Graven's while he falls between them. His sword crashes into the ground and creates a deep hole with a heavy gravitational pull. "Now, Hinata!"

"*Infinity vortex.*" She waves her blade like a fan and creates a vortex that drags down the two with the help of Graven's spell from below.

"Now Doc!" Graven launches himself out of the hole.

Having already summoned my scythe to my hand and evolved it into its second form, I cast "**Dark abyss,**" swinging my blade across the mouth of the hole and creating a pitch-black void of darkness within.

"What now?" asks Graven, looking over at me.

"What do you mean?"

"This situation's new to me. I've never had a pair of corpse shadows this strong resonate. I'm hoping you have a solution."

I take a moment to consider our environment and manpower. With everything in mind, I say, "It's new to us as well, but I'll need Carona's opinion on what to do. She has the experience."

We looked over to Carona, who's helping Sara recover. The bleeding isn't stopping as easily as normal. The chaotic nature of the energy swirling around in her wounds keeps Carona's magic from doing its job. Normal medicine likely won't have any effect for a while either.

Graven approaches her. "Sorry to interrupt you, but we need a plan. Do you have anything?"

Carona does an exasperated sigh. "We need to get their weapons from them. If we can do that, they'll be forced to use up all their energy through magic." She sighs again. "That'll make them so much harder to deal with in a populated area."

"What if we can give them false weapons?" Graven looks at the top of the building. "Something hollow, that'll absorb their magic."

Carona nods affirmatively. "I'd be grateful if you could do that. If you can…" She scans her surroundings, deciding what to do. "Leuna. Ariel."

"Ma'am?" says Ariel, stepping up.

Leuna stands at attention with her bow still drawn as she points it toward the hole housing Caroline and Naomi.

"Leuna. When we get their weapons, I need you to hold them in a stabilized vortex. Ariel. I need you to punch a hole in the ground to put me, Sara, and Leuna. Doc. you're in charge of everything after."

"I can do that," I say, placing the pole of my scythe against my shoulder.

"Good. Graven, I'm counting on you to get their weapons."

It's Graven's turn to scan the group. "In that case... Krow?"

"Yeah?" says Krow.

"Sorry, but you're going to have to do the heavy lifting.

A wicked smile spread across Krow's face. "I can do that."

9-Control

[Krow Hunt]

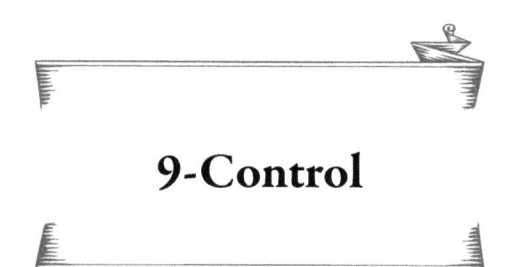

Making my way onto the roof, I approached a man on his knees with bloodshot eyes mumbling incoherently.

"Blood?... Blood!?... Blood!" He was silently slipping from sanity.

"Is he ok?" I asked the man to his left.

"If he's okay, I can't say. You might want to ask the one he's connected to, or rather, the one he's connected through,"

I looked at the girl on his right.

"He means our lady Anna Archfield." She gestured toward a small, black bat with big, blue eyes hovering over Vincent's head. "By the way, my name is Jane Walker, and he is Aaron Stage. We serve our lady Archfield as her guard. Hearing this, I analyzed them.

Jane wore capris, a short-sleeved shirt, and a small jacket. All in bright colors. Aaron dressed comfortably in all dark colors, and he seemed to speak in rhymes.

On further inspection, I could see what seemed to be the end of a dragon's tail on Jane's left arm. She covered it with her folded arms and the same could be said for Aaron's right arm, although his was barely noticeable as it barely glowed under his long sleeve. On a more detailed level, Jane's seemed to be blue and Aaron's green.

"Lady Archfield." I recognized the name, but couldn't remember where from, so I spoke according to her title.

"Yes, Krow?" The voice of a girl came from the bat.

"Glad you know who I am. We can do this fast." I motioned to Vincent. "Can you pull him back to sanity? We need his creation magic."

"I can do so briefly, but it's up to him whether or not he stays coherent." She began to glow in an eerie light that was almost blinding. When the light stopped, I saw a girl about half my height with long, wavy, jet-black hair and red eyes wearing a red and black dress. She took Vincent's face in her hands and hushed her voice. "Wake up." She tapped his face with the flat of her hand.

"Hah..." He snapped out of it. "Anna!"

"Remember your promise..." she said, lovingly.

"Yes, I'll always remember."

"And remember to keep your bloodlust in check. I don't want to have to do this again."

"It was kind of your fault; I mean you just-" He noticed her serious expression with crossed arms. "Yeah..." He stood up.

"Vincent, we need your help," I said.

"My creation magic. I heard."

"That being said, we also need the help of Lady Archfield," I said, gesturing toward Anna. "And her promising water-bending bodyguard." I gestured toward Jane. "Construct substitutes. Can you make them from shadow and water?"

"Yeah... Anna, Jane," Vincent put his hands out to both of them. Each of them put both of their hands over his. I could feel a rush of energy from both of them converging upon him and taking shape. "Done." in each of his hands, he held an opaque artificial core. One smoky black and one blue. "Here." He handed them to me. "They won't last long."

"Thanks. I got work to do." I went to the edge of the building.

"Good luck," he said.

"Good luck to you too, and try not to go crazy," I responded.

"Yeah." He looked at Anna who turned back into a bat.

I jumped and began my descent. I only had one shot at this. "Now!" I called out and a hole opened up inside the darkness of the ground. As soon as I was inside, the hole closed. There was nothing inside except for darkness and the oppression of gravity. I dropped both orbs on the right sides, stretched my hands out, and cast "***Flash***," A blinding light bound for my targets hit both Caroline and Naomi.

"Aah!" They yelped as the light hit their unsuspecting eyes.

One weapon hit the ground to my left. I swiped it and replaced it with a core from my hand. Assuming the other one also loosened her grip on her weapon, I reached to my right and cast 'pull'. A polearm landed in my hand, allowing me to drop the other orb on that side. "***Dragon's ascent.***" I became encompassed with a green glow as draconic scales fell while I jettisoned myself out of the hole through the gravitational field suppressing the area.

"Now, Hinata!" called Graven. She snatched me out of the air and over to Luna, who contained the weapons in a steady orb of air. She was the only one who could keep a constant flow of energy around them well enough that no one could sense them.

"And now the hard part's over," I said.

"I wish," Leuna moaned. She huddled with Carona who was still healing Sara.

"Ready?" said Ariel

Leuna took a deep breath. "Yeah."

"Let's go," said Carona.

Ariel punched the ground and a circle etched itself around the three. Within that circle was another circle and overlaid with triangles upon triangles upon triangles and squares within squares. The ground sank and Leuna made a pained expression as she fought her fear of the underground.

"Now, let's do this." Graven released his gravitational spell.

"Ready." Doc released his darkness spell.

After a moment of silence, both Naomi and Caroline came shooting out of the hole. The weapons in their hands were not the weapons that they fell into the hole with, in more ways than one. They infused the fakes with their corrupted magic, which changed their appearance. Even so, it wouldn't have been enough to make effective weapons. Caroline's was the same except blood-red, and the insignia on the blade was smaller. Naomi's blade was shrouded in shadows. Its double-bladed figure was gone, replaced with a single long blade and a design that appeared to be a blade within a blade. Also, it lengthened out to be about four feet from end to end. They weren't the only ones whose weapons changed.

Ariel's weapon was normally a smoothly cross-sectioned lance in a similar shape to a kunai. It was now wider, had a longer handle, and was somehow more triangular. Doc and Graven also transformed their weapons. Hinata stood ready with her guitar since it couldn't evolve. I changed my sword to its second form as well; a double-ended sword with markings on one end that resembled fire and on the other that resembled wind.

Naomi said something unintelligible, and Caroline said something as well. After a brief moment of spying on their surroundings, they began to move against one another.

"*Fireball*." I cast the spell and launched a ball of fire from my hand at Caroline, getting her attention as it bounced off her forehead. She looked down as angrily as she would have without being overtaken by a shadow.

"*Gravity ball*." Graven followed my example, except his attack was a purple orb that nudged Naomi toward him.

Since we shifted their focus, we all split up. Some of us went left, some went right, some went up, and some stayed low. Caroline and Naomi also split. Caroline went for me, but Doc intercepted her, and Naomi went for Graven.

Instead of making sounds of metal on metal, the copies made a thumping sound on impact. All Doc and Graven could do was block and dodge for fear of the girls finding their weapons ineffective and resorting to more drastic methods before they could take back control of themselves.

Twirling my weapon into the air, I conjured a weak 'fire tornado' and let it go. "Doc!" I called, as it came spiraling in his direction. He dodged, but Caroline didn't. Although the fire was weak, the tornado wasn't. This sent her high into the air and around in circles. However, she soon broke out of it and burst downward. While doing so, she extended her weapon by pulling the handle on both sides. "Here she comes!" I said, jumping back. Her weapon hit the pavement with a *bang* and Doc vanished before the weapon made contact. He appeared beside me a second later.

The ground shook, but not because of Caroline. Instead, it was because of Ariel coming from below. The ground opened and created a dome over Caroline. Meanwhile, the tornado I created affected the other side of the battle. Hinata strengthened the tornado and sent it toward Naomi, who became caught in it.

"***Gyrosphere***." Graven surrounded Naomi in a zero-gravity orb in which she floated. The tornado was then moved over the dome that held Caroline.

"Krow, heat it up," said Doc.

"Got it," I let go of my sword and it dissipated. I then put both of my hands out in front of me and cast, "***Inferno***," releasing a buildup of flames from my palms, which super-heated the tornado and in turn heated the earth and the gravity orb.

The fire could never come in contact with either of the girls so that they would never be burned. Instead, they would be baked as if in an oven. On our side what would feel like an active stove-top, was on their side what would feel like a gentle embrace. A hug that coaxed their minds and bodies into a hibernation-like state. This would not last long.

"***Suppression***." Doc cast the spell to literally suppress their chaotic energy and force them to calm down.

"Did we do it?" asked Hinata.

"For now," responded Doc.

After a while, the blaze subsided, and the wind died down. Graven went up and brought Naomi down.

By that time, the dome over Caroline had receded and Doc placed a temporary seal on her in the form of a series of black marks that spread across her body.

A moment passed. Then, a minute. Then, two minutes. Finally, Naomi woke up, followed by Caroline. A huge sigh of relief came from everyone around. Including bystanders who came to see what the fuss was about and police officers who came at the sound of destruction. There was a round of applause as Sara, Leuna, and Carona came from underground, and Naomi and Caroline were being carried back into the building.

Barely a moment passed when there was an audible *bang* from uncomfortably close by. A three-story tall humanoid with gelatinous skin and bulging eyes was summoned behind the crowd and tried to attack by reeling back to slam down its arms. Doc released Caroline onto a floating surface of darkness and turned to the giant.

"***Tracker***." He said as his gaze shifted from the giant to a member of the crowd. "Data received," I knew when he started sounding like that, he was serious and something about that giant appearing pissed him off. He reached out his hand and a stream of darkness rushed from behind him. "I have no time for you!" He said as the darkness rushed into the middle of the crowd and picked out an oddly familiar seeming man. I felt like my memory was failing me but now wasn't the time to focus on my memories. Doc brought the man closer and said, "Send it back,"

"Sorry I got nothing to do with that," replied the man, frantically looking around. Doc began closing his fist, and the darkness tightened around the man. "Okay, okay, ok... **Release**," Swish. The giant disappeared before it could do anything.

"As I thought," Doc's grip began to tighten.

That's when I grabbed his hand and said, "Stop. The police are over there," I gestured toward the men and women with their guns drawn at what was the giant. "Let them take care of him."

"Oh..." said Doc as he relinquished the summoner to the authorities.

"Let's take these two back in," I said, gesturing toward Caroline and Naomi.

"Yeah... Let's do that," he replied. Caroline and Naomi were semi-conscious and weak from fighting to take back control of themselves.

Had I not been both exhausted and preoccupied with our situation, I'd have acted when I noticed familiarity I felt from the man was similar to what I felt from the dragon we met in the Vatican. I gathered everyone and told them of my suspicions. Carona then came forward and said that while she was healing Sara, she also cured what looked like the remnants of a curse on her back. Once the reality of our situation hit, things became very apparent. Whatever would happen next was only a matter of time.

From then on, I worked closely with Vincent to develop a way to take someone's magic and turn it into a familiar that they could sustain themselves. Eventually, we were able to get something useful out of it, but our methods could only make bird-like creatures and it only worked with a few people. All in all, only Hinata, Ariel, and Doc got one.

10-Challenge

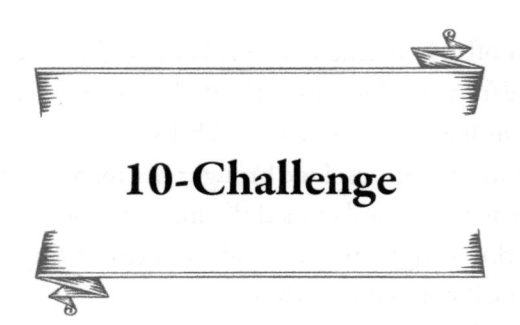

[Solo]

In the middle of dreamless sleep, I floated in the darkness of my eyelids until a presence snapped me awake. Even so, I kept my eyes closed and pretended to sleep. Regardless, the voice slowly but surely aggravated me.

"Hey, man, wake up." The voice rang in my ear. "Come on, man... Okay, it's up to you."

Something hard landed fast on my head and I heard the bonk reverberate through my head.

"Aaagh!" I opened my eyes slowly to see Conrad and Lucia. Conrad, wearing the all-silver suit that he was ever so proud of, and Lucia wearing the C.H.E.S.S. uniform. A red tie, brown khaki pants, and brown work boots. Looking up I saw the random assortment of shelved chisels and blocks made of different materials that signified my room.

"Looks like you're up," said Conrad.

A quick impact alongside a *bonk* sound forced me to open my eyes.

"What the hell are you two doing in here?" I rubbed my head.

"We're here to see if you're okay," said Conrad, feigning concern.

"We all know that's bull. Since that mess up a year ago, all you would have to do is talk to the Guile." By their lack of response and the look on Lucia's face, I could tell that something was troubling them. "Spit it out." I snapped my fingers and Lucia jumped.

She sighed and responded. "You have been requested for a hearing-"

"I don't think so." My response came quickly.

"Well, you *are* being requested." She continued, calmly. "Regarding your potential relocation-"

"Then it's not a request. They can come to me-" A second bonk was the only thing I heard; the impact cutting my words short. Immediately after, Lucia grabbed my scarf from the corner of my bed, wrapped it around my neck, and dragged me out of the room with it.

"We were assigned to escort you," she said, sternly.

"And hitting me with your staff, then dragging me there by force is escorting?"

"We were told to take you with extreme prejudice if you resisted in any way."

"You couldn't at least let me walk?" We were getting weird looks from other people as we made our way across the halls to an office on the opposite side of the east wing. The carpet and tile color changed three times and never got any more comfortable as I allowed my butt to be dragged across its many surfaces.

"Shut up, we're almost there," said Conrad, annoyed. One more left turn and we entered an open door.

"Now get up and sit down," ordered Lucia.

"Okay, no need to be so bossy," I picked myself up and sat in the first chair I saw.

"Sorry, we're late sir," Lucia spoke as if it was someone important. I looked up at her and I could see the worry on her face.

I looked across the marble white table toward the gray-haired kid sitting there, hands folded. His uniform was dark orange, and he had a shiny platinum patch on his chest over his left breast with an image of a pawn, unlike Lucia who had a gold one on her left shoulder that showed a bishop. It was rare to find a pawn with a rank high enough to have a platinum badge. This one especially. At a mere sixteen, the youngest person to ever reach that rank. His name was Nero Cursley.

"Oh, so this is the infamous Solo." His voice was flat with indifference.

"Yeah so, what's it to you," I said with just as much indifference.

"Solo don't-" started Lucia.

"No need," said Nero. "Now, onto business. Conrad."

Conrad straightened up and answered, "Yes, sir!"

"I've heard of your success with that clone from the science department."

"Yes, the transformation and destruction of the cell was a complete success. We even gathered information on some of their numbers." Something about the level of respect he put on his words irritated me.

"And their location?"

"Currently, they're in the heart of New York City, in America."

"What about that thing you've been working on?"

"It's falling in place as we speak."

"Good, Now onto you," Nero turned his gaze back to me.

"You'd better have a damn good reason for bringing me here." I turned my nose up at him.

"Looking at you now, I can see what they meant."

"That's not a reason," I said, demandingly.

"Well, it looks like your friends higher up think you lack discipline."

"I have friends there?"

"Not that you'd know."

"So, discipline. That's what you're here for?" I sat back and smiled.

"You could say that." He folded his hands on the table. "A request, more like it. Your friends requested that you take part in a mission. One where you can redeem yourself upon completion."

"My 'friends' didn't need to send you to tell me. I already have someone I take orders from."

"You don't respect your elders enough to do what they say. That's why I'm here."

I leaned forward in my seat. "Here to piss me off?"

"I wouldn't be so antagonistic if I was you." He pressed his thumb against the platinum pawn on this breast. "You never know who you're dealing with."

"You think you have authority here?" I sat back.

"Authority has nothing to do with it. You seem to have a hard time understanding that."

"You saying you're stronger than me or something?"

"There's a reason I'm a higher rank than you."

"Alright, let's put that to the test." I stood.

He smirked. "The training room, it is."

Thirty minutes later, I stood in a preparation room leading to a large chamber at a small white table waiting for the door into the room to open. I was checking my clothes for rips, tears, and signs the enchantments on them were wearing off. Lucia and Solo were with me.

"Are you sure about this?" Lucia sounded stressed.

"Kid's gotta learn manners or something. More like, something about him just annoys me."

"You're one to talk." I looked to my far right to see Conrad walking into my field of view next to Lucia. "Are you sure about this? His rank is much higher than yours for a reason."

Annoyed, I said, "What's up with you two asking me the same question?"

Lucia pressed her hand hard on the table, cracking its surface. "We just want to know what your game plan is If you lose, we *won't* be on the same team anymore. A demotion won't be the only thing you'll have to worry about."

"Said the only girl that's never cautious really, at all." I sighed. "Have some faith in me."

"It's just I- I-" Her voice was shaky.

I took her in my arms. "We'll still be together."

"It's not that..."

"You're worried they'll send me away?"

"And then I don't know how long it'll be until we see each other."

With a smirk, Conrad said, "I just don't want to lose my guinea pig."

With a smirk, I said, "Keep talking like that and I'm dragging you to a training room."

To that, Conrad chuckled. "Alright, just make sure to focus. Can't have your powers go out of control."

"That doesn't happen anymore."

"Oh, I can see it happening again. Trust me. It could make a difference. Maybe focus even if it doesn't happen."

I sighed and released Lucia. "You two can go. The door's probably going to open soon."

The two left through the far door and a minute or so later, the door near me slid down, opening. I walked into the virtual reality arena where Nero was waiting.

"Are you ready?" The kid before me seemed all too eager to begin.

"If you are," I said, walking toward him.

"You can still turn around and you might be let off with a slap on the wrist." He began moving as well.

"And you could just refuse to fight me, but we both know that's not gonna happen." By this time, we were circling each other. Just walking in circles. The VR arena was huge and blank-white with circular walls.

"Starting VR arena." The voice was coming from a command module in the control room where Conrad and Lucia were. "Location."

"Your choice," said Nero.

"Random."

After a humming noise, the machine responded. "Location set, plain arena," There seemed to be no change.

"Let's get started." He summoned his blade into his hand. It was somewhat of a standard broadsword with an arrow coming out of each side pointing out then, up. It also had a zig-zag pattern coming from top to bottom.

"Agreed." I summoned my broad sword into my hand as well.

"Ready?" said the machine's female voice.

"Yeah," I said.

"Let the battle begin," said Nero.

"Start!" said the machine.

We both jumped into the air after a running start. Our swords clashed with each other in mid-jump. As my foot touched the ground, I rushed at him. When he hit the ground, he jumped again and missed my blade. From there, he showed off by doing a backflip in mid-air and landed on his feet.

"**Blade wave**!" I swung my sword and released a thin blade of pink energy. He blocked my energy with the flat of his blade and returned one of his own.

"**Sound wave**." An actual reverberation of sound blasted from his blade. It caught me off guard, and I slid backward. When it dissipated, he pushed forward with a swing of his sword.

I stood my blade with the flat of it facing him, blocking his strike. Next, I cast 'magic missile' and shoved it into his chest by hand, blasting him back and sending him flying.

He sent out a shock wave in all directions, nullifying his momentum and stopping mid-air. "That all you got?" He seemed unphased.

"Hell of a lot more where that came from, **blade wall**." I sent wave after wave of energy after him that linked together as more waves began passing between them with him in the middle. He began to dodge every one of them, mostly in mid-air.

"That sword looks heavy," he said while still dodging my blade waves. "You must have used up a lot of energy just to swing it, huh?"

I couldn't let my emotions get ahead of me mid-fight, but he still annoyed me. I raised my blade again. "Just stay still."

Quick as a flash, he darted out of the range of my spell and put the tip of his sword in front of my face only a few centimeters away. "**Point blank**." He hit me with an uproar of sound. My body smacked into the rounded wall over forty meters away.

"That's all you got," he said, He sounded disappointed, "Well, I guess we should just wrap it up now."

I stepped away from the wall. "I'm still standing."

"Well, what do you know? I guess I couldn't really have expected you to stay down so easily. Guess I'll have to make you."

I sighed, calming myself a little. "It's unwise to underestimate me."

"What's there to underestimate? Your telekinesis can't keep up with me and you can't get close at this range." His arrogance traveled farther than his words.

I released my grip on my weapon and let it lean against the wall. Gathering my strength, I cast 'light speed' and reinforced my body against the spell as I sped to his location. He didn't have time to react.

"Huh-?" The sound left him as I was in front of him, and his feet were dangling off the ground, my hand around his neck.

"Got you." I let him go and kicked him as hard as I could. I then summoned my sword into my hand as I sprinted toward where Nero was flying.

"**Blade wave**!" I evolved my sword before casting the spell. If he stopped his momentum again, it'd hit him and teleportation would take too long. As I swung my sword down, I felt the rush of energy from my heavier blade release into the air.

He blocked it sideways and hit the opposite side of the rounded arena where he landed on his feet.

"You gonna give up yet?" I stood with my weapon at the ready.

"I guess I'll cut loose." He smiled. "I rarely get this opportunity." I could feel his energy begin to fluctuate as his weapon glowed until it disappeared. He put his hands up in front of him, and a burst of sound erupted from them.

I knew what was coming so I guided my blade through the shockwave and forced it to part so I wouldn't go deaf. Next, I heard the sound of a footstep behind me. I swung my blade behind me, using my telekinesis to keep myself from swinging around as well. I hit nothing. He vanished.

"That little bastard," I said.

This time I heard it from my left. I turned, but as I thought, nothing was there. I knew this pattern. This was a basic strategy taught to us in the academy. Next would be behind again then, either above or below, and that would be the strike. The next one did come from behind.

"*Up.*" The thought rushed into my head before I stabbed directly upward. I caught the blade of his sword with the tip of mine. He was slashing downward, hurting my ears with the sound of the collision. We were perfectly balanced, and he was pivoted on his sword mid-air.

His blade began to vibrate, and he soon began to move. The balance broke, and he began to spin vertically with his sword at his back. I turned my sword sideways to avoid being hit. This went on for a few seconds until a new sound rang out between us.

The release pushed us both apart and for a second, we just stood there. That's when I got a good look at his blade. It had a long metal handle that extended into the blade, four openings that ran up the center of the blade, and a long, thin edge but the border of the holes where emboldened. It also had several back spikes with curved edges leading to each. His blade had entered its second form.

I also had an opportunity to assess the condition of my blade which now had a crack through the center.

He took a wide stance as a rush of energy started pouring from him.

"No chance!" I rushed at him with a diagonal slash. The vortex of his energy created a boundary line my sword couldn't cross and pushed me back a few meters. His energy was radiating outward too fast to push back. He held his blade above his head as the tremendous sound escaped.

"**Kinetic burst**!" He yelled above the rush of sound. He brought his sword down. All of his pent-up energy came rushing out at me.

I couldn't react more than by blocking with my blade sideways. I was too slow to cast a protective spell. When it hit, my sword broke, and I was thrown into the air. The shards flew out in all directions.

He was behind me in less than a second and knocked me forward and up. He then knocked me left, then back, then down, then in all directions while continuously casting a spell. "**Sonic blast**." He was hitting me with bursts of sound energy that carried cutting waves. Every blast felt like a run-in with a high-speed bus on a racetrack. Until finally, he had me where he wanted me. "**Kinetic shockwave**!" Right in the middle of the room. He blasted me down into the ground and landed feet first on my chest.

The room flashed red a few times alongside an alarm. A warning that one of us was losing consciousness. The computer kept a constant assessment of our conditions, and my vision was getting hazy. Its assessment was accurate.

"I guess it's over," said Nero, disappointed as he stepped off me. "I thought we would have a little more fun before that happened. Guess it's over."

"No!" I shouted. "It's not."

"Huh?" Nero stopped and looked back. "You're still awake?"

"There's that underestimation..." I was barely audible to myself but somehow, he could hear me.

Nero turned and said, "If you think that, then why don't you stand up?"

"Then I'll stand." I forced my shoulder up and turned to stand. Putting one foot on the ground, I almost fell over. I was pushing my psychic ability to its limits to force myself to move.

This was odd. Not what was happening, but how I was viewing it. Like a top-down view through someone else's eyes from the control room high above us. It was slightly blurred. I could see myself beaten and bruised. I couldn't let this happen. Inadvertently, I let their emotions get to me.

I formed a link to Lucia by accident. It was her emotions pushing me, not mine or anyone else's. I could almost see the tremble of her lips. Her nerves were wound so tight that she would have exploded if touched.

I looked upward to a box above the room where Lucia, Conrad, and likely, a class of students were watching the fight. I took a deep breath and exhaled a whisper. "Just like this..." I almost lifted myself to my feet, but the unexpected weight of Lucia's emotions, on top of my injuries, halted my movement. I fell to a knee with my arms at my sides. I pushed one more time and a five-pointed circle of energy appeared under me. The flow of energy lifted me into the air.

"What do you know," said Nero in surprise, "A seal."

Lucia's face flashed in my sight. Her eyes were sparkly from holding back her tears and she was holding her breath.

I could feel a rush of energy. It was fast and concentrated. It ran in between my fingers into my hand. I gripped it and my sword appeared in my hand with a flash of pink light. The same color energy that I was surrounded by.

"*Break the seal.*" The voice was oddly familiar. "*Break the seal,*" I could feel and hear it as if I was whispering to myself from inside my own head. I moved my right hand, and my newly fixed sword broke into fifteen pieces. My handle vanished, and the shards circled under my control. I raised my hand in front of me. "*Break the seal, break the seal. Release it and you shall be released.*"

"How's this for getting up?" I said. "**Mind reader**," I stated the name of my sword as if summoning it. The circle shrank until it disappeared. I fell from there, landing on my feet.

Impatiently, Nero cast a spell at me. "**Kinetic burst**." The shards of my blade moved up on my command and absorbed the blast.

"Shatter," I named the form my blade now took and reached out and grabbed a shard. After which, it formed into a handle and a second shard became the blade.

I rushed at him with my sword at the ready. Even before I reached him, the remaining shards were all over him.

He began blocking and dodging the shards as they came until I got close enough to stab him.

He jumped on top of the blade. "**Blast off**!" He propelled himself into the air in a burst of energy.

I reached my hand up, and the shards followed.

He turned his body downward, put his hands against his sword in front of him, and cast, "**Sonic blast**." When it hit, it deflected my shards around the impact.

While still going up, he cast another spell. "**Sonic blast**." The move sent him higher into the air. He gritted his teeth in frustration as the rotation of my last two shards absorbed most of the blast.

I pointed up, and he looked behind his shoulder. He should have been able to sense my blades surrounding him, but he seemed too focused to notice until then.

All the shards closed in on him and he was trapped in the center. "**Satellite Impact**." The mass of blades encasing Nero glowed brightly with my spell and raced to crash into the ground.

I opened my eyes. I didn't realize they were closed, but they were. In all directions, I saw nothing but darkness aside from a large creature hovering above the ground and a gate farther away. The creature stood with its oversized glassy eyes that seemed to each cover a quarter of its head. Its skin was a clean white and its small limbs would be hardly noticeable under its tassel-like extremities had it not been the size of a truck. The pink gate had an inscription of an eye with a five-point star in the center surrounded by pink chains and a disproportionately large lock.

"Why am I here? Did I pass out?" I looked to the floating creature for an answer.

It only stared at me with its giant eyes as its tassels flowed in the non-existent wind.

"Thought so." I looked back and forth between it and the gate. "Did your head get bigger?" I walked toward the gate.

"Indeed," it answered. Its voice was high-pitched and electronic as if it was speaking with a voice modifier.

"One of these days, your head's gonna explode."

"It may."

That thought made me stop walking. "What happens if it does?"

"I don't know."

"Then why is it so big?"

"We've become stronger."

I thought for a second and said, "At a cost."

"Indeed."

"So, if I get too strong, I'll die."

"Perhaps."

"What do I do?"

"I do not know. Maybe it is best to seek wisdom from one whose powers are beyond our own."

"Guess I have no choice." I continued toward the gate.

A towering vortex of pink energy surrounded it that threatened to knock me away if I came too close. I reached my hand out to touch it, but then, a thought crossed my mind. The same thought I have every time I come here.

"What are you?" I asked, just as my hand neared the volatile energy before me.

"That again? Now is not the time."

"My injuries aren't fatal, and I won't have the mind to come back here after I leave. What are you?"

"I am you."

"Bullshit. You give me a different answer every time, but it's all the same." I turned around. "You're a part of me, we're the same, cool, what are you-!?" A sharp pain sprung from my chest and spread until it reached my head. I fell backward into the vortex of energy, and everything went blank.

"Ah-!" I awoke in pain, forgetting what was just on my mind.

"So, what do you think?" said a familiar voice.

"I think she's got more than enough potential," said a more familiar voice. I swung my head to the left and became dizzy from the pain in my chest and neck. I saw Guile, his visor shining in the light, and Nero in a blue-green hospital gown with crutches and a cast over his leg.

The infirmary had four beds. I occupied one, and the one next to mine had ruffled sheets while the other two were presumably not being used. I watched a video on the TV on the far wall of the all-white infirmary repeated. In the video, there was a girl in a white C.H.E.S.S. dress uniform preparing to fight four others who seemed to be gold rank 4,3,2, and 1 by their badge color and placement.

They looked like they were in a desert. The girl didn't seem to have a weapon, but that didn't go for the four that she was fighting. One blond guy had an ax, the taller one had a sword, the shorter one had gauntlets, and the blue-haired girl had a large, beaded chain. They seemed to start when the blue-haired girl whipped her chain at the girl in white.

The girl in white jumped, making the chain miss and hit the ground. She then moved her hands in place as if she was holding a bow and arrow. Sure enough, what materialized in her hands was an all-white bow with a matching arrow, shooting it at the chain, and it stuck into the ground. She then shot one at the girl.

The blonde guy pulled her out of the way and dodged the attack while the taller one charged forward with his sword. The next arrow flew at him, and he knocked it sideways before it could hit him as he continued forward.

The girl in white gripped her bow on one side and it reformed into a sword as she rushed at him.

Their blades clashed several times until she knocked his blade aside and severed the vital connection between his head and shoulders. At least to him, she seemed to. He dropped to his knees and fell to the side with a painfully shocked expression on his face.

PAUSE. The video froze with the word 'Pause' in white on the upper right side of the screen.

"So, what do you think?" Guile turned to me.

"She seems quite skilled," I said. "With an ability to hurt but not kill? I'd assume she wouldn't kill a fellow subordinate."

Guile smiled. "Of course. It is a rather unique ability."

"So, it's unanimous?" said Nero.

"So far, it is," said Guile.

Feeling like something was off, I said, "Wait, what are we talking about?"

"Nero here recommended that girl for our team. Rank 4 Diamond Bishop: Mary Black. Since your fight with Nero, he's joining us already and since our team is relatively small, we can afford to have a couple of new members. She's pretty new, but she's got the skill, and she got Nero's attention too," His smile broadened, and his shoulders jumped as if he was trying to hold in a laugh. The joke wasn't very funny.

"So, I won? I don't remember much on account of passing out."

"We'll consider it a tie," said Nero. "Regardless, it resulted in my rank dropping. Then, Guile came to me with an offer, and I decided to accept, that's all."

The door of the infirmary opened, and I could hear who entered before I saw them. "Solo! You're awake!" It was Lucia followed by Conrad and Vinessa. Lucia seemed ecstatic to see me as she dashed to my side and delivered a massive bear hug to my midsection.

"Ow-!" I winced at the pain, and she loosened her grip on me.

"Oh, they are a couple," said Nero. It sounded like he was joking.

"Well..." I started.

Lucia pressed her hand against my face and looked at me as if debating violence. "What have you been telling him?" She held me by the collar of my hospital gown with her other hand.

"I mean, aren't we?" After noticing the distance between her face and mine, I spoke up. "Well, in this position, it would be kinda hard to tell."

She looked at me with wandering eyes for a moment until she squinted hard, straightened herself up, and said, "Well, you two sound like you've been getting along well?"

"Of course!" Exclaimed Vinessa, twirling in her skirt. "Their hearts connected during the fight." Her theatrics didn't help anything.

"Our hearts didn't 'connect,'" I said. "Guild probably just told him some stuff."

Hesitantly, Lucia said, "It's not like I haven't seen it before, it's just weird. I just don't get how someone could go from almost a feud to... This, in a fight."

"Lucia, remember when we had that first practice battle when we started as freshmen?" asked Vinessa.

"You promised you would never mention that." Lucia was visibly red with her hands over her face. "And besides, that was different. We weren't- we didn't even have ranks yet."

"Lucia." I turned her toward me. "Honestly, it was your emotions that pushed me. It just kind of happened."

Nero spoke up. "Since I'm joining your team, I should know a thing or two about you guys, right?"

Lucia seemed taken aback by this information. Maybe it was the fact that someone who was in a higher position than her, being brought down to her level, made her feel uncertain in her own position, or maybe it was that he even agreed to join our team. Either way, the shocked look on her face was appropriate.

"So, that's why it would be no problem with you two getting along," concluded Vinessa.

"I guess so," said Nero, repositioning himself in the hospital bed next to mine.

"So, You're with our ragtag group of a team, huh?" I said, looking at the ceiling.

"Yeah, so is she," he said, pointing back toward the screen. "If you let her."

After a moment of silence, someone came to the door of the infirmary and walked through. Her uniform was blank white and she had a diamond bishop badge on her left breast. All eyes were on her as she walked in confidently and sat next to Nero.

"Okay, you can continue the video now," she said.

Silently, Guile shifted around next to Conrad and pressed the button on the remote in his hand and the video continued.

Everyone on the battlefield seemed to stare at the boy hunched over on the ground and the girl who caused such a commotion. She seemed to reassure them that he wasn't dead. From then on, they acted with caution.

The blue-haired girl yanked her beads back and whipped them forward as the shorter guy punched into the ground with his gauntlets.

The chain smashed into the ground where Mary would have been had she not jumped back to dodge the blow.

The ground rose in a straight line toward her, and she jumped at the last second as the gauntlets blasted out of the ground right underneath her supported by their chains. They opened to grab her legs and held her in place as the bead chain, glowing blue, crashed into the side of her body while growing to half her size.

Mary flew a distance and landed on her back. Slowly but surely, she got up from the dust and stretched out her arms. Her hands began to glow and it extended up her arms. Whatever her weapon was, she evolved it. Reaching up, she seemed to summon what looked like an angel appeared and a healing glow encompassed her for a moment. It then disappeared. It likely healed her.

The chain was flying again in Mary's direction. It no longer glowed but the size was still bigger but with fewer beads. This time, Mary extended her fist and stopped it completely. In her hand appeared what looked like a Roman shield and in the other, there was a sword that spelled: 'EXCALIBUR', while scale-like armor appeared to dress her. They were all pure white.

Mary bolted toward the blue-haired girl as the gauntlets blasted out of the ground again, and this time they followed her.

The blue-haired girl was ready for what was coming next as she whipped her chain directly at Mary, who ducked and slid under the chain as it scraped against her shield.

The sword and shield disappeared as their wielder slid between the blue-haired girl's legs. They reappeared as she stood and pushed the blue-haired girl into the oncoming fists using the shield. Her face stretched in surprise as everyone winced at this display.

Mary's sword ran through the blue-haired girl's midsection. It cut through her clothes, but not her body. The bottom half of her uniform top dropped as she opened her mouth in a scream, and she fell to the ground, lifelessly.

All hesitation was put aside for the rest of the fight.

Mary pushed off toward the shorter guy before he could pull back his gauntlets. She hit his legs with her blade and swept around to get him through his back. He fell with his mouth open, but it didn't seem like a scream.

Still shocked, the last one standing made a desperate move. He began to unleash wave after wave of energy at Mary in a nearly unpredictable pattern. He then cast 'blade wall' to increase the effect. Even so, he still flailed wildly.

Mary saw this and exchanged weapons into a bow and arrow. She shot the arrow into the air and swapped places with it as she teleported to its spot, and it landed where she was. She fired another arrow at him and replaced it with herself and a sword that pierced his chest.

He fell, holding his chest and the video promptly ended.

The screen now only showed the words: Promotion test - Black, Mary - Rook - 5 Gold - 1 Diamond.

"So, how did I do?" The girl in question stood and went in front of the screen in confidence.

"Eh, ya' did fine," I said. "I got no problem with you joining us for now."

"More than acceptable," continued Conrad. "I assume you'll be joining our team?"

"Fabulous!" went Vinessa. "Having another cute girl wouldn't hurt. Especially one that's so capable."

"Indeed, we'd be glad to have you," said Guile.

Lucia just nodded in approval.

"See, I told you so," said Nero, "You're in."

"I guess so," said Mary. "Thank you for having me." She gave a courteous bow.

That night we had a small celebration for the arrival of the two new members of our team.

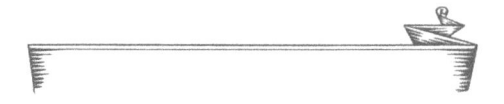

11-Guile's Afternoon

[Guile Pain]

Sitting behind his blue steel desk, Geist read over the files on the deployment and activation of the cell sent to the group of nameless Corpse Hunters. "So, it *was* a failure." He sat back in his seat. "It was expected, but catching that summoner takes more than just combat prowess. Do you think we underestimated them?"

I gave it thought for a moment and responded, "Well, given that we didn't know where they'd run to, I'd say we're on track whether we underestimated them or not."

"Speaking of such." Geist sat down in his chair. "Do you have the data on Solo's third form?" He looked at Conrad, the third person in the room.

"Yes, sir." Conrad slid a sealed envelope across the brown-acre desk. Geist opened it, briefly peering at the papers inside and then setting the envelope down.

"Would you please excuse us, Conrad? I need to speak to Guile privately." Conrad left the room and Geist looked at me with his intense eyes and an even more intense glare. "They are just as capable as I thought. All we need now is to contact them. A task that I will leave to you, but please let me know when you have a plan so I can help you."

I smiled and said. "I already have one."

"I'm listening."

In a matter of minutes, I told Geist the plan I spent the last few weeks crafting, and he helped me refine it before writing up a mission brief and drafting it to perfection. A few days later, I was in a meeting room with the people I needed to make it happen.

"Looks like we're all here," I said, as the last few people filed into the room. "Good. What I have for you here is the information you'll need to accomplish your mission."

Each of them sat in the seat with an envelope in front of it that had their codename on it.

"Let's get started. Your group assignments are in your files."

They all opened their files and looked at them, scrutinizing the contents.

"It looks like we're together on this one." said a girl with long, pink hair, nudging a man with the same color, short hair next to her.

"Don't forget about us," scoffed a man to her left.

"So, I guess this side's all one group too," said the man in pale white on the opposite side of the table.

I spoke to calm the room and continued with the short meeting. They were a rather volatile and somewhat unique group, but they were hand-picked for this mission. Normal soldiers fell in line too easily.

"Any questions?" I asked before concluding the meeting.

"Yeah, I got one," said the man wearing a soft green jacket. "Can we kill anyone who gets in our way?" The already quiet room fell silent.

"We'd like to spill as little blood as possible. But if someone who's *worth* the effort *ACTIVELY* tries to hinder the operation, then and *ONLY* then, do you have permission to kill anyone *including* the targets, and *only* if *absolutely* necessary," I stressed it enough that even the most thick-headed, bloodthirsty marauder could understand. "Anything else?"

No response.

"You are all dismissed," I said casually. As they began to leave the room, I spoke again. "Oh, and a piece of advice." Everyone turned and looked. "If you get too close to the Corpse Hunters, you may end up like the corpses being hunted."

"We'll keep that in mind," responded the one in orange. They continued out of the room, going in their respective directions.

I took a few minutes to look back into the file that Geist left me. About halfway through, I heard two knocks at my office door.

"Who is it?" I ask.

"It's Solo." His voice resounded through the door.

"Come in, I've been expecting you."

He entered as if expecting to see something that he hadn't seen in a long time. "I see you have the charts on my third awakened state." He guessed what was in the envelope.

"Yes, it looks like your telekinetic and telepathic abilities get further boosted. Proportionally, so does your speed and strength."

"I thought that was to be expected," he said, casually.

I looked up at him and said, "The only reason I have these charts is that Geist himself gave them to me. The reason for which he was counting on your curiosity to bring you here to see."

His brow rose. "And what's that?"

"I understand that you use your powers through your body instead of your mind as much as you can. Even so, you can't escape the degradation caused by them."

"My mind's fine." He tapped his temple. "You of all people should know I haven't changed."

"I know. The problem stems from the way you use your ability."

"What's wrong with it?" he asked, looking for new information.

"Nothing's wrong with how you use your power, just the conduit in which you channel your energy."

"My body?" He sat in the nearest chair.

"Usually, the biggest threat to someone like you is losing your mind. That would be if your mind was the sole conduit. However, you use your own body as the key passage between your mental prowess, your magic, and the rest of the world. That means that eventually, your body will give out on you. Just as your mind would."

Looking around as if unsure of when he took a seat, he stood. "I understand." He turned to leave silently.

"That's not the reason I wanted you to come here."

"What?"

"Your newly awakened state also increases the rate at which your body releases channeled energy to control those shards. This doubles the speed of your body's output. This also increases the rate of your body's decomposition. Because of this, your classification has been updated to devastation instead of divergent"

"In English?" He was visibly bothered by what I had to say.

"The more you use that form, the faster you die. For every second, you lose more. We're not sure how much, but-"

"I'll just have to live with it then. You know I can't give up on my goal." He reached for the door. "Not 'till I get the bastard that killed my mother," He opened the door.

"Twelve minutes," I said. "That's the limit. Don't overdo it." I hoped those words would stick with him.

"Thanks." He left in an air of mystery

"What am I going to do with you?" I said, shaking my head

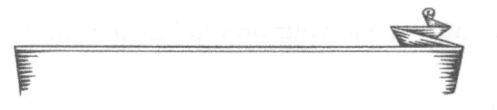

12-Magnolia

[Noah Black]

Drip-drip, drip, drip-drip, drip, drip. The sound echoed throughout the cavern. "Turn it off..." I moaned under the pee-inducing drip-dropping of the cave water.

"Sorry hun, can't do that," sighed Catt as she sat next to me.

"I wish we could because it's soo annoying..." I paused, giving in to the restless feeling rising in my gut. "Monneyyy!"

"Where'd that come from?" I startled her.

"I don't know, I just felt like I had to say something crazy."

"And that's the best you could do? Yeah, well, next time just try not to yell it out loud like that. People can hear outside of this cave," she warned.

"Well, that," I said while putting my arm around her and pulling her into a standing position with myself against the cave wall behind us. "That time was up a while ago. They followed us."

"How can you tell?"

"There is a corpse shadow attached to one of them. Chances are, they don't know of my abilities."

"And if they do?"

"Then, we're in a lot more trouble than we bargained for."

"Any chance they're Corpse Hunters?"

"I doubt it. Why would they need to come after me?"

She shrugged. "Okay, try feeling all of them out. Like, what are they like?"

"Well..." I said, concentrating. "There are two near and two afar."

"How close?"

"Can't tell, but I can say that they are all wielders. The closest one has an axe-type weapon and the other one has a hammer. Not only that... I can also see they share the corpse shadow between the two."

"What about the other two?"

"I don't know... They're hiding their presence pretty well."

"Well, I'm going out," she said, nonchalantly walking to the entrance of the cave.

"Wait, what if they-" I tried to protest.

"Then back me up, ok?" She winked.

I sighed. "Be careful. This is a threat."

She gave a soft giggle. "Come on."

"Okay then..."

She walked through the mouth of the cave into the open air. I hid in the opening's shadow. As she reached the sunlight, I was reminded of the fact that her hair color changed. At the moment, her hair was yellowish red. Her yellow leather jacket and matching gloves were shimmering in the uncertain light, and her black skirt made a dark contrast to it with a square design.

Taking a power stance, she said, "Show yourselves and come out now! I know you're there!"

Silence.

She looked back at me, and I pointed to her left, causing her to turn in that direction.

"Come out now or those trees are gonna be falling with you!" she yelled into the forest before the cave.

"They're moving," I said, just loud enough for Catt to hear.

After a brief rustling, two shapes emerged from the wilderness. One was a man wearing a dark brown shirt with a loose collar, same color pants, a red tie, and heavy-looking boots. He had short, pink hair. The other was a woman with the same uniform except hers was yellow and she had a mid-length dress. Her hair was also pink, but long.

Those were C.H.E.S.S. uniforms. They were supposed to deal with magical threats, like an international guild. They had no reason to follow us so maliciously.

The man took a step forward, weapon in hand. "In that case, let's do this as soon as possible." They were the ones who shared the corpse shadow with the stronger presence in the girl.

"What do you want?" demanded Catt.

"We want the boy you have hidden in that cave." He shifted his battle-ax in his hands. "You'd best give him to us if you don't want to die."

"Well, let's see you try." She put her hands up and summoned her weapons. They were twin gauntlets. They looked like martial arts gloves, but the color corresponded to her hair color and by this time, it was completely yellow. The attribute, however, was shown by the outlines of the borders within the gloves. This time, she chose lightning, and it was the same color as her gloves. The matching colors increased the effectiveness of her many abilities.

She rushed at him, hands ready. His axe came down at but a fraction of her speed. In a second, her fist was nestled just above his gut. Electricity arced across his body and paralyzed him in place. All he could do was arch forward on his knees in response.

"You bitch!" The girl was swinging her mallet down at Catt, who was still distracted.

In a flash, I was on the scene. My blade ran clean through the pink-haired girl I swiped at. There was a long pause before the lower half of her top fell away cleanly and a piercing scream sounded from her and echoed into the cave, rebounding off of its walls. The scream wasn't human. It was from the corpse shadow inside her. I cut and purified a part of it.

"Sakura!" It was the paralyzed man slouching in front of Catt. "What the hell did you do to her? Tell me!" He was panicking motionlessly aside for some minor rocking back and forth.

"Don't worry, she's not dead. She'll just be asleep for a while," I responded.

"You'll live," I said to the unconscious girl at my feet. "Let's go, Catt, I don't want to see them any longer." I started walking away and got a good look at my sword before it vanished on its own. It was a pure white katana with a single black thread going through the blade and handle.

The other two energy signatures faded, and it seemed like they were leaving. Apparently, they found whatever they were looking for.

"Yeah... Okay." Catt seemed bewildered as she followed. "Why are you so serious? It worked out alright."

"Any time my sword comes out, it's because bad things are happening. That was bad things."

"I know that, but... Whatever."

We continued on our way to Magnolia, a city of magic. We had found a lead to someone we were looking for and were following it until we noticed we were being watched. In response, we re-routed our path to avoid confrontation. As it turned out, that was impossible.

"What about them?" said Catt, pointing back at the two we were leaving behind.

"The paralysis wears off in about five minutes, right? We can leave them behind. We should pass into the underworld by now, anyway." I stepped up the pace, and she kept up with me.

"What happened to you, just now? Was it like before?"

"No, it was nothing." I brushed it off.

"If you say so. What about the other two?"

"They're not following us."

"Good." She nodded. "We should be close to the city." She looked up. "There it is!" Her excitement almost made me excited.

"Where?" I asked, looking around.

"Up there! There's the Scorched Ice!" She pointed at what looked like the top of a black and white pillar reaching toward the sky above the trees.

The Scorched ice was the tip of the castle that can be seen from a distance outside of the city. The castle itself, which housed the royal family, was called the Frozen Flame. It was named by appearance, like a giant fire that was frozen with a scorch mark on one side as a reminder of the flame it used to be. Looking up, I could see what looked like the tip of an iceberg that was layered with soot. That was the sign that we were close to our destination.

By the time we reached the first gate, fifteen minutes had already passed, and we weren't being followed. The gate looked like the stereotypical medieval castle gate made of steel and lifted when opened. The wall itself was ash white and lined with moss and vines from decades of standing.

"Identification, please." said the gruff guard at the gate. We each produced a card from our wallets. Mine was white with a black dot in the center. Catts was a rainbow and kept changing colors. The guard swiped them both in a machine to his right while our bags were being checked at another station by a female guard. Mine was a brown sack. Catts was a red duffle bag. "Okay, go on through." He handed us back our cards, and we entered a metal detector with no further trouble.

"So, where's our informant again?" I asked.

Catt pulled out a small, handwritten letter and said, "It says they would be waiting for us inside Wall Rize."

"Oh yeah. They must live there."

"Actually, I'm not even a resident of this city." I looked down to see an old man wearing a pale cloak under the sunlight. "I'm just staying at a friend's place until my business is done."

"Uh... old man-" I started but the feeling he carried made me stop.

"Just call me Jamie." Looking at his face, I could see wisdom that had nothing to do with his age and the mental scars of things no one should ever have had to lay eyes on. The things that man probably went through were things I wouldn't wish on my enemy. "Now, follow me please." He began walking toward an entrance into the second wall. We followed until we met a door numbered 1227.

It was an apartment room nestled near the top of Wall Rize. It had three parts to it. A bedroom, a bathroom, and a living/dining room with a small blue kitchen on the side. There was brown carpeting in the bedroom, blue carpets, green walls, and furniture made of and covered in what felt like the same material in the living room, and an all-white bathroom. We were nestled comfortably on three chairs.

"So, what did we come all the way to Magnolia about?" Catt questioned the old man.

"You came for information, did you not?" he responded.

Catt looked for me to answer.

"So, what do you know about what we're looking for?" I continued the questioning.

Jamie nodded. "I've known about the Black family for fifty years and I've been a friend of the family for forty of those."

"So, you knew my grandfather?"

"I knew your father too. And your mother. I was there when they met. Marilyn was a sweet girl, and Jessy was a man of many talents. It horrified me to hear of what had happened to them and their family." He paused after I gave him a look. "But you're not here to talk about the past, are you?"

"Do you even know what we're looking for?" I raised my voice and Cat preemptively grabbed my arm.

"The locations of you and the others of your family were of passionate debate for all who heard the news," said Jamie

"Could you stop beating around the bush and tell us what you know?" said Catt.

"I and a few colleagues of mine found one of your sisters a month and a half ago. Hariet was found dead when the police raided a major slave trade hub in Guatemala."

I blacked out. The next thing I knew was facing up toward Catts's blue gauntlet with purple trim. I came from a comfortable chair to the ground. She used gravity to subdue me.

"You back together?" she said.

"My sister..." I said, listlessly.

"I brought a picture so that you can verify for yourself." Jamie handed me a picture. "I know it may be difficult for you, but we need someone related to her to identify her."

It was a cross-sectioned photo showing a crime scene in one panel, a morgue table in another, and a closeup of the same person in the other two images as depicted in both settings. Tears slowly materialized as my eyes ran over the details of my older sister. Her long, brown hair, the blue streak in it she loved so much, and the butterfly tattoos she was so proud of on the back of her right hand and her left cheek. I sat up.

"That's her... How..." I couldn't form a cohesive sentence.

"That's not all." As I struggled to say something else, he continued. "We also found your little sister."

"Mary?" I covered my ears with my hands to ward away more heartbreaking information. I didn't think that I could take any more. Catt embraced me from my side. Her warmth put me at ease.

"It's okay." She then gently cupped her hands around mine. Feeling the comforting aura she exerted, my hands mimicked the shape.

"Okay." I let him continue.

"She's part of an organization called C.H.E.S.S."

"Really?" said Catt. "Those guys are after Noah."

A shadow of worry fell over Jamie's face. "That's no good. I investigated it myself and it turned out to be a front for a dark organization." He handed me a picture of Mary. She was older and wearing an all-white uniform with a white bishop badge over her right breast. Both Catt and I were shocked to see such a recently familiar uniform on my little sister.

"But why-" started Catt before the light hum of a temporal distortion cut her off. It was like my ears popped and all sound stopped.

"We're being watched. I stopped local time to prevent anything of necessity from being known by others," he said.

"But-" I started.

"Take this." He handed me a small notebook. "Everything we've found is inside that notebook, don't lose it." By the amount of power I felt rushing from the old man, I expected him to be heaving sighs and barely standing. Instead, he seemed not to lose even a sweat.

"I'll put it in a safe place." It just barely fit in the only side pocket of my bag. The popping sound came again as time started while I stood up.

The door burst open, and three guards entered the apartment.

"Time prophet James Rose and guests. The royalty would like an audience with you," said the first guard to enter. "They await you in the minor throne room."

The three guards moved to the side to let us through. Exiting the almost plush room into the stone hallway was a welcome change of venue. They led us down the hall and out of the complex that made up the second wall. Next was a flight of stairs down the inside of the wall and a straight shot to the third. It was a single path through the sidewalks and streets between Rize and the third wall.

"Wall Seria," said Jamie as we traveled through the red third wall straight toward the castle. "And finally, Morne," He finished as we continued through the black and white stone wall surrounding the castle.

Up to then, we had seen at least two guards wearing uniforms of similar colors at each gate. All of those guards seemed to be nothing compared to the two we were left off to by the three that were escorting us. One was a large, bulky man in heavy-looking clothes with minimal facial hair and clenched fists. The other was a girl around 160cm in loose-fitting jeans and a black and yellow jacket with piercing eyes, folded arms, and a dangerous look. What she seemed to lack in presence she made up for in raw intimidation.

"We'll take 'em from here," said the girl, stepping up from leaning on a wall near the castle gate.

Jamie put on a smile and approached the girl. "Why, Helen! I haven't seen you in such a long while. Have you reconsidered my last offer?"

"I already told you. I only work for my prince," she responded. At this point, I was questioning Jamie's residency here.

"I wonder what kind of 'work' that is," said Jamie, cheekily.

"Don't push me, you perverted old man," she scowled.

"This way," interrupted the large man with a gruff voice, breaking up their conversation. "Inside." He opened the even larger front door of the castle.

"Best not to keep royalty waiting," sighed Jamie as the large guard entered first followed by Catt, me, and the guard known as Helen last.

The entrance hall of the castle was as crystalline as the outside with decorative paintings, murals, and armors lining the walls and columns. This seemed to compliment the surrounding white, blue, and black swirl-stained walls. Like the outside, they seemed to have been frozen mid-burn.

Entering a set of shimmery silver doors that stood ajar, we turned right as we went into what seemed to be a larger corridor. Upon noticing a large table on my right with chairs on its opposite side, I looked to the left to see two high-standing chairs on top of a stair platform looking down on the rest of the large hall.

Seated and waiting were an elegantly dressed woman in a long blue dress with gold accents and a man with gold-plated armor with red accents. They were sitting on adjacent thrones. Both thrones seemed to be made of high-quality silver with the same running theme of gold accents. The man who by this time I figured to be the prince had a solid structure to his throne, while his sister had a whimsical feel to hers.

Their young faces had similar features in their air of simplicity despite their royal appearance, but that's where their similarities ended. The princess had pale skin and long, wavy, cold white hair with a solid curl at the end which she let drape over the front of her shoulder. Her eyes seemed to reflect a bit of light, and her tapping fingers signified her impatience.

The prince had a smug look on his face as if he had just soundly won an argument with his chin lying gently on his fist resting on the arm of his throne. His short, blonde, hair clearly showed through the bottom of his crown, and his sharp, blue, eyes stared down at us the way only royalty could.

"Sit." The large guard pointed at the twist-oak chairs on one side of the ashwood table. I kept my eyes trained on the two highest in the room as I took a seat between Catt and Jamie. There were five chairs in total. Enough for a small group of executives or council members to sit.

"I see your guard is as simple a word as ever," remarked the prince.

"Well, mine isn't a living stagger," Retorted the princess.

The two guards walked as soldiers to what would seem to be their posts. Helen to the prince's side and the man to the princess' side as the siblings saw to one final quarrel before getting to business.

"Christopher and Bianka Roland. Successors to the throne. For what do I have the honor of meeting with you today?" Jamie spoke with reverence.

"That's a question for you to answer, Sir. James," replied the prince, "Had we known of your presence within these walls, we would have happily accommodated you and your... Guests." His eyes swept over us as his triumphant smirk faded.

"The subject matter for which I had to discuss with my guests was deemed of little importance to your highness." He expertly avoided directly answering the question.

"The Black family is of more importance than you may know." The princess spoke this time. Her voice could carry unlike her brother, whose voice could be understood but not felt. In my surprise, I nearly fell over and stood up simultaneously while opening my mouth to ask a newly burning question. She raised her finger as my action took place. This somehow calmed me down and cooled the erupting question that was about to rise out of my gut. I wasn't sure if she cast an unspoken spell to quell my conscience or if it really was her royal influence that did this. Either way, I kept quiet. "The Black family has guarded this kingdom against the shadows for as long as it has existed." I just noticed that the two entrances and four stained glass windows were both closed and likely locked as she continued. "Noah Black. It is imperative that you see what your family has been protecting. As such, consider this your birthright."

The room began to shake slightly as it rotated so that the door in which we came in was behind us while the steps leading to the two thrones flattened to floor height and the entire room descended. No one moved as the polished gray walls disappeared to be replaced with the same colors adorning the outside of the castle. White marked with streaks of black and blue. Out of curiosity, I touched the wall behind me.

"Whoa..." The wall, despite the moving, was hot to the touch and then cold in a flash. Upon closer inspection, the heat seemed to only be coming from the scorch marks and the ice really felt like ice. There was no doubt in my mind that the entire wall behind us was actually made of either burnt ice or a frozen flame. "Catt," I said. She turned to look at me.

"What are you doing?" she whispered.

"It's real," I whispered back.

Unimpressed, she responded, "It's a wall."

"It's ice."

"Really?" Now she was intrigued.

"Touch it, it's hot."

"But how is it ice?" She leaned her hand closer to it.

"It's cold too, like a frozen flame."

"You're right, the scorch marks are still hot, and it feels like ice on the cold parts." She traced her fingertips across the surface of the gradually escalating wall as we went deeper into the ground.

"This would explain the rest of the castle, wouldn't it?"

"Yeah, this woul-ss-aah!" She brushed her fingertips across a scorch mark, jumped, and began flailing her hand about violently.

"Please do be careful as the temperature differences increase as we descend." As the princess' voice reached my ear, I turned back around to the stare of both the prince and princess landing on Catt. This only surprised me for a second as I realized that Catt was the only one here that didn't seem to belong, at least as far as the whole 'royal guard' business was concerned.

"Catt," I whispered. She looked toward me, obviously still in pain. "They're staring at you."

She turned around as if she had been caught sticking her hand in a cookie jar that had been sitting out in the sun all day and became too hot to touch.

The prince spoke. "My, my. That's not the way a guard such as yourself should be acting, is it, Miss…?"

"Catt," responded Catt, nursing her injured hand. "And I'm not a guard."

"Oh!" Resounded the princess. She then pursed her lips, slowly and gingerly smiled, and softened the look in her eyes.

"If that's so then, what is-" started the prince.

"That's enough for now, brother." His sister interrupted. "I'd rather save those questions myself for later."

"If you say so." He shrugged.

By this time, the room opened up as the platform lowered into a large chamber far below the castle. The ceiling seemed to continue upward forever as I wondered when The platform beneath my feet would stop moving. It did stop but in an unexpected way. It seemed to stop sharply but I didn't feel a jolt or any sign of it slowing down as the rate of descent seemed to increase as the distance between us and our stop decreased.

In all directions, the pattern of black and white was visible, except in the direction of any of the three doors. There was one on the left and right as well as what would have been behind us if we had not turned to face it upon notice. They were all large, metal doors decorated with art. Flowers, butterflies, and the occasional tree adorned the steel in vibrant reds, blues, yellows, and white. They seemed to liven up the otherwise gray doors.

"This is where our ways part," said the prince, walking toward the door on the right from his throne followed by Helen. "You two will come with us to meet the twins." He pointed at both me and Jamie "And you will stay here." Before Catt could object, he continued, "I don't want any outside contaminants inside their chambers. It could prove fatal." His eyes narrowed at her as he left the platform with his guard in tow.

"Be that as it may, we can't just leave a guest out here alone now, can we?" The princess spoke with a slight melody in her voice.

"I suppose," replied the Prince. "What do you have in mind?"

The Princess smiled through her pursed lips. "If you don't mind, I would like to borrow Helen from you for a while."

"What for?"

"I'd like to have some alone time with the girls, just the girls. Of course, a fair trade of this big lug here would be in order." She tapped her guard's chest as she addressed him.

"Hmm..." The prince seemed to think it over for a second. "I suppose that can be arranged." He turned back toward Helen. "Any objections?"

"None, my prince." She nodded.

Hearing that seemed to make his decision easier. "So be it. I'll accept your temporary trade."

"Yes... temporary. Take care of my Lug now." The princess waved away her guard.

"And you, her." The guards moved swiftly to their independent destinations cautiously as if crossing each other's paths would cause an unwanted confrontation.

"Oh, and tell them hi from me, would you?" said the Princess.

"We'll see. You two let's go!" The prince continued to proudly step toward the large, metal door as if it didn't really matter if we came along or not.

"Off we go," commented Jamie as he began to walk in the same direction.

"What do you think the princess really wants with me?" whispered Catt.

"I don't know, but I'll be back for you," I whispered back.

"And that's why people always think we're a couple."

"No, it's not."

"Whatever you two keep whispering about can wait. Let's go!" The prince's impatience became more obvious every second.

Catt took a deep breath. "Let's stop reassuring ourselves and just go."

"Yeah, you're right." I followed in the direction of the prince and the guard toward the door. It was already open, and they were leaving me behind. Catt just watched until the door closed behind me.

13-Separated

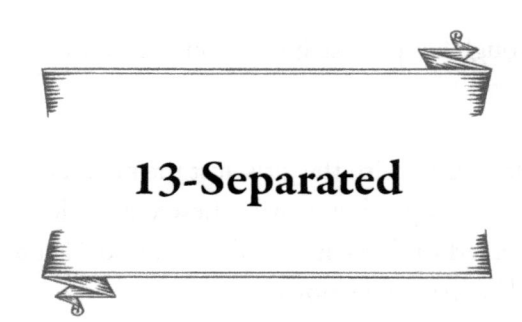

[Cattherine Lockhart]

As I watched the door close, it hit me. They were separating us. While I was Idly focused on nursing on my burned fingertips, it distracted me from most of the conversation at hand. Had I been paying attention, I would have argued that the group stayed together. Although I had no reason to distrust the royal family, I also had no reason to trust them either. This thought made me wince as the shout of the closing door hit me.

"Now that that's taken care of, follow me, ladies." The woman known as Princess Roland guided me and Helen, the prince's guard, toward the room opposite the one her brother took Noah. As she neared the door, it opened to what seemed to be a library with three sofas, two desks, four chairs, and two floors of bookcases. There was also a single white desktop computer impossibly connected to the presumably unmeltable wall in the far right next to the top of the staircase on the second floor. The walls and floor were still the same color as the room we had just exited. It also smelled like a library with a mixed aroma of new and old texts lining the walls in old wooden bookcases. There was also the taste of parchment in the air. I felt like just sitting and absorbing the knowledge surrounding me. It being a royal library, who knows the type of information one could find?

"Please, take a seat." Gesturing toward the red, white, and black sofas surrounding an ash-wood table in the middle of the room, Bianka swiftly found herself on the black seat facing away from the door. I cautiously positioned myself in the middle of the red seat on the right of her, and Helen took the one opposite me. "Now let's start." The smile on her face said 'innocent' but I felt otherwise. "So, do you prefer to be called Catt or Miss Catt?" She turned to me, teasing me as if we were already good friends.

I said, "What do you mean?"

"I, myself, like to be called by my first name, so how about we all go on a first-name basis while we're here? Is that ok with you two?"

Somehow, I knew it would become like that. She was trying to become as familiar as possible as soon as possible. Manipulation 101.

"Sure," I agreed. After all, the look she gave me was quite charming. Her silver eyes coupled with a seductive glare made it hard to resist. It was subtle but powerful magic and resisting it could have made her suspicious of me.

"And you?" She looked toward Helen.

"I have no problem," responded the guard.

"Good. That brings me to the first question." She turned back to me. "If you're not a surviving servant of the house of Black, then what is that boy to you? And don't just say a 'comrade' or a 'fellow traveler' because I saw the way you looked at each other as he left through that door and the way you two kept whispering amongst yourselves. That's a little more than just companionship." She immediately went where I thought it would eventually go.

"What's it to you?" I asked as straightforwardly as she did.

"His bloodline has known knighthood in this kingdom for generations. And as one of my potential knights, I need to know his current relationship status."

"His relationships aren't your business," I said boldly.

"Is that so?" She brought her legs up onto the seat, allowing her dress to cascade down, almost touching the ground as she turned into a more comfortable position.

"Yes, it is," I said.

"With recent events being as they are, we need every eligible knight we can find. That's why my brother is taking him to meet part of the foundation of what he would be tasked with protecting. Times being what they are, if I asked him to stay and be knighted in my kingdom, he would be obligated to comply. Both of his parents were knights. After all, I could use a bedroom guard to keep watch of my sleeping frame. All I need is a reason not to cage my little birdy, and I thought that reason was sitting before me."

The princess was bold, that's for sure. Even so, I couldn't let her coax a definitive reaction from me. I called her bluff. Struggling to find the right words, instead, I vaguely moved my still-closed jaw with a frustrated look on my face.

"No need to fret now," she said, reassuringly. "Take some time to think about it." Her stare said otherwise but I kept silent. Her eyes fluttered toward Helen, who had been constantly swapping gazes between me and Bianka while my interrogation concluded. She straightened to attention as the line of sight belonging to one of authority landed on her. "That reminds me." The Princess smirked. "What have you with my brother?"

"Excuse me, Princess-" she started.

"A-a-ah~" The Princess held up a ticking finger. "First name basis, remember?"

"Yes, but is this the only reason you wanted me to accompany you to the library?" Helen seemed completely unphased by Bianka's casual attitude.

"I won't order, nor will I force you to answer, I just want to know what you think of my brother."

After a moment of pause, Helen responded with a straight look down at her black shirt with a red, thorny cross and a slightly reddened face. "He's... Nice to me."

"Oh? How so?" Bianka's intrigue visibly increased. As had mine.

As if she had just realized her moment of weakness, Helen wiped the redness from her face, looked at Bianka with an accusatory expression, and said, "I'm done. You almost got me. I almost opened up to you and your tricks." She stood up, walked behind her seat, and rested her hands in the middle of it. "But I'm not going."

"If that's true, then how about this?" Bianka turned forward in her seat, crossed her legs under her dress, and spread her arms across the back of the sofa, then continued, "If you answer my question, then I will answer one of yours." There was a distinct pause as each of us rose a single brow after the other. First Helen, then me, and Bianka. "Of course, that goes for you as well since you had already answered my first question." She looked back toward me while saying this.

Helen drastically changed her posture and sat back down with her arms crossed. "So, I can ask you anything?"

Bianka smiled. "Yes, and I'll answer to the best of my abilities."

After another moment of pause and a deep breath, Helen began. "twelve years ago, there was an incident in Egypt where a new tomb had been discovered dedicated to the god Anubis. Have you heard of this?"

"Indeed, I have. Legend has it that whosoever can appease the Egyptian God can have one wish granted. But of course, there's always a cost."

"Your soul." Helen's solemn expression gave away her feelings. "My brother and I had found the crypt at the same time that an excavation crew came through to explore it." The slowly nodding head of Bianka told me she knew how this story ended. "It took them six days to uncover an altar at an enormous abyss at the base of the tomb. On the seventh day, they rested, and that was the day my brother planned for. He knocked me out and went to the base alone." Her eyes began to water, but not falter. "I woke up in time to find his soul being ripped out of his body and being pulled down into the abyss."

"And you want me to help you bring him back?" Bianka seemed to have spoken before she could stop herself. She closed her mouth fast after speaking.

"Not just that... There was something else." Helen seemed to ready herself for what was coming next. "I saw something akin to what I believe may be a grim reaper."

"And what was this grim reaper doing?" Bianka's intrigue seemed to reach a height of impossibility as her next question came through.

"He was carrying a soul… It wasn't my brothers… It was somebody else's. It dropped the soul into my brother's body, and it started moving." Bianka raised her head and her jaw dropped as if she recognized the scenario. "That was when my powers awakened. I attacked it when I saw it stand back up with eyes different from my brothers. It had this… foreboding feeling emanating from it."

"Like it was going to kill you?" This time, my experience led me to ask.

"Yes." She nodded in her response. "It leaped into the air and flew on wings of blackness. It even apologized… For some reason. Ever since then, I've been hunting this thing inside my brother's body so I could put him and his soul back together. After I started wandering the world in search of answers, my health began to fail. Eventually, your brother found me when I was at my lowest and allowed me to work for him in exchange for the medicine I needed and resources to find and purify whatever is in my brother's body." She turned her gaze directly into the princess's eyes. "I think highly about your brother. He saved my life." After another distinct pause, she continued. "Now you have an answer and I have a question."

"That is?" asked the Princess.

"I expect an honest answer,"

"I wouldn't dare answer otherwise," Bianka spoke with a seriousness she hadn't exhibited since entering the library.

"Have you known of any reports of anything, no matter how minor, involving a being shrouded in darkness under any circumstances regardless of implementation?" She seemed to run out of breath before calming down. "Anything that cannot be explained?"

"I have, but only in stories. Some of my comrades in the Hunting business have come across such a figure. While most have been encounters with the corpse shadow epidemic that seems to have struck the globe. A few seem to be particular to your case."

"Such as?"

"A mysterious occurrence where a man got his soul stolen in Cairo around the same time that your incident took place twelve years ago. Whatever took the man's soul absorbed it and grew 'wings of darkness' before abruptly fleeing the scene on said wings. This was in the twilight of March fifth. A month later, a group of researchers sent by yours truly to excavate the site found the chasm deep underground. That's not the only case either. There have been cases of powerful wielders like ourselves being attacked by a being cloaked in black. They call it the 'black reaper'. Few have survived, but they were all members of C.H.E.S.S."

"It's always them," I said, nearly getting lost in thought. This was the third time I came across them today.

"Yes. They seem to have their hand in everything nowadays. That aside. I have heard stories ranging from twelve years ago to last year. Witnesses also said that the black reaper wielded a black scythe."

Helen continued. "Can you think of anything that may pose or present a pattern of significance?"

"A friend of mine asked me to look into that very matter some time ago."

"And?"

Bianka shrugged. "I've come up empty-handed."

"Oh…" Helen finally showed some emotion as she seemed to be saddened.

"Are you disappointed?"

"No, I… I guess I was expecting too much."

"Well, there's your question answered." She turned her sights back toward me "Do you, perhaps, have a question for me Catt?" It took me a second to realize that she was talking to me.

"Mmmm…" I took a moment to think about what I would want to know from a princess with so much information waiting to be spilled onto the table at a moment's notice.

"No need to ask away now. I didn't expect you to have a question immediately."

"I'm looking for someone." My statement gave her pause.

"My, my. You, too?"

"The man I'm looking for is the reason for my traveling and I'd like to have anything we say on this matter kept a secret." I made sure to keep a straight face.

"You have my word as long as you keep the specifics of the rest of this conversation to yourself."

"What about her?" I nodded toward Helen.

"You have nothing to worry about," the guard responded.

"I'm looking for a man who saved me. I can't give a name, but I can give a description."

"Go on," encouraged Bianka.

"In my search, I found that he wears clothes that seem to wrap completely around his entire body except for his eyes. That aside, he's also a wielder and his abilities have something to do with matter manipulation."

"Of what kind?" she asked.

"Last I saw him was five years ago when he saved me from some dangerous people. He made things levitate with a kind of pink or purple energy surrounding them, me included. Those people are still out there, and I want to find him so I can help people the way he does."

"If those people are that dangerous, then are you sure you want to find them?"

"Not them, just him. I know I'll come across them eventually."

"Okay, I'll tell you."

"Huh?" I didn't expect her to have any kind of answer.

"There's been a story or two about a man who roams the Big Apple who fits that description. If I recall, he went by Graven."

"That's all I needed to know. Thank you for the information." I folded my hands in thought.

"Any time." Her smile was as innocent as ever. I still wasn't sure If I could trust her or the one sitting across from me, but I decided that the best way to confirm anything was to go for it. "Well, the boys should be back by now. Shall we go meet them?" Standing up, she turned and hopped over her seat one-handed like a kid on a playground. "Let's go, ladies." She waved. Perplexed by her behavior, I just went with it.

Seconds after exiting the library, we were surprised by three new faces. Two children wearing a blue and white dress and a red and yellow dress, respectively. And a rather tall man in black and white with hints of yellow beside the expected group of four. The children shyly hid behind the man. As my curiosity deepened, I wondered where this was going.

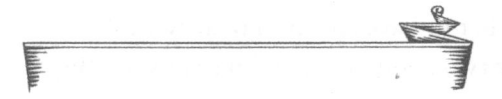

14-Deadly Premonitions

[Noah Black]

The sound that every closing door seemed to make was deafening in this castle. It resonated through the walls and echoed a little within the hall.

"You must be infatuated with that girl, huh?" The prince referred to me without looking.

"Excuse me?" His remark took me by surprise. I expected a quiet walk to wherever we were going through this oddly room-temperature hallway made of fire and ice instead of a conversation about my love life.

"Even if you don't fancy her, she obviously adores you. You must have noticed it by now."

"I have no idea what you're talking about."

"Is that so? You looked back at that door three times since it closed."

"I was only wondering how you have automatic doors down here."

"Oh really? I get those same looks from my guard when she thinks I don't notice. Either you do fancy her, or you owe her a lot."

"Excuse me, Prince, but I don't see what any of this has to do with us being here." I had to change the subject.

"There is reasoning behind these questions, is there not, dear Prince?" I forgot Jamie was here with us. Either by his sheer lack of stature or presence, he was invisible until he said something.

"Indeed, there is. My sister is undoubtedly questioning that girl on the same subject as we speak. Like her, I will get answers. Unlike her, I will give fair warning when I dig. The reason I ask is because of a question that you must answer. Do you understand, Noah Black?"

I asked, "What is the question?" getting straight to the point.

"In due time. For now, I must ascertain the status of all your current relationships." The prince seemed to dance around his true intentions.

"Is that all?"

"No, but we'll get to that once you're introduced to the people beyond that door." He stopped and pointed at the only door at the end of the long hallway. I hadn't noticed it because it blended in more with the walls than the previous doors we'd seen in the castle. This one was a light gray with dark burnt patches all over its surface instead of the whole thing being dark gray or blue. This door was also much smaller than the other doors. About the size of a house door.

The rest of us stopped walking when it started opening in our direction. On the other side looked like a living area with an open front room, a stairway up along the left side with a brown door on its side, a short hallway to a door past a kitchen in the middle, and a tall man covering the rest of the image. It seemed he was the one who opened the door. He looked more like a hardened soldier than someone who needed protection. He wasn't particularly large, just tall. His otherwise black jacket was stamped with the symbol of a white cross mirrored over the middle, with one side pointing up and the other side down. His pants were a similar shade of black, but they had small, yellow electric patterns running around them.

"Hello." He bowed deeply after scanning our group with his eyes. "I thought I heard the voice of royalty." His face suggested he was near exiting his thirties.

"Your ears are as sharp as ever I see," The Prince responded.

"I see you brought guests." The man stepped aside and back into the room. "You are welcome to come in."

As we entered, the rest of the room came into view. To the right of the door, there were two black couches. One was against the wall next to the opening to another hallway and the other was against the wall next to the entrance. Both could fit four comfortably. The entire room had white walls and a blue candle-shaped chandelier in the middle. The walls were stark white with no hint of the blues or blacks on every other wall of the castle.

As soon as we were all inside, the Prince introduced us. "Noah Black, this is Sirus Shey, direct guardian to the twins of ice and fire. Sirus Shey, this is Noah Black, the current heir to the house of Black."

"Nice to meet you," said Sirus.

"You too." We shook hands firmly.

"And of course, you know the time prophet James Rose," continued the prince.

"Long time no see," said Sirus.

"Likewise," responded Jamie. By this time, I was sure that there was more to Jamie than he wanted me to know.

"Might I ask what brings you down here, Sir?" Sirus bowed to the prince

"I came to see the twins, so, might I ask where they are?"

"They're in the playroom in a feverish contest of rock, paper, scissors."

"May I ask that you call them in? I have important business with them."

At nearly the same time as he finished his sentence, there was an audible shuffle coming from the door on the side of the stairs. Seconds later, it opened, and two girls came through. One had shoulder-length red pig-tailed hair with yellow ribbons, while the one behind her had the same-length white hair with blue ribbons braided into it. They both wore sun dresses of different designs. One was deep red with a thin, yellow floral pattern traced across its surface. The other one had a white strip through the middle of a ruffled deep blue dress. The white spread around the entire skirt near the base, which had the same deep blue on the end. The red one darted toward me with the other one behind her and grabbed my arm.

"Mine," she said.

Befuddled, I said, "Excuse me?"

"Who said you could have him?" interjected the pale one.

"I won, remember? That means that I get him."

"Girls, what's this about?" said Sirus. "Prince Roland came for a visit, and I expect you to address him."

"Hey, brobro! Whatcha here for huh?" asked the red one.

"Yes, please do tell," continued the pale one.

The Prince said, "Actually, I came to introduce you to my guest, who you are so aggressively clutching at the moment."

"Can you please let me go," I asked.

"Nope!" The red girl seemed a little too happy to be latched to my side.

"Either way, Girls, that's Noah Black, current head of the Black family." The Prince gestured toward me.

"Humph!" went the pale one.

"Nice to meet you!" Jumped the one on my arm.

"Noah, that one skulking by the door is the Ice Queen, Snow Shey," said the Prince pointing at the pale one with a bright blue left eye and a presumably blind right eye pouting in my direction. "And the one glued to you is the Red Lady, Sun Shey." He pointed to my right side. I looked down to see one unbelievably bright red right eye and a yellow one next to it. "They are the twins of ice and fire." He said it with such pride that one could assume that he was their father. "That is all, have at him."

"Wait, what's that supposed to mean?" I demanded, looking around at the satisfied faces of everyone in attendance.

"Alright, I propose one more duel!" Snow was intently pointing at Sun.

"And what is that?" Sun responded. They were both ignoring me.

"A battle."

The prince chimed in. "Now, now, that's unnecessary."

"Yeah. I got a better idea!" exclaimed Sun. "We'll let him choose for himself."

"What are you talking about? He's still clueless. There's no way he could make an honest choice." Snow sounded very adamant about her statement.

"What about our gifts?"

"What about them?"

"They could help him choose." Sun shrugged.

"Idiot, there's no way he'd be able to choose based on those."

"Hey, there's always a chance, isn't there?"

"I guess so..." Snow looked down and dug her heel into the ground.

"Seems like they made up their minds." The Prince sounded happy with this recent development.

"So, what is this all about exactly?" For a second, it seemed like my question landed on deaf ears. Looking beyond the prince, I could see that Sirus and Jamie were having their own conversation and leaving me in the confusion that was Sun and Snow while the princess's guard was nowhere to be found. Not to mention the prince who was overly accepting of the situation.

"Follow me and you'll find out." Sun began pulling me along past the kitchen, down the hallway into the room at the end. The redwood door opened by Snow into a large, empty, white room. It was like a clean white sheet.

"A training room?" I asked, looking around. No one followed us. It was just me, Sun, and Snow.

"In this room, we can have unrestricted use of our powers," said Snow.

"Unrestricted?" I asked, trying to piece together this scenario in my mind.

"Go over there and watch." Snow pointed to the left of the door as Sun let go of my arm.

"Oookay?" I obeyed and sat over next to the entrance with another unanswered question.

"Now watch us and no matter what happens, don't look away."

"But why?"

"We need your powers of observation." They stopped at what I could only assume was the middle of the room.

"Don't worry. Just don't stop looking, ok?" said Sun, looking back at me. She was pleading with her eyes.

As she turned away. It just hit me at that moment that I couldn't see age on her face, nor her sisters. Going by everything else, their age was between thirteen and twenty-two. I wasn't sure, so I assumed they were ageless. It made sense since

Snow said, "Are you ready?"

"Yep!" Sun responded.

I asked, "Uh... Can I blink?"

"Yes, you can blink, but whatever you do, don't look away or close your eyes," responded Snow. "Is that all?"

"Yeah, no more questions."

"Let's start," she said. They both cupped their hands in front of each other. "***Never-melt in the blind hues of forgotten snow***," started Snow.

"***Burn forever in the memory of the all-knowing flame***," continued Sun. After they uttered those words, an intricate circle etched itself around them. Half of it burned and the other side froze. Something was forming between them as a sound arose from them followed by an ominous wind. They lifted off the ground and levitated upward.

"The circle's set," said Sun as they clasped hands together.

"Let's begin," responded Snow. "The song of ice and fire."

The indiscriminate sound rose to an audible hum. This continued for about five seconds before a small bright light appeared by Snow. It was a ball of fire. Its light dimmed as a ball of ice appeared next to Sun. The ice ball melted before it took the shape of a small vial and rotated around the girls in tandem with the dim flame. A couple of seconds after this began, another flame and an ice shard joined the mix. All of this was followed by a sudden stop.

Everything ceased. Before I knew it, so had my heart, my breathing, and my mind. I barely regained my functions as I saw a visible shock wave come from the twins and slice all the created assets in half. The shockwave hit the wall above my head and I felt lucky that I had sat instead of standing. The lower halves of each item swam into the center as everything began floating down. They coalesced into a small glowing orb in between Sun and Snow. The glow of everything lessened as they all reached the ground. Even the one fire that remained, darkened until it looked like a moving, fire-shaped pendant. It was a moment before I realized that the humming had stopped, and time had begun running normally again. I had wondered at the moment if that was all their doing, but my question was answered shortly after that thought.

"We're finished," said Sun as they gathered the small objects off of the ground.

"What are you still doing down there? Get up and come here so that you can see what we have." Snow sounded slightly agitated.

"Uh... Sure." I moved my sluggishly weighted body to their location.

"These gifts are for you." Sun held out five small objects in her hands. I could sense the energy coming from them. It felt familiar. "You should be grateful. My sister doesn't like to do this for just anyone. She says it takes way too much energy from her and she feels drained afterward. If she's willing to do this for you on the fly, that means you're special!"

Snow grumbled, "It's not like he's really all that special or anything."

Sun smiled. "You don't mean that." She lowered her voice to a whisper. "That's her tell."

My spell of confusion seemed to lift as I came to slowly understand the situation and nod my head. "Huh."

"Anyhow, now's a good time to explain what these objects are and how they work," said Snow, pointing at the small trinkets in Sun's hands. "That one's never-melt-ice." She pointed at the blue and white ice shard. "It can freeze almost anything, including fire."

Next, she pointed at the one that looked like the slowest burning flame ever. "Next to that is forever fire. It can burn almost anything and evaporate almost any liquid."

The next one was a blue liquid in a vial. It was as blue as the sea. "The one there is heavy water. It's what happens when you melt never-melt-ice with forever fire. It can heal any wound. Just apply it gently. Also, it can never be frozen or evaporated."

The second to last one looked like it was a miniature-scale version of the castle by the same name. The only difference was at its core was a glowing red ember. "And this one here is a frozen flame. It's what happens when you freeze forever-fire with never-melt-ice. It has minor healing properties, but it's also a protection charm. It can also never be directly melted."

The last one still had a faint glow about it and was a white liquid inside a crystalline sphere coated in a translucent black that was invisible upon direct sight. "Last, but not least, is what's called 'holy essence'. It's what happens when two absolute attributes collide against each other. Like when never-melt-ice tries to freeze forever fire and forever fire tries to melt never-melt-ice at the same time. It's not actually holy, so it's usually called 'sacred essence', but it can be in the right hands. Its abilities are varied and entirely dependent on who uses it and for what purpose. That aside, each of these charms can be used for their raw energy."

I learned about what most of the objects in Sun's hands were from my father when I was younger, so I wasn't surprised about what they did. I just enjoyed the explanation. That was for all except for the sacred essence and the fact that I was being presented with all of them at once. Considering where I was, I wasn't all that surprised that they would be in one place. I just didn't expect them to be given to me so readily. If anything, I was surprised that there was a thing like sacred essence out there. It piqued my interest.

"And that's all of them!" Sun spoke up after so long of staying silent. "Now, there is one last thing for you to do."

"What's that?" I asked, unprepared.

"You need to choose."

"What?" My confusion set in again.

Sun explained, "Close your eyes and reach out. The first thing you touch will be your choice."

"She doesn't mean the artifacts. She means us." Snow saw the look on my face and clarified the situation.

"Wait, a minute... It's not like we know each other much at all and I mean, even if you're ageless, I'm-"

"What are you talking about? We are about the same age as Chris out there." Sun gestured toward the door.

"In other words, we're not that much older than you," said Snow. "Your facial perception just doesn't work with some people."

Sun's eyes darted to her sister as if she was surprised.

"Wait, how do you know about that?" I asked.

"Very well." Snow seemed very smug. "I'll tell you when we're done here. Are you ready, Sun?"

"Yep!" They tossed all five of their creations into the air.

"*Float*." The spell was cast by both of them, and we all floated alongside the trinkets.

"Now close your eyes and reach out. Whatever you grab will be your choice. The objects in this room will act as catalysts for what you choose. Now please, reach out." I couldn't tell which one said that, as my eyes had already closed in thought.

I just had to choose something, right? Be it one of the objects or one of the girls. Either way, I felt like I didn't have a choice but to choose. My mind rose in a shower of thoughts. Each blended into the next until it sounded like a crowd having a thousand conversations. My hand rose and they all stopped.

Completely thoughtless, I reached out and grabbed something. It was warm, squishy, and fit in the palm of my outreached hand. As I closed my fingers, I could feel that the object was, in fact, fairly larger than my hand.

I opened my eyes to see if the object was what I thought it was, and I saw nothing. There was nothing in my hand but air. Looking around, I saw the artifacts surrounding my hand. They were encircling it like planets to a star. I looked up to a vibrant red crossing the faces of Sun and Snow. They were both too far away to be what the object felt like, but it was so real.

"How daring," uttered Snow.

"He did it!" squealed Sun.

"What was that?" I asked.

"You made your choice," answered Snow. By the look in her eyes, I felt like I should have been red in the face too.

Looking back and forth between the two, I asked, "But what was that?"

"A lady shouldn't disclose such information," said Snow.

"Yeah! Especially because your hand was directly on-" Snow closed her hand over her sister's mouth as fast as she could as her cheeks got redder.

"As I said, A LADY! Wouldn't disclose such information." By this time, my feet had already grasped the ground, and the twins were still barely floating.

"What are you doing?" Said snow. "Grab the charms before they drop. As soon as we touch the ground, the levitation will cease."

"Uh- ok." Quickly, I gathered all the charms in my hands before they fell.

"Good. now we can return." Snow took a few steps and collapsed. I quickly shoved the charms into my pockets before catching her under her arm.

"Are you ok?" I asked.

"She really used up too much mana." Sun was visibly worried about her sister. "That must be how she got that ability."

"What ability?"

"In the creation ritual, she must have used extra power to get one of your quirks. Now her efforts have gone to waste."

Following my pattern of confusion, I asked the only question that made sense. "You mean, she knew about my ability because she got it from me?"

"There is no reason explaining now. We just have to get her to Sirus."

"Okay." I hoisted Snow onto my back, and we made our way back to the others.

As soon as we were out of the training room, all eyes were on us.

"Snow!" Sirus jumped up and rushed over to the small log on my back. He took her off my back and carried her upstairs. Jamie and the prince were sitting on the couch near the door watching.

"It's okay, she just pushed herself too hard," Sun explained and then turned her attention to me. "She must have seen something in you, Noah." Before I could ask what she meant by that, she answered. "She's clairvoyant. Well... partially." She shifted around a little on her feet. "Whenever we do that ritual we performed earlier, we can take a magic trait belonging to whoever the ritual's target is. It also allows us limited insight into their minds. One time, we did it for a psychic. I got the ability to read unhidden thoughts, and Snow can glimpse into any one person's potential futures the first time she sees them. Whatever she saw in your future must have been important. I don't know *what* she saw, but I *know* she wants you to stay."

"Why is me staying so important, anyway?" I asked.

"It's about time I told you what you're here for." The Prince spoke up. "Times are tough in the kingdom as of late, and we need as much skill and talent in our ranks as we can get. Seeing as your family has served mine from the shadows for a century, I figured it would be an easy and simple task to recruit you. But after seeing you with that woman, I knew it would be much more complicated than that. That's why the questions and that's why we're here now."

"I get it, but I have things to do. I couldn't stay even if I wanted to," I said, making sure to put conviction into my voice.

"It's a promise, isn't it?" Sun brought up something I failed to say. It was a thought at the top of my mind, so I figured she'd know what it was.

I scratched my head and said, "That's the long and short of it."

"Well, there's no helping it. It's about time we take our leave." The prince seemed more serious at that moment than I had seen him the entire time we were there. He and Jamie moved to the door, and I followed. "Give Sirus and your sister our farewells, will you?"

Sun nodded. "Sure."

Snow's voice came from the top of the stairs. "I know what you're thinking and if you leave this city, then you won't come back... Not alive anyway." I turned back to see her holding onto Sirus. "But I understand. I saw but five of your likely futures and I saw your mind. You already made your choice. You won't give up, but three to two says you die out there."

"If you don't mind me asking, what exactly were the other two?" The prince asked the only question I wouldn't dare.

"In one, he lives only long enough to succeed and lose everything. The other sees him stay here and prosper. In all the rest, you die before you can accomplish anything." Her eyes were pleading with all their might.

The prince turned to me. "Is your decision unchanged?"

"Thank you for telling me. I'll be sure to add 'change my future' to my to-do list." I said, now determined to see my quest through than ever."

Desperately, Snow said, "There's one thing about those trinkets I forgot to mention."

"Yes?" I said.

"Overuse of either one of those as an energy source can lead to your death. The only other bit I can say is that sometimes, taking a step back is the only way to proceed forward. I hope that information can help prevent the most likely outcomes. The rest... I can't help you with."

"Why not?"

"In every circumstance, you lose her and that will lead to your ruin. Nothing I could say would help."

"Well, I guess that's it." I felt like there was no reason to decipher who 'her' was.

"Indeed," said the prince.

Exiting the underground home, we found the princess's guard waiting silently next to the door outside and began the walk back.

"So, may I ask what exactly it was that you saw?" Surprisingly, the question came from Jamie.

"When?" I asked.

"The girls spoke of using their gifts to help you acknowledge your choice. If it meant what I think then, who your choice was must have solidified their resolve."

"The weird thing is, I didn't see anything. I just felt what felt like a boob," I said, nervously scratching my head. "At least... that's what it felt like."

"That spell probably showed the observers the most likely cause of your death. Whoever that spell showed must have been the woman whose end could bring about yours." Jamie always seemed to speak from experience.

"I feel that it's obvious who that woman is." The prince never averted his gaze from the end of the hallway.

"Well, I already decided to change my future. And besides, she only saw five different outcomes. I'll take the outcome that she didn't see." I hoped my resolve showed as much as I thought.

"You may be sure, but I'm not." Jamie's response sounded like it had much thought put behind it. "There was too much left unsaid in that conversation for me to feel comfortable about any of this. But maybe that's just old age."

Silence followed us until we reached the opening door. On the other side, I saw the princess followed by Helen and Catt. As I walked toward Catt, her eyes wandered behind us. Turning around, I saw Sirus with both Sun and Snow stooped behind his tall frame. I turned back to see Catt bending forward and waving to the twins.

"So, you're the girl worth dying for?" Snow raced toward Catt, stopped just before her, and began looking her over. Eventually, she began looking with her hands too.

"Uh... Can I help you?" Catt was unusually calm while being groped by someone she just met so suddenly.

"I only had a small glimpse, so I had no idea..." Snow was hugging Catt's chest. "You have my blessing." Nobody moved during this recent development. Either from shock or unwavering curiosity. In the resulting silence, Catt was glaring as if yelling the word 'help' at me. "Noah, come here for a second, dear."

I swiftly moved to Snow's location next to Catt.

"Hand me the sacred essence, will you?" She held out one hand with her other still centered on Catt's chest.

"Sure..." I looked around in my pockets, found the object she asked for, and handed it to her. Catt raised a questioning eyebrow, and I responded with a confused shrug.

"I hereby bestow upon you, **selective sight** and the skill: **strike warning**." The orb began glowing red. The glow began encompassing both Snow and Catt.

15-Flower to Fruit

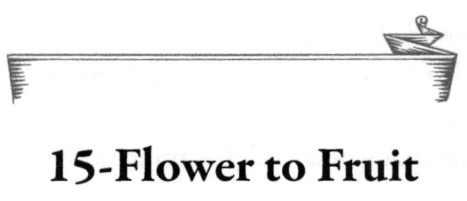

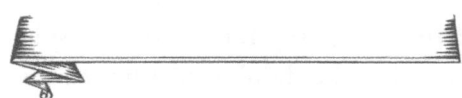

Walking out of the vicinity of the castle and through the first wall was a silent experience. Embarrassment hovered over both of our heads. Catt was rubbing her elbow with her hand, and I was staring at the sky. It showed signs of oncoming rain but it was still relatively clear. I looked down just before I almost fell down a set of stairs into the next wall. I missed the stairs and hit the wall. The sound I made, and my sudden absence made Catt giggle.

"That's not how I meant to do it, but at least you're smiling." I caught up.

"I never thought I could feel so violated by a kid," she said, looking dejected.

"She's not a child," interjected Jamie ahead of us. "She's older than the royalty."

"She's not royalty?" I said, now confused.

"Some would say so."

"Just another woman groping me?" Catt shuddered, "That makes it worse."

I said, "It could've been even worse. She could've grabbed you somewhere else."

"That's the problem. It felt like she grabbed me *everywhere*." She shuddered heavily this time. "It's like that dolphin from a while back."

"Well, whatever she did, it seems as if she had passed some abilities onto you with that sacred essence," said Jamie, "What did she give you, by the way?"

"She said something like 'selective sight' and 'strike warning'?" She put a finger to her chin. "She also whispered something to me."

"Really? I didn't hear her whisper anything," I said, rearranging the items I had attained in my pockets. The sacred essence was slightly smaller to the touch, even though it looked no different.

"I think it was only for me to hear."

"Really? What did she say?" I asked.

"I think she whispered it so that you wouldn't hear." Catt turned her nose up at me.

Sarcastically, I said, "It's okay if you're embarrassed. I'll leave it alone if that's how you feel."

"Embarrassment has nothing to do with it." She punched my shoulder light-heartedly.

"We're turning left here." Jamie turned just before one of the few crosswalks on our route. We followed.

"Where exactly are we going, by the way?" asked Catt.

"We're going to meet that friend I mentioned earlier," he responded. After a little more walking down a street full of shops, I looked around. This was the first time I had a good look at the city between the walls. This part of the city was effectively a marketplace. There were shops in every direction selling everything from food to weapons, to armor, to clothes, to potions.

I saw a wide man with a mustache selling weird mushrooms to a green-scaled dragonborn carrying an egg the size of her head. There was also a guy carrying a large sword buying little glowing orbs from a kid with the longest chain of keys I had ever seen around his neck and a man in a red leather jacket, white hair, and a sword of his own. There was also a couple armed to the tee in a gun store buying from a cloaked man in a gas mask. Almost every store had some type of large window to see through for some odd reason.

By the time we came to the next crossing, the street was clear almost completely of vehicles. What was once cars of all different makes and models, a surprising number of motorcycles, and the occasional broomstick or carpet, became nearly empty except for one kid racing up and down the street on a fume-powered enchanted bike. A couple of blocks of empty shops later, Jamie stopped in front of a store with a large window featuring a picture of a man wearing a gold cape and standing on a flying broomstick. He went in through the front door. Catt and I followed.

"Welcome to 'Whatever Moves You Enchantment' store. How may I help you?" The voice came from behind the counter on the other side of the room, filled with levitating scrolls and models of various enchanted vehicles. It was a small girl hovering so that her arms came just above the counter. She had dark skin, long, shimmering light brown hair with a green tint, pointy ears, and wings that visibly fluttered behind her. She also had a button nose and a surprised look no matter what face she made.

"Yes, is Cosmo in?" responded Jamie.

"If you're looking for my grandfather, he's in the back."

"Could you get him for me, please?"

"What's your name, sir?"

"It's James Rose, young miss."

"Please wait here a moment while I get him."

"Sure thing."

She fluttered her way around to a door behind her. Opening it, she stopped hovering and planted her feet on the ground. She turned out to be around four feet tall in a blue and black dress with matching shoes, and her hair was in a single braid along the back while the front was left to hang free. She reached her head around the edge of the door and a soft, yet loud jingle sound erupted from where her head was. It sounded oddly like a voice. Maybe it was her voice?

"What was that?" asked Catt.

"Oh, that was me," responded the small girl. "I have mediocris."

"I've never heard of that. I was kind of sheltered until recently and nobody in my family had it so, could you please explain what that is?" I decided that every time I saw something I didn't understand, I would ask questions about it.

"Have you ever heard of faery disease?"

I looked her in the eye and responded, "Nope."

"That's what they used to call it before-" She was abruptly interrupted by the harsh creaking of the door behind her and the entrance of a bald old man with a similar skin tone as the girl. Unlike her, he was taller than me. He was far into his seventies with black reflective spectacles, a gray shirt with 'Whatever Floats Your Boat' on it in bold, white, Russian letters, black work pants, and solid black work shoes. All of which were well-worn with age.

"Cosmo! Long time, no see." Jamie extended a fist up toward his friend who was walking around the counter to meet him.

"Same here." They fist-bumped. "How did that bit of business that you needed to take care of go?"

"Well, actually, they're right here." Jamie motioned to us. "Would you two kindly introduce yourselves?"

"Hi, I'm Noah, nice to meet you," I said, extending a hand.

"And I'm Catt." She extended a hand as well.

"Nice to meet the both of you. I'm Cosmo Dmitrievna, and this is my enchantment shop." He shook both of our hands.

"I'm Belle House!" exclaimed the small girl. "But I go by Tingle. I never actually introduced myself."

"My name, little miss, is James Rose. Nice to meet you."

"I'm not little. I'm here on a break from Uni," she said matter-of-factly.

"So, did you come just to have a talk? Or did you come for something else?" said Cosmo, moving things along.

"Ah, yes. Actually, I brought these two here because they might want to get somewhere fast. Do you know where you want to go?"

Catt perked up quickly at the sound of getting somewhere fast.

"That would've been a good question to ask on the way here," I responded.

Catt took a deep breath. "Well- actually there is- and trust me on this- it's great. New York City."

"Why there?" I asked.

"I caught wind that someone we know lives there."

"Is that what she whispered to you?"

"Nope, that was something else. A girl's got her ways."

I sighed, "Man, does she ever."

"What's that supposed to mean?"

"Uhh…" I couldn't think of a way to back-peddle.

"It'll take about two days to make something that'll take the two of you that far normally." Cosmo sat in a short chair behind the counter. "But I can make it two hours if you're willing to forgo certain… safety measures."

"How long would it take to get there?" asked Catt.

"It should take somewhere between four and eight hours."

"Eight hours…?" Catt and I looked at each other.

"That's insane!" We both exclaimed.

"Are you going to make an airplane in two hours?" I asked.

"You two don't know how this place works do you?" Belle's question came as a sort of surprise.

I looked her right in the eye again and responded. "Nope."

She responded by shaking her head and with a facepalm.

"I think while you two get taught by Tingle on how Magnolia works, Cosmo and I'll finish up on the specifics of your transportation." Jamie tapped Cosmo on the shoulder and they both went into the back room, leaving us. I wasn't sure if we could really trust either of them, but Jamie seemed not to harbor any ill will toward anyone and he seemed to trust Cosmo. In fact, I had already begun to trust him a little. He only seemed worried about something that I couldn't put my finger on. I decided not to say anything as they left, and neither did Catt.

"Come here and sit." Belle pointed toward a couple of comfortable-looking seats to the left of the counter. Catt and I sat. She then moved the seat behind the counter to the front of us. It turned out to be an adjustable stool. "So, which would you like to know about first? My condition or this city?"

"Can we learn about both?" I asked, raising my hand.

"I will try not to regret this." Her response told me I was already getting on her nerves. "Let's start with me. My condition is called mediocris cavea disorder or faery disease. It's a magical disorder. As I really hope you already know, anyone who uses magic has a spirit animal they coincide with whether they know what it is or not. It's almost like it's in our blood, more than just magical. That being said, Since wielders primarily rely on their spirit animals, it's a huge part of our powers. With that in mind, there are those of us whose spirit animals are mythical creatures. In some of us, myself included, there is a phenomenon that makes our magic highly unstable. Like, unstable enough to kill us."

"It could kill you?" Catt asked the same question I was opening my mouth to ask.

"When I was fifteen, I started having seizures. As it turned out, that was why. Also turns out, the effects only start once you meet two conditions. One, you have to begin using magic before a certain age, and two, have a growth spurt of over ten centimeters. I was about five when I accidentally cast a levitation spell from a witch's grimoire."

She seemed to be in thought for about a minute until she shook her head and continued. "Where was I- oh yeah- It turned out that just one of the requirements had to be reversed to fix that. I had to either get my magic sealed or, somehow, become shorter. Naturally, I chose to keep my magic over height, but there's always a cost to everything.

As that turned out, there were three ways to shrink myself. Either by keeping a spell over myself for the rest of my life, getting a permanent partial seal put on me with its own requirements that restricted my height but also lessened my total energy output, or partially taking the form of my spirit animal to balance myself out. As you see, I chose the latter. Though, I think I took a little more than a partial form. The wings allow me to hover though, and I can talk like a faery, so it's not all bad. Any questions?"

"Yeah, how do you take the form of your spirit animal?" I was very glad I asked this question later.

"It hurt a lot." she winced as she explained this. "There's a ritual involving drinking your own blood mixed with artifacts pertaining to your spirit animal. Like for a lion would be lion fur or something."

"I get it."

"Good. Next is the city, right? Oh yeah. Just to be sure, how much do you two know about this place?"

"All I know is about the castle, that people live in the walls, and some overworld coordinates for how to get here," I responded.

"Neither of us have ever really been to this place, so we're basically clueless." Catts's response was very frank.

"Yeah, pretty much." I shrugged.

"Okay, first things first. This city has three prominent walls. Mary, Rize, and Seria. As I'm pretty sure you've already seen, they each have their own distinct color. White, blue, and red. The outer wall, Mary, is a guardian wall meant for basic protection and enchanted with a sort of teleportation spell." She looked up and tapped her chin in thought for a second. "Eh, we have about two hours so, I might as well explain that too." She pressed her hands down on her dress and the seat between her legs and leaned forward. "You know, the way you came in isn't necessarily the way you have to leave out going the same direction."

My head tilted to the side.

"Man, you two always have the same reaction every time." she sat back. "I love seeing people that close." Catt and I looked at each other and shrugged. "Okay- anyway, the enchantment on the outer wall extends to the forest and mountains. I'm not sure to what degree, but under certain unknown conditions, by entering a forest or mountain range almost anywhere in the world, you could find yourself at the gates of the outer wall. Leaving the city through the woods or mountains will result in you returning to where you came in at. That being said, there is a way to cheat the system. Leaving through any other way will send you to the closest region equivalent to where you came in. With that in mind, my grandfather created his own way to alter the spell put on the wall." After a moment of silence, she continued. "Well... I really can't tell you more. It's kind of a secret, you know?"

"Yeah, I get it," I said, stretching my arms above my head. "Kinda reminds me of my dad."

"Oh really? What's he like?"

"Dead," I said, poignantly.

"Oh, I'm so sorry."

"Don't be. The one who needs to be sorry is whoever killed him, and they will be." I said it in a light-hearted manner but I regretted it anyway. I felt like I ruined the mood.

"O-kay. Is there anything else we can talk about?"

I pointed both index fingers toward her and said, "Yes."

From there we just talked about random stuff like life, the differences in growing up in different parts of the world, and puberty as a half-fae. Eventually, time caught up with us when Jamie and Cosmo came through an unapologetically loud door.

"That took so much longer than normal, yet it was only an hour and a half," said Cosmo behind Jamie.

"Just like the good ol' days," Jamie responded.

"Does that mean you're done?" I asked.

"Here it is." Cosmo raised his hand and in it was a tube around the same size as an empty paper towel roll. It was silver with horizontal grooves going around both ends and a vertical slot on what might have been a handle in the middle. "It's not done yet. To finish it, I just need to ask you one question."

"What is it?"

"Both of you, What's your color of arms?"

"Color of arms?"

"Are you sure this is ok, James?" Cosmo seemed concerned.

"By color, do you mean this?" I pulled out my card and showed him.

"Purity, huh? And with a flaw in the center. How about you?" he turned his attention to Catt."

"This one's mine." She showed him hers.

"I kind of figured seeing as your hair constantly changes color."

"Oh, it does?" she said, considerately. She often forgot about that quality of herself.

"Yours is so pretty." Belle's face was almost touching Catt's card. This is what mine looks like." She reached her hand into the side of her shoe and out came a striped neon green and black card. "I wish we could switch."

Cosmo cleared his throat. "Either way, this won't work. Not with that color at least."

"Why not?" asked Catt.

"Your color of arms. This device here works by locking in your color with your destination and transporting one to the other. Your color constantly changes. This thing here won't be able to zero in on a constantly shifting wavelength."

"What if I fed my energy directly into it?"

"The only way that could work is if you had a code of arms that keeps you in proper contact with it. Like gauntlet-type arms."

"As a matter of fact, I do." In a deep blue flash on her hand was a single glove, shining the same color as her hair at the time.

"That could work. Since that's taken care of, here." He tossed the contraption to me, and I caught it.

"What do we owe-" I started.

"Nothing, but if you want to owe me something, how about a favor?"

"Uh... Sure."

"There's a woman where you're going by the name of Hinata Schield." The quickness with which he pulled out a piece of paper and scribbled what seemed to be over one paragraph on it was astonishing. "If you see her, you'll know her. She was a cop but probably isn't anymore. She always carries a guitar and has enormous hands that she always keeps hidden by gloves. And don't let her looks fool you, she's much older than she looks. If you find her, give her this." He handed me the folded piece of paper.

"Anything else?" I asked, unsure of the task which I had accepted.

"Yeah, tell her I said it hurt like hell."

"I'll try."

"Good. Now I'll explain how you use that device there. First, after exiting the city outside of the walls, you need to insert your card into the slot and give it a moment. It will beep three times before taking off." He turned his attention back toward Catt. "You're gonna need to grab hold of it before that happens, ok?"

"Yeah."

"Good now, off you go." He ushered us out of the store and Jamie led us the rest of the way to the outer gate. On the way, I was analyzing the object in my hand. It seemed like it really was just a metal tube, but I could feel some sort of presence coming from it. I figured it might have been because it was a magical item but that wouldn't explain why I didn't get the same feeling from the trinkets I got from Sun and Snow. I decided to ask Jamie about it.

He said, "It's not a magic item, Just heavily enchanted. Just be sure not to lose it. It might not be able to bring you back here, but it might prove useful again down the line." I took his word for it. Reaching the gate, Jamie stopped walking. "This is where I leave you." He waved us off.

"Goodbye and thanks," I said, waving back.

"What he said." Catt waved as well. I got one last look around as we exited through the gate. The wall was at least twenty feet thick, stark white, with a single hallway through what I could see, and one raised gate on either side. After leaving the wall, I inspected the forest. The trees differed completely from the ones we saw on the way there. I couldn't really tell what type of trees they were on account of how dark it was. Dusk was setting in.

"It's kind of like a video game," I said, staring at the sky above the trees.

"Come to think about it... It sort of is." Catt responded.

"We came here looking for clues on missing people and we met a prince and a princess, were given enchanted items to use on our adventure, a prophecy, and a fast travel device."

"What prophecy?" Catt picked up on the part I didn't mean to say.

Trying to sound ignorant, I said, "Did I say prophecy?"

"Yes, you did. Is that what that was about?"

"You talking about what Snow whispered in your ear?"

"Let's finish talking about this when we get to where we're going."

"Yeah." I took out the device and inserted my card. "Let's hope this works." Both sides of the cylinder extended outward, and a white tail extended out of one side. It began levitating on its own. "Oh, it's a broomstick!" I exclaimed. "I get it." I tossed it to Catt. "I think you need to get on before it starts beeping."

"This is actually really cool." She straddled it as it beeped the first time. Removing her feet from the ground, she levitated with it. Summoning her weapon caused the white tail to shift to a rainbow of colors. "Hurry up, get on." I did so as the second beep sounded and held on to Catt for dear life. "Too tight."

"Does it bother you?"

"No." She seemed to relax a little. The final beep sounded as the broomstick began crawling forward. Before I knew it, it was going too fast to distinguish our surroundings properly. Everything was a blur until it wasn't. All I could see was snow and evergreens.

16-Cure for Shadows

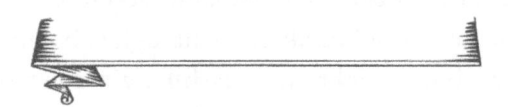

[Nero Cursley]

"You ok dumbass?" Jordan, codenamed Gale, was standing over our recovering teammates.

"Who you callin' a dumbass?" said Demitre, codenamed Bismol.

Jordan sighed. "Both of you. You both jeopardized the mission and now we have to switch with the other team."

"Oh..." A relaxed moan came from Lilly, codenamed Sakura. "And I wanted to see the inner walls of the city, too."

Annoyed, Jordan continued, "Well, it's your fault you don't get to see it now, isn't it?"

"Lay off on 'em Gale. They were just playing their roles as the unstable duo," I interrupted.

"Who you callin' unstable," They both whined together.

"Either way, we can't finish the mission like this," decided Jordan.

"No... We can do this," said Demitre.

"Yeah... I'm feeling better now," continued Lilly. "But next time I see that girl, she's gonna pay!"

"It wasn't the girl who took you down. It was our target," I said.

"Well, next time I see them, they're both gonna pay!" She excitedly jumped to her feet and nearly fell from dizziness. "Is it just me or is there a breeze?" She looked down at her uniform now converted to a crop top. "Oh, weird."

"Either way, we can't go on like this. A mission is a mission, and orders are orders." I reached to my ear and turned on the transmission. "Mission failed, we'll get 'em next time." I turned the sensitivity up so I could be heard by the receiver. "Mission control. It's team B. We were spotted and compromised."

A voice responded, "Roger. We'll need you back for a debriefing."

"Copy. I also need to speak directly with the mission head."

"Codename?"

"Noise."

"And your captain?"

"Viser."

"That can be arranged."

"In person?"

"That is not currently possible."

"Then, forget about it."

"Alright, what's your position?"

"We'll be at the corresponding location for aerial pick up between seventeen and eighteen hundred hours. Overworld coordinates are 51.844927 and -8.492792."

"Pick up will be there in a day."

"Thanks, that's all. Over and out."

"Over and out."

"We've got till tomorrow to get back," I said, turning back to the group. "If we're quick, we'll be there in time."

"You know, I actually feel a lot better. Even better than I've felt in years." As Lily stretched on her feet, this remark gave me pause.

I said, "Wait, a minute..."

"What is it Noise?" Jordan knew I was on to something.

"Sakura. The target said something along the lines of purification when he hit you, didn't he?" I asked.

"Yeah, he did," responded Demetre after eyeing Lily's confused expression to a question directed at her.

Hearing this, I came to a conclusion and thought it was right to tell. "That's it. That guy's probably a cure. It looks like he can purify dark entities, including corpse shadows. It's like he killed off a bit of it without directly harming you. Good reason to catch him, even off the books."

"I don't know about all that... All I know is that I was trying to hit that girl with my mallet and then, I woke up and that's it." She began looking over herself.

"No pain or anything?" Demitre began poking at Lily's side where she should have been cut.

"No, it was a dreamless nap though." She seemed certain that she was fine.

"You're not catatonic, so that's proof enough right now," I said. "Besides, any of you need any more time to rest?"

"I'm ready to go whenever," responded Jordan.

"I feel like I got enough rest. I'm full of energy too," Lily's response was predictable.

"And you, Bismol? You seem to have gotten the worst of it." Demetree looked up at me from a rock beneath a tree he was leaning on.

"No, just surprised and paralyzed me for a bit is all. That chick was fast."

"Alright," I said, "Let's get moving."

The journey to the rendezvous point was fairly smooth, even though it took the rest of the day. Pit stops were brief, and the weather was forgiving. There were minor quarrels between the aforementioned unstable duo like always, but they didn't dull the refreshing country atmosphere or the beauty of our surroundings. This was the kind of thing I had always wondered if I'd be doing with my own family if I had one. I had dreamt about it many times. Me, my sister, and two faceless parents. We'd be walking a trail through the mountains, swimming at the beach, or even just sitting at home watching TV together. It wouldn't matter. As long as we had the family that we felt was so important to have. That family was impossible now.

"Are you ok, Echo?" The look on my face must have given her pause because Lily was staring directly into my eyes from approximately a few centimeters away, walking backward as I was forward. "You're just staring into space."

"It's Noise, not Echo, and I wasn't 'just staring into space.'" I waved her away.

"My bad. You two seem so similar. You both command sound and you both wear orange."

"So does Whirlwind, but you didn't compare me to him."

"You two are nothing alike. He does wear orange, but he doesn't use sound; he's just noisy. And the way he's all over Blossom. He knows how she feels about Eye."

"Hey, I don't want to hear about the love triangle in team Forty-seven."

"Oh, how about the one in team S.O.L.? They really need to rethink that acronym."

"No. We're almost there."

"Well, I heard something about the unknown members of the seven virtues." This would normally interest most others as the seven virtues are a team directly under the Boss as the right hand and are normally a public group, but some of their members never seem to show up on record whenever anything happens involving them.

"I don't care." By now, we could see an airport in the distance. It was dark, but the runway was well-lit.

"What about the seven sins?"

"I don't think it's a good idea to talk about them at all." Jordan pulled her aside with a word of warning.

It was taboo to speak about anything that might be considered a secret involving the seven sins. Even the identities of the team that worked directly parallel to the seven virtues as the left hand of the Boss were kept a secret. The only thing that anyone officially knew about them was that there were seven of them.

"You're so concerned, maybe you're one of them? Anything I say will just be considered rumor anyway-"

"Sakura, stop messing with them," Demetre said, with a warning note in his words. He was slightly ahead of the rest of us, with me and Lily behind him and Jordan bringing up the rear. "You don't need to pick up whatever the rumor mill spits out. That's the last thing we need."

"Anyway... Do you really think that that boy was a cure?" Lily changed the subject.

"Probably not. Just a theory. Let me get back to you on that."

She hummed to my response as if I was really going to give her any information any time soon.

Arriving at the airport, there seemed not to be many people. This wasn't unusual for an airport at night, but with it being such a major airport, there seemed to be very few cars parked outside and we saw almost no one around. I didn't have time to ponder over why when the receiver in my ear activated on its own and a voice came through.

"Noise, if you can hear me, give a simple response."

"Yep," I said, folding my arms and sitting in an empty seat.

"Alright, we're on the runway and have already contacted security to let you out for pickup. Go out the south exit and get on." The transmission ended.

"This way," I said, getting back on my feet and heading down toward a terminal.

"Are you sure?" asked Jordan.

"Certain." I kept walking.

"Alright guys, follow the leader." The other two rose from their seats and followed.

Reaching a door that read EXIT above it in green, it led to a series of runways. Rolling in our direction was an all-black jet. A door opened and stairs came down as it neared us on the runway, and we climbed aboard. Making sure we left no one behind, I boarded last and found myself in the nearest comfortable seat.

After finding ourselves off the ground, a voice came through the intercom. "Attention passengers, if there is a Noise present, the pilot would like to see you."

"I guess that's me." Getting to my feet, I waddled to the front cabin, entered with my hands in my pockets, and closed the door using my heel.

"I suggest locking that door." A familiar voice came from the captain's seat, and I obeyed, locking the door.

I said, "I call, and you came to me? That's rare for a captain."

"You've never had me as a captain." The seat rocked slightly with a creak.

"That being said, I have questions about this mission."

"Just questions? Or do doubts come along with them?" The seat rocked again.

"Captain Viser, I know that there are things about this mission that you didn't tell us that we need to know." All of my thoughts and theories were bubbling to the surface.

"This room is completely sealed from the inside," he said, "We can address each other by name. That also means that no one can listen in on what I'm about to tell you."

"I prefer codenames on missions." I leaned back on the wall to my left.

"Codenames it'll be." He made it sound like whatever he was going to tell me would have made a bigger impact without codenames. "I assume you met with the target?" He swiveled his head around to face me before looking back out toward the sky.

"That's what I called to talk about."

He clasped his hands. "In any case, I'm pretty sure you saw his powers firsthand. What do you think?"

"That capturing him alive is the only priority. He's too useful."

He nodded. "What if I told you that this was originally meant to be an extermination mission?"

"What?" That revelation only brought up more questions.

"That was my first thought too. Until I considered the alternative. Only a handful of people know this, but there is a part of the main base known as 'the shadow zone.'" He seemed to pause to let what he just said sink in.

"And that is?" I asked.

"The side of this organization you have yet to see." He shuffled around in his seat, leaned back, and continued. "Have you ever noticed someone you normally see every day just disappear? Anything from a week to months' absence without explanation or clear reason."

"I assume you're asking me this because the reason isn't special ops like my current mission?"

"No, in these special cases, they come back with some previously unknown abilities or an odd or sinister air about them."

Just then. I remembered someone from the first team I was ever assigned to. His name was Bastion and he was part of the science department. He used to make all kinds of equipment for stealth and recon. One day, he just went missing. He turned up three weeks later and was completely engulfed in negative energy. After that, he began arguing with anyone he could and crying inexplicably. He was never the same after that. I thought he might have been taken over by a corpse shadow, but that didn't add up. Eventually, I was assigned to another team. I later found that he had died on a mission hunting for the Black Reaper.

I took a breath and asked, "And that had something to do with this 'shadow zone'?"

"That's where they go when they disappear. It's an area composed of centuries of negativity. It also acts as a nest for corpse shadows. Do you understand what I'm saying?"

"I figured every major organization had a few demons living in their closet, but that's ridiculous." Despite that, I was inclined to believe him.

"I wouldn't be telling you this if it weren't true. I also wouldn't be telling you this if there weren't more to it. It seems the organization wants to reduce all threats to its plans by either assimilating them or destroying them. That goes for your target as well. As far as the Boss cares, he's a corpse hunter. They just can't risk giving him that title."

"Why not?"

"His bloodline has deep connections with the Rolanites. Putting a price on his head guarantees he'll be protected by them. That's why you were supposed to capture or kill him. Of course, it's my responsibility to give that order and I chose capture."

He seemed all too smug even with things in his favor and all the things he told me. Something felt off about it. "You actually planned this-"

"As you know, you will switch places with team A. Our informants tell us that your target is heading the same way, so your teams will just merge instead. Here, you'll be getting a second try. If you choose not to let him go, at least try to convince him to join."

"I have a choice to let him go?"

"That's up to you. I assume you know the consequences of killing him if he doesn't comply?"

"I can figure. After all, this mission was an extermination initially."

"You also know what it means to let him go, right?"

I shrugged. "I have a hunch."

"You're more straight-laced than most others, so no one would be on your ass immediately but stay alert." I couldn't see the look in his eyes, but it felt like he was worried about something.

"If it ever comes to that," I said, reassuringly

"Exactly."

"So, you planned his going to Magnolia, his escape from us, and this meeting after. Probably even where we're going to find him. Is there anything else?"

"Nothing that I can tell you now. Meeting adjourned." He swiveled the seat back around.

I returned to my team and briefed them on our next move. Whatever powers Guile had to make things go his way was terrifying. His aptitude for scheming was unnatural. It was hard to believe I was ever ranked higher than him.

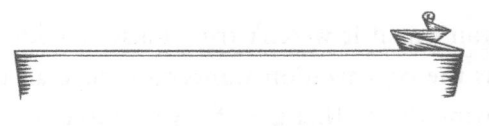

17-What Matters

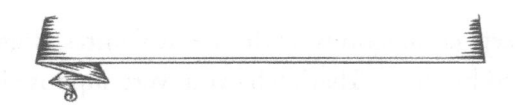

[Cattherine Lockhart]

 With all the wind and scenery whipping by, surprisingly, I couldn't hear any of it. All I could hear was my own minute movements as well as Noah and his breathing if I listened hard enough. "Can you hear me?" I asked, using my indoor voice.

"Yeah," he replied. "It's like we're in a bubble. The air inside here is too calm compared to the air we're flying through. I don't even feel cold despite the outside environment."

"Come to think of it, I don't feel cold either." We'd have to thank Cosmo if we ever saw him again. "Since we're going to be here for a while, mind telling me what that whole 'prophecy' thing was about?"

"I thought you forgot about that."

"That quickly?"

"I guess not. Uh, before I tell you, um, how long has it been since either of us went to the bathroom?" He had just made me realize I hadn't been to the bathroom in at least nine hours. "And... I'm hungry."

"Just get the dried food out of your bag."

"I would, but I'm too afraid of falling." He sounded like a child.

"Can you reach mine? It should be right in front of you."

"No, do you think you can get it?"

I took a quick look back down and said, "Do you think I wanna fall?"

"But I just realized how hungry I am. I'm so hungry that I feel like nibbling on anything I can find."

The thought sent a shiver down my spine. "If you even THINK of nibbling on me, we will both be spiraling out of the sky going who knows how fast and probably die from the impact before exposure, got it?"

"Just a little?" Now, he was getting on my nerves.

"I will elbow you right now," I jerked my shoulder in his direction.

"Oh, never mind, I think I can reach it." I felt one of his arms release from around my waist and rummaged in my bag behind my back. "Got it." I heard a tearing sound as the sound of munching erupted from behind me.

"You're eating chips?"

"Crisps? Yeah," he said, ever so nonchalantly.

"Not any of the actual food?"

"It had to be something I could eat with one hand."

"Half of the things in there could be eaten with one hand."

"Really?" If I didn't know any better, I'd have thought he was an idiot at this point. An impression he hadn't made in a while.

"Did you turn into a five-year-old since we got on this thing? Or are you just afraid of heights?"

Smugly, he said, "I'm just a five-year-old."

"Oh, really, because I-... Wait a minute. Weren't we talking about something before all this?" I tried to get us back on track after realizing how far removed we were from the subject.

"Really? I don't remember."

"Ugh, whatever." I sighed.

He was trying hard to distract me from talking about the 'prophecy' thing. He let it slip once, so I at least knew something was up. I would have to find out what I was embarrassed for, eventually.

Once he was done eating, he replaced his arm around me and said, "I'm sorry."

"Don't be. You'll tell me eventually, right?"

He stayed silent.

Everywhere I looked was almost a blanket white. Dots of green and blue poked through the white though, only for a split second at a time. I couldn't tell how fast we were moving but I could tell it was fast. It seemed regardless of the speed or distance, the snow was the same when I looked at it. All it was at night was a second sky in reflection of the gray and white that fell even though there was no snow falling. It was just clouded over with a silver lining reaching all the way across the horizon. The sun had to have set before we left for the night to have set to the degree it had already. There was no orange, red, or blue fading light in the distance, just blank gray. It further proved the fact that we were teleported to a different part of the world.

After a while of staring into the night, my eyes began to droop, and I was getting sleepy. That was when I noticed a dead weight behind me had gotten heavier, and upon closer inspection, I could hear a soft snore. I resigned myself to making sure we both didn't fall until I found myself being tapped awake by Noah.

"Catt," he said, "Wake up. We both fell asleep. We're out of the snow area. I think we're close." He was right. Below us was farmland and long stretches of road as far as the eye could see. The sun was beginning to peak up from the right.

"How long was I asleep?"

"I was gonna wait till you woke up, but I thought you might hurt your back by then. You were in a bad position for sleeping and you were very tense"

"I wish you had woken me up sooner."

"Nah, besides, you needed some sleep. It can't be healthy to stay awake that long while draining your energy like that."

The flow, surprisingly, hadn't stopped, yet I felt no worse for wear. I just hoped it wouldn't hit me like a stack of bricks when it was over. After a while, a cityscape passed below us, and the number of roads exploded. There were also more cars. That's when I noticed that we were climbing altitude.

"Aren't we too high up?"

"We'll probably go back down when we get close." He sounded calm yet he tightened his grip around me. Eventually, there was a noticeable decrease in altitude as another cityscape appeared in the distance. By this time, we were over a river. There was no noticeable turning until a riverbank came ahead and we followed the curve. There was no feeling of motion, and the river was close enough for me to see the larger waves on its surface.

"I think we're almost there," I said, noticing that the sun was nowhere to be seen once again. We must've been so high up that the sun was visible where it should not be. After barely a moment of following the river, there was a sudden stop. It was more like a sudden change in scenery. We were hovering over a large patch of grass in between encircling on and off ramps. There was a single tree in the clearing, and we were hovering over a square bit of concrete.

"I think we're a little closer than, almost," said Noah. Slowly, the broom descended with us on it and our feet touched the ground. It stopped levitating and Noah moved his arms from my waist. Instinctively, I grabbed his arms. "You want me to keep holding on?"

"Stop it... Just let go." I released him and he let go. There was an odd popping sound and whatever bubble we were inside of was gone. It came from relatively warm to freezing in less than a second.

"Are you ok?" said Noah, noticing my shivers.

I shook my head. "I should have thought of what I was wearing before we came here."

"You cold?"

"My legs."

"Do you need help with that or...?"

"I'll get used to it soon" I brushed my hands across my skirt. "Hopefully."

Noah went toward a sidewalk next to one of the roads. "We should get moving then."

I started following him and then I stopped. "What happened to the broomstick?" Looking around, I saw it nowhere.

"Right here," he said, waving the retracted pole in his hand. He then, promptly, dropped it in his bag. "And look what popped out of it." He held up his card and the color was slightly faded. He then slotted it back into his wallet.

"I should've dressed the way you do," I said, following his direction. Noah only had two outfits, which he wore back and forth. The one he was wearing at the time consisted of navy blue cargo pants, a dark gray long-sleeve, and a black short-sleeve shirt over it. He seemed relatively comfortable compared to me.

"I said that once, and you said, 'That's not my style.' After which you promptly fell into a hole, and I had to save you."

"I think you forgot who fell into that hole."

"Yeah, whatever. So, where to now?" I somehow didn't expect his question. By this time, we were at a crosswalk at a red light.

"You know, I didn't really think about that. Let's improvise."

He smiled. "I feel like I'm rubbing off on you too much."

"Too late to stop now."

"I agree with that."

Noticing a glow on Noah's leg, I asked, "Hey, has your pocket been glowing this whole time?"

"I don't think so." He reached his hand into his pocket and out came a white, glowing, folded piece of paper. "This is what Cosmo gave me."

"It might be enchanted like the broom," I said, getting a closer look.

"Yeah, probably so that we can find the person this letter was for." As he opened it, I saw a glowing arrow and a matching compass. The arrow was pointing south.

I thought for a second and said, "This might be perfect. If we can find her first, maybe she can help us find the other person we're looking for."

"Who is that other person, by the way?" By this time, we were already following the arrow by turning left and walking by a chest-high stone wall that protected us from a drop onto the freeway.

"Oh, just my brother," I said, brushing hair off of my shoulder and locking it behind my ear, immediately regretting it, and putting it back. Ironically, my hair was blue.

"So, you found out where your brother was and just now decided to tell me, huh?"

"You are way more laid back than I thought you would be hearing that."

"Of course, I am. You told me he's stronger than both of us combined, right? That means I can leave you with him and continue on my way, right?"

"Nope, you're stuck with me. I told you that we were going to find everybody we're looking for, and I meant it. I just desperately wanted to confirm for myself whether or not he was still alive. If he is, maybe he'll come with us."

"Somehow, I'm happier than I thought to hear that." He failed at hiding a smile.

"Then we'll both be saving you the trouble of fighting everybody you meet."

"That was once."

"Three times." I held up the number three, smiling.

"Okay, maybe more than once."

I wiggled my three fingers a few times.

"Okay, maybe three." He smiled more openly this time. Reaching a crosswalk in front of a small, gated park, we stopped again. There was nowhere to go forward. Just apartment buildings. "Let's turn right. It's better to take as short and few turns as possible on something like this." He was right and I agreed. The right way led straight into the freeway and a bridge, yet also an almost immediate turn back to our current direction. Unlike the left, which led farther down before a turn the same way. Roughly halfway across the sidewalk before turning, Noah folded up the map back into his pocket and turned around sharply. "Who are you?" He was too fixed on looking past me to notice my confused expression.

"Well, look what we have here." I lost my breath as I turned around in shock. I didn't notice the new presence. "I follow a sudden spike of power in this area, and I find two strangers. It's the overworld, you know?"

"That didn't answer my question," said Noah.

"My name is Nero, stranger." Everything he wore was a matching army fatigue orange and brown except for his baseball cap, which was solid orange, blue, and white. By voice alone, he didn't seem very old. Probably younger than us. He stood next to a nearby tree in the twilight. "I'm part of a sort of neighborhood watch that looks after this city at night and when the police can't. I just thought something was wrong and came to see. Since you two are obviously new here, need directions or some help?"

He seemed friendly enough. It didn't seem like he was here to hurt us. It didn't seem like he could. He was right in front of us, and I couldn't sense any energy at all coming from him.

"No, we're good," said Noah. moving in front of me.

"What?" I said. His response caught me off guard. I was usually the one to respond the way he did.

"Then, I'll have to assume whatever you're doing here isn't good and call the others in to question you on the spot. Won't take them long to get here." Nero motioned toward his ear.

"Alright. We're looking for a wielder. His color of arms is a dark pink or purple." The pause before Noah's response was disconcerting.

"Oh, that makes perfect sense." Nero seemed to relax. "He always talked about how he left someone behind that might come looking for him."

Believing in Noah's suspicion, I asked, "If you know him, what's his name?"

My question seemed to give him pause. "Never trust anyone. Just like him. His name is Graven, and I can take you straight to him right now. He's on patrol just like I am. I'll just call him back to the rendezvous point and you can follow me there, deal?"

I stepped forward with my arms crossed. "Deal."

Noah put his hand on my shoulder. "Are you sure?"

"Yeah." I nodded. "Lead the way."

"You guys were actually going the right way. If we take a left here, all we have to do is keep going straight and we'll be there in no time. Now, I just need to call him there." Nero reached his hand up to his ear as he passed us. "Code D.N.A purple, I repeat, D.N.A purple. Respond to rendezvous." This was followed by barely audible static and a muffled voice. "Copy that." He turned back to us. "He should be on his way, but it might take a while. He has his hands full right now in lower Manhattan. Let's start moving, shall we?"

"You couldn't sense his presence, could you?" Noah and I were walking at what felt like a safe distance from Nero, and Noah was whispering.

"No," I said.

"He came in, not hiding anything. I felt his presence as soon as he came within range."

"I still can't sense anything. I figured he was powerless. It's not hard for a normal person to feel the kind of energy he mentioned. If he uses ki, like I do, it would be even easier."

"But can you sense his ki?"

"Hmm…" After a moment of concentrating in his direction, I found that I couldn't see the shifting aura that should have been surrounding him. I couldn't feel its presence either nor from anywhere else. "That's weird."

"What is it?" Noah sounded more concerned by the second.

"I can't see or feel anything from anywhere. Not even you." I looked at my hands, wondering what happened to me.

"That's what I'm worried about. I think he noticed it too. If he turns out not to be on our side, I need you to be prepared to run. This is a threat. Don't summon your weapon. I don't want to know what'll happen if you do."

Sarcastically, I said, "You think I'm gonna hurt myself?"

"Worse. This happened to one of my older brothers once. Your power might have sealed itself from overuse. If you had any other powers, it'd probably affect those, too. I don't know what'll happen if you try to squeeze out more than what you have."

"Fine, but whatever happens, I'm not leaving you." He knew that there was no way he was going to talk me out of my decision and decided not to argue, yet still handed me the compass map and what looked like a glowing ember inside of a fire-shaped ice casing.

"That's the frozen flame. Concentrate on it and it'll protect you."

Our walk was a silent one. The route we were on took us down an endless block of apartments on one side. After a park, they appeared on the other side too. The road wound back and forth as we continued. I barely noticed it, but there was also a mostly glass building hidden in between them.

The apartments mostly differed in color and design. Most of them were red or brown and others were gray, yellow, or orange. I couldn't really tell. We were still in the dark. The building designs, on the other hand, were wildly different to the point where it didn't matter how dark it was. The streetlights were on, so visibility was no problem. After a while of just being distracted by the scenery, I heard a voice ahead of me.

"Here we are." Nero was talking. "Our rendezvous point is over there." He was pointing in the same direction we were already going. It was a parking lot between a few connected buildings that formed a sharp left curve ahead of us. "It's a pretty outta-the-way spot at this time a day." We continued walking in toward the building at the back in the middle. "That's why I'm glad I could get you here."

"Catt, run!" Noah pulled me behind him by my shoulder. Stumbling back, I hit a wall.

"What?" I slammed the side of my fist on it as I turned around. "Come on." The wall was invisible. I looked up from squawking overhead and saw a bird had also been caught. I tried punching it harder and found myself powerless against it. The stone seated in my fist did nothing.

"Don't try, girl, you're already tapped. I can tell."

"Says you." I tried summoning my gloves, but that just resulted in me flailing my arms at my sides.

"Use the flame and run through the wall. I'll be right behind you." Noah stood ready.

I looked at the stone in my palm. "That's the problem. I already am."

"Don't worry," said Nero. "I just set that barrier up so that you wouldn't run so blatantly. If I wanted to kill you, I would have done it when I descended upon you earlier. As it stands, I mean you no harm." Even if he was telling the truth, I didn't care.

"What do you want?" Noah took a wide stance between me and Nero.

"I just want you to come with me to my company, that's all," said Nero, concentrating his gaze on Noah.

"And that's C.H.E.S.S. I assume?"

"Yes, it is. It would be better if you both came quietly. Either way, you're coming with me."

I stepped forward. "We're gonna have to fight him on that."

Noah put his arm out in front of me. "Catt, don't. I can't sense any power from you, even with the flame."

Noticing what was in my hand, Nero said, "A frozen flame, huh? Neither of you have the energy or the control to use that thing to get out of here. As it stands, no one would be able to tell if anything's happening here if a fight breaks out. Even if you did get out, there are more of us than just me. Trust me. Most others wouldn't give you the option of coming quietly. Moreover, there's no way to break this wall without strength."

"So, we just have to kick your ass and get out of here." I took another step forward.

"Catt," warned Noah.

"Don't worry, we got this. I can pull energy from the flame, right?" I gripped the object in my hand harder.

"I don't think that's a good idea anymore."

"I'd listen to him If I were you." Nero's words fell on deaf ears.

"Okay, let's go." I concentrated as hard as I could on the frozen flame in my hand. "**Meteor**." I called the name of my weapon, and my hands began glowing multiple colors at once, but then stopped. I lost all feeling in my body, and I found myself face-first on the ground. My hair had faded from bright green to its natural black and I dropped the frozen flame. My knees started hurting after a second. They were bleeding.

"Damn it, Catt!" Noah bent down next to me.

"You know what'll happen if you move her, right?" said Nero. "You can't even run if you wanted to, and you're not even strong enough to beat me. Not that I would let you. I learned my lesson in going easy on the 'try hard underdog'. You're not getting the benefit of the doubt."

"Stay still and rest for a while. By the time you can move, it should be over." I heard Noah's footsteps in front of me and the sound of a sword being drawn. Without seeing it or the feeling behind it, a wielder's weapon being summoned just sounds like someone unsheathing a large blade. A second later, I heard his feet move quickly, followed by a volley of concussive blasts.

"Yeah, why not?" said Nero, right before a bigger blast rang through, and the sound of a body hitting the ground hard followed. "All I want is for you to come with me. You're a cure to the corpse shadows. We could use your power."

"Nah, you really want to control this power. Otherwise, your people wouldn't have tried to kill my family." Noah spoke with the clarity of someone who wasn't just flung through the air.

"And who told you that?" Nero sounded more serious than before.

My efforts in moving had also become more serious as it became clear what information was inside the book Jamie gave Noah, I concentrated on myself. I tried to feel anything more than I could at the time. Anything. I already closed my eyes and focused, slipping into a meditative state. I hadn't been in one in months.

Reality became silent and what pain I had was gone. Everything was pitch black. Snapping my fingers, I noticed I couldn't feel that either. The resulting sound, however, made me feel at peace. Getting a feeling of familiarity, I turned around, realizing I was on my feet. What I saw was a rainbow door surrounded by a visible and constantly color-changing aura. The door was covered in rainbow chains with a lock the size of my head, and it had a four-pointed seal over the chains. Beside the door was a giant bird. It had a blue face, a green chest, and wings that were spread apart. It was yellow from there down. I had never seen this while meditating any time before.

"Is this really what you want?" It spoke softly.

"I'd find myself hard-pressed to say no," I said.

"Is that so?" It cocked its head to one side. "As honest as always, aren't we?" This confirmed my suspicion. It was my spirit animal. "It's true. The boy might get himself killed if he keeps this going alone. That being said, You overused our power without even thinking once about the consequences."

"But that-"

"And attempted it further, this time, knowing the consequences could be dire. I see your reasoning, but I have my own."

"Self-preservation," I responded, solemnly, remembering my past grievances with the phrase.

"Correct. That is a stigma which you have been overcoming as of late."

"Excuse me?" I was starting to question the bird's logic.

"You have not the strength to break the seal, yet I can grant you as much power as we can use right now." It straightened its head.

I lowered my head in a bow. "Thank you."

"No need to thank me, thank yourself."

"I thought I just did?"

"Indeed, true, you did." Everything began to fade away.

"See ya later," I said before it faded completely. It responded with a soft murmur before disappearing.

I opened my eyes to Noah being blasted into the barrier. It took a solid second before he hit the ground.

"Alright, let's try this again," I said, picking myself up. "***Meteor***." This time, I felt something as my hands were engulfed in a warm glow of many colors. It felt nice. Like I had just dipped them into a steamy bath. My gloves appeared and this time, they were constantly shifting between colors. My fingers began to take a shape resembling talons and when I checked, my hair was shaped like feathers and changing colors just as fast as my gloves. "She wasn't kidding when she said 'we.'" I looked over at Noah. "What's his deal so far?"

Noah was back on his feet as well. "I can't get close. He's trying to tire me out. He's got a straight sword with prongs near the base, but he hasn't summoned it yet, and he uses sound."

"Okay, let's see if this works too," I said, looking at my fists. "Booster." My gloves extended slightly past my wrists and tubes opened from them. "Good, second form."

"That's what I get for playing nice." Nero put both of his hands together. "**Sound wave.**" An actual sound wave blasted from his palms. It was fast and powerful as it rippled through the air. Both Noah and I dodged it in different directions "**Serene Echo**, Tuner." He summoned his weapon to his hand as we both began closing in on his location. Instead of what Noah described, his weapon was basically four bladed circles with spikes and the handle going through all of them. "**Sonic wave.**" He swung his sword sideways, and a more encompassing pressure wave followed.

I punched the shock wave with the color of earth and broke through it. Noah, unfortunately, did not. He ragdalled back into the barrier.

I continued onward, forcing energy out of the boosters at the back of my gloves. I reached him before Noah hit the ground again.

"**Shockstate!**" Before he could move his sword to block, I hit him straight in the chest with lightning. There was a shock wave of electricity on impact. He stood there, unmoving after I hit him as hard as I could.

"That's not gonna work," he said as he grabbed my arm, pulled me down toward him, and kneed me in my diaphragm, knocking the wind out of me. "I'm shockproof."

I tried to change attributes to fire and counter with my other fist, but he stopped my arm by stabbing my bicep with the butt of his sword. He then disoriented me with a headbutt and as I fell, began blasting sound at my head with his sword hand while still holding my arm.

The continuous blast was so concussive that my shoulder hurt from my head being pushed from it. That went triple for my wrist where he was holding me. The pressure alone prevented me from moving. The pain made it impossible. He was spending a lot of energy to make sure of that. From there, I couldn't tell what was going on.

All I could hear were muffled voices out of my right ear. My left was being blasted with sound. I was trying to concentrate on his wavelength. If I succeeded, I would've been able to cancel out his sound with mine. Unfortunately, the crushing pain and pressure combined made that impossible as well. As the muffled voices continued, the intensity increased dramatically. My sense of time and balance was virtually non-existent at this point, so I had no idea how long this lasted.

At some point, a massive energy ripped through the barrier and came spiraling in my direction. Nero jumped to avoid it and I was left lying on the ground. Everything from there on was slightly muffled with a constant beep in the background.

There was a man cloaked in black energy falling from the sky. He landed on a shorter building connected to the others nearby.

"The Black Reaper!?" Nero sounded surprised and on edge.

"And you're C.H.E.S.S." The man cloaked in black moved so fast, I couldn't find a trace of him as he went. I scanned my surroundings and found that he was behind Nero with a black scythe at his throat. It landed between his hand and the ear with the communication device in it. "**Pressure**." An enormous energy came from him all at once and Nero went limp on the spot. Shortly afterward, the bird that was flying around inside the barrier landed on his shoulder. The bird turned out to be a black, pigeon-sized vulture. "There's no time, I'll take you." He lifted both Noah and me off the ground and encased us in a cocoon made of his darkness. I could see Noah clearly, even though the space was pitch black.

"Can you hear me?" asked Noah.

"Yes," I said, barely hearing either of us.

Noah looked down at himself pitifully. "We should've run as soon as I sensed him coming while you couldn't use your power."

I sighed. "No, that fight was one-sided. He could've killed both of us if he wanted. He wouldn't let us get away no matter how hard we tried."

"I don't want to admit it, but I guess it's true." he slouched into the wall of the space.

I pulled him close, hugged him from the side, and said, "You know, while I was faced down on the pavement, I talked to my spirit animal."

"Really? What was it?"

"A very colorful bird. While I was talking to her, she helped me understand something."

"What is it?"

"I think I really like you. I wanted to protect you so badly that I nearly killed myself to do so."

He tried and failed to hold back a smile. "I guess that goes for both of us. The only problem now is that some random guy is taking us somewhere and I don't think we could fight him at all."

"That's fine. I think he's friendly. I heard that he only kills C.H.E.S.S. operatives. And look." I had already taken out the compass map. The arrow was pointing at a glowing dot that was getting closer.

He breathed a heavy sigh of relief. "I'd ask how you know that, but I'll just take the good news."

In seconds, the arrow overtook the dot and disappeared.

18-Reunions

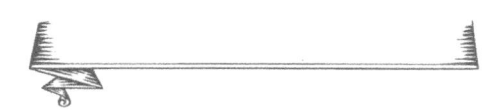

[Noah Black]

One second, it was like flipping through a multi-color page book. The next was like having a psychedelic color dream on steroids. "Your hair makes me feel like I'm gonna barf."

"Why? Is it still changing colors that fast?" Catt responded, looking at her hair. Putting her hand over her mouth, she continued. "I know what you mean." She set it back behind her ear. "I'm glad I don't have to deal with it."

"Yeah, but you still have to deal with that," I said, pointing at her no longer bleeding knees.

"Good thing you said something. I was going to grab my knees in a second." She sat back and smiled.

"Maybe that would teach you about being responsible with your own body," I said, shaking her gently. "And actually, listening to someone for once." I rocked her more aggressively.

"I get it, I get it. Don't make you worry about me, right?"

"I'm serious."

"Man, my life is like an action comedy." She looked up wistlessly.

"Do I need to tap your knee?" I put my hand near her knees.

"No, no, no, no, don't do that." She waved her hands frantically at me. "I can't even straighten them out as they are. You and I both know you can't heal."

"Oh, I wasn't going to heal them." I smiled deviously.

"You jerk." She pushed my hand away.

I sighed. "As long as I know you're listening."

Less than a minute later, the bubble we were confined inside opened up at the top. I was blinded by lights reflected by the pearly white walls, ceiling, and floor. Beds made of wildly different materials of different colors draped in white lined the closest wall, and the other wall was home to a variety of vials and medical equipment. I had little time to discern what kind because of the striking yet slender figure blocking the view. He was around a meter tall with dark skin, short, black hair, and eyes that seemed completely devoid of light from the pupils. He was wearing a long, black cloak, a gray long-sleeved shirt, and black sweatpants with the same color tennis shoes. There was no sight of any birds, but it was obvious that he was the man who rescued us from our predicament.

I started, "Thank-"

"Don't," said the man, "Just consider yourselves lucky." I was dropped through the darkness below onto one of the beds. Shortly after, he released Catt onto one next to me. "You especially," he said, pointing at Catt and relinquishing the darkness he was carrying around.

"Hey, Doc." Another man came through a set of double doors on the far left of where we were. He was of a similar height and skin tone. Unlike the first guy, he had long, curly hair and wore all black except for the red on his otherwise black cloak. "I heard you found some trouble." He raced in with an excited expression on his face. Like the twins, I couldn't see any age on the first guy, but the second guy was similar in age to me.

"That way," said the guy called Doc, pointing at the corner to the left of the doors. "He might be conscious by now or have called backup even."

Still excited, the other guy said, "Cool. On a scale of one to-"

"Six," said the one who brought us in, "He knows advanced spells. Otherwise, five."

"Alright!" The other guy dashed out of the room even faster than he entered, trailing an enormous pressure of energy behind him. His weapon was a katana. The image almost shoved itself into my eyes as soon as I saw him. He had a powerful presence in his excitement.

"So, the Black Reaper is a doctor?" asked Catt.

"No, That's just my name. By the way, what are your names?"

"My name's Catherine Lockhart and we're looking for someone."

"I'm Noah." In my surprise at how fast Catt gave her identity, I gave my own. "Can you help us?"

"If you're looking for Graven, He's on his way. I was able to pick up on your whole conversation with that guy from C.H.E.S.S. because of my bird. Until he gets here, How about you both dismiss your weapons and power down? You may not feel fatigued now, but when you do, you'll probably sleep for at least a full day."

"Is it bad that I don't really know how to do that?" I said, reflecting on the fact that I never really knew how to power up in the first place.

Doc nodded. "Given what you've just been through, yes."

I shrugged. "It'll happen eventually. That's what happens every time."

"Okay." Catt was holding her wrist and looking at her left hand as her gauntlets disappeared and her hair color changed to black.

"Hold on a second." Doc left the room for a minute and returned with a small vial filled with an electric blue liquid between his fingers. "Drink a quarter of this now and whenever you wake up, drink the rest."

"What's this?" She asked.

"A mana potion," he answered.

"Is that a raw mana potion?" I asked. "They stopped making those. How do you have one?" It was my turn to ask a question.

"Those are made by condensing fae particles and adding an attribute value to balance it out. A raw potion is created without a balancing attribute. Most places banned the harvesting of fae magic and in other places, there is a lack of people who can actually condense that sort of magic effectively. Here, neither is a problem."

"Yeah, that makes sense," I said.

"You sound like a doctor to me." Catt had just downed a quarter of the vial and re-corked it before speaking.

He smiled. "Well, I was training to be a nurse at one point."

"Are you a *Corpse Hunter*?" The answer to my question seemed all too obvious, yet he seemed happy to answer any questions we had.

"Officially no, but that's the life of a hunter."

"Does there also happen to be a reason that you're answering all of our questions so honestly?" I was probing for anything he wasn't willing to tell.

"What can I say, the truth is the easiest way to earn someone's trust."

A new voice rang from the hallway behind the doors at the end of the room. "So, those are your methods."

"I don't have to hide anything if I make myself transparent on the first impression," Doc responded, still turned my direction.

"That would just make me paranoid." The cracked door began opening slowly.

"That's because you were trained to interrogate, Graven."

The man who came through was wearing a white turtleneck, blue jeans, gray shoes, purple gloves, and a mask of the same color that only showed his green eyes. He was far shorter than Doc and likely shorter than me. He paused for what felt like a year and then unmasked himself. He had short, black hair, pale skin, and a pronounced scar across his right cheek.

"Karasu." Catt jumped out of the bed and nearly fell as she made her way to Graven. He caught her before she almost fell again, and they hugged as her hair began changing color again.

"Catt, what are you doing here?"

"I've been looking for you for the past two years."

"And you only found me now?"

"What do you mean?"

"I haven't been that hard to find for a while."

"I suck at this ok." She was beginning to choke up on her words.

"I was really hoping you forgot about me before then."

"That's so selfish of you." She began sniffling.

"I know." He shifted his stance to keep her balanced.

"Then, why didn't you come back for me?"

He held her away from him by her shoulders. "I would've, but you were better off without me."

She began wiping her tears. "That's what Mom and Dad said. Even though they supported my decision to find you."

"And what about everybody else?"

"There was so much support..."

"That's good to hear." He picked her up and carried her back to the bed she was in. It looked odd given how much taller than him Catt was. "Right now, you need to rest."

"Oh yeah, that's Noah. He's a friend I met that I've been traveling with while looking for you. He also has someone he's looking for," she said, gesturing in my direction.

"I'm looking for my remaining family members. I belong to the Black family of Twilight Village. Do you know about it?"

"I understand what happened with your family and I'm willing to help." His glassy eyes were just beginning to dry up.

"That reminds me, I have something to discuss with you when I wake up..." Catt's eyes began to droop. The physical and emotional toll of what happened that day finally hit her, and she snapped out of consciousness. The same was slowly happening to me.

"Thank you." I reached into the pocket on the outside of my bag. "I trust you with this." I handed him the book as my eyes finally drooped closed.

My eyes opened to the dark surroundings. There was a soft hum in the background and the only things I could see clearly were my hands as I sat up and put my feet to the floor. Slowly, I reached down to where Catt was sleeping and found no one.

"That means I'm alone then." The double door was vaguely visible at the end of the room. Walking through the doors, I was greeted by a morbid sight. The sky was red and there were large masses of corruption in all shapes, colors, and sizes. Inside of them were people calling for help. "What the hell are you?"

"Those are corpse shadows and the people they inhabit." There was a girl to my left. She seemed to be floating on her own black mass of corruption. I couldn't exactly see what she looked like. It was almost like she wouldn't let me see her.

"So, will you help us?" Another girl appeared on my other side. "After all, you're the only one who can." She was completely surrounded by a blue bubble of corruption, coated in chains and seals. I saw no details of her either.

My thoughts flashed back to an incident I didn't want to remember. "I tried to cure someone once. They died. I'm not doing that again."

"I can tell you're a sweet kid." The one on my left spoke again. "You just haven't realized the true potential of your power. You can do it. You just need to control that strength of yours."

"I had a feeling that was the case." I hung my head low at the thought of my weakness. "What happens if I try again and someone else dies?"

"That's a selfish way of thinking," said the one on my right. "Do you think these people would rather suffer than try, at least, try whatever it takes to put an end to this?" She seemed to be speaking for herself as well.

"Just try… You know what? I like the sound of that." I brought my head back up and scanned the crowd of suffering souls. "Whatever it takes, I'll try."

"Good. Let's just hope you can keep that conviction."

My surroundings blinked out of existence, and I opened my eyes. I was lying down again, and the room was the same except this time, I saw Mary at the end of my bed.

Quickly, everything shifted, so that we were in my room back home. The dull yellowish walls matched the faded grayish carpets as years of abuse and sunlight shone through like the wrinkles on the face of an elderly person. I couldn't make out most of the room, but I could tell that it was all the way it was before the incident. The one large, black dresser next to my closet, the TV with its accompanying stand, the posters of foreign bands I came to like, a single lamp which I kept on a nightstand on my left, and a handheld game and a phone on top of the other one on my right and a waist-high chest that stretched from one side to the other at the base of my bed.

"What are you doing in my room?" I asked, forgetting that I was dreaming.

"Come find me." Her tone alone filled me with sadness and dread. Not to mention the blood that began streaming out of her eyes. "You don't want the same thing to happen to me that happened to Hariet, do you?" As she said that, Hariet's body manifested on top of the bed. She was in the same position as she was in the picture I saw. "Or would I end up like Roger, or Allison, or Sean, or Mavis, or David, or Mom and Dad?" With each name, she dropped came the corresponding family member on a cross, covered in bloodied wounds, and slightly writhing. "And who knows what happened to Frederick and Melonie." Two more crosses with their names etched on them began floating at her sides. "Please, come for me before you lose us all." She began floating up into the darkness with the crosses and family members in tow.

I opened my eyes once more to the sight of my hand reaching into nothingness. I sat up, still reaching forward. Looking around, I put my hand down. This time, the sight I was greeted with was the same as when I left it. The room was the same, the lighting was the same, and Catt was still there. She was sitting up and staring at me with a worried expression on her face. She was also dressed differently. She had on a yellow sleeveless shirt over a light blue long-sleeve and blue jeans with a yellow lightning design. Looking over myself, I was still wearing the same thing I fell asleep in.

"It was a nightmare." I thought telling her that would make her worry less, but it seemed to have the opposite effect.

"You were talking while convulsing in your sleep and crying. Mind telling me what you saw?"

I wiped my eyes and reluctantly explained what was in my dream.

"They're getting worse again, huh?"

"I don't know. I think this time, it was more like... A message? Like I need to do something now or nothing's gonna change."

"Do you know how long you've been asleep?" She asked.

"Doc said it would be about a day, right?" There were no windows, and the room was still as well-lit as when I fell asleep.

"That's about how long I slept. You slept for around three days."

"Seriously? How was I knocked out longer than you?" I just noticed that her arm was in a sling. "Was that from... when that happened?"

"Don't worry about it. It's about healed, anyway." She slowly got to her feet, and it looked like her knees bothered her as she only bent them slightly as she moved. "You need to eat something." She walked across the room toward the shelves on the other side.

I started moving to follow.

"Don't get up," She said, hearing my movements. She reached into a warming oven on the shelf and produced a bowl and a pack of crackers on a plastic tray. "There you go," she said, sitting it on my lap, single-handedly.

"Uh... Thanks." It was regular chicken noodle soup and Ritz crackers. The soup smelled good like it was homemade. There was also a plastic spoon and fork. After taking a moment to look over the tray, I noticed Catt staring at me with a weird smile. "Catt, are you ok?"

"No- I mean, yeah. I'm fine, why?"

"You're kind of weirding me out," I said, beginning to sip on my soup. "I'll be damned if this is a dream too."

"Your dreams were that vivid?" She sat beside me.

"Too vivid. Almost lucid but not quite."

"I got an idea. Stay here and whatever you do, don't get up." She stood again.

"Why?" I asked, still looking down at my soup.

"Oh, I forgot to ask you. Apparently, your fatigue wasn't just from that battle. Doc said that you must have been through some kind of life-changing ritual. Is that true?"

"I guess so," I responded, thinking about what happened underground.

"Is that what happened while we were separated?"

"I don't really know how to explain it."

"You don't have to right now if you don't want to. Just don't get up until you finish your soup." She skipped to the door and disappeared out the other side.

"And thus, I sit in silence." After finishing my soup and crackers, I sat and thought about all the things that happened before my sleep. Everything from what happened at that cave to the fight where Catt's arm was injured. That was the first time I summoned my weapon at will. With any luck, I could do it again. I reached out my hand and tried to go back to that feeling of when I summoned it last. Nothing happened. "Come on..." Still, nothing as I grabbed at the air for a minute. "Alright...Sword." I had never learned the name of my sword, so I just called it a sword. According to Catt, the name of her weapon just came to mind the first time she summoned it. That didn't happen to me. It would just come to me on its own and leave whenever. It was like it only came when it knew I needed it.

As far as I could tell, a weapon's name, regardless of how recognizable, was unknown even when called. It seemed more like a hidden curse or spell that had to be cast by calling it out than a natural form of magic. Maybe it was the opposite? Maybe we were slowly breaking a seal on our own powers that were set either subconsciously by ourselves or by someone else, and the name was just a code word to trigger it.

I turned my legs off of the bed and stood up. I wobbled on my feet and almost fell over. I caught myself. Feeling a little silly about almost falling, I shook my head with my hand on my temple and stood up straight. Next, finding my balance, I stomped my front foot forward. The shock up my leg somehow made me feel more stable. The next step I took was in confidence.

I walked around the room. The tiles on the floor were uniformly square and the wall that housed lines of shelves had a multitude of devices and appliances yet, none of them were medical. They mostly seemed to be common house supplies. Toasters, microwaves, lamps, TVs, etcetera. Most of them had a strange presence coming off of them. They seemed to be very strongly enchanted. More so than the broomstick and paper that led us there.

That reminded me to look through my pockets. I did, and the note was in my lower left pocket near my knee. Catt must have put it there. Opening it, I saw a giant red dot pulsing on and off in the center of it. Wherever this place was, the woman the note was for was still there.

I paced across the room in circles. It seemed more like a storage room than a patient room. The bed frames were made of everything from redwood to steel, to what seemed like some sort of foam-like plastic, and even glass. They were of many different designs as well. Before I had a chance to remark on them, Catt came through the doors.

"Oh good, you're walking," she said, holding the door open. "Let's go."

"Okay," I ducked under her arm through the door. "Such a gentleman."

"Whatever." She rolled her eyes.

"So, where are we going?" I inspected the hallway. The hall was a light gray, the walls had a grimy texture and the floor was the same as back inside the room.

"We're going up," she said, pointing down the hall, leading to an elevator at the end.

"You've been awake here longer than I have. Where is this?"

"It's a basement complex under a bunch of apartments and businesses."

"Cool."

"I also found the woman that note was meant for. She's waiting for whenever you wake up to read the note. Apparently, she wanted us both to be there when she read it, so I put it in your pocket for safekeeping."

"So, does that mean that she's straight up there?" I pointed up as we came near the elevator. There were pathways to the left and right leading to more halls and doors.

"She should be, albeit asleep."

"Just to be sure, are we going up or down?"

"Up, why?"

"Do you know how tempted I am to press this button?" My finger was hovering over the 'down' button.

"Stop, I don't want to get in trouble here." She pressed 'up'.

"There's no trouble if there are no floors below this, but they might just have stairs down. I doubt it though."

"We really do rub off on each other," she sighed. "Now I wanna see if there are any floors below this."

"Don't worry about it. I'm just glad I could get you curious."

"Are you trying to be a bad influence on me?"

"What if I said yes?" The elevator door opened. On the other side of the door was a hallway. "Wait... What happened." I looked around to see the inside of a mirrored elevator. "When did we get here?"

"I figured you wouldn't notice," she said, between hard giggles. "We walked on and rode all the way up and you didn't notice." She stepped off the elevator and I followed.

The floor was still the same, except with a black square every meter or so. The wall was divided in half at a little over waist height with a redwood wall border. The bottom half was black with a brown diamond pattern, and the top part was white with a black diamond at around the same spot as the corresponding one on the bottom part. The diamonds seemed a little off, and I couldn't tell what it was. The end of the hall housed a staircase that led up and down, made of the same wood as the wall barrier.

"Like the wall and floor pattern?" The female voice came from an open door down the hall. She seemed to have noticed me analyzing the pattern. "The diamonds are kinda off just to fuck with people with OCD."

"Excuse me?" A random lady just stepped out of her apartment just to tell me about the hallway decor.

"Seriously. The contractor that renovated the hallways in this building and I had a past, and he knew I lived here, so he did that just to fuck with me. Gets on my nerves every time I come through here."

Confused, I said, "Umm... Hello?"

"Oh yeah, come in. I'll feel better once we're all back inside, anyway." She turned and walked back into her apartment.

"Was that her?" I turned back to Catt and pointed at the open doorway.

"That's her." Catt moved toward the empty doorway, and I followed.

"Hey, close the door behind you, ya?" Hinata called back to us.

Catt closed the door behind us as I looked over the room. There was a short hallway from the entrance that led to a larger room with one door on each side, and the walls were green with a deep blue floral pattern. The exit to the hall opened up to a living room on the right and a kitchen on the left. The floor was a plain square tile until it reached the living room area, which transitioned to hardwood. One green sofa patterned in deep blue stripes and two accompanying armchairs that were next to each other surrounded a square clear glass table on top of a square rug of the inverted design of the furniture. The walls were light gray in the kitchen area and faded into light blue in the living room. On the far wall stood a flat screen TV surrounded by shelves housing small, decorative trinkets.

"Hey, boy." She was sitting on the sofa and pointing at me with a comically oversized and gloved hand.

"Me?" I pointed to myself. "Yes. I am boy."

"Don't get cheeky with me." She cracked a smile. "The bathroom's to your left. You've probably been holding it in for three days, you need to go before you have an accident."

"That actually sounds like a good idea." I reached for the doorknob and entered a porcelain room with a white shelf behind the door, a toilet, and a sink facing each other on either side on the way to a green-curtained bathtub. I was tempted to open the curtain and see what was on the other side, but the immediate urge to release three days of waste overpowered the temptation. The room smelled of strawberries until what felt like an hour later. The sink, however, had strawberry-scented air freshener resting next to hand soap with the same scent. I felt thirty pounds lighter exiting the bathroom.

"So, how'd that feel?" said Hinata as I exited the bathroom. "I hope you used some of that air freshener in there." Catt was sitting next to her with a glass of water.

"Yes, I am still boy." I gave her a smile and a thumbs-up.

"I see what you mean," she mumbled to Catt.

"What's that about?" I asked. "Catt?"

"You're crazy, you know that?" responded Hinata.

"Was that a compliment or...?"

"Come to think about it, we all are a little bit," she mumbled aloud to herself. "Just sit down." She patted the seat on her other side.

"Okay." I shrugged my shoulders, took out the letter, and sat next to her. "Here you go," I said, handing it to her. "He also wanted me to tell you 'It hurt like hell'."

She smiled solemnly while looking down at the paper, followed by a soft giggle. "Yep, this is from Cosmo alright. I thought he had forgotten all about me by now. Of course, it's hard to forget about someone when you've had their child." A long awkward pause ensued as Catt and I each decided on how to phrase our questions.

Catt sat her glass on a blue coaster and clasped her hands together as I just stared with my hand out questioningly and an expression to match.

"How... I mean, how?" Words were escaping me.

"Okay. You is girl and he am boy, so how do boy does what only girl do? Is that about right?" Catt summed it up perfectly.

"Exactly." I nodded.

"Magic, my dears, magic. You can't do everything with it, but you can do just about anything." She had already opened the letter completely and began reading it. "Oh, I even have a granddaughter." She continued to read down the page. She paused for a moment, and she seemed to catch literal fire for a split second. Catt and I jumped at the same time. The look on her face told me she was angry enough to kill. It also revealed her real age. Normally she looked to be in her twenties, yet now she seemed to reach as high as eighty. She looked like an angry old lady or a hag.

"Are you ok?" I hurried back to her side.

"Yeah, what's wrong?" Catt did the same.

"You've heard of C.H.E.S.S. by now, right?" Her eyes never left the table.

"Big organization, kind of everywhere, maybe evil? Yeah, we've been hearing that name too often recently. Does it have something to do with them?" Catt held her by her shoulders while saying this.

"Nevermind. I'm going to need you two to leave for now. I'd appreciate it if you lock the door on the way out."

"Are you sure you don't need any help?" I asked.

"Yes, please just…" She sounded greatly saddened.

"Alright Noah, let's go." Catt rose from her seat, ushered me out, and locked the door behind us.

"Did you see what was on the note or something? Your reaction was pretty different than normal for things like this."

"C.H.E.S.S. has their eye on Belle. Apparently, she's her granddaughter."

"Oh, that makes sense. Damn. I'd be angry too if I was in her position. Even if she went to them and told them what those people were about, that wouldn't change that they have an eye on her." I followed Catt silently back to the elevator.

"Remember that thing I left the room for earlier?"

"Yeah, what was that about?"

"You'll see." She pressed 'up' again on the elevator, and we entered.

"Where are we going this time?"

"Like I said, you'll see." She had already pressed the button for the top floor. The ride was short because the building wasn't very tall. "Follow me." She made a B-line straight for the stairs on the other side of the hallway.

"Are we going to the roof or something?" I asked once we came to the stairs.

"No, we're going to a magical half-floor between this floor and the last one," she said, sarcastically.

"Really?"

"No, but it does sound plausible, doesn't it?"

"Yeah, I thought you were telling the truth for a second."

"The roof it is."

The way to the roof seemed like a short gray hallway made of stairs to a door of the same color. She opened the heavy door, and the rising sun blinded me for a second.

I walked onto the roof with Catt, and she moved as a wave of corrupted shadow energy came my way. My instincts kicked in and I instantly purified it with a swipe of my blade as it was summoned.

"That get your adrenaline pumping?" Graven stepped out of artificial darkness. He still wore the mask, but he was also bound in a close-fitting purple jumpsuit.

I looked around wildly and asked, "Uh… What's the meaning of this?"

Graven folded his arms and answered, "As of today, I will be training you."

"Uh, Catt-" I looked toward her on my right.

"I asked him to." She folded her free arm around her bandaged one. "It's the only way for you to get skilled enough for you to completely rid anyone of a corpse shadow, let alone get your sister back."

After a moment of consideration, I responded. "Alright, I'll do it."

"Really? I thought it would take more than that to get you to say yes." She seemed fairly surprised.

"You're right, I do need to get stronger..." I clenched my fist. "Much stronger."

"Alright then. First lesson. Stay on the ground." Graven pointed up. "Start." My hair stood on end, and I became overcome with a feeling of weightlessness as my body began ascending into the sky.

"Waaah- boof!" I came from slowly floating upward to careening into the ground from about seven meters. "Hey! What the hell was that about!" I said, getting up.

"We have a lot of work to do," said Graven with certainty.

I moaned, "What did you expect me to fly or something?"

"I'll be leaving you two to your training." Catt left through the only door down.

Graven nodded and said, "I said to stay on the ground. It was your first test. You failed."

"How was that a test?" I rubbed my aching jaw.

"I'll tell you if you ever pass, but now onto actual teaching. By your reactions a minute ago, I assume you only react to immediate danger. When a wave of corrupted energy flies at you, you react on a dime. But when you begin floating up toward the sky with little explanation, you hardly react at all. That being said, you need to learn how to summon that thing at will." He pointed at my sword.

I didn't argue. It sounded like he knew what he was talking about, and I was more than ready to get started.

19-Pure Spirit

[Graven Lockhart]

"First of all." I summoned my sword to my hand. "To make sure you know everything you need to know so we can start with the real training, I'm starting at the basics as they pertain to wielders. These are called wielder's weapons, but their technical name is 'code of arms.'" I let my sword hover behind me and I sat on top of it. "When it comes to wielders, that's the only defining surface factor that we all have in common. In terms of internal factors, we have access to an 'inner space' like any other magic user. Unlike other magic users, however, ours holds a gate and a creature unique to the individual. Any questions?"

Noah responded, "I can't summon this thing at will, and I don't know its name. Are you gonna help me with that?" He was pointing his sword squarely at me.

"Have you tried asking it?"

"Yes, once. I got like a hum or something. No real answer and I still couldn't summon it."

"Well, since you have it out now, try asking it again." I stood and stabbed my blade into the ground in front of me. "Except this time, try concentrating on the weapon. Close your eyes and visualize what it looks like in your mind. Once that's done, ask away."

Normally there would be no reason for a code of arms to keep its name secret from its wielder, but this turned out to be a special case.

He stuck his blade into the ground facing him. After a moment, the contrast of his weapon reversed. The pure white blade faded to an inky black, and the black line in the center brightened to a pure white. The handle never changed. He opened his mouth slightly and breathed out rhythmically. He was speaking directly to it. It responded with vibrations that could be felt through the ground. He said something else, and it responded again. This pattern repeated a few more times before he opened his eyes.

"So, how'd it go?" I asked.

The look on his face was something between a scowl and stark confusion. "Well, I know the name now. It wasn't as hard as I thought it was. There was a giant, white tiger, and a door. I think that was my spirit animal?"

"It should be. You don't look happy about your experience. What happened?"

"The door was open, and the tiger told me it was because I had nothing holding me back, but I don't believe that."

"There's never been a case that I've heard of where someone's gate had been completely unlocked before they even saw it for the first time. If it was going to happen, it'd happen after they've seen it at least once. The gate's supposed to have chains, a seal, and a vortex of energy around it. Was any of that present?"

"No, I could barely feel any energy from it either." He furrowed his brow. "And the inside was just a solid black surface. It felt like stone bricks and there seemed to be, like, a room on the other side."

"I'll be frank," I said, standing my sword behind me and leaning on it. "I've never heard of what you just described. Your case is special, so I don't even know what to tell you."

"That reminds me. Have you ever heard of a phantasm?"

"Is that something your spirit animal told you about?"

"It said something like 'beware the phantasm.'"

"That may have something to do with your sword inverting like that." I pointed at his sword, and he took notice.

"That's never happened before." He took a good look at the seam in the center. "I wonder... If I cut something, would I corrupt it instead of purifying it?"

"There's only one way to find out. Hey Krow, could you get me a fruit?"

Krow had been sitting on top of the roof of the rooftop entrance and calmly concealing his presence. He was just far back enough that he could only be seen at a certain distance. Noah turned and looked up in that direction as well.

"I got something better," said Krow, standing up. He hovered one hand over the other in a spherical shape. "*Sacred flame: phoenix feather.*" A golden glow of purified flame appeared between his hands the shape of a bird feather. "Here you go. Be careful, it could explode if handled too roughly. I haven't done that one in years." He tossed the feather, and it spiraled down to Noah's open palms. "Drop it on the floor and go to town."

After a second of intense examination, Noah turned back toward me and dropped the feather on the ground. It fell slowly but was unphased by a brisk wind that came through and landed in front of him. Slowly, he raised his sword over the feather and quickly plunged it into the ground below it. In less than a second, the color came from a radiant yellow to pitch black and dissipated with a poof.

Before either Noah or I had a chance to comment on what just happened, Krow said, "Wait a minute." and saw Krow landing beside Noah. "Where's the boom?" He crouched down and examined the feather. "That's peculiar." Noah removed his sword from its position and bent down himself. I would've followed suit, but a hand on my shoulder prevented that. "It looks like it was corrupted so thoroughly and so quickly that even the magic couldn't react in time."

I grabbed the hand on my shoulder and walked forward to see the feather closer for myself. "It looks like that phantasm you mentioned is the second part of your spirit animal." I scrutinized the corpse of a black flame left over from the feather. "Phantasms are ghostly creatures that inhabit some of the darkest places in the world. I've never fought one, but I've heard that they're like wraiths but more dangerous. It's up to you whether you embrace this side of yourself or not. It's a part of you, so I'll help you learn how to control it in case there's a chance that you can go on a rampage because of it. That being said, it looks like the classification of your color is still purity. Be it pure white or pure black."

"Uh... Graven?" Noah sounded concerned.

"What is it?"

"Who's that?"

"If you mean the girl with the scowl behind me, that's Naomi. She, along with Krow here, will be helping me train and teach you. She just doesn't like to be taken out of the shadows so suddenly." The gentle tug of her hand in the opposite direction became a harder pull, and I let go. "Do you have anything to say, Naomi?"

"You two are the same, yet different..." I could hear the distance in her voice as she began floating back into the darkness. "One an innocence writhing in cruelty and the other, a white canvas splotched with blackness. Both accompanied by a figure of ruin. A maggot and a rorschach." I looked back to see her vanish into a void. "I look forward to watching your development."

"Wait, you seem familiar somehow." Noah reached out to her but quickly retracted his hand as she disappeared.

After a short pause, I said, "Speaking of development." Stepping back a few yards, I traced a line in the ground with my blade, and I evoked a spell. "***Wall***." A solid purple wall sprang from the divide. "I want you to break this," I said, moving away from it. "I'll gouge your strength with it."

"I guess I'll be over here then." Krow turned around and jumped back to his perch.

"Okay." Noah slowly moved in front of the wall and tapped it with the blade. The instant he did, his sword's appearance blinked back to its original color.

"We'll figure that out as you go, don't worry," I said, as he looked at me and then back at his sword.

"I'll take your word for it." He raised it high over his head, slammed it back down, and sunk his blade a couple of centimeters deep.

"Well, I'll be damned." I surveyed the damage. "I expected it to be strong, but this is ridiculous." The blade was slowly digging deeper into my spell.

"Did I do better than you thought I would?" His sword stayed embedded into the wall.

"You could do better. I was referring to the pure attribute of your color of arms. It's like it's eating away at the impurities of the wall I created."

He removed his blade from the wall and shifted around on his feet a little. "What next?"

"Noah, do you know any spells?"

"Nope. I was a couple of weeks away from learning any sort of magic before I had to set out like I did."

"That explains a bit. If that's the case, have you ever done some sort of action regarding the sudden release of massive energy and debated naming it?"

"Not even once."

"Alright, try going back to your space and talking to your spirit animal again. This time try asking it about any powers you can use. It should know something."

"I'll try." He closed his eyes and stabbed his blade into the ground, concentrating once more. Within seconds, his blade color inverted again.

I snapped my fingers softly behind my back and whispered, "Get close."

The form of a small black snake came around my side and slithered up to Noah. It began closely examining his sword, but before it could touch it, the blade's color blinked back just as it had before, but this time, it began glowing in a white aura and he did too.

This wasn't a spell that he was consciously casting. It seemed that something else cast the spell from within him. The snake was erased by the light, and I could hear Naomi sink to the ground as an exasperated moan escaped her. I kept my attention focused on Noah. His eyes opened to reveal a solid black color and with it came the feeling of fear. It wasn't natural fear. This was another spell. Tears began streaming down his eyes as if a dam had been breached in his mind. This lasted for about five seconds then, everything went back to normal.

Noah fell to the ground, still clutching his sword. "That... was a lot to take in." He stood.

"I'll say. First 'sacred aura', then 'nightmare eyes'. There's a fine mix of light and dark. Although, they "

"I was talking to the tiger about spells when he disappeared and was replaced with a giant shriveled-up corpse shrouded in smoke."

Krow, from his perch, said, "Sounds like a phantasm all right."

"Was it frightening?" I asked.

"It particularly wasn't, no. There was something else about it that looking directly at it scared me for some reason."

"That explains it then." I leaned back against my sword. "Your blade is normally white because the tiger suppresses the phantasm. When you enter your space, it pushes the phantasm out so that it won't come into contact with you and your blade turns black. In other words, the tiger doesn't want you to have anything to do with the phantasm."

"But I just talked to him, and he seems relatively chill even with his predicament."

"It may be the darkness. While you were in there this time, I had Naomi send a familiar to you and it was destroyed by what was presumably the tiger casting 'sacred aura', a spell meant specifically for protecting one from darkness. While the tiger was occupied, the Phantasm probably took the opportunity to show itself to you. It also happened to cast 'nightmare eyes' while doing so. That's where the fear most likely came from. It might've been trying to keep the tiger out as long as possible before it took control again."

"Did ya get any spells?" Krow got us back to our original track.

Nearly forgetting, I said, "Oh, that was the reason I had you go in there this time. Did either one tell you anything having to do with that?"

"Actually… Yeah. They both kinda gave me a spell for lack of a better term."

"Would you mind showing us?" I took a step back.

"Alright, the one the tiger showed me went kinda like this." Noah leaned his sword against his leg, put both hands in front of him, palms forward, and stared intently at them. "**Purify**." A white light began emanating from his hands. "Huh, I did it."

"Good job. That's a basic variant spell. That means its multi-purpose. It can also be used as a basis for more advanced spells. Now, what's the other one?"

"Well…" He said, banishing the spell and staring at his palms. "The other one was from the phantasm. I don't know if I can trust it."

"Remember this," I told him, "Dark and light don't necessarily mean good and bad. After all, the basis of my power is darkness. It has more to do with their personality and circumstances than who they are as a person. Take Naomi, for instance. She's a little standoffish and very secretive and likes to toy with people a little too much, but that doesn't necessarily mean that she's a bad person."

"Let me hear you say that to my face." Naomi was hovering menacingly next to me.

"Anywho, you see where I'm getting at?" I pulled the floating menace close by her shoulders and gestured toward her.

"Whatever." She rolled her eyes, escaped my grasp, and floated back into darkness.

Confusedly, Noah said, "I guess? It's just, he said, the spell will double my output but will throw me into madness."

"Yeah, I see where you're coming from," I said, " Madness is an effect that can make one go temporarily insane."

"I don't know what that'll do to me." He looked down at his sword still at his side.

"Can you at least tell me what it's called?"

He hesitated the most I'd seen from him so far before he said it. "He said it was called 'Hell soul'."

"Hey Krow, you ever heard of a spell by that name?" I asked.

"Nope," he responded. "Doc might know. He tends to gather information about spells that have to do with the soul more than anything. I'll ask him later."

"And there we have it. Now we can move on to the next thing." I moved back over to the wall and put my hand on top of it. "***Wall***." I recast the spell and fixed the wall. "Take that spell you just did and this time, focus on the edge of your blade."

"Okay." Noah took his sword out of the ground and stared intently at it. The blade began glowing.

"Now, let it build until it feels like you can barely control it." After a few seconds, there was a noticeable shift in his energy. His presence had gotten stronger. "Now, swing your sword and cast the spell at the same time."

Eyeing the wall, he did as told. "***Purify***." A pure energy wave escaped the tip of his blade and cut into the wall.

"Good job. One more of those and the wall will be in two. Give it another go and let's see what you can do."

"Alright, I think I got a handle on it now," He said, holding his blade at the ready.

"Just this time, don't think of it as the spell 'purify' and think of it more as a wave of purity that you're sending out. It's a blade wave, so just call it a blade wave."

"Okay, got it." His energy began building up again and his blade began glowing much faster this time. "***Blade wave***." This one was enough to split the wall in half. The pieces fell to the ground and dissipated.

"And there you go," I said, "Now, you can use two spells. A few more and you can start your own grimoire."

Noah relaxed. "My dad had one of those. It was all white and had a picture of two snakes eating each other in a circle with a shield in the middle. Wait, that's a separate spell?"

"Yeah, when you transform one spell into another type of spell, be it by changing its shape or completely altering its properties, it usually counts as a different spell. Reason being is that it's a sort of shortcut to get the results you want. You don't want to take the time to recast a bunch of low-level spells just to cast a higher-level one every time. Aside from that, a grimoire can just help you keep better track of things than your mind can alone. After you master a few more spells, we can talk about making you one."

"So, what's next?" asked Noah, eager to continue.

"Hold It." Krow landed between me and where the wall was. "Graven, do you mind?"

"Go ahead." I stepped away.

"Okay, try to break this one." He pressed his hands onto the ground. "***Wall***." From the ground sprang a red wall of energy. "Light eats away at darkness. It won't do that with fire. Take your best shot. When you can break this in one shot, I'll consider you a master of the 'blade wave.'" He leaned an elbow against the wall. "Got it?"

Noah smiled. "I'll take that as a challenge."

"Good." Krow moved away from the wall.

"One more time..." Noah readied his sword.

"Try doing the concentration part before you take a stance. That way, you don't have to wait so long to fire it off. You might even get a little more power out of it that way."

"Okay." Noah's power swelled again.

"But above all else, don't forget to calm down and relax."

"Yeah." Noah relaxed his shoulders and swayed on his feet a bit. His power saw a minor spike. "Any other tips?"

"No, you're a natural."

"Okay... ***Blade wave***." The words flowed with his breathing as a substantially stronger energy wave crashed into the wall. It cut a tenth of the way through.

Krow was now beaming and looking my way. "Waddaya say, Graven? Nine more goes?"

"Sounds about right," I responded. "Nine more at that strength should be able to cut it completely in half. That is if you're accurate enough."

Noah looked closer at the chipped wall. "I should have more than enough accuracy. I used to juggle knives and throw them at targets. I was good at it."

"Alright, hit the wall, and let's see it," said Krow, hopping back to his perch.

Noah readied himself again and after a few seconds, let another one loose. This one came within a hair of the first one.

"Keep going until you break through. You got this." Krow encouraged him.

Noah tried again another twelve times. His accuracy began to wane, and so did his output. He'd been shelling out a lot more energy than he'd ever let out a day in his life all at once, and it was continuous.

"Tired yet?"

"No."

"That's the spirit! Keep going."

Seeing this, I said, "I guess I could teach him a defensive spell tomorrow."

"Sounds like a plan," Krow responded happily.

I hoped that I would be able to teach him the basis of defensive spells before we were done for the day. Taking things into consideration though, continuous training on one skill would build him up to master it and reduce the chance of confusion. By the time the sun came back up after going down, Noah was unable to stand properly and was on the verge of exhaustion.

"Think we overworked him?" I said as Krow and I carried Noah back down to the basement.

"Nah, he's improving pretty fast. At this rate, he'll have mastered at least five basic spells and an intermediate or two or maybe even learning advanced ones in about three months tops."

"You sound like you speak from experience."

"Maybe I am. With my memory this non-existent, I could be, or I could have no idea what I'm talking about."

Krow picked up Noah and tossed him over his shoulder. We made our way back down to the basement where Catt was waiting.

"So, how'd it go?" Catt had taken up residence on one of the beds as we entered. She seemed restless.

"He'll be fine, he just needs rest. Whenever he wakes up, we'll start training again," I responded.

"Sounds harsh," she said, looking over Noah as Krow laid him on one of the other beds.

Krow responded this time. "That's how it is. Besides, to be built up faster, you have to be broken down faster. Aren't you in training too? I figured you'd know that by now." He propped Noah's head up on a pillow. "Besides, I believe in extremes when it comes to training." He pulled the bed off of the wall and sprinkled a vial of red sand around it in a circle. He then placed both hands on the ground and cast a spell. "*Wall.*" The bed became surrounded by a red wall up to the ceiling in the shape of the sand. "He'll have to cut this down when he wakes up. He should be able to use what he's practiced."

"You sure that's necessary?" I asked.

"Oh yeah." he pushed his finger against the surface of the wall and pushed a hole through near the top and bottom. He repeated this a few times on each side. "That should be better."

"The hard way is the best way, they always say." I looked back toward Catt. "So. how are you doing?"

"Pretty good. My arms and legs are still tired. I was running around a track all day with weights on them. They just finished healing, but that's training, I guess."

I looked at her and Noah and said, "I'm pretty sure it'll only get harder from here on for the both of you."

"Can't say I'm looking forward to it." She placed a hand on her shoulder and wound up her arm.

"Whelp, Imma get some sleep." Krow walked past me and out of the room. "I don't use that spell often enough to do it that many times in a day."

"I need to sleep too, actually. Good night... Morning... Whichever." I went forward, moved the bottom of my mask, and kissed Catt's forehead. "Love you. Be sure to take care of yourself, ok?"

"Love you too, bro." She hugged me.

"We're getting a place for you to stay by next week, so try to take care of yourself until then, ok?"

"What about him?" She let me go and pointed at Noah.

"Him too."

"Thanks for everything."

"No problem. See you later."

"Yeah."

Waking up late in the afternoon, I found myself back on the roof meeting with Krow and Naomi, who happened to be having a conversation. They were sitting next to each other on the edge of the roof. Unintentionally, I eavesdropped.

Krow was looking out at the sky wistfully as he said, "I just see a lot of myself in him. He'll get strong real quick. The problem is that eventually, he'll run into something that'll mess with his mind. Not sure someone like him can handle that. That's not something you can teach. Through warning is necessary though."

"What about you?" said Naomi. "Those memories seem like a key to uncovering something so big it might eclipse the life you have now. Do you think you'd be prepared for that?" She sounded genuinely concerned.

"Talk about a real mind fuck now that you mention it. It's one of those things I can only answer by fighting. I fight just to understand myself."

"Are you serious or are you just being cool?" If I didn't know any better, I'd have thought she smiled just then.

"Well, I like to fight, but moments like this are just as good."

"Agreed." She placed her head on his shoulder.

Krow chuckled. "You sure you don't like me?"

"Not like that, no."

"Alright."

This was the first time in a long time I'd seen Naomi comfortable enough to have a normal conversation with someone. This was good for her. She seemed to have a warmer presence about her.

Without warning, Naomi whipped her head around, "Ninja." Her presence turned cold once again.

"Turtles?" Krow turned as well, and Naomi gave a questioning look. "Ninja turtles." He shrugged, "New York, Ninja Turtles."

"Sorry," I said, "I didn't want to interrupt your bonding."

"There was no bonding," said Naomi, threateningly.

Krow shrugged. "I mean... Wasn't there... Kinda a little?"

"No." She pushed his face away and phased through shadows to another edge of the roof, standing.

Krow simply sighed, "Girls."

"Krow," I said.

"Yeah?"

"Let's take a week on the blade wave."

He smiled. "Perfect timing. My spell just broke. Let's do that."

20-Training

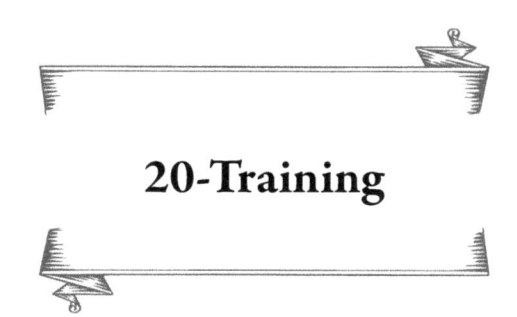

[Krow Hunt]

Noah stumbled onto the roof and walked up to me with both hands up. He looked at me with raised eyebrows and wide eyes. "Krow- why?" He had taken the time to wash up and change his clothes before coming up to the roof.

I shrugged. "Why did I put a wall around you? Or the thing about the wall aside from the holes?"

"Both- wait, what other thing?" Noah's expression changed to one quizzical in nature.

"Wasn't that one any harder to destroy than the others?"

"No, not really, why?"

"I made that one twice as strong as the ones I had you break before. The fact that you didn't notice means that you're growing pretty fast."

Noah looked down at his hands. "Cool."

"And Graven gave the go-ahead to do this for a week. It will only get harder and there will be a little test."

He sighed. "Great, another test I have to worry about."

I shrugged. "Well, we need some way to see your progress."

"I guess..."

I proceeded to create another wall for him to break. This one was as strong as the one I put around his bed and after he broke it, I made another. Every time it seemed like he improved, I made the obstacle slightly harder and by the end of the day, he'd run out of mana and pass out. Slowly, he learned to pace himself and not tire out by the end of the day. Eventually, he learned how to swift-cast the spell and send out two blade waves almost simultaneously. With his new skill came strength and by the end, I was putting in as much effort as he was just to make a wall that wouldn't be destroyed in under a couple of seconds. By sundown on the last day, I was more proficient with the 'wall' spell than I had in a long time.

"Good work. Tomorrow's the test. How do you feel?" I said through the buffeting wind.

"Okay, sure." He turned around onward the door and hesitated before turning back. "I want to try something." He had an earnest look in his eye.

"Go ahead. We'd all be learning something." I gestured over to Graven and Naomi watching from the side.

"Alright, let's see..." He held his sword in a ready pose and closed his eyes. He began the rhythmic breathing that indicated his speaking with his spirit animal, and a smile bridged across his face. His blade colors swapped. "I wanna try it like this."

"There we go!" I said excitedly, clapping both hands together and creating another wall as strong as the last one. "Have at it."

"**Blade wave**." The black wave careened at the wall and crashed into its surface. It had the same effect as its counterpart and the weapon's color didn't change back afterward. It seemed that between training sessions, he'd managed to convince his light half to loosen its hold on his dark half. "Blink." The weapon changed back to its original color.

"Now, I have to see." Graven stepped up. "*Wall*." He created a wall of his own. "Hit this with that negative blade wave."

"Alright, I'll try." Noah seemed a little hesitant.

"Don't say it this time," advised Graven.

"What?"

"Every time you've cast that spell, you called it out loud. By not calling out the name of the spell, it loses some of its strength. If you're feeling nervous, do it that way."

"Okay, blink." After turning the blade black again, he wordlessly sent out another wave. The sound was like a whip crack, and it was almost deafening. There was now an open groove in the ground where the wall had moved a few solid feet toward Noah.

Naomi was also snatched off her perch in the darkness and slid across the floor where she landed a few feet behind Graven.

The wall had seen about half the damage mine had but the reaction was wildly different. It wasn't as if we weren't expecting anything, but the cause and effect seemed almost disconnected. Upon closer inspection, Graven had to force himself backward at that moment to prevent himself from being pulled forward as well. I was the only one not affected.

I couldn't hide the visible smile on my face. "What the hell was that?"

Graven responded first. "It felt like I was being pulled in, but only toward the wall."

"The corpse shadow jumped at the boy." Naomi's response was muffled by the ground. She sounded like she was giving her all to not lash out in anger, so I went to her side and lifted her off of the ground in my arms. The 'dark shroud' that she kept over the entirety of the roof had faded when she hit the ground, and the setting sun could be seen over the buildings.

"Oh look, the sunset." I turned Naomi so that she could see it.

"I'm not a baby, put me down." She pouted.

"It's okay, just relax." I ignored her request.

"Stop cradling and put me down." I was, in fact, cradling her.

"Come on, just a little?"

She reached her hand toward my face. It turned black and began producing a sulfur smell. She cast 'necrotic hand'. I moved my face to the side before she could touch me and ran around in circles. She tried again and nearly succeeded. This time, I spun in a circle before continuing to run.

"Stop, you're making me hate you."

"I don't care, this is too much fun," I called her bluff.

"Now I feel sick." She held her other hand over her mouth.

"Whoops, sorry about that." I had only stopped for a second before her shin met my face. I was prepared for impact once I saw her leg move and didn't falter. Taking the opportunity to launch herself with her kick, she levitated away and recast 'dark shroud' over the entire roof before landing as the sky went dark again.

While this was happening, Graven went and talked to Noah, who seemed to be affected the most. Visibly shaken, he fell to his knees, wide-eyed and staring at his sword. "So, that's why." He was actually shaking.

"You mean the warning the tiger gave you?" said Graven.

"It looks like the light side purifies and can pass through living things… While the dark side can corrupt and pull in other darkness." His eyes never left his blade. "Yet, I'm supposed to cure someone of a corpse shadow when I'm basically half one? How am I supposed to do that?"

Graven sat down next to Noah. "As you already know, you're a wielder. You weren't born with that power, but you were born to inherit it. What resides inside you is a conglomeration of your will and the collective will of your lineage for you to have and use that power. At least, that's what I think it is. As you grow as a person, so does your power. Look." He summoned his sword and evolved it into a guillotine shape. "This is what happened when I decided to leave everything I knew and loved at home and do something that I thought was right. My weapon grew with me. In this case, literally."

"So, will that happen with me?"

"No." As soon as Graven said that, Noah's face began to droop. "That's because you're different. Krow, show him."

By this time, Naomi was free of me.

"Okay, sure." I held my hand out. "**Black Flame**." I summoned my sword by calling its name. This time it was in a black sheath. Pulling it out, the color and pattern could be seen.

"Are you like me?" asked Noah.

"Not exactly," I cast a spell. "**Burn**." I picked up a rock by stabbing it with the tip of my sword and it caught fire.

I tossed it into the air and returned the blade to its sheath.

Pulling it back out, I cast another spell, "***Whirlwind***," cutting it in half.

The rock was carried by a strong current higher into the air and landed in more pieces than it was cut.

"See?" I showed him my blade.

Instead of black with red markings, it was silver with black marks. "My spirit animals are a wind dragon and a fire angel, believe it or not. Fire is my default, yet unlike most like us, I can use the power of both at the same time. wielders like us, with more than one spirit animal are called multi-wielders. Graven is a common wielder, but we're special. However, there's something you are that I'm not."

"You mean the whole 'curing corpse shadows' thing?"

"No, I think it'll be better to show you than to tell you." I stabbed my sword into the ground, reached into the pocket inside my jacket over my heart, produced my grimoire, and opened it to a page that read 'Inner Gate Illusion'. It had a magic circle around a depiction of a door with a smaller magic circle on it. "There we go." I touched the larger circle with my finger and activated the spell. "***Inner gate of the mind.***" A bubble formed around the book and expanded over the whole roof. The rooms on the last two floors technically didn't exist, so I figured it wouldn't bother anybody if it reached them. My spell nullified Naomi's, but the sky stayed black. To my right appeared a giant red gate with a curvy green pattern on it. It was surrounded by red chains with a green lock and a combination wind-fire seal. "That's my gate," I said, pointing at it. "And that's yours." I designated Noah as the spell's target and his gate appeared to my left. It was wide open with a white frame and a series of black marks across white doors. The brick-like surface Noah described was clearly visible. They were both far away enough to be beyond the edges of the roof. "See the fundamental difference?" He stood and began walking toward his gate. "Be careful, it's only an illusion of what's inside you and you could still fall off the roof."

"The inside of my gate is literally stone black. Do you know what's on the other side of yours?"

"I don't know what's inside mine, but that's why you're special. Common wielders only have one spirit animal and a locked gate, and I already explained multi wielders. There are, however, two other wielder types. They're called closed and open wielders. Sara's a closed wielder. It's more like a condition than an actual category. Have you ever heard of Mediocris Cavea disorder?" Up to this point, I had been pacing back and forth between the doors. I stopped when I asked the question.

"Yeah, I met a girl with that while I was in Magnolia," he answered.

I began pacing again. "That is what you call a wielder with that condition among others. They're closed because there are restrictions on their access to their full potential in one way or another. You are an open wielder. Your door is always open after the first time you see it. You have no restrictions on your potential from then on. Normally, a weapon will grow in stages but in your case, there are no stages. As you grow, so does your weapon, and at the same rate." I stopped pacing again. "Because you're open, whatever attribute you have at your base is gonna be what we call 'absolute'. If it's fire, it'll normally burn forever. If it's ice, it'll normally never melt. If it's wind, normally it'll never stop shifting. In your case, the light will never dim, and the dark won't brighten. There's a lot you can do with that. Oh, there's also one more called a 'divergent' wielder. You might be one of those, but they're very rare. It's a little tough to describe what they are, but their powers are unique, to say the least. Anybody else need any exposition?"

"You nullified my spell, put it back." Naomi was standing off in the distance, trying to recast her spell. Mine was too strong, so all she got was a black bubble in front of her face.

"Oh yeah, I forgot this spell makes me a little loopy. It's more of a ritual spell, really." I placed my finger back on the circle on the levitating book. "**Release**." everything went back to normal and Naomi recast her spell.

"Basically, he's saying that your light acts light, and your darkness acts dark. No in-between. Get it?" Graven was standing again and dismissed his sword.

"Yeah, I just need time to figure out what I can do with that, you know?" Noah looked at his hands.

"Don't be afraid to ask if you need help, okay?" I made my way to the door on my way back downstairs.

"I'll try," he responded as the door closed behind me.

The next day, I walked onto the roof only to find Noah shooting off blade waves into the sky while switching between light and dark. He was concentrating heavily, and Naomi was watching from afar. "I like your dedication. How long were you up here?" My words seemed to startle him as he wasn't expecting me.

"Oh! Krow. When did you get here?"

"Just now."

"I was training with Naomi to see how far I could shoot this spell."

"And how far is that?"

Naomi spoke up. "Around seventy feet silent and ninety feet spoken."

"Come to think of it, I never paid much attention to how far mine goes at max," I said, summoning my blade. I then slashed upward and cast the spell. It cut upward and continued until it dissipated on its own. "How far was that?"

"One hundred, ten feet." Naomi seemed adept at keeping track of things, so I believed her.

"Okay then, ***blade wave***." I sent up another. "How far was that one?"

"One hundred, forty feet."

"Cool." I gave her a thumbs up.

"So, we're measuring distances now?" Graven stepped out of the doorway downstairs.

"Oh Graven, now we can start." I put my sword away.

"This is your first real test, so be ready." Graven positioned himself in the groove where the wall had moved. "**Horizon**." Stretching his arms out, he surrounded himself in a bubble. The base of the bubble was pitch black, fading into purple with a wave pattern on it as it reached his waist and became clear from there. "Now hit me with everything you got."

"He means everything," I said, stepping back. "Don't hold back in any capacity. Hit him with absolutely everything."

"If you're sure about this, I'll do it." Noah took a pose.

"Oh, we're sure about this alright." I took another step back. I couldn't see her, but I felt like Naomi was behooved to do the same.

"Okay... **Blade wave!**" His voice echoed as he built up a mass of energy and released it at once. On contact, a large swarm of dust was kicked up, and the spell dissipated instantly. After the dust settled, Graven could be seen standing there with folded arms and still inside his bubble.

"That's not all you can do. Try to hit me with as many attacks as you can. You don't need accuracy for this either. Don't aim. Just will them to all hit me at once. From all angles if you can. Just don't hold back or you'll never be able to pop this bubble."

Noah looked at me confused and I just gave him a thumbs up. He got a determined look on his face and began shooting the spell wildly and at varying strengths. Most of them went right past and only a few hit head-on. As he continued, his eyes narrowed, and he went faster. In his attempts, the waves that were missing began curving ever more slightly toward Graven. He was actively learning how to control the direction on his own. I took another step back and was caught by Naomi as I was unknowingly near the edge.

"Oops, I almost fell. Thanks."

"No need. What you did yesterday actually helped me. It gave me a moment of clarity to calm down. I actually had a little fun."

"You know, I always find that some good, wholesome comedy always helps with stuff like that. Well, that and I just like picking up chicks, you know?"

"Never mind, fall." She pushed me by my shoulder off of the roof and I caught myself on the ledge and stayed there with my head resting on my arms. By now, I knew this was just her way of being friendly.

Noah stopped. Slightly winded, he let his arms fall to his sides. "How am I supposed to do that?"

I spoke up. "Think of it like this: every new thing you do with your powers is considered a new spell. Also, consider this: have you ever tried stopping and redirecting the spell yourself?

And above all, just believe that they'll all hit at once." Naomi was slowly edging me off the roof while I was saying this. She put up a valiant attempt to hide a smile while doing so.

Noah shook his head hard. "Alright," He said, getting ready. "**Blade wave**!" He closed his eyes and swung wildly in almost every direction at full power. He opened his eyes and relaxed completely. Time seemed to stop as he aimed one more directly at Graven. "All. At. Once." He sent it, and the ones surrounding Graven began passing smaller waves between each other. The spell was only active for five seconds and faded away in a second. The moment this happened, Graven dispelled his bubble and teleported away. "Did I do it?" Noah was wobbling on his feet and nearly fell when I went to catch him.

"Not only did you do it, you mastered it," said Graven

Making sure he could still stand, I said, "That was an advanced spell. One you can normally only cast it if you mastered the one before it. In short, you mastered 'blade wave' and learned 'blade wall'. Can you stand?" I patted him on the back and stood him up straight.

"Yeah, I'm good." He wobbled a bit more but stayed standing.

"Good job, you passed." Graven came up with his hand out and Noah accepted the handshake.

"Great, are we done for today? I'm tired."

"Nope," I said, "It's time to teach you a bunch more important stuff."

"Like what?"

"Combat type, Magic type, and affinity. Take it away, Graven."

"Alright." Graven stepped away, stretched his palms outward toward the ground, and began levitating. "Do you know what type of magic I use, Noah?"

"Gravity?"

"My attribute attunement and thus my code of arms is gravity. My type is spatial magic. Because I use gravity, I excel at utilizing my surrounding space and so that's my type. My affinity, on the other hand, is manipulation." He moved a finger, and a rock levitated up to his hand where it stayed. "I like to use my surroundings to any advantage I can find. It's a result of my training before I learned to use my powers." He stopped levitating and let the rock fall. "Magic type and affinity are necessary for personalizing what spells you learn to better fit your style. Also, it allows you a medium in which to create your own. That, among other things."

"So, what does my attribute say about my magic type?"

"Attribute has very little to do with magic type. There used to be a few tests that determine your type, but they all turned out to be inaccurate. Like concentrating on a leaf, sitting one on a full glass of water, or even bringing someone to the edge of death and watching their reaction."

"I think I did that last one," I said, feeling as if I was remembering something. "What were the different outcomes?"

"If objects began to levitate, then it would be spatial magic. If their soul could be seen visibly leaving their body and returning, then personification magic. If their soul leaves and comes back without being seen, then it would be power magic. If the surrounding area explodes, then it's force magic. if they come back in a berserk state, then that's where they lose categories. Also, none of those outcomes could really be trusted."

"Hmm…" I tried as hard as I could to remember and all I got was a feeling of dread followed by rage. "I'm sure I was pushed to near death, but not for that purpose. I think I could already fight by the time it happened"

Noah had a surprised expression from my little revelation. "You mean there's someone strong enough to put someone like you in that state?"

"I don't know, but I would love to fight whoever could…"

"Anyway," interrupted Graven. "I think it would be beneficial to learn what your magic type is. I have a nearly foolproof way of finding out what it is. It'll have to wait 'till tomorrow though. Until then, I suggest finding something to do for the rest of today."

Time passed and noon came quickly. I found myself wandering around the park and into some sort of ruins between heavy foliage beside a pond. There, I unexpectedly fell asleep. I awoke to a feeling of total calm. Lying awake in the middle of the structure, I remembered a conversation I had with Naomi before I took off.

"I know I made you stay up here with me, but don't you really want to go out and explore some?" She sounded like she was afraid to ask the question.

"I'm fine where I am," I said, with folded arms.

After a long, hesitant pause, she said, "You should go out and find something to do before you get too attached to me. Maybe find somebody?"

Finally understanding what she was saying, I responded with a sigh. "I wasn't trying to-" I sighed again. "I'll just go."

A few hours later, I was staring up at the sky wondering what was going through her mind. As far as I was concerned, we were only friends. Even so, I couldn't help but think about her making an exception.

"Do you like me?" I rolled over to my side and stared at a rabbit that happened upon my corpse and was staring at me. "Maybe if I stick around long enough, you'll start feeling a thing or two. Maybe you already have. Am I an exception or not? Maybe I'm just talking to a bunny that I just wanna pick up and hold. Yeah, that's it."

Springing to action, I slowly inched toward the animal. Steadily while keeping direct eye contact. Eventually, I found myself up close to it. I reached out to touch it and it bounded in the opposite direction. Finding itself landing on my palm, it tried to hop away only to be caught around its midsection. Hugging it close, I petted it. It stayed strangely calm even when I lessened my grip on it. Before I knew it, the sun had begun to set. I released the rabbit and met up with Naomi on the roof.

"Why are you back up here?" Naomi was finishing off a cookie on a pink lawn chair in front of a red tent. The tent had enough space for five people and was what Naomi called her home. It was filled with her belongings and had more than enough space left for her to sleep. No one knew what she did with it when not in use.

"I don't know." I shrugged. "I just happened to gravitate in this direction."

"No doubt." She reached her hand out toward me. "But you're not who I was talking to."

A black orb appeared behind me, encompassing my hood. It raised with Naomi's hand movement and levitated in front of me. In it was a brown rabbit with a white tail. The same one I was petting. I didn't notice it hop in there. The bubble began to shrink before it popped, and a woman came out of it. She was tall and pale with shoulder-length straight orange hair, a navy blue sweater with a star-shaped opening at the top, a thigh-length skirt, and leg warmers of the same color.

"Hey, were you really trying to kill me just then?" The woman feigned scorn.

"I don't need to answer that," said Naomi.

"Oh, how cruel." The woman put her hand over her heart as if she was hurt.

"Uh... What's going on here?" I asked.

"Allow me to introduce myself." The woman turned to me. "My name is Fantasia, a witch. I also happen to be Naomi's best friend-"

"Acquaintance." Interjected Naomi.

"And lover."

"No..." Naomi facepalmed while shaking her head. This was the first time I had seen this kind of reaction from her.

"Nice to meet you." Fantasia held out her hand.

"You too, I guess." Wondering what was going to happen with the information she eavesdropped from me. I went to shake her hand only for her hand to disappear. Naomi grabbed her by the wrist and held it behind her back.

"How forceful!" Fantasia was bent forward, and a blue mass could be seen on her palm.

"You're one to talk. What's in your hand."

"Oh, nothing-"

"*Identify*." Naomi cast the spell and pulled a little harder. "Did you really intend to use an infertility potion on this boy?"

I quickly pulled my hand back and into my pocket.

"That was just a prank. It would wear off in a month."

"Not with *nightshade* as an ingredient."

"Okay, you got me, could you just let me go? You're hurting me." Fantasia received her hand back, and she carefully removed the blue patch on her palm. It burned in bright blue flames and dissipated into nothing. "But still, it's nice to meet the little cockblocker who's been getting under my girl's skin."

"Are you trying to piss me off?" Naomi's energy began to fluctuate but settled back down.

"See, you're irritating my love." She waved her hand, gesturing toward Naomi as theatrically as she spoke.

"That's enough outta you." Naomi put her hand on Fantasia's back and after a surge of energy, she flashed gray and vanished. "Good riddance."

After an awkward moment of silence, I spoke up. "What was that about?"

"That was an acquaintance of mine. She's an info broker. She just also happens to be a little obsessed with me."

"A little? Honestly, I would be too." I joked.

"I sent her to the crawl space between the asphalt and the ocean where do you want me to send you?"

After a moment of thought, I decided to speak my mind. "I'm curious-"

"Don't be. She means nothing to me."

"No, not that. You said you'd tell me more about yourself, remember?"

She paused like a deer in headlights. "I did say that, didn't I? I didn't think you'd remember." She seemed to relax as she sat on her lawn chair. "Of course, no information is free."

"Alright, what do you want from me?"

She looked down as if she was going to regret her words. "I need you to stop visiting me in your free time."

"What?"

"You don't understand." She smiled softly. "I'm too used to using people. You're a sweet guy. Not the kind of person I want to take advantage of."

"I'm a corpse hunter. People have used me for any number of things. What would make you any different?"

"Don't make me feel bad."

"You saying you were already using me?"

She nodded and started playing with her hands. "Well, your presence kept people like her away for a while." She nodded her head to the side. "I have a pretty long history of leading people on. I was a bard for a long time. I made uh... friends. And some of them don't want to leave."

"Like Fantasia?"

She nodded. "They're not like you."

What she said brought me to a conclusion. "Is that what you meant by making exceptions?"

She forced a smile away from her lips as her cheeks became slightly more rosy than normal. "No, that's not it. I just need you to stay away from me a bit, alright?"

I scoffed. "So, you *were* leading me on?"

She seemed to freeze for a second. "I- That's not-"

"It's fine." I stopped her before she could stutter out an answer. "Just consider it a joke. I'm just glad I could see a different side of you. Friend or not."

She looked off toward the city lights, barely visible through the darkness she kept over the roof. "Shut up. Just go."

I started walking toward the door. "Alright, but if you decide what you mean on the whole 'exception' thing, you might want to let me know before someone else does."

She smiled solemnly and waved me away.

The next morning, I woke to find Fantasia hovering above my head. She was staring silently and whispering threats.

About as casually as I could, I said, "What are you doing?"

"Oh, you're awake," she said just as casually.

"And so are you. Why and how did you get in here?"

"Just so you know, I'm never going to give up on Naomi so, you'd better back off."

"She's not mine, but she doesn't want you, either. You're just a weird stalker lady."

"If you think that will fool me, then here's a taste of what's to come." She pulled out a blue book with a depiction of a tree with a keyhole in it and began opening it.

In a split second, I had my grimoire in hand and opened to the last page it was on. "**Open, gate of the soul**." This time, the bubble only filled the space between the floor and the roof. It was centered around Fantasia.

"What Is this? Where are we? What is this?" She was looking around and shaking like a leaf.

"Sorry, I don't feel like dealing with someone else's stalker." I put my finger on the page and turned it around the circle as if it were a dial until the circle shrank to only encompass her. "Here's a taste of what happens when you mess with someone like me."

What she was seeing was an ancient dragon and the true form of an angel. Just the sight of either would be enough to take the fight out of most people, let alone both. Her levitation cut off, and she fell onto her knees on the bed. I moved out of the way and made sure the bubble followed her.

"And here's for extra measure." I placed my hand on her head and cast another spell. "**Mare**." It was a fear spell. It tricked her mind into seeing something that would terrify her. Whatever she saw next caused her to ball up in the fetal position and pass out crying as a small puddle formed underneath her. I went to Vincent, informed him of my problem, and he assured me he'd handle it.

After that encounter, I was the last one on the roof. Graven was already instructing Noah on how to make a bubble, and Naomi was in the shadows as usual. I felt her presence and walked straight toward her. She was standing near the far edge and looked at me quizzically as I walked up to her.

"Fantasia came to my room last night."

"What did she do?" She had the sourest face I had ever seen on her.

"Not much. She's passed out on my bed right now. I didn't feel like moving her after her little uh... 'Experience'. She might be out for a while."

"Krow... You didn't... Oh my god. How could you?" She sounded genuinely disgusted.

"Yeah, she has a fear trigger imprinted in her mind now. Next time you see her, can you tell her that I don't take kindly to intruders."

"Oh..." She relaxed. "That has nothing to do with me."

"You just had two completely different reactions. What did you think I meant at first?"

"It doesn't matter. I'll deal with her later."

"I think Vincent's already on it."

"I can't allow that. Where's your room?"

"I never really could tell where it was by the room number. I just remember the code number is 714."

"Alright." She began fading into the darkness.

"Wait, if you're really going down there just know that I have a roommate."

She faded completely and her spell lifted from the roof. All that was left was a bright gray sky on a cold fall day and two others whose attention I had garnered.

"So, what was that about?" asked Graven, "Is there anything I need to be worried about?"

"No, just girl problems. That is unless there's a problem with Naomi going into the building."

"Not really. She's been having a more positive air about her recently. If she wasn't stable, she wouldn't go inside. In fact, this might be the first time she's been in there since she came here."

"Really? Nothing seems to have really changed. She's just as distant and aloof as always."

Graven scoffed as if he was suppressing a laugh. "Maybe to you. From the outside looking in I saw a change. She's definitely warming up to you if she hasn't already."

I couldn't help but sigh. " If you say so. I'm sure warm's an overstatement. She's been pretty cold. Anyway, she's not here now so there's no point talking about her."

"Alright, I won't pry." He nodded slowly.

"So... Back to training?" asked Noah. He had his hands cupped and was looking back and forth at me and Graven.

Graven nodded. "Yeah, it's just like when you channeled your energy and cast 'purify'. Except this time, it's not a ball, it's a bubble."

"Okay, I'll try." Noah's hands started to glow, and a light began escaping his palms.

"Now, try to close it around as if it was your fist closing around a ball. Imagine a firm grasp over an empty space."

"How am I supposed to imagine that?" He looked back at Graven quizzically.

"Well, you said you were about to start learning magic before everything happened, right?"

"Yeah, why?"

"What did you know about magic before we started this training?"

"Not much, just magical creatures, magic users, and organizations. Well, aside from wielders. My mom and dad always played it safe and waited until my sisters and brothers were Fourteen to teach them anything having to do with magic directly. Since we were all pretty much guaranteed to become wielders, they waited until then to teach us about that, too. They were going to do the same with me." He looked back down at his hand. "But they died before I turned fourteen."

"I'm sorry to hear that but thank you for telling me. That just means that we have to teach you with the base assumption that you know nothing. That being said, do you remember the feeling of summoning your sword for the first time?"

"Am I supposed to use that feeling to help me make a ball? Because I've been doing it and trying to make one for a while." Noah shrugged.

"If that's the case, then I have one better for you. Have you ever squeezed a boiled egg and tried to crush it with one hand?"

"Hasn't everybody?"

"Good then, use that as a reference."

"Oh, I get it." He almost made a fist with his right hand. "***Purify***." The glow from his spell occupied the entirety of the inside of his hand. "Like an egg." He relaxed his palm and gently opened his hand until his fingers just stopped touching. "Let's see if I can stop the spell." The glow from his palm began to dim until there was only a bright white ball in his hand. "Is this it?"

"Toss it to Krow and I'll tell you." Graven looked at me and nodded.

At the time, I was pacing back and forth from the door to some arbitrary spot and back. I stopped and opened my hand. Noah tossed the ball to me, and I smacked it to the ground. It landed and didn't shatter. "Yep, that's it, you did it." I picked it up and tossed it back to him.

"Thanks?" Noah sounded confused.

"Now, take that ball and try to expand it to cover your entire body," said Graven.

"Am I supposed to like, stretch it out or something?" He started grabbing at it with his fingertips.

"It's more like putting on a jacket, except the jacket's your skin."

I spoke up before Noah could ask what he meant. "Just act like it's a part of you and put it on."

"Like it's a part of me?" He proceeded to stretch it over his head, and it conformed to his entire body. "This feels right."

"Can you try expanding that to a bubble?" said Graven.

"I think I can." He stretched his arms out, and the bubble expanded to surround him. "There you go."

"I'm curious. Can you shape it into an elephant?" I asked.

"An elephant?" an elephant formed from the bubble.

"Thanks. You made an elephant."

"No, I did... How did I make an elephant?" He looked around and saw the shape of his bubble.

"You seem to have a strong affinity for free-form magic." said Graven.

"So, it's free-form?"

"Yes, It looks like your magic can be easily shaped into anything you can imagine. Now we just have to find out your magic type."

"How do we do that?"

"Up." Graven raised his hand. Noah's hair began to stand straight up, followed by the rest of his body as he fell up toward the sky.

"Wha- not again!" His bubble popped, and he began flailing his arms while turning upside down in a vain attempt to get back to the ground. "Hmm..." He furrowed his brow and seemed to be deep in thought while he cleared ten feet in distance. "***Push***!" With a boom followed by a crunch, his boots exploded off and brown chunks of rubber and fabric flew into the air as a stream of white energy came from his feet and rocketed him toward the ground. Graven snapped his fingers and Noah hit the ground so hard that pebbles flew into the air, and he made a hole into the building. "Oww... What was that for?" Half of his torso was dangling into the attic space.

"I'll explain that in a bit." Graven walked over to Noah. "But first." He placed his hands on the ground next to Noah. "***Repair***." The hole closed with Noah on top of it, relatively unharmed.

Noah patted around his body, "No pain." He stood up. "Okay, cool."

"Aura magic. That seems to be your type," said Graven, "You manipulate your aura to a greater degree than anything else when you use magic. That became more evident when your shoes exploded when you used a spell you hadn't learned yet."

"You mean that was an actual spell?" Noah was dusting himself off. "I just used the energy I put into the bubble and pushed off of it."

"Good job," I said, "Now we don't have to teach you that one from scratch." As I said this, a shroud of darkness reinstated itself over the roof. The door into the building opened while I was pacing toward it and Naomi came out. "So, how'd it go?"

"Oh, you're cruel." Her response took me a bit by surprise.

"I know?" I tilted my head to the side in momentary confusion.

"I couldn't have done better myself."

"You sound a little too happy about that."

"I know."

"So, what did you do about her?"

"Now, wouldn't you like to know?"

Graven spoke up, "Can we get on track?"

Naomi vanished as she spoke. "Do what you wish."

"Anyhow, It's time we get to figuring out your combat type," said Graven, breaking the tension. "I'm going to start with an explanation."

"I got it," I said, starting to pace back and forth.

"I assume you know about the six different combat types, but I'll tell you about them anyway."

I stopped and crouched down, hovering my hand over the ground "***Illusion***."

I conjured the image of a shield the size of my torso on the ground.

"Obvious one first. Defense types are usually sturdy and despite usually having really slow attacks, hit really hard, but their strength is, well, in the name.

Of the people you probably met, Vincent fits that bill, but he fights with a dagger; a quick, slashy weapon instead of something like a hammer."

"That would offset the speed difference, right?" Noah picked up on it quickly.

"Ah, you get it." Next, I swapped the shield for a bow. "Range is, well, range. They mostly fight from a distance and want to stay that way. If you ever met Aren or Leuna, you met a ranged type. Aren uses razor-sharp string mixed with sound magic to reach anywhere for an attack while Leuna uses a classic bow."

Noah just nodded.

Next was an arrow pointing down diagonally. "Speed types are obviously fast, but their attacks are usually really weak. Even so, they can overwhelm you quickly. Catt's a speed type. Unlike most speed types though, she hits hard since her gauntlets and natural strength can compensate for her lack in power."

"Oh, I see, she... Yeah..." Noah seemed lost in thought for a second before shaking his head and returning to the moment.

A heart now stood where the arrow was. "Support is more tricky to quantify because they come in so many variants, but usually they're healers or just good at backing up other fighters. I was raised by a support type. It really helps when you don't have to worry about breaking your neck falling off a tree."

"I met an old man in Magnolia that could stop time. Wouldn't that count as support magic?"

"Oh, you get it better than I thought." I stabbed through the illusionary heart with my sword. "Then there's power types like me. I'm not usually the fastest, but I hit harder than most with enough speed to make me a constant threat on the battlefield. That goes for me and Graven."

"That sounds like me," mumbled Noah with a nod.

I removed my sword and the illusion changed to a set of scales. "Last, but not least, there's balance. They're kinda swiss-army fighters. They can do a bit of everything and mostly act as vanguards if they're in a group. My brother's pretty much that. He can do pretty much anything without sacrificing any of his attributes, so he just kinda does whatever."

"I think I am a power type." Noah was peering at his sword.

I snapped my fingers and the illusion disappeared. "Yep, otherwise, you wouldn't have mastered an attack spell like that so quickly."

"Now we can do more extensive training," said Graven. "That's all going to start right now."

21-Teamwork

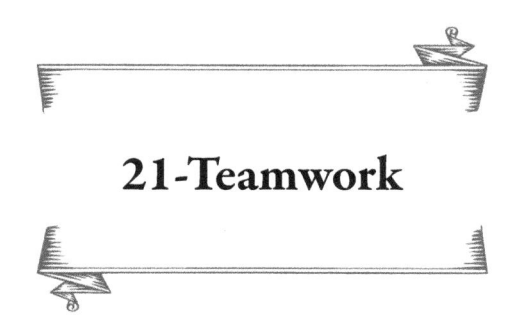

[Solo]

Walking into the large room, I traced my gaze over the blank white panels that made the floor and walls up to the ceiling where Guile was in the control room high above. This was my first time back in a V.R. arena since my fight with Nero but he wasn't there this time. This time, it was a test. With the available members of my team, we were being tested by our leader and strategist who sat idly above us.

"Arena type: Location," sounded the robotic voice.

"Forest preset," I said.

"Random practice forest selected. Opponent type."

"Accurate copy."

"Accurate copy type opponent selected. Prepare for combat."

I watched as an identical clone of myself materialized before me, raising my sword at me. Even its aura was familiar, but not totally the same as to not be confused for the real me. Same for the rest.

Next to my clone was a clone of Conrad in a silver three-piece suit. Regardless of how talented the person inside of it was, I'd scoff at the absurdity of it. On the other side of my clone was a Lucia clone in a brown skirted uniform with a wooden staff and a Mary clone in a white uniform and fingerless gloves. The only visual difference between us and them was that their colors were dull and muted in comparison. The clones were a copy of data from a set of tests each C.H.E.S.S. agent underwent each month.

"Are you sure that this is a good idea?" asked Lucia on my right.

"Nero's likely on a mission and Vinessa's dealing with sick people. If the four of us can't be a team, then that makes this an even better idea," I said, summoning my own sword.

"Are you guys ready?" asked Guile from the observation box.

"About as ready as we'll be," I said.

"No support and no vanguard," continued Lucia, "Are you sure this is a good idea?"

"You still have a knight, a bishop, and two rooks. You'll be fine. Besides, against clones, it equals out regardless," Guile responded.

"Yeah, you still have me," announced Mary.

"If you say so." Lucia still sounded apprehensive.

The ground began moving and trees began jutting out. They were tall and slender oak trees. They didn't hinder much visibility and seemed rather fragile but looks could be deceiving. Roots and foliage followed by uneven ground shaped from the floor while a blue, yet slightly cloudy sky appeared overhead.

"Just thumbs up whenever you want to start," said Guile, waiting patiently.

I put my thumb up and stood ready with my sword. Conrad did as well with his claw, followed by Mary with her gauntlets. Lucia took multiple steps back, summoned her staff, and hesitantly raised her thumb.

"I'm pushing the button... Now." A click could be heard and the sound of machinery starting up filled the room. One beep sounded followed by another, the final beep signified the start of the battle.

Both Lucias began by throwing her serrated staff, which separated into seven identical pieces.

All except three crashed into their counterpart as they were spiraling toward each of us and our clones in turn. One from each was still being held by their respective Lucia and the few that missed, spun counterclockwise from either side around each other toward the other Lucia.

The clone dodged into the air and out of the way while aiming the last one at us.

Our Lucia, on the other hand, twirled the one in her hand and caught the remaining two, converting their forward momentum into rotational momentum. She then flung them back before throwing her last one. It was a risky move, but she pulled it off. Her clone was caught off guard and it didn't have enough time to make an effective shield.

My clone jumped in to intercept, and that's when I acted. I cast 'push' and jettisoned myself at them with my psychokinesis. The clone Conrad, or Clonerad, began creating a bubble shield around them.

"***Orion shield!***" Clone Mary created a shield large enough to encase all of them. The clones' staffs dissipated on impact and Lucia's bounced off. I caught it and tossed it back to her.

"*Magic missile!*" Both Mary and Lucia sent the same spell at their respective targets. Lucia threw her staff again, and Mary shot an arrow into the air. They both took a detour around the shield and seemed to reach their locations until a silver dome expanded to cover the entire shield in front of them. It had large spikes sticking out of it and was nearly clear. The spikes bashed away nearby trees and came at me before I could move out of the way. I had to block with my sword and was pushed back, nearly hitting a tree and landing next to Mary.

Conrad called out to us. "Don't attack recklessly. The spikes on the shield have minds of their own. They can change direction and attack in formations."

His warning went unheeded as Mary and I decided to put a new plan into action. She jumped onto my sword as I swung it at the spiky bubble. She rode on a blade wave I sent with her. The spikes spiraled at her, and she cast 'flash step' to teleport herself above it as more spikes came up to meet her. My blade wave redirected one of the spikes into a tree.

"**Sagittarius Scutum**." Her bow morphed into one with a shield wide enough to cover her completely except for a single hole to see through as she readied a charge shot. The first spike hit the shield and sent her farther away. The next one went into the hole and pinned her to a tree. "Ah!"

Conrad acted by turning and running in my direction. "Solo, fastball special!" He jumped, feet toward me.

"Oh, now you wanna call it that."

I caught him and threw him in the same manner as I did Mary. He rotated and began spinning as more spikes came to intercept him

Lucia threw her staff and redirected it. She had been throwing 'magic missile' staffs alongside her original staff at any new spikes going for Mary. She did no damage, but they changed direction aside for the one pinning Mary.

Inside of the dome, the shield moved over to face Mary, and I could see what looked like a bleeding Mary clone trying to heal a bleeding Lucia clone next to a meditating Clonerad. It seemed that he was doing it to keep the spell going. My clone had taken a running position and was getting ready to move. Meanwhile, Conrad crashed into the spike poking through the hole in Mary's bow and it broke off.

"Shoot now!" yelled Conrad as the sight in Mary's bow opened up again.

"Got it!" She adjusted her aim. "**Star blast!**" The area directly in front of her lit up like a Christmas tree as a beam of white energy struck straight through the barrier. Just before the barrier broke, my clone shot out of it.

"**Blade wave**." He shot the spell at Lucia and came my way. I went to meet him, and we clashed. It being a clone of myself, it felt like I just ran into a wall using my sword.

Lucia jumped back while aiming at my clone. She threw the staff at full power as the blade wave hit her arm. My clone tried to disengage and block the staff, but as he was doing so, I found my opportunity to lean in with my sword while he was distracted. My blade landed squarely in the middle of his torso, and he melted into a puddle, dissolving through the ground.

Rushing to Lucia's side, I called, "Mine's down, and Lucia's hurt!"

"I'm fine," she responded, "It's just a flesh wound."

"What flesh?" I came to her side to see a gash in her underarm. "It didn't hit your chest or anything."

"Ha, ha. Very funny. Just focus on what's happening over there." She gestured toward the other side of the battle.

I turned back toward the action. Mary had pushed off of the tree and was on top of the giant shield, pulling back again on her bow.

"Everybody, get ready!" said Mary, "I'm about to break this one too!" The shield quickly moved down to face us, and she jumped to not be shaken off. "Now!" Just before she could shoot, the shield came back to bash her away. In doing so, the three inside were totally exposed.

Deciding to throw caution to the wind, I evolved my weapon to its third form and rushed to the scene as it split into pieces. I rode on one shard as they all levitated under my power. Surrounded by the rest, I aimed at the Mary clone and three shards flew in a line toward her. Before the shield could block them, all three shards cleared under it. A couple of seconds later, the shield dissipated, and the clone could be seen with one shard beside her, one in her leg, and one where her ribs would be. She sank into the ground and disappeared.

Clonerad and clone Lucia were left. Both were barely standing. Clonerad was greatly weakened and was getting to his feet and clone Lucia was staggering with a serrated staff while still leaking dull red blood from her arm.

"***Forest of death***!" Clone Lucia stabbed her staff into the ground, and all the surrounding roots from the trees began spiking upward from different spots. Each root sharpened to a point and their tips changed color to indicate what effect would take if they hit someone. A red one whizzed past me and singed my scarf. I had to dodge so many roots that by the time I was done, I couldn't see the clones, but I still knew where they were since I could feel the presence of my shards.

I called them back and they cut through the roots until they came to me. They were red hot, frozen over, electrified, and covered in poison, but I could see my destination. The only problem was that Clonerad had evolved his claws into longer, curved claws and was literally flying in my direction. He was met underneath with more spiky roots. They came before either of us knew it, and he melted into a blob before falling to the ground and vanishing. Lucia had cast the same spell that her clone had.

I continued my way to the only clone left. By the time I got there, she had collapsed with a red puddle by her. She had lost what would have been too much blood for her real self. I slapped her back and she dissolved into the ground as half of the standing roots vanished. Sometimes it was uncanny how realistic the clones were. With the exercise over, the arena returned to its normal blank state, and the remaining roots sticking upward went along with the trees.

Conrad was carrying Mary, who was unconscious, outside the range of the 'forest of death' spell, and Lucia was far behind me holding her arm. Once outside of the VR arena, we used the first-aid kit in one of the rooms leading from it to bandage up Lucia's arm and Mary's head before traveling down the hall to the nearby infirmary.

It was empty aside from the on-site nurse. He was stout, albino, and wore the typical nursing uniform. A long white coat and a tag with 'Sinbad Clover, RN' on it. He used a basic healing spell on Lucia while Mary was laid down on one of the beds and would be examined soon after.

"Hey nurse, why did you put another bandage on my arm after you healed it?" asked Lucia, picking at the cloth wrapped around her arm.

"Because," he responded as he began looking over Mary. "I only closed the wound. There's a chance it'll open back up so, please stop picking at it." This was new to Lucia, whose recovery speed is more than twice that of a normal person, so whenever she was hurt or injured, she'd always go to Vinessa who'd heal her up completely with her magic without needing anything more.

"Oh, ok." She continued to pick at it. The next day, she would become slightly ill due to an infection.

"Looks like this one only has a minor concussion. She should wake up in due time, but I'll see if I can get her an x-ray in the meantime just in case."

Mary's eyes fluttered open. "Oh, my god... I didn't know I could hurt so much."

"Good, you're awake," said the nurse. "Try not to move around much. You have a concussion."

"I can feel it."

"I'll be back." He left the room and Guile entered after.

"Good job," said Guile, taking a small roller chair from under the nurses' desk near the door and sitting. "I honestly expected the simulation to last much longer than that." He clapped his hands together. "You've all improved. Mary: this may have been your first trial as a part of this team, but you were quick on the draw and acted as an anchor and point of reference for the rest of the team to rally behind. However, it's best not to forget your role as a rook. In actual combat, if someone loses a shield, they're more likely to die than if they lose a sword. That goes for you as well, Conrad. I admire your teamwork, but throwing yourself into combat will leave your team with little defense to fall back on. Solo: your teamwork is improving too, but as a knight, you were holding back too much throughout the exercise. And Lucia: your reaction timing has gotten better, and you have gotten considerably stronger, but never downplay an injury. It could mean the difference between life and death. All in all, good job, but everyone could stand to improve."

"How about you go into one of those with us and lead like you're supposed to?" I said, "Then we could all learn together as a team."

Without skipping a beat, Guile said, "Did you forget that I'm not in the system for the simulator?"

"For us," responded Conrad. "I've heard that, because of an error on the computers, your rank was false and that you're much stronger than you seem. Somewhere around the rank of 'left hand' and that's why your access code is locked off to personnel under ruby rank."

"You of all people should know not to entertain rummers, Conrad," said Guile.

"I don't know about that. I've checked, and there is a locked file with your code number on it. Not only that. You seem to disappear at random intervals and show up out of nowhere without warning. An example would be last year when you showed up with Solo on your back after falling back on your own while we were on that mission in Japan. How did you get so far ahead of us when you were so far behind so quickly without any of us noticing? Better yet, my question is, are you one of the Seven Sins?"

"Is that all?" asked our leader.

"For now."

"For your second question; I'm not, and even if I was, I wouldn't be able to tell you, I presume. And as for your first question." Guile got up, turned around, and stuck his head out the door. Returning, he locked it and turned back to face us all. "Most of you have known me long enough to know that I'm a very suspicious person. That's who I am. Because of that, I've developed a teleportation spell on my own and without the notice of most of the higher-ups. One that can't be picked up by technological or magical means. The few that know about it made sure to make it so that my records don't make it to the training arena to prevent anyone from finding and learning it. As one would assume, if the wrong person got their hands on something like that, It'd upset the entirety of the magical world "

"And you're still with C.H.E.S.S, why?" I asked, "And what's the point of sharing such secret information with us right now?"

"Because I feel something big coming. I know you all feel it as well, otherwise, there would be no questions to begin with and no one would be waiting for me to answer. Normally you all are too rambunctious for all of that."

He had a point. Being suspended for a year has allowed me an understanding of the facilities that I wouldn't otherwise have. I had that same ominous feeling for a while before he said something about it. Things seemed to have gotten much more serious around the campus in the last month or so. At first, I thought it was because of the World Magic Tournament. It took place every January between the different domains of the wizards, witches, warlocks, summoners, enchanters, and wielders. The upcoming one would be set in the main C.H.E.S.S. campus. Even so, it was like the entire corporation was in a panic. That was unusual, even for a time like this.

"I feel something coming all right, my lunch," remarked Mary. "Just kidding, I didn't eat lunch yet." She put her hand to her forehead. "Sorry, I'm just a little nauseous and I felt like we all needed some humor to lighten the mood."

"I appreciate that," said Lucia, patting her shoulder.

"Come in," said Guile. I turned back to see that he had unlocked and opened the door before anyone noticed.

"I didn't even have to knock," A familiar voice rang through the door. She walked in wearing the same uniform the nurse was wearing except her tag said 'MD' on it and she had a large pink heart sticker on her chest. "So, I just get through taking care of like, fifteen patients and I get called as I'm leaving to come look at a girl with a concussion and here you are." Vinessa walked confidently to Mary and began asking her questions. "Do you feel nauseous or sick?"

"Yeah, a little," said Mary.

"On a scale of one to ten?"

"Five."

"Do you feel dizzy at all standing, sitting, or lying down?"

"I haven't stood since it happened, but I haven't felt dizzy either."

"Good, do you feel any kind of tiredness or sleepiness at all?"

"My eye is having a hard time staying all the way open but that's all." Mary gestured to her left eye.

"Have you had any changes in mood or mood swings since it happened?"

"No, I've been all mellow since then."

"Okay, can you tell me your name?"

"Mary Black."

"And your birthday?"

"February 8th."

"And what's today?"

"Wednesday, September 23rd"

"Can you move your head?"

"Yeah." She turned her head to face our direction and winced.

"Do you feel any pain or discomfort?"

"A lot."

"On a scale of one to ten, how much does it hurt?"

"Fifty and a handful of dynamite blowing up in my face."

"Is that what happened?"

"No... It was a shield... My shield... Clones."

"So where exactly does it hurt?"

"All of this hurts." She gestured to the red and swollen left side of her head.

"Any spot particularly?"

"No, all of it hurts the same."

"Okay." She gently gripped her head on either side of the swollen area.

"Ow!"

"Sorry. Just hold still for a second while I take a look at it up close." She leaned in and kissed the wound. As she did so, the swelling decreased dramatically, and her lips turned blood-red. It looked as if she just put on fresh lipstick. "This is going to need bandages."

"What was that? It felt good, and it hurts way less now."

"A 'vampiric kiss'. It helps make the swelling go down faster." Humming, she began casting another spell. "***Healing flame~***." The side of Mary's face lit up as a bright yellow flame engulfed the red area. As moments passed and as the red faded, so did the flame. "I'm going to have to ask you guys to leave the room for a while." Vinessa turned around with a pink clipboard that seemed to have come out of nowhere. "There are a few in-depth tests I have to run and there can't be any distractions."

"Alright," I said, getting up, yawning, and stretching. "I'll be back at my dorm if anybody needs me."

"Same." Conrad walked out of the door first, followed by Lucia and me.

"Did you get any of that?" asked Guile as he was leaving behind us.

Vinessa responded, "Some of it,"

"Come see me later so that I can fill you in."

"Alright." The door closed, and I found my way to my dorm. It wasn't far, but it felt like it. Just entering 'Shatter' as a form was more draining than I had thought. My movements were sluggish, and I had almost fallen over before reaching my bed where I fell asleep on contact.

22-Testing

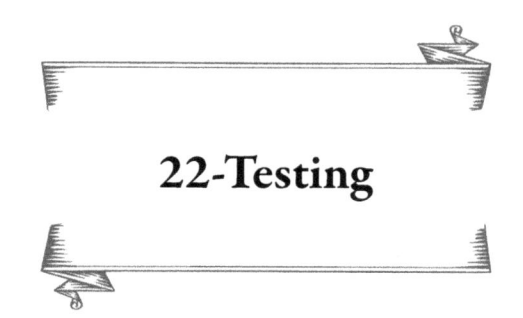

[Noah Black]

After months of learning how to use my power, I had a solid grasp of what I could do and a clear view of what I could achieve. Of course, I wouldn't be sure of what I could do until I did it and it was time for me to do a lot.

"Get ready, this will be your final proper 'test' before you can go do your own thing," said Graven, stepping back and casting 'horizon' on himself. "For the next minute, cast every spell I say to the best of your abilities, do each spell only once, and make sure you do each one as strong as you can." He pulled out what looked like a small blank sheet of paper and set it against his barrier. It created ripples across the surface. "If you fail then we're going to have to start all over from the beginning."

"Okay." Getting ready, everything training taught me ran through my head like a glass bullet. It was so fast, yet so clear.

"Summon your weapon by calling its name."

"***Pure Spirit***." I summoned my blade to my hand and a stream of what felt like its essence began flowing from it to the paper. It lasted for a second and stopped.

"Next, 'bubble shield.'"

I cast it and was surrounded by a slightly opaque bubble, and the same thing happened to the spell that happened to my sword

"Now 'purify.'"

Turning my blade sideways, I cast it and the same thing happened again.

"'Push.'"

It happened again, and every time afterward. We cycled through every defensive, attack, mobility, and support spell including the negative blade and the subsequent dark spells that came with it. All aside for a single exempt spell. At least, that's what I thought.

"'Hell soul,'" he said.

I didn't hesitate.

"***Hell soul***." My vision faded, and I heard voices. I couldn't tell what they were saying and their languages were unfamiliar, but I understood them. They offered me secrets and knowledge of my desires in exchange for my sanity. Remembering that the spell would drop me into madness by default, I agreed on the condition of having complete control of the spell itself. I left it vague and open to interpretation just in case something went wrong while using it.

"Kill the shadow within a vessel and the vessel shall die too." This time a single voice stood out among the rest. It sounded raspy and ragged as if they were out of breath but steady at the same time. "Weaken it and the vessel shall not be harmed unless it is killed. Then so, too, will the vessel die. Remove it, and the result shall be the same. Take the shadow onto yourself and destroy it before old connections die and after new connections are made and there will be no consequence."

My vision returned. Apparently, I had just been standing there with my eyes clouded over. Unsure of how to describe what happened, I explained what I experienced.

"It was a contract," explained Graven, "I figured a spell like that would have one attached to it. They're pretty common for high-level spells. What it told you might be something that phantasm wanted you to know. The question is: why tell you through a spell?"

"I don't know. Something feels off about it, though."

Krow hummed. "It might be because it's something that it didn't want the tiger to know. Another question would be how it even knew."

"I think it's something I already knew, adherently. Magic by birthright."

Graven pointed at the white sheet floating in front of his spell as his bubble popped. "Whatever the case, I need you to come and plunge your blade into this."

"Got it." I walked up to the sheet. It seemed less like a piece of paper and more like a blank void in space. Cautiously, I leaned my blade into it, only to find that it was much deeper than I thought. I could fit my entire sword into it.

"Put the whole thing in and let it go."

I did so, and the paper started glowing. After a second, it started levitating toward me and a pattern emerged across its surface. it was a simple dual magatama symbol except the tails left out of either side and seemed to reach around each other. Both sides also had a smaller outline of the opposite color inside of them.

"Take it, it's yours."

I reached forward and it fell into my hand. I caught it with the other hand as well to make sure it didn't fall. I figured I knew what it was, so I opened it. The first thing I saw was a page that read: *'Blade wall'*, at the top with a description in words I'd use to describe it and a depiction of what it looked like beneath it.

Reading through it, I said, "Is this a spell book?"

"A grimoire and yes, it is," responded Graven. "It's also my gift to you as we're done with your training. From here on, you can train on your own. That makes us equals."

"Wow, thank you."

"I believe Krow and Naomi also have something for you."

I looked over at the pair.

Krow smiled with his arms folded. "I'ma let Naomi go first since my gift'll blow your mind."

"If I must." Naomi stepped out of the shadows and walked up to me. "Stay still." She reached her hand around my head and put her forehead to mine. For some reason, a new spell popped into my mind. I could see it being cast as if I just did it myself.

"What was that?" I asked.

"'Mental convergence'. I gave you what information I have on a certain spell. Now you can teach it to yourself. I think it'll come in handy."

"Thanks. I feel like I can do a lot with it... I think."

"You're welcome." She stood back.

"My turn." Krow stepped up and handed me a letter. It was blue with a red 'KZ' seal stamped on it.

I opened it. On the white paper inside it read: *'You are cordially invited to the WORLD MAGIC TOURNAMENT!'* It was an invitation straight into C.H.E.S.S. headquarters, and it was addressed directly to me. It said that the only requirements were to have a grimoire of my own and to have the letter.

I looked up at him. "There's a tournament?"

"Yeah, you know what that means?" He smiled.

"I can get to my sister."

"And we get to test out your skills in a real fight."

"How and why is this...?"

"They sent a messenger to wreak havoc nearby. Ariel took 'em on and they left a few of these behind. They like to use events like this to recruit corpse hunters or decide who gets the label. It's probably a trap, but it can't be one they'd spring until the event's over. Besides, I'd like to meet the people who decided I needed a bounty on my head."

"Ariel was one of the girls training Catt, right?"

"Yep. My oldest sister."

"Oh, I met her while they were training."

"I figured you would meet at least one of them. Both Ariel and Sara were in charge of training her."

"Is Sara your sister, too?"

"Yep. So are Leuna and Caroline. Doc's my brother and Carona's mom."

"Oh, I guess I met your whole family already." I thought back on how I watched them push Catt to her limit on days I rested from training. "They're all really strong."

"No way they could be any less."

Graven spoke up, putting us back on track. "There is still one other thing we haven't tested yet, and I think you've figured out how to do it already."

I clenched my fists so hard that I thought my hands would start bleeding. "You mean corpse shadow extraction."

Naomi stepped up, having not slipped back into the shadows like normal. "I've been ready since before you came here." She took a deep breath. "And I'm not the only one." She took both of my hands together and looked me in the eye. "Do whatever you need to. I believe in you." Just then, I felt like I could do absolutely anything, although I was still apprehensive.

"You mean, right now?" I said, looking around nervously.

"It can only be right now. You have every spell you know fresh in your memory, and so are the instructions on how to get this thing out of me. Please..." She looked desperate and not thinking straight, but I agreed.

I slid my grimoire into one of my leg pockets along with the letter. Next, I summoned my sword. "***Pure Spirit***." It appeared in its dark form. "I don't know how this'll feel but bear with me."

She smiled, and I was put off completely. "Go for it." Her smile faded away.

"Okay, here we go." Shaking like a leaf, I aimed my blade at her chest, and she closed her eyes. I quickly thrust the blade through her. The spell of darkness she kept over the roof faded. I thought I had killed her until I saw her eyes open. They were blood-red and piercingly so. I froze. I was too scared to do anything. I couldn't move.

"Noah, now's not the time to get cold feet," said Graven.

"Yeah," added Krow, "Remember, she believes in you."

That comment brought back the fleeting feeling I had before. It felt less like confidence and more like inspiration. Shaking out of my daze, I looked Naomi straight in the eye, or the corpse shadow within her. "Come to me."

"As you wish." The voice that came out was not just hers. It was layered over with a deeper, more gritty voice. "You are suitable." a black mist-like creature began climbing out of her and around my blade. It had no defining features, just a black mass moving along the blade. It reached my hand and a sharp pain shot through my palm. I nearly let go, but instead, I took a sturdier hold.

Naomi's face began losing its color and her eyes changed back to their natural brown. The corpse shadow was slowly crawling into me. The pain extended up my arm and to my chest. Once it reached there, the pain spread around my entire body at once. It was tearing away from Naomi, taking her life force with it and attaching itself to me. It was then that I acted.

"Blink." My blade turned white. "*Arklight*." A white light extended from and around my chest, around and down my arm, around the blade, and around Naomi. I stopped the corpse shadow from moving. It began struggling, and I tightened the spell to make sure it couldn't free itself and jump completely into me or Naomi. "*White pillar*." I used the spell that Naomi showed me, and a white circle appeared on the ground, surrounding her. I hadn't figured out exactly how to use the spell yet, but it was worth a try. This spell required me to have my catalyst for casting it either pointed up, down, or touching my target. The spell took more out of me than I thought. It seemed like that was what happened when using a spell you haven't properly learned. It explains why Graven didn't teach me that way.

The circle wouldn't expand until I felt like I exhausted myself. When it did, it was barely so. I kept at it until it was safely around both of us. I then allowed the spell to be completed and a beam of light encompassed both of us. A deathly scream began coming from the surrounding space. It sounded like a dying banshee. My ears began ringing and a heavy weight lifted off of my shoulders as the sound stopped. Both Naomi and I crashed to the ground.

Opening my eyes, I scanned the space in front of me to see a host of worried faces. Krow, Graven, Catt, Hinata, Sara, and Vincent were all around me when I woke. Krow was the first to notice me looking around and didn't seem very worried at all. He gave me a thumbs-up. I couldn't get a read on Graven's face. He was stoic as far as I could tell, and the others were in conversation about what to do if I didn't wake up. After a second, I could hear a loud beeping sound coming from next to me. I was hooked up to a heart monitor.

I looked back at Krow and Graven. "Where is she?" Everybody stopped their conversation and looked at me. Nobody said a thing. The three that were talking froze like deer in headlights. A moment later, Sara darted out of my field of view. I could then hear a door open and close.

"About time you woke up," said Krow. "I was wondering how long we'd be waiting."

"So, you're still alive," said Vincent, before getting elbowed by Hinata.

"Please don't scare me like that again..." Catt gripped my hand to her face. She was close to tears.

"Where's Naomi?"

She clenched my hand harder. "A couple hours after you both went unconscious, her heart stopped." I tried to get up, but she pushed me back down and held me in place. "You need to stay down."

"No, I'm fine, I need to see her. This is all my fault."

"She's not dead... Yet... I don't know. Her heart kept starting and stopping back and forth last time I saw her. You have to wait for my mom. She's in charge of taking care of both of you."

I met Carona once while exploring the building and again while watching Catt train. She was a nice lady who always seemed like she knew what she was doing no matter what it was. I stopped struggling and waited. A minute passed and Sara, followed by Carona, entered the room. Not wasting a second, Carona brought out a small flashlight.

"I'm about to shine a light in your eyes, ok?"

I nodded.

"I need you to follow it." Shining the light in my eyes, she began moving it left and right and I followed accordingly. Putting the flashlight away, she put one of her hands over my arm. "Can you feel this?" There was a radiant heat coming from her palm. It was more like electricity than anything.

"Yeah, it's kinda electric."

"Good. We avoided the worst possible outcome. If you can stand and walk, you should be fine." As soon as I could, I stood and made for the door. I paid no attention to my surroundings as I opened it and followed my gut to find Naomi. Krow was beside me so quickly he startled me.

"This way." He ran straight down the hall and took another left by kicking off of a wall and jumping. I followed as best I could. Based solely on the walls, floor, and ceiling, we were back in the secret basement.

Halfway down another long hall and a right later, we came to a door. Krow opened it and I walked in. Inside the room was a hospital bed surrounded by medical equipment and a few seats. Standing next to the bed was a woman I'd never seen before. She had medium-length red hair, wore dark clothes, and her eyes were glittering from tears. Behind her on a chair was Doc in his black reaper form and holding a scythe. When the woman looked up, she saw me, and sadness changed to pure rage.

"YOU!" She walked around the bed in my direction. "You did this." She sped up.

"Dragon." Krow's voice rang as the door began closing. The woman jumped back in fear about a meter.

"Krow..." The woman was shaking like a leaf. "I don't like you."

"The feeling's mutual. I thought you might've dispelled that little charm I placed on you by now." He sounded very satisfied with himself. Even so, there was a hint of guilt behind his words.

"I tried, but you know what happened? After our little 'encounter' the building's owner came with a cleanup crew and told me to get out. Then, Naomi came to me laughing and told me how permanent your little 'charm' really was. "

"She did?"

"Yes... You win... for now. I won't quit being around until she wakes up. After that, though, you won't see me again." She was now shaking with a combination of anger and fear.

Krow simply folded his arms. "I'm surprised. The way she talked about you, I'd have thought it'd have taken more than that. She deserves better than that. Well, regardless, I think you should go face your fears or you'll be afraid forever."

Without another word, the woman swiftly and cautiously made her way around him and out the door. By this time, I already made my way to Naomi while the woman's eyes were trained on Krow.

Naomi was hooked to a heart monitor like I was, except the beeps would fall farther and farther apart, then grow closer in the same manner. The height of the beeps seemed to be very shallow. There was also a blood pressure monitor on her finger.

"Doc, how's she doing?" asked Krow.

"She's on the edge. It could be worse, but it could be better. She could go at any second."

"What about her soul?"

"It's clean of anything foreign. There's no trace of a corpse shadow. It's just missing something." He shed his dark cloak and sat down. "Now, it's up to you, boy."

I felt vaguely like I knew what to do, and it seemed that Doc did too. I put my hands over her and cast a spell. "**Necrotic aura.**" The spell I cast was one that would normally surround someone with a withering effect that would decay anything close to them they chose. Instead, I felt like I was giving her what felt like the missing pieces of her soul back.

What damage the corpse shadow did over however long it persisted was partially reversed. I pumped as much power as I could into the spell. When I was done, her eyes flared open, and she lurched forward, coughing. "What happened?" She sounded like she had a desert for a throat.

"You were unconscious for five hours and at death's door," explained Doc, "Noah relieved you of your corpse shadow, then essentially, brought you back to life."

"I'm sorry I put you in that situation-" I started.

"What the hell are you apologizing about?" She took both of my hands into hers. "Not only did you save my life, you saved my future." Her voice became shaky as tears started streaming down her face. "Now... I can actually show emotion... and be around people regularly without the thought of r-randomly snapping and... and... massacring everyone near me..." She looked me in the eye. "Thank you... I literally can't thank you enough." The beeping on the monitor was more steady and much less shallow than before.

"You're welcome?" I had no idea of how to take gratitude for something I would've done earlier if I thought it would help.

"If you need any kind of favor in the future, don't hesitate to come to me. I owe you my life."

"Uh... Sure?"

"I'm back with Carona." Krow was at the door and Carona was behind him. I didn't notice him leave, but with the speed he had, I wasn't surprised. "See? Told you she was awake."

"Okay, get out. I need to conduct some tests, and everyone needs to leave."

"Whelp, I'm out," said Krow.

"That goes for all of us," commented Doc, getting up.

"Before you go anywhere, I need you two to be by the door in case something happens." Carona pointed at Doc and me.

Waiting outside of the room, I was approached by Krow. He was smiling broadly with excited sparks of flame bouncing off of his open palm. "Pull out your sword; I just realized something."

"Uh... Sure." I summoned my sword, and he summoned his.

"Look at this." He showed me the handle of his sword. It was dark red and wrapped in what looked like fabric that was almost as black as the blade. It wrapped completely around from near the base to just under the hilt. "See how it's wrapped?"

"Yeah."

"Now take a look at yours."

Mine was wrapped in a diamond pattern except for the spot where I held it. "What about it?"

"You see; the thing about a katana is that the diamond pattern is mostly for looks and not strictly functionality. That means the more your weapon evolves, the more combat-able it becomes. It'd be a good thing for you to look out for in wielders. Now that you can train on your own, I suggest trying to get your hilt more like mine if you want to be taken more seriously." Even if he wasn't completely right, he was excited enough to believe.

"If that's the case, can't we just train until the tournament starts?"

"You know what, sure. I love fighting and we could always do with some getting stronger. Before that, though, there's still one person among many that needs to be cured of corpse shadows. I'm wondering if you feel up to the task." He looked very hesitant to ask. "It's one of my older sisters. Her name is Caroline. That's all I'll say." After a few silent minutes, Carona followed by Sara and Naomi came out of the room.

"If anybody needs me, I'll be taking a nap." Carona made her way to the nearest elevator. Naomi had a smile the likes of which I never thought I'd see on her. She looked genuinely happy. It was as if her personality had completely changed.

"Did everything come out okay?" asked Krow.

"Just some fatigue, but I'll be with Nurse Sara for the day just in case." Naomi's voice was back to normal.

"That's good, high five!" Krow gave each of us a high five. His excitement was infectious.

"I guess It's time for us to go," said Sara, "This way!" She pointed down the hall in the same direction that Carona went. Then, before I could ask how she got in the room, she jumped into the air surrounded by a pink and golden glow. She changed form and a small black scorpion landed on Naomi's shoulder, still in the fading glow.

"Thank you again," said Naomi to me one last time. Smiling, she went along on her way.

"So, where is your sister?" I asked Krow. Looking around, I noticed Doc was already gone, though I didn't see him move once.

"This way." He bolted back the way we came and continued down the hall to a different elevator and I followed. "You know, It's kinda funny. It seems like Naomi was a really happy person before the whole 'corpse shadow' thing." By this time, we were in the elevator.

"I don't know if you noticed or not, but she cast a passive spell on you before you extracted the corpse shadow. It's called 'inspiration', and only certain types of people can really use it passively like that. You know about bards, right?"

"Yeah. They use music as a tool, right?"

"And a weapon."

"I always wondered about that."

"Well, it doesn't just have to be music. They use anything that can get your attention. They rely on natural harmony to run their magic. They like to use illusions and status ailments as a staple of their spell repertoire." The elevator door opened, and we stepped out. "If you're up to it, we can start there."

"With status effects?"

"And illusions. But we can work on building up your resistance to things like various poisons, blindness of all types, burning, freezing, drowning, increased and decreased gravity, confusion, nauseousness, fear, love, and especially rage and madness."

"Love?"

"Yeah, there are spells that can sway your emotions. Usually to the benefit of whoever caused the effect."

"That's possible?"

"Yeah, I put a near-permanent fear trigger on that girl that left that room earlier. That's an emotional effect. She probably won't be rid of it even when it wears off."

"When does it wear off?"

"It should have already if she wasn't still traumatized. If she can't get over it in a month, it might be permanent." He sounded a bit guilty. "Caroline should be over here."

I just noticed that the hallway never changed. We were still underground. There was a door at the end of the hall that we were walking toward. It opened to a large, open white room with smooth panels for walls and floors. In the middle of the room was a girl in a blue turtleneck and blue jeans with a blue scarf and short dark hair. She was meditating in levitation. She turned around in mid-air. Something about her seemed familiar, but I couldn't put my finger on it.

"Is it time?" She sounded emotionless. "My only positive vision may just well come true." Her feet touched the ground. "Shall we start?"

Krow tapped my shoulder. "Now that I think about it, I might've just rushed you into this."

"It doesn't matter," I responded, "I was planning on doing this as soon as possible anyway."

"Yeah, but this is delicate, and I know you know that, but…" His apprehensiveness was understandable.

"I'm glad that even you can get worried." I put my hand on his shoulder. "But feel this." I let a rush of energy go between me and him. "I'm confident this time. I can feel it. It just takes timing."

"Alright, I'll just be here just in case. Like last time."

"Okay." I let him go.

"So, we doin' this?" asked Caroline.

"Yeah." I walked up to her and summoned my blade in its dark form. "Could you let me know how this feels?"

"Sure."

"Okay, starting." I rammed the blade into her chest. Her eyes went blank, and all the color drained from her face and clothes.

"Sharp pain… Bearable… Compared…" Her voice trailed off.

"Who are you?" another voice escaped her. This one was similar to the one from Naomi. This was different in the feeling it gave off. It was like it was trying to take my breath away. It was making it hard to breathe.

"I'm here for you," I said.

"Then, free me." A series of circles appeared, coiling around her. Some had words in what looked vaguely like an ancient language, but I couldn't figure out what it was.

"Let me handle this." Krow walked up. "**Heaven**." He created a golden flame. "**Hell**." The flame turned a dark red. "**Earth**." The flame dissipated and was replaced by a small vortex of wind. "*Trifecta release*." A larger seal in the shape of a triangular prism appeared around her and shattered. "The rest is up to you." He stepped back and all the rest of the seals broke in tandem.

The force of the shock wave nearly pushed me back. There was so much power being held back that once the floodgates were let loose, the room began shaking and my senses were shocked for a second. The energy began expanding exponentially until I felt like I was in a bubble of water, and I nearly held my breath.

"Be careful," said Krow. "Drowning is an automatic effect in this situation."

"This is drowning?"

"Never mind, you're fine since you can talk. If you can't fight the feeling and hold your breath, that's when it takes effect."

"Good to know. After the fact."

"I forgot." He shrugged.

"What are you waiting for?" said Caroline.

"Come to me." This time, the black mass crawled up my blade much faster and Caroline's eyes closed slowly. The pain was worse as well. It was as if someone took a white-hot spike, stabbed me in my palm, and ran it up into my chest to my heart. I nearly fainted at that moment. It was like it was trying to get to me before I could change my mind. Her color came back all at once just to fade again. I acted once a larger mass began running up my blade. "**Light coil**." I caught it with my spell and it began trying to wiggle itself free. It almost succeeded, but I layered the spell twice to prevent that after turning the blade white. An unnatural groan-like roar came from the blackness. It was angry. Unlike the last one, it was powerful enough to audibly convey intent. It wanted me, dead or alive. "**White pillar**." I figured out the spell, yet I still had to strain myself to make it powerful enough to completely eradicate it. It went out screaming and the pain slowly faded away until it was gone. Caroline collapsed as her color returned. I was still standing. Removing my blade from her chest, I could feel the piece of her soul that was taken resonate. "Uh... I don't know any water-based spells."

"You need one to do the same thing you did with Naomi?" said Krow, keeping a close eye on what was happening.

"Yeah. Just to be safe, it should be one that covers her entire body."

"You're sounding like you know what you're talking about now," he said, walking forward again. "Funnel that energy into me. I'll cast the spell."

"Okay." I placed my hands on his back as he took position next to Carline.

"**Aqua ball**." He seemed to have no problem casting a spell that was his polar opposite. She was surrounded by a blue bubble. "Now." I channeled the pent-up energy through my hand and into Krow. After a moment, Caroline opened her eyes and stood up with a bit of help.

"I feel much better." She began stretching, and a multitude of popping could be heard from various joints all at once. "Thank you."

"Don't mention it." My response felt a little too overthought.

"So, how do you feel now that you're free?" asked Krow. I meant to ask Naomi the same question myself, but I lost my opportunity.

"I feel... so powerful. Like there's something welling up within me." She took a step back while looking at her hands. "Excuse me for a moment." She reached her hands out and an image of a crescent moon flashed in my mind. "**Deep Sea**." A blade shaped exactly like the image in my mind popped into her hand. "Shimmer." her weapon grew slightly bigger, attained blue accents and a second handle parallel to the first. "**Glacier**." She turned around, held it out, and a large block of ice crystallized in front of her. "**Heavy rain**." She reached up and a bubble of water came off of her hand into the air. It then scattered into many smaller droplets and rained down hard enough to completely shatter the block. "There was so much excess." Her weapon began pulsing. "Is this what I think it is?" A six-pointed seal appeared below her feet. She looked at her blade and let it go to levitate in front of her as she had already begun to levitate as well. "Let's see... I'll name you... Blood-edge." Her weapon shrank back to its original size, turned completely blood-red, and the universal symbol for water could be seen on its side. She was back on the ground in a second.

"That's what a weapons evolution looks like," said Krow as Caroline turned around and walked toward me.

"There are more people who need what you can do. Please, if you can, help them," she said.

"I plan to," I responded, honestly.

"Thank you."

"You're welcome. I can't think of literally anything else to say," I said, looking around. "What is this room, anyway? Like a meditation room or something?"

"It's a VR room." Caroline spun around and spread her arms out.

"Like with those headsets?"

"More like a training room," said Krow. "We've been on the roof up till now because of Naomi. It was to see how you two would react to each other as you evolved during your training. Since that's over now, you can come here from now on." He walked past Caroline and me to the middle of the room. "We can start whenever you're ready."

"Oh yeah, I've been in one of these before," I said. "There was one in my basement back home."

"I want to help," announced Caroline, "As thanks for curing me. This is the least I can do."

"You just made this so much easier," said Krow, "I wanted to see what you can do now, and I don't have to ask. We can start tomorrow. For now, we need to get you to Carona so we can be a hundred percent sure you're ok."

Caroline smiled and made her way out. "Alright, we should get moving."

Krow followed. "So, Noah, just let me know when you want to start."

I followed behind them. "Tomorrow sounds good."

From: W.M.T association
To: Black, Noah

We cordially invite you to the
WORLD MAGIC TOURNAMENT!

Mages from all over the world will converge in one location held this year in C.H.E.S.S. headquarters off the coast of Athens, Greece near the isle of Macronissos in the Aegean Sea. You are invited to either spectate or join in on the action. The only requirements to enter are that you have a grimoire of your own by the start of the tournament and have been sent this letter. By entering the tournament, you are opening multiple opportunities for yourself. Scouts from all over the world will be there looking for people like you to join their Guilds, Covens, or even job offers from the likes of The World Mage Organization. As a spectator, you can watch the spectacular performances of all the talented mages the world has to offer. This is not an event to miss.

Gate opens January 4th at 6:00 am
The event starts January 4th at 9:00 am
Event ends January 12th

✕

On-site room and board included for competitors and family
Sincerely *FKZ*
Ferris Kaizer, CEO, and principal

23-Magic Qualifiers

[Caroline Hunt]

Imagine, if you will, a creature created of hatred and anger as black and red as dried blood. Its piercing fangs and claws gnaw at your very being. It holds onto you, clutching your existence within its spines. It drains you until you pass out and lashes at everything that moves while doing so.

The pain and suffering drown everything else you know into a sea of numbness. You wake up every so often to see the carnage of what's become of your friends, family, and yourself. You try to put an end to it but find that you're too weak to stop it, so you seek help. It snaps and you fall back to earth with a poor man's now broken tie dangling around your neck.

You come back to consciousness again to find the man dead and unable to help anyone anymore. You wander around under the same repeating pattern until someone finds you. They have kind eyes and a gentle tone despite how engrossed in blood you are. They embrace you and the creature shows itself only to be met with understanding eyes and a blanket. The creature, for once, hides itself away only to be sealed within a maze of doors, locks, and chains. Every so often, it would grow impatient and attempt to break out. Only to be locked behind tighter security before it could cause more damage. Every time, it does. To you.

Now imagine that somehow, some way, someone comes and offers to take it away. Accepting the offer, you awake for the last time with the pain of most of your existence as a distant memory. That's me. I still awake every once in a while in a cold sweat from nightmares of a time long since passed.

Oh, you want to know about my time training with Krow and Noah as well? And the tournament too? Sure, I'll tell you. Besides, it was fun. At first.

It didn't feel like two months. The only noticeable change in anything aside from the weather was the attitude of the city as well as my own. Everything felt much cleaner, and the people seemed much happier too. Noah was steadily improving at a rapid rate. He was a natural at pretty much everything except dealing with people.

Like Krow, he was a power type. Unlike Krow, he had a more orthodox fighting style and only resorted to tricky tactics when cornered. A real 'heroic' type fighter, you know? Anyway, nobody really had anything to teach him that he didn't either already know or couldn't easily figure out on his own, so the only thing left for him was combat. That was the only field in which he still had anything fundamental to learn.

In that time, I learned a thing or two about myself though. It turned out that my spirit animal was a mute mermaid. It took some time to get her to reveal herself to me. She was three shades of deep blue that shined different colors depending on what angle you looked at her from. She had sharp claws and teeth as well as red marks on her tail, arms, and neck that looked like it was made by chains. She couldn't speak but I would know what she tried to convey to me at any time. I spoke to her often. She was shy and wouldn't converse with me at first. It took some time for me to convince her otherwise.

It seemed that the reason was that the corpse shadow took over by convincing her that it was me. It took her prisoner inside of me. It was why she was mute. A mermaid would lose her voice if... Since then, the red marks faded to pink and are still there. I think it might be symbolism. I still have PTSD and all... Oh yeah, back to the first thing.

I honestly never fought like that before, and I wasn't all that apprehensive to start. I went against Krow in a demonstration of how it looks when someone inexperienced in magic-based combat fought someone who was. My water almost completely nullified his fire, and he had to switch to wind. I felt like I was learning more than anybody else at that time. While low-level training with Noah, he took the time to teach me the basics of fighting with magic as well. Since I normally only fought only when I had to, and only with overbearing strength. Now, I could control myself. Now, things would be different.

There was an entire stack of letters inviting each of us individually to the magic tournament. I decided to use mine to enter.

Before long, Sara and Ariel were done with Cattherine's training, and they all joined in as well. All she needed was basic training and some schooling. She had already had basic spell-casting experience. Now that I think about it, it all went past pretty fast, didn't it? Of course, time did slow back down during the whole tournament thing, if you know what I mean.

Since we didn't have permission to take the normal avenues to get to Greece, we went by conventional means. We arrived by bus at Kennedy Airport. Thankfully, Mom always made sure each of us had a passport for most major countries, so we had no problem. Hinata was able to help Noah and Cattherine get their own before the deadline. I fell asleep on the flight and Leuna woke me up as we landed on the day before it was set to start. Vincent and two others went on an earlier flight, and we met them after getting off.

Before going to where the tournament was being held, we went and toured around the city. The people were decent, the food was great, and the scenery was to die for. Did I mention the food? There was a fish spot that I can't remember the name of- oh yeah, back on track.

We got to the island the next day by boat. It looked like a city on the water. It was circular and had what looked like buildings jutting out of it. It turns out that it was actually just a large wall shielding the inside from storm waves and icebergs. Apparently, it was meant to be a mobile city on the ocean. Instead, it somehow became a mobile base of operations for that organization. There was a large, icy blue, rectangular platform in front of the entrance about the size of a football field. The ferry dropped us off there. Up close, the wall was smooth and slightly reflective. It looked like stone and felt like steel. I heard from Doc later that it was perma-steel, an 'absolute' attribute like Noah. I had never seen it myself before then. The gates into the place were gigantic and almost as wide as the platform.

The gate began to open a few minutes after we arrived. The big gate didn't move. A more person-sized door opened on the side, and someone looked out. After a second of looking around, they darted back and a minute later, the ground began to shake, and an outline of a door appeared on the gate and slid open in the middle. The opening could pass around ten people through at a time.

We entered a giant courtyard that had a mural of a woman with long bright red hair and piercing blue eyes wearing a white gown and no shoes. She had a nub on one side of her back and a strikingly white angelic wing on the other side. She was on her knees crying and holding six different colored artifacts in her arms. A silver gear, a white snowflake, a green feather, a blue orb, a red crystal, and a black crucifix. Krow knelt on the image and touched the feather.

He said, "I'm sorry," as a single tear fell from his eye. I asked him why later and he said that he didn't know why. He just knew that the woman's name was Faramosa. He also had no idea why he knew that. Faramosa had come up when we were researching C.H.E.S.S, but we never saw an image of her. It was odd that he recognized her, but for some reason, I wasn't surprised.

We were ushered via guide rails along a gray marble pathway to a sandstone-colored coliseum far away from what looked like a residential district. The coliseum itself was absurd in how large the stands were compared to the center arena. The entrance of the coliseum was a series of arches. Under each of the three main arches was a pedestal with enchanted plaques that read: *'main entrance', 'bleachers',* and *'contestant entry'*, respectively. I followed the arrow for the contestant entry area, pointing right. The gray pathway led to a set of stairs that led underground. At the base was a guy with long blue dyed hair in a uniform. He was checking everybody's letters and making sure they had a grimoire.

I showed him mine and kept going. It was a pocket-sized book with a translucent light blue circle taking up the top left of the cover with a curved line leading to another of the same circle on the lower right side. The book itself is a glittery deep blue and shimmered in the light.

The stairs opened to a large ballroom. It still kept the sandstone motif but had a spiral pattern that led to the center of the room on the floor of gray tiles. The large room filled slowly, so there was more than enough time to admire it. Looking at it for a while gave me the sensation that the room was spinning. I couldn't break the feeling until the sound of someone being slapped snapped me out of it.

Not too far from me was a tall woman in a blood-red jacket that fell to her ankles glaring at a boy with gray hair and an orange long sleeve who was then rubbing his hand on his face. They were talking discreetly about something that I couldn't make out completely. All I got were their names; Nero and Rachel, and the fact that Rachel was mad at Nero for joining something dangerous. Maybe it was the tournament.

After a little more talking, she turned around and ran straight into Krow who, after introducing himself, seemed to ask what the whole scene was about. They conversed a little, and he gave a courteous bow before saying something that made her giggle. She gave him her hand, and they shook while passing each other. He watched her go, and she looked back before finding her way up the stairs. Not at him, at Nero. A second later, Krow walked up to him and said something while putting his hand on his head. He swatted his hand away and said something along the lines of 'She'd never!' before looking Krow up and down. Krow's response seemed to calm him down and they talked for a bit before parting ways.

Krow came my way. "There are testers in the crowd," He said. "Be careful. I already told everybody else."

"You mean like this psychedelic floor?"

"Yeah."

"By the way, what was up with that woman? You like her?"

"Yep, she's tall and cute." He could have been joking but I wouldn't put it past him. "She's also a famous bounty hunter. That was Rachel Cursley, the Blood Rose. She retired years ago, though. And she's almost twice my age. It turns out that boy over there is her son. He's also the same guy that roughed up Catt and Noah. I'm kinda hoping they get a rematch." After maybe five minutes, he spoke up again. "So, how are you doing? You feeling okay?"

"I'm doing fine," I told him, "I just wanna test myself. If anything, I just kinda wanna see if I like this kind of thing you know?"

"Yeah, I get it. I'm usually the odd one out on stuff but you never really fight with magic even though your fists do a lot of talking already."

"You really think so? Thanks."

"Yeah, like that time you drop-kicked me in the face off of my bed and made my nose bleed because you lost to me in a fighting game."

"That's because you kept cheating."

"I didn't cheat, I just grabbed you a couple times at the end and you kicked me."

"Okay, my bad. It was forever ago anyway."

"That's okay. I probably cheated anyway." He gave me a hug, and I patted him on the back.

I gave him a word of warning. "Be careful going after cougars."

"Don't worry about me, I'll be fine." He faded into the steadily growing crowd.

However much the crowd grew, so too did the room. I noticed it after a while because no one ever ended up closer than a foot or two from each other while everyone was piling in one by one. Eventually, the steady stream of people slowed down and the wall on the opposite side away from the stairs opened up to reveal a wooden stage and a man standing on it with an award-winning smile. His smoothed-back brown hair had a sliver of gray in it, and he was wearing a light blueish-gray uniform with an emblem of a red king chess piece on his gloved left hand.

"Good morning, ladies and gentlemen." The man held his arms out in greetings. "I see many of you have come early. The event doesn't start for another hour and a half. As a precaution for boredom, if you look around you, there will be seats and confectionaries."

He was gone and the wall was back to normal so fast that I thought I blinked. It occurred to me that the entire display could've been a mass illusion. It made sense, but what bothered me was that I couldn't tell when it started. While thinking it over, I found myself sitting on a blue and silver stool holding a cookie. It seemed that I was sitting there with a cookie in my hand the entire time. I had been gingerly taking bites out of it since I sat down. I hadn't been able to finish it because of my interest in the commotion from earlier, my conversation with Krow, and my confusion as to whether or not I was still under the influence of an illusion spell. I couldn't come to a conclusion and the more I thought about it, the more I felt that something was off. I still hadn't finished my cookie. It never seemed to get any smaller, so I took a larger bite and before I could look into it more, the wall opened up again and the same man appeared once more.

"Hello again, ladies and gentlemen. I have yet to introduce myself. My name is Geist Kaizer and I'll be your guide and peacekeeper, if necessary, for this upcoming tournament." He took another bow. "I know all of you have been called especially for a tournament, but there seems to be a larger number of contestants than we can fit into our timeframe for the tournament so, we'll be whittling down the number to a more... Manageable size. In other words, these will be the qualifiers. Please, listen closely and carefully, for I will only say this once.

This course you all will be undertaking is split into four parts: each with an objective. The first part is the infinite desert. The only goal of this part is to reach the next section in under three hours from when we start. This is the only part with a time limit. The second part is the black forest. The objective there is to avoid the ground until you reach the other side; simple enough. After that, is the underground cavern. The objective there is to bypass the testers stationed there and make it to the other side. The last part is a surprise. That is all." He looked down at his wrist. "Oh... And we start... Now." He disappeared again, and the wall didn't return.

The only thing on that side of the room was a wide expanse of a desert, complete with an open blue sky. I stood up slowly as those closest to the opening began walking through the space. While most began walking in uncertainty, others took to the air and either jumped or flew to where the wall was. They all seemed to go through, and any attacks sent at it passed as well. I made my way through with everyone else. After a few minutes, I found myself alone. I looked down at my hands and didn't see a cookie. I spat and still no cookie. I hadn't been chewing since I took the large bite.

"This whole thing is a god damned illusion." It didn't matter what was or wasn't an illusion from that point on, as long as I got out of that desert. Knowing that inside of an illusion, I could have just been lying on the floor and the whole thing could have been over already, I took out my grimoire. The pages were blank. That's when I figured out when I was pulled into the illusion.

I put my hand on my head and tried to remember any spell that could help me out of my situation. At that moment, I remembered one. "*Calm.*" I cast a spell on myself and my surroundings became hazy. The spell was meant to calm my mind and succeeded in allowing me to see what made everything feel off, to begin with. "*Nullify.*" I reached my hand out and cast that spell on the space around me. The air began breaking apart and shattered like a mirror. I wasn't standing in the underground room like I thought I was. Looking behind me, I saw the stairs that led up and no room.

There was a group of people spread far apart from each other who were marching in place. There were more of them off the ground, either hovering or slowly descending from a high jump. I didn't see anybody I recognized, so I turned back around. The desert was still there, but the sand was white instead of yellow like it just was and everything had a blue tint as everything seemed to be at the bottom of the ocean inside of a giant bubble with the city floating as a ceiling above us. There was no sign of any flora or fauna. Looking farther, I could see what seemed like a forest in the distance.

I looked back down at my Grimoire and all the spells were there. Just in case I was in a larger illusion, I cast 'nullify' a second time before finding my way to the forest. The edge of the desert was just a drop-off. The trees came from so deep into the ground that I couldn't see the bottom. Jumping to the first tree that I saw; I found a trail of sprung magical traps and shattered illusions. I followed it until I reached the other side.

There was a twenty-foot gap between the last of the trees and a hole in the side of what looked like a sheer cliff face. I made a mad jump toward it and nearly fell because I lost my footing on the run-up. I cast 'levitate' in time and floated the rest of the way. Feeling weary, I cast 'nullify' once more just as a trap sprung and a bubble filled with water came up from under me. It popped before anything happened.

Making my way through, I could hear the sounds of fighting coming from different sides of the tunnels. I silently made my way through each one that I couldn't hear anything through. In one tunnel, there was no sound even if I tossed a rock down it, so I avoided it and kept going. Somewhere between entering the cave and exiting, I realized that even though I didn't mind fighting and sometimes actually looked forward to it; it wasn't the thing I wanted to do.

Because of that decision, I decided not to fight in the actual tournament. The sounds alone, and sometimes the lack thereof, convinced me of it. The fact that I later found fresh blood on my shoe helped solidify that choice.

24-Selective Sight

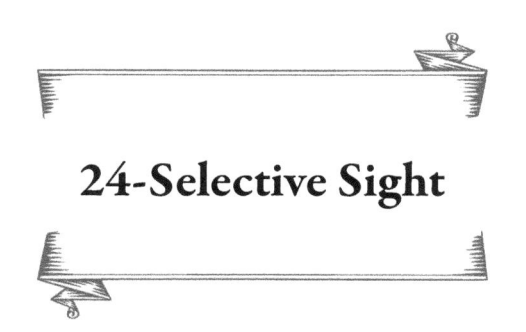

[Noah Black]

I stood from the small metal-worked chair as the opening appeared. Looking back, I saw it had a white velvet cushion on the seat. In a moment of random curiosity and nothing more, I picked it up and carried it with me.

The desert was odd in that it wasn't hot or dry. I tanned easily and noticed no difference in my skin tone between what was exposed and what wasn't during the twenty-plus minutes that it felt like I was walking. I had also found myself alone, and the desert seemed to be missing an ending in sight. By casting 'push' I boosted myself high in the air. On the way up, I noticed a distinct lack of weight, and the chair that I was holding onto was no longer there. The muffin in my mouth had also become non-existent. Making up my mind, I cast 'awakening' on myself to make sure I wasn't asleep. Nothing happened. I then put both of my hands in front of my face and cast 'flash' hoping to shock myself out of the fog I found myself in.

I succeeded only to find that jumping was a bad idea as I was spiraling toward the ground at an increasing rate. By the time I noticed, I was already too close to the ground to slow down or stop. At that moment, I saw a yellow flash and felt someone sweep me away. I looked around to find Catt. She had a mixed look of relief and anger on her face. Her hair was black, but her gloves had electricity running through them. I barely recognized her without her yellow jacket. She had foregone it in favor of an autumn-inspired combat outfit that Hinata made for her. It had flowing red and orange patterns.

"Thanks for tha-"

Stopping, she dropped me sternly on the ground. "You almost died, you know that?"

"What?" I said, getting up.

"I saw a vision where you died pulling that stupid stunt and what do I see straight afterwards? You falling to your death. You're lucky it snapped me out of the illusion thing in time to come and save you. This ground is much harder than it looks or feels on the surface. It may be sand but it's compact." She stomped her foot to demonstrate. The sand barely moved aside for a shallow layer on the top.

"Well, thanks for keeping me grounded." I stomped my foot as well.

She sighed and said, "Let's go," as she began walking toward the forest in the distance.

"Thanks for saving me though. I'd feel pretty stupid for dying from just a fall."

"Don't mention it. It's why I'm here."

"Really?"

"No, silly, let's just keep going."

We walked until we both almost fell into the vast chasm that waited for the unobservant. It was a black abyss with a multitude of trees sticking out of it with wide branches seemingly for transversal.

I bent down on one knee. "Catt, get on my back."

"What are you gonna do?" She had already gotten on my back before she asked. "Then again, why'd I ask? It's gonna be reckless, isn't it?"

"Did you even have to ask?" I responded as I backed up for a running start. She held on tighter. "Here we go!" I began running.

"Now I wish I didn't!" she screamed as we picked up speed.

"**Push**." I jumped with the spell, and we flew high into the trees and almost immediately hit a branch. It broke on my face, and we continued upward, only landing after hitting a thicker branch and falling back down a couple of meters where I landed on my feet.

"Are you okay?" she asked.

"If I said yes, would you worry less?"

"No, let me see your face." She had already freed herself from my back and was trying to look under my quivering hands at my face.

"No, I'm good."

"I don't think so." She tried to pull my hands away and I wouldn't let her. "Let... Me... See!" she yanked my hands away and the look on her face told me it was worse than it felt. "Can you feel that?"

"No, should I?"

After hearing my answer, she went pale. "Yes, you should and I'm going to do something about it before it scars." She put her hands up to my face and her gloves began glowing green. "**Regenerate**." After about thirty seconds, she stopped. "That should just about do it. Let's get going."

I asked, "What'd it look like, anyway?"

"I'm not telling you."

"Why not?"

"Because you'd be upset that you won't have a *cool* scar across your face."

"It was gonna be cool? What was it? Was it an X or a big scar over my eye or something? You could have just left it."

"I just prefer your face without a scar alright?"

"You do?"

"Think about it this way: do you really want a scar you got from bashing your face against a tree?"

"It'd be cool because it wasn't on purpose."

"Never mind, I never should have said anything."

"I don't know about that. I was just thinking about how badass you'd look with a scar."

"You know what, just forget I said anything." She jumped to the next branch, and it fell causing her to leap to another one which caused acid to be sprayed from the trunk of that tree. Screaming, she jumped to another one, which didn't cause any additional problems.

"Are you okay?" I said, almost moving toward her but unsure of what I'd have to deal with on the way.

"I'm good. I just didn't expect this place to be booby-trapped."

"Heh, you said booby."

"Now's not the time for that. We have to figure out how to get through here without getting knocked all the way down or killed. Keeping up a nullification spell would be too taxing here." She took a single leap and landed back on the branch I was on.

"Okay, get back on my back." I turned around and showed her my back.

"No."

"Come on."

"No, you're gonna hit something again."

"Come ooon~." I slowly beckoned her toward me.

"Crash again and I'll give you a scar myself," She sighed.

"Really?"

"No, that was just a joke."

"Oh."

"Just shut up and bend over,"

Krow's voice rang from close by. "If it's like that, then you two need to get a room."

Catt looked up and said, "Why are you here? I thought you would've been farther along than us by now."

Krow landed on the branch Catt was just on. "I was but I stopped to chat with Doc. He was looking for any of us who might need help when we heard your scream and I decided to heed your call. But what do I find but one demanding that the other bends over."

"I get It." It struck me when I thought about how she phrased it. "Ew," I said, pointing both of my index fingers at Catt. She gave me a tired look and folded her arms.

Krow walked along his branch. "Anywho, follow me and I'll help you two through this if you want. Besides, I was heading straight through to the end, anyway. Care to come with?"

"Sure," said Catt, "Just know that I can't take both of you making jokes at the same time. I don't feel like being worn out before I can actually do something."

"Okay, got it. Light on the jokes." He gave a cheeky thumbs up. "This way."

He turned around and shot a fireball toward our destination. It fired past the trees and tripped every trap that was set. Some branches fell, others spat poison, fire, exploded, electrified, froze, or even shot out blades. The few that were harmless became singed. Each trap seemed to only trip once, so we followed behind Krow to the edge of the forest.

The gap was no problem. Krow levitated across and I offered to carry Catt across with mixed results. I successfully boosted us across but slipped on the landing and awkwardly fell on her. She never let me live that one down. Krow's laughter didn't help. He apologized after he caught the angriest look I'd ever seen on Catt's face.

It was clear that even though she still went through with my shenanigans, she wasn't having much of it that day. We had been through many trials and difficult situations. We always laughed our way through every struggle. I thought that this was no different, so I asked her what was wrong.

She said, "I might as well tell you. That girl, Snow. She gave me something called 'selective sight' and another thing called 'strike warning', remember?"

"Yeah."

"I think I figured out what they do specifically."

"What is it?"

"I'm certain that their purpose is to keep you alive."

"Are you sure that's what it is?"

"I saved you earlier, remember? I think that was it activating."

We followed Krow to a room that closed us in after entering. On the opposite wall was a small opening in the shape of a circle with four protruding right angles at opposite ends. To the right was an angular mass of rubble and on the left was the same except rounded.

"Damn." Krow put his hand on his head and turned toward us. Catt, did Sara ever teach you the shrinking spell?"

"Yeah, why?"

"It looks like we have to shrink this rubble and fit it into that hole," He said, pointing at each pile and the hole. "Also, It's a spell I don't use, so I don't have it written down or committed to memory."

"Leave it to me," said Catt, stepping up, "And you." She pointed at me. "Try not to die while I do this, will ya?"

"Sure..." I had a comeback, but I felt a lot of danger coming my way if I let it slip. "Okay."

"Let's see." She took her time shrinking and growing the pieces until they fit perfectly into the hole. "There we go." The door slid up with the newly installed puzzle pieces in place.

On the other side, all any of us could see was a girl in a black C.H.E.S.S. uniform pinned to the wall with fragments of stone. She had a gold rook badge over her heart. There was also a puddle of blood underneath her and she was staring blankly right at us. After a moment of absorbing what we were seeing. Catt unleashed a blood-curdling scream. I jumped in front of her to shield her from what felt like incoming danger.

"Hey, you down there!" A man was sitting on a small outcropping on the wall high above us on the other side of the room. "Care for a fight?" His eyes were glowing a dangerous blank yellow. Even considering the distance, I felt like I was in front of a wildcat that at any second could tear out my throat.

"I know those eyes," said Krow, moving ahead of us, "Those are eyes that kill. Is it a thirst, or a compulsion? What's the chance you're here for the tournament?"

"I'm just here for some fun. How about you?"

"Same." Krow took another step forward and summoned his blade. "I just don't like killing if it's avoidable."

"That's no fun." The man dropped to the ground, and his surroundings exploded. The ground turned to sand as pieces of it whipped by. "I like watching my prey die slowly. That one hasn't even passed out yet." He pointed back at the woman pinned to the wall. "And now I have more prey to torture right in front of me."

"This guy obviously isn't a tester. Stay back, I got him." I felt like Krow was only talking to me.

I was going to step forward to help him when I remembered Snow's advice. 'Sometimes, taking a step back is the only way to proceed forward'.

"Ok, be careful." I took a step back and right into Catt's arms. She was looking at me with a deathly fear in her eyes as she was shaking her head.

Whatever vision she saw this time must have spooked her more than the grizzly scene before us. She would never tell me what she saw and any time I ever brought it up, she'd go silent and not talk to anyone for hours. It scarred her for life.

Krow responded, "I won't. I don't like being careful. Besides, that kind of bloodlust makes people predictable. Just be sure you keep watching all the way through alright?" He looked back at his opponent. "Watch and learn. This might be a fight to the death."

"Alright," said the man, "I'll take you on first then the small fry for dessert. I already had my appetizer. She put up a hell of a fight."

I had just regained my nerves enough to get a good look at the man. He was just above average height and was built like a monster truck. Anything that could cause harm was amplified to a scary degree. His knuckles were the size of marbles and each of his arms were the size of my head at least five times over. He had wild blonde hair and a goatee. His clothes were covered in blood and were mostly loose-fitting aside from his steel boots, which seemed to fit all too well. It was like he was made to murder.

Looking at both men objectively there seemed to be little difference in that matter between them. Krow was over a meter and thin, yet solid, and his arms were like snakes, long muscles with sharply angled knuckles. They were both perfect killing machines. At least, as far as I could tell.

"Are you gonna keep talking or are we gonna do this?" I just realized that Krow had never had a serious look on his face since I met him, and now he looked like a completely different person. The look of excitement in his eyes was gone, and the slight smile he always kept was missing as well. He looked like he was going to work.

An image of two round bucklers marked with yellow fracture patterns crammed itself into my head so forcefully that it hurt for a second.

"Krow... His weapon-" I forced my clenched jaw open to convey the message and I almost bit my tongue as the man shifted his gaze to me.

"What is it?" asked Krow.

I clenched my fists and loosened my jaw to speak once more. "He's got twin shields with a forward spike in the middle of each one."

"Well, there goes that surprise!" The man summoned his shields and rushed at Krow with both spikes.

Krow blocked the attack by holding his sword sideways, but there was a simultaneous and unexpected explosion that knocked both Catt and me back. Almost falling over, we caught each other. Krow, however, was unharmed and standing strong.

"Neither you nor your weapon broke on impact. This'll be good." The man smiled excitedly through the wafting dust.

Krow pushed the man back, but he rebounded quickly and missed his strike as he only phased through a wisp of flame. Krow teleported.

From the right, Krow appeared in a second wisp of flame and dashed at the man with his blade gleaming red.

The man used both of his shields to block, and this caused another explosion on impact. Krow wasn't pushed back by this one either, even though he was sideways in the air. While he was in this position, he pushed something behind the shields.

"Let's see how you handle it." Krow was back on his feet and out of the way as a ball of wind with a small flame seated inside expanded around the man and exploded.

"That actually kinda stung." The man seemed relatively unfazed. "Let's see what else you can do."

Krow jumped back at the man as he moved his shields, and he just barely caught the blade pointed at his chest between his hands.

The man swung Krow around and let him go then hit both of his shields together. "**Kinetic shockwave.**" An uproar of sound rushed outward.

Krow landed near Catt and me then moved directly in front of us and made a bubble around us all. "**Horizon.**" When everything turned red, I was a little alarmed at first, but it was just the color of Krows horizon. It faded from deep red to a fiery yellow.

"Nice. Now I really wanna break you," said the man, laughing, excitedly.

"Chopter." Krow evolved his blade, and it became a dual blade with wind on one side and fire on the other side.

"Scizor." The man evolved his weapon as well, and both spikes extended to rounded blades, but they still kept the shield base.

They raced at each other and clashed. The explosion that formed between the two rocked the cavern. Dust and debris seemingly appeared out of nowhere as cracks formed in the floor and walls. Even though I couldn't see them, I could feel them.

The two moved briskly through the debris as more formed from their collisions. They weren't particularly fast, but their strikes made me think even lightning would be deterred from their collisions. Few words were uttered, but none of them spells. I heard more than I thought I would over the consistent booms, but I didn't pick up anything in particular.

This wasn't a battle of strength. Too much power from both of them would have caused a cave-in. Instead, they gauged each other's reactions and worked to outmaneuver each other. Krow aimed for the space around his opponent's shields and occasionally between them as he continuously unleashed a flurry of strikes that kept the man on guard with little chance to counterattack. The man, on the other hand, seemed to be aiming for the point of impact to parry Krow's blades and go on the assault himself. Whenever he was successful, Krow would back off to reset his pressure.

Despite this back-and-forth, it looked like they were just attacking each other, flailing in the throughs of battle until one of them fell inexplicably to one of many blows. While this lasted only a few brief moments, it felt like I was watching a movie of just combat. That was until one of the man's counter attempts was countered itself. Krow allowed his blade to be pushed aside while he used his free hand to grip the man's face.

"Got ya!" said Krow as the pair was surrounded by a spiral of fire that blew away the dust and debris. Still surrounded by flames, they were lifted from the ground and rocketed to each wall three times while the man was slammed into them each time before rising to the ceiling, all in a split second. "***Fire drop.***" They picked up speed as Krow smashed the man's face into the ground in an explosion of fire with the flaming spiral becoming longer as it followed them. "***Blazing funnel: collapse.***" The spiral flame bypassed Krow while it closed in where the man was and carried him all the way back to where it started, coated in flames. As the man was carried back from the ceiling to where the spiral started, Krow hopped back up with another spell. "***Reach.***" His hand temporarily turned into a flaming talon and hit the man head-on. The impact sent the man into the ceiling, and he flew back into the room he came from.

With only a second's delay, the man recovered and stood back up. Every impact of what I just saw carried enough heat to make me think that I just walked into a jet engine, and he just stood up from being hit by all of that. I thought I might've caught sunburn on the arm I used to shield my eyes from the light.

The man beamed with a smile. "I like that."

For the first time ever, I could feel the presence of what I saw in someone. It felt feral and disturbing. There was a purely murderous energy coming off of him. It was so intense that I felt sick and Catt gagged.

"Let's skip the torture and just kill each other!" The man sounded way too excited for anyone's good. "I won't hold back. Ripper." The man evolved his weapon again. His shields began glowing and shrank around his hands, appearing almost like gloves. They were scizzorhands-like gauntlets and seemed like blades attached to a thin frame on his hands.

"Divide." Krow evolved his weapon as well. His sword shifted so that half of it was a handle, and the other half was the blade. The whole thing was about the length of his height and both the blade and handle were reminiscent of its first form. They clashed before I could take in the moment, but they stayed in place this time. "***Enfeeblement.***"

"A weakening spell, huh?" said the man, still beaming. "You're going to have to cast that spell a million times before it does you any good."

"What do you think I've been doing this whole time?" Krow began pushing the man back into the ground.

"Damn it, really? How?" The man seemed to struggle more as the seconds passed. His arms and legs were shaking like jelly.

"***Dead cells.***" I could feel a buildup of energy as Krow cast one more spell, and the man went limp on the ground. His weapon dissipated and all he could do was moan angrily. "You two, I need you to see to that girl. If she's still alive, try your best to heal her as best you can and get her down. I need to make sure this spell holds, so I'll carry him."

"O... kay." said Catt as we were both still in a shell shock from what we had just witnessed.

"Today?" Krow sounded hurried.

"Okay." We hurried to the woman's side and looked for a pulse. Catt found it and she waited a couple of seconds to make sure there actually was one while I cast 'sacred healing' to the best of my ability. I was never really good at healing, but the spell held up fine. The pulse was there, and we both kept the spell on her after we took her off of the wall until she regained consciousness. She couldn't walk so I carried her.

It turned out the man's name was Dagon Wong. He was a criminal who was lured there with an invitation, and he somehow ducked under security. He found his way to the underground cavern where he waited for anyone to come by. Apparently, he already killed three more people before we found and stopped him.

It took a while to get out and meet someone else who could help with our situation. The officials took over from there and they questioned us about what happened in the tunnels. While there, Krow inquired on how and why they sent a letter to the criminal to lure him in instead of just sending someone after him since they knew how to contact him. He then asked where the guy who said he was a peacekeeper was while all of that was going on and about the lack of communication between the testers and everyone else on the outside.

After a long run of questions and non-answers, they sent us to the last part of the qualifiers. It took place in a small gray building away from the exit of the cave. Upon entering the building, we were each given a pen and paper. It was a questionnaire. At the top was a disclaimer, to tell the truth. I had no problem with it. I had nothing to hide. The only part of the whole thing that seemed off about it was the last question. It read: *'What is your weakness? (combative)'*. I assumed it meant something my opponent could take advantage of during a fight. Regardless, it seemed like a trick question. I didn't think much of it and answered honestly before turning it in. It wasn't like I had any weakness I was aware of, so my answer meant nothing, anyway.

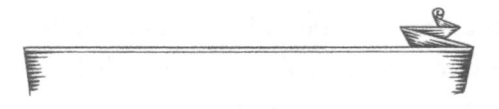

25-Magic Tournament

[Krow Hunt]

Walking into the stadium in front of expecting eyes, I was hit with a feeling of déjà vu. I had been there before. Not that specific place but somewhere just like it. The thought of it gave me a headache and I pushed the thought aside. If I was going to remember anything, this wasn't the place to do it.

Everyone entered from a gateway that led up from underground. The number of people left from the starting number was dramatic. The original number looked to be in the hundreds, now it was less than fifty. Not long after we all entered the field, the man who appeared in the trick room now appeared on a large, levitating stadium screen over the middle of the center area.

He re-introduced himself as the son of Ferris Kaizer and a member of the Seven Virtues, then made a point of thanking everyone for being there. He also spoke of the history of C.H.E.S.S. and what 'good' they have done in the time since they opened their doors until now. I zoned out for most of it but at least an hour passed before it was over.

What caught my attention was the picture that showed up after his face went away. It showed a thirty-man bracket. Looking carefully; I found my name, Doc, Noah, Catt, and Mary; Noah's sister. It didn't say a last name, but it didn't seem coincidental. I still wasn't paying any attention to the voice coming from the screen. Looking around, I spotted Noah doing the same until a gate opened to the left.

After entering the gate, a few uniforms ushered us to the bleachers and down to the first two rows, which had a yellow line behind them going around the entire stadium.

Everyone sat in a single file in the front row. The next thing to show up on the screen was a picture of Rachel Cursley on the left side of a slash vs screen with another recognizable person on the right side. He had short, dark hair cut into a fade, dark brown eyes, and dark skin. His name was Grem, and he was the one who gave me the heads up on there being testers in the crowd. He was also a public member of C.H.E.S.S, known as Moderacy. I followed my gut and took him at face value but I met no testers in the crowd myself. Maybe that was a good thing. Like Rachel, he went back upstairs before the qualifiers started. The bottom of the image read: *'Exhibition'*.

Less than a minute after the image came up, the gate to the left opened, and Grem walked out as Rachel came from the right since that gate was already open. The screen overhead changed to show the field below as they walked toward each other, shook hands, and walked back away from each other. A countdown appeared and started at three on the screen and they seemed to stare each other down until it reached zero.

The first thing they both did was shoot a fireball. A deep red one from Rachel and a bright yellow one from Grem. They collided and the red one overtook the yellow one, then dissipated.

Rachel's next move was to put both hands in front of her and fire two more fireballs.

Grem retaliated by creating a white ice wall to block them and jumping back a distance. The wall was opaque and both sides were presumably blind to the other. It held up well from the impact

Rachel propelled herself forward with two more fireballs that followed after her.

Grem prepared an ice ball for when the wall was broken. The fireballs broke the middle of the ice on impact.

Rachel ducked around the wall as the ice ball was thrown and opened her mouth, firing a wide stream of flame, melting the ice ball mid-air and meeting Grem with a hot surprise. The attack didn't reach him fast enough to prevent him from escaping, but it singed his clothes.

Grem shot six magic missiles at once from his hands. They were all white orbs each surrounded by two rings of bright yellow.

Rachel dodged three of them and counterd two of them by casting 'burning palm' on herself and setting both of her hands on fire then catching them. She then threw one into another and the last one at him spiked with a flaming trail.

Grem cast 'ice mirror' and created a literal reflective surface of ice between him and his spell. The magic missile bounced back and hit her head-on. The next thing he did was freeze the ground in her direction.

It didn't slow Rachel down. She was levitating at running speed toward him with fire trailing from the side of her mouth.

He threw an ice spike at her and created another ice wall, this time backed up with a firewall.

She ate the ice spike as it melted in her presence. She turned blue as she began frosting over before a heat wave rose from her and melted all the ice.

Grem jumped above the wall out of the way. That was his mistake.

Rachel changed tapped the ground with her foot and changed direction while picking up speed and coated herself in flames. She tackled him out of the air. Landing on top of him, she readied another fireball and pointed it at his face.

Grem put both hands up in defeat.

Moving off of him, she put out her flames and helped him up. The battle comprised a show of skill while only using basic spells mixed with natural abilities. Shaking hands again, they exchanged a few words and parted ways back to the opposite sides of the arena and through the gates.

Geist had been talking for a while by then, and I hadn't noticed until people started standing and leaving. I stood and wandered around until Doc found me walking back and forth between the seats.

"Are you okay? I haven't seen you like this in a long time."

"Not since you found me like forever ago, right?" I looked out to the rest of the emptying stadium. The sandstone and marble-colored arena nagged at something in the back of my mind. It was like finding a faint light in a pitch-black room. You know it's there and you're just waiting for your eyes to adjust to where you can see it. "There's something about this place. It reminds me of something. I don't know what, but I think that mural in the courtyard has something to do with it."

"You think so?"

"I think I cried when I saw it. Tears fell. I don't know about you, but I stopped crying a long time ago. I think I have memories here. Deep ones."

"So, what else do you think?"

"I think this curse won't break no matter what happens. Everything is so far out of reach that I'm starting to feel a disconnect from reality. I feel like I'm trying to chase a dream and every time I close my eyes, someone calls my name and wakes me up. Not my name, that other name. The one I can't remember."

"How about those pages in your grimoire that you couldn't read? Can you read any of them now?"

I opened the book and flipped to each page of unidentifiable text and symbols. None of them had changed. "Nothing." I put the book back in my pocket. "Too bad. More than anything, I just want to know what those spells are." Every time I talked to Doc about something like that, I got the feeling that he knew more than he let on. Maybe it was because every time I looked at him, I got a feeling that I was forgetting something important, or maybe it was that he never really had a name either. The name he used now was only what I came up with as a kid after he found me. In essence, I named both of us, but it seemed like he'd be thinking back on his own past whenever I talked about remembering mine. "So, what do you think?"

"Same thing as always. It'll come to you, eventually. That said, I think we should be going." He pointed at the exit. The stadium was almost empty. The only people left were a few security guards in black with the word "security" across their chest and backs in white and a few late-going audience members. I walked toward the exit and Doc followed. The girls were waiting for us aside from Carona and Sara. They had already gone to see about the on-site room and board.

Caroline told us of her decision about not fighting in the tournament. Ariel, Leuna, and Sara didn't try. We began walking together via more guide rails to the housing district that could be seen in the distance. We caught up with Carona and Sara, who were waiting for us in front of a small black gate guarded by three security guards. Carona was pointing at us and talking to a guard.

It turned out that proceeding past that point meant that you had to be on the list of combatants or an important guest. Both Doc and I were on the list, so they let us all through. They handed us a card with an address on it and were told to follow down the first street until we found it. The address was to a house. It was blue with a driveway that could fit two cars and bushes in the front yard. It was an actual house in the middle of what looked like an actual neighborhood. There seemed to be enough room for an entire city on the floating base.

The inside of the house had white walls and was furnished with beds and dressers in the four bedrooms and a sofa in the living room with a TV on the adjacent wall. It was nice in its own way. The TV had local channels and a special channel for broadcasting the arena in case someone stayed to watch from there.

Later, I let Carona know where I was going and found my way back to the mural near the entrance to the island. She was concerned about me, but I assured her that it'd be fine.

I spent my time sitting and staring at the trinkets the woman was holding in her hands. For some reason, they reminded me of all the fading dreams I had that I still couldn't remember.

After staring at the crystal for a while, a glow began shining through my coat. My grimoire was shining bright red. I sat it on the ground and opened it. Every page was glowing, but one was brighter than the others. The glow brightened until I attempted to read it. It was one of the pages I couldn't read before. The words became tangible, and I gained meaning from the symbols. The more I read it over and over again, the more I felt like something was going to happen until it finally did.

A small red sphere formed over the book, and smaller particles formed around it until it culminated into a small red crystal. It looked the same as the one in the mural. The book stopped glowing and I could no longer read or remember the spell after that. Putting the new crystal next to the one in the mural, they were exactly the same.

"No way," I said. "I can't be that important."

"Believe it." Rachel was behind me on a bench. It seemed that she'd been there a while.

"So, you reconsidered my offer for a date, or am I still too young for you?" I put my grimoire back into my pocket.

"If you are who I think you are, then I might be too young for you instead of the other way around. Besides, I heard you gave my idiot son a lot of trouble a while back."

"What makes you so sure it was me?"

"I can't think of many others who'd leave him alive."

"That's pretty specific insight." I shrugged. "Well, if it *was* me, if I knew he was your kid, I would have done more to find out what he was made of."

"You may yet just get that date." She crossed her legs.

"Is that a yes?" I wasn't particularly opportunistic, but I like to believe my smile said otherwise.

"If you win this tournament, I'll consider it. I want to see what you're really made of."

With a scoff, I said, "Who do you think I am, by the way?" before standing.

"Some legendary corpse hunter who defeated an all-powerful warlord over half a century ago. That sound about right?" Her laid-back tone didn't give her away as a liar.

"Oh, is that so?" I turned around to face her.

"Yeah, my mother told me all about it when I was a kid. That's her right there by the way." She was pointing at the mural.

"Faramosa... That's your mom. I don't see the resemblance."

"Yeah, I take after my dad. She founded this place and ran it before she died. Her second in command took over shortly after and turned it into this. I was away at the time, so I had no say in anything, and it was too late by the time I came back."

"I'm sorry to hear that. Was that why you were pissed to find out that your son joined the organization?"

"Damn right. I took in that orphan. I warned him specifically about those people and he still found his way here... Who the hell am I kidding? I might've never joined those guys, but with the amount of jobs I did for them... I might as well have. That's how I got this scar on my face." The scar in question was across the bridge of her nose in a jagged crescent shape. "It's what I got for trusting people."

Sitting next to her, I said, "That's pretty unusual to divulge to someone when you're not at a bar." I looked around at our empty surroundings. "I don't see a bartender."

She chuckled. "It's not all that much. Besides, I thought you wanted to get to know me better."

I shrugged. "Well, I'm prone to blindly trusting people myself, so I would be in the same position if I didn't know any better."

She sighed. "I *did* know better." She sighed again.

"Well, do you want to talk about it?"

She smiled and the conversation continued until well after sundown. We then parted ways.

The next day, I awoke to Ariel handing me a letter with my name on it. It read "TOURNAMENT RULES" and listed off a set of rules and restrictions, as well as exceptions for the tournament as it proceeded.

To make things interesting, the rules stated that during the first round, only basic and intermediary spells were allowed as well as any natural abilities regardless of perceived rank. There were also restrictions for specific types of magic. Only minor and moderate enchantments, mild curses, and humble and familiar summons were allowed. Even wielder's weapons couldn't be evolved to their second stage.

I read the letter and clinched my other fist. It was shaping up to be a fun event.

We all made the trek to the colosseum, where Doc and I were shown back toward the front rows. After maybe forty minutes, Geist appeared on the screen. This time, he was calling for attention and then explaining the basic rules and restrictions of the tournament in a visual format. Noah and Catt found and joined us before the presentation ended.

"So, how you two doin'?" I asked, "Do anything special?"

Noah squinted at me. "There's a joke in there somewhere... Isn't it?"

I shook my head. "You'll never know."

"Noah," said Catt, "You're first." Looking back at the screen, we could see Noah's name next to someone named Mortimer. Noah stood to his feet and found his way to the space between the isles and onto a small marker that indicated a teleportation pad. There was a small popping sound, and he was gone.

About five minutes later, the gates on either side of the field opened and Noah entered through one side while another figure entered through the other side. He wore a jet-black, broad-brimmed, pointed hat and a shadowy cloak. The epitome of a black mage in faery tales. They both stepped toward the middle and shook hands as was written in the letter. The black mage said something, and Noah nodded and responded before they walked back away from each other. The screen counted down from three and the battle began.

The mage pulled down their hat in the front, and it morphed into a hood on the cloak. They then stretched out one arm, and a disk flew out from their wrist.

Noah dodged it on what looked like pure reflex, and it made a small hole in the ground where it hit. His ranged training with Leuna was already paying off.

The mage shot two more times, and Noah dodged them both by running toward them in a circular pattern.

He was fast enough to continue dodging, even when he had to change direction to avoid getting hit. Once Noah was close enough, he grabbed the arm that they were shooting from and aimed it away from himself.

Before he could do anything else, they aimed the other arm at him and he grabbed that one with his other hand, then he put both of his feet on theirs and headbutted them.

The hood flew back, revealing nothing. The clothes were empty.

Noah hadn't noticed that when the mage pulled on their hat, they stepped backward and phased out of their clothes. They then cast an invisibility spell on themselves and waited.

The invisibility dropped and there stood a red-haired man in a gray short-sleeve and black shorts aiming two wrist shooters at Noah. Next to him appeared a nearly ten-foot skeletal giant oozing negative energy. It seemed to be composed of vengeful spirits.

The man was likely a witch, and that was a portion of the being he was linked to by contract. This kind of creature would normally be immune to physical attacks of all kinds, but it could be purified, and Noah was perfect for that job.

The man started shooting again, and the skeleton bound forward. Noah dodged the shots and summoned his sword. Next, he cut the skeleton in half and then stabbed it through its skull once it fell. It disappeared in a white light.

The other guy seemed to panic a bit and calm back down. His shooter began glowing darkly as he began shooting more at the ground all around. He was creating a mana field to turn the battle in his favor.

Noah took heed and rushed at him before a wall of darkness rose to block his path. Instead of cutting it down, he jumped over it and was met with another giant skeleton.

Around five materialized from the ground. The one in front raked at him.

Noah blocked it with the flat of his sword and was knocked to the ground. Standing back up, he traced his hand across his blade, and it began to glow.

The other four skeletons started moving toward him around the wall. Each of them reached into the darkened ground, pulled out a club-shaped lump of earth, and began swinging.

Noah retreated and readied his sword. The first one to reach him tried to slam its club down on him to find it cut in half as well as itself. It fell with a white light escaping it. He cut through the other three as well.

Instead of staying down, they reformed and stood back up. The white light turned to a gray fog, then into a black smoke, and stopped. They were being fed darkness through the ground, which nullified Noah's purifying.

He backed off farther from the skeletons, stuck his blade into the ground, and cast the spell one more time. It made a wide circle in the darkness but didn't purify the entire area. The other guy was saying something as he sat down, pulled out a small ordinary book, and began to read.

The skeletons got to Noah, and he was forced to retreat further. The spot that was purified turned back to a near pitch-black. Noah stood back further and inspected his surroundings. The entire field had turned black, and he was being descended upon by four gashadokuro.

He took a hard look at his sword and stabbed it into the ground again. This time, instead of purifying anything, he began absorbing it. The darkness began fading from the ground and Noah's sword inverted.

It took the guy a few seconds to realize what was happening. When he did, he put his book up and began another summoning spell.

The next skeleton to attack was swiped in half and the air around Noah darkened. He was overflowing with energy. He cut down the rest of the skeletons and moved on to the one protecting the mage in seconds, absorbing all of their energy before going for their creator.

The man was scrambling to cast a spell when Noah tapped his shoulder with his white sword.

The man put his hands up in defeat and fight was over. The screen changed to show it. Noah's name went up on the bracket. He sent his sword away, walked straight back toward the gate, and left. His opponent did the same after retrieving his clothes. A minute later, Noah appeared back on the teleportation sigil and came back to sit with our group.

"That was definitely something," said Noah, sitting down.

"You did a good job, I'm proud of you," said Catt, punching his arm.

"Uh… Thanks." He responded.

"Now I don't have to worry about protecting you all the time."

"That goes for both of us." The next match that showed up on the screen struck a chord with Catt and Noah. "Look, isn't that Hinata's granddaughter?" He was pointing at the screen.

"She has a granddaughter?" I asked.

"Yeah, we met her in Magnolia. Her name's Belle. It looks like she's going up against someone named Kim."

"Looks like a girl fight. Unless Kim is a Korean dood."

"I guess we'll just have to wait and see," said Doc.

"I can't wait to see how she fights," said Catt, "She doesn't seem like the combative type though."

After a couple of minutes, the gates opened again, and two new figures emerged. Neither of them looked female. One looked like a short man in brown armor with deep blue plating and a matching helmet. The other was obviously a guy around seven feet in blue jeans and a dark green jacket. He was so big; it was a wonder why I didn't see him earlier.

"Neither of those people look like the tiny girl that we met," said Noah.

"The short one could be her. They're wearing full armor," said Catt. "She seemed smart enough to have something like that prepared. After all, she did look a little too squishy for direct combat like this."

"That could be, but the chest plate isn't shaped for a girl," said Noah as the two combatants came to shake hands. The smaller one had to tilt their head all the way back to see eye to eye with the larger one.

Once they moved back away from each other, the timer started from three again and the fight started.

The smaller one jumped into the air, wings appeared on their back, and they began flying. The wings were a wielder's weapon and looked like wind chimes. They were blue diamond-shaped shards dangling from a thin blue frame on their back and each of the two wings had about five shards dangling from them. They began flying over the large man while shooting the shards in a rapid-fire fashion.

All the shards were blocked and shattered by a single forearm. This went on for about thirty seconds. Every time they shot a shard, it was replaced quickly. With every other shot, they gained speed, a common strategy for ranged types.

Eventually, the big guy swung his arm to knock back the shards and counter his attacker. The flying one took the opportunity for a dive kick with a gust of wind behind it. The guy was unguarded, at least, that's what it seemed like. They struck fast, but they weren't fast enough. Their entire torso was caught in one hand. Wings included.

The big guy started talking but the smaller one was struggling too much, so he squeezed them, and they stopped. The big guy then continued talking. After he was finished, the small one shook their head and said something back. What happened next clicked something in my mind.

The big guy quickly tossed the smaller one into the air. In doing so, they flew so fast that all the shards on the wings broke off and fell without direction. Before any of them could regenerate, the large guy jumped to meet them nearly twenty feet in the air.

I came to some type of realization that I didn't understand as he grabbed them and fell to the earth with them in his grasp. Noah and Catt winced as he landed, and his arm swept the other person close enough to the ground to kick more dust than had been already.

The large man began speaking again.

"They need to give up," I said, shifting in my seat.

"What? No, she can't just give up like that," said Noah.

"Yeah, she could turn this around at any second. If she gets thrown in the air again, she can just fly away." Catt agreed.

"No," I said," I feel like I've seen this exact scenario before. They need to give up now or it won't end pretty."

My suspicion was confirmed with the small person struggling some more while speaking in response. The man then turned and circle-tossed them around a hundred feet into the air in under a second. He followed up by jumping to meet them for the descent.

"Say goodbye!" The coarse voice of the larger man was heard clearly over the roaring crowd, followed by a scream and the boom of a crater being made.

The match ended there. The one still in the hole stayed unconscious as a new timer counted down from thirty to zero.

Afterward, the name 'Belle' was shown going up in the brackets. Shortly after, two medical personnel came out to the field with a gurney and carried away the loser. Once everyone was out of the field, it reformed itself to get rid of the crater. It did so after every match in which the field itself was affected.

"So, neither of them was her?" Catt sounded disappointed.

The next couple of names that came up were me and Nail.

"I'm up, let's go!" I stood and made my way to the small marker. "This is gonna be fun." Everything in my sight shifted as I was teleported. I was now in a white room with one exit. The door had a sign that read *'preparation room'*. There was also a blue chair and an empty shelf with a sign to leave overly enchanted items behind. The only thing I carried that was enchanted at the time was my cloak, and it only provided minor elemental resistance.

After a few minutes of sitting in the chair, a man in a yellow uniform walked in to escort me to the field. It was a ten-second walk to the gate. It opened a few seconds later and I walked to the middle of the field and toward my opponent. He had dark skin, ear length straight, black hair with red highlights, and wore a red elbow sleeve shirt with ***"DEVIL"*** written in bold, black italics and darker red pants of unknown material. He reached his hand out and smiled. I shook it.

After we shook, he said, "I heard you took down that serial killer yesterday without getting hurt or getting someone killed. You must be really skilled."

I shrugged. "Not particularly. I just didn't want anybody to die. Enough killing happens outside these events already."

"If you can do something like that then, I won't hold back."

"Please, don't." I was walking backward, and a line appeared in front of me. I stopped and looked back up at Nail. I was shaking with excitement. This was a fight for fun and a test of my abilities, nothing to do with the usual grim dark world outside of a flowery tournament. I was eager to get it started.

The timer came back up on the screen and counted down from three. As soon as it ended, I rushed at him.

I kicked up loose dirt behind me in the first step, delaying my start. I found myself going at half speed from my miss-start. He reached into the air, a sword appeared in his hand, and he threw it at me. It looked like it was made of raw elements like melted stone or lava rock and sharpened to a point.

I summoned my own sword and knocked it to the side as I continued my assault.

He summoned one more sword in each hand before I got to him and blocked my strike. It was a simple tactic, but an effective one. He was on the defensive.

Keeping the pressure on, I pushed him harder. He brought up his knee toward me and I brought up mine to counter and grounded his foot by stepping on it. Doing so meant that I had to let up my pressure a bit.

He took the opportunity to move one of his blades from under my sword and swipe at me from the side. I moved my blade to block that one one-handedly and attempted to knock the other blade away with my other bare hand.

I succeeded in blocking the strike, but when I went to knock the other one away, instead of just knocking it away; It shattered when I hit it with the back of my fist. Based on the surprise on his face; he wasn't expecting that. I wasn't either but I still took the opportunity to do damage.

I caught him with a solid left in the face. He rocked back, but my foot was still keeping him in place. Before the next one came, he had dropped the remnants of his sword and hit me with a fireball. It pushed me back and nothing else.

"I guess I gotta up the ante. ***Burn***." He summoned another sword and cast the spell on both of them. They flickered red and began glowing.

To use an attack spell like that as an enchantment meant he was a summoner or an enchanter. Either way, it didn't matter. I just had to beat him.

"So, are we just going to be using fire?" I conjured a fireball into my hand and smiled. I threw it at him, and he cut it with one of his blades. "Because I'm not against testing out whose is hotter."

"Good point," he said, stomping the ground. "***Rock toss***." a boulder about the size of a van popped out of the ground and flew at me. Normally, earth has a slight advantage over fire. This time, however, the fire had wind feeding it.

"***Burning touch***." I had coated my hands in flames and jumped to meet the rock. It was coming at an angle and I had to change my positioning to make a straight line to him. "***Gust***." I used the spell to fan my flames onto the rock and send it back at twice the speed. I cast 'push' silently so as not to give away my plan as I rocketed behind it.

He cut into and broke the boulder in half. When he saw me close behind it, he tried to block with the bladed side of his swords.

His defense meant nothing to me. I brought down my fist and shattered both blades before making contact with his face again. I figured another hit like the first one would put him down, but I was wrong.

Something hit my chest hard. It was his fist. Whatever power he was holding back, he used to hit me. He couldn't pull that punch or else, he'd likely have been knocked out.

I lost all of my breath, and my lungs began to sting. I flew over his head and landed on my back. He was wobbling on his feet while I regained my breath.

"What happened to not holding back?" I asked, getting to my feet.

"You're right," he said, as the ground began shaking and energy began to flow out of him at an alarming rate. "***Lava flow***." The ground exploded and lava flew everywhere with enough force to toss me into the air. Molten rock cascaded over the entire field, and me as well. This was unexpected, but I went with the flow.

"***Fire tornado***." A wind kicked up, and a tornado coated in the flames of the lava cut through the sky and freed up space around me. Finding myself still in the air, I turned toward my target. "***Dragon strife***." Coating myself in draconic wind, I jettisoned myself straight at him as fast as I could, leaving behind green scales that dissipated as they fell.

He watched me fly into him at full speed and didn't react. It was either because he wasn't expecting it, or maybe it was something else. Either way, it seemed like I knocked him out of the sky as I carried him through the lava covered ground and into a new crater. As soon as I could, I moved away from him in case he awakened with a counterattack. Instead, he uttered a single sentence.

"That's enough, I give up."

"Really?" I said, surprised.

"I can't go any farther than this without breaking any rules and I don't want this battle to be drawn out, so I give up."

"I really wanted to keep this going."

"We can finish this fight later. It's a double elimination, remember?"

"I never really paid attention. Need help?" I reached my hand out to him.

"No, but I'll take it." He accepted my hand and I helped him up.

"Because I like you, I want you to take this." He reached his hand to his head and pulled out a small reddish-brown bubble from his temple. "It's a spell, take it. Not many people can make me resort to attacks like that."

"What spell?"

"It's a ranged spell that I doubt that you'd know already. It's called 'ballistic fragment'. Its primarily earth based but works well with lava and in turn, fire."

"Alright, I'll give you one too. I reached to my temple, cast 'mind bubble' and pulled out a green bubble of my own. "It's the spell 'fierce roar'. It can throw off your opponent and lower their defenses from a distance. It works fine with any attunement and can be used as a blueprint for the creation of new spells."

"Fine, then it's a deal." We both took out our grimoires and opened them to blank pages. His was jet-black with red streaks running through it with a deformed crucifix in the center.

We dropped the bubbles into each other's grimoire. Words and symbols appeared that I vaguely understood. In time, I came to understand them and was able to cast the spell at will.

We went our separate ways and after a couple of minute of being examined by a doctor, I was teleported back to the marker I stepped up to initially.

"That was awesome," I said, sitting down.

"So, what happened at the end there?" asked Noah.

"We exchanged spells."

"What spell did he give you?" asked Doc.

"'ballistic fragment' and I gave him 'fierce roar'."

The next couple of names that came up were Sofia and Mary.

"Let's hope this one's actually a cat fight," I said, turning to Noah. "So, if your sister is here, what will you do?"

"I'll find a way to talk to her."

"If you need any help with that, let me know."

"Will do." He nodded, seemingly nervous.

A few minutes later, two people entered the field. One was a girl who was sitting near us. She was petite with medium length blonde hair and wore a black combat suit complete with metal knuckles and boots. She had a reflective silver sword and shield on her back. She was taking notes on what was happening on the field with a notepad that seemed to be slightly burnt after my battle. When I asked her if I could help with it, she scoffed at me. The other girl had long brown hair tied into pigtails and wore a white combat skirt with matching boots and top.

"That's her," said Noah, pointing at the one in white.

"Alright, let's see how this goes down." I sat back in my seat.

After the handshake and the countdown, the battle started. Mary summoned her weapon. There was a faint white glow around her wrists and a bow and arrow appeared in her hands as she drew back and shot.

"That's an interesting weapon she's got." commented Doc.

"It looks like her weapon is a set of bracelet bands." Said Noah "They probably create constructs based on her own imagination. My mom and one of my older brothers had similar abilities except theirs was a necklace and a chain, respectively."

"That's a unique weapon type indeed."

The fight continued as Sofia pulled out her shield and reflected the arrow back. It was dodged and Mary shot two more arrows. One up and one forward. She waited until the one she shot upward began to fall before shooting the other one.

That's when Sofia made her move. She rushed forward after taking out her sword and reflecting the arrow. She avoided the one from above and countered the one in front. This, however, seemed to be Mary's plan. She and the falling arrow switched places, and a sword constructed by her passed through the back of her opponent.

Killing was against the rules, but more than enough of the audience seemed to be shocked. Mary leaned in and whispered something, and Sofia dropped her weapons.

It was a quick end to a quick match. She removed her sword and Sofia patted down her midsection. After a sigh of relief, she hung her head low, picked up her weapons and left the arena. Mary moved up the brackets and a few minutes later, the next couple of names came up. Cattherine and Anatoly.

"You're up." Noah patted Catt on the back.

"Yeah, I got this." She got up and moved to the marker. A few minutes later, she entered the field with another person. The other person was a large man with a shaved head and a large black orbed staff in a gray trench coat.

As soon as the match started, his entire body became surrounded in flames and the orb in his staff turned red. As this happened, small, orange and red faery-like creatures began appearing out of embers in the air. He was definitely a summoner.

Tilting his staff forward, he shot a fireball and the faery creatures followed close behind. Catt created a wall of water in front of her to block it. Before the fire could hit the wall, the fairies caught up with it and converged upon it.

Out of that convergence came an ifrit. It was red with curved horns and sharp teeth with large butterfly wings. It towered over the wall that was a little over Catt's height.

It brought its arm down, shattering the wall. She dodged the blow and retaliated. She sent a solid punch right through it. Steam erupted as the aqua bubble surrounding her fist fizzled away. Her hand was stuck inside of the beast and no matter how hard she pulled, she couldn't set herself free.

Anatoly was behind the ifrit in a few seconds with his staff held high above his head. He swung it down through the ifrit and before Catt could block it properly; it landed squarely at the top of her head.

The blow didn't seem to faze her as she grabbed the staff and attempted to free herself with it. It caught fire and seemed to singe her fingers before she let go.

Next, the ifrit leaned down and transformed into a fire bubble around her. Catt's biggest weakness had come into full effect. She was immobile. Most people would've given up at that point, but she didn't.

Her hand was free, but she was surrounded by fire. She tried casting 'aqua barrier' to shield herself from the flames, but the spell just evaporated in seconds.

Anatoly said something to her, and she responded by punching the barrier. It began shrinking and her attempts became more frantic. It soon became too small for her to stand, so she sat.

Licked by the flames, she meditated as her opponent watched on. It stopped shrinking after it became small enough that it just surrounded her in her sitting position; he said something else to her, and she didn't respond. She was still concentrating.

He quickly grew impatient and began attacking with his staff once again. He didn't hit her, just the barrier however, every contact he made with the flames seemed to affect Catt directly.

He hit one side of the barrier and she slammed into the other side while holding her ribs, breaking her concentration. As this happened, more tiny ifrits appeared from the embers trailed by his staff and phased into the bubble, fueling the flames, and making them stronger. Whatever those attacks were, she had no way of defending against them. She went back to meditation and toughed her way through the numerous impacts and the steadily increasing temperature of the burning flames.

Another decisive strike came down at the top and was caught by Catt's hand. Her hair was now a solid red and yellow mix, the same as the flames surrounding her. She stood up through the flames and punched him so hard that he bounced up a bit and was forced to let go of the staff. She then made a mad dash for him, punched him a few more times, finishing it with an uppercut that sent him into the air and another punch that sent him maybe ten feet away. All while coated in flames. The best part was that each time she made contact, tiny red and yellow birds formed from the embers and chased after where she made impact.

Getting up, he called back his staff, but Catt caught it as it zoomed past her. She cast 'nullify' on it and threw it to the side. The red glow it once had now faded.

She rushed at him again, fist at the ready. He created a bubble shield around himself for protection, but it failed when her punch phased straight through it. His face hit her fist then, the ground.

He pulled a stone out of one of his pockets and held it up. A shield of a brighter flame surrounded him. He had summoned power from a different being. This one must have been stronger than the last because it pushed back Catt on creation. This didn't last long, however, because her arms began faintly glowing. She had cast a strength spell on herself and in a couple of hits, shattered the shield. She then brutalized his face until he gave up.

"She just kept punching his face until he gave up," said Noah after a relieved sigh.

"Don't expect your opponent to hold back," responded Doc. "He did, and that was his downfall."

"If Ariel or Carona entered, you'd see worse melee carnage than that," I said, shaking my head.

"Women are scary," continued Noah.

"That's a good thing. It keeps guys like us in line," laughed Doc.

"I never thought you *could* laugh. I'm not sure whether to laugh with you or be scared."

Laughing as well, I said, "You've been traveling with one this whole time and you haven't noticed?"

"You'll be fine kid, just take it slow," Doc reassured him.

A few minutes later, Catt returned.

"Are you okay?" Noah was clearly worried. Catt's clothes were mostly singed, and some parts were burnt off entirely. Both of her hands were bandaged as well as most of her body and as she approached, her knees buckled, and she nearly fell with blood newly trickling down her face.

Absent-mindedly, she said, "I thought they tried to do what they could with the time they had, and I felt fine when I left. I dunno what happened."

"Sit tight ok, I'll take care of you. *Sacred healing*." He sat her down and put his hands over her head as a white light crept across her temple.

"I'll help with the burns," I said, putting my hands over one of her arms, "*Soothe*." The swelling wasn't super apparent at first, but she shrank by half of her size by the time I got to each limb. "This spell won't last long, so we need to get her to Carona as quickly as possible."

"Can you stand?" he asked.

"Yes," she responded.

"Damn, that's what you look like up close, and you won?" It was Sophia who now had a blade shaped slit in the front and back of her suit. "I'm not surprised. Those guys are only concerned with making sure you can walk on your own. Other than that, they don't care."

"I'm not surprised," Doc and I said at the same time.

"I can help with that by the way." Sofia reached into a pocket and pulled out a talisman. It was blank aside for three lines at each corner. "This should last for a day. *Ameliorate*." The lines turned pink as she laid the talisman on Catt's chest.

After a moment, Catt perked up and looked around. "I feel so much better." Right after she said that she gagged a bit and spit out a small object. "I need water. What is this?"

"Let me see," said Doc, holding his hand out. She handed him a small, red, shimmering stone. It was slightly translucent and shaped like a creature's claw on one side and a feather on the other. "This is interesting." He held it up to the light and his fingertips caught fire. He quickly dropped it into his other hand and blew out the flames in one breath. "It's an ifrit's summon stone. I suggest activating this for the first time in private." He passed it back to her. "It came out of you, which could mean one of a few things. Either the stone contains your essence, or you were gifted the essence of an ifrit because you tapped into the power of one."

"What does that mean?" She asked.

"I don't know," he said, "That's up to you to find out."

The next match was between someone named Edna and Shane. One was a girl with short, light brown hair and pasty skin in a navy-blue school uniform and the other was a guy with ear length black hair and light skin in a long sleeve blue sweatshirt and white jeans.

As soon as the match started, the ground within the entire arena froze. The ice was knee deep and cold enough for the audience to feel. So much energy was put into the spell that it began snowing.

"Whoa...," said Catt. She, Noah, and I began shivering. I let off some heat to warm everybody back up. This caused a steam cloud to form over our heads. There were clouds floating above multiple parts of the stands and some of them began raining which, thankfully, ours didn't.

Back in the match, the girl tried to move her legs and failed miserably as the guy walked calmly toward her through the ice as if it was soft snow. She reached into a pocket and pulled out a small stack of cards, throwing one.

He threw it back after catching it. She caught it back and threw three more while letting one fall behind her back. One card landed directly in front of the guy and the other two landed on either side of him. Out of the cards sprang gargoyles of varying shapes. All of them were made of some type of earthen material of slightly different shades of gray, but the one to his right was shaped like a griffon and was generating wind, the one on his left was a winged snake generating electricity and in front of him was a rounded creature with one big eye.

As he continued to walk forward, it morphed into a wall, blocking his path. Before he reached it, both the snake and griffon began glowing blue and green respectively with their mouths open before shooting charged blasts of elemental energy. Small chunks of ice flew into the air and before they settled back to the ground, all three gargoyles were frozen solid.

He then walked into the wall in front of him and shattered a person sized hole into it in the process. As he neared his target, she threw another card at him and this time, he ripped it in half and threw the pieces away when he caught it. That gave her the opportunity to let the dragon gargoyle that was melting the ice behind her jump at the guy.

He tried to freeze it in place, but it exploded in flames, forcing him to back down. The girl escaped out of the ice, leaving behind her shoes, socks, and skirt but maintaining her black shorts and held another card up to her chest.

The dragon dove into her, and they merged. Her arms, legs, and torso were covered in the gray earth and resembling draconic armor, while a mask of a dragon's face sat on top of her own and a twenty-foot wingspan appeared on her back.

The wings barely got her ten feet off the ice before she was met with an ice ball, which knocked her out of the sky. She stood up quickly to be met with a damaging gut punch. She fell to her knees as the armor broke away and as this happened; the guy tapped the ice, and it all disappeared. That caused her feet to hit the ground before the weight of her fall could completely register on her body. He then placed his hand on her head, and she turned blue.

In a second, she snapped back to reality and grabbed his arm, attempting to put him in a hold. She lifted both of her feet off of the ground and attempted a kimura lock to little effect. This lasted for a few seconds until she gave up and began screaming while trying to pry his hand away while the rest of her body went limp.

He said something to her and she screamed something about giving up before he let go.

The name "Shane" went up in the brackets.

Catt had fallen asleep between matches and Noah decided to stay and take care of her instead of going to find his sister and citing that he could always find her later.

The next names to show up were Einn and Sean. One was another giant man near seven feet with spiraling orange hair that draped down his back and a beard to match. He wore a white tank top and dress pants, which seemed to be bursting at the seams with pure muscle. The other was of average height with short blonde hair and wore a black turtleneck and slacks.

The match started with the larger guy taking steady steps toward his opponent, who didn't move until he came within ten feet of him. That's when the smaller guy stretched out his arm and out came a laser.

The blast was large, but most of it was deferred around its target. The force of the blow still pushed the man back a few paces, but he seemed largely unaffected. Instead, he seemed to actually move faster.

As he came within reach, the smaller guy's arm started glowing and in the last second a bright flash came out and blinded most of the audience. The sight was accompanied by the sound of a shattering pane of glass.

Between the flash and the sound, I caught a glimpse of a weapon in the smaller man's hands and in mid-swing. It was a crescent blade seated on a square frame that seemed to serve as a handle. As quickly as I saw it, it was gone.

As soon as the flash subsided, the larger man could be seen laying down with a tattered shirt in a groove made from him sliding across the ground.

He stood surprisingly fast only to be met with another laser and this time; it carried him into the closed entrance that he came through and embedded him into the door. He couldn't get unstuck thanks to a binding spell that was placed on him at the same time and was counted out.

The name "Einn" went up in the brackets.

After both fighters left the field, the words "30min INTERMISSION" popped up on the screen and Geist's accompanying voice confirmed it. He also said for anybody still in need of medical aid to report to the medical personnel in the facilities located next to the bathroom and repeated it three times every ten minutes.

Doc and I took the opportunity to find where the rest of our group were sitting. It turned out that they were six rows behind us. They could only see us when we walked into the isle and while in the field, but we couldn't see them at all. Noah and Catt would've been with us, but Catt decided to wander off and Noah went to look for her. They somehow made their way around the entire stadium with ten minutes to spare.

Carona took a look at Catt and determined that she should be fine with some rest and a bit of medicine.

It seemed that the majority of the damage she took had been healed completely. After a needed bathroom break, we found ourselves back at our original positions.

The very next name to come up was Doc's followed by Jonas. Only a few minutes after he sat down, he stood back up. As he walked past, he ruffled my hair and continued to the marker.

A couple minutes later, he entered opposite a man that had dark skin and a long, black beard wearing a red turban and red and yellow robes. When the match started, they stood there staring at each other. This lasted for nearly a minute. Finally, Doc raised his hand and the entire area around himself, and his opponent became shrouded in darkness.

'Dark shroud' was his go-to spell for disorienting his opponents and disguising himself. Less than a second later, Jonas came backing out of what looked like solid black smoke with two chakrams in each hand. The chakrams were three-pronged and bladed completely around with red accents. He threw half of them into the inky blackness and the other half; he held at the ready.

The two he threw came back and began rotating around him. After a couple more seconds of nothing, he decided to throw the two still in his hands and the couple surrounding him followed. Multiplying in mid-air, they began moving in a similar pattern to the 'blade wall' spell with flames following each one. As soon as this happened, they were all knocked away in different directions from the center of the cluster.

Where there was nothing now stood Doc with one of the chakrams in hand. He said something and threw it at Jonas, who caught it and threw it back as the rest of the chakrams came back and converged upon Doc. It took less than a second for all of them to reach and fly right through him. His form melted into black smoke and dissipated.

The fake had done its job as the real one was standing beside Jonas with his hand on his throat. Both of them turned near pitch black for a split second and the flying chakrams all fell to the ground. Doc let him go and walked away as the man fell to the ground. The counter started but stopped halfway through.

Jonas had gotten back to his feet. He had been hit so hard with a wither effect that his skin was gray. His fallen weapons spun back to life and converged upon Doc once more. This prompted Doc to send out a single black ball of energy in Jonas' direction.

He tried to dodge it but nearly fell over before colliding with the spell. He and his weapons fell once more. The timer started over and concluded before he could rise again.

When Doc came back, he ruffled my hair again before sitting back down.

"Can you stop that?" I said, trying to smooth my hair back down.

"Nope," He said, ruffling my hair again, "That's my good luck charm."

"It's not like you needed it..." I shook my head aggressively to reset my hair.

The next names up were Anjelica and Lynch.

There was a guy that sat farther away from us that stood and made his way to the nearest marker. His skin was light with short, smooth, brown hair and he wore a green short-sleeved shirt under a gray vest with dark green slacks. As he entered the arena, his opponent did as well. She had short, red hair that was just visible under a brown wide-brimmed hat with a matching tailcoat and pants.

As soon as the match started, the girl pulled a crystal ball out of nowhere and the guy pressed his hand on his chest. He flashed green and made a mad dash straight at her.

She shot a fireball that connected and seemed to slow him down slightly. In retaliation, the green aura returned, and a green fireball exited the glow. It followed the same path the original took to get there except; it turned to meet the one who shot it when she dodged.

Thorns were always difficult to deal with. She began running away but he was gaining on her. While this was happening, her ball began glowing red and intensified until it became blinding. She then stopped and shot a powerful fireball that was twice her size.

The guy ran straight into it and didn't stop until he hit a wall of fire that the girl set up. That didn't stop him either. Instead, a giant green fireball flew straight at the girl and found its mark.

She fell, clutching her left arm with the crystal ball seated in the crux of her right. The guy caught up and sat on top of her chest. What followed was angry yelling from the girl, followed by explosions. Red, then green. The final red explosion came when the girl freed one of her hands and punched the guy with a nearly white-hot supercharged fist. He took the whole impact to his face and returned it in kind.

The timer started almost immediately after. Ten seconds in, her hand shot up, and she said something that caused it to stop. The guy stood and Lynch went up in the brackets.

He reached out a helping hand, but she just laid there, with an arm over her face and a hand reaching toward the sky.

Lynch didn't leave until the medical personnel came to pick up Anjelica.

The next names to come up were Robin and Leon. One guy had spiky dirty blonde hair with an islander complexion in a yellow button up, blue jeans and fingerless gloves. The other guy was dark with black, neatly cut hair, a red shirt with one long and one short sleeve and black pants.

When the match started, the one in red put his hands in front of him and shot a fireball. It missed its target as it dove straight toward the ground halfway and fizzled out. Next, he shot two more to the same outcome.

He took a wide stance and shot one that took the shape of a lightbulb. This one, instead of meeting the ground, dipped down and continued toward its target. It was a magic missile. It came within five feet of its target and exploded as it seemed to meet an invisible barrier.

The red guy took that opportunity to make a dash for his opponent and go around the spot where his attacks failed before any dust could clear up. Summoning a weapon and swinging it down, he was met with so much resistance that he was knocked in the opposite direction.

It was a wielder's weapon and a straight sword with a tapered point and a rectangular cross guard. It looked devoid of detail and kind of blank, as if it hadn't been personalized. He hadn't been a wielder, of any kind, for long.

Landing on his feet, he went for another attack. This time, he was surrounded by a yellow glow before being thrown around thirty feet into the air. Reorienting himself, he charged and shot three more magic missiles before readying his sword to strike down. Two of the attacks hit the invisible barrier before the sound of glass breaking echoed out and the third one made it down.

The guy in yellow hadn't moved the entire time and just watched what was happening until then. He jumped out of the way just before it reached him and it landed at his feet, singeing its surroundings, including him. He seemed to nearly throw off one of his gray tennis shoes in surprise. The red guy was still falling and picking up speed with his sword held over his head and ready to strike. The yellow guy reached into his shirt pocket, pulled out a clear object, put it on his face and looked up at the red guy who began picking up more speed than he should have while being surrounded in a yellow glow again.

Stabbing his sword into the ground, the red guy stopped himself and released a wave of raw flames that spread outward while scorching the earth up to sixty feet away from himself in a circle. The yellow guy jumped before it could reach him and began levitating while keeping his eyes on his opponent, who began sinking into the ground. Struggling halfway to his feet, the red guy shot three more magic missiles that were countered with a big, yellow laser originating from the monocle that the yellow guy was wearing.

The blast wasn't magical, it was a psychic attack. It hit him straight on and he was thrown about five feet away while still sinking into the ground and making a straight line in the process. The timer started and stopped as the yellow guy found himself back on the ground just before the red guy somehow stood back up. His long sleeve was now gone, as well as part of the actual shirt to reveal wrapped bandages across most of his body. It looked like he had been in a serious battle before coming to the tournament.

The yellow guy extended his hand outward and pressed his palm toward the ground. This seemed to increase the pressure on his opponent, but not faze him aside for sinking him into the ground faster. The red guy seemed to start concentrating on his sword before pointing it at the yellow guy who had one hand on his monocle, which began glowing bright yellow.

This was their final standoff. This time, five missiles came from the tip of the red guy's blade and were completely countered again by a narrower laser that hit its mark. Instead of being blasted away this time, he blocked with his blade and held it before back-turning out of the laser sight and throwing his sword.

The rectangular guard struck the yellow guy's throat which caused him to fall back followed by a boot which made him hit the ground. The red guy had teleported to his sword in a wisp of flame. The sword landed next to one side of his neck and a boot landed on the other side with a fireball in front of his face.

The battle ended there, and Leon went up in the brackets.

The next names to come up were Mike and Evgeny. One guy had long, light brown hair and full blue leather armor adorned with the Gaelic word for water on his chest and a seashell necklace. The other guy had short, black hair with a corner of it dyed dark-blue and was wearing a navy-blue cloak.

The match started with the cloaked guy flinging coin sized projectiles. The air coiled around them as they flew, signifying the wind attribute. In response, the armored guy reached to his waist and released what looked like a decorated belt.

With a flick of a wrist, he blocked all the projectiles at once with his whip. As each one fell, they caused miniature concentrated whirlwinds that bore holes into the ground. As the assault continued, he struck the ground with his whip and created a wall of water to block the piercing strikes. He then struck the ground on either side of him and opened two blue, swirling portals. Out of one popped a man with wild, dirty blonde hair, no shirt, and blue shorts, and out of the other came a woman with long, brown hair that nearly met her feet in white robes accented in blue.

The armored man spoke with them briefly before clasping hands with the woman who grew wings and took flight with him as the guy in shorts ran around the quickly diminishing wall toward his target. Seeing this, the robed guy stopped throwing his projectiles and instead, scattered them on the ground around him, creating a tower of wind that was immediately rammed into by the guy in shorts. The barrier seemed not to faze him as he ran into it continuously from different angles, picking up speed until he became more blur than person.

The wind mage was unable to strike him with any direct or scatter shots while this was happening. Above them, the summoner and the woman were conversing before she let him go and dove directly into the ground. He landed and created a bubble shield that deflected the projectiles while he took a seat in a meditative position.

The wind mage began concentrating his fire on the one meditating to little effect. The shield remained unscathed for the majority of the time, and whenever there was a noticeable crack, the caster would just recast the spell before it could break. Between concentrating on keeping up his own barrier and breaking his opponents, the wind mage seemed to be stretched pretty thin. He couldn't charge any single attack, and only focusing on defense was unlikely to change anything.

This situation lasted for almost five minutes until the winged woman came spiraling out of the ground surrounded by a geyser of water. In seconds, the water was waist deep and in a minute; it was too deep to stand. The woman's feet were replaced with a tail fin and the shorts guy came from running to swimming with one too.

Both main combatants were still dry. Over time, that began to change. Water was entering through the cracks in the wind barrier, and it was rapidly filling it up. He was forced to drop the spell when he couldn't hold his breath any longer and jettisoned himself out of the water in a column of wind.

The merman leaped up and missed his target before the winged mermaid tried from the air, only to find a projectile in her chest before falling to the waves below. The summoner perked up when this happened.

He had begun to glow green from the amount of energy he was stockpiling before dropping his bubble and pushing both of his palms toward his opponent as the water crashed upon him. At the same time, the wind mage began levitating while charging and releasing two projectiles that carried a swirling mass of smaller projectiles behind each one.

The attacks reached halfway to the water as the surface began rippling and an upward current formed and met them. There were a couple of small flashes and the water swallowed both of them before impacting the one who sent them.

He was knocked out of the air and dragged into the water. Two more flashes went off and his opponent was sent quickly flying about ten feet back through the water before slowly floating in place. I had to lean forward in my seat when the merman transformed into a horse with a large fin for a tail and a dorsal fin for a mane. I had heard of; and even met a kelpie, but this was not one. As far as I know, kelpies can't transform into humans.

He quickly raced at blinding speeds to the wind mage and seemed to adhere to him while dragging him, struggling, deeper into the water until he slammed him into the ground, forcing the air out of his lungs. The winged mermaid took a moment, but trailing blood from her chest, she swam to the also bleeding water mage and darted to the surface with him before taking flight with him in her arms.

Two separate timers started. One from when the summoner was knocked out in the water, and one when the water horse grabbed the wind mage and swam down. While trying to resuscitate her summoner mid-air, the winged mermaid began glowing bright blue; as did the water horse and in seconds, they both disappeared in a flurry of particles. The wind mage floated to the surface and the water mage fell back into his own element as the water drained back out on its own, leaving them both motionless on the drenched earth.

Not long after, the summoner reached one hand upward and grabbed his other arm. It was bleeding badly and there was a hole in his chest plate. A few seconds later, his opponent coughed up water and failed at attempting to sit up. He was drained of energy and couldn't even lift himself. Both timers continued until the summoner struggled and limped to his feet.

Ten seconds later, Mike went up in the brackets and he limped out of the field.

Two more names came up in due time. They were Riolu and Phenom. One of them had medium-length light brown hair with light green highlights in a ponytail and wore a brown fur jacket and white half-shirt with a sword and shield printed on it and black ripped jeans. The other had short, black hair and wore a full-body purple combat outfit lined with bits of chain mail over the joints and purple goggles.

The match started with both of them shooting a ranged spell. The ponytail girl stomped the ground, a head sized piece of earth rose in front of her, and she punched it forward. The purple girl put her hands together and shot a purple ball of energy with a short trail behind it.

When they collided, the purple energy eroded the rock while they both fell to the ground to form a smoldering, poisonous puddle.

The earth mage reached into the air. In a flash, a small axe appeared in her hand. The poison mage reached behind her back and pulled out a black quarterstaff decorated with a purple spiral from the base to the silver spider that adorned the top. Neither was a wielder's weapon.

The earth mage threw the axe while ducking and running around her opponent counterclockwise in the same move. The axe was matched with an acid ball from the end of the spider staff that was followed by three more going clockwise while the earth mage stayed low, etching a circle into the ground with a newly summoned hand axe.

Before the circle was completed, the task of avoiding the poison projectiles came first. She achieved this without breaking stride by putting her hand out and forcing the surrounding ground to part so that she could bypass the ranged assault above her head and finish the circle. Upon its completion, whatever illusion that was held seemed to disappear because the poison mage took notice and snapped toward her opponent, who had just stopped and stood back up.

Realizing she had been fooled, the poison mage readied her staff and let loose a ball that looked to be surrounded by rotating blades. The earth mage quickly took her axe to her hand and pressed the blood onto the ground, completing the ritual she set up. The ground following the line on all sides rose to meet the blast, but it dove over and continued until it was finally stopped by a spear summoned and thrown by the earth mage. It struck through and carried the magic missile into the ground where it dissipated, leaving a half-eaten pole staked into the melted dirt.

Upon seeing her surroundings rise around her, the poison mage raised her staff and began firing shots off in every direction. The walls remained relatively unscathed as they steadily rose higher until they reached about twenty feet on all sides. She stopped shooting and took the opportunity to sit and concentrate with her staff at her back until the ground began to rise around her.

She stood and was surrounded as if she was in quicksand. It didn't happen very fast, but it seemed to surprise her when she couldn't move her feet or her staff. Struggling, she tried hitting the rising earth with blasts from her palms, channeling energy through her staff, which was already nearly buried, to no effect, and even beating it with her fists. All of this came to a head as she took a deep breath just before being buried herself. The timer started as the earth rose to create an egg-shaped dome over the walls.

Before it could reach zero, however, half of the entire dome changed from light brown to deep purple. From it, emerged the woman, dripping with poison. In front of her, stood a large, silver spider that was once a quarter of the size and sitting on a staff. It was moving and reacting like a living creature, which either meant that it was the result of an enchantment or that it was a familiar.

The earth mage stepped back until she was near the arena wall and began charging a spell with her hands on the ground again while her opponent stepped off of the failed trap. It seemed like she was using her own blood as a catalyst since the ground took a slightly reddened tone in front of her.

The poison mage took this opportunity to pick up her spider and kiss it on its head. It then turned around in her arms and the silver coating melted off and a solid purple spider with glowing red eyes could be seen with both it and its master glowing purple before it shot a jet of purple venom from its mouth straight at their opponent. The earth mage pulled from the ground a solid chunk of what looked like light red marble in the shape of an axe and threw it using her entire weight as well as a thin trail of earth rising behind it.

The attacks collided and stalemated with both combatants remaining stationary. The earth mage fell to her knees, unable to move, and the poison mage stayed in place because of her spell. It seemed as if the poison would erode the stone before the realization that the trail of earth continued past the projectile hit everyone at once.

Before anyone knew it, the poison mage was on her side on the ground, motionless. She had been hit directly between the legs. She bounced straight up and to the side before she reacted. As far as I could tell, everybody collectively winced except for her. Her attack was interrupted, and her spider shrank back to its original size and color, also immobile.

The axe that was flying in her direction continued until it passed by and landed into the ground before melting into sand. The timer started. Ten seconds later, she reacted. First, rolling around holding herself and kicking her feet with the most pained expression I had ever seen on a woman. Then, she found herself on her knees while shouting loud enough to be clearly heard and digging into the ground with the side of her fist. Finally, she stood with wobbly knees and walked with a hard limp. Grabbing her quarterstaff without the spider. Using it as a crutch, she meandered toward her immobile opponent.

Using what was left of the reddened soil, the earth mage created a smaller axe with a longer handle and used it to push her way back to her feet. Using what strength she had left, she took a step forward and brought the axe down on a wide, overhead swing. It was blocked with the quarterstaff, but was followed up with a kick to the gut

The poison mage was slightly staggered, but also enraged. She retaliated by pushing both weapons aside and delivering a solid headbutt that knocked the earth mage to the ground. Next, she bound her with a spell that consisted of simple ethereal wraps around her torso, arms, and legs. She then turned and stamped her foot in discontent before she threw her quarterstaff across the air in anguish. She started limping harder.

The timer ran out as the earth mage couldn't break out or even move from her position. Phenom went up in the brackets before slowly limping out of the arena.

The next names were Winry and Loch. One was a giant woman with a bald head, a green tunic, and half chain-mail armor. The other was a guy in a gray cloak with short brown hair, black pants, and a slightly lopsided walk.

The battle started with the man reaching out and summoning a wielder's weapon. It was a stone-gray metal spear, and the pole thinned out from the base until it reached the blade, which was a trident in shape where all three blades combined at the end to create a triangular structure. The total design was reminiscent of a key.

He stood with it at his side and didn't move. The woman seemed to analyze the man for a moment before pulling out and throwing a simple dagger in his direction. In response, he shifted his spear so that it blocked the dagger, which then fell directly to the ground.

Seeing this, the woman took a deep breath and let out a torrent of air that turned the ground in front of her into sand, creating a smokescreen. The guy simply twirled his spear and seemed completely unaffected while the woman disappeared at blinding speed.

The smokescreen shifted continuously until it was gone to reveal one sided clashing. The woman was attacking the man but he was blocking and parrying her attacks one handedly. She now had a short sword with a large, green gem in the hilt. She was fast, but he was able to match her speed with simple movements and even when she came up behind him, he just twirled his spear and parried her attack.

Once the dust cleared up completely, the woman made a full-frontal dash. Just before reaching striking range of the spear, she ducked over to the right. The man took the opportunity to strike whatever illusion was in front of him with the back end of the handle before swiping upward and hitting nothing.

This opening was more than enough for the woman to embed the back of the sword hilt into his gut. It seemed to stagger him as he released his weapon.

That couldn't have been farther from it.

She did hit him hard enough to stagger him, but he reached out and grabbed her before she could escape.

She cast a spell to jettison herself away from him, but he also cast one that kept her in place. A huge gust of wind whipped most of the dust back into the air just before a long spike exited the newly formed cloud.

When the wind died down, I saw the metallic spike coming from the middle of the man's palm. It was through the woman's shoulder.

At the same time, half of the man's cloak was blown off to reveal a gray sweatsuit with one sleeve cut off and an arm missing.

The woman brought up a leg to kick the unguarded side but she was sent farther away as the spike lengthened with her still on it. She tried to cast another spell, but he retracted the spike, pulling her close before pinning her to the ground, breaking the spike off of his palm and aiming his spear at her face.

She had no choice but to give up and the match was over.

Next was the last match of the day and the quickest. The names that appeared were Rwanda and Hiyaku. One was a woman in an icy blue shirt and shorts with matching shoes, gloves, and jacket with her long, black hair tied into a bun on top of her head. The other was a thin man with a brown vest and a red bowtie over a white-collared shirt and khakis.

The match started and ended at nearly the same time. The guy walked forward until he was within object throwing range and the girl took a dash at him with an oversized dagger, freezing the air as she went. Just before she reached him, there was a flash. Her weapon was in the ground across the field, and the man had a wielder's weapon at her throat from behind.

His weapon was similar in design to the last wielder except his was a straight sword that took more from clockwork hands with an arrow-shaped tip and a guard that circled around the entire handle.

The girl's momentum was completely stopped, and she was forced into an impossible position immediately. She seemed utterly shocked for a moment and didn't seem to know what to do until, slowly but surely, she put her hands up in defeat.

After both combatants left the field, Geist appeared on the screen again with a short speech about sportsmanship before a song played that signified the ending of the event for the day.

With that, everyone who still needed medical attention took to the medical staff and everyone else left the stadium.

26-Second Round

[Docter Ganger]

The first round of matches is over, and the stadium empties of its inhabitants. Catt and Noah stay with Graven's group, and they split off as soon as we enter the residential district.

Soon after entering our temporary residence and making sure none of our stuff has been tampered with, Krow takes the opportunity to disappear again and only tells Carona where he's going.

I shadow him like before and rest in the dark side of a nearby tree behind the benches. Krow takes a meditative seat before the mural, closes his eyes, and doesn't move.

Hardly five minutes pass before Rachel Cursley appears from the residential district, walks right past him and sits, wordlessly, on the bench in front of me. She wears a soft pink tunic that reaches down to her knees with a wide, red belt and a straw hat. She watches him intently and never once seems to look away. More than an hour passes and Krow stands back up.

"Rachel," says Krow, "Are you still watching?"

"I never stopped," she responds.

"Good, I want you to see this." He takes out his grimoire and opens it before reciting an incantation. "**Open, gate of the soul.**" The resulting spell encompasses just the two of them in a translucent black bubble. "Don't be afraid, they're both harmless."

"A dragon and an angel? What is this?" she asks, looking around.

"I wanted to see what you thought of this spell. It's one of many I don't remember putting in my grimoire."

"I don't think I've ever seen this spell in person, but I might have heard about it. These are your spirit animals, correct?" She stands and takes a couple of steps toward him.

"Yeah." He turns around. "If I start acting a bit weird, just know that it's a side effect of this spell."

"What do you mean, weird?" she says.

"Like, off." He shrugs.

"Off?" She takes another step forward.

"Like... Have you ever heard of the 'See's all complex'?"

"Yeah." She nods slowly.

"It's like that except instead of feeling like I can see everything that happens all the time, I feel like there's this 3rd wall, like in movies, that I can edge toward and possibly break. That and blatant emotional coldness. If I happen to be over-explaining, then please stop me."

"I get it and it's fine." She feels around for the bench and sits back down. "This spell is the 'wielders core visualization ritual' right?"

"Do you know anything particular about it?" He sounds hopeful.

"I only know that there are three parts to it. The mind, soul, and body. The mind shows the gate, the soul shows the spirit, and the body makes everything physically intractable. It's an incredibly rare spell, and my mother was one of the few I knew that could cast it without falling into complete madness."

"So, you 'only know' everything about it?" Krow ends his spell and comes to sit next to Rachel.

"Not really. I know the spell, but I would never attempt it myself and if I did, it would take me weeks to work up the courage."

"Why is that?" He asks.

"That spell already takes so much mental fortitude without the madness effect. Fortitude that I don't have." She sits up abruptly. "Speaking of which. I just remembered something."

"What is it?" asks Krow, scooting closer to her.

"While teaching me, my mother told me of a kid who could handle the spell just fine. I think she said his name was..."

As soon as she says the name, my mind flashes back to my own past and a trial having to do with dream eaters in a lost underground city. Krow, however, seems to cease functioning and slumps down completely. This has happened before and I'm not worried.

"Krow!" Rachel worriedly attempts to shake him awake before looking into his eyes with a small flashlight she pulls from her purse. She then put her ear to his chest. "No pulse." Replacing her ear with her hand, she casts a spell. "**Electric palm**."

There is a visible shock and Krow's eyes flutter open followed by slight heaving. "So, it *is* a curse," he says gasping.

"If your memories are locked behind a curse so strong that it could kill you just from remembering your own name, then you should have died a while ago. That name is pretty common." She sounds much calmer than she seems to be, but she's panicking.

"In that case, it wasn't the name, it was your voice saying it. You probably sound just like her... I think. I blanked out as soon as you said it, so I didn't exactly hear the name, but I would appreciate it if you didn't say it again."

"I won't, but what about anyone else who might figure it out like I have?" She seems visibly concerned. "You know as well as I do that magic can do some crazy things."

"I'm always prepared even, and especially if, I'm not ready. Like I was prepared for a moment where we'd end up in this position." He smiles wryly as she looks him up and down.

"You move fast for a man who was dead a second ago." Rachel smiles back while moving her hand from his chest to the bench.

"You moved first." He leans up as she leans down, and their faces come within inches of each other before they're interrupted by a stone careening toward Krow's head. He catches it as if he's expecting it. "Just when things were getting interesting."

"Mom, get away from him." I've seen the one who threw the rock before. He still looks the same without the hat barely covering his gray hair. I'm getting ready to leave before this development but I decide to stay and watch.

"You choose now to start calling me that?" Mumbles Rachel as she lifts herself off Krow and steps in front of him. "Nero, what are you doing here? You said you'd leave me to my own business."

"That guy is not your business and doing him on a bench in public isn't either." His face spells murder.

"I- we weren't... Right?" She looks back at Krow.

"I wasn't going for it if you weren't." He had fully readjusted himself and stands up.

"Mom, move out of the way." His sword is already summoned in his hand.

"No. I'm not going to just stand by and-"

"Rachel," says Krow, "It's ok." She moves out of the way, and Krow holds his hand out to shake. "It looks like we got off on the wrong foot. Hi, my name is-" Krow quickly shifts his weight and leans back as the orange-tinted blade comes within a hair of his throat. "That's not nice." He says, sitting back down. The blade trails down to his throat once more only to be blocked with his own, causing a pressure wave to fly in my direction. "Are you sure you want to do this in front of your mother?" he asks with a serious tone.

"Die." Nero shakes with anger.

"Alright then," says Krow, dryly, "I won't hold back this time."

"*Negative space*." Rachel has her grimoire open and casts a spell. A gray bubble materializes around Krow and Nero, expanding to include most of the courtyard and surrounding trees. I move to avoid it by teleporting into the shadow of a more distant tree. "Stop. This is not the time or the place."

"It doesn't matter if you nullify my magic, I don't need it to kill this guy." Nero jumps back and holds his sword at the ready.

"If you're going to be that overprotective, it can't be helped." Krow stands up and readies his blade.

Nero makes the first move by rushing forward and thrusting his blade.

Krow sidesteps it, takes a step forward, and elbows him in the face.

As Nero's head rocks to the side, he tries to swipe at Krow only to have his blade parried followed by a kick to the chest. He falls back only to return with a strike at Krow's sword.

The blades lock together, and Nero pushes his blade forward until Krow's is seated between the prongs, then he twists it until Krow lets go and his sword flies out of his hands and lands a few yards away.

Krow is weaponless and dodging sword slashes until one aimed at his neck comes close. He bends backward and twists his body so that his foot arcs into Nero's ear, guiding him to the ground.

Rolling around the foot and standing up, Nero holds his ear for a second before shaking his head and rushing back in with the same attack.

Krow ducks and charges forward, tackling Nero to the ground. Someone of his height flattening himself so fast likely caught Nero off guard.

The size difference is obvious and Nero can't push Krow off. Krow, on the other hand, takes the opportunity to punch his arm. He aims for pressure points. After a few strikes, he does the same to the other arm.

"Had enough?" asks Krow, standing up and stepping back.

Nero does a kip-up with no hands but Krow simply sweeps his legs and he falls again, shouting obscenities.

Rachel comes over and helps her son up. "I'm sorry about this." She puts Nero over her shoulder.

"Don't be. It's obvious that he loves you too much for you to be sorry about it. Besides, I'm sure that if it was anyone weaker, he'd have held back more." Krow smiles as he responds.

Rachel nods slowly as both she binds Nero in thin strands of magic while dismissing her nullification spell. "See you around." The pair are surrounded by flames and they vanish in an instant.

Krow heads toward the gate for the residential district, and I follow. "You know, I didn't think I'd actually get that far with her, but I guess I did a good job." He raises his hand for a high-five, and I step out of the shadows to reciprocate it. "So, were you going to stick around if we did end up doing it?"

"I was about to leave before that boy came in," I say.

"And what do you think about her and the stuff she said?"

"She's either really into you or something more sinister is going on, and it seems like she knows a lot more to do with your past than we thought. I don't think you should let this one go." I pat him on the back. "After all, she has a sure-fire way to kill you if she ever turns on you."

"Maybe, but I don't think she'd do that."

"You also didn't think that a trip to the Appalachian Mountains would result in fighting wendigos," I point out.

"Not really. I figured we were going there for something. Just not cannibalistic, shapeshifting, humanoids," he says, matter-of-factly.

"This is the same. We know she's into you but not the reason."

"You think she was put up to this?" His question seems more like a statement.

"All I'm saying is that you can never be too careful. We're dealing with C.H.E.S.S. here, remember?"

"But they're dealing with us as well," Krow says, putting his hand on my shoulder. We both stay silent from there until we get back.

The next day begins round two of the tournaments. The first matches to take place with the loser's rounds. Surprisingly, none of them seem any worse for wear. Most of them seem pretty high-spirited as well, despite some of their crushing losses.

The first match is between Nail Smith and Kim Seol. Nail's loss against Krow doesn't seem to slow him down at all. He matches all of Kim's wing shards by throwing his summoned swords until he overpowers him and knocks him out of the sky into a binding spell that keeps him in place until the timer runs out.

The next battle was between Sofia Hernandez and Anatoly. Anatoly starts with a volley of magic missiles that Sofia reflects until they dissipate.

His next move is to summon Ifrit. Sofia ducks it and closes the distance. He backs off and lets her run straight into a circle that he carved into the ground.

As a column of fire erupts under her feet, Sofia uses her shield to ride to the top of it and slams back down on top of Anatoly's head before he notices, knocking him out. He awakens to a sword at his throat and the battle ends.

Next are Edna McLaughlin and Sean Kowalski. Edna wins by outlasting Sean by keeping her distance and using her gargoyles to run down his defenses until he can't resist being captured until the time runs down.

Jonas Abdul and Anjelica fight next. It's obvious that Anjelica's in over her head when she can't keep up with Jonas' chakrams and fails to dodge, block, or counter one too many. She finds herself bleeding out too much to continue.

Robin Moore and Evgeny make a spectacle as initially, neither can hurt the other through projectiles alone. Both of their defenses hold until Robin displays a burst of speed he hadn't in his last round. In doing so, he breaks Evgeny's shield up close by telekinetically moving the coins on the ground out of the way. Next, he fires a laser spell at his opponent's face to knock him out and win the battle.

The final battle of the losers' rounds of the day is Riolu and Winry. Riolu can't keep up with Winry's speed, leaving herself wide open in an attempt to keep her opponent in place. This gives Winry the opportunity to quickly close distance and catch her off guard with a short sword pointed at her throat, ending the battle.

A thirty-minute break signifies the ending of the loser rounds. The first thing to show up when the break timer runs down is a notice on the screen about the winner's rounds. The restrictions are loosened, and advanced spells are allowed as well as major enchantments, brutal curses, and colossal summons.

The next names to show up are Charls Meyhem followed by Noah.

Noah stands and makes his way to the nearest marker. A minute later, he emerges and so does his opponent. Charls looks like a sailor in a long blue tailcoat and a bandanna on his head with a blue and gray striped shirt and gray pants. They shake hands and back off from each other.

The match starts with Charls throwing a blue tinted scimitar from his waist at Noah, walking backward into an oncoming mist and vanishing with it. Soon after, his sword disappears in the same way before it can reach its target.

Once the sword and its thrower are gone, Noah jumps into air where he hovers around ten feet up, until the sword exits the mist the same way it entered behind where he was before he jumped.

From the same mist, Charls catches his sword before it can get away from him. The mist he walks out of spreads across the field and becomes opaque. Looking up at Noah, he throws the scimitar again while backing into the mist.

Noah sends a blade wave the moment Charls throws his scimitar. The blade wave splits the mist in two and sends the sword flying outside the mist.

After a moment, a torrent of water shoots from the mist.

Noah waves his hand and creates an orb of pitch-black void that absorbs the torrent of water.

More torrents of water escape the ever-spreading mist at different angles, forcing him to rise higher to avoid them. In doing so, he starts circling the battlefield as more torrents follow.

While dodging the attacks, he takes a particular path, as if he's following something. Likely his opponent.

Tracking his opponent is a talent of his. His above-average sensory ability allows him to out-maneuver most and force them into direct combat, his specialty. Even so, he has to guess where his opponent is going, not where he was in this case.

With the flick of a wrist, Noah sends a ball of light down into the mist. It returns from another direction, where it fizzles out before it can reach him. Next, he hovers along, avoiding more attacks before sending a volley of his own. The balls of light whizz into the mist and back from different angles, vanishing before they can return to him.

After a moment of this, he swipes his hand at an incoming torrent of water and casts 'reflect', creating a white mirror between him and it, sending it back. Even so, it just vanishes into the mist and comes back out from another direction, causing him to dodge again.

It looks like things will drag on until he gets worn out, but he stays calm and continues the pattern of following something unseen in his movements.

Charls sees this too. He responds by sending many torrents of water at once. They close in from different angles. Even so, some seem like they're slowed down by something. It's subtle but noticeable.

Noticing the discrepancy as well, Noah dives down at an angle. He points in another direction and an orb of darkness appears within the mist where he's pointing. It disrupts the mist and pulls some of it in. Next, he puts his hand out in front of him, creating a black surface that he barely touches before darting off of it toward the black bubble.

He vanishes into the blackness, and a white light ascends from it in an instant. Seconds later, a distinct sailor pattern on a person comes flying out of the bubble of darkness hoisted by the column of light.

The mist coating much of the battlefield vanishes and the column of light disappears.

Charls, now hovering in the air, surrounds himself with a blue bubble and summons more mist to surround himself.

Noah, appearing from the vanishing black bubble on the ground with his sword in hand, swipes his blade upward, sending a 'blade wave' at his target. This both shatters the bubble and disperses the newly formed mist.

Reorienting himself, Charls traces his fingertips across the area in front of him and a slightly blue-tinged mist appears before him. He does it a second time below his feet and lands on the cloud as it appears.

Noah, still racing up from the ground, slashes at the solid cloud in his way, cutting it in two.

Charls jumps to make distance and Noah taps the remaining cloud with the tip of his sword, casting 'white pillar' and engulfing his target a second time in a column of light.

At that moment, all of Charls' momentum stops and he descends slowly toward the ground.

Noah catches him and sits him down gingerly. Eventually, the time runs down.

Noah returns to cheers and high-fives.

"I forgot to ask earlier," says Krow, "Did you ever catch up with your sister?"

"No. She went through a gate and I needed identification or something to enter and there was no way around it. I didn't want to seem too suspicious, so I didn't call out to her either." Noah's obviously torn between something but doesn't want to say.

"Remember, I'm here if you need help," Krow reassures him, only getting a nod in response. The next names to come up are Belle and Krow. "I'll be back," says Krow as he excitedly jumps to his feet and makes his way to the marker.

He walks with confidence through the gate to meet his opponent. He speaks to the giant as they shake hands and seem to strike up a conversation. They don't talk long before backing away.

The match starts with Krow rushing at Belle unarmed. They try to grab him with an open palm but he ducks it and lands a solid punch to the chest. There's no physical response to the impact aside from a follow-up grab with the other hand.

He ducks that one too and jumps back to find his leg in the grasp of the first hand. He's slammed into the ground twice and kicks himself free before it can happen a third time. Relentlessly, he dashes back toward his opponent. This time, instead of ducking the oncoming hands, he decides to jump off of one and is caught by the other only to be circle-tossed into the air, anyway.

Quickly reorienting himself, he summons his sword and shoots a blade wave down only for the attack to be broken as Belle jumps to meet him. He's grasped tightly and held close as they become a dot in the sky before plummeting with the realistic force of a meteor.

Before long, they produce embers that turn into an arrow-shaped flame. Krow had cast 'fire drop'. The heat from his flames only intensifies as the trail following them lengthens. Before long, a large bulk of the mass within the flames can be seen flying off in another direction before landing and rolling across the ground.

Bell just barely stands up as Krow reaches the ground. It looks like he's grown wings of flame before landing on his feet, still surrounded by glistening embers created by the scorched earth below his feet. The wings are visible for only a split second before all the flames disappear. Summoning his weapon again, he points it at his singed opponent and says something. Belle's response is to hold their hands up in defeat.

The match ends and Krow returns with an unusual smile on his face.

"What happened?" I ask.

"I have a new spell. It's called 'angel's descent'. It's an old one, but I remembered it." He takes a second to look at Sofia, who decides to sit near us again. She's giving him a sharp glare. "What's wrong?"

She holds up a small spiral notebook. It's almost ash in her hands. "I was writing."

"Oh, sorry about that. I guess I'm just too strong." He only toots his own horn when he's particularly proud of himself.

"We'll see about that." I can't tell if she's angry or just annoyed.

The next match is between Mary Black and Cattherine.

"Is there anything you want me to tell her for you?" asks Cattherine, standing.

"Tell her: I never stopped looking for her and that I'm glad she's alive." He pauses. "And that there's more stuff I want to talk to her about when I get to see her." Noah's looking up at the sky with a smile on his face the whole time.

"Will do," she says, giving a thumbs-up and a wink. Just before she teleports away, they both look at each other as if they have more to say, but neither makes a sound and she's gone.

Mary and Cattherine enter the field and shake hands before striking up a conversation. They talk for nearly a minute before going to their starting positions.

The battle starts with Mary summoning a bow and shooting a volley of arrows one after another at and around Cattherine.

In response, Cattherine summons her gauntlets and punches the ground. Her color changes to that of the ifrit, and red and yellow flames appear around her, producing small red and yellow birds.

The oncoming arrows turn black and fade into ash. She then takes a stance and readies herself. Although Cattherine's a speed type, she can easily pass herself off as a power type. It makes sense for Mary to attempt a sneak attack by shooting one arrow into the air and swapping places with it while concealing an invisible arrow falling behind Cattherine and outside the range of her spell.

She shoots one arrow that turns into an orb of light surrounded by a rotating halo. A magic missile. Replacing herself with the invisible arrow, she attempts a quick dash at Catherine from behind.

Her attempt fails as Cattherine takes notice of her strategy at the last second. Cattherine turns around, punches the sword that Mary summoned out of the way, leaps over her shoulder behind her, locks her arms under her pits, and lifts her in place while the magic missile makes impact.

Mary takes the whole blast and seconds later, her situation only seems to get worse. The flames surrounding them lick her feet and slowly rise up her legs. The small birds scatter themselves around her body and scorch her clothes and skin.

The timer starts a few seconds after she starts struggling to get loose. She lifts her legs and casts 'push', sending herself and Cattherine out of the circle of flames and freeing herself.

The timer stops as she turns around with a glow from her wrists that leads up her arms to her elbows as she summons a halberd into her hands. Cattherine dodges the first couple of swipes and blocks it with the back of her fist as it comes for her neck.

Getting closer, she blocks a similar strike only for the sickle edge to extend to a full scythe and rake at her from behind. She ducks and slides across the ground until her feet hit a shield Mary placed there as the halberd strikes from the same direction.

Cattherine pushes off from the shield and lifts herself into a summersault to avoid the edge of the polearm.

The halberd morphs into a sword with the word 'EXCALIBUR' on its side. Mary picks up her shield and her weapons at the ready as her opponent draws closer.

Cattherine punches at the shield and Mary retaliates with a sword swipe that gets ducked before her feet are swept and she finds an uppercut on the way down.

She blocks with her sword arm and the impact still sends her flying. Rising to her feet, she reaches upward, and an angelic figure appears above her. It strings a harp that makes the bruise appearing on her arm fade nearly as fast as it appears.

Cattherine already took the opportunity to rush back in, only to be blocked by the shield that had grown large enough to cover her entire body. The shield pushes her back, but she just keeps punching it until it cracks. Once the angel is done, the shield pushes even harder and knocks Cattherine away.

That isn't before her hair and gloves cycle from light blue to pristine, empty white. She locked on to Mary's color and can now, fundamentally, use her powers.

The shield disappears to be replaced with a spear that narrowly misses its target and lands behind Cattherine. She turns to kick it away and her foot is met with a fist.

Mary now sports gauntlets that rise and fall with a jagged edge pattern across the entire back of her hands and fingers. They both seem fairly even in raw power.

No weapon used by Mary is able to put a real dent in Catterine's defenses, but that doesn't change the fact that something is amiss. She should know that using the same weapon would only put her at a disadvantage. This, however, isn't the case. They still look evenly matched.

The first real collision is fist-to-fist, and they both buckle, holding their own hands before getting back to it.

Of all the blows blocked and parried, only one hit carried through on both sides. They catch each other in the jaw. I'd say it's scripted if I hadn't seen it myself.

Mary gets knocked back, and Cattherine hits the ground quickly. She rises back to her feet in a few seconds as Mary seems frozen in time.

Once she sees her opponent has gotten back up, Mary speaks a few short words, and they shake hands again and hug. Cattherine goes up in the bracket and they both step out of the field. Catherine comes back with a smile on her face.

"What happened?" Noah asks.

"Your sister's pretty cool and she's a nice person too." Cattherine sits back in her seat.

"So, what'd she say?" Noah mimics her posture.

"She warned me about which people in the tournament were testers and who to look out for. She said that Nail, Einn, Lynch, Loch, Shane, and herself were testers in order to gauge the strength of the competitors. I think it's safe to assume that some of them were still in it to win, though. There was also something about the criteria that they were looking for. A specific power that I didn't have."

Krow looks at me and says, "What do you think that means?"

"That depends on if she said anything about the other competitors or not." My response seems to resonate with Cattherine.

"Oh yeah, she said to stay away from Krow and to give up immediately if I happen to face Doc. She said I should do fine against anybody else." She looks at us with a confused look.

"I guess that makes us the target," I say, sitting back in my chair.

"Good," says Krow. "No holds barred."

"She also said that she has things to talk to you about too when she sees you." Cattherine grips Noah's arm and shakes it vigorously.

"That's good." He smiles.

The next match is between Shane Road and Einn Finnic. Two of the testers are fighting each other, which proves that the bracket at least isn't seeded.

The match starts with Einn teleporting in a flash behind Shane with his weapon summoned. Shane blocks the oncoming strike with his own weapon. It's a crystalline blue double-edged straight sword with a diamond pattern running up the blade and across the guard.

A counterstrike results in ice crystals rising from the ground and snow falling from where the blade slices through the air. It doesn't seem to faze Einn as he dodges the strike and spins with his blade pointed outward, tracing a circle around himself that turns into an expanding energy wave.

Shane cuts through the part coming toward him and stabs his blade into the ground. The wind picks up and a flurry of snow appears out of nowhere. He casts 'hailstorm', and the field snows over in a dome accented by shards of ice reflecting light from the inside.

Not much can be seen from the outside aside from the occasional laser exiting the cloud. Nothing can be heard except for blades clashing.

This lasts until Einn, covered in frost, emerges from the top. He turns and throws his weapon down. The half-moon blade seems to become a full moon as it spins.

Upon impact, the hailstorm subsides. Shane is at the bottom, blocking the still-rotating blade. He redirects it to the ground and jumps toward his opponent. Einn's weapon stops spinning and follows Shane back up.

Twisting himself around and dodging it, Shane shoots a blade wave which boosts it past its owner. He then clasps both of his hands together and casts another spell. The area around both of them turns into a giant snowball. It falls to the ground and explodes.

Shane stands and looks at the respective spot on the ground where his opponent is in the air. Einn stands up shortly after and waves himself out of the field.

The next name to come up is Maxwell Blue followed by mine. I stand and ruffle Krow's hair. He tries to slap my hand out of the way, but I move too fast and do it again.

"Next time, I'm just gonna move out of the way," he says, waving his hands above his head.

"Yeah, yeah," I say, moving past him to the marker.

The room is the same as before, except mirrored. I'm on the opposite side of the stadium than I was last time. I remove the few items in my pockets too heavily enchanted to bring with me and place them into a black bubble. I then proceed to enchant the walls to alert me in case anyone enters after me just like I did before.

Walking into the field, I see my opponent. He has short, black hair, a long gold and white trimmed hooded robe, and light gray sweatpants. Despite the aged look in his eye, there is a lack of wrinkles.

We shake hands and go to our starting positions.

I start the battle by creating an illusion of myself standing still while I step five feet to the right and walk toward my opponent. He pulls out a bulbous wand made of cherry oak with a silver engraved depiction of a primrose and releases a ball of light surrounded by a rotating square. A magic missile. It flies through my illusion and then toward me afterward. I counter it with a 'shadow ball', but the illusion is broken.

He aims at me and shoots four more.

I run and jump over all of them before casting 'dark abyss'. I make sure that more than half of the field is covered in a solid sheet of darkness. The darkness should completely blind anyone caught in it aside from me, but it doesn't seem to succeed to the degree that I want.

The magic missiles disappear, only to be replaced by a beam of light that clears some of the surrounding darkness. I'm within the circle of light and get pushed back into the dark, where I decide on my next move.

Casting 'extreme speed' on myself, I dive out of the shadows before diving right back in. I do this multiple times until I get behind him, where I cast both 'mare' and 'necrotic hand' before touching him once and triggering the effects of both spells.

It doesn't seem to dawn on him until it's too late. After enough time, I step out of the shadows in front of him. He attempts to cast a spell in my direction, but the light at the tip of his wand dims and fades until it's non-existent.

He staggers before noticing that more than half of his body has turned gray. The look in his eyes flicks from old and experienced to young and fearful before he hits the ground. I walk out of the field thirty seconds later.

I decide not to ruffle Krows hair when I sit down because he covers his head with his cloak and doesn't uncover it until the next match begins.

The next match is between Lynch and Leon. Leon's shirt is still destroyed, but it's now cut to look like it's supposed to be that way, and his bandages are gone.

The match starts with Leon summoning his sword and sending out a blade wave. The attack hits Lynch directly and a green wave flies back at him. He takes it head-on and doesn't seem phased. If anything, he just smiles before dashing at his opponent. Before he can get there, green fog forms around Loch. It balloons until visibility into the cloud becomes difficult.

Leon rushes in headlong. His sword catches fire and can be easily seen in the poisonous fog. They clash and a brilliant yellow flame erupts from the haze. The entire cloud catches fire.

It seems this battle is nature versus fire, and fire has a clear advantage.

Out of the yellow flame comes a small green one. Lynch's 'thorns' spell triggers from the fire and surrounds him in a similar form. He's holding an emerald-colored two-handed tower shield with spikes on the front that seems to split down the middle.

Leon chases down Lynch who's backing himself toward the wall. Stopping before his opponent reaches his destination, Leon pushes off at high speed. His body is engulfed in a red and yellow flame, and draconic scales are trailing behind him as he crashes his target through the wall and out of the match.

Leon reaches his hand into the hole and helps out Loch. They shake hands and say a few words before Loch leaves the arena, followed by Leon.

Next is Mike and Phenom. Phenom still shoulders a heavy limp that's barely hidden at all, even though she walks with confidence.

Mike pulls out his whip and strikes at Phenom's feet. The whip itself doesn't reach, but a wisp of clear blue extends from the end to make contact at an extended range. Phenom jumps in what seems more like a fear reaction than combat sense and dodges the attack.

His next strike hits the ground next to him, and the merman from his last match comes out of a portal that's created. Phenom pulls out her staff and fires three magic missiles from the spider end. One of them knocks the merman off balance and spreads a purple mark across his chest. The other two are blocked by a wall of water.

The merman takes a running start at Phenom who, instead of running, shoots more poison at him. He dodges it but only seems to turn more purple.

With the merman steadily getting closer and the constant threat of being distracted, Phenom puts her hands together and casts a spell. Before she can complete it, however, the water whips at her, and she jumps back to dodge it. She lands awkwardly but is still able to cast her spell.

She's surrounded by a purple rotating ball and levitating with her staff in front of her. The merman rams straight into it and is sent flying in the opposite direction. The purple coloring on his body spreads quickly and immobilizes him to the point that he can only go at walking speed.

Phenom turns her full attention toward Mike and quickly travels in his direction while leaving a groove in the ground.

She gets halfway there before the water wraps around the entire sphere and lifts it up thirty feet with her inside it. She puts her hand against the bubble and the water turns purple but doesn't stop moving.

The look in her eyes as she reaches an equal height with the crowd would make you believe that she's going to cry. Any one of many landings could put her out of commission with a critical injury already poorly hidden.

She lands in under a second and the bubble disperses instantly. Finding herself on her back, she squirms for a couple of seconds before somehow getting back to her feet with her staff in hand.

She kisses the spider at the top and it comes to life while growing past the size it was last time. Little does she know, she's still wrapped in the water whip. She's lifted into the air by her hips, back up to audience height. Before she accelerates back down, there's a look of absolute terror with tears in her eyes.

There's no crash this time as she stops less than five feet from the ground. She's gently laid on the ground and let go as she already passed out.

The match ends, and she awakes as she's being taken out on a gurney.

The final winner's match of the day is between Loch Steel and Hiyaku Otanaki. As soon as this match starts, I make sure to focus on Hiyaku. Last time, I was late in noticing a temporal disturbance. This time, I can see exactly what he's doing.

Loch wastes no time in summoning his weapon, stabbing it into the ground, casting 'horizon', and creating a silver and gray dome that turns clear over himself. Hiyaku dashes toward Loch with his sword summoned as well, just before a light shines down from the sky and a meteor the size of a car comes racing down on top of him.

Time stops at that moment. No, that's inaccurate. Everyone's perception of time stops except for Hiyaku and many audience members, as far as I can tell. A twelve-foot area around him seems to actually stop in time, however, and he ducks around the rock before it can touch him.

Time continues, and the resulting explosion is a perfect cover. The 'horizon' spell requires the caster to concentrate in order to keep it up. Hiyaku takes a moment to carve a rune onto the surface of the bubble with his sword. The other side of the rune creates illusions that cause Loch to disperse his own spell and he's open to be caught from behind with a sword at his throat.

The match ends here.

27-Chain Reaction

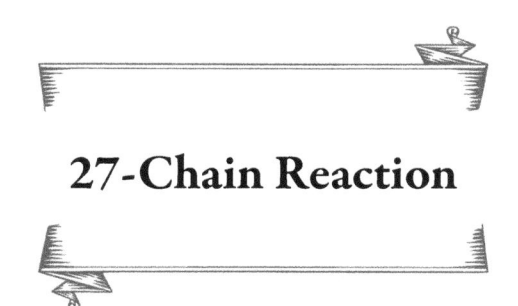

[Krow Hunt]

Target or not, instead of contemplating what to do next, I decided to continue my pattern of telling Carona where I was going and finding my way to the mural near the front gates.

As I'd done before, I sat and concentrated on my grimoire. Before long, it began glowing and levitating in front of me. It opened to the page with 'Angels Descent' written on the header. I inspected it closer, and my surroundings began glowing a golden yellow in a circle around me. Some of the words and symbols on the page were still blurred over, and I couldn't understand them. I tried to touch one of the symbols and the glow intensified.

As this was happening, I noticed a presence from the same direction I had come. It was faint, but I was drawn to it so intensely that I could feel its exact location. It went past and stopped behind me where the benches were. The entire page began glowing but died down quickly. Nothing changed about the page at all.

I got an idea and reached into my pocket to pull out the red crystal. It was translucent, so I decided to look through it while attempting to read. I started with one of the most curious symbols and as I began, the book fell to the ground, the glow disappeared, and I froze. It felt like someone sat the sharp end of an ax on my head and hit it as hard as they could with a sledgehammer.

I couldn't move and became frustrated quickly. Minutes passed, and the pain wasn't going away in any capacity. I was experienced in ignoring pain to get things done, but this was different. I decided that pretending that there was no pain would be the thing to do otherwise, my surroundings would suffer the same. Picking up my grimoire and pocketing it with the crystal, I stood.

"Rachel," I said.

"Yes?" I heard a book close. She must have been reading.

"Could you come here? I don't think I can move too much." I put my hand on my head and removed it quickly. The pain got worse when I touched it.

"Sure." I heard her footsteps this time and saw her appear in my right peripheral before stepping in front of me.

"C-Can you feel my forehead... Please? Something's wrong... And I don't think I can figure it out by myself." The pain began interfering with my speech.

She touched my forehead for a brief moment. "Oh my god, you're literally as hot as a furnace." She shook her hand to cool it down and took a closer look at my forehead.

"I figured I looked good, but how's my temperature?" My remark made her pause, and then she flicked my forehead. I froze again, and the look in my eyes gave her a clue as to how I was feeling.

"Sorry. Jokes because of pain, right?"

I gave a soft whimper to confirm her theory.

"It looks like the curse from before. I suggest we stop trying to dig into your memories. I don't want you dying on me again."

"How can you tell that it's the curse?" I was just able to speak again.

"There's a symbol that appeared on the same spot last time." She traced the image in front of me before pulling out a small notepad and sketching it.

"My forehead?" I said, trying to see what she was drawing.

"Yeah. I don't know why I didn't do this before." She turned it around, and I saw what looked like a stylistic M with an elongated S through the middle that connected with the base of the M on one side and the top of it on the other side.

"That doesn't look familiar in any capacity," I said, reaching for the notepad. She ripped the page out and handed it to me. Carefully, I folded it and put it into my pocket.

"Okay, I'm going to try something." She put both of her hands up to my head. "*Tranquil mind*." The pain began receding a little. "Is it working?"

"A little bit," I said. It was becoming easier to move and concentrate.

"This curse is so strong that I didn't think that this would work at all. There is so much resistance that I feel like it could break both of my arms. There's no way to completely nullify something like this."

When the pain lessened to a point where I was confident that I could function, I spoke again. "You can stop now, I'm fine."

"Alright." She lowered her hands and almost fell over. I caught her, and we helped each other to the bench.

"You must be really drained," I said, gently rocking her back and forth.

"Of course, I am. We were standing there for hours," she said, between gasps.

"Hours? That felt like a few minutes. I guess that's just pain and magic for you." I sat back and looked at the sky. The sun was close to setting. "I don't know if you realize, but you lied to me yesterday."

"I did?" She seemed to lose her fatigue quickly as her eyes became more alert.

"You said you never saw it but you might have heard about the spell. You then told me that your mother taught it to you. You definitely know more in-depth things about it than somebody who never did it themselves, even considering Faramosa probably showing it to you." I whispered, "So, I wanna know; who's watching you?"

"What did you say?" She didn't seem surprised but she did seem a little panicked.

"It's not your son. This feels like a totally different thing." I stood, returned to my normal volume, and faced her. "It couldn't be a coincidence that nobody shows up here in the afternoon but us."

"That's not what's going on here, you don't understand." She attempted to get to her feet and then fell back to the bench.

"Here's the deal. I get rid of my watchdog and you get rid of yours. Then, we talk honestly and in private. No ears, just us, deal?" I stuck my hand out to shake, and she just sat there for a moment before she responded.

"Here." She took a small, enchanted microphone out of her ear and handed it to me.

"And the other thing?" I said, finding the tiny hatch to the batteries and extracting them.

"What other thing?" she said, tiredly.

"You don't know it's there?" As I said that, the other presence I felt from her faded. "Never mind."

"What about your watchdog?" She shifted in her seat while keeping eye contact.

"Oh, yeah. Live. Die. Repeat." I recited the code phrase and a murder of crows flew out of the tree directly behind the bench Rachel was sitting on and disappeared into the night. "Now, we can talk."

"About what?" She seemed much more comfortable now that all eyes were averted.

"You don't want to be here, do you?"

"No, I'd honestly rather be anywhere else in the world right now."

"I know that I'm a target, just not what kind or priority. Do you know?"

"No. I was handed a list of participants to look into, and you seemed the most interesting. You're also the first one to come up to me personally."

"About that list, who else is on it?"

"Why not see for yourself?"

She reached into the air, and a piece of paper appeared in her hand. She handed it to me, and I read it. It was a list of names with numbers and X's by them. The names I recognized were Belle, Caroline, Catt, Doc, Dagon, Hiyaku, Leon, Mike, Maxwell, Noah, Phenom, and myself.

"What does this mean?" I asked.

"All I know is that the X's mean that they are no threat." She took a more solemn tone. "The numbers are meant for someone above my pay grade."

"That explains why Dagon has an X by his name. I took care of him myself. Because I could take out someone like him alone, it would make sense that I would be a higher priority level than most."

My name had a 1 next to it. As did Doc, Hiyaku, and Leon. Belle, Mike, and Noah all had 2. Maxwell, Phenom, and Catt had 3. Caroline had an X.

"Here." I handed it back to her. "So now that I know, are you going to erase my memory?" I sat down.

"How did you know?" It sounded like a weight just left her shoulders.

"We wouldn't be able to go on that date if I skipped out on the tournament." I smiled.

"I'm sorry, but I have to." She turned so that her whole body was facing me.

"Can't you not and say you did?" I leaned forward and back again.

"It doesn't work like that." She looked off a bit to the side.

"But it does." I turned to face her as well. "How about this: in five seconds, I'll try to kiss you. I'll lower my defenses completely and you can use the opportunity to do whatever you want. If not, we can just let things keep going as they are. How does that sound?"

She stared into my eyes, speechless for the next five seconds. I reached around her waist and pulled her closer. Our eyes stayed locked as our faces touched. Her tongue touched mine, and we stayed locked for almost a minute. I pulled away as I needed to breathe again.

"I'm sorry, we're not going to meet after this." She placed her hand on my cheek. "Don't get me wrong, I like you. I just can't risk it." I gave her a soft smile, and she forced a frown. "*Evanescence*."

I awoke the next day with the majority of my memory intact. Whatever she erased had to have happened after the kiss, but before she actually erased anything. It took me a while to figure out what it was, but I haven't ever regained those memories. Doc was sitting at the end of my bed with a letter.

"Anything I need to know?" He was definitely concerned.

I told him about the priority list and my theory about Rachel herself.

"You were there. Any clues about why she doesn't just leave?"

"Nero. They have him under their thumb. She calls him her son for a reason." I reached for the letter. "What's that about?"

"Apparently, targeting us isn't the only mistake they made." He handed it to me, stood, and walked away. I opened the letter and read it. Looking around, I was startled as I found Sara standing off to the side in my peripherals. I didn't even sense her presence until then.

"Hey, Sara. What are you just standing there for?" I turned to stand up, and she jumped and squeezed me in her arms.

"I'm so sorry, I didn't know." She was tearing up.

"What are you talking about?" I put my hand on her head.

"I was there the whole time. You sent Doc away, but you didn't know that I was there."

"Curiosity killed the cat. How many times did you sneak away?" I hugged her back.

"Just this once. When were you planning on telling us that you could die at any given time? I don't wanna see you in pain like that ever again." Her tears began dropping down one by one.

"It's ok, don't worry about me. I'll be fine," I said, attempting to lift her up. She held on tight, and I couldn't get her loose.

"Stop trying to shoulder everything yourself. You and Doc both do that. We used to tell each other everything. We used to be inseparable." She buried her face in my chest.

"We also fought a lot," I said, as she let me go.

"What changed?" She was looking at the floor.

"We got too old to share a room, and we drifted apart, maybe?" My sarcasm didn't make anything better even though I tried.

"What are you going to do about that woman? You can't just let her go after all that." She stopped crying, but her eyes were still glassy.

"That reminds me, did you tell anybody about what you saw?"

"No. I wanted to talk to you about it first." She sat next to me. "Part of your memory was erased, right?"

"Before that; I don't want to know what I forgot this time. I have a feeling things will only get harder if I remember now and could you not tell anyone else, please?"

"But what about the things you said… and did? I'm scared for you."

"It's fine. Nothing's going to happen and if it does, I'll be ok."

"I don't believe you, but I'll still take your word for it."

She left the room, and sometime later, we were in the stadium. The big screen showed a revision to the schedule that was also in the letter. There were supposed to be longer breaks between rounds.

The losers' rounds started with Charls and Mortimer. Charls used his teleportation and speed to great effect against Mortimer's skeletons and took him down quickly with a direct blast that knocked him out.

Next were Belle and Nail. The match started with Nail summoning a wielder's weapon. It was a jagged broad sword that was reddish brown around the edges. He used the sword to impale Belle before they could react.

I almost jumped out of my seat, but Doc put his hand on my shoulder to prevent that. The giant frame of the man dissipated quickly to reveal a small girl in his chest. She had long brown hair and small features aside from her eyes, which were huge.

She was wearing what amounted to a black bodysuit with a glowing green techno pattern over it. She was floating for a moment before she fell with the blade still seated between her ribs. The crowd fell silent.

"That's her, that's Belle," said Catt, covering her mouth with her hand.

"That black suit she's wearing is her weapon." said Noah, "What's going on...?"

"She's not dead, just knocked out," said Doc. "She's not bleeding either." His eyes were glowing blue, indicating his enhanced sight with a spell.

There was movement from Belle. She stood and removed the sword herself before the timer could reach half, losing a lot of blood in the process. She began wobbling drunkenly before hovering a couple of feet off of the ground and glowing green as a huge volume of electricity expanded from her. It wasn't a spell, just raw power.

Nail called back his weapon too late and didn't create a barrier in time either. He was sent flying and crashed into the wall. He limped out of the hole that was created to find Belle being lifted out of a puddle of blood in a gurney by paramedics and Geist himself waiting for him.

They walked out of one side while Belle was taken out of the other. Noah and Catt jumped up and ran down to where Belle was taken, only to return less than a minute later with their heads hung low.

"They said we weren't allowed to see her, but her grandfather and Hinata were already there before us so it should be fine," said Noah. Catt stayed silent.

The matches continued as if nothing ever happened with Mary and Sofia. This was a rematch. Mary confused Sofia with a mix of speed, omnidirectional attacks, and teleportation to win a second time.

Next were Einn and Edna. Edna had little defense against Einn's laser attacks and was beaten before she could activate one card.

Maxwell and Rwanda. This match could have gone either way, but Rwanda left an opening that Maxwell took advantage of, to blind and capture her in a spell she couldn't find her way out of before the timer ended.

After that, Loch and Jonas battled. Once again, it was nature versus fire. Loch's defense was tough, but Jonas out-strategized him with a mix of ranged attacks and constant self-recovery until Loch gave up on his own.

Next were Phenom and Robin. Phenom seemed to have mostly recovered, but Robin seemed to have the upper hand until his barrier was covered in poison so that he couldn't see. Using his speed, he found himself on melted ground that acted as quicksand and covered him in more poison. His strength drained until he was stuck crawling and Phenom won.

The last battle was between Loch and Winry. The match seemed even in skill and despite the overwhelming power difference, Winry found enough openings in Loch's defenses to force him to give in.

During the thirty-minute intermission, we all went to see how Belle was doing. She hadn't regained consciousness yet but was breathing regularly and seemed to respond to stimuli. She suffered from severe blood loss and required a transfusion. Thankfully, her blood type was common enough that more than one person in the room was a match. The intermission ended, and we were sent back to our seats.

The first name to show up was Noah, followed by me. We stood and looked at each other. I put my fist out to him, and we fist bumped.

"Don't hold back," I said. "I don't want to injure you on accident. I also don't wanna hold back myself."

"I'll try not to, I guess…" he said, nervously.

"I want you to do your best so that I can see if you can actually beat me." I placed my fist on my chest.

"You think I can beat you?" He sounded more optimistic.

"Don't act like you didn't. If you go in expecting to lose, you will. I go in expecting to win. How about you?" I turned and went to a marker farther away from the one we all had been using.

"I'll try my best," he said, slightly more confident.

"Don't try. Do." I stepped onto the marker and teleported into a small room one more time. A moment passed and someone came to get me. I faced Noah across the field and shook his hand before stepping back to the starting marker.

The match started with me putting my hands together and sending out a fireball large enough to cover my approach as I charged at full speed behind it. He cut the fireball in half, and I dodged to the right to strike with my sword.

He blocked and guided my sword to the ground with his own before springing back and guiding his blade to my throat. I dodged by arching backward, going onto my hands, and kicking Noah to the side. He swayed a bit but didn't go anywhere, so I created an explosive ball and released it between us.

He jumped back and sent a blade wave at me. I dodged it and continued toward him.

We clashed, and I began pushing him back right before he cast a spell. The ground below me began glowing white, and a rush of energy hit me all at once.

I waited until the attack was over to see what he would do next, but he was just standing with a peculiar stance. His positioning wasn't anything unnatural, but he was holding his sword one-handed with only his ring finger and thumb. It seemed like he could drop it at any time, but the look in his eyes told me that he was serious.

I stepped toward him with my sword stationary before me and struck forward. He tightened his grip and reinforced it with his other hand as we collided. It created a sort of spring effect and pushed me back a bit. He then took a full step around me and guided his sword around mine while keeping up the pressure.

I kept my blade sturdy and followed his, turning in the process. He released the pressure and stepped back. I took a few steps back myself, suspecting a trap.

"I have a question," I said, "All the power you've seen me use in this tournament. Did it seem like I was stronger than you in any way? Do I seem like any more of a challenge at this point? Or have you not improved as much as I thought you did?"

"Honestly, no," he said, "When I first saw you, I thought you were one of the strongest people in the world but now, all I know is that you're holding back."

"I like to match my opponent's strength so that my skill speaks for itself," I said, extending my blade. "Chopter." My blade began glowing and morphed into its second form. "Let's start with this." I raced toward him and used the fire side to clash against his blade.

Embers jumped from my blade to him and turned into flames as they went. He stepped back and tried to disengage, but I swung the wind side and created a whirlwind to fan the flames at him. I caught him in it, but he didn't catch fire himself.

I continued my pursuit only to run into four blade waves. He sent them all at once and they crashed into my arms and chest. They hurt, but I didn't falter. I stopped and swung the wind and fire side, in order, to create a small fire tornado and send it toward him.

He ducked to the side and avoided it just before I cast another spell. I opened my mouth and released the most inhuman roar I could muster. The air shifted, and he caught fire. 'Burning shout'.

His resistance made sure there weren't many flames, but they were still there. He retaliated by throwing his sword at me. I tried to parry it, but it weighed enough to cause me to drop my own sword.

He took that opportunity to drop-kick me. His feet landed directly in the middle of my chest and sent me flying farther than I thought I would. I landed on my back and rolled onto my feet to find myself in a circle that was etched into the ground.

Another rush of energy hit me all at once. Unlike the first one, I felt like I just jumped off of a house and hit the ground straight on. My vision flashed red, and I decided to get out as quickly as possible. Summoning my sword in a whirl of fire and wind, I jettisoned myself toward Noah at full speed.

The flames on him were all gone, and he was back in his stance. He dodged the attack, but not the next one. I stabbed my sword into the ground and left it there as I dashed toward Noah again. A flame erupted from the sword that encased over half of the entire field.

When I turned toward him, he reacted as if I was striking with my sword. Instead, I watched where his arms were going and knocked the sword out of his hands with a single strike. I grabbed it by the blade and threw it at my own where they made contact and began burning together.

Reinforcing my fists, I punched Noah. He blocked it with his arm and sent his leg up to kick as he fell. I caught his foot, spun around with it in my hand, let him go toward the wall, and followed.

He surrounded himself with a white bubble of energy and released it in all directions to stop his momentum. I took that opportunity to drop-kick him, and he hit the wall just outside of the flames.

"**Heat coil**." I cast the spell, and Noah was pinned with flaming ropes that appeared from the wall. "You're still holding back. Where's that dark side?"

"Behind you." His eyes had turned pitch black, and it wasn't a spell. I dodged to the side and his sword flew past me. It was still on fire, but the flames were black. As soon as it reached him, the bindings turned black as well and dissipated.

He had become a blur in my vision as he dashed toward me. I jumped back into the flame, but instead of a warm embrace, I felt like hay in a needle stack. All the flames turned black, and my sword was still in the middle of it. Moving was difficult, and all of my surroundings felt like pins and needles whenever I did.

I anchored the spell to my sword to make the flames stronger, so I had to touch it myself to deactivate the spell.

Before I could do anything, a blade wave came at me, and I had no choice but to block it with my arms. The attack carried me through the entire width of the black flames and past my sword.

I fell to one knee and pressed my hand to my chest.

"**Body of sacred flames**." I cast the spell as well as I could while detached from my weapon, and I was surrounded by golden yellow flames before charging back for my sword.

The blurred image of Noah was coming toward me through the flames, and I cast 'blast off' to jump high enough into the air that I could see the entire burning area and my sword. "**Fire drop**." I was encased in more flames as I descended to the ground at breakneck speed. Noah jumped to meet me and was met with another spell. "**Reach**." Part of the flame surrounding me morphed into a large talon that swept him to the side. He landed quickly and sped to where I was trying to land, but I got there first.

The entire stadium was hit with divine light and raging winds as I retrieved my sword and sent it to its third form at the same time. The blades combined to make one white and emerald-colored sword and the handle lengthened so that half was the blade and half was the handle with a black eight-pointed star in the circular guard.

"Sorry Noah, I was still holding back too," I said, slightly levitating before landing.

The black flames disappeared, and Noah wasn't standing too far from me. His eyes were still pitch black, and he was silent. Before I noticed, the ground had turned completely black, and my feet began sinking into it.

My sacred aura purified the ground around me, and I was pushed back to the surface. In response, Noah jumped back and shot around fifteen magic missiles. I countered them all with a single blade wave that he was forced to match with his own and with it; he cast 'blade wall' around me.

I dodged what I could while calmly walking forward, and the few that hit me only scraped by. As soon as I was out of it, I found a large ball of darkness in front of my face, and it was followed by a ball of white energy. I dodged it quickly, but before I could do anything else, they collided together and exploded in raw energy that pushed me a little to the side.

I found my focus back on Noah to see that half of his body was surrounded in shadows and the other half in light. He was charging two separate spells that he was pushing together at the same time. One white and one black. I couldn't help but smile. Next, I charged toward him while pulling out my grimoire and opening it to a certain page to cast my own specialized spell. As soon as I came within five feet of him, he released both of his spells together.

"*Pure blackness*." He faced both of his palms toward me, and the opposing elements clashed in an array of color and energy.

"*Palm explosion*." I had created a single flame in my hand, enveloped it in a micro whirlwind, and condensed it using all the air in a thirty-foot radius.

The air fed the flame, and it grew uncontrollably in its tiny confines until it made contact with something. The result was an incredible reaction of an instant vacuum that pulled everything together and an explosion to push everything apart.

The space in front of me turned into a giant spherical fireball that then exploded in the most violent reaction I could imagine at the time. The bubble expanded around Noah and his attack before detonating, and I had to jump back before I was caught in the blast myself.

When the smoke cleared, Noah was lying in a pit on the ground, unconscious. I went in to pick him up.

"Hey Noah, I don't know if you can hear me but if you can, I want you to know something. I can tell what's going on in there. There's something buried deep down under the surface and you're fighting yourself to keep it in. You might not know it, but she notices it too. Don't hide your struggle. Let the people that want to help, help. Don't succumb to the curse of the powerful or they'll fall to the curse of the powerless."

I carried him out of the hole and took him out of the field myself. It turned out that we were both severely injured.

Noah had multiple second-degree burns and impact fractures along his arms and ribs while I had a severe nosebleed, four large gashes that opened up in my chest, six fractured ribs, and one broken one.

We both were covered in numerous cuts and suffered from advanced fatigue. I was able to convince a nurse to get Carona who was able to help with most of our injuries. Noah was still out of it, but I was able to get back to the stands after being basically mummified with bandages.

"Where's Noah?" asked Catt, looking around after I sat down.

"He's still knocked out. Carona's looking after him right now so no need to worry. So, what's going on?"

"Nothing really," said Doc. "Just waiting for you."

"He seemed like he had a lot on his mind. I thought helping him let off some steam would help him focus," I said, sitting back and waiting for the next round.

The names that came up were Shane and Catt. As Catt stood, she seemed to be in thought.

"No holds barred, remember that," I said. "I suggest not holding back against this guy."

"Yeah…" I wasn't sure if she heard me as she went to the marker.

A minute later, the battle started with Catt attempting to dash around Shane in a circle only to have one of her feet frozen and the other slip on ice. She landed in a perfect split as the entire floor of the field was coated in ice.

She thawed herself using a fireball on the ice around her foot and sent a magic missile.

Shane reacted by freezing the attack mid-air. He moved out of the way for it to just slide across the ground and break apart.

Catt attained a bright red glow that melted the ice below her feet before using her speed to circle her opponent. She was moving carefully, yet quickly while increasing her speed as she went. She then took a series of sharp turns that resulted in a decagram being melted into the ice, causing a shift in the battle. All the rest of the ice melted and was replaced with fire rising out of the ground.

Shane hadn't moved until then. In less than a second, he had summoned his weapon and closed the distance between Catt and himself. She just barely had enough time to block with one of her fists when his sword came down on top of her.

There was a bright flash the instant they made contact, and Shane was sent flying. His movements from there seemed to become sluggish. His weakness to fire was definitely hard to ignore as he constantly had to fight back the flames that were too widespread for him to freeze.

His only choice was to disrupt the ritual spell that Catt had placed. He boosted himself high over the field and turned down to face the ground. He put his hands together, and the temperature dropped dramatically. I was able to see my breath as a ball of ice large enough to fill the entire field materialized in front of him and began to fall.

Catt, standing among the flames and surrounded by electricity, switched back to fire and did a superhero jump at the glacier. Her gloves evolved and shifted to include boosters on her wrists that she used to increase her speed while rising to meet the challenge.

The heat coming from her intensified, and her color changed to resemble my flame. In response, the crystal in my pocket began glowing and floating in her direction. When she hit the ice, she disappeared into it, and it stopped falling. Three seconds later, she appeared from the top surrounded by a spiral of flames, and tackled Shane.

He used his sword to block, but she was still able to punch him in the gut with both fists. Once she found herself above him, the flame collapsed around Shane and carried him down into and through the glacier all the way to the ground before it started falling again. There was a thunderous crash as Ice filled the entire field.

Catt then careened down into the hole she made in the glacier while surrounded by wind with draconic scales falling behind her. When she landed, there was a pillar of white light shining from inside that shattered and melted the ice. The ground that she stood on had lowered by ten feet, and the water was being evaporated by the flames that survived the impact.

Shane was floating on the water until the timer ran out, then he stood and left on his own. Catt returned with Noah in tow. Apparently, he had woken up during Catt's fight.

"Hey Noah, you feeling ok?" I asked as soon as I saw him.

"Yeah, how about you? Did I even hurt you? I felt like I was hitting a brick wall," he said, sitting down.

"Well, you broke the hell out of that wall." I showed him my ribs. "So, when did you wake up?"

"I woke up when the giant piece of ice crashed down. It was insane."

"That means you missed the part where Catt did a perfect split at the start. A. Perfect. Split. Mind you," I said, looking back and forth at them both.

"I'm not surprised," said Noah before noticing the smile creeping across my face. "That's not why though," he said, with a quick look at Catt. She seemed to still be deep in thought. "What's wrong, Catt?"

"Nothing. I'm just thinking." It seemed that she didn't hear any of our conversation.

"About what?" Noah put his hand on her shoulder.

"I'll tell you when I figure it out." She was staring at the ground with a blank expression.

"Ok." He shrugged and sat back. "Oh, Krow."

"Yeah?" I said.

"I heard you. What you said at the end there."

"I was hoping you did."

The next names to come up were Leon and Doc. Before Doc stood up, I put both of my arms on top of my head and all he did was put his hand on my arms before walking to the marker.

The match started with Leon running forward, disappearing into a flame, and reappearing behind Doc with a kick before getting his leg caught. He tried to shoot a fireball at Doc's face before being slung in a circle and thrown.

He teleported again as soon as he landed. This time, Doc stepped out of the way as Leon came flying out of more flames with his sword. Doc reached his hand out and Leon slammed into the ground.

Leon seemed to struggle for a bit before covering himself in flames and standing up. The flames extended around ten feet away and Doc moved to avoid it. Leon rushed at Doc and the flames followed with him at the center.

Instead of dodging, Doc stood and waited for his opponent. He dodged the sword and punched Leon in the face. As that happened, the surrounding space turned pitch black and stayed that way for around ten seconds before it combusted into more flames. Normally any opponent Doc faces would be overtaken by wither and be on the ground by that time, but that wasn't the case. Doc's clothes were smoking as he exited the flames before they died down.

Leon was standing with a new sword in hand. It had a more stylistic handle that curved in a flame pattern; the guard curved slightly back on both sides, the blade shape changed to look like seven different blades fitted onto each other, and the whole thing was tinted red. Based on the immense rush of energy, that was the first time he was able to use that form.

The flames came back shortly as Leon dashed at Doc for the last time. In the blink of an eye, Leon's sword was across the field. He was back-to-back with Doc, and the business end of a scythe was pressed against his throat. He had no choice but to give up.

When Doc came back, he put his hand up and I high-fived him before he could ruffle my hair. He sat silently for a minute and said something unexpected.

"We can't let that kid join C.H.E.S.S." He sounded as serious as usual.

"What?" I said in surprise.

"He's got too much potential. If he's corrupted, nobody could stop him easily."

"What about me? Or us?" I said, gesturing toward myself, then spreading my arms to include our whole group. Doc was always confident that no matter what happened, we'd be able to handle anything that came our way, but that one hypothetical seemed to shake that belief a bit.

"You see, you used to… You'd need every encounter to be life or death against ever stronger opponents and consistently break your limits to get the way he is. I know you think you'd be prepared for something like that, but I know you're not." Doc chose his words carefully and methodically.

I stood and said, "Oh yeah? Try me."

"I will." His response was calm and cold.

"Ok." I wasn't expecting him to accept my challenge so readily. I sat back down without another word.

The final match was between Mike and Hiyaku. The match started with Hiyaku walking calmly toward Mike who was digging a small hole in the ground before a thunderous sound erupted from the sky followed by dark clouds, heavy rain, and a shark-like creature that was bigger than the entire stadium. It was a dark blue from below and nearly pitch black on top with large, black, beady eyes.

The creature began a nosedive before opening its mouth with thousands of rows of teeth, each the size of at least two people. At that moment, Hiyaku summoned his weapon and stabbed it into the ground. The area around him began glowing in a rainbow of colors before spreading outside of the stadium.

Time stopped again. What little resistance I had to the phenomenon only afforded a five-foot bubble where I could see things in real time. This was far beyond the effects of the last two times this happened.

A few seconds later, the creature was gone, and Mike was unconscious on the ground. The battle ended there.

After the round was over, we all went to see Belle. She had woken up and began walking around when no one was looking, and it took a few minutes to find her. She was roaming around the stone underground tunnels of the stadium looking for food and was caught with six hotdogs, two burgers, and four nacho plates in a basket. Apparently, massive weight loss and extreme hunger were side effects of her summoning contract with the mechanical man that she housed herself within.

We were making our way back outside when an explosion that was so loud that I thought my ears would bleed sounded off. It came from the facilities on the other side of the island. The few who stayed behind to find Belle were me, Doc, Catt, Noah, and Hinata as well as Belle's grandfather. Doc split off from the rest of us early and he never reconvened with us. He likely would have had events not unfolded the way they had.

Less than a minute after the explosion, most of our phones chimed at once. It was a text from Carona. It read: '*work to do. Scatter 9642*' That was our code for radio silence. It turned out that Catt, Nero, and Hinata all got a similar text from Graven.

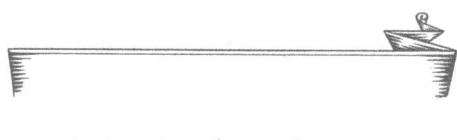

28-The Tale of Titania

[Carona Hunt]

The explosion rocked the entire island from the base to the top. Everyone just barely managed to keep their balance in the sway. I knew what was going on and wasted no time giving orders. Ariel, Leuna, Caroline, and Sara were with me at the time. Sara and Caroline were to stay together as a precaution and everyone was to scatter as quickly as possible, leaving me behind. They knew their roles and what to do from there. They were to gather information to understand the situation and act according to what they found.

No one questioned me and left the island following a lockdown command that sounded over speakers across the entire base.

I used the confusion to find my way deep into the residential district and into a series of unmarked storehouses. In the back room of one of them hid a hatch pipe that led into a network of tunnels.

"I'm not who we are." I said the password, the hatch opened without sounding any alarms, and I descended into the passageway. It was always dingy down there, but now, it was decrepit.

The foundation was relatively untouched aside from the copious amounts of graffiti across the walls, but the ceiling had seen better days. There were no cracks, but mildew had settled in layers on the insulation, and it was hanging down in strands that threatened to entangle me.

The tunnels were originally part of an emergency evacuation plan but were only used by new recruits to sneak out past curfew. The fact that the password still worked was proof that someone was still using it.

I traveled to an opening that led to an elevator shaft and climbed to the bottom before reaching a maintenance room through a hatch. If I was lucky, nothing had changed. There'd be no security cameras and the room would be as cluttered as always.

I opened the hatch slightly and peered through the crack. There was everything from sports to lab equipment, electronics and decorations once stacked high with dust, now toppled all over the place from the shaking. The light was on, but the debris likely triggered the motion sensor. Any people that were around would've responded to the lockdown call.

As silently as I could, I left out the hatch, climbed over the unstable mountain of stuff, and found my way to the door. The light turned off halfway there and made it more difficult, but I was able to get to the door with no problems.

Before I could reach for the handle, it opened by itself, and I froze. There stood a face I still recognized. His black hair was longer than it used to be, and he had grown taller as well. None of his changes were natural, but that visor he never took off was still in place. Guile stood before me alive and well.

"Hello, De'Reece," He said, with a smile, and folded arms. "I didn't think you'd come alone."

"I'm not putting any of my kids in danger for something like this and that's not my name anymore, and It's Carona."

"You consider even the Black Reaper one of your own?" he said, stepping out of the doorway and down the hall. The walls once were blue and white, but the colors faded to a uniform gray and the black carpet had been eroded in place of the stone foundation.

"You got a problem with that?" I said, following him at a safe distance.

"Somehow, I expected no less." He reached a double door with a keypad and stopped in front of it. The door led to one of four internal observatories that linked all communications in and around the base.

"So, what kind of job did I have to come all the way here to do?" I was becoming a little anxious.

"You know, you're much bigger than you used to be." He said, leaning against the doors.

"You callin' me fat?"

"No, just different. On the outside anyway." He took out a cigarette and lit it in his mouth. "I got a feeling that on the inside you're the same old De'Reece."

"It's Carona."

"I heard. That was your daughter's birthplace, right? You got yourself a nice little group of soldiers under your command."

"They're not soldiers, they're my children and if you know my name then use it."

"It must be nice to have someone to take care of you when you get old. Not that I'd ever have something like that."

"Because you don't grow old."

Mildly surprised, he said, "Oh, you knew?"

"It took a while, but I figured out what you really are and that you led me to figure it out on purpose. Why?"

Solemnly, he said, "It was for Arin. You two were always close and I couldn't tell her directly myself. That would have made her a target. In hindsight, I didn't have to worry about that, you were all pegged for execution, anyway."

"That reminds me," I said, moving swiftly in front of him with a punch that sent him to the ground. His cigarette went out, and he sat looking up at me from the floor. "That was for Arin. I couldn't help her when she needed me most, but you weren't there at all. You weren't there for any of us."

"I know." He stood back up. "That's why, before we enter this room, I want to know what happened that day."

"I guess it's only fair that you know." Taking a few steps back I recounted the experience.

There were eight of us in our team. Toriel 'Glitter' a rook, Beatrix 'Pix' the other rook, Micah 'Hobb' the pawn; Arin 'Fay' the bishop, Marroon 'Oberon' the king, Guile 'Spriggan' the Knight and leader, not to mention me, De'Reece 'Titania' the queen.

We were sent on a mission to seize a warehouse selling illegal goods and Hobb was sent in alone to scout.

"That was a bad move," said Guile, solemnly.

"Well, you weren't there. We only had our strategist and no leader with no plan." I continued.

Hobb never responded, so Glitter went in after him. She also didn't return. Shortly after, Pix was hit out of nowhere and she was gone just like that. A sniper was on the prowl, and we couldn't tell where the shot came from, so we were forced to retreat. We barely got away, but not before Nymph went down, protecting the rest of us from the shots that seemed like they could come from any direction.

"Then there were just the three of you left?"

"Yeah, I thought we were safe until Marroon slit Arin's throat. I Heard her muffled scream, and I turned around and I saw her just staring at me. Her eyes were so blank, and his knife was still in the middle of the motion, you know?" I choked back the urge to cry and continued. "Somehow, I managed to fend him off and take her with me, but it was too late." I fought to resist the welling tears. "So, where were you the whole time?"

"Now it makes sense. As it turns out, you weren't the only one to figure out my identity, and while I was busy dealing with that." He snapped his fingers and re-lit the cigarette still in his mouth. "They moved in on convincing her to join their cause. When she refused, they decided to wipe our squad completely, save for myself and Marroon. The only question was: Why would they decide to do something so drastic?"

"It could've been because they figured that she'd tell the rest of us," I said, knowing that my theory wouldn't mean much now.

"That's unlikely. Based on my intel, if they succeeded in convincing her, they thought they would've had an easier time convincing the two of us and the rest in turn. The real problem is how did they know our dynamic? It was Marroon." He typed a code into the keypad and the doors opened. "They got him, and he gave us away."

On the other side was a black-and-white room with control panels and monitors showing live camera feeds from around the base. There were around twelve people scrambling between monitors and speaking quickly between each other and two people conversing at the main terminal roughly twenty feet away and up a set of stairs to hover over the middle of the room.

"Welcome to the resistance," he said with open arms. "We never really had an official name, but if all goes well, we won't need one."

"So, this is what me coming here was all about?" I was hesitant to follow him into the room, but I did.

"Indeed."

"I'll assume you called Graven, too. I heard about your encounter."

"I did."

"I don't think he's coming."

"We'll see." He turned around and went up the stairs. Interrupting the conversation between the two people, he pointed me out and they followed him back down the stairs.

"Hello, Miss Hunt, my name's Dr. Soliman Cruz. I'm a head researcher and scientist in the phenomena sciences department." The man held his hand out and I shook it. He had short and curly brown hair, thick-rimmed glasses, and a white lab coat.

"And I'm April Cartwrite," said the woman, followed by another handshake. "I believe we're in a similar position." She held up her left arm, which had a jagged scar from the top of her shoulder down to the back of her hand. "Prior to three years ago, I worked under C.H.E.S.S. as well. I was codenamed 'Stamp', a rank five platinum rook and part of team Mid-twinight. We were part of the special ops division. And you? That is, if you don't mind me asking." She wore a navy-blue sleeveless cargo jacket and matching jeans, and her eyes glowed faintly behind long black curls.

"I was Codenamed 'Titania', a rank four platinum queen and part of Faery, a team under central command."

"She was a part of my squad," said Guile, moving back to the terminal. "We don't have all that much time, so let me tell you what's going on."

He pressed a few buttons and all the screens changed to depict a map of the facility with the front gate as the south point with a short list of names with faces next to them on the left-hand side. Among the names and faces was Graven with his mask on. "The list on the left is the names and known faces of those we invited here ourselves to help with the resistance. So far, you two are all we have on that front," He gestured back at me and April. "Unfortunately, due to unforeseen circumstances, we had to meet early, and most others were unable to make it. What just happened was a premeditated strike by an outside group that has uncovered the truth about what C.H.E.S.S. is really about."

He pressed his finger onto the console and dragged a red circle over the advanced training facility in the middle of the base. "The explosion happened under this facility. The reason is likely because underneath that building, like the rest, is an underground facility of equal importance except in this case, that facility's function was made secret from everyone under the rank of ruby aside from a few personnel. That facility houses the very basis for what has become of this organization. The resurrection of the Shadow Master."

He paused for dramatic effect and continued. "Sixty years ago, at the end of the secret wielder's war, everyone thought he was killed, but that's not entirely true. While his body was mostly destroyed, his soul stayed attached, allowing him the opportunity to regenerate from his fatal wounds. This is a recent picture of him."

He pressed another button, and the map disappeared in place of a picture of a man with unusually pale skin and alternating black and red eyes with short, slightly curly, black hair, and a full beard. "The good news is his natural power was sealed away permanently as a result of his dealings with the devil. The bad news is People here are working to restore his lost power and bring him back completely. How they plan to do that is with this."

He pressed the button again and the picture changed one more time. Now, it was what looked like a wielder's gate. It looked to be made of stone with a sprawling black pattern across the surface and six small holes around a seventh in the middle. "When the Shadow Master 'died' his gate materialized in the physical plane and his spirit animal split itself into innumerable pieces referred to by the world as 'corpse shadows'.

This gate, until eight years ago, was securely guarded underground by a family of vampires known as the Archfields. The majority of whom were left deceased after C.H.E.S.S. moved to retrieve it. They plan to restore the gate and empower him once more. They also seem to be gathering corpse shadows together in a bid to restore his spirit animal as well. If they succeed, I doubt we'll have another miracle like we did last time. That's why we'll have to stop them. Most of our forces are outside helping with or taking part in the lockdown, and some are gathering new recruits.

Our job is logistics support. We need to make sure that our people can make moves under the radar without getting caught. If anyone comes under the shadow of suspicion, this whole operation could be a bust. To that end, I've swayed the higher-ups into thinking I was gathering a set of outside associates for scientific tests to create a potentially elite unit within the ranks of C.H.E.S.S. and they gave me permission to utilize discontinued codenames. We will use our original codenames for this operation. Any questions?"

"One," I said, "Is there any insurance in place for if we're found out?"

"Unfortunately, no. There are, however, contingency plans but those are just shots in the dark at this point. If something goes wrong, I advise you to get out as quickly as possible and leave this island. If you choose to stay at that point, there's very little I can do for you."

"What are the contingency plans?"

"There are two." He was ready for my obvious follow-up question. "One is to kill Ferris Kaizer, the leader of C.H.E.S.S. The other is to break deep into the center of the island and destroy the astral gate held there. Both require a lot of luck and a tremendous amount of power and skill, seeing as the gate is unscathed despite the bomb and the boss is constantly surrounded by elite soldiers." He changed the screen back to a map with a dot still focused on the center.

"So, you were betting on me bringing that power and skill with me, right?" I folded my arms in accusation.

"You weren't the only one. There were supposed to be more than sixteen of us here. Somewhere in the thirties, but we'll have to work with what we have. You three are the most experienced people here aside from myself, so I need you to watch over everyone else while I inspect the rest of this abandoned wing for allies and rogues." He stepped down from the terminal and left the room.

"It's such a high probability that we could all die... Why did I come back here..." April seemed to have just realized how much danger we were putting ourselves in by coming here and was having a little breakdown. She reached to grab my hand, and I pulled away. "Do you trust what he said? You used to be part of his team, but don't you think that this could be a trap or a setup?"

"If this was a setup, we'd already be dead. I came to see the tournament from the start, believing that it was a trap. After all, I received an invitation." I pulled the letter out of my purse and showed it to her before putting it back.

"I got one too, but I don't know what I was expecting coming here. I was just looking for someone." She took the same letter out of her pocket and stared at it.

"And who might that be?" I asked.

"I was looking for the remaining members of my team. Despite appearances, I'm pretty hapless without someone to help me, you know? And I was trying to find as many of them as I could. I honestly don't know how I survived without any of them." She sounded as if she was just dropped into an empty room with a ghoul.

"You didn't see any of them on the list?" I said, leading her to the nearest console and finding the command to bring up the list of names and pictures.

"I'm fuzzy with remembering faces, so it would take me a little time to recognize any of them; not to mention they likely changed their faces, and the text is in a cypher I'm unfamiliar with." She was, indeed, hapless.

"It's in Greek," I said. The alphabet and language systems change with every place the base stops at. Don't you know that?"

"No. my team was always off base. Covert ops, remember?" That statement alone raised more questions than I had time to ask in a day.

"Ok, what were the names of your teammates," I said, zooming into the list and scrolling through.

"They were D'angelo Martinez, queen; Hope Jackson, king; Blare Sharp, pawn; Azrael Laitin, rook; and Karasu Lockhart, knight, and leader." She sounded very proud reciting their names and positions.

"Graven," I said, shaking my head.

"Do you know one of my teammates?" she asked, excitedly.

"Yes. Karasu changed his name to Graven. I know him."

"You do? How?"

"He's dating my daughter."

"Oh..." She sounded disappointed. "At least he's alive."

"None of the other names ring a bell though, and none of them are on this list either."

"Are you sure?"

"Here, take a look for yourself." It took a minute, but I was able to find a Greek-to-English alphabetical translation in the database. I brought it up next to the list of names and left her to it.

The next thing I did was go to another terminal and draw an updated map using the one I found there. Afterward, I spoke with the people constantly shuffling about and found that they were mostly scientists and low-ranking soldiers who could barely cast intermediary spells.

None of them had any management skills, so I took charge, divided up responsibilities, and made sure everyone knew how to communicate effectively. Eventually, the chaos on the surface died down and Guile came back. Instead of new allies, he had a warning.

Apparently, most of the prisoners held in the on-site prison were released and more than a few of them have yet to be found. They were all extremely hostile and very capable. It would make our job more difficult not only because we'd have to watch out for the criminals, but because that aspect caused security to tighten even more. Thankfully, we could open and close certain passageways to confuse most of the prisoners we found to lead them outside. Leaving them inside the base would have only complicated things. Some of them found the living quarters, however, and made themselves comfortable in empty rooms.

In time, I came to understand all the others who were part of the resistance. It went all the way to the top.

29-All of the Truths

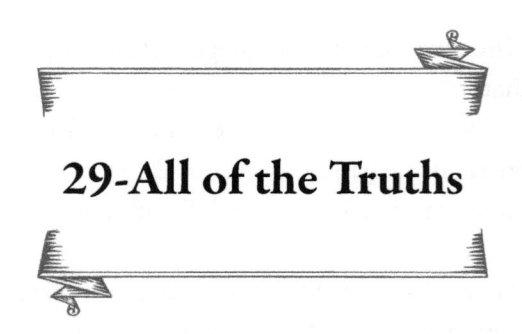

[Nero Cursley]

The lockdown saw all personnel aside for a few select units gathered in their respective dorms and awaited orders. For a few minutes, the halls were bustling with the sound of foot traffic. It eventually died down, followed by the alarm going silent as well. The silence was eerie, and the wait was foreboding. I felt like eyes were watching me from every corner and no matter what I did, the feeling persisted. Eventually, I decided to say something.

"What do you want?" I said, nose-deep in a book I've read too many times to count. "This has been too consistent for this to be just a spell, and we don't have enough personnel for this to work everywhere."

The feeling disappeared after the sound of paper sliding under the door. It read: '*ANSWERS -10 0 5*'. They were coordinates pointing to a location within the base. I looked at a map and found that it was where the entrance to the detention center was. I had never been there and had never heard any stories about it either, so this made me curious.

I followed the map and found that a spot that was normally a stone wall had moved, and a dark walkway had opened up. The ground was solid, but there was a gentle sway as I reached the other side and another open door.

There was a counter to my left with bulletproof glass reinforcement and steel benches on my right. Everything was white and there were two doors leading away from the room; both of which were open. One opened directly to a visitors' room, which was also reinforced with bullet-proof glass, while the other led deeper into the prison. The place felt empty, but it was an odd kind of empty. As if there was a major commotion and then nothing.

"I'm here!" I called out, not expecting any particular response. There was a faint voice and I followed it down the hall and into a large room with cells lining the walls up to three stories. The voice sounded again, this time, unprompted. It was less faint and a voice I recognized in stress.

I was sprinting by the time I realized it. Far in the back of the prison, I found a solid wall with a slit in it at waist level and small holes near eye level. "I'm here, Is that who I think it is?" I said, trying to peek in through the holes and finding near darkness on the other side.

"Nero?" Mary was on the other side of the wall.

"Do you need help?" I asked, looking around for a handle or release mechanism.

"Yes, it feels like my leg is broken and I can't get out."

"How did you get in there? I can't find a way to open this." I banged on different parts of the wall and stomped around to find a pressure plate.

"That wall opens. I don't know how and whatever they have on me is nullifying my magic. I don't know who it was, but she was really strong. She used a rapier, was really pale, had black, spikey hair, and a creepy smile. I couldn't tell what kind of magic she used, but it felt like she attacked my soul directly. If you see someone like that, run as fast as sound can take you and get away. You can't beat her. She only had to glance at me to break my spirit." I could hear the rattling of chains followed by pained groans. "So, I couldn't run..."

"Are you directly behind the entrance?" I asked, preparing a spell.

"No, I'm next to it."

"Good, **shatter**." I cast the spell, and nothing happened. No wind picked up either. I tried it again and nothing happened again. I put my hand on the wall and tried casting another spell. It was clear that the prison walls were enchanted with magic-nullifying properties. I successfully summoned my sword, which meant that either the space between the walls was unaffected or it didn't work on non-magical energies. "Hey, Mary."

"If your magic isn't working either, you need to get out, I don't want you to get caught because of me." She sounded tired.

"No, my magic works. It's just the walls that nullify it. I'll try the strongest spell I know. If that doesn't overpower it, then I'm gonna go get help." I charged the spell with my grimoire floating in front of me as I read it.

"If you do, try to find my brother. He might be able to help."

"You have a brother?"

"His name's Noah. He was in the tournament. He's friends with Catt, the girl I fought; Krow, the guy with the crazy fire; Doc, the darkness guy; and there's more too. They're a whole group that might be able to help."

"What about our team?"

"There's a conspiracy. I've seen it myself. Honestly, I don't even know if I can trust you right now, but as it stands, you're my only hope."

"Here I go. **Chorus of maleficence**." The area before me glowed, and the wall remained unchanged as a pressure wave that amounted to a slight breeze blew back at me. I touched the wall again and felt that the enchantment had gone nowhere. "Damn it!" I punched the wall as hard as I could, and my fist bled. "I'll be back," I said, before turning and running to the nearest exit, making my way above ground, and out to find Noah.

I didn't notice at the time, but all the doors I went through opened on their own and closed behind me. The sun was down before I made it to a port town on the mainland.

There was no presence of anyone following me and there seemed to be no movement directly around me the whole way, despite guards being present. They were either waiting for me to drop my guard or someone helped me escape undetected.

On the way, I had time to contemplate what Mary meant about a conspiracy, and it brought me back to the conversation I had with Guile on the jet. Now I was certain that there was more to it than he let on.

"**Farsight: echolocation.**" I scanned the area in front of me and saw a multitude of different magical wavelengths. They looked like dense bubbles that could be seen through solid structures that were all nearly invisible and very small, which made them hard to spot. I took to the air and wandered toward a few that looked similar to what I thought Noah to be, from when we met.

I had to get within a certain distance to know for sure, so I also looked for one that was constantly shifting. I came close enough to a group of four to feel their presence and confirmed that it was them. The moon was now high in the sky. They were in a small house on an unnamed road. I wasted no time landing in front of the door and knocking.

There was cautious movement and heavy breathing inside. A minute passed, and I knocked again. Another minute passed and the door quickly opened. Cattherine was inside, ready and waiting to fight.

"Noah's inside, I need to talk to him." She rushed toward me, aiming for my face. I put my hand up to block and she was gone. Immediately after, something came in contact with my back, and I was knocked to the ground.

Before I could get up, someone pulled back both of my arms and placed their knee on my spine. I ended up far enough from the door that it could close, and close it did.

"What do you want?" said Cattherine, sending fire up and around my arms threatening to burn me.

"It's about Noah's sister. She's in trouble. Mary told me to find you."

Noah stepped out of the shadows. "Catt, let him go," he said, looking me in the eye.

"You sure I shouldn't pull his shoulders out of the sockets?" She began pulling harder.

"Catt, please." He walked back into the darkness, and she let me go. The lights came on and he could be seen sitting at a small table in a wooden chair.

I stood and explained the situation. The girl stood behind me the whole time. Once I finished talking, he took a minute to respond. While that was happening, I concentrated on my hearing and found that everyone who was in the house had an increased heart rate, and all of their breathing aside for one was deep and calm.

"There's something you need to understand," said Noah, as he stood up and began pacing. "C.H.E.S.S. isn't the good guy. Most of my family is dead and so are many others because of them. They tear apart small towns just to find anyone who awakens to any powers and recruit them to do the same to someone else. They kill ruthlessly and indiscriminately. They numb you to the experience and when you're too far in, they show you what you've done and expect you to do it more. If you don't, they kill you if not worse. Do you understand?"

"I don't know anything anymore. I just want to get her out of there before that 'worse' comes to pass," I said, shifting my weight back and forth.

"Ok guys, you can come out," said Noah, standing back up. Out of a doorway behind Noah came Leon, one of the contestants in the tournament. Down a set of stairs to the right came a girl.

Her eyes were yellow, her black hair was neatly braided with one distinct yellow braid in a zig-zag pattern, and she wore a jean vest over a gray long-sleeve and black pants. She came within a foot of me, smiled, and then hugged me.

"Do I know you?" I asked with undeniable confusion before I noticed that I was tearing from my left eye.

"Yes, you do." She took a few steps back. "Maybe this will jog your memory." She reached out and summoned her weapon. It was the same as mine, but it was tinted yellow, and the spikes were reversed.

"You're... My sister..." I stumbled forward and hugged her. "Of all the people I thought I would run into, it happened to be someone I thought was dead." We were both sobbing.

"My name's Carrie," she said, hugging me back. "I thought you were dead, too."

"You finally found a name you like, huh..." I said, between sobs.

"So, your name's Nero, huh?" she said, calming down. "When I heard about you, I thought it was too good to be true, but now that I see you in person, I know it is true."

"Wait, so you two are related?" said the girl behind me.

"We're twins," said Carrie. "And we have a lot to catch up on."

She sat me down and we caught up with each other. The first thing she told me was that there would be no way to get back in after getting out in my position. She was well-informed and knew a lot of secrets beyond my rank.

It turned out that she was part of an outside faction that had infiltrated C.H.E.S.S. to take them down from the inside out. Mary was a part of it as well. The explosion was their doing. There was also an inside resistance composed of more experienced people that started within C.H.E.S.S. They were most likely who helped me escape, and it turned out the pair lost any way to communicate and were forced to improvise. That's how they met and joined with Noah and Catt.

It turned out that when we were separated, she was inside the orphanage when the fire broke out. As a result, she had a burn scar up her left arm. She was saved by a firefighter who took her in and raised her beside Leon. I told her about how I was raised by Rachel and joined C.H.E.S.S. myself. Eventually, we came to the present.

After we finished catching up, I went out to see if I could find any way to sneak everybody into the base unnoticed. It turned out to be impossible as the entire island was on total lockdown.

It looked like a villain's fortress with a forebodingly dark cityscape and eerie silence surrounded by a sheer wall to keep everything in and everything else out. I decided to check again to see if I was being followed, and I found Carrie.

"What are you doing here?" I said, sharply turning toward her.

"I'm worried. We just found each other, and I don't want to lose you again so quickly." She stepped out of some nearby brush.

"I won't be killed off so easily. I can handle myself," I said, sitting at the edge of the water bank.

"I know. I just want to be there in case something does happen. Two of us are stronger than one, right?" She lightly punched my shoulder.

"As long as you have my back, I'll have yours. Just let me know next time you stow away, ok?" I punched her shoulder back.

"Sure." She punched me back harder.

"You know, those bushes were poison ivy," I said, lying back and looking up at the stars.

"You're messing with me." She leaned over me and stared into my eyes to see if I was lying. My years of experience apart from her had made me a better liar, and I gave no hint to the contrary.

"Wait... You are messing with me, right?" She began squirming around and checking to find any bumps on her arms.

"Glad to have you back," I said, with a giggle as a tear started rolling down my cheek.

30-Bounty Hunter

[Krow Hunt]

Being among the first to leave the island, I wasn't taking any chances on leaving in a group. I did, however, spot a building where people seemed to be gathering. I had entered the main city to hide in plain sight.

I ran my fingers along my collar to activate the enchantments on my cloak. It shortened into more of a jacket so I wouldn't be as easy to point out in a crowd. I wandered around the city looking at landmarks until I noticed what looked like ripples in the sky converging on one tall building. It was easy to notice because the sun was setting by that time and the color spectrum of the sky was being visibly disrupted.

Assuming the building was a hotel, I entered as if I belonged there and went directly to the elevators. Finding the one that went to the upper floors, I entered. Allowing my cloak to return to form, I exited the elevator and made my way to the stairs.

The roof door was locked, but I burned through the chain to open the door. Thirteen people were staring at me when I stepped out, five girls and eight guys. I recognized a few of them. Phenom, Charles, and Sofia from the tournament.

"Ok, whose dumb idea was it to use invisibility at sundown? I could see all of you from the ground and I just so happened to be looking up."

"It was my idea." I found a serrated wielder's blade in front of my throat and a female voice with a Scottish accent from my right. "It was so we could catch people like you; knowledgeable and curious."

"No, he's cool," said Sofia, stepping up. "I sat near him in the stands, and he doesn't like them either-"

"Intel says he's friendly with that bounty hunter." said the voice. "Very friendly."

"Oh…" Sofia stepped back.

"Get out here." I felt a hand grab my collar and pull me out into the open while the door closed behind me. The blade was still at my throat, but I could at least see who it belonged to. At that point, all I could see was her face. She had long, red braids, big blue eyes, and freckles dotted across her nose. "Tell us what you know about C.H.E.S.S."

"For your information, she cut ties with me last night and I don't know any more than you guys probably do," I said, leaning against the door behind me. I was pulled toward the blade again.

"Try us," she said with a murderous look in her eyes.

"I was under the assumption that the invitation I got was a trap, so I decided to at least use it to have some fun. Getting to know Rachel was just a happy accident, that's all."

"What do you mean, 'fun'?"

"I like fighting, ok? Call me belligerent. Come to think about it, this ain't all that bad either. I've never had a…" I recounted the number of potential opponents. "Fourteen-on-one fight before. This could be fun." I was pushed against the door with the blade pressed directly against my throat. "Okay, if you don't want to fight, we don't have to. I wasn't trying to intimidate or anything."

"*Light coil.*" A rope of light wound around my whole body and held me to the door. "We wait till dark and move out." said the girl after removing her blade from my throat. It turned out that the blade was curved around the bulbous structure of a round shield on her arm.

Darkness came quickly, and so did her next order. "Starshe and Patty, scan the area and report back." One guy and one girl closer to the edge cast invisibility on themselves and jumped off the building in opposite directions.

More than ten minutes passed, and they didn't return. By then, there was more than one worried face. I tried silently casting a spell and nothing happened.

"If they don't come back in five minutes, I suggest letting me go or you might have more problems," I said, scanning the crowd in front of me for varied reactions. The shield embedded itself in the door next to my head.

"What did your people do?" The girl was seething, and her face was red.

"My people did nothing. This is textbook. We're either surrounded or they sent someone highly skilled. You send out scouts and they take them out silently. You send someone after them and it's the same. Soon there will be a surprise attack and if you don't let me go, more than a few people here will die."

"And what? You'll vouch for us so that we aren't killed? As if I'll believe that." A couple of seconds after she said that, a shockwave in the center space between the crowd flung most of them directly off of the roof and down. The rest had some leeway but seemed unable to cast spells as a familiar figure appeared in the epicenter of the blast.

"So, this is where you went." Rachel came walking toward me with her sword in hand. It was a straight sword with a slightly curved handle and what looked like two more curved blades hugging the base of the main one.

"I'm guessing they sent you after me?" I said, hoping she came of her own accord.

"Unfortunately, yes." Every step she took seemed to be slower than the last.

"To kill me?" I asked.

"Worse," she said.

"They need me alive, and you don't know why," I guessed.

"But I have also been ordered to kill you if you resist." Just then, a shield flew in out of nowhere she parried it with the flat of her sword. The girl that stuck me to the door didn't land too far away and caught her shield as it came back.

"Way to go, Captain America! Now, could you let me go?" My question went unanswered as she put her hand up to cast a spell and nothing came out. "She used a spell that negates spell casting. You can only dispel magic that's been already cast and anything that's not magic."

The woman rushed toward Rachel, and they clashed for less than a second as her shield was parried again and she was sent to the ground with a heavy roundhouse kick to the head. The spell holding me in place was released as the caster was knocked out. "You know, I like strong women, but this is just overkill."

"Are you coming or not?" Rachel reached her hand out.

"No," I said, reaching my hand out and tracing a line across in front of me. As surely as I did, my sword appeared from the outline. "You're going to have to kill me."

"Of course," she said as if she knew that would be my answer. "You don't want this fight."

"Neither do you. It's just like last time. There's always a choice to not and say you did."

"We'll see," she said, charging toward me.

I moved away from the door and something else hit it. One of the smaller blades hugging her sword popped off and flew in my direction. I didn't know I dodged it until it smashed through the door.

I went on the defensive as I blocked the next blade that came my way. Both blades began swarming me until I found my way to the edge of the roof where they stopped, and Rachel made her move.

She charged one more time with all three blades at the ready, but before she could reach me, both the Scottish girl with the shield and Sofia with her mirror shield came to block her assault. They had gotten the rest of their people down the stairs and stayed behind to help as the only ones left with available weapons.

I took a step back. "What are you two doing? I don't need help."

"You 'Don't need help' my arse. You're on the edge," said the Scottish girl.

"That's what I wanted." I leaned back and let myself fall.

The world slowed down as my fall was followed by an explosion, and the two people who tried to help me began falling too. In the blink of an eye, Rachel was following me down on her levitating blades and I made my move as we exited the vertical range of her spell.

"***Heat coil.***" I cast the spell out of both of my palms to catch the two as they fell and pull them to me before casting another spell. "***Angel's descent.***" Surrounded by soft golden flames accented with angelic wings, I landed gently with the other two in tow on a nearby building. "Well, I do love picking up chicks," I said under my breath before letting them go onto their feet. "You two can leave. She's not after you."

"Hell no," said the Scottish girl. "The enemy of my enemy is my friend. I'm helping."

"You heard the lady," added Sofia.

"Put your pride away. If she was here for you, she'd already have you."

"Whatever you say," said the Scottish girl before charging forward. "C'mon Sofie."

"Got it," said Sofia, following close behind. Rachel hadn't landed yet, and they began acting before she could. The Scottish girl threw her shield and used Sofia's as a springboard to follow it up.

"***Nova blast.***" Positioning herself sideways, The Scottish girl shot a large blast of yellow light back at the shield. The shield glowed yellow as it absorbed the blast. Her other hand was held open until Rachel deflected it. She caught it only to clash with her target in mid-air. She was then flung down and created a hole in the roof of the building.

Rachel landed behind Sofia toward me.

Turning around, Sofia released the blast that was sent into her shield. The blast dissipated as Rachel's sword passed through both it and the shield it came from on its way to the person holding it.

As soon as I saw what was happening, I swift-cast 'flicker' and teleported to catch the blade before it could pierce its target. I was too late, however. It had gone through her arm and into her chest, but it missed her heart.

The blade began emitting flames, and I quickly removed it from its position before it could cause more damage. Sofia fell to the ground, but there was no blood. She began using her functioning arm to retreat to the hole that was made by the other girl.

"Ok, we need to talk," I tossed Rachel's sword back to her. "You said you were going to kill me. Why didn't you? It wouldn't take much effort on your part, what's stopping you?"

"The same reason you didn't just overpower my 'anti-magic field'. You should already know the answer to that question." She placed her finger against her ear and then trailed it down to her chest. She was wearing all black, but I understood where exactly she was pointing. Someone was listening.

"It's gonna be one of those, huh?" I took a stance and pushed off as hard as I could with my back foot. I went fast enough from there that I didn't need to touch the ground. Instead, when I pushed off, I did so in such a way that I spiraled through the air straight forward.

Rachel followed my blade with her eyes through my rotation and blocked the strike to guide it with her sword so that it would cut only what was necessary. I found my footing behind her, and she gave an exasperated gasp.

She stomped on a small marble-like object that fell to the ground. "You got it."

"Good." I grabbed her sword arm and pointed it away. "So, would you mind telling me what happened to the people you knocked from the roof? At least a few were unconscious and none of them found their way back up."

"You know I'm a hunter, not a killer. That shockwave from before was 'transit dreamscape'. It's a spell I use for dispersing crowds. Anybody knocked beyond the spell's boundary with me as the center is automatically teleported into the dreamscape until I undo the spell." She snapped the fingers on her other hand and six people appeared unconscious on the ground. "The other two are sitting on a building that way." She pointed to her left.

I let her go. "Tell me what's going on."

"All I know is that there was an explosion deep inside the island and I was sent for you after you fled. Now, I'm going to go find Nero and go home. Don't wait for me." She walked toward the edge of the roof.

"Does that mean this is the last time we'll see each other?"

My question made her stop. "Last time was supposed to be the last time, so yes." She cast invisibility on herself. Now, all I could see of her was a faint silhouette.

"And see, here I was getting all attached," I said, tapping the toe of my shoe on the ground and looking down at my feet.

"Don't flatter me." I thought she left after that statement, but she continued a couple of seconds later. "Who knows? We might see each other in passing out there somewhere." There was a spark of flame near the edge of the roof, and she was gone.

"Damn, two in less than a year's time," I said.

Sofia was too injured to move the other girl whose name I learned was Rose. She had taken multiple big impacts in close succession, and they took their toll. It didn't look like she'd wake up for a while. I carried her on my back and made a tourniquet for Sofia from spare cloth I carried with me.

There wasn't enough for both her arm and chest, so after using our combined healing aptitude, it turned out the hole in her arm was worse than the one in her chest so that's what it was used on. Eventually, the rest of the group re-converged on our location and the people sleeping on the roof woke up. I had just passed Rose off to one of the people who wasn't groggy from their nap, and she held my arm so I couldn't get away.

"And where are you going?" she mumbled, loudly.

I stopped dead in my tracks. "To find answers. If I can find some here, I don't mind sticking around for a while."

"There's war coming... Stay... Talk..." She was fading in and out of consciousness.

I decided to listen to what she had to say and before I knew it, it was daylight.

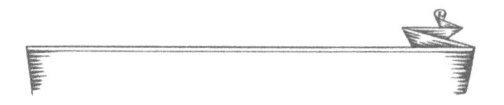

31-Faerie's Retreat

[Scarlett Hunt]

The group felt strangely calm when the island swayed from what felt like a blast from deep underground. Ariel, Leuna, Caroline, and I were with Mom when she gave the signal. Immediately after, we scattered and only a few seconds later, she sent the text on what to do next.

Caroline and I stayed together and dove into the water to escape. Leuna took to the air and cloaked herself with invisibility like many others and Ariel dove down with me and Caroline before tunneling down and away.

Making it to land a few minutes later, we trekked from a rocky beach into a grassy plain by a small town. We figured more people would show up, so we went into town and kept a low profile at a small inn.

Caroline was anxious the entire time after getting to land and only calmed down once we enchanted the walls of the room for privacy. She sat on the bed with her arms wrapped around one of her knees. "Do you think Mom's doing alright?" Her emotions fluctuated a little as she spoke. "I had another vision. I thought the visions were gone with the corpse shadow but they're back."

"Well, given how corpse shadows draw out your power by force, maybe it's just a magic trait you would have had regardless." I sat next to her and placed my hand on her shoulder. It didn't help calm her down, but I felt like removing it wouldn't help either.

"Yeah, I'm thinking the same thing, but that doesn't mean the visions are getting any better."

I sensed that she only started feeling worse, so I said, "What was the vision about? You know we've always survived everything that came our way, and we'll survive anything else that comes."

"The thing is, I don't know if this vision is bad, it's just never happened to be so uncertain." She sighed. "There's this guy and he's dead, but he's not... I'm not sure what it means."

"Well, is there anything about this man you can point out?"

"He was wearing all camo and there was this dangerous feeling coming from him."

"So, nothing specific?"

She tossed her hands and said, "He was wearing shorts, ok?" Her emotional state didn't change.

"Alright, alright. It's fine. We'll deal with it. We need to find out what's going on and regroup. First thing's first, where should we look?"

We found ourselves touring around town, keeping an eye out and an ear to the ground for anything resembling the explosion that rocked the C.H.E.S.S. headquarters. Eventually, we found a guildhall in the center of town. Given what it was and the waves of emotion emanating from it, it was safe to assume more than a few patrons were at the tournament during the explosion.

Entering the smooth-stone building, we made for the bar opposite the door and sat in a pair of empty seats. More than half of the occupied tables on the way carried the same irritated feeling emanating from them. Either they were weary of new arrivals in such a remote town, or they were aware of the current situation and cautious of subsequent visitors.

"What can I get you lovely ladies?" A man behind the bar stood with a notepad and a pen. "Or are you looking for work?"

"Information," said Caroline in a low voice, tapping her finger on the counter.

The bartender tilted his head to the side then smiled and lowered his voice as well. "What kind of information?"

"Something close to the base."

"That just happened. I feel like you'd have more info on it than me."

After gauging the emotional levels of everyone in the guildhall and determining none of them as a threat, I said, "There's not enough space to breathe if you're screaming underwater."

The man furled his brow and then used his fingers to smooth it out. "Alright, I'll get someone who understands that." He turned around and went through a door to the back. A few seconds later, he returned with another man. This one was familiar, however. "Here you go." The bartender walked off.

Standing before us, dressed as a bartender, was Grem Rose, also known as Moderacy of the Seven Virtues. "Can I do anything for you?" He gave a courteous bow.

I swallowed hard and said, "The current must really go places. There can't be much to fish up around here, can it?"

"Only the stragglers. Sharks attack and the schools scatter."

"Did you catch any? Or do you still have a full stock of bait?"

"I'm not here for the fish. They're good, but the current is bringing much larger game our way."

"So, that means we'll all be eating good?"

"Not if we get eaten first. A simple rod won't be enough. We'll need something bigger."

"So, you're saying I should make myself hungry?"

"If you're not already. The captain will be casting the first line in due time. Evening is fast approaching, and the beast appears at dawn."

"Thanks for the forewarning. I'll gather my gear then."

"Best of luck to you." He bowed again.

Caroline and I stood and made our way out of the guildhall. Once we stepped outside, we collectively heaved a sigh of relief. We happened upon someone with information who was both willing to part with it and non-hostile. I was sure I just used up all of my luck for the next year. Back at the inn, we went over what we had just heard.

"So, whatever's going on at C.H.E.S.S. is going to affect everyone and we just have to figure out how to deal with it?" Caroline looked at the one window covered by blinds, nervous.

Putting my hand on my chin, I said, "It seems like we got way too much information way too fast from probably one of the most reputable sources we could... He could always be lying... But it didn't feel like it."

"Do you think we should go back?" Caroline was now turned toward the window.

"We already got lucky. I don't think we should push our luck at this point. At least, not today."

"I meant to Mom."

I sighed. "I don't think we can."

"It's on the water. I think we can do it."

"This is why Mom has us together. We're not going back, not now. You just have to be patient."

Solemnly, she said, "You think Krow's gonna be patient?"

"He will if stays as carefree as normal. I hope."

"I think we should go back to the guildhall tomorrow. If that guy is still there, we might be able to get more out of him, lucky or not."

"Yeah, you're right. We should take a few jobs as adventurers as well. It'll just make gathering info easier. What do you think?"

"I think you read my mind."

The next day, we made our way to the guildhall and up to the bar table. The energy this time around was much tamer. It almost seemed like business as usual. As if yesterday's energy was barely an afterthought. At the bar, this time was a woman who was busy pouring drinks at the far end and Grem Rose himself with his arms folded behind the closer end.

"You've returned," he said with a nod. "What can I help you with?"

Wasting no time, I hopped up onto a seat and said, "I came for a game. Got any ideas?"

"We can play chess but I'm afraid we have limited pieces."

"Does that mean we get special moves?"

"It means I can only make so many. You'll have to take your turn first."

"That's a little forward," I said, breaking the code talk.

"We haven't been speaking strictly shade, to begin with. Just take a commission or two. You'll see."

I scoffed. "Alright. Any recommendations?"

He flipped through a large nearby rolodex and stopped on one of the papers for a second. "There are reports of movement from a sleeping ancient hill giant that threatens to disrupt a local dairy farm."

"So, we just have to make sure it stays asleep?"

"That's the plan."

I turned to Caroline. "What do you think, Sis?"

"That's doable," she said.

I turned back to Grem. "We'll take it."

"Alright, here you go." He plucked the paper out and placed it on the table where we could read the specifics of the request before formally accepting it.

After reading it over a few times, Caroline and I decided to formally accept it and write our names in the logbook alongside the commission we took. An hour or so later, we were face to face with a large hill with goats grazing across it.

We took a few steps onto the hill and the ground gave an ever-so-slight sway that told us something was loose under there. A mild rumbling sound confirmed that it was the ancient hill giant slowly waking up. The terrain was so natural that looking for the giant's head would yield no results and digging for it would likely wake it up instead.

In the end, we decided to use magic for the entire process. Since we already knew where the giant was, finding it wasn't a problem but finding how deep underground it was, was a mild challenge. Standing at the peak of the hill and fending off any goats offended by our presence, Caroline pressed her hand against the ground and cast 'aqua pulse' to send her mana into the ground as if it was water trickling down as far as it could go.

Eventually, we learned the giant was a little less than half a mile below the surface. With that in mind, we used her trail of mana as a highway for our spells to reach down below. I cast 'sleep toxin' and she cast 'sleeping tide'. With both spells combined, the giant was bound to fall back to sleep and within a matter of minutes, the hill shrank to less than half the size as the giant calmed down and relaxed back into its long slumber.

We made our way back to the guildhall to turn in the commission, but we stopped at the door when nervousness overtook me. It seemed like something was going to happen, but I wasn't sure what.

With this in mind, I said, "On second thought, we don't have to turn in the commission today, right?"

"I think we have to," said Cattherine, seemingly sensing something I wasn't.

Entering the guildhall, we made our way straight to the bar on the other side where Grem was waiting. I would have stood like Caroline but took a seat so I could see over the counter. Barely a moment later, an ornate glass mug slammed down between me and Caroline. A presence I didn't sense until then made itself known.

Another woman a little taller than me sat beside me on the seat Caroline didn't take. She wore studded leather armor with a full breastplate, and I noticed the glint of a metal shield on her back and a sword on her hip. "Barkeep, fill me up." Her pitch-black hair was barely long enough despite the curl to cover the side eye she was giving me. Under her breath, she said, "You two are a little colorful for your average adventurers, don't you think?"

Softly, Caroline said, "If you have something against colorful adventurers, then don't come to a guildhall." She started tapping the counter with her finger. She was irritated, and for good reason. Blue was the only color she wore for her whole life and changing it wasn't easy.

Feeling equally irritated, I said, "We don't have time for haters, move on."

Grem placed the mug he took back on the counter with a sweet-smelling yellow drink in it. "Here you are."

Taking her drink, the woman kept her voice low and said, "Hey, barkeep. Is it just me, or do I smell a corpse shadow?"

At those words, Caroline flew into a silent panic. She didn't move and her fingernail dug into the counter. I was already weary of the woman, but she just proved I was right to be.

Grem's eyes quickly darted left and right. "I'm sure it's just you."

"Is it? I'm sure it's illegal to purposefully conceal a corpse shadow so no one would dare attempt it in a guildhall, but my nose doesn't lie. Let me see the corpse shadow registry, I'm sure neither of my new friends' names would be on it if I'm wrong." She tilted her head at me and Caroline. "What did you say your names were again? Jill and Blue? Nah, those are codenames... Who are you really?" She lowered her voice to a whisper. "Corpse Hunters."

By now, I was gripping a dagger underneath my top so hard my knuckles turned white. While it was illegal to kill in a guildhall, I was prepared to do so. I had done even less legal things before so this would be no different if necessary. Besides, being wanted for murder would be less problematic than for her accusations while surrounded by who-knows-who in a guildhall.

The woman whispered again. "Calm down, calm down. I'm not here to hurt you. Just to let you know how serious I am." She took a swig of her drink. "There's a commission from Melonie Black on the board. Take it." She hopped off the seat and walked out of the guildhall.

Caroline started tapping the counter much faster than before. "About that commission..."

"We'll take it," I said.

Caroline shot me an uneasy glance.

"Do you have a better idea?"

"We have a job to do. Let's do it."

Grem placed the commission in front of us. "Here you go."

Caroline and I looked at the commission, then at each other, then back at the commission. After some time, we found ourselves back on the rocky shores near a shallow cave. Within the shade sat the woman from before on a rock.

"Hello there," said the woman, with a smile and a wave.

"So, you're Melonie Black?" said Caroline.

"In the flesh. I didn't think I'd see a couple of notorious Corpse Hunters here, especially not your kind, but now that I have you, I have a proposition."

"What 'kind'?"

"The kind you can't refuse."

The fact I couldn't read her emotional state put me on edge. Not being able to read the flow of emotion and pinpoint what exactly she was feeling was one thing, but not being able to feel any emotion from her at all was another. She likely knew of my abilities ahead of time. Even if she didn't, it was a safe assumption to make. Nervous, I prepared to take a step back, but Caroline placed her hand on my back, reassuringly.

"And if we refuse?"

"Are you really in a position to do that? After all, an intentionally undocumented corpse shadow is one thing, but a couple of Corpse Hunters with one? I wonder what kind of bounty would be put out for such a thing."

Deciding it would be easier to just leave and wait until Melonie came after us once she found herself desperate, I pulled at Caroline's arm, intending to make my intentions known. Besides, there was no hidden corpse shadow, so Melonie had nothing to stand on. In response, Caroline sharply yanked on the back of my collar as if to pull me back. She most definitely sensed something I didn't, and whatever it was, was likely dangerous.

"Why us?" said Caroline.

"Aside from you being Corpse Hunters? I've seen what company you keep despite your dynamic, so I figured you'd be worth it."

Caroline scoffed. "Our 'dynamic'?"

"Yeah, the loose cannon and her suppressor."

Caroline and I looked at each other and shrugged. She could have been talking about either of us given how little she knew.

Melonie frowned. Her emotions were still unreadable. "If you don't know which is which, then you're not worth it."

Caroline said, "Alright, before we even consider the job, mind telling us what it is? We can't trust what we don't know."

As she talked, I readied myself to stop her if she reacted negatively to any answers given. It was an instinctive response on my part; being used to her being unpredictable on account of the corpse shadow she was afflicted with until recently.

Melonie locked eyes with me for a moment before turning her attention back to Caroline. "Before I answer, tell the little one to calm down-"

"Don't worry about her," Caroline interjected. "Just answer me."

Melonie seemed to think for a moment. "Alright, I need you to help a friend of mine."

"Too vague." Caroline took a step back, pulling me with her.

"Alright, we need you to infiltrate C.H.E.S.S. headquarters." Melonie seemed to panic for a split second, and I was able to glean a bit of emotion from her. She was surprised.

I scoffed. "Really? And you think that's possible?"

"We only need you to get in on one of the lower floors, get something, and get out. Real ninja-like."

Apathetic, I said, "I'll assume you've had no luck getting an actual ninja for the job."

"If everything went to plan, a ninja should already be inside."

With a shrug, I said, "You shouldn't need us, then."

"What do you need us to get?" said Caroline.

"It's a registry," said Melonie. "A list of sorts. We're not exactly sure what's on it, but we know where it is."

"First, why is it so important? And second, where is it?"

"Can I take your questions to mean you're in?"

Caroline shrugged. "Sure."

"Both of you?"

I folded my arms decisively. "Depends." Caroline tugged tightly on the back of my collar. Whatever it was she was sensing put her on edge, but I couldn't sense it and that put me even more on edge. "Alright, I'm in." As soon as I said that, I remembered Caroline wanting to go back for Mom.

Melonie reached her hand out and a clipboard appeared in her hand. "Alright, now, if you'd sign that in blood, we can get underway."

"Why? So you can kill us if we fail?"

"Or get caught, or go off-script, or any number of things that could go wrong when involving a Corpse Hunter."

A new presence made itself known accompanied by a voice. "No need for all that." A man touched down behind us outside the cave. He had piercing blue eyes with a scar trailing from his right and short blonde hair in a black turtleneck that had seen a lot of active wear and matching pants riddled with little pockets. "I believe we can trust them farther than we can throw them."

"Got evidence to back that up?" said Melonie.

"Yes, actually." The man gestured toward us. "They're standing right here." He paused as if for dramatic effect. "Do you think a couple of Corpse Hunters would walk into what smells like a trap from a mile away for no reason?"

With a smirk, Melonie said, "To avoid a bounty being put on their heads in a foreign land, probably."

"They're Corpse Hunters," remarked the man. "No matter where they go, there's a bounty on their heads. If we include the corpse shadow, it's just insurance to make sure anyone looking to cash in would give them a wide birth, at the very least."

Melonie huffed. "Have it your way."

"Are you done talking about us like we're not here?" said Caroline folding her arms.

"Ah, yes," said the man. "I go by Ray. May I ask what you'd like to be called?"

"Jill," I said, giving my codename.

"Blue," said Caroline doing the same.

"Ok, I know I said we can trust you, but We are risking a lot by sending you in. I'm going with you, and I need to know you can hold your own if things do get dicey."

Making sure I understood correctly, I said, "Some type of assessment?"

Ray nodded, "I've seen members of your group in action. If you're as capable as them, we have nothing to worry about, but I'm not willing to risk it without proof."

"Alright, how are you trying to test us?"

"Well, I could send you on a bounty hunt, but first-hand experience will show me more than watching you kill something." He reached his hand into the air and a wielder's weapon appeared in his hand. The black crescent-shaped sword. Its curved edge was accented with unusually shiny silver that reminded me of a blinding laser. "You can come at me one by one or together."

Caroline and I looked at each other and shrugged simultaneously. She felt very reluctant, but I wasn't sure what for.

I turned, drawing a dagger lightly enchanted with piercing and course-correcting. One of twelve I had at my disposal. "How about just me? She's far stronger than I am so this should be enough."

Ray smirked and said, "We'll see about that."

I joined him outside the cave, and we took positions across from each other away from the shoreline.

Once I was comfortably in place, I swiped my dagger through the air in a single fluid motion to make a golden X, casting 'checkpoint', before throwing the dagger through it with a gold hue.

Turning to the side, he dodged my dagger and swiped his blade at me to send a black blade wave my way.

Turning to the side, I dodged his blade wave as my dagger reappeared in the space where the X was and continued forward as the X vanished. Once my dagger appeared, I cast 'magic missile' on it, giving it a gold blade and a pink handle as it curved mid-air to meet its target.

Ray swiped it aside with his blade, gripped the handle of his sword with both hands, and took a step forward. My dagger curved back toward him as he became engulfed in an orb of darkness bordered with white light and vanished.

I swift-cast 'pull' and 'mine seed' then delay cast 'faerie's retreat' and waited. My dagger returned in a straight line and the golden hue of my magic seed blended in like a pebble with the sand at my feet.

Instinctively, I ducked to the ground and rolled to the side as another black orb rimmed in white appeared where I was standing and vanished, leaving Ray behind. At the same time, my dagger came back around, and the trap I set triggered. The explosion masked the oncoming blade with a burst of gold.

With a swipe of his sword, Ray spiked my dagger into the ground and turned his blade toward me in the same motion.

I was running out of time on my 'faerie's retreat' spell before it activated so I jumped back and cast 'wall of thorns', causing a solid wall of golden bramble to spring from the ground between us as I backed off further while charging a 'light ball' and making sure the glow was bright enough to see past my wall.

Less than a second later, I teleported as 'faerie's retreat' activated on its own. I let the light ball float above me then leaped into the air when I did and found myself on Ray's back. He took a step forward just like I wanted and gave me the space to teleport on top of him. Placing another dagger at the back of his neck, I said, "Do I pass?"

"You got good instincts at least. I was expecting you to show a bit more power, but skill works fine."

I hopped off his back. "Thought so."

"Okay, now that's taken care of, we need to go over the plan."

Back in the cave, Melonie said, "Back to the guildhall?"

Sometime later, we were back at the guildhall. Grem was no longer there but in his place was the woman that was on the other end of the bar before while her spot was taken by someone with a spiny black fish swimming in the air at their side. The woman in front of us had a yellow tattoo that trailed down her right side and gave off a white hue while her white hair literally flowed like water with a yellow hue coming off it.

Ray walked up to the bar. "We need a quiet room."

The woman nodded quietly and gestured for us to follow her before making her way toward the staircase to the right. We followed her up the steps and down a series of halls until we reached a door which she opened, leading us inside.

There was a single hardwood table surrounded by six cushioned seats. At one of the seats sat Grem with his hands folded drinking what smelled like tea out of a mug. He looked up and said, "What do you know? You didn't scare them away."

"So, they're your hounds?" I said, reconsidering my understanding of the situation.

Grem scoffed. "No. My only hound is here." He placed his hand on the woman's side, and she began glowing bright white until she was perched on his hand in the form of a small bird feathered in white and yellow. "More like a parrot. Regardless, I knew as soon as we talked the first time that you'd be scouted."

I took a seat. "Alright, you got us, so what's the plan?"

"Simple," said Melonie as she sat across the table from me. "We secured a route into the base underwater." She laid out a hand-drawn map toward me. It featured a series of rooms of various sizes as well as corridors traced between them. "The C.H.E.S.S. base is split into a grid of interlocked sections that can move independently. This is just one section near the middle. You're going in from here." She pointed at one of the corridors at the border of the map. "You'll make your way through the marked rooms and hallways. None of them have cameras or surveillance since, for some reason, it's reinforced with strong anti-magic properties."

"So, how are we getting in?" said Caroline standing behind me.

"Underneath. There's a mechanical hatch on this section that opens with a rather elaborate puzzle of all things. We think that part was constructed as part of a test or obstacle course for C.H.E.S.S. recruits but we're not entirely sure. We do know that it's a vulnerability we can exploit to get in. From there, you're making your way to the prison in the center of the base. It has its own dedicated security system but the anti-magic there is much stronger. It's full of defectors, claimed bounties, and only a few guards. That's where your first real obstacle lies. There's a control room somewhere inside and we don't know where it is. Our intel points to the list being kept there since it's the most secure part of the base."

Skeptical, I said, "Points to? No proof?"

"Our source is reliable enough to risk our lives on. Regardless, if you get caught at that point, you'll have a bit of a failsafe. The control room is also where you can release the prisoners. That way, you'll have a distraction to make your escape."

"And if we can't get out?"

"Consider your lives forfeit. Nothing here is guaranteed and if you get caught, you will be left behind, but that's a given. You'll be leaving the way you came since it's the only secure route we know about."

"Are we really doing this?" I looked up at Caroline and she nodded in response. I looked back at Melonie. "Alright, when are we doing this?"

"As soon as possible."

"That'll be sunrise tomorrow," said Ray standing by the table.

Caroline and I took some time to memorize the map and route before taking our leave since there was nothing more to discuss.

We regrouped at the cave on the rocky beach the next day. The sun was barely peaking over the island offset to the east and the C.H.E.S.S. base looked as quiet as always off in the distance.

"Looks like everyone's here," said Melonie scanning our small group from the shadows of the cave.

"I guess one of us just isn't coming?" I said, noting Grem's lack of presence.

Melonie responded, "He's only our benefactor. Besides, I'm not going either. My job was planning and liaison. I planned it out and recruited who I thought best. I'll also be here when you come back. I just hope my choice wasn't the wrong one."

"Are you two ready?" Ray stood by the water, constantly scanning our surroundings. "We should go as soon as we can. The later we get there, the more likely we run into someone."

Caroline walked up to the water's edge, and I followed. "Then let's get moving." Reaching out her hand, she cast a spell. "**Bubble**." A translucent blue bubble appeared around all three of us with Caroline at the center. "Lead the way."

We walked into the water with the bubble holding it at bay barely more than an arm's reach away. This was the same way we reached the shore. After some time, we routed our way to an area with a bulkhead door barely visible against the flush gray silhouette of the seemingly organic metal of the base hovering high above the sea floor which overshadowed everything as far as the eye could see.

While Caroline and I stopped for a moment, Ray continued until he nearly pressed into the bubble surrounding us. "Now's not the time to be in awe. Our objective is still up ahead."

"I'm sure it is. How are we going to see it?" I said, scanning the vaguely metallic surface high above.

"How big is this thing?" said Caroline, looking with me.

"When we get there, it'll be obvious. It's over thirty kilometers across and swirling with vortexes of mana. What we're aiming for is a spot of calm somewhere in the middle."

Continuing on, we wound our way around turbulent waters underneath the base for hours. The surrounding waters hummed with movement as the current carried fish and seaborne debris in every direction. Even so, the ecosystem somehow didn't look affected, and it actually looked more vibrant than I thought it would.

Ray stopped below one of the many sections pressed flush together and pointed up. "Here we are. The turbulence here is much less dense than everywhere else. No mana flows from the section directly above us."

Feeling out our surroundings, I found that he was right. The hum was virtually gone, and the fish swam freely. I felt like a pressure lifted from my chest and I could finally breathe after suffocating the whole time.

"How sturdy is this bubble?" asked Ray, pressing his hand to the base of it.

Caroline responded, "It can take the pressure of the whole ocean as long as you don't poke at it."

"Can it take a trip straight up? We need to fast enough to trick the sensors into thinking nothing's there when we get close."

"How fast is that?"

"Somewhere around the speed of a bullet. If it's not strong enough, I can reinforce it."

Carolyne pressed her hand against the bubble. "***Crystalize***." The blue bubble gained a white sheen. "It'll be fine now."

"***Blastoff***." Ray cast the spell and a soft *pop* sent us straight up and we traveled for around five seconds.

Everything was a blur as we raced toward the shadowy surface above us until a soft *tink* accompanied by a sudden stop put us against the hull of the base where the bubble stayed. Since we were close enough now, we all simultaneously cast 'darksight', causing our eyes to glow with night vision.

Ray examined what looked like measurement markers ever so slightly eroded from what was likely decades of erosion. "It should be this way." He pointed behind where Caroline and I were looking.

Caroline pressed her hand against the bubble. "Do we still have to move fast, or are we safe?"

"We're past the sensors. Since we didn't trip them on the way, we're safe."

Since we couldn't walk on the ground, Caroline moved us with the bubble along the gray metallic surface above us. Eventually, the markings lead us to a bulkhead door flush with the rest of the metallic surface as if it was only painted on.

Pushing his hand out of the bubble, Ray traced his fingertips across the door. "Now the puzzle. This is the part I need your help with."

I spoke up. "What do you need us to do?"

"Put simply, I need you to solve it."

Taking a look at the mechanism flush to the door as everything else, I saw a complex series of grooves and dials pointing in odd directions. It looked like it was supposed to make some type of pattern. Instead of questioning it, I pressed my finger onto one of the dials and tried to turn it, but it stayed as solid as the rest of the door. Next, I ran a bit of magic from my finger into it and the dial started glowing but not turning.

Assuming this really was a low-level test for recruits, I cast a spell. "***Pick***." With a grunt, the dials and grooves started turning but stopped once the spell ended a second later, incomplete. I cast the spell again and this time, I fed more mana into it. All the while, the grooves filled with a mix of pink and gold as my mana ran through them to each dial, turning them as per my spell until all the dials and grooves turned to make a five-point star. Once the star filled with color, something clicked, and the door sank slightly inward. "I think it's open."

"Push the door open."

"Alright, but before I do that, why couldn't you do it? The 'puzzle' war really simple"

"I guess it's fair I tell you. The difficulty of the puzzle is dependent on rank. Since this is the start of a gauntlet made for members looking for a promotion. It's only someone not registered in C.H.E.S.S. has a chance of getting through it easily."

"And what rank are you?"

"Virtue."

"Alright." Making a fist, I pressed my knuckles into the door and pushed. It opened easily and light flooded outward from an empty room.

Caroline maneuvered the bubble against the doorway and Ray climbed in first followed by us. As soon as we were all in, the door closed on its own and a soft hum came from everywhere at once. Weary of this development, Caroline and I readied ourselves for conflict.

"Calm down," said Ray. "The rest of the trials should amount to nothing more than basic mechanical puppets and traps to get new recruits accustomed to training. The less magic we use, the easier it should be."

The room we entered was little more than a well-lit hallway with blank white walls, floors, and ceiling. At the end was a white door with a gold scorpion with pink butterfly wings inscribed on it.

"Mind explaining that?" I said, pointing at the door.

"Your insignia, I take it? The excess mana you poured into unlocking the door also went into customizing this trial. There shouldn't be much to worry about since the anti-magic should take full effect after we get through that door."

His explanations seemed to leave out details of what was to be expected every time. I only made a mental note of it as we continued.

Making our way toward the door, I noticed illusionary flowers start blooming at our feet. Knowing they were illusions allowed me to see straight through them but something else seemed off, so I concentrated on keeping track of Caroline's presence in case any more subtle illusions appeared. Soon enough, I started hearing faint voices off in some direction as an expansive field of vibrant flowers littered with butterflies settled in place within my field of view.

Refusing to let myself be lulled in, I followed Caroline's presence, and we all made it to the door in moments. It appeared as if it was through a fog. I reached out to touch it and someone patted my back harshly, thrusting me forward and breaking the illusion. We were barely a few paces from where we started, and Caroline just nudged me from behind. Ray was on the other side of the room beside the door.

"Don't let your guard down," said Caroline. "This was made based on your magic, remember? Even a weak illusion can get you easily." She reached her hands out to me. "Should I carry you?"

After a moment of consideration, I nodded. "That's best." I grabbed her hand and lent more mana to the sigil imprinted on my chest and allowed myself to transform and shrink surrounded by a golden glow. As I shrank, I climbed onto her hand and ran along her arm until I settled within the folds of her jacket where I could peer out. I was now a black scorpion the size of a thumb.

As we continued forward, Caroline would jostle me slightly to make sure I wasn't taken in by any illusions. It also helped that I was enveloped by her natural aura of calmness.

Once we reached the door, the sigil vanished in an instant and the door slid down through the floor. On the other side of it was another room with what looked like a humanoid puppet carved from pink wood with golden grain. We didn't have long to observe it before it was replaced with an orb of darkness surrounded by an aura of light that vanished soon after with the puppet. The next door fell open momentarily. Grem destroyed it with a spell.

The next room housed only a blank white table and beyond it was a push bar door. We followed Ray past the table and the door into the void behind it where another door stood and walked through it into a long hallway housing similar doors. We marched past them and onto our pre-planned route.

The rooms and halls were eerily devoid of energy. Some of them were abuzz with activity in the form of large turning gears that could be heard within the walls but even that felt dead, for lack of a better word.

Every minute felt more tense than the last despite being assured ahead of time that there were no cameras and almost no chance of running into personnel. Even though it felt more like a normal commission, something seemed more eerie about it. I couldn't put my finger on it. Ulterior motives would have been easy to sniff out and a trap would have felt more obvious. Even those who could hide their emotions wouldn't be able to for long around me, but Ray seemed to just be resolved toward his own goal. Nothing about him seemed devious. Of all things, that was what made me nervous.

Eventually, we entered a room resembling a marble office. Ray walked straight up to the desk, summoned his sword, and cleaved the marble in two. The strike sent vibrations through the ground and things started moving with the same sound of gears grinding that we were hearing the whole time. The door closed behind us and the center of the room starting from the desk, all the way to the far wall started raised in a stair-like pattern until it reached the ceiling, which opened like a sliding hatch.

We traveled up the marble steps and into what looked like a storage room that was empty aside from a sink, a couple of buckets, and a mop. Much like every other place, we went through in the base up till then, it felt dead, but in this case, it was more like the calm after a storm. Something happened recently and it likely wasn't the explosion.

Ray propped himself against the side of the door and gently pushed it slightly open. As soon as a sliver of light from the other side glanced through, the door seemingly flung itself open and we were all snatched out of the closet and out into the open.

Two men stood in front of us. One was clad in reds and browns with red highlights in his otherwise black hair. I recognized him as Nail from the tournament. The other stood in a gray uniform with silvery gray eyes and silver rings on his fingers.

"Look what we have here," said Nail, with a smirk. "We came looking for missing prisoners and found new ones."

Not missing a beat, Ray said, "We found this route while also looking for escaped prisoners. It seems they used the promotional chambers as an out. We're not sure how many got out, but they're long gone."

"Good work," said Nail.

Less than a second later, a spike appeared from the ground where Ray was standing and he was standing beside it with his sword summoned, having dodged it. There wasn't even a hint of intent or mana flow. Caroline didn't seem so surprised, but I most certainly was. She only took a few steps back toward the door we came in from.

Nail raised his hand and a multitude of different bladed weapons appeared above us, all seemingly made of molten rock. "Ironically, it doesn't even matter what you were doing here. We still need to take you in, and I know you won't go without a struggle."

My vision faded as white mist with a blue tinge to it swallowed my field of view. Once it cleared, I was back in the hallway leading to the marble office. Caroline teleported us. She was sprinting at full speed using magic to go even faster. Our surroundings were a blur of white and gray since those were the only colors of the walls and floor.

We didn't travel long before Caroline tripped, and I was thrown onto the ground. I stood and scanned my surroundings to see her struggling with a pale white light wound around her legs and wounding up higher.

I drew power away from the sigil on my chest and grew from a little black scorpion to my larger form, putting me roughly the same size as Caroline. With this transformation, my full power was at my fingertips, and with it, I pointed my finger at the light coiling around my sister. "*Nullify*." The spell didn't break but the light seemed to distort enough for Caroline to slip out.

Someone was coming after us and we weren't waiting to find out who, so we started running again. I cast 'poison fog' behind us as we ran but the anti-magic properties of the walls made it dissipate before we were more than a few paces away from it.

The way back felt infinitely longer than the way there. Every so often, I'd see something out of the corner of my eye as flashes of light flared up behind us. I heard Caroline cast a multitude of spells during this time, so I trusted her to keep our pursuers at bay.

Eventually, we made it back to the trial room. Breathlessly, we beat on the door open. It opened instantly after I cast 'pick' and we fell into the water.

Caroline reached out and pulled me close. "*Aqua jet*." A turbulent bubble of magic surrounded us, spinning like a drill. It carried us fast and far, leaving a vacuum that disrupted the turbulent water around us and pulling fish in its wake to fill in the void. We jettisoned straight back where we came and onto land, diving out like a dolphin and landing with Caroline holding me in her arms.

Melonie was peeking out of the nearby cave and approached us after scanning our surroundings for a moment. "What happened?" she said.

"We happened to run into someone," said Caroline. "The way was clear and then it wasn't. They wanted Ray and I think they got him. They didn't seem to care much for us though. That's why we could even escape with our lives."

Melonie sighed. "Did you at least get the list?"

"No. They caught us as we entered the prison."

"Damn, I guess that's it. It's best we scatter before someone comes looking. Let's meet at the guildhall." Melonie vanished in a flash of light as she finished her sentence.

Caroline and I went further inland and left town. We wandered around until we found another and made sure to keep a low profile at an inn. The next day, we found a note under the door. It read: '*I guess I can't tell you in person since you skipped town instead of meeting me, but we found out what was on the list. It's the names of wielders that have an ancient dragon as a spirit animal. C.H.E.S.S. needs them for some reason. I'm telling you this because I believe you know someone who has one. If I'm wrong, ignore this message.*'

Deciding to trust the message, Caroline and I texted everyone in code what was going on. Moments later, Ariel responded with a news dump. She found a group associated with the people who set a bomb in C.H.E.S.S. headquarters and what she had to report made my heart sink. Mom was in the base and what was soon to go down wasn't something I was willing to leave her alone with. Krow reported something similar which confirmed it. With that in mind, we came up with meeting coordinates so that when the time came, we could regroup and go together.

Even with a plan, Krow said he intended to fly straight in through the front doors as soon as he could.

Doc never responded but I assumed he was following the conversation.

32-Planning Phase

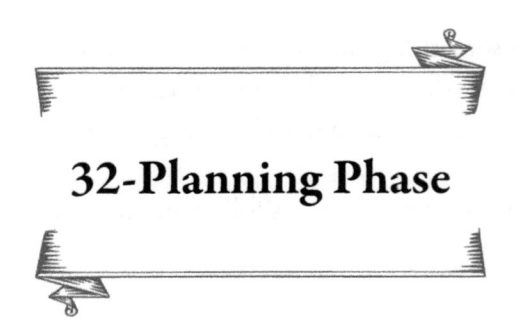

[Graven Lockhart]

I received a summons from Guile that appeared before me in an envelope after the first rounds were over. I was untrusting of a summons from anyone related to C.H.E.S.S. so I was already considering the idea of leaving the base, but when the explosion happened, that was my cue.

I messaged everyone I could to split up, leave, and regroup at a designated location in two days. I left a single line of one-way communication open between myself to Naomi just in case.

Taking to the air, it was apparent that I was being followed. There was an unwavering intensity following me I couldn't shake. I didn't have to look to tell who it was. I landed farther east on the island between the mainland and the base.

Coming close between a few trees, I cast invisibility on myself before tossing a flash grenade into the air behind me. It was made of a ping-pong ball filled with flash powder and enchanted with a silencing spell. It would cause anyone except myself to go temporarily deaf if they had low resistance to sound-based magic and blind them with a non-magical flash. If it didn't hinder either of their senses, it should at least confuse them.

I jumped back into the air to observe the results while setting a trap. As I thought, Solo was close behind me. He seemed a little bothered by the flash, but otherwise nonplused. I used the time he was looking around to levitate away. Before I could get to a safe distance, I heard a voice in my head.

"*There you are.*" He had strengthened his telepathic pull and was trying to force me out of my invisibility. I quickly weaved a few hand seals to calm my mind and force him out. It was too late, however, as he came charging in my direction with sword in hand.

I stopped going forward and went straight up. After I did so, he followed suit. He was running, then he jumped directly below me. He was locked on and trying to force me into combat. I intended to be a decoy anyway, so I obliged. Dropping a handful of small smoke bombs, I followed up by dropping some caltrops enchanted with explosive properties.

The smoke bombs did their job, and the caltrops exploded soon after. I used the opportunity to teleport to the ground and assess the situation while setting up another trap. He jettisoned himself toward me soon after, and our swords clashed.

The pressure plate I set up below my feet triggered a small explosion that set a thin wire net covered in oil under it on fire. The net was made of a special steel that pulled taut all at once when heated up. It was enchanted with a binding spell which made it triple effective at catching enemies and intruders alike.

I teleported out of it before I could get caught and unfortunately, so did he. Teleporting to a spot directly in front of me, he shot a blast of telekinetic energy at point-blank range. I was caught off guard and my invisibility faded. I didn't take any damage, but I was pushed back.

I was looking for a sword swing next, but there was a kick instead. Barely dodging it, I caught his leg. On it, I placed an explosive marker before pulling him closer to land a strike to his chest before retreating and allowing the marker to explode. He didn't seem too phased by the explosion and continued moving.

He got closer than I thought he would and reached to grab me by my collar. I tried to bring my sword down to make him back off, but he stopped it with his own before wrapping his fingers around my cuff and throwing me in the opposite direction of where I was going.

I landed on my feet after a complete flip in the middle of a circle that I was trying to avoid. Solo placed it when he jumped after me. The ground quickly flashed pink and 'ethereal chains' emerged from the ground, tethering themselves to me. I could still move normally and in fact, that's exactly what Solo wanted.

Since he still had to draw a circle to use the spell, it meant that he hadn't mastered it, but it wouldn't detract from its strength. Once chained by the spell, if the one chained moved a certain distance one of them would snap and the momentum from the movement would be multiplied and returned as physical damage. There were ten chains instead of the normal three, and it was safe to assume that the movement requirements were altered as well.

Instead of pursuing further action, Solo stopped in front of me and said, "I finally caught you. Had I known that you actually were a ninja instead of just looking like one, I wouldn't have been so straightforward. I wonder why you decided to use your tricks now instead of the six other times we fought."

"I had time to entertain you before, not now. Besides, I'm not a ninja anymore. Otherwise, I wouldn't use this massive sword."

"You seem more conversational now." He stabbed his sword into the ground and leaned against it.

"So do you. Less megalomaniacal as well." I folded my arms and stood still.

"I was a little too excited before. Not now."

"Every single time? What's different this time?"

"Nothing much. You know, the giant hole in my home." This was an obvious lie.

"Well, that's unfortunate."

"Unfortunate or not, that's not why I came after you." He tapped his sword, and it transformed. "We've tried to kill each other six times before. Do you know why now is different?" He seemed intent, yet hesitant to do something.

"For one, you seem calmer. You're not just pursuing me for no reason."

"That's right." He clenched his fists. "Since you're not going anywhere, I want to ask you something. Why did you defect from C.H.E.S.S?"

"Are you only now harboring doubts about them?"

"Answer me."

"Alright. I wasn't the only one from my family to join them. I had a younger brother who joined before I did and was approached after he recommended me. Back then, I was working as a freelance corpse hunter and they offered me stability, so I took the offer. It was a few years later that I found out what they were really about. I stumbled upon a strange area within the main building where people were being experimented on with corpse shadows. It was a place I wasn't supposed to find, but my curiosity brought me back until I saw my brother strapped down while a corpse shadow was being forced into him. I would have done something on the spot, but knowing where I was, I involved my team instead. We planned to grab my brother and anyone else we could and escape. That plan was never executed as C.H.E.S.S. had already known about it and sent an extermination squad after us. Most of my team was killed in the raid and the rest of us scattered. Does that answer your question?"

"Ok, I've decided." Solo gripped the handle of his sword, and it started glowing. "You're a liar."

"If I'm a liar, there was no point to your question then." I felt that my chance to convince him was fleeting.

"Shatter." His sword broke into multiple pieces that began levitating around him. I held my sword at the ready as he began directing them at me.

There were too many shards to keep track of at once and deal with without moving too far from the spot, so I closed my eyes and tried to sense them instead. Each one held a tremendous amount of energy as they shot toward me.

I blocked the first three normally and was almost knocked over as I swayed from each impact. For the rest, I stabbed my sword into the ground and leaned into it to block them. Next, I had to deal with them surrounding and moving in on me.

"*Gyroball*." I cast the spell and was surrounded by a rotating orb that deflected some of the shards before the rest broke through.

I dodged the few I could and blocked to the best of my abilities, somehow avoiding all of them before turning my attention back to Solo.

He was unmoving while his shards began moving again. This time they circled around me repeatedly. He was trying to find an opening to take advantage of.

Instead of waiting for that, I decided to take a chance and act. I waited for an opening behind me and leaped in that direction. Two of the chains snapped and I almost hit the ground, but I caught myself.

The pain started at my shoulder and raced down my arm, followed by the warm sensation of blood. Having weak defense against spirit-based attacks didn't help. I decided not to teleport because I'd get the same result with the rest of the chains at once.

At the very least, I got a sense of the distance I could now move safely within the boundary. With that in mind, I dodged the shards with increased speed and fluency. The shards were taking most of my attention, so I barely noticed Solo closing in while trying to hide his presence.

He put two shards together to make a small sword and was ready to run me through. I reached toward him and cast a spell, "***Pull***." He raced toward me even faster, and I dodged to the side. His attack missed, and he flew past me uncontrollably.

In that second, I put my hand on his back and cast another spell, "***Ethereal chains***." Twelve purple chains came from the ground and latched onto him.

One of the chains snapped before he could stop himself, but there seemed to be little change in his demeanor. We were both bound by the same spell now. I dismissed my sword and replaced it with a short sword I had tucked behind my thigh. As long as he held back his newfound power, I had a chance to beat him.

We clashed and continued to push each other back until I noticed a distinct lack of blades hovering through the air. They were all sticking out of the ground around us and before long, they began glowing. The ground soon followed and not long after, all the chains disappeared.

To free himself without me noticing, he had to free both of us. Now that we were both free, Solo tried to back off, but I was quicker on the draw. "***Fall***." I cast the spell, and he hit the ground.

Struggling, he tried to send his blades after me, but they were grounded as well. It took a lot of mana to cast the spell in an effective range to hit all targets, and it continued to drain me to keep it up.

I intended to keep it going until he passed out from the pressure, but that wasn't going to happen. The power that he was holding back erupted from him and forced me to drop the spell. I took a couple of deep breaths and before I knew it, I had gone through nearly ten hand seals just to calm down and focus.

I summoned my sword in its second form, but the difference in power was still great. He stood from a depression in the ground and moved. I saw but couldn't react as his foot made contact with my ribs and he sent me through a nearby tree. I stood as quickly as I could before his blades began descending on me again.

Spreading my arms, I cast another spell. "**Horizon**." The spell drained much of the stamina I had left, and the bubble deflected the blades as they converged, but Solo was in front of the barrier in an instant and cut through it in a single swipe.

The fact that he could cut through that spell so easily meant that if he cut me, I'd die. That thought sent me into a panic. I didn't have time to calm down as he continued advancing from the front with his blades coming from the rear. I had almost zero time to make a choice, and I did.

It was a choice I made all too often in the past. I charged forward to swing my sword down with an intentionally wide arc. In response, he sent his sword between my ribs and ran me through. Before I could succumb to the pain, I grabbed him and twisted around so that he was in line with the rest of the blades barely a foot away. I heard multiple impacts before I blacked out.

I opened my eyes to the image of a large black tanuki hovering its snout over me. His fur was closer to purple than black, and his wide eyes were rimmed in purple as well. My surroundings were pitch black in every direction as far as the eye could see aside from the one large, purple, sealed gate off to the side.

"Long time no see," said the tanuki.

"Am I finally dead?" I asked.

"Not yet," he responded.

"If not now, then when- scratch that, I can't be here right now. I have work to do." standing, I began pacing. I thought my mind retreated to my core to cope with the physical backlash of what had just happened.

But that wasn't the case at all.

"If you leave here now, you will die." He sat back and began stroking his chin. "Perhaps you will finally get your wish if you go back now, but is that something you really want?"

I clenched my fists and stopped pacing. "How long do I have to stay here?"

"That depends on you." He gestured toward the gate. "Come with me if you want to live." He turned, took a single step, and landed right next to the gate. It was purple with three black spots in a triangle around a larger black spot in the center.

"Will it open?" I asked after following and standing in front of the gate itself.

"No, but if your will is strong enough, you may get a glimpse inside. I can't, however, guarantee your survival based on will alone."

"And If I'm not strong enough?"

"You will die." It sounded like a promise more than a possibility.

"Not today," I said, reaching my hand into the swirling energy surrounding the gate and walking into it. "I have too much to do right now."

Once I stepped completely within the boundary surrounding the gate, my entire body began tingling. The deeper I went, the more the tingling turned into pain and the closer to the gate I got, the more intense the pain became.

It started with the most recent pain I could remember. It felt as if my arm was on fire, but it didn't stop there. It spread across my entire body, and I nearly stopped moving, but it only got worse from there. An onset of new pain originating from the stab wound in my chest added a dynamic element to what I was feeling.

More still followed.

Every bit of pain I've ever felt for as long as I'd known myself to be alive emerged in layers, submerging me in an unprecedented feeling that I had never felt before. It wouldn't numb or dull, just accumulate and intensify. I couldn't put it into words or action until I finally reached my destination after what seemed like an eternity.

I reached the space between the vortex and the gate and stopped. All the pain I felt disappeared, and that's when I realized something. Turning back around, I looked back into the vortex.

It seemed at first like it was some type of trial to overcome, but it was the opposite. It was the cumulation of all the suffering I was willing to endure to get where I was then. Up until then, I was only looking for a way to end my own suffering. I was fighting just to fight, but somewhere along the line, that changed. I was fighting for more than just a goal. After all, what use is there in saving someone if I can't spend any time with them?

The old me would have been ready to die.

Not anymore.

I turned back to the gate. It was tightly chained and sealed. I reached for the chain and pulled to no avail. I felt all of my strength drain at once, and I nearly collapsed.

Taking a closer look at the door, I saw a small gap between the doors. I leaned in to peer through and saw nothing. There was a black void on the other side. That was what I thought until I realized that the blackness, was in fact, something.

I slid my hand up the door before trying to pry it open. I couldn't tell what it was made of, but the door was smooth and warm. I felt intense fatigue but kept pulling.

I pulled for what felt like an hour and the door finally creaked with no indication of movement whatsoever. That was when I noticed movement on the other side. The darkness moved upward, and a bright purple rim followed it, then whatever it was blinked.

I looked around and saw the tanuki still sitting in the same spot as before. I heard the door move, and I turned to see the chain rattling and the eye pushing against the inside of the door, followed by a brief wind that sounded like a sharp breath. It moved to one side and disappeared until another eye took its place.

All of this was followed by a deafening rumble of unintelligible words before the gate shut closed too fast for my mind to register until a second later.

My eyes opened on their own. The sky was dark, even though the sun was only close to setting before I passed out. Time passed while I was bleeding out. I stood despite the pain. It was nothing compared to what I had just experienced.

Solo's blades were gone, and I was bleeding out. Solo himself was on the ground with multiple stab wounds in his back in a puddle of our combined blood that I was standing in. I was still holding my sword, but it was different. It was no longer curved, but triangular. It came to a point and was sectioned into quarters with the upper left and lower right sections colored purple and the other sections were left uncolored. The hilt housed a purple gem and small tassels dangling from the ends, while the handle recurved

I couldn't admire it for too long before my knees buckled and I had to use it for stability. Blood loss was a real problem. I put my hand on my chest and was going to cast a spell when I heard a voice.

"**Restore**." Both Solo and I were surrounded by a blue light. The hole in my chest closed painfully and my insides realigned in the same manner. I looked and saw Guile standing beside me. "Can we talk?"

"I have no choice, do I?" I said, exhausted.

"You do." He nodded.

"Ok... Let's talk." I found a newly fallen tree and sat on the stump.

What he told me next drew a complete picture of C.H.E.S.S. and their plans as well as their goals. Not to mention their enemies. There were many major players involved and every one of them had their own part. The series of events led all the way back to the advent of the Shadow Master around sixty years prior.

While talking, Guile put Solo, who was still unconscious, on his back and we made our way to the mainland. We landed not a moment too soon.

"What was all of that?" I said, mostly unsurprised.

"It's the truth, believe it or not."

"Despite the absurd amount of information you've given me, I'm mostly unsurprised."

"Mostly?"

"If you are what you say you are, why is it that you haven't stepped in and stopped this already?"

He sighed. "I cannot interfere with turning points in human history, but I can influence them. That's all I have been doing to prevent the catastrophe that may come."

"Fair enough. The only part I didn't see coming was about Krow. His disposition is alarming, to say the least. Do you have any plans to resolve that?"

"The plan would be to kill Rachel." His response was blunt.

"Based on what you told me thus far, that might have to be the case, but she'd have caught up with him by now. Either he's dead or worse."

"I see what you mean." His statement snapped me out of my thoughts. "But the likelihood that she's on our side can't be overlooked."

"Even if she's not, that shouldn't be a thing we should worry about. He's strong. It'll take more than one of anything to put him down for good."

"Are you sure about that?"

"Based on the stories I've heard and the accounts I've read, everyone involved in that incident should be dead. Even the Shadow Master perished. If Krow really was a part of that, I don't think anything can kill him at this point."

"That may be true, but only time will tell." He nodded.

"So, where are we going?" I asked. The lights of a small town could be seen some ways away, and we were walking past it.

"And here I was following you," he said. We were heading directly to the emergency meeting point that was set up in case we had to scatter.

"Do you know what's in this direction?" I asked, suspecting that he knew the answer.

"A short mountain with an unmarked building at the top, but you already knew that." He kept looking straight ahead while responding.

"So, what are you going to do when he wakes up?" I asked, pointing at Solo while in the midst of deciding what my next action would be.

"He's been awake the whole time. I've just been keeping him passive up till now." Guile snapped his fingers and what looked like blue faery dust lifted off Solo's face and his eyes opened. "What do you think of all of that, Solo?"

"What about my mom?" He was visibly holding himself back from any action as he painstakingly uttered his response.

"I've looked into that some time ago and I haven't found anything that confirms the story that you've been given. Graven didn't murder your mother. It was a member of the seven sins. Your mother was a powerful psychic and a talented summoner capable of summoning an Asura. They saw it as a threat and an opportunity to-"

"Who was it?" Solo pushed off of Guile's back and began walking in the opposite direction.

"I was never able to find any specifics because the job was off the books." By the end of Guile's sentence, we had all stopped walking.

"So," I said. "Is that why you've been trying so hard to kill me this entire time?"

My question went unanswered.

"Never mind. If you're not after me anymore, then you're one less thing I have to worry about." I started walking again.

Guile followed behind me. "Come on, Solo. If you're thinking of going off on your own, then don't. It's a death sentence if you do. I have a plan."

Solo listened to Guile and followed unwillingly.

It wasn't long before we reached a lone mountain and the single building atop it. The building was gray, desolate, and rundown. The windows were mostly shattered, there was no front door, and the graffiti was visible from every angle.

The building itself wasn't the destination, but underneath it was. There was a single hatch that led to a straight drop that went down four feet. From there, you'd enter a code by tapping out a pattern on each of the four walls inside. Afterward, the floor would drop, and an enchantment would activate that carries you down to a hidden base far below.

After inputting the pattern and allowing the floor to drop, we exited what was essentially a magic elevator shaft. Stepping out, I was greeted with a familiar sight. The walls were the same gray, but the floor was duller, and some tiles were loose. The lights were emitting a dull light, and the bulbs needed changing. I pulled out a small, black button and pressed it. A sharp sound echoed through the halls and after a few seconds, Hanna as a small bat could be seen rounding one of the corners followed by Vincent, Aaron, and Jane.

"Who's all here?" I asked.

"Everyone you see here," said Hanna.

"Alright, these are allies and guests," I said, gesturing to Guile and Solo. "I trust you can show them to some rooms."

"What about you?" said Vincent.

"I'm going to wait here for the rest of us." I allowed my sword to levitate behind me as I sat on it.

Fluttering away with everyone else following behind, Hanna said, "Alright, let's leave him to it."

I sat and waited with little distraction for hours until the elevator door opened and Noah, Catt, and three others entered. They quickly explained their situation, and I told them that all we could do at the moment was wait. Next was Hinata with Cosmo and Belle. They had been laying as low as possible until they could reach the base. The last to come was Naomi and someone I hadn't seen in a while.

Kirara was present. She had been out gathering information abroad for anything she thought we'd need. She came out with a piercing stare as she walked up to me and bent forward even though we were at eye level with each other.

"Long time, no see boss. I brought something for you." She began zipping down her heavily enchanted dark blue and red jacket. Out popped another familiar face. He was dazed and looking around as if he had no idea what was going on. Hiyaku was standing before me after being ejected from the dark recess of Kirara's jacket, in which she held too many items to count. Around his neck was an enchanted spiked collar that seemed to cause his state of mind.

"I'm not your boss and what did you do to this kid?" I said, nonchalantly.

"It's the collar. like it? It took both of us to get it on him, though. Man, feminine wiles only get a girl so far," she said, poking at the collar and zipping her jacket back just high enough to still see cleavage past her blue button-up. "Hard work sucks."

"You got that right," I said, sternly. "Take the collar off."

"What? He'll just stop time and escape, and we won't be able to catch him then. Did I mention how hard it was to catch this one?" Her whining was only getting on my nerves.

"Naomi," I said.

"Yes?" she responded.

"How does this thing work, how did you get this on him, and why?" Kirara scoffed after my line of questions but still let Naomi answer.

"It works by forcibly slowing down his mental processing and putting him in a dream-like state. I distracted him with some provocative chatter and Kirara nabbed him then. We did it because of what that Guile guy told you. He seemed reliable enough. With that time spell he cast during the tournament, it made too much sense."

I sighed. "Take the collar off him. If he wanted to stop time, he would have already done it. As soon as he realized that anything was slowing down, he'd have sped himself up to compensate. He should be completely conscious right now."

"Fine." Kirara reached forward and took the collar off of him. As soon as she did, time stopped instantly. Both Naomi and Kirara stopped moving completely while I was left unaffected.

"So, you want to talk to me alone?" I asked in the wake of this turn of events.

"Tell me. What part do you play in all of this?" His eyes were focused now, and his clockwork sword was summoned. "Depending on your answer, I'll act accordingly."

"Is that a threat?" I stayed as laid-back as I could despite my mood.

"No, it's a promise." His energy fluctuated and my legs up to my hips became frozen in time.

"Before I answer, did you stop time at the tournament so they could plant that bomb?" I folded my arms.

"Of course, I did, now tell me what I want to know or else." The time dilation traveled up to my neck.

"Listen, kid." I stood and stabbed my sword into the ground next to me. All of our surroundings turned purple, and what little debris there was began levitating as well as the two girls frozen in time. "Because of your actions, there will be a war. I've had a bad enough day as it is without you trying to strong-arm me, and that's what I have to look forward to on the horizon."

Reality seemed to crumble away as my space manipulation interfered with his time manipulation. He was visibly shaken. It was likely that he never met someone with spatial control before.

"Now, I was always ready to fight no matter what. What about you? Are you willing to fight this war and finish what you started?"

He seemed to only regain himself enough to answer, "Yes."

"Good." I sat back down on my sword and reality flashed back into place with time flowing normally. "Kirara."

"What is it?" She hadn't noticed a difference.

"Will you see to finding him a room?" I said, exasperated.

"Sure. Follow me." She began walking down the hall and Hiyaku followed.

"And kid?" I said.

"Yes?" His response was quick.

"Next time, I'll leave you there," I said, folding my arms.

He nodded quickly and hurried behind Kirara.

After they were out of sight, Naomi spoke up. "Wow. You gave a threat. I haven't seen you that angry in a while. You even lost control of your powers for a second."

"If you had awareness during that, why didn't you do anything?"

"I felt like you had it covered. He's *definitely* scared of you now."

I sighed, "This would've been much easier if the most powerful bard I know *actually* acted like a bard for once."

"Don't take it out on me. My singing days are over. However, I do miss the limelight every once in a while, though."

"You could always try an instrument."

"I could. There is a fine instrument chaperoning our guest at the moment. What do you think, percussion?"

"Please don't make any moves on Kirara. I know we haven't seen her in years, but she's hard enough to deal with without her becoming another one of your stalkers."

"You don't need to worry about that. I know how to keep my girls in line." She gave a mischievous grin and turned to look back down the hall in the direction Kirara and Hiyaku went.

"Just... Please... Don't." I shook my head and stroked my brow.

"Alright, I won't. I was just joking anyway." She gave a sharp turn and walked off down another hall.

"Sure, you were." I said as soon as she was out of earshot.

Everyone I was expecting had arrived, so after a short rest, I gathered everyone in one room and Guile explained his plan, albeit slightly altered considering all who showed up.

His plan wasn't perfect and had too many working variables, but with the group's combined knowledge we were able to further alter the plan and determine the best course of action. Now all that was left was for C.H.E.S.S. to make a move.

33-First Assault

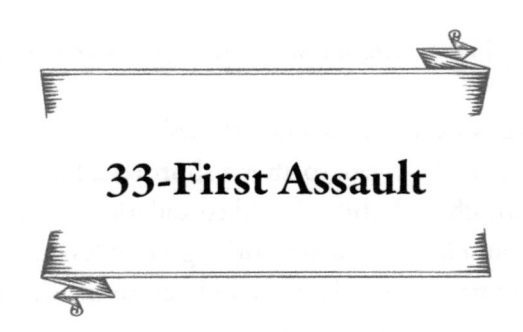

[Princess Bianka Roland]

The morning of the attack was a few weeks after the whole fiasco at the World Magic Tournament. I dreamt of myself standing on a glass floor high above the kingdom at dawn. It was a peaceful dream until I got a shaking feeling. It was accompanied by the sudden fear of falling, which woke me up.

My eyes opened to Angelo, my royal guard, gently shaking me awake. Normally, I could never imagine someone of his stature doing anything gently, but he was sure to learn as my notorious frailty demanded it. In the coming moment from my awakening, I regained my senses and shivered.

The room was unusually cold. While winter had come a month earlier, the inside of the castle was kept at constant room temperature and never dropped noticeably low. Even so, I could see my breath, and the windows were frosted over more than they should have been.

"My lady, there seems to be an intruder," said Angelo, eyeing the bedroom door.

"I believe so as well," I said, sliding out of bed and quickly getting into an outfit that had been prepared and folded on my nightstand. A white long sleeve shirt accented in red and matching sweatpants. Placing my tiara on my head, I went for the door only to be stopped by Angelo.

"I don't think that is a good idea, my lady." He stood unmoving between me and the door.

"Oh, it'll be fine, you big lug. I'll just take a peek and assess the situation. If anything happens, you'll protect me like always, won't you?"

"I will, but the enemy is too far away for me to sense, yet they're powerful enough for us to feel the effects of their magic from a long distance. Either that or they're close by and skilled enough to prevent me from sensing them. If something happens-"

"I know. If there's danger, I'll step back and let you handle it. Don't worry, I won't lift a finger this time." We both knew that I was lying, but he turned around and opened the door, anyway.

The temperature on the other side of the door was much lower than inside. There was a piercingly cold wind coming from the stairs at the east end of the hall. The emerald carpets were frosted over and the windows were close to shattering from the chill.

A deep breath hurt my lungs and I could feel the cold seeping down to my bones. Angelo took the first steps out, and the carpets shattered beneath his feet while I followed closely to the same effect.

All I could hear as we walked was the crunching of a normally soft and relatively malleable material below our feet. Neither of us took our eyes from the direction where the wind was coming from. As we both made our way to the middle of the hall, the most terrible thing I had ever felt came rushing up the stairs. I couldn't hear it or see it, but I felt it. It was as if I was between the teeth of an enraged beast and just waiting for it to close its jaws.

Angelo said, "Run," and for once, I did what he said. However, I only took a few steps before I fell to the floor with my tiara barely hanging on. All of my leg muscles seized up and an advanced chill began creeping through my body. I tried to move my legs, and they screeched in pain. The cold had a vice grip on me and wouldn't let go.

The sound of footsteps coming up the stairs made me turn over and look. A brown-haired woman in a blue and white fox mask and a long, white coat traveled with the freezing wind.

She was a gnat next to Angelo, who took a stance and summoned his sword. His broadsword had no consistency. The edge was spiked all around at different lengths and thicknesses. He stepped toward her to strike and was blocked by a light-blue morning star shaped like a snowflake.

In an instant, the woman was sent flying into the wall behind her. At the same time, Angelo turned completely white before multiple layers of ice shattered off of him. I wasn't sure if it phased him or not, but he continued with a follow-up attack. He pointed his blade and fired a translucent ball of force from its tip. It completely missed its target as the girl moved to the side.

A flurry of snow ran through the hall, blinding me for only a second, when it died down, the woman appeared a meter in front of me. Behind her, Angelo seemed completely frozen. Even so, he looked like he was vaguely in motion.

"So, you're the 'Glass Princess', Bianka Roland?" She spoke in shade, the language of thieves "I'm LeBlanc, a lady thief, and I've come to steal the both of you. That is to say, you and your guardian. Apologies for no advanced notice."

By the time she finished speaking, the frost surrounding Angelo broke and he freed himself. He was now behind her with a downward sword strike.

LeBlanc caught his blade with her bare hand and was nearly crushed by his delayed gravitational pressure, but in the process, she had completely frozen him again. This time, the temperature rose through the rest of the hall only to drop further around him.

LeBlanc hit the ground like dead weight but stood up as if nothing had happened. If it wasn't for the material the castle was made of, she'd be through the ground.

She dusted herself off and turned back to me. "You should be much easier to take than him. Now, come with me willingly. I don't like the idea of harming my targets more than this."

I reached my hand out and summoned the reflective ornate fan that was my weapon. The instant I did, the cold feeling in my legs raced up my body before a beam of light struck the ground between me and her.

"It's impressive you got this far, but I believe it's time you leave." It was Christopher, my brother, and the last person I thought I'd see at that moment.

"Very well." LeBlanc placed her hand on Angelo and they both faded into a snowy mist before anyone could stop her.

"War comes," said Christopher.

I was shaking like a leaf from the cold as he came to my aid. Placing a jacket on me, he helped me up and escorted me downstairs, where the bodies of many guards could be seen strewn about, mostly frozen and some dead.

"Where's your guard?" I asked, barely keeping my speech from stuttering and my knees from buckling.

"There was another one that went for the twins, but Sirus held them off long enough for me and Helen to get there. She's with them now."

"Did she manage to mark them?"

"No need. I know where they came from." He looked me in the eye briefly and looked away as if it was hard to meet my gaze.

"Brother, what have you been hiding?" I said, suspecting secrecy.

"I'll tell you everything I know when we reach the basement." He had a look of determination with a hint of rage as we entered the throne room and lowered ourselves down to the basement. The first thing that caught my eye was that the emergency exit close to the platform was wide open with the doors blown inward. Whoever it was, they were skilled enough to get in through a secret passage that was sealed from both sides. After a bit of investigating, we found Helen, Sirus, Sun, and Snow together in the library.

"Princess, how are you faring?" Sirus came to my side.

"I'm fine," I said, "How are you?"

"The intruder used electricity, so I had the advantage with my magnetism, but he was powerful enough to nearly wound me before the guard showed up."

"We're fine, too," said Sun, "It was a bit scary, though."

"Speaking of scary." I turned toward Cristopher. Helen was by his side, bowing toward me on her knees. "Didn't you say you'd tell me something when we got down here?"

"Yes." Christopher took a deep breath. "Those people were from C.H.E.S.S. I found out years ago that they had a shadow organization when I bumped into some of their representatives at a... morally questionable event. Ever since then, we've had some... questionable dealings."

"Like what?" It was difficult to hide my anger as I asked.

"Yeah, it's time I come clean." He took a hesitant step back and continued. "It started off small with items on the black market and eventually became something much bigger. I gave them questionable tasks, among other things, and they requested secrets about the powers of our guard as well as ourselves. They particularly wanted to know of any outstanding magic traits among other things."

"Oh, I see." I stepped toward him, and my left hand raced to slap him as hard and fast as I could make it. He saw it coming and didn't dodge. The sound reverberated through the room despite the presence of books and sofas that dampened the sound. In an instant, my hand stung, my palm turned bright red, and my fingers hurt just to move. There wasn't a mark on his face.

"Are you done?" he said, looking down on me. "You're hurt-"

The next sound was my right fist making contact with his face. Many of my knuckles popped at once and the pain rushed up my arm to my elbow so fast my knees almost gave out. Christopher swayed a bit in surprise but was ultimately unharmed.

"It's one thing to have shady dealings with them, but it's another thing to keep me in the dark about it. I don't even care about what you didn't tell me. You should have at least told me something sooner. The point is that you betrayed my trust and the people's faith." Cursing my frailty, I walked past him and began making my way back to the platform. That was when I realized Helen was bowing the way she was because she believed she took blame as well and saw fit to do so. "Helen," I said, turning back.

She turned around on her knees and looked up.

"You are not to blame for anything he did or ordered you to do. I'm sorry you had to deal with his selfishness, and I appreciate you for doing so." I turned around and went to sit in my throne seat to wait for everyone else. The basement and underground passages by extension were compromised and unsafe.

I looked at my arm and found that all the way from my pinky to my elbow was swollen and my knuckles bled a trail from the library to my seat. Because I was always a frail child, Christopher never failed to tease me about it. I'd bruise from bumping into walls and if I fell, I'd break a bone. I bled countless times just learning how to use my weapon when I awakened to my powers. In time, I became less fragile, but the moniker 'Glass Princess' stuck. A detrimental magic trait.

Taking a moment to reflect brought me back to a time when we were in grade school when I was being bullied for being excused from all physical activity because of my condition. Back then, our father requested that no one know about us being royalty. He didn't like favoritism, so we were treated mostly like normal kids.

The bullying lasted for almost a week and unexpectedly stopped. It turned out that the reason was that Christopher became the leader of those bullies. They still bullied everyone they could, but he wouldn't allow them to bully me. I asked him why and he responded, 'You're an important part of my future kingdom. I'll deal with the devils personally to make sure that the kingdom prospers. Of course, that includes you.' I didn't know what he meant at the time, but now, I think I do.

I had calmed down considerably by the time everyone else joined me before beginning the ascent. The ride up was silent until Sun said something.

"So, where are we going?" She was shifting around and swinging her legs in her seat.

Christopher looked toward me. "Despite the unforeseen circumstances, there was always a contingency plan for such an occasion."

"If the underground offered no protection, the sky might," I said, pointing up and wincing from the still lingering pain. I was the one who knew what the contingency plan entailed aside from our late father and a few others, as my brother saw no need for such things at the time and never inquired about it.

"You might want to get that looked at, sister," Christopher pointed at his palm. "And you have something along this area." He gestured along his knuckles. "Surely it pains you?"

"I'm fine-!" I clenched my fist and was forced to grit my teeth. "What you've done is much worse than this. I'll bear it."

Upon reaching the minor throne room, I stood quickly and made my way up the nearest set of stairs. I continued to the next set and the next until we were as far up in the castle as we could go. The top floor was a relatively plain room. It was twenty meters across in a circle with three windows on opposing sides being the only decoration alongside the stairs leading to it. I went to the middle of the room and pressed my knuckle into the floor. They had just barely begun healing and my wound reopened, dousing the spot with fresh blood.

"*As royalty, I shed blood for the people.*" The spell laid in place by my father years before activated. White circles of text in a lost language that only a few people alive knew appeared on the floor and began spinning slowly. The walls seemed to vanish and the floor followed soon after. Before we knew it, we were high above the castle.

Anyone on the inside would be invisible from the outside, and the entire room was invisible, to begin with. It was designed to hold however many people entered and expanded to accommodate any who entered after its activation. Shortly after the spell completed and the text disappeared, an image appeared far below us yet high above the people. It was the face of an elderly man. His face was wrinkled with the shadow of a gray beard and he wore a stern look despite his usual smile. His crown was worn and slightly dented.

"Hello," he said, "In case those of you don't know who I am, my name is Cerillo Roland, formerly Cerillo Vermillion and former king of Roland. I say 'former king' because if this message is aired then I am deceased, and an emergency has arisen. This is likely because the flames of war have met our gate on short notice and we have little time to prepare or, an unavoidable disaster is upon us, but I digress. The reason you see me now is because a member of the royal family wished it, for they have spilled their own blood to protect their people. Please understand that what is about to happen is for your safety."

His face disappeared and a similar text to what was inside the castle appeared glowing throughout the city and along the walls. The text then began rotating with the castle as the focal point, and in a flash, all the people were gone. All vehicles that were still running stopped and the open gates closed. I looked up to see that the entire city's worth of people were standing before me. Men, Women, and children alike as well as a few pets stood in the otherwise empty space.

The sounds of confusion, panic, and crying children were cut through by the sounds of alarm from those closest to me as many rushed to my side to assess my condition. In moments, almost every doctor in the city surrounded me.

Despite my protests, the royal doctor, ahead of everyone else, began assessing my condition. She pushed through the crowd with her medical bag over her shoulder and got to work.

Amidst my continued protest, she expertly placed a gauze into my mouth and reset my dislocated elbow in a single move. I bit down as hard as I could and screamed. She continued by doing the same for my knuckles and applying ointment to my wounds. She then put my arm in a sling and wrapped up my various injuries, including a scathed knee that she discovered in the process. She had one arm around me that kept me from falling over as she carried out every action with one hand.

After putting her tools back in her bag, she placed her hand on my forehead and cast a healing spell. I was enveloped by a coating of mud that started from the top of my head and ran down to my toes before fading away. The pain subsided, and I relaxed.

She didn't realize how embarrassing the whole ordeal was until she was already retrieving the gauze from my mouth and let me go. After assuring her for the last time that I was okay, I looked back at Cristopher. He nodded one slow time, a sign that he was waiting for me to speak. Turning back, I waved my hand over my throat and cast 'echo' to make sure my voice reached everyone.

"Excuse me, residents of our fair city. Though many of you may not see me, I hope that you may hear me. I am Princess Roland and I have urgent news to share with you all." I paused, took a deep breath, and continued. "The situation we currently find ourselves in is a direct result of the organization known as C.H.E.S.S. Two of their operatives have infiltrated the royal castle, successfully kidnapped my closest royal guard, and attempted to take me as well. These actions are a declaration of war and both my brother and I fully intend to reciprocate. I ask that all able-bodied warriors step forward.

Many young men and women stepped forward alongside their older counterparts. Around a quarter of the total populace stood directly before me. Upon closer inspection, the number of people who moved to the front outnumbered the number of able-bodied combatants taken in a recent consensus.

"I see many more of you here than I thought would be present and for that, I'm happy, but know that it only took one of theirs to overpower and kill many of the guards in the castle and take Sir Write by force. Although we need as many soldiers as we can get, there are other provinces under this kingdom's rule. I will not ask those untrained to join this battle."

No one moved.

"Please, I am only asking for the warriors among us to step forward." This time, more people stepped forward. "So be it," I said, raising my hand. "Step forward at your own peril." Everyone who had taken to the front had also taken a knee. "So be it," I said, slowly lowering my hand to touch the invisible floor. "*Together we fight for the people.*"

More scripts appeared and this time, it was only after we teleported. Unaware of the full capabilities the complex mechanism of magic held, I was surprised to see the number of potential soldiers drop from unexpectedly high to predictably low. It seemed that anyone under a certain age or weak of will was excluded from the transportation.

The spell took us to the soldiers' hall on the eastern side of the castle. From there, we devised a strategy to confront and defeat our enemy while keeping the people safe. Messengers were sent to our other provinces to relay the news and help them prepare for the coming events.

34-Father, Son

[Geist Kaizer]

The total lockdown and subsequent clean-up resulting from the bombing of the gate at the center of the base is tireless and consuming. Nearly half of the staff and all the enrolled students are sent off base until further notice following the incident. All that's left is soldiers. After playing my part until the lockdown lifts, I decide to visit my father. I come to his door and rep twice, pause a second, and deliver one more.

"Enter." I hear his voice faintly from the other side. The few steps between the hall and the office are a shift in atmosphere. It shifts from a neutral office environment to the homey library of an old man. There are bookcases filled to the brim standing on both sides of the door leading all the way to the respective corners. The rest of the room is dimly lit by the sunset shining through the row of windows along the far wall.

The old man in question is sitting at his desk near the far right of the room. He's only just entering his grays with short, spiky silver hair beginning to overtake the black, minimal wrinkles, and a surprisingly soft demeanor. His dark, tired eyes slowly wander up from a pile of papers to meet mine. "So, what brings this pleasant surprise?"

"I just came to see how you're doing. You must be tired after all that's happened." I approach and sit across from the desk in a wooden chair.

"Not so much as tired but bored, really." He begins organizing the papers into stacks. "I heard you've been keeping in contact with your mother. How is she?"

"That's part of why I came to see you. She's worried."

"She is, is she?" He gives a soft smile and nods thoughtfully. "Tell her I'm glad she still worries about me, but I'm fine."

"She's coming personally to make sure of that." As quickly as the words leave my mouth, his smile fades.

"That's fine. I hadn't seen her in a long time... But speaking of family I haven't seen in a long time, how's your sister? I haven't heard much about her since a member of her team was suspended, 'Solo' was it?"

"Lucia's doing fine. I've learned that she and Solo are quite the item."

"Ah…" He nods slowly. "It looks like she took after your mother more than I thought she would; always going after the dangerous ones. I used to be a little dangerous myself once upon a time. 'The demon with the heart of gold', they called me."

"I know, Dad. You told me the story." I sit back and chuckle.

"It's true, you know." He chuckles as well. "So, is anything new happening with you?"

"Actually… Yes. I've had my eye on a lady recently."

"What's she like?" His eyebrows rise and a smile spreads across his face.

"Well, she's smart, confident, and does whatever she puts her mind to. She's also considered the most beautiful woman where she's from."

"Where she's from? Do you know how she feels about you?" He's now past the initial excitement and his smile fades.

"While I can't be certain, she did seem to have a passing interest. I met her at the Magic Tournament, so I wasn't able to talk to her for long. The real problem is that she's a princess."

"Royalty? Of what kingdom?"

"Roland." Once I say the name, he falls silent for a moment.

"I don't believe- no that won't work." He has a stern look on his face.

"Why not?" I ask. "Is there any particular reason?"

"I just don't think she's a good match for you."

"You think so?"

"I just think she's a little too much for you."

"I guess we'll see soon enough. She's coming for a visit."

The look in his eye morphs from a man having a conversation with his son to a dead-eye stare. He is clearly displeased, and although I've never known him to be fearful, maybe a little scared. "Did you invite her?"

"No, you did." I retrieve a blue and white letter envelope embroidered with a seal depicting a red butterfly surrounded by black feathers from my pocket. "Because it wasn't directly addressed to you, it found its way to me first." I sit the letter on the desk, and he stares at it. "I don't know the specifics, but I suggest sending an apology and request for reconsideration."

"I can't do that. We are on the verge of something tremendous. This is just the tipping point for what's to come."

"If that's your choice, I can't support your endeavors anymore. This letter is a declaration of war and apparently, we started it." I stand and step away from the desk. "Tell me it's a mistake."

"No, war is inevitable. I'm sure the contents of this letter made that apparent, but do you really like that woman enough to let your feelings sway you?"

"That's not the reason. I only said that to see your reaction, and that told me everything I needed to know. While your right hand was busy cleaning up from that attack, your left hand went out under the guise of plausible suspicion to infiltrate Magnolia and kidnap the princess. Was the attack during the tournament even done by outsiders? Are you some kind of supervillain? I can't support you on this without answers."

"Is this coming from you as my son or a member of the Seven Virtues?"

"It's coming from me as Geist Kaizer: a man who doesn't want to see war in my lifetime."

"What happens if I give you answers and you don't agree with me?"

"I'll be taking my leave if that's the case. Mom will be here by next week and depending on what you have to say, I might be leaving with her."

"Do you remember the goal of this organization, son?"

"To help make the world a better place in a way that others will accept even if they don't agree," I answer.

He opens a drawer and pulls out a large, folded sheet of paper. It unfolds to a map that I've never seen before. It's old, faded, wrinkled, and made of parchment. The lands on the map are sequestered into five territories with stretches of no-man's-land in between. "Do you know what this is?"

"An ancient map?"

"Indeed. This is a map of a land that existed before, after, and during civilization as we know it. 'Directionem', as It's called. Legends tell us this land is real but at the same time, is spoken of as if it either never existed or has yet to exist in the first place. This was a land I had sought after for years out of pure curiosity until I met your mother and settled down. That was until the passing of my late mentor. She handed off the organization to me and that's when I received this."

He pulls out another map from the same drawer. This time, of the overworld and on it were markers showing the current position of all capital cities in the underworld in relation to it. They're positioned as if they're in the overworld. There was a filter over it ranging in between white, yellow, and purple with a key showing saturation percentages of void density with white being above 30% and purple being above 70% with yellow in between. "You know how these cities are built, right?"

"Every country uses a different method, but they all use magic."

"And how do you think those cities stay standing the way they do?"

I search my mind for a believably definitive answer and can't find one. It feels like he's trying to subvert my expectations.

"They use voids. If ley-lines are rivers of naturally occurring mana, voids are lakes."

"What does that have to do with anything?"

"Like many things, magic is temporary, so we often use it sparingly in place of more permanent solutions, even in medical applications. Those cities are no exception. Even so, Voids are ever flowing with energy from the natural flora and fauna that inhabit them. Adding people into the mix, especially powerful ones, further strengthens the voids. So, to keep themselves functioning independently from the outside world, they use the natural mana in the ground to alter the ecosystem and supply a continuous flow of power to their facilities."

I feel like he didn't hear me the first time and ask again. "Again, what does that have to do with anything?"

He ignores my question and taps a rhythmic pattern on his desk with his finger and a screen on the wall behind him turns on, showing the C.H.E.S.S. headquarters from a distance as the screensaver. He taps a much longer pattern on the desk and the screen changes to the same map of the world as was on the table. "When I saw this, I knew there was something about it that was... off, to say the least." He turns around and double-taps the screen. The world map disappears, leaving behind the filter on a black background. "Out of curiosity, I played with it for a bit and found this."

He pinches his fingers on the screen and the blotches of color come together in the center. As the borders combine, I see what he means. I find myself looking back and forth between the ancient map and the image on the screen. They are nearly identical. "The points with the highest void density coincide with what seemed to be the capitals of the territories shown on the ancient map. When I saw that, it hit me."

He swipes left on the screen and the ancient map comes in from the right behind the overlay. He swipes again, and another map comes up while the previous one shrinks to a quarter of the screen; he does it twice more, and every corner is filled with a different map containing similar points. Each is from various locations and eras of time. One is from the Zou dynasty in China, another is of major settlements in the early Americas, and the last is a projection of void spots as they would have been before Pangea separated. "Do you see what I mean?"

"What does this have to do with your reasoning for war?" I ask the only question still on my mind.

"Of all the legends associated with Directionem, one tells of an extinction event that did, will, and is wiping the land from existence. From my research, the likelihood that it is a phenomenon that can destroy all life as we know it is far too great. What I've set in motion is to prevent that outcome at any cost. This war isn't for nothing. It's to force the city of Magnolia to relocate and prevent a worldwide catastrophe."

"How can you be sure this catastrophe hasn't already happened? What about the trigger? An event like that would have a trigger."

"I know it hasn't happened because we're still here and the trigger was set in place in the advent of the Shadow Master. Since his defeat, one thing is certain. His being was split into five pieces. His body, gate, weapon, mind, and soul. One way or another, they will all come together and ignite the apocalypse unless we stop it. The only problem is that the only way to stop it is to bring all of the pieces together. A self-fulfilling prophecy, maybe, but on the off chance that that's the case, I needed one of the key locations to be inactive. That meant forcing the migration of one of the cities here." He traces his finger around Europe and part of Asia.

In that broad location sits Forstad, capital of Gullanda, a country founded by wizards and situated in Sweden; Gratamal, capital of The United Coven of Streghaven, a country originally founded by witches and situated in Italy; Trollvei, capital of New Feskog, a country founded by summoners and nestled near the western edge of Russia; Zamkrev, capital of Velzed, a country founded by warlocks on the border of Czechia and Poland; and Magnolia, capital of Roland, founded by wielders and placed on the southwest side of Ireland. Despite those only being their relative placements on the overworld map, a pattern emerges that seemingly applies to the underworld map as well.

"I see," I say. "An empty void must mean an inactive one and of the five countries, Roland was founded most recently. They have the least ties to the current location of their capital. I still want to know why you need to strong-arm them. Why not use diplomacy? They were the people hit hardest by the advent of the Shadow Master. I find it hard to believe they wouldn't comply if we told them the situation."

"It's because they were affected the most that they wouldn't comply. Their prince knows of our original plan and outright refused any proposal we made on the basis that bringing those pieces together would resurrect someone who was already nearly impossible to kill from the start."

"Speaking of. What's the chance of that happening?"

"In the best possible scenario, I would like to say zero but it's more like forty percent, but even if he does come back, we have more than enough manpower to take him down."

"What about the pieces of the Shadow Master? I know we have the gate, but what about the rest?"

"I can't tell you." It made sense. If I was to oppose his plans at the last minute, I could put all of his efforts into ruin.

"Okay. I'll inform you of my decision before Mom leaves next week." I walk toward the door and stand for a moment.

"I'll be looking forward to it." The screen changes to blank, and both maps are securely stored back in his desk in seconds.

I open the door and return to the neutral office environment before heading home to end the day.

35-Wargames

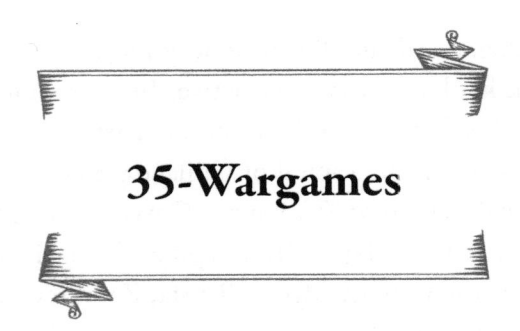

[Princess Bianka Roland]

A week after my attempted abduction, all of the injuries I sustained healed completely. Word spread through the kingdom, and we were able to organize an army of nearly six hundred in the next two weeks with more due to arrive soon. During that time, figuring out the ancient magic put in place by my father took equal priority. After another five days, we were able to move the entire capital to a presumably safer spot and retrofit the newly open space for war. It was essentially flat grassland with few trees dotted around. There were small trenches and tunnels as well as magical, non-magical, land, and aerial traps laid around. We were also putting the finishing touches on a large-scale transportation spell that could take the entire location with the surrounding void and teleport it to our pre-ordained destination. At the moment there was only a one-way peephole in which we could see the C.H.E.S.S. headquarters.

I spied my destination with a determination I had not known myself to possess in such a long time that I barely recognized myself when a small hand mirror overtook my line of sight.

"If you make that face too often, you'll look like that when you get older," said Christopher, slipping the mirror back into my pocket where he picked it from.

"Sneaky as always, are we?" I glanced at him for less than a second to see his usually smug demeanor replaced with unprecedented worry.

"It was a good way to relieve some of the tension, besides, it wouldn't be hard to cut it with a spoon at this rate." He was trying to get me to relax, and it didn't work.

"Do you have someone?" I asked.

"That's a sudden question," he said. "What do you mean?"

"If I perish here, you will be crowned king. I want to know before that could happen if you have someone in mind to be your queen."

"Don't be silly, there's very little chance of that happening."

"Then our nation will have two kings? That's fine." I held not a hint of sarcasm.

"That's not what I..." He sighed. "What about yourself? Surely, you have someone in mind to keep you company should I fall."

"I do not," I said. "And I doubt I ever will."

"Don't say that. I have a bad enough feeling about you being here instead of with the people. You haven't been in the capital since it was moved."

"I know how you think, brother. If I entered the city, you would've locked me in a tower or something to make sure I wouldn't leave... I'd be the princess in the tower..." I scoffed.

"But I assure you that you don't need to be here-"

"Oh, I assure you that I do, and you can't stop me."

My retort came faster than he expected as he paused before responding, "I will not, but I will also not allow you at the front lines."

"You have no choice in the matter. I've made up my mind and you're not changing it."

"On the contrary, I do have a choice." He softly put his hand on my shoulder and gently turned me around. "I'll fight in your place and even deal with the devil personally to ensure your safety."

"You've told me something similar before," I said, finding myself thinking back once more.

"I have? Well, that should tell you how important you are not just to me, but to anyone who calls themselves a Rolanite."

"I'll take your word for it, but I still refuse to simply sit back and watch."

"Then, how about this?" He held up a small silver amulet embroidered with a butterfly surrounded by five feathers. The royal crest. "Put this on and I'll always know where you are. I'll have one on as well so that we can keep track of each other."

His efforts seemed sincere, so I accepted it. "I can agree with that." Opening it, I found a small screen with a map of our surroundings and a blinking beacon directly in front of me.

"I also have one other request." He took a step back.

"What is it?" I said, expecting a proposition that would keep me out of the fight.

"I'll be taking command of the front lines and I want you to head the back lines."

"Should I break this right now?" I clenched my fist around the amulet, threatening its destruction.

"No, you shouldn't." His reaction was as close to panic as I've ever seen in him, and it caused me to open my palm in surprise. "While I won't stop you from joining the battle, I also don't want you to fight any more than you have to." His voice was layered with desperation.

"I'll think about it," I said, pocketing the amulet and turning to continue my watch through the ethereal window.

"I hope you do," he said, leaving me to my devices.

In a couple of days' time, the transportation spell was complete and ready to activate. As the final preparations were near complete, I was confronted once more by Christopher. His usual gold-plated armor was replaced with a shimmering silvery metal that looked much less bulky and more streamlined and a matching helmet. He wasn't the only one though. I personally commissioned armor for myself long before in case war ever broke out. It was as blue as sapphire and white as marble made of a thin layer of silver woven over layers of steel with Kevlar threads. It was designed for mobility and protection from piercing attacks. The silver was enchanted with defensive magic and the steel was naturally magic resistant. The headdress held a gem that was enchanted for physical defense as well.

"What do you think?" he said. "Today's the day. Have you thought over my request?"

"Do you intend to protect me forever? You've discussed it enough at strategy meetings for it to seem expected by now."

"I will protect you if and when I must, but if it's against your will, you're more than welcome to let me know."

"Does that mean you'll stop if I do?"

"That depends on the circumstance."

"How about now?"

"The only thing I intend to protect you from at the moment is yourself. I can't have you rush into battle without first thinking of your actions. I don't want to lose the family I have left."

His words hit deep and forced me to take a moment to reflect on my recent actions. "You won't," I said, reaching for his hand and grasping it tightly. "I'll take the middle lines. That's my compromise. You head the front."

"Thank you." His eyes softened as a weight seemed to lift off his shoulders.

After a final strategy meeting with our generals, our plans were finalized. The army was to be split into nine groups of roughly sixty-six each headed by a general.

Even though we each had a starting position of equal distance apart from the nearest squad in a box formation, given the foreseen chaos and the likelihood of communication interference within the heavily magically charged environment, each squad would act independently from the rest. With that in mind, each soldier was placed in a squad befitting their abilities and the style of their commander.

Christopher's squad consisted mostly of speed, range, and balance type soldiers to maximize his adaptability and mobility while mine was mainly power, defense, and support types for long and stationary assaults as well as a generally powerful defensive line, though it didn't matter much to that end.

As promised, I was set in the middle while Christopher was in front, and the others were set accordingly to make up three lines. We couldn't see each other, so each squad moved to position and shot a white flare to signify that they were ready. Each flare was enchanted to be a part of the key to trigger the transportation spell.

Once all of the flares went up, the ground began glowing a bright white with symbols and words before the peephole hanging in the air expanded over the entire sky. We were instantly transported to the Aegean Sea off the shore of Athens and pushed against the walls of the C.H.E.S.S. headquarters, forcing it to be landlocked. We successfully transported part of the underworld into the overworld. A moment later, a yellow beacon of light was flying high into the air and exploded over the base, a warning shot.

There was no reaction for more than five minutes, so I ordered my troops to move forward in an arrow formation. Not long after, a bright blue light could be seen hovering over the base before it began moving at alarming speeds straight toward the battlefield while shrinking in size. I thought it was only a confirmation beacon before it gained definition and began spiraling straight toward the left of the midline where I was.

Without a moment's hesitation, my troops put up a collective barrier before I could give an order. Many colors mixed in a giant bubble around my entire squad and culminated in a wavy rainbow pattern. At that moment, the projectile sped up and crashed straight through as if it wasn't there. It changed trajectory and homed in on me directly.

"*Reflect*." I summoned my fan and cast the spell. A reflective surface of magic appeared between me and the object. I thought the object was simply a spell that I could send back to whoever cast it, but I was wrong. The projectile turned out to be a person as he broke through my spell and tackled me to the ground.

When I opened my eyes, I was on someone's shoulder and tied with blue electric bounds while high in the air. We were moving too fast to make out any geography despite the majority of the battlefield being flat ground. I was still clutching my fan in my hand but couldn't move as the air pressure was too great to resist. The sound of the rushing wind was deafening, and my head felt like it was split in two from hitting the ground so hard.

I tried casting a spell but was shocked across my entire body the moment I tried it. It hurt but not enough to keep me from trying. I was able to cast a sleep spell that seemed to have no effect and actually backfired as I was overtaken by drowsiness despite my situation.

Everything went dark and I hadn't noticed until my eyes already adjusted to the indoor environment. We were going down a hallway free of but a few office doors to other halls with black and white floor tiles and white walls. I tried to cast a spell but found that I had been silenced. It was too powerful to resist. Even thinking of a spell made my mind go blank. I tried to move but the effects of the electric binding left me paralyzed and I could only do slightly more than twitch. Voices awakened my other senses and I realized that they were the reason I was able to regain consciousness to begin with.

"Looks like she's becoming restless," said a female voice ahead.

"You should have seen her on the way back." The man carrying me yawned. "She managed to cast a sleep spell on me while bound and moving at mach two."

"So, that's why the silencing spell?"

"Yeah, if it was anyone else but me, they'd be asleep right now…" The man swayed to the side and almost dropped me before finding his balance again.

"I don't know about that, Sloth, you seem more drowsy than usual."

"Nah, I'm just not used to being this active. I went on a mission with Greed recently and her 'phantom thief' act was a pain in the ass to deal with. Not to mention that the mission was botched and that's why we're in this mess."

"Look on the bright side. There are so many delightful souls out there to take… For me anyway." I could hear the delight in her voice as she talked.

"Listen Glutton, our orders were to take who we need and standby at our posts. If any of us go out there and start wreaking havoc, it would end too quickly."

"I think you overestimate our sins." She giggled.

"I think you're just looking for an excuse to wreak havoc. Besides, the battle already started. All that's left is for us to do our jobs."

"If you say so. I'll be at my post." The woman's footsteps became more distant until they were made inaudible by the sound of a closing door. What I saw of her was that she wore a black T-shirt with holes in it, black knee-high skinny jeans with the same design, combat-grade heels, and short, spiked black hair. At the last second, she looked back with the most unsettling smile I had ever seen before leaving my field of view.

From there, I was taken through a few office doors and down a staircase before a large metal door. The door opened on its own and I was taken into a room reasonably sizable to a stadium and more than nine stories high. I was dropped briefly to the sound of my armor clacking against the ground before being grabbed by the scruff and tossed into the air. I expected an impact before my momentum slowed and I came to a stop. The binds dissipated and I tried to free myself from whatever new force held me against my will with all of my strength.

"I wouldn't struggle so much if I were you." The man was now around four stories below me. I stared daggers at him but the look on his face was of someone who couldn't care any less if he tried. He wore a yellow shirt under a navy blue blazer with matching pants. That was the last thing I saw before everything went black.

36-Castling

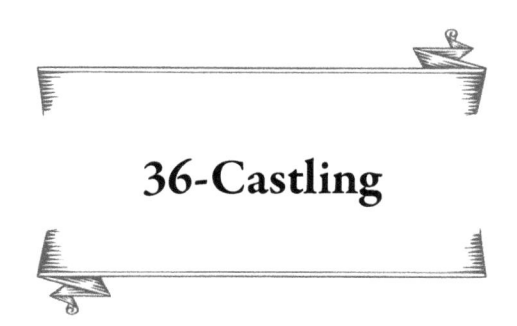

[Geist Kaizer]

A few days after speaking to my father about his recent decisions and advising against war, I find myself in my office staring blankly at one recommendation page of many. I'm contemplating whether to accept any of them. The applications are to join the special academic curriculum held within C.H.E.S.S. headquarters. I feel like I'm wasting time, despite my carefully laid plans being carried out with no outstanding delay or difficulty. My contemplation runs long, but eventually, I decide that no matter what happens, there will be no new students. I let the stack of papers rot on my desk while I take a stroll around the building.

I'm near a window when I feel it.

The entire island rocks as if another explosion went off. The ground tilts twenty degrees and settles back in place. Less than a minute later, a yellow light explodes over the buildings after arcing in from outside the walls. A warning beacon.

I make my way as quickly as I can to my father's office and open the door. Inside, I find a woman in a blue and white sweater with matching pants and boots. Her blue-dyed hair is tied into a single loose braid in the back.

She seems to be looking out the windows in the direction of the landmass that appeared and beached part of the base. I only recognize her once she turns toward me, and I see her face. She's as blind as they come.

"Mom, you're here late." My eyes dart between her and my father, sitting at his desk as usual. "I believe the Rolanites are here."

"Don't worry, all preparations have been made." My father folds his hands and sits back in his chair. "Everything has already been taken care of."

Taken aback by my father's words, my mother says, "What do you mean, 'everything'? What were we just-"

"It's too late to change plans. They've already made their move and so have we." My father speaks with finality, as if he has no control over what happens next.

"We? I refuse to have anything to do with this," says my mother, frankly.

"I know. I meant to keep you out of this, but you came here of your own volition and it's too late to change that."

"What about Lucia?" I cautiously take a step in while leaving my other foot outside. "Is she a part of this?"

"No, I never intended for her to be a part of this either. She should be in a safe place and away from all of what's happening by now." He seems to be telling the truth, but something in the way he says it rubs me the wrong way.

I quickly step back into the hallway but I hit something that feels like a wall blocking my retreat. Knowing the door is still open, my only conclusion leads me to turn around and face what's there. What I see is non-uniform gray and two blotches of red and black. I don't realize what I'm looking at until the blotches turn gray for less than a second and return. I instinctively take a defensive stance as I realize it's a pair of eyes set within stone-gray skin.

"Hello Humble, Kind." The man acknowledges both me and my mother by our titles, respectively. "I'm Darkside." He speaks with no emotion, signifying his incomplete nature. I know who he is but saying anything would give me away, so I hold my poise, unsure of what to do. "Does my aura upset you?" He says, looking past me.

I looked to see my mother trembling. Despite her total blindness, she has the uncanny ability to 'see' the energy given off of everything, as if she has sight, and her reaction to Darkside is in line with my assumptions. Cautiously, I step back until I stop in front of my mother, shielding her from his presence. It's said that anyone weak of will, will fall at his glance. My mother had the strongest will of anyone I know, but whatever she saw in him made her tremble. Any longer and it would get to me as well.

"Are the preparations ready?" My father stands and speaks, taking Darkside's attention off us.

"Yes. Shall we proceed as planned?"

"Lead the way." My father follows the hollow man out of the room.

The door closes, and I turn back to my mother. "Mom, why didn't you let me know when you arrived?"

"I was caught up in the scenery and decided to take a look around Athens. I've never been here before, so it took some time." She has a soft look in her eye despite her stoic demeanor.

"If you were lost, you could've called and-" I'm interrupted by a coughing fit. It's bad enough that I fall to my knees.

"Are you ok?" My mother rubs my back until it's over.

"I didn't think it was that intense... But as soon as I relax, this happens? Was it because I looked him in the eye?" There's a small pool of blood in my hand where I coughed. "I'm fine now."

"Are you sure?"

"Yeah. We need to call in all virtues. There's no time." I go to the door to open it, but it's sealed shut. There is only one visible lock, and it's unlatched. On closer inspection, the inner frame is bolted on all sides. I try the windows and find that I can't force them open or break them. All magic does is ricochet back or dissipate entirely. Breaking a window will take much longer than we have. All electronics are jammed save for the one-way communicators embedded in our badges that only give emergency information. I take my badge off and press the switch to send the emergency signal for five seconds, then drop it on the floor and stomp it to pieces.

"What did you just do?" My mother is standing against a window and isn't looking in my direction.

"I sent out a signal that should get to the right people who would know what to do. Aside from that, I'm waiting to see what happens."

"It may be too late to stop this war, but we should still be able to stop your father."

"Although he is a priority, Dad's not what I'm worried about right now. It's the thing that was with him. That's the body of the Shadow Master. The pressure he exerted was unreal, and that was just from his presence alone. I don't even want to imagine what would happen if he was completely resurrected."

A moment later, the floor shudders and begins to lower quickly but smoothly, leaving the walls behind to change from brown pebble cobblestone to solid concrete. The bookcases and the rest of the furniture don't follow, instead seeming to stand on a non-existent floor. The movement ceases a minute later and an opening in the wall created by the shifting floor leads to the catacombs in the deepest parts of the base.

I go into the darkness first and cast 'darksight' to see. After a few minutes of walking, my field of view is obscured by an unnatural mist that blinds me to the way ahead. I stop walking, perplexed, until my mother taps me on my shoulder.

"Maybe some type of mana field?" she says. It has to be magical in nature for it to blind her.

"There shouldn't be anything like that down here."

"That's what I thought. Can you see at all? The fog's too thick for me."

"Looks like we're both blind. I'll see if I can push it around." I extend my arm and cast 'push' to force the stagnant 'fog' into motion so it would thin out and dissipate on its own. Nothing happened.

My mother puts her hand on the nearest wall and snaps her fingers, causing the surrounding walls and floor to glow white. We had just entered a large chamber, and the air is thick with a light green fog. "What do you see?"

On the other side of the room is a man standing against the wall near the opposite entrance. His long, sprawling hair is an unnatural leafy-green and his skin has an oddly tree-like texture.

His muscles are well-defined and can be seen through the green sweatsuit he wore while his hands rested on a wooden quarterstaff wrapped by a metal snake.

Not expecting someone down this far waiting to stop us, I take a step back and summon to my hands what's more like a kusarigama except the sickle is replaced with a square saw-patterned blade. "Who are you?" I say, fully knowing that he's a man who betrayed his closest comrades on a whim and became a Sin. Marroon Crest. I'm not supposed to know who he really is, no one is, but I know each and every one of them.

"They call me Lust of Sin, and based on appearance, you are Geist Kaizer and Courtney Riddles, is that right?"

"That is correct." I try to continue, but Lust says something else.

"That's unfortunate. I was told to stop anyone who came through here and capture a select few, and that includes family. Boss's orders."

"I guess that means we have no choice."

I throw the weighted end of the chain and he only moves forward a bit and slightly to the side to dodge it. That gives me leeway to yank the chain and cause the weight to begin wrapping around him.

He lifts his quarterstaff to guide the chain over his head and escapes. He then taps the ground with his staff and the mist spreads out while a root the size of a truck grows from the ground in front of him and twists my way.

I catch the weight, cast 'blade wave', and split it into fourths before it can reach me.

Sensing the power he's holding back, I evolve my weapon to its third form and send my strongest attack at him before he can react. At least, I try to. My weapon begins glowing blue as usual and then stops. This is followed by another coughing fit and a sizable puddle of blood spilling onto the ground this time. I look into the puddle as a feeling of weakness washes over me and I slump to the ground.

"Geist, are you ok? *Purify*." A faint white light spreads across the entire room and the fog only slightly thins out farther.

"Mom, get back. Don't come into the fog." My voice is raspy, and I can barely move, but I still find myself on my feet.

"That's not me doing that to you." Lust is now directly in front of me, and I hadn't noticed until he said something. "It looks like you met Darkside. His aura'll do that to you." He opens his palm toward me to cast a spell, but before he can, a bright white spear comes whizzing past and lands on the ground behind him.

"It lifted enough that I can sense you both." My mother's voice comes calmly and clearly through the building noise in my own mind. "*Omaerith*."

She does the same thing I tried to do; call in my strongest weapon. Being a summoner, she doesn't have the pension for combat that most wielders possess. Instead, she summons creatures to help and do most of the fighting for her. The strongest of which was a guardian angel that she made a contract with the day I was born. The spear levitates from the ground and a hand materializes holding it, followed by the rest of a winged figure bathed in a warm light.

The spear comes slicing through the air and Lust ducks to the side to avoid it. He engages the angle. By this time, I'm struggling to stay standing as my mother lays her hands on my back and attempts to heal any wounds that could be found. The problem is, there are none. I'm not injured in the least, I'm cursed. And I can feel it.

"Is my will truly that weak…?" The last words I utter begin floating in my mind, and within moments, the growing darkness surrounding my vision finally overtakes my sight.

37-Capture

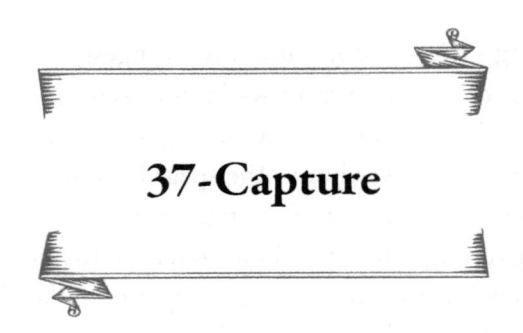

[Noah Black]

I was deep in meditation beside Catt in one of the empty basement rooms. I was contemplating how best to use my purifying ability and she was just going along with me. Since helping Naomi and Caroline, I was able to get around to helping a few other people. Even though I wanted to help everyone I could, keeping my ability under wraps was a priority. I hoped to distill the process even further into something I could teach to others or have it be otherwise replicable. I'd just be putting myself in danger if I went around curing everyone in sight.

Two I remembered well were a witch and his adopted son who lived in one of the underground residences of New York. They were both taking care of each other and barely keeping the corpse shadows at bay through a combination of makeshift seals and sheer willpower before I helped them.

Despite helping only a few people, I was able to boil what little experience I had down to a reliable method of coaxing the corpse shadow out, making contact with it, and purifying it before it could react. The problem now was doing it as fast as I would need to in a combat setting. Hopefully, one I could teach. I had just come upon what felt like the start of an answer when the ground trembled.

In less than ten minutes, we were all at the water's edge. Nothing seemed to be wrong aside from the large base that could be seen across the water, having completely disappeared in less than that time. It was obvious that something more was off when a seagull appeared from nothingness in the air near the edge of the water. Now, we just had to wait. There were a lot of people with the organization that Leon and Carrie belonged to, and we were waiting for them before going into what was essentially a warzone.

Nearly a minute passed before a pressure met us from behind. It was as if something huge was coming our way, but upon second notice, the energy was familiar. A moment later, I saw Krow flying at high speeds with fire at his feet as he soared toward our location. He was followed by at least ten people at a considerably slower pace. He swooped in and landed next to me.

"So, it's started." He looked wistfully at what was presumably an illusionary barrier in front of us.

"Yeah, how are you doing?" I felt that something was amiss, so I asked.

"Rachel came after me."

"Rachel?"

"The bounty hunter. There are some insanely powerful people out there and some of them are right in front of us."

"Is that right?"

"She took out the small army behind me almost instantly and could have given me a run for my money if she didn't hold back as much as she did."

"You calling us useless?" A red-headed woman landing behind him objected to his statement. "We were caught off guard."

"That's not my point." Krow stuck his hand out over the water, and it disappeared. "There are people here that can do that with a full day's notice, people she was afraid of." He looked around a bit and scanned the crowd. "I guess I'm the only one of my family here." He took a step forward and his foot disappeared before he was stopped by the woman at his side, grabbing his wrist.

"Everyone's not here yet, you can't go in." She tilted her entire body away and grunted in her attempt, but he wasn't budging.

"My mom's in there, I'm going." He flicked his wrist and shook her off before stepping in completely.

"Damn it, I'm going in after him. The rest of you follow after everyone else arrives." The woman gave hurried orders to the rest of her group before jumping in behind him.

When I saw Krow go in, I took a hesitant step forward and my toes curled inward at the prospect of walking into a war zone. I couldn't understand how Krow could just walk in, and that woman could just follow. I had a reason to step in as well; a good one. I just couldn't.

"I'm ready any time." Catt patted me on my back. "What about you?"

"I think so. I don't sense any corpse shadows nearby, but since we're dealing with C.H.E.S.S, there are probably quite a few in there." I stepped closer to where the illusionary barrier seemed to be. Scrutinizing it further, there were slight ripples in an otherwise seamless illusion "I think we should go now and not waste any time."

"I agree." Catt stood closer to the barrier as well. "Let's go in, I'll back you up this time."

"Took you long enough." The voice came from above. Looking up slightly, Hanna was hovering above Catt's head. "Shall we get going then?" The small bat settled herself on Catt's shoulder and raised a wing toward our destination.

"Sure." My hesitancy faded as I stepped into the barrier, but the situation was not immediately apparent.

There was a mostly flat battlefield stretching from the barrier's edge all the way to the base in the distance. I couldn't tell what exactly was happening in multiple areas as they were mostly too far away to get any details, but I could feel a constant influx of negative energy from almost everywhere. It was as if the warzone was saturated with corpse shadows. They were everywhere, and I was being drawn to them. Looking around, I was able to see what looked like a fireball flying across the sky far ahead, followed by a ball of light. It was likely Krow as more than a few airborne soldiers tried to intercept him, only to spiral straight downward shortly after making contact.

"Do you sense anything?" Catt was close beside me.

"Yeah, everywhere. I think we should head for the center. They're drawn to me as much as I'm drawn to them."

"So, we're putting on a show." She popped her knuckles and stood at the ready.

"You took the words right out of my mouth."

"Be sure not to get ahead of yourselves, you two," warned the bat.

"No promises." I summoned my sword, held it flat at knee height, and jumped onto it. I hovered forward while Catt followed closely on foot.

Despite how much faster we'd gotten, the middle of the battlefield only seemed to get farther away. I was too focused to notice, but Catt was keen to shoot a fireball in front of us and shatter the illusion. Before us stood a slender man in a black suit and red tie. The air around him constantly shifted colors between red and blue hues.

"Shadow." Catt got ready to cast a spell while the man's eyes clouded over in black.

"No, he's not." I pulled out the frozen flame and held it up. While there was something 'dark' about him, it was no shadow; at least not the kind we were dealing with. "I'm Noah, of the house of Black."

"What proof do you have?" The man's voice was layered, and I was having a hard time keeping focus on him. "More than just a frozen flame, I hope." I understood his skepticism. In a warzone, you don't take chances.

"I'm sorry, we don't have time. Catt, can I see your arm?" I put away the frozen flame and reached my hand out.

"Sure, why?" She put her hand in mine.

"This will hurt a lot." I pulled her sleeve back.

"Ok?" She tensed herself and winced as I passed my blade clean through her flesh and out the other side. There was no damage whatsoever. "Ah- that hurts like hell!"

"Do you see? The magic trait of the house of Black." I let go of Catt's hand and she cradled her arm.

"If that's the case, then you're late. The battle hasn't made it here, but someone like you should be near the middle ranks." He pointed ahead and past what was likely his unit. "I'm General Phishbac by the way. The platoon ahead of this one is headed by General Rose. If he asks, tell him I sent you."

"By Rose, do you mean James Rose?" The term 'General Rose' brought back my curiosity about the old man.

"Have you met him?"

"Yeah, he helped us out once." We began making our way in that direction. "Speaking of helping out, we have reinforcements coming this way. That includes the two flying across the battlefield right now, but the rest should be coming sometime later."

The General pulled out a flare gun, loaded a blue shot, and fired into the air. "Now everyone else should know that, too."

We continued on our way and despite the distance, made it in a short time. As soon as I could see any details of the people, I focused on pinpointing any nearby corpse shadows. There weren't any as far as I could see, but the feeling I had persisted. Many of the soldiers noticed us as we neared them, but they seemed oddly relaxed even for receiving reinforcements, and the reason became clear soon. The familiar sound of a temporal distortion surrounded us, and everything seemed to stop, including us. I decided not to fight against it, and it seemed to only last a split second before time resumed and Jamie appeared in front of us.

The old man sighed. "I can't say that I expected to see you here, but then again, I didn't expect myself to be here either."

"Jamie, we came here with a plan," I said, hopping off my sword before explaining as much as I could about it.

"It looks like the good surprises keep on coming." Without a moment's delay, Jamie sent out a messenger to the other units, and we began preparing to execute the first phase of the plan.

Jamie created a magic circle made to draw in large amounts of mana into one point, and I stood in the middle. Most of the soldiers spread apart in the circle facing away while Jamie, Catt, and a few others stood closer by and waited.

I started by putting my sword in its black form and stabbing it straight down in the center of the circle. "**Dark world**." The spell warped our surroundings as far as the eye could see with a shadowy blanket. This would have taken around half an hour to cover the entire area, including the full battlefield and C.H.E.S.S. base had it not been for the others around adding to the spell. They funneled some of their mana into me through the circle on the ground. It only took a minute instead. The fact that it didn't take long to complete was a blessing as amorphous humanoid figures began popping out of the ground around us.

They rose like zombies and hobbled along the ground toward us until they met the edge of the circle and stopped as if they were waiting for something. They were different colored elementals with a visibly black core in their center. Those were the source of the negative feeling I had. Everyone should have been able to feel it as well now.

Curiously, one of the soldiers touched a yellow one near them and was rejected with an electric shock. Immediately after, a green one jerked toward them before jumping at them, sweeping up a small whirlwind.

I acted quickly, removing my sword from the earth and soon from the figure on top of the soldier. My blade was now white, and the figure dissipated completely, leaving behind the black core to fall to the ground. The core produced more slime-like substance and reformed as the same entity. Based on what happened, it was easy to surmise that they were humanoid slimes with shadows as cores and were only interested in people of a similar attribute. Even so, I knew it was only a matter of time before they became less picky.

Jamie took the initiative and created a time bubble around us that froze the slimes. "Everyone, retreat into the circle and hold your ground." He barely finished his sentence before many of the slimes began moving despite the time stop.

Before one near me could begin moving, I stabbed into its core and my blade turned black instantly. In the process, the core blinked out of existence. I turned the blade back to white to the sound of distant screaming in my head that faded quickly. I did the same to a few more within my immediate reach. After each one, I had to turn my blade back to white, and each time, there was a slightly longer delay. I didn't notice it until just after I attacked a brown one when a completely black one jumped at me. I quickly swiped at it while changing the blade from black to white, but the delay caused me to use the black blade instead. The shock of making contact with a being of pure darkness caused a shock wave that pulled in around six of them at once with more, close behind. In a flash, Cat grabbed the back of my shirt and tossed me behind her before punching the ground. The resulting debris knocked back the rest that were still coming.

"Are you ok?" she asked.

"I think so." I took a moment to scrutinize my blade as it slowly turned white again. Now, I couldn't hear the screams of the corpse shadows anymore as I purified them.

The time bubble was gone. It was no longer preventing the corpse shadows from moving. The corpse shadow-slimes were unmoving once more by the edge of the circle.

I looked at my hands, and they were shaking. The adrenaline rush was subsiding when I felt a pull at my hair. Looking up, I saw Hanna hovering above me.

"Give." She slowly fluttered down until she landed in my outstretched palm. I reached into a pocket and pulled out a vial of red liquid. Uncorking it, I gave it to her. She downed it all down in seconds despite the vial being the same size as her. Once she was done, she dropped the vial and looked up at me. "What? Is there something on my face?"

"I was just thinking about what it would be like having a familiar."

"That's insulting."

"No, I didn't mean like *you're* a familiar-"

"Backpedal as you wish, but I've got work to do." She jumped out of my hand and glided a few feet away. She began emitting an eerie light and appeared as a small girl with bright red eyes, short jet-black hair, and a black and navy blue dress. "***Door***." Before her rose a red door framed in black from the ground. There was no handle, yet it opened seconds later, and people walked through. The first was Vincent followed by Aaron, Jane, Graven, Guile, Solo, and soon many others who were waiting to be summoned. There were around twenty of them. The rest would have to travel like me and Catt.

"So, it's already started." Guile was taking an agnostic look around.

"Not quite," said Hanna, "Those things emerged as a response to our preparations and were likely buried within the ground long before the call to war. It's unsurprising when you consider what lengths they went to get to this point."

"Does anyone have any ideas as to how we're going to stop this many if they decide to attack?" Graven proceeded cautiously to the edge of the circle.

"I might have an answer to that as well." The door closed and disappeared as Hanna gave her theory, already back in the form of a bat. "They seem to only attack anyone who shares a similar attunement to them and if what I'm thinking is correct, they may be easier to kill if purified, just like any other fiend. Light spells alone might be enough." She fluttered over and nudged Catt. "Would you mind giving it a try?"

Catt cupped her hands together with her gloves glowing white before throwing a white ball of light into a crowd of gelatinous corpse shadow-slimes. It hit a blue one and sank into its body before reaching the core, causing an explosion in its center and disintegration of the whole thing. Shortly after, an orange one came to fill the space.

"Did you see that, soldiers?" Jamie rallied his troops. "We now know what to do. Anyone with confidence in their light magic, step forward and destroy the enemy. Aim for their cores." The soldiers split off with less than half staying in the center and the rest spreading out to attack on all sides.

There were flashes of color, primarily yellow and white, in all directions. Despite the steady increase in corpse shadow-slimes wandering in from farther away, their presence seemed to dwindle. Jamie himself got in on the action, creating clear time bubbles around some of them that held them in place until they shattered into pieces.

A few seconds after this began, some of the creatures began to undulate before thinning out and appearing like a stream of water jetting themselves into the air where they hovered in a spherical shape.

"It looks like they're getting ready to retaliate." Said Graven. "We need to get moving before they cover the sky." He created a purple orb around himself and a couple others before hovering in the air and speeding off with them.

Everyone who came through the door with him followed suit and scattered in a similar direction, toward the base in the distance. Each of them used some type of invisibility or cloaking on their way up. Hanna was also gone since she couldn't spend much time away from Vincent. Catt and I joined in on destroying as many corpse shadows as we could before they had a chance to fight back.

38-Archfield

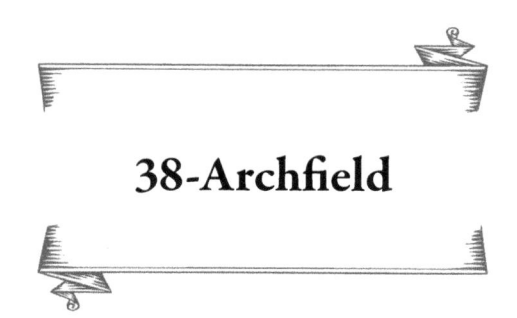

[Vincent Cornello]

Not many people ask me about my backstory. I think most people are too afraid to ask and the few that do, tend to regret it. I honestly don't know why. My story isn't any worse than most. Seeing as that's the first thing you ask, I'll tell you. That being said, I'll leave out some of the more... detailed... Never mind.

I don't know where I was when it happened, and I couldn't remember if I tried. All I know is that I had been wandering through some sort of jungle or woodland for some time. I only knew that I had been a while because my clothes were tattered, I couldn't feel my feet, and I was starving.

I couldn't remember where I came from or what I was doing, but I eventually came upon a large tree with a cross nailed to it and passed out under it. I awoke in the back of a car next to a guy with long jet-black hair and a black suit with an angel embroidered on it in red. He was smiling a fanged-toothed smile, and his eyes were slowly shifting from blood-red to light brown. I was too tired and starved to move or talk, so I just stared at him.

"Don't worry, you're safe," he said.

I didn't have the energy to react, so I closed my eyes and passed back out.

Next, I awoke on a bed with a bowl of soup in front of my face, held by the same man. He was no longer in a suit, but a casual button-up and slacks.

"Eat," he said, and I did. I was too weak to move my arms, so he fed me. After I ate, I slept again. I couldn't tell how many times the pattern repeated itself, but it did until I could move well enough to feed myself.

Again, I awoke. This time, I was alone for once and sat up unconsciously. The walls of the room were light blue, and the carpet was red. The room was well lit with a light near each corner and one in the middle of the ceiling. Neither was on as there was a large open window overlooking a courtyard and a forest. I was in a queen-size bed with satin sheets and red blankets.

I was still too weak to stand, so when I tried, I hit the ground with an audible thump. Less than a minute later, a blonde woman dressed as a maid entered the room through a large oak door and lifted me back on the bed before calling for someone. A minute later, a girl that looked around the same age as me entered. She had brown eyes and long black hair, wearing blue shorts and a white blouse. With her were two silent figures. One was a man in a black and neon green hoodie with matching jeans and short black hair. The other was a girl in a pink and blue skirt with a blue short-sleeved shirt. They seemed to be dressed for different seasons.

The girl spoke. "You must be a guest of one of my brothers. I wonder which one. Do you know his name?"

I shook my head.

"Can you speak?"

"I don't know," I said, in a barely audible whisper.

She came to me and placed her hand on my chest, then gently, she lifted my hand and gazed into my eyes. Her glittery eyes were such an odd shade of brown that I'd have mistaken them for red. They reflected my face so well, it gave me chills. I was drawn in by her charms even though she only looked at me in concern. Her gaze alone was enough.

She looked pained to see me. As if I reminded her of someone she never wanted to see again. Maybe an event that scarred her. Perhaps something even she didn't remember.

"I'll take that as a 'maybe.'" She said. "In any case, you are too weak to stand, so I suggest you lie there for the time being." She left the room with her group close behind.

I took her advice until I fell asleep again.

I awoke once more to the same man who had been taking care of me for who knows how long. He handed me a tray with the bowl this time. It was some type of chowder with a couple of bread slices. I looked down at it for a moment and looked back at him. He grew a warm smile as our eyes met.

"Where am I?" I asked. My voice was still but louder than a whisper.

"Oh, you can talk. I was beginning to think you were mute." He sat up and put his finger to his chin. "I guess before we get to that, we should formally introduce ourselves. My name is Sandor Archfield. What might your name be?"

"Vincent Cornello." It was the only name I could remember and the first thing to come to mind. Not one I would consider 'mine' but one, nonetheless.

"Well, nice to meet you." He gave a courteous bow. "We're in Archfield Manor. It's considered a relic of a forgotten era, but it's where I live."

"Thank you for saving me... How long ago?" I reached for a piece of bread and dipped it into the soup.

"It's been six days, but you shouldn't be thanking me yet. I haven't told you the reason I saved you."

I was about to take a bite and stopped.

"Do you know where you collapsed when I found you?"

"A cross...?"

"It was a grave that belonged to possibly the greatest servant this house has ever had. That alone inspired me to save and groom you to be a servant of this house." His eyes wandered to the window. "In truth, you are a gift. Once I've groomed you, I'll be sending you to my younger sister. I believe you've met her already. Her name is Hanna. She's kind of cold and standoff-ish, but she means well. She's been of age for some time and hasn't made any attempt at accepting a suitor. I believe you could change that."

"Me?" I took a bite.

"Yes, I'm not just going to groom you to be a servant worthy of this house, but a suitor worthy of my sister."

What he said sounded far too good to be true, but I didn't question it. In my position, I couldn't do much on my own, anyway. I figured I'd cross that bridge when I came to it.

In the coming days, I regained my ability to walk, and my speech became clearer. A week later, my training started. First were general lessons on what it meant to be a servant.

The classes were long and taxing. The other servants took turns teaching me everything they knew. I also had to memorize the names of everyone who lived in the manor, including the other servants and many other things that would have been impossible had it not been drilled into me regularly. Next was cleaning, courtesy, and catering. I was a natural at the first two, but the third took multiple dishes being dropped and either broken or barely saved until we could move on. From there was combat training. This was one I was particularly scrutinized for.

It was established early that I was prone to temporary memory loss, but muscle memory seemed to stay. That being said, I either got my butt handed to me on a silver platter or I found my instructor on the floor inexplicably with no memory of how I did it. The frequency of the events earned me the nickname 'Blackout'. Eventually, that moniker spread to the other parts of my learning which caused it to stick.

Six months later, Sandor stopped my training abruptly and started training me himself to become a suitor for Hanna. This involved everything from language and linguistics to etiquette and business as well as specialized weapons training. It turned out that some of that training was unnecessary as I had known four different languages fluently and I could already wield a dagger with deadly accuracy. Once he saw what I could do with the training dagger, he took it from me and handed me a silver one that was decorated with a black and red briar pattern around the entire thing. It felt natural despite its heavy weight and unevenness.

"Okay, be honest with me. What do you think about becoming a servant of this house and eventually, a suitor for my sister? I'd prefer you to be as brutally honest as you can." His question was sudden but not uncalled for. I never voiced my opinion about any of it and only did as I was told up to this point.

"Honestly... I feel like I'm getting a pretty good deal. I get a free place to live and a potential wife in exchange for temporary servitude. All after getting my life saved. For a guy with nothing to his name, there's not much that can top that. Despite the steep learning curve, that's what's been pushing me to meet your expectations." I was staring down at the dagger the whole time.

"Thank you for telling me how you feel. Now it's my turn to be honest." He reached under my chin and tilted my head up to meet his gaze. His eyes were bright red. "Can you tell what I am?" As he spoke, I could see the rows of daggers that were his teeth. They weren't so sharp before.

"A vampire?" I wasn't sure of my answer as I had seen him in sunlight not bursting in flames, yet it was the first thing that came to mind.

"Correct." He let me go. "Everyone who lives here save for most of the servants are vampires. Do you know what makes a powerful vampire?"

I thought for a second and my mind came up empty. "No."

"It's love. The more direct answer is a donor. Someone who willingly gives their blood to a vampire directly contributes to the exponential growth of said vampire. Willingness is key but affection pushes it a little further. That's what I want you to do for her. She has always refused to drink and has always been frail because of it. She's been starved for years and can barely keep herself together. I believe you can convince her. With your blood, I'm sure that she would become stronger than any of us."

"Is it really just my blood or is it because I'm the one you found that you think that?"

"Because I'm a vampire, I have an excellent sense of smell. You smell strikingly similar to my late husband. His blood was special, and I believe yours is too. It can't be a coincidence that I found you on his grave."

"So, that was your husband's grave?"

"Yes. He started out as a servant, but he and I grew close and eventually got married. I wouldn't put so much belief in you had I not found you there. Even so, you still have a choice as to whether you want to do this." Despite this being my first time hearing this, it didn't strike me as odd that he never wore a ring. What struck me as odd was the choice.

"I have a choice?"

"You've always had a choice. Forgive me for not making that clear from the start. You can choose to decline my offer. If so, you can name any place in the world and I can send you there, no questions."

I took a moment to think. Looking at the dagger, I saw the reflection of a clean, well-dressed man ravaged by sorrow and desperation. On his back, he held a boulder, and he stood on a bed of thorns. He was groveling in front of a shirtless man standing on a bed of straw holding nothing.

"I don't have a good answer and I don't think I'll find one. I think if she'd accept someone like me, it's worth a try. I'll do it." I wasn't one hundred percent sure of myself, but I had found some resolve.

"Alright, let's see what you can do with that dagger." The look in Sandor's eyes made it seem like a weight on his shoulders lightened a bit.

My training continued with the later inclusion of hunting, ballroom dancing, vocal lessons, and driving lessons. Between how much I was learning and doing, the traffic of things going through my mind wouldn't allow me a moment of clarity. A part of me was glad since that meant I didn't have to think about the meaning behind what I was doing. I was busy for the next six months until Sandor made an announcement while we were taking a lunch break in his study.

"Hanna is turning sixty-five next week. I believe we're ready to give this a shot." I was eating a sandwich and almost choked on it. He patted me on my back until I stopped coughing and continued. "There will be a party and we'll make our move then."

"Ok, what's the plan?" I said, taking another bite.

"It's a surprise party. She always declines parties in her honor, so a surprise party is thrown every few years. Usually, she tries to avoid mingling by sticking close to either me, one of our brothers, or our parents. The plan is: She'll stay by my side, and I'll bring her to you where you can try to converse with her. If all goes well, I'll be able to leave discreetly while she stays with you for the rest of the night."

"I don't know..." The image of Hanna from when I first saw her flashed in my mind.

"Are you having a change of heart?" said Sandor, "That's fine as long as you're honest with yourself."

"No, I just wonder if it's the right thing to do. I feel like we're trying to force something on her that she might not want."

"We'll never know if we don't try." His words put me at ease.

"Then, I'll try."

Everything went as normal for the next week until the day came. Everyone seemed to act completely normally. There was no sign of a party or anything brewing underneath the surface. As soon as the sun fell, Hanna began avoiding every large room in the mansion. I was looking out for anything suspicious, and I saw her and her two servants trying to avoid the empty foyer at all costs while trying to get to the front door. She was distraught and kind of jumpy. I didn't watch her for too long and went back to my business.

Not too much later, I was visited by Sander in my room with an outfit for the party. It was a casual suit in the colors of amber and turquoise. The outfit matched my hair and eyes and gave me a regal look despite how casual it was. He then ushered me to a ballroom I didn't know existed until then. It was decorated in deep red and purple. There were balloons, streamers, set tables, and an open center.

The chandelier hanging overhead was antique, like most things in the mansion, and adorned in gold with each light surrounded in its own crystalline case. The walls were stark white, and the floor was checkered in two different types of wood, one light and one dark.

The room was already filled with guests and residents alike while I found my way to an open spare seat near the far wall and sat until the door opened again. In the doorway stood Sander and Hanna. They were dressed similarly in jeans and button-up jackets. There was hardly a moment of silence before there was an eruption of voices saying the same thing, 'surprise!' before classical music began playing from a radio positioned high in a crevasse on the far wall.

Hanna was visibly displeased as she folded her arms and began walking away before Sander put his arm around her and led her in the opposite direction down the hall. They returned a few minutes later dressed for the occasion. Hanna wore a straight dress in the same colors as the decorations with her hair down aside for one braid wrapped around her head like a tiara and Sandor wore a vested suit in black and navy blue with his hair in a single long braid down his back.

True to the plan, she stayed on his arm as they entered. In less than thirty seconds, they were swarmed by young men. All of which were vying for attention and holding some type of flower or gift. Letting go of Sander, she respectfully bowed and shook her head before speaking. She then went back to her brother. They were persistent, however. Eventually she accepted the flowers before darting off in another direction with Sander in tow. A few minutes passed and out of the corner of my eye, I saw them approaching me.

"Hanna, this is a close friend of mine," said Sander, stopping next to me.

"Hello," I said, standing. "My name is Vincent Cornello. Nice to-"

"Whatever my doting brother told you, I apologize in his place." She gave a courteous bow. "I am currently not looking for a suitor at the moment."

"That's fine," I said, giving a bow as well. "I only wanted to thank you."

"Is that so?" She seemed surprised.

"You may not recognize me, but we've met before."

"Yes." She looked me up and down. "I believe we have. You were Sander's guest, and now you're training to become a servant, correct?" She seemed more at ease.

"Yes, he found me dying in the woods and nursed me back to health. I'd like to thank you for the moment of kindness you showed me that day."

Hanna folded her arms. "So, how far along your training are you?"

"I'm unsure. You see, I have amnesia and-"

"*Amnesia*, huh?" She reached forward and grabbed my hand. "Sander, I'll be taking him with me, stay here."

"I'm not one to take orders, but I'll do as you say for now." He waved as Hanna darted off while dragging me behind her. We went through a small door near a corner, down a small hallway, and into a stone stairway that led down to a small room with only a dim light and a barred window. She let me go at the base of the stairs and stood between me and the door.

"I am aware of what you and my brother have been doing." Her eyes turned bright red and began glowing.

"I figured you'd find out. There are so many people under one roof that it would be hard to keep a secret."

Her eyes narrowed at me. "So, you admit it?"

"Yeah, since I met you, I couldn't get you out of my mind. You were kind enough to help me, even with just a few words."

"I don't believe you." Her eyes began glowing more intensely. "**Tell me the truth**." Her voice was layered onto itself, and I was compelled to do as she said.

"It was your eyes." The words flew out of my mouth before I could stop them.

"What?" her eyes stopped glowing, but I continued as I stared into them.

"They're deep, beautiful, and so full of emotion. You look so hurt but so strong. I don't know what your burden is, but I feel like I want to help you lift it. I thought that if there was a chance that I could make that happen, I'd give it a shot."

"What do you know about me?" Her voice slightly wavered.

"I heard you were starved from your brother, and I thought that maybe I could help you that way." I held out my arm. "Please."

In less than a second, the sound of her hand swiping my face sounded through the room and into the hall outside the door. My face stung and my neck popped.

"Insult! You know nothing about me!" She ran out and slammed the door. I tried to follow her, but as I opened the door, I saw she hadn't gone anywhere. Her eyes were red again. "Let's see what's really in there." She grabbed me by my temple with both hands and peered into my eyes.

My vision went blurry and then I blanked out. I regained consciousness after some time with a fleeting feeling of remembering something. Hanna was still there except she now had her arms wrapped around me and was sniffling like a child.

"What happened?" I said, bewildered.

"I saw… What you don't remember." She squeezed tighter. "I don't think you *should* remember."

"You can do that?" I had forgotten that we were on the stairs and almost fell backward. Her holding onto me kept me from falling.

"Yes, and now I wish I hadn't. I'm sorry." Her sincerity spoke loud and clear.

"No, I'm sorry. I said too much." I hugged her back.

"Don't hug me back. I'm just keeping you from falling."

"Oh, sorry." I let her go.

"One condition." She let me go as well and looked into my eyes.

"Excuse me?" I said, bewildered.

"Your blood. I'll accept it on one condition." She wiped her tears with a handkerchief.

"What is it?"

"That we get to know each other like normal people." She went out of the door and left it open. "Follow me."

"Agreed." I followed her and closed it.

Getting back to the ballroom, Hanna took a brief look in and walked past the door. I followed her down a now familiar series of halls and eventually, to unfamiliar halls. We were in a part of the manor I wasn't allowed in. Where the residents slept, away from the servants. The closest I'd gotten to this area was Sandor's study.

Keeping my nerves in check, I tried not to raise my expectations. We stopped at one of many doors. Hanna swung it open and invited me in. The room had purple wood flooring and a black rug across the entrance. There was a large desk piled with what looked like study materials to the left and what looked like a closet door next to it. On the right, there was a mural of a sunset on an otherwise bare wall. The paint looked recently touched up. Against the far wall stood a queen-sized bed with deep red curtains draped around it. The blankets were pitch-black and fluffy.

Hanna sat on the bed. She crossed her legs and pointed at the chair sitting at the desk. "Bring it over here and take a seat."

I swallowed hard and did as told.

We sat across from each other and after an awkward moment, we began to talk. Hanna was surprisingly open with the topics we spoke about and willing to share more than I expected. My nerves slowly smoothed out as she told me about herself. One of the topics she brought up herself was why she was starved.

"I'm not actually starved, you know?" she said. "We vampires aren't required to drink blood to sustain ourselves. Some of us consume mana. Some, memories. Some even consume emotions, like succubi. The vampires here mostly all consume blood. I'm no different, but feed off the mana of my servants, as well. They'd both be wizards if they weren't warlocks through our contracts. I consume their excess mana and they take on my vampiric attributes."

"Oh, are your eyes slightly red because you don't drink blood even though you should?"

She giggled. "No, it's a magic trait. Useless aside from terrifying visitors in the dark. They glow ever so faintly that it's only noticeable in the complete absence of light."

Over a few short hours, we had gotten to know each other. There wasn't much for her to learn about me given that she saw through my memories, but she seemed amused every time I shared a bit of my personality with her. Of course, we did more than speak, but relevancy is an issue.

After some time, Hanna stopped speaking and looked up, alert. "It's quiet."

"It is? I looked up and strained my ears. "I guess there's less of a hum than before."

"Something's wrong." She stood and made for the door I followed.

We made our way back to the ballroom to find nobody there. The music had stopped, and everything was clean and tidy. The party was beyond over.

Hanna started sniffing around in the air like a puppy. "I smell blood."

Darting back out of the room, she followed her nose to the foyer. What we found was a gruesome sight. The front doors blasted off of their hinges and the bodies of six servants. There were holes in the walls and floor. A battle had taken place. The assailants were nowhere to be found, and neither were anyone else. Afraid of where the next trail would lead, I continued following her until we found an opening in a wall at the end of a dead-end hallway. It led to a hidden set of stairs.

We followed them down until it opened to a sprawling catacomb. Many openings led to many other rooms and dead ends alike. Hanna moved hesitantly, but she kept going. I'd be lying if I said I wasn't a little scared, but I followed, nonetheless. Hearing footsteps, we stopped and hid. Peeking from behind a corner, we saw Hanna's two closest servants: Aaron and Jane. They were both in normal outdoor clothes, but they were scuffed and torn beyond recognition.

"You two, what's going on?" Hanna jumped out and approached them. They both wore expressions of fear that shifted to relief when they saw her.

"Lady Hanna, there are two intruders in the inner sanctum," Jane explained. "They took Lord Sylvester and made him open the passage. The rest of us followed to try to stop them, but during the battle, we were told to come back and protect you."

"They took father? I've seen what they did in the foyer. Why would they need him to come down here?" Hanna tried to make a mad dash past the two, only to be stopped by both of them. They crossed their arms in front of her and caught her between them.

"I'm sorry but we can't let you go through," said Aaron. "We have protecting to do. Now come with us, will you? We don't know the details and were just told to turn tail."

"I think we should do as they say," I said, gesturing for them to go the way we had just come.

"Where is everyone else?" Hanna paid me no mind.

Jane answered, "They're in the inner sanctum fighting, but they began having troubles and that's when we were ordered to see to your safety."

"Who gave the order?" Hanna was still trying to get past, but they weren't allowing it.

"It was Lady Elizabeth who told us to take you away, now would you please do as we say?" Aaron tried to pick up Hanna, but she slapped his hands away.

"I'll walk on my own," she said, turning around and walking past me. We almost made it back to the stairs before we heard footsteps behind us. We turned around to see a man in a gray cloak not far away. He was radiating an aura of calmness. It was enough to make me slightly drowsy. Aaron and Jane began pushing me and Hanna up the stairs.

"Why such a hurry?" As soon as his voice reached my ears, I fell to the floor and was unable to move. Shortly after, I felt a prick in my butt and could move again.

"Get moving!" Jane lifted me by my collar and tossed me up a few steps before I could continue up on my own.

We ran up the stairs and through the mansion before being stopped by an invisible force field at the front door. It wouldn't budge, no matter how hard we pushed or how many spells were cast at it. I couldn't use magic, so I just banged on it to no avail. It only started moving when the sound of footsteps echoed from the stairs. They were purposely loud enough to be heard. He appeared again at the top of the grand stairway and began walking down. The barrier moved through the open doorway and into the courtyard, where it dispersed on its own.

"You can't get away." The man was following us at a leisurely pace. He stopped at the base of the stairs and reached his hand out. In a dull gray light, he summoned a two-handed crescent moon blade in front of him and threw it to the middle of the room. It stopped and flew up at the sound of wire tightly wounding around it echoing through the area. "Nice trap, though."

"That's not all we can do, take one more step and you're through." Aaron raised both of his hands to reveal a ring on each finger with a small wire stemming from each one.

"We'll hold him off, you take Lady Hanna and go protect her with your life." Jane pushed me toward Hanna before walking up next to Aaron. I took Hanna's hand and ran as fast as I could into the forest.

"Be sure to find us when this is over, ok?" said Hanna as I dragged her away.

"We'll try," said Jane, just before an explosion erupted from within the manor.

Everything moved quickly from there. The forest was expansive, so we took a route that zig-zagged between barely recognizable landmarks in the darkness. Before long, we had gotten to the point of there being no sign of any civilization. It had only taken a couple of minutes running at full speed, but we soon ran into a problem.

"Aaah..." Hanna screamed while clutching one of her arms. She rolled up her sleeve and a large imprint resembling a feathery wing was burning away and leaving a smoldering wound. It started from her palm and spiraled up her arm past her shoulder. "Aaron..."

"What happened?" I asked, panicked.

"He's dying. This mark connects us. It's our contract between master and servant." The mark stopped burning halfway only for one on her other arm to be a concern. "Not you too."

"Jane as well?"

"Yes, we need to get as well hidden as possible. We can't get much farther in the middle of nowhere."

"Do you know of anywhere this far out that we could hide?" I looked into the inky blackness to find any sign of a place to hide.

"No, I've never been this deep in the woods before." She looked on as the marks on both of her arms continued to smolder away. After a few minutes of searching for a hiding spot, I found a tall tree that grew over a well. There was still an opening large enough for a person to drop in.

"Hanna, are you ok?" I asked because I thought she was shivering. Instead, it turned out that she was shaking in rage.

"I'll kill him. Whoever that was, I swear I'll kill him myself." Her eyes began glowing bright red and then stopped as she wobbled on her feet. She was barely standing.

"Hanna!" I caught her before she could fall over. Despite how she looked, she felt like a corpse. That wasn't the case when her body was pressed against mine earlier. I couldn't feel any warmth, just cold skin and bones.

"Looks like I don't have to do much to this one." The voice came from nearby. Looking up, I could see the man in a slightly more tattered cloak on a tree. His hood was missing, and his face was visible. His eyes were bright silver and there were a few fresh cuts on his face. "She must be starved."

I instinctively reached into my pocket and found the ornamental dagger. Sander must have put it there, just in case. Pulling it out, I held it at the ready.

"*Sleep*." As soon as he said that, everything went black.

I awoke with my dagger clashing against his blade while he was against a tree. He pushed me back and kicked me into another tree.

"*Arklight*." Rings of dull gray light closed around me and the tree. I struggled but couldn't get free. "You're not a servant or a vampire, so I'll leave you alive for now. You might be useful if you're that powerful alone." He turned around and was met with a fireball that he promptly knocked to the side with his hand before it fizzled out.

"Die... You..." Hanna was up and panting heavily. Her face was sunken in, and her figure had diminished. She looked like a walking corpse.

"Lie down." The man raised his hand and a beam of light sprung from his fingertip, piercing Hanna's chest. She promptly hit the ground like a sack of bricks.

Seeing this, I closed my eyes and concentrated. I tried to tap back into that unconscious state. If it was a magic trait, now was the time to control it. The result was almost instant. It was as if I just woke up from the middle of a dream. I knew what was going on, even though it didn't feel like I experienced any of it. I broke the light, binding me before lunging at the man. He dodged, but he wasn't my target. I made my way to Hanna. Before I could get to her, his blade met my back.

I didn't fall until I reached her. In this state between lucidity and unconsciousness, memories of things that I had forgotten came rushing back and with it, came unfounded, yet fleeting strength. I ran the dagger across my palm in hopes of my blood seeping into her wounds and reviving her.

"That won't work. She's already dead." The man tried to pull me away, but I swiped my dagger at him and held it steady. "You don't believe me? I'll prove it."

I swiped at him again to stop his approach but after a flash of light, I found myself face down on top of Hanna. A numb feeling through my gut told me I was run through with a blade. There was no reaction from Hanna. The man was beside us, looking down indifferently. His sword pierced us both, pinning us to the ground.

"You know what? Just in case I'm wrong." He took a nearby stick and replaced his blade with it so that we were still pinned. "*Purify*." The stick began emanating light. "If she is alive, that'll make sure neither of you escapes before dawn. A true vampire can't survive in the sun without some type of immunity, and all of her servants are dead. She won't last a few minutes in that condition." He began walking away. "And neither will you." There was an audible beep followed by more talk. "Wrath to Sloth, extermination complete."

I was starting to feel more than numbness and I felt the dreaminess of it all start to fade. I held out in that dream-like state for as long as I could before the aching pain forced me back to full consciousness.

I reached into my wound and lifted some blood onto my fingertips and looked at it. My swirling memories brought a spell to mind. I was never taught magic but through these memories, I saw glimpses of it. "*Thread of life*." The blood took the form of a strand of thread and extended to Hanna. I wasn't sure of the exact nature of the spell, but I felt like she'd survive as long as I did. Not long after casting the spell, my vision went dark.

I awoke to Hanna's face. She was carrying me in her arms, and it was broad daylight. I was paralyzed and couldn't move, so I just let her carry me. Her face was more flush than before and her eyes were bright red. She sat me down next to two other bodies. They were Aaron and Jane. Both looked lifeless with grave punctures in their chests.

"I hope it's alright if I could use more of your blood," she said, leaning over me.

I smiled and responded, "Yeah." My voice was but a whisper.

"Thank you." She sank her teeth into my arm. I could feel the blood leaving me. It was very surreal, like she was draining a river that was flowing inside of me. She pulled her mouth away and began casting a spell. She began a chant that made Jane's body glowed a bright blue. The only part I could grasp were the last two words, "***True resurrection***." Jane's wounds all closed at once and she opened her eyes, heaving with a panicked look on her face. Shortly, Hanna did the same to Aaron, and he had the same reaction, except with a green light. They both sat up slowly and began looking around.

"Didn't I just die?" said Aaron, getting to his feet.

"Me too," confirmed Jane, following suit.

I was so amazed at what had just happened that I didn't notice what became of Hanna. She had shrunk, grown wings, and began fluttering about. Her red eyes faded to blue, and her fangs refused to recede. She was now a bat.

"What did you do?" I asked.

"I brought them back to life," said the bat. "That spell requires a high level of proficiency or tremendous life force. That's why I had to borrow your blood, and of course, I had to sacrifice my form in order to do it. Sadly, this is as much as I can do for now and I'll be stuck in this form for some time." She landed on my chest and stayed there until I could move again.

Sitting up, I could see the result of last night's events. The mansion was gone and replaced with a hole in the ground filled with rubble. Aaron and Jane were busy looking for survivors to no avail. Eventually, we left the place as a burial ground and went into hiding.

Months passed, and Hanna never returned to her original form. It turned out that she became reliant on me to sustain herself. While she renewed her contract with her servants, whatever happened when our blood mingled kept her bound to me. Eventually, we formed a proper symbiotic contract. Not as master and servant but as equals.

Hanna, being as studied as she was, recognized the danger we were still in. The ones that attacked were from C.H.E.S.S. and they could easily finish the job if they knew we were alive so we stayed hidden.

Within the shattered foundation of the manor was still a heap of wealth, but we couldn't let anyone know who we were. Eventually, we found a haven for people of the underworld who were displaced by unfortunate circumstances. We were able to flee the country and fly to America with their aid. The murder of the Archfields made many vampires living in New Feskog seek safety and we were just some of many. There, we used the wealth we still had to make a living helping others like us.

39-Duet

The moment Hanna, Catt, and Noah went through the barrier, I noticed from the immediate feeling that I was missing something and began looking over my shoulder for who wasn't there.

"She's gone," said Jane, surveying the space ahead of us. "This barrier seems to completely erase the presence of anyone who enters. Leaving back out might not be possible before this whole thing is over."

"I don't doubt it." shifting my gaze to the barrier as well, I subconsciously stepped toward it.

"Don't go. Our job is to sit and wait, you know." Arin put his arm around my shoulders and looked into the barrier alongside me. "I have something that could put that theory to the test. It's best to do it now before we end up in a of mess at our lady's behest."

"I agree." Jane grabbed both me and Aaron by the scruff and pulled us back. "But can we do that a little farther away from it?"

Aaron pulled a throwing dagger from his bandolier and said, "Can do. All I need is to throw this through." He unwound a wire from one of his rings and wrapped it around the dagger by hand. He then brought it close to his face "**Sight**." The spell caused his left eye to disappear and be replaced with a black void, while the imprint of an eye could be seen shifting across the surface of the dagger. He threw it in one swift motion, and it disappeared into nothing. "I can see it stuck in the ground where it hit." He went on to describe what the battlefield roughly looked like from his limited perspective, which amounted to a grassy flatland with the base in the far distance. He gave the string a sharp pull, and the dagger reappeared before landing neatly between his fingers. In the process, his eye and dagger went back to normal. "It let me pull it back, but it also dispelled the enchantment it held."

Graven walked up nearby. "So, magic can go in but not out? Good to know."

"I don't think so. In fact, that's a no." Arin's dagger began glowing green. "**Airblade**." It released itself from his grasp and raced toward the barrier only to be stopped on contact, fade from green, and lose all magical presence before falling to the ground.

That display made it clear what kind of barrier it was. It was likely intended to cause as little damage as possible to the surrounding environment by weakening any magic that passed through it, but while generally weaker magic wasn't affected much, the stronger the spell, the more aggressively the effect triggered. The only question left was whether that affected transportation magic. Either way, that question would be answered in time. After finding this out, we made sure everyone else knew as well.

In the coming minutes, small groups ranging from around ten to thirty people began accumulating around us. They were all from the New-Hunters, an organization hell-bent on stopping C.H.E.S.S. As each group came in, we explained the situation and what our plan was.

After hearing that we sent in someone from the house of Black, the first group looked nervously at each other as if unsure how to respond. When questioned about the nervous looks, we were surprised at the response. A member of the house of Black was apparently their leader. Despite the new information, we couldn't verify it before a black door appeared behind me and opened.

I didn't hesitate to walk through to find Hanna. It wasn't often that I could see her in her human form outside of emergencies. Whenever she did transform, she would make sure I was asleep, for that was when she would feed. I went to her with open arms, but she dodged me and shrank back down. She was in the middle of explaining something, but I didn't pay much attention until she bit my hand. Being used to her bite, it didn't hurt much, but it was expressively more aggressive than normal. It seemed she was saying something, and I wasn't paying attention. At first, I thought it was because the blood vial didn't have enough in it, but she didn't draw any blood and instead lifted my hand toward where everyone else was going. Arin and Jane were waiting patiently to start moving as well.

"Oh yeah," I said, angling my hands toward the ground in front of me and closing my eyes. What I saw in my mind was a wide-rimmed teacup, black and solid. The handle curved like the wavy mane of a mare and large enough to hold four people. Hanna fluttered onto my shoulder and held on tight. After a few seconds, I opened my eyes, and before me was what my mind's eye had seen. Arin and Jane were already climbing in. Hanna and I followed.

As soon as we were all inside, Arin pressed his hands to the lip of the cup "***Levitate***." The whole thing began levitating under his command.

"***Hidden mist***." Jane pressed her hands against the teacup as well and we were surrounded in a blue mist that rendered us invisible. To us, it appeared like a slight translucent haze over everything in sight.

As per the plan, we headed to the west side of the base. There was a gymnasium that hid a secret passage into the depths of the base. It went straight to the room holding the Shadow Master's gate. Once we made it on land, we exited the teacup and entered the surprisingly stout blue building with a similar interior littered with rooms and hallways. It was a recreational building with the floors in reverse. The gym itself was over five stories underground through multiple stairways. The lights were on and although it was relatively pristine, it had no doors. It was large and empty aside from the bleacher seats neatly folded into the left and right walls. There was also a man standing against the far wall from the main entrance.

We couldn't feel his presence until we already entered. His gaze lifted from the floor to us despite the invisibility still being active. He had black hair with red highlights, a black and red shirt of unknown material with matching pants, and a long open red jacket with matching fingerless gloves. His clothes were heavily enchanted with a faint red glow. I recognized him as Nail, the contestant from the magic tournament that Geist himself reprimanded, and a confirmed member of C.H.E.S.S.

"Welcome. Is there anything I can help you with?"

None of us responded in hopes that he was just talking to himself.

"Where are my manners? I'm Pride, a member of the Seven Sins, and if you don't leave now, the last opponent you'll ever face. Maybe even the last thing you'll see. Would you all like to introduce yourselves?"

We continued to collectively hold our breath.

"No response, huh? I'll take that as a challenge." He flicked his wrist and what looked like a shard of black glass shot from his palm.

I reacted before I knew it and caught it just before it would have hit Hanna sitting on my shoulder. The attack shattered the bubble of invisibility. The heat permeated through my glove and I dropped it. My glove was partially melted so I took off the pair and dropped them.

Without a moment's notice, a gust of wind spewed forth from Arins forward facing palms, pushing Jane ahead into the room to land on seemingly nothing. Her crystalline dancing shoes and accessories sparkled in the dim light, offering a distraction from the razor-thin wires pulled taut and seamlessly anchored to the walls. They traveled through the air the same way she did.

Dancing upon the wires, she leaped, glided, and twirled while slowly casting a spell that would hopefully end the battle before it started. Nail just stood there and watched from the wall, scrutinizing her every move. Eventually, he tried to fire off another shard at me, Hanna, and Arin, but Jane intercepted it by kicking it out of the air without breaking stride.

Nearly a minute passed before the spell's completion. Once it was done, she stopped for a split-second to activate it, resting on a wire with her hands clasped around a pendant resting above her breast. Once she did, a molten spear was resting in her appendix and out her back. It happened in less than a blink of an eye. The slightly melted point landed far behind her while the burning black and red rod was left penetrating just above her abdomen. She began slowly leaning backward still on top of the wire and somehow still cast the spell, resulting in the entire inside of the room becoming flash-frozen and encased in ice aside for the doorway. What little blood there was became still.

Despite the shock of what happened, Arin expertly maneuvered his wires embedded in the ice to carve out a path and removed chunks of the ice while avoiding Jane despite them being literally frozen in place. He stopped when a faint heat began radiating toward us through the ice from the other side. Quickly, he carved a sphere holding Jane and moved her into the open hall and out of sight before much of the ice melted. The same spell once used to stop an active lava flow and quell a volcano had completely diminished in moments.

"Ok, you got me cold and a little wet." Nail never moved from his position with the heat escaping him evaporated all the resulting water in the room. The hallway wasn't affected, but it became nearly impossible to breathe near the doorway. "Now, I'm all dry. Anything else you wanna try before my turn?"

"Arin. Speak." Nothing less than unquestionable authority could be heard in those words from Hanna.

"Say less, princess." Arin leaped into the room similar to Jane before him, but instead of landing on the wire, he seemed to disappear completely. As he did, a strong wind kicked up and persisted. The wind carried sound as if a barely audible voice was flowing through the air and permeating through the room.

Nail reacted by summoning a sword into his hand and swiping upward, resulting in the blade falling cleanly in pieces. His reaction afterward was to summon another blade before the pieces of the first one hit the ground. The second one wasn't made of solid or molten rock. It was a much stronger weapon, a single-edged, serrated long sword. It looked like it was chipped into shape like a piece of obsidian.

He held it steadily against the encroaching wires before lifting his blade to bypass them. He then did the same to his left before taking a short hop, replanting his feet onto the ground, and continuing to parry the multiple attacks from multiple directions.

I was pulled by my sleeve back into the hall where Jane was still frozen. Letting me go, Hanna hovered close to the encapsulated face of her wounded servant. "She's still alive in there."

"Ok, let's help her out while we still can." I laid my hand on the ice near the handle of the spear. It still kept its color despite the lack of the orange glow it once had, every detail still in place.

"We have to be careful. There's a chance she could still perish. Do you remember that spell you used to save me way back when?"

"Only its name and sort of what it does, not how to do it."

"This is where you regret never having a grimoire."

I sighed. She was right.

"Then we're lucky I took the time to learn it." She fluttered into the ice then phased through it and Jane, trapped inside. Once out the other side, a scarlet thread-like line could be seen between the two, from Jane's chest to Hanna's back. "Now I just need you to…" She trailed off as a slowly rising feeling became more noticeable. "Do you feel that as well?"

"Yeah, I don't think we have the time-" A chill went up my spine and I turned abruptly.

Hanna sped to the open doorway just as fast, her wings barely able to prevent her from crashing into Arin on the other side. He seemed relatively unharmed aside from the open cauterized wound on his broken right arm dangling at his side. The space he faced was littered with broken wire still floating in the air, surrounded by a green hue.

The other side of the room housed Nail squatting with his arms on his knees and a familiar man carrying a black body bag was standing next to him. His silver rings gleamed with a dull blue light similar to his eyes, in little contrast to his tanned skin and casual suit. The scars on his face and hands denounced his ability to avoid harm. He came out of an open trapdoor large enough to fit a car starting from the wall with stairs leading down. They were talking between themselves, and it ended briefly with the man handing the bag to Nail and staying behind while he escaped down the stairs and closed the trapdoor.

"I see you survived." He gestured to me. "But you didn't. So, why are you here?" He gestured to Arin. "I also feel the presence of that vampiress. You all should be dead. But since you're here and you survived our last encounter, I'll introduce myself this time around." He took a brief bow. "My name is Oliver; mostly known as Envy of the Seven Sins. -not just a title by the way-."

Hanna fluttered behind my ear and whispered, "Evoke our contract."

Instinctively, I nodded despite not knowing what she meant. The only contract we had was symbiotic. The way she said it made it seem like I had control over something she didn't. I laid my hand on Arins's shoulder and nodded when he looked back at me. He nodded in response and stepped back to where Jane was, but his attempted escape was almost cut off by a nearly instant movement from Oliver who summoned his moon blade. It soared through the air in the blink of an eye.

Hanna hopped in front of me. She glowed as she returned to her original form. At the same time, she parried the weapon with one of her own. She held a collapsible wizard's staff outfitted with four uniformly curved sickles that pivot out at the end, creating an elongated mace when folded and an umbrella-like weapon when unfolded. Each sickle was inscribed with a corresponding elemental symbol of wind, fire, darkness, and blood.

Hanna whispered once more, "Now," before standing at attention.

I placed my hand on her head and this time we both began to glow. A sigil appeared on the back of my hand of four ovals overlapping each other in the shape of a cross within a pentagon, the Archfield family crest.

The girl before me bolted from my grasp toward the target of her ill will. I ran to catch up with her. She slowed down and whispered, "Go." In response, I aimed at the man's throat with my dagger and jumped at him.

He parried my attack and I sailed over his head. Even so, I made space for Hanna to strike.

Oliver's attention shifted from me to Hanna. As they collided.

Hanna pushed him far enough back that I could swing my foot around and kick the side of his face on the way down.

I landed in a handstand before rolling into the wall and pushing off, sliding across the ground, and swiping at his heels.

He lifted a foot and tried to stomp me, but Hanna pushed him back further and he was forced to jump to retreat.

Hanna lunged after him. In response, he pushed the mace to the side with the moon blade's edge.

Holding my dagger steady, I stood ready below Oliver and jumped at him at the last second, right when he began descending.

He swung his weapon down in a cartwheel motion to counter my blade and send me back to the ground. I had to switch from offense to defense in an instant to keep my head.

Hanna fanned out large, black wings on her back to hover in the air until I hit the ground and rolled away before dive-bombing with the wind and dark sickles unfolded. A black cyclone formed around her and tore up the ground, sending Oliver careening to the wall with a thud.

He dodged as I sprung to surprise him with a frontal attack, and he nearly cleaved my head off in response had it not been for Hanna intercepting. She nearly did the same to him.

Dodging the attack, Oliver moved away from the wall, swiped his blade toward us, and sent multiple blade waves.

Hanna erased them by summoning a bubble of darkness that overtook the whole room. The attacks broke against the outer edge as if it was a barrier. She then sent bolts of fire from the tip of her rod.

Oliver dodged most of them before sending dim balls of light back, distorting the bubble and forcing it to dissipate.

The light balls were difficult to dodge, and I was hit in my left arm and leg before they stopped. Hanna was better off as she flew to avoid them before diving back down to strike at Oliver. Their weapons clashed a few times this way.

Oliver took to the air as well, with balls of light under his feet.

After seeing to my wounds being no more than bruises, I prepared to take to the air. Before I could, Hanna's weapon was parried to the side and she was kicked toward the ground. I tried to catch her but she hit the floor too fast for me to get to her. The resulting shockwave sent me back a bit.

Instead of reverting back to a bat like I thought she would, she stood and coughed up blood into her palm before promptly licking it back up.

Oliver burst down in a moonlit glow and crashed down between us. I moved to jump out of the way but I would have been blown back had Hanna not grabbed my hand and fanned out her wings, catching the wind and carrying us into the air. Next, she spun and threw me at our enemy.

Not having much time to dodge, Oliver attempted to counter instead. His blade met mine twice. Once when I was flying toward him and again once I managed to slide past him. I wasn't able to cut him, but that wasn't my job.

Hanna followed behind as soon as he was distracted and tried to impale him with her unfolded umbrella-like weapon.

Oliver dodged and only suffered a minor cut to his arm. Next, he landed a solid punch that slammed Hanna into the ground with a deafening crunch. Cracks permeated through the floor from the impact. He then took her weapon and impaled her into the ground with it before turning toward me.

I stood at the ready, watching Hanna grab her weapon and start pulling to free herself.

Oliver raised his hand and cast a spell, "***Nova blast***." His entire body became engulfed in light, which took the shape of a ball and left him to careen toward me at blinding speed.

I was grazed after trying a dodge roll and began bleeding from my temple. The heat also burned at my sleeve, leaving it to smolder.

I quickly cut into my palm with my dagger and let my imagination loose with my blood as a catalyst. I wanted to create a weapon with a wide range, but instead, I decided a single weapon wasn't enough. I needed something that couldn't be dodged. To that end, I created a fine mist of blood that covered most of the surrounding area and obscured visibility with some of it. The rest of it condensed above and fired down with enough force to shatter stone, let alone the wooden floor.

In a literal flash, Oliver teleported to me while visibility was still clear. As we were bombarded with the blood hail, I lunged at him with my dagger. He caught my wrist but was still knocked off balance. Falling backward, he swung his blade toward my throat.

Since he still had my wrist, I couldn't pull away. I was, however, able to use my knee to flatten the weapon onto him where it stayed. The hail stopped since I only used so much blood to use to make it.

Our ground struggle only lasted a couple of seconds before Hanna, having risen from the ground and fueled by the fallen blood, raced in from the aid. She snatched me off Oliver with one hand and began flying around the room where we watched him on the ground. The crimson haze was gone as well as the hole in Hanna's chest, leaving an open tear through her blouse where the same crest as on my hand shone brightly.

During that time, Oliver seemed to talk to someone while on the ground. His face lit up and he stood with a kip-up, dusting himself off before looking up at us with a gleeful smile.

"Are you ready?" Hanna was lifting us higher in the air.

"Yeah." I put my concentration on the rod in her hand and the sickles extended with black, green, and two different shades of red trailing off each element, respectively.

Making a short upward loop, she tossed me into the air where I landed so that we were foot to foot. I was standing upright and she was upside down. We both pushed off simultaneously and she spiraled down at Oliver.

I did another flip so that my feet met the ceiling and I pushed off back down. Returning my dagger to its scabbard, I reached my hands onto a pair of thick black gloves housed in custom leg pockets. They were inscribed with multiple seals created to suppress my consciousness while preventing me from falling asleep. They allowed me to tap into powers I normally couldn't. Aside from that, my nerves deadened, and my reaction time accelerated.

Watching as Hanna descended toward him in a rotating cone of color, Oliver took a stance and in one wide stroke not only clashed with her but also pushed her far in front of him.

Hanna struck the ground with her rod to prevent herself from flying too far away. Her momentum carried her upside down until she stopped.

In turn, I came down like a meteor and struck the edge of Oliver's blade with my fist, forcing it into the ground and following it up with a punch to the face that sent him backward while I rested on my newfound perch.

He slid back on his feet and tripped on a crack, causing him to fall, yet still finding his footing quickly. Next, he reached his hand out and summoned his weapon resulting in it slicing through the ground toward him and leaving me behind where I chased after it. He gripped the handle and tried to slash me.

I dove over him to avoid it. He seemed to be looking for that and turned a hand toward me, sending a blast that nearly sent me to a wall where I instead landed on my back.

By then, Hanna was soaring toward Oliver at the ready.

He threw his moon-blade as it had begun to glow and transform. The half-moon became a full moon as it raced through the air.

It was quickly parried to the side by the incoming vampiress as she closed in, but what seemed like no time later, it was back in his hands and Hanna was on the floor facing upward, unmoving.

I was back on my feet, but I soon found myself unable to move as well. It took a moment to register that I was pinned to the wall by a sword. The blade was the same shape as the half-moon blade, but with a hilt and handle seated to one end. Oliver was also standing before me, holding it.

"***Drown***," he cast a spell.

I got the sensation of my airways being engulfed in a torrent of water. The effect was so strong, I started gasping uncontrollably. I refused to hold my breath so the effect couldn't fully set in.

Pulling the sword out, Oliver sent a blade wave that cut cleanly through the wall that housed Arin and Jane on the other side, followed by the sound of shattering ice.

Falling to the ground, I continued struggling to breathe while trying to stop my rampant bleeding.

After a moment, Oliver spoke. "I don't have time to hold back on you guys anymore. You won't get anywhere in your condition."

I followed his voice. Since my vision was blurring, I blinked a few times but it didn't clear up. Eventually, I touched a limb. It was slightly twitching and I heard Hanna screaming in my head. It was blood-curdling and chilled me to the bone. It was non-human yet, totally understandable.

The man who caused this spoke again, "You managed to come back to life, and that's how you did it? I have nothing to be jealous of here anymore. And here I thought that wouldn't be enough to put you down this time." After that, he went back to the trapdoor and headed down.

My vision cleared enough to see and I reached for Hanna's hand. As soon as I found it, she squeezed my hand and the screams in my head died down. I squinted to get a better look at her. I didn't want to, but I did. I had to see her for myself.

She was in half. a deep puddle of red was constantly leaking from both horizontal sides of her form. It was quickly diminishing into black particles and floating away.

Piece by piece.

The voice in my head returned, "Don't cry for me... I'll be back. I don't know when, but hope you remember me when I do..." She completely vanished into nothing, leaving behind a scarlet puddle that cradled my consciousness as I drifted off.

40-Death, Glutton, and Lust

[Docter Ganger]

While everyone is looking for Belle, I split from the group early to investigate everything I can. I notice a path made of gray stone instead of blue concrete. Entering the hall, I see no cameras but can't shake the feeling that I'm being watched. I keep it in mind as I continue to explore deeper into the unknown.

I come upon a fork and take a left. The gaze I feel on me intensifies in that moment and I reconsider, taking the right path instead. The feeling lessens as I proceed on this alternative path. Continuing on, I come upon another split, but this time; I don't have time to choose as the walls and floor begin shaking. I turn and leave, but just as I start, everything goes black.

I try to open my eyes, but they're already open. The feeling of being watched is gone. I can't sense anyone around and I can still move so I figure the shaking caused the lights to cut out. I cast 'illuminate' so I can see, but instead of light shining from the walls and floor, it only comes from the floor. It's pitch black and now emitting an almost silver-gray light as a result. The walls are gone and the floor is no longer made of stone.

The space feels similar to a wielder's core, except my real body is here. As far as I know, there's only one spell capable of doing something like this, and this isn't it. I begin walking in a line to see if I get anywhere with the glowing spot in the ground as a marker as to where I'm going. To that end, the light quickly becomes too distant to see. I create another beacon and continue.

I walk for hours until a feeling shoots up my spine; fast and strong. It isn't just any feeling either. There is a strong sense of foreboding and a stronger sense of danger, as if whatever lies ahead could easily end me on a whim. It feels more like an empty promise than a real threat, so it comes as no surprise when the feeling begins slowly fading as I continue.

Eventually, I notice a light in the distance. It's larger and brighter than the lights I created. As I draw closer to the light, it takes the shape of a towering open double-door and when I finally come within its glow, my senses seem to come back all at once. With the light comes the sounds of moaning and groaning associated with the souls of the damned.

For a moment, I think I'm pulled back to that realm, but those thoughts are laid to rest as I enter. Standing between the doors, I notice a large creature watching over a multitude of floating humanoid souls. They number somewhere in the hundreds while all cowering before this creature. It appears to be a nude female humanoid seemingly suffering from kwashiorkor malnutrition with a bulbous gut, long, thin, deteriorated limbs, and long, thin, sickly hair draping across its pale and wrinkled skin. Every so often, it grabs armfuls of souls and consumes them, decimating the populace. It then regurgitates all of them simultaneously. The creature then sits back and continues to monitor the spirits as they cower.

Taking a look at my surroundings beyond that, I find that the doors I entered through are inscribed with a six-point star and surrounded by a layer of gray chains on the ground. As I realize where I am, I look back through the Astral Gate and wonder why it's empty.

As I continue farther in, the creature finally notices me. At first, it just stares as I analyze my situation, but then it slowly reaches out a hand in my direction. It pauses as I stop and look toward it.

"Where am I?" I ask.

"My realm. The realm of the damned and departed. Now, come so I may assess the worth of your soul." Its voice is ragged and horse as if it's been starved for decades.

"I've been to that place, and this isn't it." I begin walking toward it, and the crowd of souls part before me. "You appear to be a preta, are you a spirit animal? And if so, who is your wielder?"

It looks at me wordlessly before disappearing in less than a puff of smoke, followed by the accompanying souls. Shortly after, a voice rings out from the same direction.

"I've been waiting for you, 'Black Reaper'. You arrived in record time and completely intact." A woman appears before me with black, spiky hair, pale skin, and dark eyes that seem to pierce the void. She wears a black, sleeveless top riddled with bullet holes that seems to always be on the verge of falling off her shoulders, skinny jeans that mirror the effect, and a silver ring on the right side of her lower lip. "It usually takes a few weeks at least for a soul to reach here, and when they do, they're usually broken and weak." She seems a little too excited about my presence.

"Since you know who I am, do you mind telling me who you are?"

Her face lights up when I ask the question. She seems ecstatic in all the wrong ways, and her face more than shows it. "I thought you'd never ask! I'm Rin Takamine, also known as Glutton of the Seven Sins. Nice to make your acquaintance." She gives an excited bow.

"Since you're so excited about answering my questions, mind telling me why I'm here and how?"

"My magic attunement is death, and my magic type is 'soul' and I've been collecting souls as far back as I can remember. I can interact with a soul directly and yank it into this space just like I did with yours. It's a magic trait. Except your body followed and even your clothes. Curious."

"Thanks for the information, now I can take my leave." I attempt to summon my scythe to my hand, but nothing happens.

"Sorry, no can do." She leans sideways and begins floating as if lying on her side, supporting her head with her arm. "You're one I've been wanting for a long time." She licks her lips. "An immortal soul."

"I'm not as immortal as you think I am."

"Immortality is immortality. After all, your body follows your soul when it's moved. That's immortality as far as I can tell."

"How would you know? Believe me, you don't want the problems of an immortal."

"What, don't think I can handle it?"

"Maybe at first you can, but soon, you'll start to lose interest in things you enjoy. Even well as simple desires. Not to mention the voices... But you'll see soon enough if you keep it up."

"I can deal, besides." She reaches her hand out and my scythe materializes between her fingers. "Now that I have this, there should be no problem."

"Oh, if that's the case, enjoy the next couple of days. You'll be begging for me to take it back."

"I'll try to remember that." The last thing I see of her is the wicked smile she wears as she vanishes from sight, caressing the jagged edge of her new toy.

As she fades, the preta and accompanying souls return the same as they left as if frozen in time.

"The devourer... One who eats..." The preta starts moving again and responds to my earlier question simultaneously. "Not one to trifle with."

The hand still hovering in the air comes down in a burst of speed and the sickly skin nearly caresses my side as I step out of its path. Many souls are thrown far from the force before it brings the hand back to itself and continues to stare silently.

"No need to tell me who your wielder is, I already know. I just talked to her."

It doesn't respond and only stares attentively for the next few minutes before returning to the cycle of devouring and regurgitating the souls it oversees.

I take to wandering around between the masses of souls and listening to their voices like white noise to an old TV set. Some of them murmur fallacies and others, curses of wrongdoings, and more still of loss and regret as well as sadness and rage being common among them as they crowd, shuddering before their ghastly caretaker.

The more I advance between the souls of the dead, the more I come to notice something. The preta only devours areas of high emotion, causing them to calm down, and rarely acts upon those devoid of commotion. I begin wandering away from everything and into the distant darkness. In doing so, the hushed whispers are replaced with a familiar screaming in the distance. The closer I get to the darkness, the louder it becomes.

I hear movement behind me, and shortly after, I feel a large presence as well. I dodge far to the left, and a hand sweeps across where I was standing.

"Not the void... All is lost in the void..." The raspy voice now carries a sense of urgency.

"Into the void I go," I say, ready to take another step.

"She's right, you know." Rin returns, appearing over the hand this time. "Once you cross that boundary, you'll be lost to eternity."

Ready to take another step, I say, "I've been to eternity. I can go there again."

"I believe you. Over the past few days, I've been able to relive some of your memories through the soul link that was made when I took you. I gotta say... It's humbling... And haunting... Even for me."

"I take it, that means you'll let me go?"

Her eyes narrow. "Not on your lives."

"To the void I go." I take a step forward and the distant wails sharply rise in volume. The gleam of my own blade before my eyes stops me and the screams die back down. "What's wrong? Since you have that, you don't need me, right?" I give a knowing smile. "Have you run into any of the problems I mentioned earlier?"

In less than a second, I'm surrounded by a gray bubble floating inches off the ground. "I'm going to need you to stay away from there." Instead of the smile she wore before, a grimace stretches across Rin's face.

"Is it the voices? They're different from the hushed tones of this place and they're not as docile either." The bubble holding me travels quickly over the center of the crowd of souls with Rin close behind me, hovering in the air.

The screams become silent.

"Much better." Rin seems to relax to the point of nearly falling asleep. Her face shifts into a more subdued position with her eyes coming to a near-close and her mouth hanging open like an exhausted athlete. Rolling over to her back, she stays that way for half an hour before finally speaking again. "How do you do it...? I knew becoming an immortal wouldn't be easy -guaranteed to be harder than I thought- but how do you deal with this?" She sounds as if she's near the point of passing out.

"That doesn't really matter. If you let me go, you won't have to deal with it anymore."

"Don't play with me... That's not happening." She sounds exhausted. "If a nobody from nowhere can do it, so can I."

"So, how many days has it been?"

"A few... It's Wednesday."

"Two days, huh?"

"What!?" She re-orients herself to a standing position before disappearing for a second and coming back. "It has..." There seems to be more she wants to say but she doesn't.

"Either way, I think you've learned your lesson." I tap once to pop the bubble and levitate myself toward the darkness where the screams peak to an inhumane screech.

"No, you don't!" Another bubble appears around me, and this one is thickened with many layers as it drags me back to where Rin wants me. She holds her head in one hand with a pained expression on her face. "**Soul restriction**!" Marks that look just like the chain lying around her gate swarm around my body and hold me in place, making it surprisingly difficult to resist. "Tell me what I want to know or else."

"Or else what? It's clear you can't finish what you've started," I say, dryly.

She growls in rage and reaches her hand through the bubble and chains only for her hand to crash into my chest. A flicker of surprise races across her face, but before she can pull her hand back, I break the chains and catch her arm. Instead of her reaching into my soul, I reach into hers.

What she said about taking souls is true. She also used her spirit animal to rob them of both their magic and spirit energy. She was planning to siphon all the information she could out of me through our soul-link, then do the same to me. She began having trouble on account of being caught off-guard by the screams of the past. She was quickly put at the edge of insanity when I went toward the darkness and was forced to confront me. I'm unable to find out too much more before she pulls herself from my grasp.

She looks at me with pure fear in her eyes before blurting out, "You're a Legendary Corpse Hunter?"

"In the flesh." I spread my arms out while responding.

"Not the flesh, not yours." Out of the fear comes resolve. "It doesn't matter what you show me. You're ultimately powerless here. THIS IS MY DOMAIN!" She rises high above the spirits with me still in the bubble "*Frozen hell, ethereal chains, soul restriction, soul lock, death grip*." Once she's done casting spells, I'm covered and surrounded by a multitude of frozen chains from all directions, as well as an embrace from skeletal arms coming from the ether and a twin-headed snake with a keyhole in each head. "And for extra measure, *inverse horizon*." The bubble changes so that only the top is gray and fades to clear halfway down. "Have fun." As quickly as she gives her parting words, she's gone.

Based on the information I got from her, all I need to do was wait, and I do. Time passes, much less inside than outside, but time passes. I stay, eyes closed, waiting.

The Shadow Master is coming, and so is Krow.

After some time, what feels like a rush of heat rises from the tip of my toes to the top of my head. Time to strike.

I summon a weapon into my hand. Not my scythe, a sword. Its once familiar handle is now foreign in my hand and its short yet broad edge now unfamiliar, protruding from the maw of the now dull ornamental dragon head. The once green wielder's weapon is now a black husk of one. One swipe cuts through all the chains, the skeletal arms, the snake, and the bubble.

I make for the darkness and as predicted, Rin appears before me, scythe in hand. We strike each other at once and she falls from the air as I continue with my scythe returned. Just beyond the veil of darkness is a solid wall.

What looks like solid entropy at first is actually hundreds, maybe thousands of artifacts from different magic users. Wielder gates stand beside summoner eyes etched into the nothingness alongside wizard emblems and enchanter sigils, as well as witch threads dangling between the gaps. If warlocks had anything to contribute to this monstrosity, there would likely be just as many as the others.

I open a hole in one of the gates with a wave of my scythe to find my way out followed by the quieted wails of immortals' past.

A white light shines from the other side when I go through and as my eyes adjust, I see small, barred rooms lined with beds, reminiscent of a prison. The large room and gray magic-resistant walls and floors confirm it.

"Where do you think you're going!? **TaKe ThE vOiCeS wItH yOu!**" Rin writhes on the floor behind me with her head in her hands. She sits up and stares at me desperately.

"I did. If you're hearing them now, it means you got what you wanted, immortality. Those are the testers; the wailing voices of past immortals who willingly gave it up and now serve as voices of reason against obtaining it." I turn to her. "I can take it away if you want." I sit the blade of my scythe behind her head. "Then, you'll be free."

She closes her eyes and slumps forward while I prepare to end her, but she acts before I do. Her hand finds its way into my chest and out the other side. "You know, I almost gave up and the voices just stopped. I deserve to be immortal. I deserve this!" With my beating heart in her hand, she begins laughing hysterically.

I put my hand around her throat as I lift her from the ground and proceed to snap her neck.

She doesn't seem to notice and she doesn't stop laughing. Instead proceeds to pull my heart out and squeeze it.

I respond by twisting her wrist with my free hand, breaking it, and forcing her to release my heart before letting her go. I then return my heart to my chest before the hole closes. Rin stops laughing as her neck and hand snap back into place and return to normal. She really had become immortal. She's no longer a normal threat and I need to kill her permanently.

"If you can take this away, then I don't need you to exist." Lost in ecstasy, she quivers with every word. She summons a rapier with a gray skull-shaped guard to her hand and strikes at me simultaneously. It's a wielder's weapon.

I sway to the side and swipe my scythe at her head.

She ducks and her rapier morphs into a black chain tipped with a gray sickle. It winds around my leg and pulls me to the ground before morphing into a halberd which she tries to land into my chest.

I roll to the side and stand, casting 'dark abyss' and shrouding the entire room in unnatural darkness that only I can see through.

My opponent quickly waves her hand over her eyes, and they began glowing bright green before looking directly at me.

Turning my wrist, I send a 'blade wave' in her direction.

She ducks it while barreling toward me with a gray pitchfork aimed at my head.

I parry it to the side and nestle my blade under her jaw in one fluid motion. It carries her over my head before I pull her to the ground headfirst on the other side. In doing so, I'm able to tug at her soul and dislodge a piece before absorbing it into myself.

She stands from sliding across the floor while holding her jaw, which is slow to regenerate. The look in her eye tells me she understands what I'm doing. She bites into her hand and draws blood, casting a spell that dispels the shroud of darkness I placed and replaces it with a red blood mist that makes it difficult to see even with enhanced sight.

The surrounding area becomes saturated with magic similar to hers, making a mana field and rendering it difficult to sense her. The mist is heavy, making it hard to tell what I'm touching, and all I can smell is blood.

"*Horizon*." I cast the spell and erect a bubble I can't see around myself despite the border being at arm's length. As soon as I do, I hear a bang to my left, closely followed by one above me. I'm in the middle of casting another spell when I see a sliver of steel-like material sliding out of my chest from behind.

"*Soul-drain*." The voice coming from behind makes me realize that I cast the bubble around both of us, and in that moment of vulnerability, Rin struck.

I feel the bond between my body and soul weakening as bits of me drain through the blade on which I'm impaled. I send away my bubble and cast 'numbing field' over the entire room. My habit of picking up and learning every spell I can find finally comes in handy. This self-explanatory spell from Sara will do more than numb the body if given enough time. Next, I swing my scythe quickly behind me, forcing Rin away and relieving me of her blade. I decide that I've been holding back far too much for far too long. My hubris and complacency allowed this event to take place, and now it's time to set things right.

"*Celestial*." While not a spell, it carries the same weight as one. My entire body becomes shrouded in a visible aura of darkness that pushes the nearby fog away while my eyes glow a piercing red. Releasing my scythe from my hand, it begins levitating to my side and each of the four forms appear hovering around me before three of them disappear, leaving me with the fourth: a double scythe with a wide, flat blade and a needle-like back spike on each end.

I spot Rin backing into the fog and throw my scythe, spinning toward her. After going a distance, it comes back to no avail. There's a presence behind me and striking in that direction yields no result. Rin comes through the fog shortly afterward in front of me. A flick of the wrist makes the illusion of her shatter, and I can hear footsteps clearly behind me as I feel another presence above. I also sense at least eight advanced spells activating around me simultaneously.

I bring my scythe high above my head and swipe upward as another illusionary woman comes through the mist. Continuing the motion, my blade strikes true with the sound of metal striking flesh and bone sounding behind me. With all signs pointing at different outcomes, I decide to trust the one sense that hasn't yet failed. The footsteps, which seemed more like a distraction, instead, turn out to be a red herring.

I turn around and pull her closer. Her skin is now gray and her eyes are sunken in, to the point where it doesn't look like she has any. Her clothes look decayed and her skin is pulled taut against her bones. She had gone into her celestial form as well, taking on attributes of her spirit animal and boosting her power beyond what should be its limits.

The blade is struck through her forearm and into her ribs. She attempts to stab me with her rapier, and I knock it aside with the back of my fist before opening my hand toward her.

"*Astral chain.*" A black rope appears around her and tightens to the sound of more snapping bone and ripping flesh as it lifts her off the ground. "*Soul reaper.*" I retrieve my blade from her as an ever deeper puddle of red builds up beneath our feet. A formless gray wisp eeks out of the blade wound and winds itself around the scythe, down the handle, and into me. It isn't as instantaneous as I'd like. Her resistance is strong.

I watch her limp body for any signs of life as the mist still hasn't gone away despite her soul being taken. Even if I can't take all of it, there should be some difference, but there isn't. Something isn't right.

I realize too late what's wrong when gray blades pierce my back and chest from below as they hoist me into the air. With everything moving so fast, I didn't expect us both to have a similar idea.

"*Heaven*," I say, focusing on the spell binding my target, its ethereal properties lending to a sacred aura; imperfect, yet incorporated, nonetheless. "*Hell.*" My aura visibly thickens as I lend its hellish properties to my spell. "*Earth.*" The 'numbing field' spell begins to glow, causing the room to turn green. "*Trifecta.*"

The magical blades shatter, and the red mist condenses, then dissipates under a triangular prism set around Rin. The prism itself is transparent, light green marked with a ring of muddy yellow and a shadowy black texture. The 'numbing field' and 'astral chain' spells are gone, having been used to cast the spell.

I stand at the sight of Rin standing in the prism, barely on her feet. All of her senses are numbed down yet still, she persists, banging on the walls of her containment with what strength she can muster as her wounds heal completely. It's as I thought, the soul I ripped from her wasn't hers, it was one of the many souls trapped inside of her. Had I not weakened her ahead of time, she'd have already gotten out.

I cast 'light speed' and dash past her, setting my scythe into her flesh on the way, leaving it behind. I do it again from the other side with another scythe, summoning each one in turn and doing the same results in the conditions being met for another spell. The 'trifecta seal' shatters with my first movement, but Rin stands helpless to my assault. I continue placing and replacing the four scythes. Each time, faster, cutting a little deeper, tearing out a soul. The faster I go, the more I pull. The more I cut, the redder everything becomes until finally, a brilliant silver orb is uncovered, gleaming with life. I continue cutting until it becomes nothing more than small, dust-like particles barely held together in an orb shape.

I take it into my hand and squeeze, shattering it, aside for one marble-sized piece in the center which I keep.

Her immortality.

The scene before me leaves no resemblance to a human and despite the room's magic-resistant properties, scars of blood and blade soak into the floors. I use magic to restore the deceased back to a tangible human form as far as appearance and leave her in a cell bed.

Reverting to my normal form, I take a moment to take in my surroundings and find that the prison houses two others deeper in with an exit far to the other side. I travel deeper and find a plain wall with a slit that I have to crouch to see through. I barely get close to it before someone speaks.

"Is that the Black Reaper?" It's the voice of Geist Kaizer. I recognize it from the tournament, and he doesn't sound well.

"What are you doing here? Aren't you too important to be in prison?" I tap on the wall to find that its magic-resistant properties are over ten times the area I just left.

"I was until I wasn't." His response tells all too well how he feels about the situation.

"*Decay*." I place my hand on the wall and cast a spell. The wall turns black, then gray, and falls to dust under the weight of my palm.

Both of the cell's inhabitants wear cuffs, chaining their hands together and restricting their magic. Geist is in dire straits with a heavy cough. A dark cloud hangs over him as a curse drains his life force. Behind him sits Mary, rubbing her leg before standing with wobbly knees. There's a clear cut through her soul that's nearly fully regenerated on its own. She comes to me and holds her cuffs up.

"Can you do the same thing to these?"

"Sure." I tap the cuffs and they rust over and fall apart.

"Thanks." She continues down the hall and out of sight at breakneck speeds.

I do the same for Geist and he struggles to his feet. "Is it my time, Grim Reaper?" He coughs.

"Not yet," I respond honestly.

"How long?" His voice quivers, afraid of the answer.

"I can't answer that. I can't tell how long anyone has definitively."

"Well, can you do something about this curse?"

"I'll see what I can do." I place my palm on his forehead. "**Identify**." As soon as I cast the spell, it's as if I'm looking at my own death. I'm taken aback but remain calm. The Shadow Master caused this.

"Is this as bad as I think?"

"I can delay the inevitable, but I also have a favor to ask." I summon my scythe.

"You need my soul?"

"No," I pull my phone from my pocket, "I need you to follow the signals and offer assistance in any way you can to my family. I'm sure you're familiar with this type of magitech."

"I am and I will." He takes the phone. "Magitech like this doesn't work here, so we'll have to wait till we're out of the prison."

"Thank you." I Let my scythe fall into his shoulder enough to penetrate his skin "**Soul reaper.**" A blue wisp escapes through the opening. Mixed onto it is a growing black mass. I absorb the blue wisp and the black mass falls to the floor where it dissipates. I then return the part of his soul I took. "I rid you of as much as I can."

When the process is over, he stands more easily and walks with me out of the prison. On the way, we find Mary gazing upon Rin's corpse inside the cell I put her in.

"She's dead," says Mary.

"I know," I say, "I killed her."

"How?" She comes to me, holds fast onto my sleeve, and tugs lightly like a child wanting a treat. "I have to know. I don't want to be helpless like that again."

I look away toward the area the fight took place in. The imprint of what happened still lingers, and likely will for some time. I go over and pick up a stone-sized piece of debris with Mary following close behind. I focus some mana into the stone before I hand it to her and say, "Study this and you'll know."

Wide-eyed, she takes it and says, "Thank you." before making her way to the exit of the prison.

"Was that a good idea?" Geist asks a question that I will hear repeated many times, and despite what becomes of the girl, my answer is still the same.

"That remains to be seen."

We make our way closer to the exit to find Mary closely hugging a wall next to a doorway that holds a sinister presence behind it. Knowing what I'm facing, I activate 'celestial' and summon my first scythe. Thanks to the soul I just absorbed, the beast-like toothed edge is considerably more vicious-looking than normal.

Walking through the doorway, I'm met with a large reception room filled with a green haze. It seems like spores of some sort but heavily saturated with magic to the point of muddling the senses. I snap my fingers and summon a small, black flame, which I toss before me to explosive results. The room lights up like a lightbulb for a couple of seconds before the flames die down instantaneously. I dust what little lands on me off and walk further into the room.

The sinister feeling fades as someone else comes through a door behind the receptionist's desk on the other side of the room. With his leafy-green hair flowing behind him and brandishing his quarterstaff, my next opponent rears his head.

"The wooden man makes an appearance," I said, taking a stance.

"I take it that you killed Glutton and made off with a bit of information?" Marroon, the Sin of Lust walks to the middle of the room.

"I did."

He sighs, "That makes it my job to put you down now." Small plants begin rapidly growing beneath his feet before he lunges at me atop a large vine. I jump back through the doorway, and he follows closely, landing less than five feet away from me.

Wasting no time, Geist summons his weapon and begins hacking away at the vines, now barring the exit.

Marroon turns toward him with his hand outstretched. Before he can do anything, I reach my scythe around him and swing him to the other side of me where he falls out of my grasp and slides across the floor. He stands as both Geist and Mary get through the doorway and out of the prison.

"We don't have to fight," I say, standing my scythe at my side. "If this war continues at the rate it's going, no one's going to leave the victor and the world will only be worse off as a result. I'm not asking you to join me or anything. I just need you to stand down so I can do my job."

"Did you say the same thing to Glutton?"

"I offered her a way out and she refused. Violently."

"She wouldn't give up on being immortal for anything in the world. If you killed her that means she either got what she wanted or found a way to guarantee she would, and you killed her as a result. Interesting."

"Are you going to let me pass?"

He holds up his staff. "Do you know what this is?"

"Asclepius' staff. A symbol of medicine."

"A human symbol of human medicine. I don't know if you can tell, but I'm not even part human. I'm a wielder. That's a human thing. Do you know why I'm like this?"

"No."

"One day, while looking over the myths and legends of old, I found a story of a great tree that was dying thanks to human pollution and sent an avatar of itself to warn the humans of the dangers the wildlife faced because of their actions. Instead of heeding the warning, the humans feared and hunted what became the last remnants of a dead forest. To survive, it disguised itself as human and lived among them until the truth of what it was came to light and it was killed. It died not long after producing its own offspring, only a few of which were left alive. That's when I realized what I am and what I'm here for."

"It's not to help them, is it?"

"No."

"I don't need you to help them, just not to be part of the cause of their destruction."

I notice a green tint in the air that fills the room. Before I can create a flame, I'm surrounded by roots that carry me into the air and converge into a tree that holds me in place. The mist is now gone, but I can't move easily.

"I'm sorry, but you'll have to go the way of the forest and burn." Marroon takes out a lighter and flicks it on before throwing it into the tree's base. "Cauterized wounds don't heal."

The tree catches as if it's made of fire, and the blaze engulfs me with enthusiasm, the flames of which lick at my clothes and bite into my flesh. The light blinds me and the change in my pocket begins to melt.

I close my eyes and cast 'decay'. This makes the now rotting tree burn faster and hotter. The wood is also now weaker so I break the rotted wood and throw my scythe in its fourth form. It lands behind Marroon after severing his arm, causing it to fall to the floor. It then returns to my hand and I begin rending the tree around me to pieces.

Marroon calmly picks up his arm with his other hand and reattaches it. His blood looks more like brownish sap than anything. It flows more like syrup than blood before hardening and cementing the severed limb back into place and returning its function.

I cast 'dark abyss' and make for my opponent as quickly as possible.

Marroon surrounds himself with an opaque barrier.

I cut the barrier in half only to be met with acidic gas that filled the bubble. It forces me to back off.

He strikes at me with the sharp end of his quarterstaff and I back off further.

By this time, my blade is already closely seated behind him and drawing toward me. Having to be careful about cutting into him given what he is, I place the edge against him as gently as I can before sharply closing the distance myself as I dodged around his quarterstaff.

He seems as if he's attempting to cast a spell, but I catch him before he can with an uppercut before grabbing him by the throat and casting my own spell.

"*Gospel of darkness*." The spell renders the targeted soul intangible by magical means. I can now fight without further affecting the ancient spirit dwelling within him.

His foot veers toward my head and makes contact, causing a green glow to radiate quickly outward before stabbing at my face with his quarterstaff once again and missing. His movements also drastically slowed as if his limbs are weighted. He's wide open.

I rend the leg he kicked me with as well as the arm holding his staff. They fall to the floor with a thump as I cleave through each of them. Finally, I land the toothed edge of my scythe in his heart.

He goes limp, and I drop him. His body crumples in on itself and forms a small ball. As a result of his plant-based physiology and his magical nature, every time his physical body dies, he's reborn as a child. More knowledge I gained from Rin. I pick up the orb and take it with me.

I create a reflective surface of magic and examine my face where I was kicked to find some of the flesh eaten away as it regenerates at a considerably slower pace than normal. My burns haven't completely healed either and my singed clothes are riddled with more holes than they have been in a long time.

I step out of the prison and make my way toward the strongest unfamiliar energy signature I can.

Making my way deeper and deeper into the structure, I'm careful not to move too briskly between the halls. I don't want to gather more unwanted attention as I pass rooms full of gears and steel as well as rooms full of desks and chairs.

Not long after, I notice the feeling of someone watching me. I already have the impression that I am, but this is different. It's like a hawk eyeing a rabbit in the distance. Someone else is coming for me.

Moments after the feeling settles in, there is a distortion. I figure no one would try teleporting into the base because of how noticeable it is, but I'm wrong. The residual mana in front of me begins twisting into knots before a person appears before me. She stands chest-high in light checker-board black and white bulletproof armor. She has black and white pistols each nearly three times the average size in her hands. The Roland crest is displayed prominently on her vest and helmet.

She fires off a shot, and I recognize her. She's someone I only met once before, and very briefly. I dodge the shot, but with speed and agility fueled by rage, she finds her gun nestled closely to the back of my head just as quickly.

"Give me my brother back, you monster." Seething would be a gross understatement in her case. Despite her calm demeanor, I see a bottomless pit of rage and despair seeping out of her pores.

"I can't do that," I say, "You can talk to him if you want."

"Until I see you leave his body, I won't believe anything that comes out of your mouth." She clearly made up her mind about me before this encounter; before approaching me.

"You don't have to," I say, calmly taking a step forward. The sound of my footstep is interrupted by gunfire. The impact on the back of my head is faint, to say the least.

"That was a warning shot." This is a lie. There was no essence behind the shot, warning or not.

"Your brother's wish. Do you want to know what it was?"

I hear a click and now both guns are aimed at my head. "Tell me."

"I inherited his memories so I know what you two have done in pursuit of the fantastic and magical, but I know you really wanted an escape from your world- a world that would allow two children-"

Another shot rings out and this time, there is a real impact which makes my head sway. "Hurry up." I can hear the soft whirr of a charged shot.

"As well-read as he was, he knew the risks of getting a wish granted and did so anyway. He wished for you to join this world- the world of magic and legends. He thought that even without him, you could live a happier life with the powers you'd attain."

"If that's the case, where do you come in all of this?"

A good question and one I'm not entirely ready to answer. I begin thinking back on everything I've done in my 'life'. "I suppose we have time."

41-Wrath en Passant

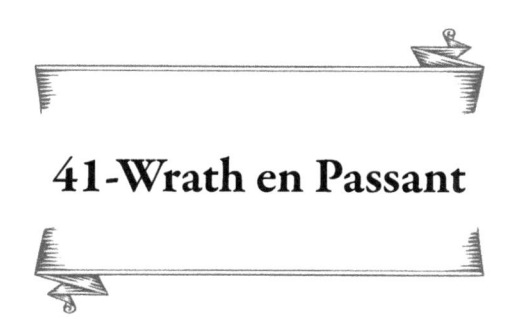

[Carona Hunt]

Lazily, I swept the multitude of video feeds coming from around the base and inspecting each one for activity. The base was split in a forty by forty-by-forty-by-forty grid with half of it below ground. There were roughly fifty security cameras in each underground section with varying amounts above ground depending on location. Guile never returned from when he left and it was impossible to reach him or vice versa without completely bypassing the emergency comms restrictions and giving away our intention, so Dr. Cruz, April, and I shared leadership responsibilities. I was almost done sweeping the buildings when what felt like an earthquake rolled through.

As alarmed as we all were, it didn't take long to find the source. The entire lower base through the front sections was either crushed completely or saw minor flooding resulting from a landmass that appeared from nowhere.

Panic was quelled quickly as this was the signal we had all been waiting for. The time of war had begun. As this realization set in, we began scanning all cameras that we could manually from our terminals with the wall monitors set to motion sensor mode.

War was here.

All soldiers and operatives were recalled since the bombing within the base. After the land mass appeared, they were rallied together in minutes and ready to march out at a moment's notice. The battle would start soon.

It didn't take long to find all seven of the Sins, Darkside, and Ferris Kaizer congregating inside the gate room where there were no cameras. After a few minutes, the Sins left the room and scattered.

Sloth went outside where visual was lost after he flew toward the soon-to-be battlefield. Next, he returned with Princess Roland in tow before taking her into the gate room. Finally, he took residence in the lobby of the first building in the city district. It served as part of the academy and had a direct line to the gate room.

Lust went down into the catacombs where there were no cameras and returned a few minutes later with what looked like liquid gold splattered on him and based on what I know, it was likely angel blood. Geist was draped over his shoulder and Courtny Riddles was in a bubble made of vines that wound around her arms and legs, floating behind them. They went into the prison and returned without Geist before going to the gate room. The prison had a dedicated security system so nothing could be seen from the outside.

The rest of the Sins went to separate locations that all had direct routes to the gate room until Glutton took off from her post in the grand library and made her way to the prison as quickly as possible. All the cameras she came past flickered and glitched as she went.

All soldiers were deployed onto the battlefield by then. The cameras pointed that way were disrupted and I couldn't see what was happening.

That was when a short-range missile siren went off. Instead of a missile, the cameras showed a familiar red soaring through the sky, followed by a straggling yellow. Krow was on his way, but the second person was swiped out of the air by someone else who went up to meet them.

Reaching the base, the first thing Krow did was enter the building Sloth was in. He took only a few steps in when the entire room erupted in blue, and all cameras ceased to work. I would have already gone to that location had it not been for another situation unfolding elsewhere.

When I saw Krow, I looked at my phone. It looked like everyone else was already within the base aside from Doc. His signal was missing. Everyone else was near the crushed area. I looked through the cameras and saw a small black creature scuttling around and a brown one gliding between rooms before those cameras abruptly shut off. Sara and Ariel were cutting them off and making their way to me. They only showed up briefly each time, but I was sure it was Sara as a scorpion and Ariel's familiar.

The problem was that someone other than us noticed. Wrath began making his way to that location, only stopping to listen to the communicator in his ear before continuing during the short alarm.

It'd take too long to get to Krow, but the girls were coming toward me, so that's where I went. The only one to react when I headed for the door was April. She reached out a hand to stop me, but didn't, nervously pulling her hand back and shaking like a leaf.

Hesitantly opening her mouth, she said, "Like me, I'm sure you're already considered dead." She took a shaky breath. "Death was only the beginning for me. Now, I'm just looking for the end. How about you?"

I chose not to answer and cast 'invisibility' on myself before running off to where I saw the last camera cut off. Looking around, I could see the surrounding cameras were still functioning. That made sense because the next area in that direction was a large room for open use. It was one of few rooms big enough to use large-scale magic and so anyone was allowed to come and do anything they wanted as long as it wasn't against the rules.

There were multiple entrances in all directions and a relatively high ceiling balconied by the next room up. Because of the frequency at which the room was used, there was a constant mana field even twenty years later. A mana field this strong would overpower any weak magic introduced into it. My invisibility wouldn't last, and I'd have to release it and cast a stronger version to make it through the room without detection. I wasn't going to take that chance seeing as Wrath could be anywhere nearby, so I stood and waited.

I didn't hear any footsteps or feel any kind of presence aside from the mana field until a man landed silently from an entryway next to the one I was in from the above floor. Dressed lightly in camo shorts with a matching short-sleeved shirt, black kneepads, and military boots. He stood in place for a moment, seemingly to adjust to the room's atmosphere. That's what I thought until I felt the mana field beginning to expand and strengthen.

I tried to move back and stay ahead of it, but it expanded too fast to do so without drastic measures and then I realized; I was in a hallway, the easiest place to hit a fleeing target. He wouldn't have known about my being here, so my daughter was definitely nearby and in the same situation.

I turned around and charged forward. My invisibility faded in an instant and I summoned my axe to my hand. It was a normal-looking double-sided war axe with slightly longer blades than normal and a volatile pattern reminiscent of whatever elements I was using at the time. In this case, lightning and wind. I dual-cast 'whirlwind blade' and 'lightning blade', coating in a mix of splitting winds and striking electricity. To make sure the spells were silent, I dual-cast 'tailwind' and 'lightning flow', using the runoff of the two previous spells. Both gave me a considerable speed boost. Next, I made use of my one opportunity to end the battle before it started.

Bolting forward, I swung my axe as hard as I could. The strike landed between his head and shoulders. Even so, it stopped a few inches shy of his neck and couldn't get any closer. It was as if a steel beam was in place of air.

I pulled back, but before I could strike again, he turned around and removed the object resting between his cheek and shoulder. The thing he used to block my strike.

He feathered a nearly translucent arrow into a glassy light green short bow and fired it at my face at nearly point-blank range.

Having already increased my speed with the wind/lightning combination, I dodged easily but the pressure of it passing by pushed me off to the side.

Stumbling, I caught my footing and slammed my axe into the ground, electrifying the floor. He stabbed an arrow into the ground in response, whipping up a whirlwind that diverted the lightning around him.

While he was distracted, I evolved my axe into its second form. The elongated and rounded edges shortened on both sides. One side kept the outward curve and refined a second outward curve at the end while the other side adopted spikes that resembled the spread wing of a large bird. I called it 'Thunderbird'.

"**Sandstorm**." I tapped the ground and made the top layer of aged stone around me crumble away. It whirled around in a sandstorm strong enough to break away more stone to add to its power. It grew despite the limited space. I was hoping it would hold him long enough for me to get in close enough to strike or evolve my weapon again and try to match his strength.

I was afforded neither option as another arrow blew through the sandstorm, causing the rubble to disperse and fall to the ground.

Barely dodging it this time, I was blown away again and landed harshly on my side. "Shoot!" I exclaimed, hearing a hard pop from my shoulder followed by an accompanying pain. Thinking I'd have to dodge again, I stood as quickly as possible to a sight I hadn't considered.

He was surrounded by what looked like a shell of green thorns so thick that I couldn't see him, and his legs were covered with what looked like a mound of sparkling white fabric or snow. Upon further inspection, I saw that nearly half of the thorns were in fact arrows and the other material was silver or crystal in a shell of ice anchoring him to the ground. It looked like a bulbous Christmas tree ready for decorations.

Leuna stepped out of the doorway opposite where I came in with her evolved bow, shimmering metallic green, drawn and focused on Wrath. She was closely followed by Caroline wielding her evolved moon blade, Although blood-red instead of blue, it was the exact same as the one she used when controlled by the corpse shadow. Next was Ariel with her thrice evolved lance, managing to shorten the handle, flatten the edge, and employ a mesmerizing pattern that made it hard to follow when used. Last was Sara. She stood tall in her natural state with her evolved dagger in the second form. It looked similar to a kodachi except with the ability to fan out both sides of its dual edge. Despite overflowing with energy, I couldn't sense any of them before they entered the room. An effect of being in such a strong mana field.

Sara and Ariel came to my side and stood readily.

Sara touched gently my arm. "Are you ok, Mom?"

I dusted myself off and checked my shoulder to find it working fine even though it hurt. "I'm fine now."

"Thank goodness," said Ariel. "We need to get out of here now."

"No, not yet."

"You think he won't let us go?"

"I believe he'd let us go, but this is too big to turn back now." I concentrated through the pain and evolved my weapon into its third form. Smoothing out the pointed edges, my blade fanned out on both sides to take the shape and design of butterfly wings. "You can go back if you want, but I'm staying here. Besides, we could just be wrong, and he could be sitting there waiting for us to turn our backs."

"Truer words have never been said." Wrath's voice echoed through the room as an isolated vortex spun around him, breaking through the layers of spells meant to keep him inactive. He opened his mouth to speak again, but before he said anything, he reached his hand upward to the space near his head and caught a bright green arrow.

Leuna shot as soon as she saw his head. She drew her bow again, ready. Her arrows were faster than a bullet and so they were never dodged or blocked, never caught until now.

"I was waiting for you to decide. To be honest, all of that kind of stung, and that pissed me off." Leuna shot another arrow and he blocked it with the one in his hand. "Now to get a shared habit out of the way before it bugs me... My name is Jordan Isles, also known as the Sin of Wrath."

Stealthily, Ariel left an illusion of her standing beside me and found herself behind Wrath. She drove her lance forward to pierce him from behind. Her illusion vanished as she struck.

Wrath turned and guided the point of her blade to the side, making it look easy. Next, he teleported in a gust of wind behind her. In his hand wasn't the short bow. Instead, there was essentially a shotgun with a rifle barrel integrated on top. This was followed by a bang.

Ariel had time to turn around and blocked much of the shot spread with the flat of her lance. Part of the blast still caught her leg, causing her to stumble back with blood running to the floor.

Sara left my side before I heard the sound. Although she couldn't stop it from firing, she made it there before the shot landed. Carving a glowing pink cross in the air, she traveled through it. Next, she jumped to swipe at the throat of the gunner. Although she missed, she forced more distance between him and Ariel.

In response, Wrath pressed the barrel against Sara's sternum, lifting her higher off the ground before firing another shot.

Sara exploded in a mist of gold and pink. She reappeared from the cross in a pink glow, still moving at full speed.

Systematically, Wrath turned his gun to where Sara returned to where she was before three arrows struck him and his gun simultaneously. The one that hit his gun forced it to turn to the side while the two that hit his arm and torso seemed to have no effect. Before he could fix his aim, Sara had already made it to Ariel, picked her up, and was making her way back toward me.

I had only taken five running steps forward between when Sara left and when she came back with Ariel. As soon as they came within reach, I grabbed each of them by the hand and enveloped them both in a 'healing breeze'. The wounds in Ariel's leg closed quickly in a blue glow and she took back to her feet. The wounds would open back up in little more than a few minutes, but it'd do for the moment.

As soon as they were clear of Wrath, Leuna began rapidly firing from the hallway to prevent him from acting. She dashed away from the hall, picking up speed as she dove into the air. Her arrows caused turbulent winds as she shot them faster and faster. She used that wind to add to her speed as she became a blur in the air.

Wrath moved to dodge the much faster shots but he couldn't dodge all of them. Some of them made visible contact but did no visible damage. Taking aim, his gun started glowing. It reshaped into a rotund, yet compact firearm. A rocket launcher. He aimed it at Caroline, the only one still in the hallway.

A translucent green orb raced from the barrel. As soon as it was visible, it was intercepted by one of Leuna's arrows, causing a premature explosion that, despite the surprise, only seemed to entertain Wrath as a second orb raced along the path of the first. He probably fired them both at the same time but the explosion of one somehow didn't affect the other.

Not fast enough to leave the hall in time, Caroline stood her ground as a wall of water sprouted between her and the exploding ball. Even so, the force of the blast destroyed the ball and sent her careening down the hallway and out of sight.

Wrath fired again, still bombarded by arrows.

Ariel dashed to intercept the shot but she was too late. The shots that came out this time were multiple small, high-speed orbs that zoomed along.

Sara dashed, carried by gold that glittered around her legs, to the hallway before the shots could pass by. She held out her hands and her blade in them when a golden film appeared before her. Most of the projectiles punctured and bypassed the flowing thin sheet of magic but the few that didn't, returned to sender almost instantly, carrying a golden trail of poison behind them and making contact.

Even getting hit by some of his own attacks didn't seem to faze Wrath. He just stood there, aiming another shot.

This time, Ariel got to him first, putting the flat of her lance directly in front of the barrel as he fired. The resulting explosion this time forced them both back as the lance acted like a lid keeping in the expanding pressure.

Sara caught Ariel. She sped to prevent her sister from falling back while Wrath blew himself a short distance. He could only correct his footing before the pair was on top of him.

Ariel with her strength and broad yet precise strikes and Sara with her speed and acrobatics kept the gunner busy despite not seeming to give him any real trouble.

Leuna stopped firing shots and instead, started charging a single arrow. It started glowing and the glow intensified as she held it.

I made my way to the hallway. I felt like I was moving in slow motion the whole time, but I got there. In the hall, Caroline was unharmed behind a mostly destroyed wall of ice. There was also a trail of blood from where Sara stood to reflect the attack. As soon as I saw that, I acted.

Holding my axe flat in front of me, I conjured three blue orbs and sent them toward the three fighting. Each one hit a target, and all three gained a slight blue glow. The glow around Wrath began pulsing. I cast 'harming aura' on him. It was a spell meant to force open any wounds over time. The other two persisted as a healing spell; 'healing aura'. I cast the same healing spell on Caroline to make sure she was fine.

Working in tandem, we slowly overwhelmed Wrath. He began moving more sluggishly in time. With the blue pulse, a few gold marks appeared on his body and spread until he was both gold and blue. Sara's spell was starting to take effect.

Any time he could free himself from the three-woman assault or cast a spell, Leuna would take a shot to prevent it. Unlike with her normal shots, he dodged the charged ones.

Whenever one of the girls got hit, my spell would heal them before they could falter. Even so, I held my axe ready and kept a keen eye out in case something bad happened.

The thing that concerned me the most was that he would change what form his weapon would take between the three forms with no noticeable difference in power output. While we were fighting for our lives, he was holding back and probably enjoying it.

This all came to a head as a shot from Leuna forced him down to a knee before charging another shot. She cast a spell with this one, causing a torrent of air to surround it.

Ariel tried to impale Wrath while he was down with her lance.

Wrath blocked with the rocket launcher, followed by a shot that landed squarely in Sara's chest with the resulting explosion, pushing the others back and allowing the gunner back to his feet. At that moment, Leuna released her arrow.

A streak of green shone through the air and into the ground far behind Wrath, where it drilled through and dissipated. He didn't block or dodge it. He only landed after following the green trail for more than half the distance to its resting place. The arrow missed his heart, and it was likely that he wouldn't be down long. There was no guarantee that he was vulnerable at that moment.

Leuna landed nearby and her knees buckled. She had been releasing a consistent stream of mana firing her arrows while keeping up her rapid movement. The amount of concentration she needed to do that took its toll. It looked like she was also grazed by shots I didn't see fired.

I helped her stay balanced and cast 'healing aura' on her like her sisters. When I did, the glow from the spell around her faded quickly. Her bow in her hand started glowing bright green instead. It morphed into a more rounded shape with a tube extruding from the front where she fired her arrows. It had evolved and she was getting stronger.

The healing spell on Sara already faded and the rest were soon to follow. She was my biggest worry, having been hit directly. A glancing blow from the same attack left her bleeding. This was far worse.

She was unconscious in her smaller stature There were a series of deep lacerations across her chest and her top was riddled with holes. The blood hadn't begun flowing yet. At least she was breathing.

Aside from her wounds, her ears became pointed and her hair seemed longer and pinkish. Even her eyes, which were slightly open, were big and gold compared to their normal brown. She had pushed herself beyond her limits. She was taking the form of her spirit animal, a faery.

I placed my hands over her. "**Regenerating discharge**." A current of electricity ran from my hands and spread across her body. I was watching for any sign of consciousness.

As I looked around, I could see that Sara wasn't the only one to transform. Through Ariel's hair, I could see small horns protruding and her eyes were morphing into slits. Signs of the ram. Leuna's ears became softly pointed and her stance shifted to make her seem bow-legged. Signs of the lion. Caroline's arms obtained a soft blue scaled pattern and her hair gained a bluish tinge. Signs of the mermaid. They were all pushed past their limits and so was I. I couldn't see my own changes, but I was sure they were similar to Sara's.

"What? Can't someone else?" The voice came from across the room. My head snapped in that direction to see Wrath sitting up with a hand to his ear. He pressed his hand against his chest and the golden poison spreading across his body dissipated with a green glow. He was already free of my 'harming aura'. "He just does whatever he wants. What about Glutton? She should be... Ok, how about Envy?" Whatever response came through his earpiece made him stand abruptly. "Alright, I'm on my way." He turned to us. "Ok, playtime's over. Time to put you down." He aimed his missile launcher.

Ariel stabbed the tip of her blade into the ground and shards of crystal grew around Wrath's feet.

They broke as he raised his foot.

Caroline unleashed a spell that caused rain to fall from the ceiling and shatter the ground top layer of the ground around Wrath.

He faced his palm upward to block it with a barrier. It quickly started cracking. He looked up at it and reinforced it with a thicker barrier.

I waved my axe over my head. "**Rain lightning**." Adding my lightning to the falling rain, they fell together and shattered the first barrier. Hopefully, it'd keep him occupied long enough for us to gather our bearings.

Leuna was charging another arrow. It was surrounded by a tightly condensed vortex of wind. She was trembling too much to aim properly. I sensed that she was having a hard time with the stress her new form and partial transformation put on her body. Charged arrows took considerably more mana than uncharged ones. Casting spells alongside it compounded the required output. She already broke her limits during the fight, but now, it looked like she was trying to push her new limits too.

Caroline took charge while I was occupied with Sara. "Wait 'till my spell's over and shoot it, it doesn't have to hit," she said. "Ariel, when she fires, do you think you can cast 'compound restriction' on your own? I have something up my sleeve."

"Sure, I'll take a moment to cast though." Ariel clasped her lance with both hands, and it began to glow a soft orange while still pointed into the ground.

"I don't need it to be complete, 'heavy rain' is almost up, and I can't have him moving before I cast my next spell, he's at the perfect range right now but we have one shot."

I said, "My spell should keep going for a bit longer so hopefully that keeps him pinned as well."

Sara's eyes opened, and she was able to stand with my help. Normally I'd protest moving with freshly healed wounds that severe, but the situation could turn at a moment's notice. She grew and I lent her my shoulder while we watched as Caroline's plan played out.

When the rain stopped, Wrath let his barrier dissipate. He was unconcerned with my lightning. He didn't see me as a threat.

At that moment, Leuna let loose her arrow. It shined bright as it whistled through the air, trailing a visible vacuum behind it as the air distorted to fill the space it left behind.

The arrow flew past Wrath's head but he didn't seem affected much, even as a secondary shockwave rippled the air around him. He only moved his head to make sure it missed.

"*Compound restriction.*" Ariel cast a spell and a multitude of crystals sprang from the ground in layers. The horns on her head grew longer and curled slightly with each layer added.

At the same time, Caroline was bursting to the seams with power. Her hair lengthened and turned a shimmering ocean blue while the scales on her arms spread to cover most of her body. Her ears flattened, taking a fin-like appearance. She was pushing herself harder than ever.

Her mouth moved, but no sound exited as the air around her and all of us by proxy attained a blue aura. What sound had carried was akin to the ocean- a soft murmur accompanied by a gentle rocking, as if we were in the arms of the sea. This was accompanied by the smell of saltwater.

All of it fell silent at once. No sound, motion, or smell. Nothing.

I almost thought I went deaf before the blue aura that surrounded us wasn't. It was sent hurling at Wrath and soon surrounded him. Next, it expanded to cover half the room and filled completely with water. It turned from clear blue to translucent black in less than a second.

The crystals keeping the man in place shattered instantly, leaving him floating in what was essentially an artificial abyss. All we could do now was watch and wait.

Caroline took a deep breath. "Attack spells won't make it through...." She seemed like she was on the edge of hyperventilating. "We should have... time..."

Wrath was on his feet, seemingly unaffected by the spell that was certainly meant to kill him. By now, the wound in his chest finally started bleeding. The blood began floating in front and behind him. He aimed his gun and tried to shoot. The small orbs stopped a few feet away from their origin and dissipated as if crushed by an enormous pressure. He tried again and when it didn't work, he inspected his gun and its shape changed to a new form. It now had a thin, square, elongated barrel and a trigger hidden inside a square stock. The gun split in two with one in each hand connected with what looked like a large power cord between them. He now had twin railguns. They were accompanied by a huge power spike that reverberated outward and shook the entire room. The mana field he generated thickened. I could feel a pressure building on my shoulders.

I pointed my axe at him. "*Electric field.*" A blanket of electricity spread around him. It lasted for barely a moment before dissipating under Caroline's spell. I was hoping it would do more.

His guns began glowing bright green through the barrels and he shot one directly forward. The resulting laser nearly punctured the outside of the enclosure. It didn't reach the outside, but it didn't need to. He teleported to the open space made by his shot and pushed his way out from there. While he aiming his next shot, he teleported again.

I couldn't follow his mana trail through the mana field. My mind filled with panic as we all scanned our surroundings, our senses sharpened to detect him.

Ariel was the first to move. She carved a line in the ground as she moved in front of Caroline. "*Upheaval-*"

Wrath appeared in front of her with a railgun raised above his head. In less than a blink of an eye, he slammed Ariel into the ground with the other. She didn't have time to finish her spell. Despite the force behind the strike, he fired at Caroline's head from point-blank range.

She hopped back in surprise and the resulting blast carried her out of sight.

Leuna drew back her bowstring and separated from the rest of us, gathering speed.

Wrath followed her motions and fired his other railgun.

She spiraled through the air and the ground not too soon after.

Next, he aimed each gun at me and Sara, respectively. "There goes my only real threat."

It all happened so fast that I couldn't react before I was staring down the barrel.

A blue light appeared where Wrath stood. It sent him backward through the air. He had his guns crossed in front of him like he was guarding from an attack.

Sticking out of the ground was what looked like a handsaw blade with a bright blue pattern etched into it. It was attached to a chain. It led up to the balcony where I heard someone shuffling around. I couldn't see who, as I didn't dare take my gaze off Wrath.

"Geist Kaizer, I see you're doing well." Acknowledging his assailant, Wrath put his guns to his sides.

"Don't patronize me, stand down." Geist's voice sounded labored despite the high amount of energy radiating from him.

"You were watching for how long and now you want me to stop? Or were you just resting because of that curse?"

Geist leaped down to where his blade was and picked it up. He assumed a stance. His navy blue suit was ruffled and torn, suggesting he had been fighting similarly to us.

"Very well, I won't hold back on a dying ma-"

At that moment, a blue streak flew by and dragged Wrath back into the spell Caroline cast. He was left suspended in the center.

"Friend... or foe...?" Caroline came staggering behind Geist, holding her chest with one scaled hand and drops of blood between her fingers. The other hand housed a newly transformed moon blade. The general shape was the same, but the blade was sectioned to look like a razor-sharp fin and the handle took a triangular shape with a silk-like ribbon wound around her hand trailing the end. The whole thing had a light and dark blue pattern reminiscent of the ocean.

"I was sent by Doc. He saved my life for the time being and I owe him... Even though I'm going to die soon." He sounded like a man at death's door, so we were inclined to believe him.

Ariel Jerked upward, freeing herself from the ground. She stood with a sigh of relief when she saw Wrath back inside the abyssal wall of water.

"Ariel, can you get Leuna?" I asked, staring dead-eyed at Wrath, still floating in the perpetual sea. I couldn't move away from the group, as uncertain as I was.

"I got her." Ariel placed her hand on the ground and Leuna came sliding across the floor on a slab of stone. Her face was grazed, but only on one spot as if she took the whole shot. She was still breathing but unconscious.

"*Pacific inferno*." I cast the spell and yellow flames sprang from the ground, enrapturing everyone nearby and closing their wounds. "*Rejuvenate*." This second spell mixed into the flames and gave everyone a second wind, helping them ignore their fatigue.

"So, you're Carona?" Despite my healing, Geist still seemed to toil in his condition. His fatigue wasn't receding.

"Yes, I am." I nodded.

"So, you're the queen of faeries, the storm faery herself, Titania?"

"I don't like that my reputation precedes me."

"I heard about you from Guile. You're the only person he ever spoke so highly of."

"Caroline, what's the deal with that spell?" I said.

"I call it 'black depths'. Inside that space is basically a super condensed ocean. It's supposed to be like the bottom of the sea, but the pressure won't come all at once. I couldn't figure out how to make it that way in time for us to come here, so instead, it's gradual. So, the longer he's in there, the more he hurts and the longer he has to fight the urge to hold his breath. He's bound right now, but I don't know how long that'll last. There's also this thing that makes it so attack spells can't pierce the border and I don't know how I did it."

"Well, you're in luck," said Geist. "He's the Sin with the least defense. The only problem is that his power only increases the angrier he is. The more he hurts, the stronger he is. Pain pisses him off. Thankfully, he doesn't have a celestial form. How long until your spell stops?"

"A few minutes." Caroline removed her hand from her chest once the bleeding stopped. The shimmer of blue scales could be seen across her skin.

"Well, we're going to have to be ready if he's not dead by then." He closed his eyes, and his weapon began to glow before taking a second form. It looked like a wood carving chainsaw with circular saw blades on the band. It lost the chain in place of a cloth-wrapped handle. His concentration broke, and he opened his eyes, panting before doing it again. The handle and blade shortened drastically. A squared archaic chain dangled from the end. Now his breathing was ragged and he was wobbling on his feet. He was still standing while the gray streaks in his dark hair seemed to increase in number.

Leuna soon woke up and after a brief explanation, we all listened as Geist explained how his particular magic worked. He could add to the potential force of anything, including magic. His magic traits included heightened matter manipulation and minor telepathy without needing to cast a spell. We each explained our powers to him and came up with a plan in case Wrath survived Caroline's attack. There was no way we could just escape if he came after us, and there was no way he would let us go at this point.

Time passed, and the ground rumbled a bit before the 'black depths' spell receded and the water covering half of the room seemingly melted into the stone, leaving Wrath on the ground. He was no longer bound but also wasn't moving.

Geist and Caroline moved toward him at once. They moved quickly yet cautiously.

When they did, Wrath sprang to life with a gun in one hand while swinging the other readily.

Geist reacted by throwing his chainsaw, which whirred to life as it flew at its target.

Dodging it, Wrath aimed Caroline, who closed the distance as quickly as possible where they clashed before he could fire a shot.

Geist followed his chain and engaged as well.

Despite the two-on-one, Wrath was more than holding off both of them.

Leuna was taking any shot she could at him while Sara and Ariel stayed with me, creating a defensive line in case we were targeted.

Wrath dodged none of the shots and seemed to lean into each hit while avoiding strikes from Caroline and Geist, the immediate threats.

Like Leuna, Caroline took a passive role while Geist tasked himself with creating an opening for a decisive strike.

I continued my role as a healer and kept their wounds in check. Even so, Caroline's chest wound started reopening as every time she got hit chipped away more and more at the healing that was already applied.

Wrath took the opportunity to push Geist away and aim both railguns at Caroline and shoot.

He didn't get the opportunity as Geist's chain wound around him and pinned his arms to his body. Geist made sure he couldn't move.

Seeing her opportunity, Caroline charged forth. "***Arctic spire.***" Her blade pierced Wrath through his chest and he was encased in a column of ice.

"***Heavenly tempest.***" Leuna's bow shattered as she fired a spell that launched her backward.

The arrow pierced clean through Wrath's head and continued into the ground, where it continued to who knows how far.

What felt like hours passed in that moment where nobody moved or even so much as breathed.

The ice shattered and Wrath hit the ground as unceremoniously as a body could. Lifeless and silent. The twin guns he held dissipated into nothingness while the high energy in the room seemed to subside instantaneously. His mana field was gone.

The chains holding him disappeared and Geist stumbled back before meeting the ground himself.

I was able to treat Caroline's wounds before any bleeding could start and went to Geist. His hair was now completely gray and his skin had grown pale. His body was visibly withering away and he was barely breathing but was still conscious.

I took his head under my hands. "What happened to you?"

He shuttered and spoke. "Cursed.... Healing doesn't work... Don't try. The world is at risk... and you might be the only healer on our side here..." His eyes gained a spark of life that the dead couldn't have. "I don't want to die..." The spark became blinding for a second and his weapon appeared floating above his corpse, unmoving and dull. It was no longer bright blue. It fell to his chest. As it landed, it transformed. The chain morphed into a second chainsaw with a wider, flatter edge with a lengthened handle that connected both ends. It resembled a chain in appearance. The light from both his weapon and eyes his eyes faded, seemingly all at once. Soon after, his eyes closed on their own as his weapon crumbled away. "Was I a good man? On second thought, don't answer that." Those last words didn't seem directed toward anyone present.

"Is he dead this time?" Caroline was looking down at Wrath. She was breathing heavily. "I had a vision a while ago that he wasn't dead when we killed him."

I walked over to her and pulled her away from the body, slowly. "He's dead. Nothing short of resurrection can bring him back to life."

42-Sloth and Envy

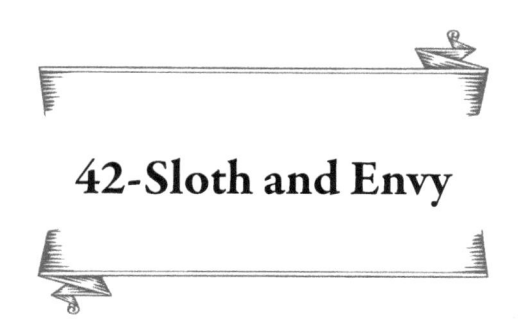

[Krow Hunt]

What time I had leading to the war was spent with a group called the Fireflies, an offshoot of the New-Hunters, a conglomerate guild, and the group that planted the bomb that went off at C.H.E.S.S. headquarters. They were using the top floor of the building I found them on as a base until the signal that called everyone to gather.

During my stay, I had gotten close to a few of them. One was Eric, the bookkeeper. He never fought but loved analyzing and trying to understand all things magic. He even helped me develop a few new spells. Having previously met Sophia, it wasn't hard to get close to her, Charls, and Phenom who made a trio of best friends.

The one I found myself closest to, however, was Rose. She was their leader and the one I spent the most time around. According to her, It was initially because she still had suspicion and reservations about who I said I was, and she wanted me as close as possible to make sure I didn't start any trouble.

Whenever Rose wasn't hiding outside my field of view, her presence would take over the room and everything seemed to have serious undertones as far as her group was concerned, regardless of the overall feel of the moment. She seemed like a well-respected leader, but despite having such a strong, outspoken personality, she seemed very timid whenever I shot her a glance. This dichotomy intrigued me, and I paid closer attention to her as well. I even tried to strike up conversations with her. Whenever I did, that timidness would fade as if she built a wall around herself just to communicate. That made it hard to find the softer parts of her personality she kept so well hidden.

One night, I managed to slip from her watchful gaze and onto the hotel roof, where I rested on my back, staring up at the stars. After a few minutes, I heard the roof door open and for the first time, Rose spoke to me first.

"Isn't it a little cold to be lying on the roof?" Her voice cut through the wind like a knife.

"As long as I got my cloak and hood, I'm fine." I flared my hood a bit with my hand.

She closed the door. "Is it enchanted or something?"

"Kinda. Minor magic resistance and such. Other than that, It's just comfortable."

"And what happens when you get sick?"

I smiled and said, "You'll take care of me, right?"

"In yer dreams."

"Luckily, I've been dreaming this whole time." My smile faded. "More like a nightmare."

"You said it."

"So, what are you doing out here, anyway?"

"Looking up at the stars."

"What stars? All I see is clouds."

"Yeah. It's a habit. One I can't seem to break. Care to join me?"

"No. I don't need you disappearing on me, and I'm only here to make sure *you* still are."

"Really? I didn't know you liked me that much. Don't you worry, I'm not going anywhere."

"But we'll never know that for sure, will we?"

"C'mon, I've seen the way you stare all narrow-eyed, and you even lean into it. How am I supposed to leave when you look at me like that?"

"I'm just watching you in case it turns out you're not who you say you are. Nothing romantic, I assure you."

I sat up and turned to look at her. "You're doing it right now."

She was leaning forward with her back against the roof door and peering at me with narrowed eyes. Upon noticing, she stood straight and widened her eyes a bit.

"You know, if you like me, just come out and say so, and who knows? I might like you, too. Never be afraid to tell someone how you feel... I know I'm not..." I trailed off at the end, realizing I might've said too much. Feeling a little too exposed by my own words, I laid back down and stared back up at the sky.

"Ok, I'll say it. I like you alright?"

Surprised, I said, "Wait, for real?"

"Yeah, an' I'd like you more if you stayed indoors where I kin keep an eye on ye."

"So, staying close enough to touch me isn't enough?"

She scoffed. "Who'd wanna touch you?"

"I couldn't answer that, but you sure did a lot of touching when we first met."

Threateningly, she said, "Oh, I'll do a lot more touching in a minute."

"Oh, so, you *do* like me?"

"I'm *shakin'* my fist at you."

I chuckled. "Well, I didn't think you'd be shaking anything else at me. You don't strike me as the fast and loose kind."

"Damn right."

"And that's why I like you."

"What?" Her confusion was hard to miss. "Did ye hit yer head or somethin'?"

"You seem like cool people. I feel like I can get along with you when you're not antagonistic."

"So, now, I'm antagonistic?"

"It's kinda hard not to be antagonistic against someone you don't like, right?"

She scoffed. "Yeah, sure. I don't like you." For some reason, this sounded like sarcasm.

"Maybe if you spend more time interacting with me instead of just watching me, you'd grow to like me a little."

She sighed. "You know what, sure. If it'll get you to shut up and go back inside, I'll stare up at the sky with you."

"Be my guest. I stretched my arm out toward her."

Surprisingly, she sat by my side with her arms wrapped around her knees and looked up at the sky with me. Whenever the wind died down, I could hear her breathing and I strained my ears to listen. At some point, everything went silent as my senses were tossed high in the air and I was looking down at the city from above. As I fell from nothingness, I scanned the clusters of lights until I spotted myself and Rose sitting on the roof. We looked like a peaceful couple enjoying a silent night.

"Huh, we look pretty good together." I could barely hear my voice as it sounded distant.

"What was that?" Rose's voice grounded me, and I was back within my own body.

"What?" Realizing she heard me, I tried to gather my thoughts. "I mean, we look like total opposites. I heard opposites attract, you know?"

"Wait, so, you really *are* hitting on me?"

"What, you thought I wasn't?" I held my hand out to her. "Give me a chance?"

"Hmm... Well, I could do worse than a mysterious wisecracking supposed Corpse Hunter who seems to have won over my crew."

"Is that a 'yes'?

"We'll see."

From that day on, it felt like Rose, and I were on much better terms. Regardless, she seemed to keep her distance and sheepishly watch me from the shadows. Since I never went anywhere other than the roof, neither did she, so we found ourselves alone often. When we did, we wouldn't talk or anything, just enjoy each other's company. Instead of using a spell to keep watch over me, she'd enter whatever room I was in and just sit with me. It was as if we were mysterious strangers forging a bond of nothingness.

One night, the clouds cleared up and I raced to the roof to watch the stars twinkle in the sky. Soon enough, Rose joined me as I heard the roof door open and close again.

"Where do you think you're going!-" She paused and gave a surprised giggle. "The stars? I guess they are out tonight."

"Yeah," I said. "It's a bad habit, like I said. Regardless, I want to watch them with you."

"Are you really serious about this?" I could hear her shuffling on her feet.

"About what?"

"Me giving you a chance."

"Why wouldn't I be?"

After a long silence, she said, "So, you really weren't joking?" She was now speaking with a softer tone compared to her normal brash one.

"I mean, I could joke about it if you want. It's not like you're really considering it, right?"

"No, It's uh..." We both remained silent for a moment.

"Hey," I said, sitting up and allowing my gaze to fall upon the horizon, where the city lights and the starry sky converged.

"-What?" Despite a moment's delay, her response was sudden.

"Have you ever looked up at the night sky and had, like, a shift of perspective where you can see what it's like to fall from such a great height in such a dark abyss lit only by the stars above and the city lights below?"

"No... You have?" She took a few hesitant steps while talking.

"All the time. I've been up there myself, but what I'm talking about is different. I read a book once where the stars in the sky were each a representation of a person and the stronger a person's life force, the brighter the star. In that vein, I feel like me and my star switched places, you know?" I reached up toward the sky and then moved my hand to the ground.

"I don't quite get it, but I understand where you're coming from... So, what's this book called?"

"I think it was something like 'Twi-Life' or something."

"Huh, isn't there a spell with a similar name?" she said, with a vague sense of wonder.

"I think there's a spell with a similar name to everything." I paused. "If not just ripped from it. Do you know what the spell's called?"

"No, it's one of those spells no one ever talks about. The kind that's only learned spontaneously, you know?"

I cast 'phoenix feather' and the long, red feather-shaped flame appeared between my fingertips as I stared into it. "Magic by birthright?"

"Likely. It was in an old book I retrieved on a job once. I don't remember much about it because it was so long ago."

My eyes darted to her for less than a second then back to the sky again and the feather in my hand vanished. "So, you were an adventurer as a kid? Were you in a guild?"

"Not really. I grew up poor, so I used to do odd jobs with my sister to get by."

"Same here, except I had a broth... Wait, I still have a..." Out of nowhere, a pain shot through my temple. Likely spurred on by the realization of memories long forgotten, the pain was lesser than what I experienced with Rachel, but not by much. Unlike before, this one was sudden. Before I knew it, I was lying down with both hands on my head.

"You okay?" Rose came and crouched by my side.

Through clenched teeth, I said, "Yeah, I just realized I had a brother this whole time."

"Realization or not, you don't look okay." She reached out a hand. "Here, let me help you up." I took her hand, and she helped me to my feet. "What's that about, anyway?" She pointed at the crest that appeared on my forehead.

I took a deep breath. "It's the curse. I think these memories triggered it."

"Are you, like, going to die or something?" She pulled her hand back as if afraid to touch me.

"Not this time, it's not as bad as before." I rubbed my forehead.

"Oh, do you need help or anything?" She seemed hesitant to reach for me again. "Wait, what do you mean 'this time'?"

"No, I just need to rest... I think." I went back in and laid down on a bed, eventually falling asleep.

Since then, Rose seemed to watch me with a more worrisome expression.

The day everything shook, I was asleep on the staircase. I was on my way to the roof the night before when I was ambushed by Phenom and Eric trying out a new sleep spell. I humored them and closed my eyes when I felt only slightly drowsy after about five minutes. As soon as I did, I awoke to Rose violently shaking me and screaming at the top of her lungs at both of them and me. Behind her, the stairs were packed with Fireflies waiting for orders.

"What's going on? Did I die again? Or was it someone else this time?" I spoke with clarity and I wasn't groggy despite just waking up.

"No, I've been trying to wake you up for the last ten minutes. It's started."

"What's started-" I got a bad feeling in my gut and stood. I reached into my pocket and looked at my phone. All the dots that represented Ariel, Leuna, Caroline, and Sara were moving toward the C.H.E.S.S. base. "**Burning step.**" With flames at my feet, I took off up the stairs, out the door, and off the roof at full speed.

"What're you doing? You're too conspicuous." Rose was close behind me.

"Doesn't matter. I got work to do."

"I've seen Corpse Hunters. This isn't how they work. It's like yer going in guns blazing."

I didn't respond. Instead, I made it to the shore and encountered Noah before entering the same way I got there, at full speed. The air above the battlefield was riddled with traps that sprung one by one. The traps ranged from illusions and capture spells to summoned creatures and time spells. Even people came up to intercept me alongside already airborne soldiers. I busted through all of them straight over the front gate and toward the city district. Rose was tailing me, but I lost her along the way.

I looked at my phone again and saw all the markers that were moving before at a crawl nearby and likely deep within the base already. Assuming what Rose's group told me was true, I'd find a direct route to the center of the base in one of the buildings. It looked like a school building, but it could've been anything.

I sensed a lot of mana inside the building but it was expected. There was also a buzz in the air like electricity. I found my way to the front door and opened it. Walking in, the door closed on its own behind me. I continued into the spacious lobby opposite a shady figure on the far side. Before I could get any detail of their appearance, a bright blue light flashed before my eyes. The light was all-encompassing as if it was coming from everywhere at once.

I momentarily lost my sense of time and place. I couldn't even tell if my limbs were still attached. Despite the obvious danger, I was at peace. It was as if there was nothing to fear and none of my problems ever existed. I was comfortable. That was when I could feel- just barely- three tactile points on the right side of my chin. A fourth appeared on the left side shortly after. There was no sense of danger or intent. I wasn't sure what exactly was going on, and I wasn't sure I could react fast enough to avoid whatever could happen in a flash of light.

My instincts kicked in and my left arm flung upward, hitting someone else's arm, and breaking the contact their fingers had with my face. Had I acted any later, I'd be facing the door without turning around.

"You're fast," I said, as the flash faded and the person from across the room was gone.

Not even a second after the words left my mouth, something struck my right side and carried me half the distance to the wall on the left before I hit the ground.

Landing partially on my feet, I stood to another strike, which I jumped back to dodge. Another blue light flashed, but this time, I could see the faint edge of a blade through the light.

It wasn't too soon after that I felt a pressure along my lower back. The sudden feeling made me arch my back and with the motion happening so quickly, it made my feet leave the ground resulting in a standing backflip.

I didn't have a second to breathe. A second hadn't even passed yet. I was still blinking from when the first burst of light touched my retinas. As the motions continued, I followed along by pure instinct.

While flying into a wall from another impact, I saw him traveling far ahead of the electricity following him. His entire body was surrounded by a blue glow and his short hair was spiked back. There were three straight swords of different types following closely at his sides and one in his hand. Based on his movements, he just hit me with the blunt edge of his blade and followed up with the front edge.

Finally summoning my sword, I blocked a strike to my side and was carried diagonally up the wall where I felt something give. Jerking my head to the opposite side, I narrowly avoided decapitation as my blade broke in two. The following kick sent me to the middle of the room with a deafening *thump*.

I tried to evolve my weapon to its third form. I settled on the twin-blade second form as three blades came spiraling in my direction. I rolled to avoid them.

A fourth blade came quickly in the hand of the person who sent them.

I just barely parried the sword. It would've pierced my heart, causing it to enter the ground instead but shattering my fire blade in the process.

I kicked both of my feet up to make contact, but all I hit was air while the blade I just avoided began moving again.

I dodged it as the remaining wind blade I used to block lasted just long enough to use as a springboard and launch myself across the floor. In the same motion, I used the momentum to kip up and evolve my sword into its lengthened third form.

As soon as I was back on my feet, I etched a circle around me with my blade.

I was unable to cast anything as another blue flash brought two blades scissoring toward my throat. I ducked and swiped my own blade upward at the same time.

Knocking both of the scissoring blades upward, I cast 'dragon's ascent'. The spell launched me skyward with green translucent wings. Draconic feathers and scales fell around me as I rose.

He followed me upward, still ahead of the lightning he produced.

I cast 'angel's descent'. The translucent green scales turned to bright crimson feathers and the emerald wings were replaced with golden ones as I spiraled back downward. The blaze was so hot that it seemed to even burn the air as ashes began to form around me.

He was pushed back down and landed on his feet. In one more flash of light, he approached me.

Since I could keep track of his movements now, I swiped my sword at him.

He knocked my blade to the side with his as he approached.

I responded by taking a full turn and swiping back at him, using my extended range to my advantage.

He watched me as if I was moving in slow motion and struck as my movement came to rest.

I watched as a saber bathed in blue light charged toward my chest with the same speed and precision I'd seen since the start. Arcs of lightning failed to keep up with it as it traveled closer to its destination.

My hand reacted again. This time, I was in complete control. I struck his blade to the side with the back of my fist and stepped closer.

Seeing this, he tried to back off.

I cast 'reach' and grabbed him with the red talon.

There was a different kind of flash this time. I sensed him arc through the air like a stream of energy. He teleported.

I reached out and cast 'fire shot' to make sure the attack reached him in time. A condensed ball of flames jettisoned from my palm in the direction he was teleporting.

The man appeared and cut through my spell as if he already knew it'd be there. In the process, he dashed from the right to the left side of the room, too fast for me to hit with a projectile.

"That's enough." He finally spoke from near the only wall scarred by collision. "You can go."

"What?" I was visibly confused.

"This fight is over. I was tasked with either killing or capturing anyone who enters here- especially you- but you kept up with my speed. There's nothing else I can do. Your name's Krow, right?"

I tightened my poise, ready in case he decided to strike again. "That's right."

"That means your real name's Jasen...." He paused for a reaction. "Nothing, huh? Well, I tried." He pointed to the flat wall opposite the entrance. "There's a hidden door over there, just heat up the wall with magic and it'll disappear to let you through."

I wasn't sure if he was telling the truth, so I sent a fireball. Nothing happened.

"Obviously, that wouldn't work. You have to touch the wall. Look- I'll just stay over here, and you can just go."

I dashed to the wall with fire at my fingertips and as soon as I made contact, it was gone and a staircase leading down appeared. I followed it with no hesitation.

The stairs were a blur under my feet as I descended the seemingly endless staircase. Looking at my phone, I found it had a short. I didn't have enough time to gauge the strength of my opponent, but it would take nothing less than a direct lightning bolt to cause such damage. I slipped it back into my pocket and continued until I reached a blue landing with a heavy steel door that led to another large room. This room looked more mechanical with steel floors and walls. Gears the size of cars sat stationary high overhead and sparsely around the walls.

With my phone fried, I took to sensing my surroundings; something I was never very good at. With my senses heightened from combat, I was more adept at it now than ever. Far behind me was the man I just fought. He stayed up top like he said. Farther to the right was a mix of familiar and unfamiliar energies clashing, and in the same direction was someone closing distance toward me rapidly. There was also a dense ball of energy hiding far below that I could just barely sense.

I watched as a door to the right side of the room slammed open and a man in a ragged gray suit covered in dots of blood with scars adorning his face and a fresh cut across his arm. He wore a broad smile and a look of glee.

"You're Jasen? You really are young. What magic do you use for that? No, a better question is- how did you get past Art?" The man's words came at lightning speed, but they were still paced and coherent. "No, don't tell me. He just let you pass."

"Yeah, kinda." I shrugged.

He nodded as if my answer was predicted. "That's just like Sloth. He never puts up a fight. But I'm not like him. I'm Oliver, the Sin of Envy, and I want what you have."

"Youth?" I guessed.

"Power. Whatever you used to kill the Shadow Master, mostly." He sounded more serious than I was willing to bet.

"That's ridiculous." I blinked, and a moon blade backed by a dull blue glow was soaring toward my face. I parried it with a wave of my sword, and it flew behind me, only to return as a spinning blade. Sensing the danger, I side-stepped it.

"We'll see if that's ridiculous or not." He caught the rotating blade by the inner edge, and it began spinning around his arm before he rushed toward me.

As he did so, I stabbed my blade into the ground between my feet and cast 'fire tornado'. I hopped into a handstand atop my weapon, masked by the flaming whirlwind.

He crashed into it blade first, and the fire and wind parted as if he cut all sides at once. His blade clashed with mine and I took the opportunity to flip forward and land a kick to the back of his head. Doing so forced him into the hilt of my sword before the blade snapped and fell to the ground.

All forms of my sword were broken now, but I was strangely comfortable with the situation. It was as if this was what I wanted. Aside from magic, I was unarmed.

The kick I gave seemed to daze him, so I took a deep breath and cast 'Fierce roar'. A primal sound filled the room and it made him jump but seemed to be otherwise ineffective.

He turned and struck at me with a curved broad sword.

The speed he was moving was far too slow. I watched his blade pass by as I dodged. As soon as it was clear of me, I cast 'infernal rush', coating my fists in dense flames and striking him repeatedly. With every blow, the flames died out and reignited even stronger. The stronger the flame, the stronger the strike.

He flew back, dotted with flaring crimson as he landed squarely on his back. As he went, he knocked into the remnants of my blade still sticking out of the ground. It flipped out and landed on his chest.

As I watched the blade fly, my chest began to burn. It wasn't long before I realized the source was my grimoire. It was glowing with deep red flames through my cloak. My hand had taken the position to snap my fingers and I was inclined to do so as if by instinct. My fingers slid past each other and the resulting sound triggered something.

A series of explosions went off at once. Many small explosions took place on the spot where my sword broke. Two much larger explosions took place where my hilt lay and where the blade sat on top of Oliver. The room lit up from the blasts and shook as the metal floors vibrated violently.

Once everything calmed down, my sword was completely gone and Oliver was unmoving with deep wounds scorched across his now shirtless chest.

I looked at my hands and re-summoned my sword. A soft red glow in the shape of a sword appeared, hovering over my open palms, slowly solidifying, and refining in shape before falling into my hands. There was something different about it, but I couldn't put my finger on it.

Having never broken my sword before, I wasn't sure how long it'd take to regenerate one. The general consensus was between a week and five years, with a couple of months being average. Being able to regenerate it in moments was more than lucky, as there was only so much my fists could do against bladed weapons.

Before I could waste any more time, I exited the room into a maze of halls and doors. I couldn't tell which way led where I was going, so I followed the mass of energy deeper in. Nearly getting lost multiple times to dead-ends and closed passageways, I finally found a straight path and followed it. On the way, I spotted Doc traveling quickly with someone at his side.

I went fast yet silent behind them and said, "Hello there."

The girl responded with a gunshot over her shoulder. It was a pristine, white gun nearly the size of her forearm with a magic shot to match. I watched the orb race past as I dodged it, nearly daring to catch it as I reached out a hand and pulled back.

"Took you long enough, Krow," said Doc, never breaking stride.

"Yeah, I got side-tracked. There was this guy who was going at like, faster than lightning and this other dood who was like 'power!' but then I beat him with a spell I remembered when my sword broke."

"So, one guy let you go, and the other one underestimated you?"

"Pretty much. Oh, and I remembered I had a brother."

"So, you're starting to remember now?"

"That was before I came back here." We went for a bit until I remembered a question I forgot to ask. "Oh yeah, What's up with the girl?"

"I'm here on behalf of my prince," said the girl.

"Oh, so you're a Rolanite? Cool."

We continued onward into the base.

43-Greed

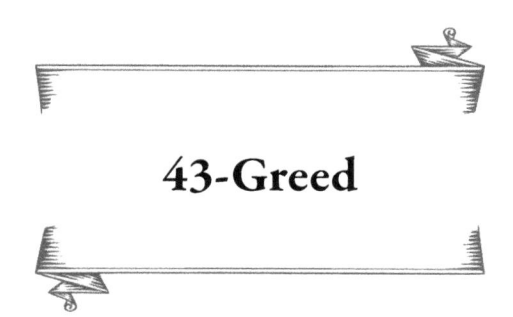

[Nero Cursley]

Despite the gravity of the situation, my goal didn't change. I had to get in, get Mary, and get out. I didn't want to be in the base for any longer than I had to. Carrie and Leon were with me in the air over the battlefield. I surrounded us in an orb of sound, Carrie used an invisibility spell on us and Leon levitated us at rapid speeds. We followed a trail of tripped traps left behind by someone else and landed with little trouble.

The quickest way to the prison from the outside would be from the catacombs below, but seeing how prepared they were for this war, it'd likely be heavily guarded. We decided to enter through an office building near the school. I didn't know what the building looked like from overhead, so we landed and walked.

On the way, we spotted a woman dragging someone up the school steps. I recognized who was being dragged by her bright orange hair held tight in a fisted grip and yellow uniform. A woman with a similar hair color in braids was dragging Vinessa up the school steps. They were both bloody, but only Vinessa seemed to be injured. I couldn't tell what injuries she had, but she didn't seem well.

"Hold up," I said, running to the base of the stairs. "Let her go."

The woman turned and said, "Vi, who's that?"

"Nero..." Vinessa's voice was hoarse.

"Oh, you're Nero? I heard yer mum's been looking for you." She waved me away. "Beat it, kid, it's dangerous out here."

Carrie spoke up from behind me. "Rose, what's going on?"

"Oh, you two. Didn't my people fill you guys in?"

"No," said Leon. "We had our own plans and I guess we got a little tunnel visioned."

"Well, I followed somebody here, but I had to stop and get something. Now, I'm going to go stop him from getting himself killed if he didn't already." Rose continued walking up the steps dragging Vinessa along helplessly.

I spoke up again. "Can you at least release that girl? I know this is war, but she's not an enemy. I know her, she's from my team and she just likes to help people." I wasn't sure of Vinessa's condition, but I couldn't act. Instead, I used reason.

"I think I know my sister better than you do." The captor violently yanked the captee's head upward, and Vinessa audibly moaned. The amount of joy she seemed to take from such a barbaric action disturbed me. I never thought she had that kind of side to her.

I winced at the display. Too many sounds I didn't want to hear emanated from my teammate. I swallowed hard.

Leon spoke. "We know where Mary Black is, can you help us get her?"

Rose shrugged. "You can follow me if you want. We are on the same side, after all." She reached the top of the stairs. "The more, the merrier." She opened the door and entered with the rest of us following behind.

The lobby inside the school felt unusually energetic despite being uncharacteristically empty. The front desk was gone and the open halls leading into the school were replaced with walls that looked as if they were always there. The gray marble floors and blue walls were scuffed and scarred from spell and blade alike, as well as what looked like a series of small explosions that took place in various spots. leaning on the left wall was someone I was surprised to see.

Prof. Haddock, a field strategy teacher, stood out of his usual vest and tie and instead wore an electric blue gloved uniform. The blue hair clip usually seen in his hair was gone and his straight brown hair was spiked mostly upward with a blue hue.

"Prof. Haddock?" I said, both confused and surprised.

"That isn't my name, never was." He responded as if he was expecting this kind of reaction. "My name is Art, and I'm the Sin of Sloth. What brings all of you here?" His demeanor was laid back and devoid of hostile intent. If anything, he seemed more like he wanted to help.

"I'm looking for a guy. Tall, long black hair, black cloak. You seen him?" asked Rose.

"He burned that hole in the wall and went down to the astral gate." He pointed at what I thought was just a large scorch mark in the wall that was instead a burn-shaped hole of charred and melted stone.

"Thanks." Rose walked through the hole and down the steps.

I was hesitant to follow.

"So, what are you here for?" asked the Prof, noticing my reluctance.

"I'm looking for the prison," I said, stopping in my tracks to answer.

"Quickest route is two buildings that way and down to the basement." He pointed toward the wall behind him. "From there, you should know the way."

"Thanks." I took him at his word and rushed out of the school to a glass building. The doors were blocked by debris from the inside. It took force to get in but the way down was unobstructed.

As we traveled deeper, I picked up on sounds from different sources with new sounds reaching my ears at almost every other floor. The upper levels of the underground part of the base consisted mostly of living quarters and recreational facilities. The prison was below that. The sounds came from between those levels and lower. Most of them sounded like battling but the two closest were of explosions and quickly approaching footsteps. As they got closer, I recognized a familiar breathing pattern.

I sped up. "Mary's being chased and they're coming this way."

"How can you tell?" Carrie kept pace with Leon close behind.

"I can hear it. There's a lot going on down here." I nearly jumped down the next stairway we met, down two floors, and through the door.

There was an icy chill and rushing winds coming from down the hall. As we followed it, an explosion kicked off from around a corner and I saw Mary running for her life from the same direction. Despite hosting a slight limp, she sprinted with enthusiasm away from a wave of cold that followed closely after her.

She passed by me, and I turned to run as well, putting me at the back of the group as everyone else did the same. We went at full speed up the staircase we just entered, down a series of halls, and up another staircase to the building where we initially came.

Even if we were going to stay and fight, a hallway wasn't the place to do it and the entire way was backed with an encroaching cold, followed by aggressive explosions and a frightening energy encroaching from a distance.

As soon as we were out in the open, we all jumped into the air, summoned our weapons, and flew east toward the nearby island and away from the battlefield. We needed to gain our bearings before joining whatever fight was going on there. We all looked at each other in readiness. It felt like whatever was chasing Mary was going to catch up soon. Even so, we kept flying as far as we could.

Barely a moment after we took flight, the ground froze over, and a woman shot out of the building, shattering all the windows in the process. Close behind her was a man followed by more destruction as the building collapsed and shook the rest of the foundation. The woman wore a cracked white fox mask with a white C.H.E.S.S. uniform that looked more like a business suit under a long white coat. The man sported a wild head of golden hair and clothes so disheveled that I couldn't tell what it originally was aside from the metal shoes on his feet.

It seemed like they were on the same side until the woman jumped up toward us with a morning star in hand. When she did, the man caught her leg and slammed her into the ground, fracturing the pavement.

Taking it as a sign to escape, we all continued on our way. When I felt we were far enough away, I turned my eyes toward our destination, the nearby island. Our escape seemed assured until the alarming energy from before raced toward us. Turning back, I saw the woman in white accelerating toward us while the man was encased in ice that rooted him in place.

"**Burn**." Leon raised his hand and the woman burst into flames.

It was promptly extinguished by a 'chill wind' that made me catch my breath as it raced up my body. The woman nullified the spell with one of her own.

"**Blaze**." This time, the fire surrounded her in a ball of intense heat that overpowered the cold. "You guys go, I'll take her on." Leon seemed unaware that we were all prepared to stay and fight.

"**Bead lightning**." Carrie's spell surrounded the flaming ball with small orbs of yellow electricity that rotated around it while closing in.

"**Atmospheric shockwave**." Swiping my blade, I sent a literal shockwave of sound. I cast my spell at the same time as the orbs made contact and the resulting explosion created a smoke screen from the elements colliding.

"Now go!" Leon summoned fireballs under his feet and used them to hover while brandishing his sword.

"Doofus," said Carrie. "Do we look like we're leaving you?"

The smoke didn't linger long as it crystallized and fell like snow followed closely by an ice ball that emerged from the dissipating cloud. It grew exponentially before being pierced by a spear thrown by Mary. it didn't stop but it slowed down enough to dodge. In doing so, it forced us to split in separate directions.

As the ice ball flew by, I could hear blades clashing from the other side of it and saw Leon falling down from that side, followed by a trail of ice behind him. He was followed by Carrie, who spiraled downward at an angle and collided with him on the way down. By this point, I realized what was happening and acted.

Evolving my weapon to its second form, I cast 'skyfall' on the ice ball and the surrounding area. The ice stopped moving forward, fell straight down, and crashed into the ground, but there was no one to be seen nearby aside from Mary who dodged in a similar direction to me. Even the terrifying energy faded a bit.

Leon and Carrie were already on their feet and looking to make their way back up to meet us. The only problem was the shifting debris from the ice ball revealing the woman in white, surrounded by a white bubble that quickly expanded around the entire area followed by an instant drop in temperature. The air froze and snow began falling.

I said, "Trust shot," before casting 'blast off' and diving toward the woman with my sword at the ready and trusting that Mary would follow my plan. My surroundings only got colder while rapidly nearing my target. I nearly lost feeling in my hands before my sword clashed with the morning star held by the masked woman as she lifted it to block my strike.

The instant we collided, my entire body became encased in ice before being slammed into the ground by a strike to my temple. The impact broke the ice which ripped the flesh across my body.

Since the ice broke, I could stand, so I shot back up to my feet as fast as I could, and in doing so, I could see a white spear sticking out of the masked woman's shoulder. She caught it in with her other hand, but it still found its mark in a spot of red amongst the white.

The temperature spiked as Leon created a ball of fire the size of a truck over his head nearby.

The masked woman freed the spear from her shoulder and dropped it before disappearing in a flurry of snow. Knowing where she was going, I gave a sharp whistle and Mary switched places with the spear on the ground before the woman appeared behind a now-falling spear that dissipated soon after.

"*Echo void.*" I cast a bubble of highly destructive sound around the masked woman. She tried to teleport out of it, only to cause a small swirl of snow and nothing else as she covered the sides of her head with her hands. This was proof enough that the spell took effect on her.

Leon threw the flaming ball he held ready over his head at the masked woman, now stuck in place. I watched as she was engulfed by the flames and began falling to the ground.

We all went back to the air and flew around the ball. Instead of going to the island, we headed to the battlefield. There was a quick consensus to the fact that the woman was holding back. Not to mention the dangerous man. He freed himself of the ice before anyone noticed and was watching from the side. Heading into the battlefield was our best chance of fighting one or both on equal terms if they weren't slowed down by the conflict.

We were soon flying over the front gates at top speed. Mary would've stopped in her tracks had I not grabbed her hand when she began slowing down. "What's going on out here?" She seemed frightened.

Both sides were fighting multi-colored shadow creatures. They were in disarray as the corpse shadow-slimes multiplied and converged on people. It looked like a losing fight.

"Corpse shadows," I said. "Noah drew them out so they wouldn't be a late surprise. He's straight in the middle of this mess." I pointed far ahead to the center of the battlefield.

"If that's the case, we need to get to him as quickly as possible." Mary sped up and stayed ahead the rest of the way.

44-Pride

[Solo]

The creature stood like it always has. Its oversized glassy eyes which seemed to each cover a quarter of its head focused on me and the space around me. The tassels dangling from where its neck would be completely covered its limbs to make it look like an odd wind chime. "What is it that you want to know?"

"What are you?" I levitated myself to meet the creature eye-to-eye.

It spoke with a cryptic garble of sounds I somehow understood. "I am, as you see, a part of you." It looked over to the pink gate inscribed with an eye and a five-point star in the center surrounded by pink chains and a disproportionately large lock.

"That's not what I meant. What are you?"

"You call my name when you summon me yet, you know not the answer?"

"Stop with the nonsense! We've been through this before, **Mind Breaker**. Just because I can pronounce your name doesn't mean I know it. Your name and what you are, are two completely different things. I need to know what you are so I can specialize my spells to better fit my magic. I still can't even control my own magic traits well."

"And I've told you many times before. My name and what I am are one. The same as you, Solo."

"As long as you're still kicking around here, I can't be alone even if I want to." As soon as I said that, both the creature and the gate disappeared.

I opened my eyes to the purple orb created by Graven, and I could hear the wind whipping by outside as we raced through the air toward the base in the distance.

"You're sweating, are you okay?" Guile was standing next to me while I was sitting and meditating.

"I'm fine. How long 'till we get there?" I stood.

"A few seconds," said Graven.

We were soon over the base and above an empty library. Most recreational buildings above ground were empty, and the library was no exception. All the books that would have been held there were held in underground libraries scattered throughout the base.

We were lowered to the entrance, and the bubble popped. Guile went a few buildings over and teleported without a trace. His job was to get to a command center inside the base and rally the resistance there. We'd make our way directly to the astral gate and try to stop the Shadow Master's resurrection.

Graven cloaked himself in invisibility and we walked in together. Hopefully, I'd seem alone. The library was emptier than I thought it was. I thought there would be a member of the Seven Sins guarding the entrance. Instead, there was an open hatch leading down. I approached it and checked for traps. None. Next, I took a step down and was met with a feeling of a powerful energy rapidly approaching from down below. I backed off and stood behind one of the few pillars as a man carrying a body bag stepped out of the hatch.

"He was right, that is the fastest way to get around," said the man, grabbing the doors to close the hatch. "You know what? I'll leave it open. That way, it's a challenge." He released the handles, and they landed back open with a thump. "I'm Nail, the Sin of Pride. Now, come at me!" He shouted into space. "I know you're there. There's two of you and one of you is..." I heard a heavy impact on the other side of the pillar on my back. "Right over there."

I stepped from my hiding place and faced the man. "I want to talk."

"That's a first," said Nail, squatting down with his arms resting on his knees with the body bag lying behind him. "So, what are we talking about?"

"Well, that was easier than I thought." I leaned back on the pillar under the molten spear that ran through it high above my head.

"You'd be surprised how hospitable we are. Well, except for Greed."

"I want to know why you're a Sin. How'd you end up in such a messed-up situation?" An honest question, but not one I thought would be answered.

"You want to know my life's story, do you?" He smiled.

"I want to know how you rationalize doing something that's so obviously wrong."

"I don't. But I used to. I once thought I was a hero, killing the root of all evil. It was all pure romanticism until I was shown the nature of my often-bloody missions. Now, I've embraced this path of self-destruction: Being a villain. It's even fun sometimes."

"So, you're just having fun while most of us are still being tricked into killing innocent people?"

"That's not all. It seems nobody told you yet. Or you didn't believe them. Any single entity caught disobeying orders or planning a coup was liable to be hunted down and dispatched. If they survived, they'd be branded a corpse hunter and placed at the top of the most wanted list. Be it a rank one copper or even a Sin."

I looked down at my hands. "That explains everything. C.H.E.S.S. was going to fall eventually. We're just helping it along."

"That sounds reasonable, but remember what I said about being caught?" He picked the body bag back up. "You're a member of Guile's team, right?" He unzipped the bag that he held up and a familiar body came into view.

"Lucia!" My mind raced toward so many outcomes that my body wouldn't move until I decided on an action.

"That's right. Who'd have thought Boss's own daughter was part of a resistance?" She wobbled as he stood her up next to him by the back of her neck, her blank stare landing on nothing. "I was supposed to keep her safe, but rules are rules."

I tried to make a mad dash or teleport or both to get between them and force him away. What happened, however, was the opposite of what I wanted.

As soon as I could gather enough energy to do anything, Nail roared, "***Don't move!***" and at that moment, despite the all-encompassing urge to move even a finger, cast a spell, something, anything, I was held in place by something more primordial than any urge. Fear.

I stood, frozen by the effect of his auditory spell. My limbs just twitched as I ignored my nerves screaming at me to run away.

Nail summoned a molten sword from thin air and ran his blade through Lucia's chest from behind.

She dropped to the ground with a hard thump and a clack from both her body and the blade colliding against the hardwood, a shallow puddle bubbling underneath her from the heat of the molten glass.

"NO!" I broke out of my trance and tried to rush to her side.

Nail pushed me back with a simple spell and a flick of a wrist.

"Keep your pants on, she's not dead yet. I *was* ordered to keep her safe. She just won't be walking anytime soon. Can't have her helping with any silly resistance. Who am I kidding? I don't really care."

I summoned my sword in its third form, Shatter.

A blade appeared beside Nail and came flying in my direction.

I cleaved the molten spear with precision and it split in two, hitting the floor.

My floating blades disappeared from sight, but I could feel them under my control.

Nail began blocking the blades that were circling and striking at him too fast for even me to see at a distance. Some he didn't block missed completely as he moved. Others seemed to be diverted by his aura alone. None of it mattered much as long as he stayed distracted while the blade etched a circle under his feet.

"***Banish.***" As soon as the circle was done, I cast a spell, and Nail was gone in a pink flash.

I made it to Lucia's side in a hurry. This was the second time I cursed my lack of recovery spells. I was always so preoccupied with chasing down my enemy in the name of revenge that I never thought of defending what I still held dear. My regret was mounting.

It was a relatively simple wound but I couldn't heal more than bruises and cuts myself. Nothing I could do would help so I decided to take her and find someone who could.

Reaching to my ear, I was going to turn to the emergency channel when I heard a voice come through. "Solo, are you there? I don't hear anything on my end. What happened?" It was Graven. I was unsure of when he began listening in, but his timing was perfect.

"This is an emergency. I've got someone impaled and unconscious. The wound is mostly cauterized, and she's breathing but there's still blood and I don't think she'll make it if I leave her." I picked up Lucia in my arms and stared down at the spot where Nail disappeared to make sure the spell was still holding.

"Don't panic. This is a medical emergency, correct?"

"Yes, I can't stress this enough. She may never be able to walk."

"This may be hard to hear, but if it's non-life threatening, find a safe place to put her and meet the rest of us at the Astral Gate."

"No, I can't leave her." My arms were shaking as I looked down the open staircase.

"Ok, then make your way down with her if you can, I'm on my way there with probably the best healer I've ever met. She can help, but you'll have to be fast."

"I'll try the emergency channel first." I tried to turn the dial, then I realized there wasn't one. Everyone else was either too busy to respond or out of range. "Never mind, I'm on my way." I jumped down the stairs. "**Lightspeed, fullsend**." With a combination of the two spells and the tremendous power given by my fourth form, I traversed blindingly fast into the depths of the base.

The opening at the bottom of the steps barely came into view when I lost my balance and spiraled uncontrollably down to the landing and into the doorframe. The cause was a sharp pain greater than almost anything I ever experienced finding its place in my chest. It was as if someone took the sun and ran me through with it. I put my hand to my chest and looked at the result. There was no blood or injury of any kind, only pain of an unidentified origin.

It took me a second to realize that I dropped Lucia, and when I did, I looked around wildly for her. She was sprawled out in the room leading from the staircase. Behind her stood high stacks of sheet metal and gear-shaped scrap. She was facing me when her eyelids began twitching. I crawled toward her and the closer I got, the stronger the phantom pain became.

I came close enough to touch her when her expression changed from a cold, blank stare to one of shock as she writhed in agony with tears flying down her face. Her movements began slowly but quickly intensified as the paralysis subsided.

I made it to her with the ever-increasing pain only serving to slow me down. Placing my hand under her head and my head on her chest, I listened to her rapid heartbeat and felt the warmth of her skin. I tried to stand and lift her again, but as soon as I budged her an inch, the pain intensified, and I fell back to the ground.

I was feeling her pain. And I couldn't turn it off.

"*Solo...?*" Her mouth didn't move, but as I looked into her eyes, I realized she could see me. She looked me dead in the eye and said, "Solo... I... Sorry... Didn't... Listen... Cold..."

"Don't talk, just think. I can hear you," I said quickly, with the mounting pain stifling my speech.

"*Hurts so much. Can't think straight.*" Her mind was a jumble of words and phrases floating around randomly with a few comprehensible sentences in between. Through her eyes, I could see the blurry silhouette of myself as well as three other figures behind me that were in focus. One was a small boy, and the others were a grown man and woman, each resembling her in different ways.

"Just try to stay with me. I'll get you to a healer."

"*No. I feel it. I'm too far gone.*"

"No, you're not." I pulled a small sack of flower seeds from my back pocket. "Can you heal yourself with these? I can't heal anyone even if I want to."

"*I can see them. My family. They're waiting for me.*" She tried to move her arm and only got far enough to twitch her fingers.

"No..." I succeeded in lifting her this time but stumbled forward at walking speed; the fastest I could go. I had to fight a slippery puddle under my feet with every step.

"*Did I ever tell you? I was adopted.*" She smiled, but only with her eyes. "*My original family is dead. My brother died in an accident and my mother took her own life in grief. Not too long after, my father died of a broken heart. Could you imagine that? Death by a broken heart?*"

"No. It won't happen if I don't lose you."

"*I love you too.*" Her eyes lost their light and the pain in my chest quickly faded to nothing.

"If that's how you feel then live..."

I felt helpless as her body became lifeless and cold. I was unsure of how long I held her in my arms. It reminded me of when I found my mother. I laid her on one of the stacks of metal sheets and laid a seed on her chest. I traveled silently back up the stairs, gaining speed as I went.

"Graven, I won't be joining you," I said, as calmly as I could.

"Why? What happened?" He was just as calm.

"She's gone, I didn't make it in time."

"Wait, we still need your-"

"Don't worry about me." I tossed the communicator before reaching the top of the stairs.

I stepped back into the library and took ample note of my surroundings. The floor was solid wood with a layer of steel or stone underneath it. The pillars were made of a mix of marble and sandstone, and the ceiling was three stories high but only for half of the visible area while the other half was two stories high.

"What do you know," I said, finding the spell I cast on Nail unbroken. I snapped my fingers and released the seal, only to find nobody there. He wasn't caught in the circle.

"So, you came back." I heard him before I could see him. He was up near the ceiling behind a pillar near the entrance. "You know, that other person was pretty impressive. They left an invisible marker to slip past me. They were probably already down the stairs before we started talking and I didn't even notice." He dropped and faced me. "Judging from your demeanor, I'd say she didn't make it. Am I right? Jostle someone like that around enough and maybe they bleed out. Maybe she just gave up?"

My blades surrounded him and closed in while he was talking.

He summoned a wielder's sword, a wide cutlass with a sharp curve, and swiped some of my blades away while dodging the rest.

It looked like he reacted before he knew they were there. He opened his palm and sent a black shard that landed in my wrist as I tried to parry it. I felt nothing, just the impact.

My sword fell from my hand and was caught by my other.

Nail teleported in a wisp of flame and appeared behind me, swiping at my side.

Keeping track of where he was going, I summoned my blades back to me to absorb the strike. The shards acted as an extension of my blade but were not helpful when I missed. They were better as a defensive barrier.

He struck again with a heavy sideswipe.

My blades absorbed the initial impact but they slammed into me, flinging me across the room. Skirting across the floor, I landed at the door.

Limping to my feet, I nearly slipped on the puddle leaking from my wrist and used a blade pressed on each side as a tourniquet before I could bleed out.

Nail exchanged his scimitar for square twin blades and swiped it through the air, unleashing a volley of red and brown blade waves interspersed with more black shards at me.

It was all I could do to block with my sword shards forming a wall before me. Mounting pressure from the projectiles pushed the blades out of place, and I was struck more than a few times before they stopped coming.

I gathered my concentration and teleported behind my opponent. I had a second spell ready for when I made it there.

Instead of casting my spell, I was backhanded through the air and into a wall.

Before I could catch my footing, Nail swept my feet from below me and stomped my injured hand to the wall.

I summoned my blades back to me. They glowed as they streaked through the air.

Nail flicked his wrist and blew my shards away. They wouldn't return as their glow weakened.

I aimed and stuck with the tip of the sword I had on hand.

He parried my blade into the ground with his. "What's wrong, reached your limit? Your weapons aren't coming back and you're getting a bit slow. Must be a time limit."

"***Mind Breaker.***" I called the name of my weapon and everything went dark.

"You called?" It appeared with an enlarged body balancing the oversized dome between its now visible shoulders.

"Yep, you're still here. I'm still not alone." I turned and walked toward my gate. The creature followed. "Yeah, myself and I" I took a running start bashed my way through the vortex of energy surrounding the gate, and grasped the chain. It took but a tug to remove it and it fell to the ground with the lock and an ear-splitting clack.

I tried to push my fingers between the cracks and open the door. The chain came to life and wound itself around me, pinning my arms. The weight was suffocating, and it constricted painfully. Breathing became painful and I couldn't move.

I didn't struggle. Instead, I accepted it. The weight I've been dragging behind me was now square on my shoulders and my body had been dragged down. Now the only thing I had was my mind. Yes. Just me and my thoughts. My reason for fighting was plain and clear.

My eyes opened to the scene of Nail fending off my blades from all sides with a barrier while they quickly encroached on us.

The blades easily perforated the lazily placed bubble, coming in with enough power to glow brightly on their own.

Nail teleported, disappearing through the floor. He reappeared on the other side of the room.

My blades all gathered around my bloody mess of an arm, glowing brighter until it became blinding.

When my eyes adjusted, my injured arm was no longer there. In its place was a pink mass of metallic material running the length of my arm. Five bladed digits sprang from a bulbous point centered on my palm and moved with dexterous authority.

Nail snapped his fingers and launched another volley of black projectiles at me.

I shielded myself with my new arm. It was large enough to cover my torso. It held up despite every other strike pushing me backward.

I cast 'speed' and pushed forward through the projectiles. Gaining speed, I closed the distance.

Giving up on projectiles, Nail struck at me with his cutlass.

I swiped it to the side with my claw.

He summoned another sword and swiped at me.

I closed my metallic fist around the man holding the blade before it could get anywhere. He looked helpless in my grasp as I squeezed with all my might.

Despite my efforts, he seemed unfazed.

"***Ethereal chains***." Around twenty chains appeared anchored between Nail and the ground. Next, I cast 'blast off' to take us both to the ceiling. The distance ensured all the chains snapped. I bashed him against the ceiling before slamming him into the ground.

Nail's expression didn't change.

"***Ethereal chains***." I cast the spell again and more chains appeared.

A wave of intense heat flowed from Nail and disintegrated the chains.

Dizziness overtook me and I quickly lost my balance. Breathing was difficult and my arm became too heavy to keep aloft. Involuntarily, I released Nail from my grasp.

"I was right. Weakening spells really do the trick as long as you're exerting yourself." He kicked the side of my head and I promptly rolled onto the floor. "Can't get up, can you? Every bit of your strength is already gone. Good news is I can sense your friend from earlier coming back up the stairs. Maybe I'll get a good challenge from them when they see your body." He lifted a broad sword over my chest. Its width would guarantee something important was hit, and the curved back spikes would ensure maximum harm.

Unable to move, I knew I could rely on my thoughts. Waiting patiently, I already prepared a spell to cast in this kind of scenario.

As the sound of hurried footsteps came from the staircase, I cast my spell.

Nail dropped his sword at the same time and it collided with hardwood immediately after.

Instead of Graven entering the doorway, he was next to me. The sound of footsteps continued, never getting closer. Nail nodded in surprise.

"That's the best spell you had for the situation?" Graven stood on his sword with me hovering next to his outstretched hand.

I was inside a bubble of constantly rotating energy. It'd push back and damage anything that got close. "Regular teleportation's too easy to counter," I said, barely able to speak.

"Fair enough. ***Rejuvenate***." I became enveloped in a purple light, and I could feel my strength return. "We should go. There's a bigger fight down below."

"Not for me." I released my gyroscopic bubble and continued to levitate. "Did you see her on the way up?"

"Yeah, who was she to you?"

"A girl from my squad." I found myself involuntarily shaking my head.

"At least you're honest with yourself. That arm's new."

"My old one's busted." I tapped the metallic surface coating my arm.

"If you're sure about continuing this fight, I'll help. The less of these guys around, the better."

"No, I don't feel like having you die with me."

"Please, I was a ninja. All I do is survive. Besides." His sword glowed and changed to become much shorter, flatter, and more triangulated than its other forms. "We've tried to kill each other enough by now for me to see the will to live in your eyes." He looked down at Nail, who was now looking up at us. "Shall we?"

I asked, "Can he see us?"

"We're in an invisibility bubble, but it's safe to assume he can."

"Okay, drop me and follow my lead. We'll be using the assault tag formation."

"Smart, but are you sure you trust me enough for that?"

"Do I have to?"

"Good point." He dropped me out of the bubble.

Nail swiped his sword and assaulted with a volley of ranged attacks.

I blocked with my metallic arm and charged forward as soon as I touched the ground. I pushed onward until I felt the distinct impact of a blade colliding with the back of my hand.

"*Point blank*." I cast the spell and sent a shockwave directly in front of me. Immediately after, I cast 'blade wave' and raked my claw through the air, followed by a blade wave from each finger at once.

Nail was pushed back by my spell and dodged the blade waves.

I sent more and he dodged those as well.

I cast 'blade wall', causing the blade waves to spread out and begin passing between each other.

"*Blast furnace*." The air turned red spreading out from Nail and the temperature skyrocketed. The floor began bending under our weight and the walls became pliable, sagging under the strain of its own construction. The surrounding pillars turned red and molten while the air became dry. The sweat on my brow quickly evaporated. Next, he advanced between the raging blades, soaring around him. One crashed into his arm, and he moved with caution from then on.

As he was dodging my spell, I readied another one. I picked a seed from my pouch and sat it on my palm. "*Floral cannon*." The plant sprouted and a daisy the size of my head emerged from the tiny seed before a flood of pink energy exploded from its center.

Unable to dodge both spells, he was thrown into the far wall by the blast.

I smirked. "Everyone always wants to walk through that spell, never teleport."

"I did." Nail's voice came from behind me.

As those words reached my ears, I realized his spell created a mana field and I couldn't sense him as easily. His illusion was enough to fool me.

I whipped around to face him, but I was too late. His sword was inches away from my throat.

In an instant, I was back floating in the bubble of invisibility and Graven was in my place confronting Nail.

Their blades clashed.

Graven tossed a small device between them and backed off. It exploded and caused a blue mist to spread outward. Lightning filled the cloud like water to a cup before the mist succumbed to the heat and dissipated, leaving the electricity to swirl around Nail like a liquid.

Nail didn't seem phased, but something was different this time. He wasn't moving aside for twitching in his arms and legs. The lightning paralyzed him.

Graven raised his sword and pointed it squarely at his target. A purple orb formed at the tip of his blade. The orb grew to the size of his torso with the debris surrounding him levitating. Nail levitated as well. "***Anti-gravity cannon.***" A bright flash followed by a large blast of purple energy shot from the tip of his sword. It overtook his target, continued into the wall, and bent it inward before it crumbled down. There was now a hole leading outside.

After his spell concluded, Graven retrieved two handfuls of caltrops from the folds in his clothes and threw them toward the wall where they hovered in the air like a minefield.

There was a hint of movement among the debris and the caltrops exploded.

The blast was drowned out by a flood of lava that replaced the floor. The force of the lava was so great it popped the invisibility bubble I was hovering in.

Levitating under my own power, I watched Graven get swept away in a river of red and black. He shielded himself in time, but the lava began to rise above his head.

I reached toward Graven and cast 'pull' to get him out of the pool he was sinking in before diving at the source myself.

Nail rushed upward in a pillar of flames.

This caught me off guard and pushed me back.

Nail raced toward me on a stream of flames, grabbed me by my scarf, and swung me into the molten sea below.

"***Faerie's retreat.***" The spell teleported me next to Graven, who cast it.

"I like what you did there," said Nail, lowering himself to the ground. The lava dissipated as he landed. "Looks like this is going to be more fun than I thought." He raised a hand. "***Blast inferno.***" The red hue of the air and accompanying heat disappeared. It was replaced by flames that spewed from the walls and ceiling. Every lick of fire lashed out at us with deadly determination and conviction. They were like living spikes thrusting at us relentlessly.

We were forced to land where Nail was waiting for us.

"Running away won't help you now." He stood leaning against his back-spiked broadsword.

Graven took a running start and left an afterimage. He reached Nail quickly with a glowing blade and a diagonal strike.

Nail parried the attack with a kick to the broad side of his sword. He followed up with another one that sent Graven off to the side and into a flame-covered wall.

I traveled close behind and swiped at him with my claw.

Nail knocked my claw toward the ground. He pivoted himself onto the handle of his sword and continued with a flurry of kicks.

I bounced from the ground multiple times before he kicked backward.

Graven appeared above Nail. His double was eaten by flames against the wall and vanished. He accelerated downward surrounded by white particles that shimmered in the light and struck down at our opponent.

Nail lifted his sword with enough force to launch Graven in my direction.

The white particles became bright sparkles before exploding in a flurry of snow, trapping Nail inside a block of ice.

I forced my feet toward the ground and slid to a halt. Opening my hand wide, I caught Graven and wound up to throw him at the block of ice.

He spiraled through the air, ready to cleave through everything before him when his momentum came to a dead stop.

Before I knew it, fire sprouted from his back and leaked onto the floor like a river.

"You were hard to catch-" Nail started.

"Solo, now!" Graven interrupted him. A purple orb expanded, then shrank back down on the pair, following a massive outpour of energy. "***Event horizon.***"

Neither moved an inch.

I teleported next to them with my fist high above my head. I slammed it down on top of Nail. "***Phantasmal geyser.***" I hit a new limit with the power I released in that second. It was enough to drill a hole into the layers of steel and stone below the wooden surface and through the ceiling as a swirling ethereal column of energy eclipsed its target and raged for a minute.

The flames leaking from Graven extinguished. I picked him up in my claw and escorted him farther away. He was vaguely responsive, but the light in his eyes was far from going out. He wasn't injured aside from third-degree burns that carried through his chest to his back. His wound was cauterized so he didn't bleed. Upon closer inspection, I could see short tufts of purple fur sticking out from beneath his clothes. He was beyond his limits.

I sat him down and looked myself over. My skin had lost its pigment, my digits appeared stubbier, and my peripherals had increased in scope. I was in the same position.

"Looks like you're already at that point." Nail's voice rang loud and clear from the hole he was slammed into. He was levitating slowly out of the abyss. His form had changed as well. His skin looked like black plates, separated by glowing red grooves. His eyes were swirling vortexes of magma. "Is that all the power you have?" He gave me a second to respond and continued. "Before you answer that, no. It's not." He was now standing before the hole surrounded by each version of his sword as they rotated around him.

"Most people think a wielder's power peaks when they reach that fourth form, but that's not true. Having all your weapons available like this is called 'perfect converation'. The transformation you're undergoing is the last step known as 'celestial' when you perfect it. Trying to reach this level early can kill you. Ironically, that's also the only way to attain it. Just like your friend there." He pointed at Graven. "I can feel it. He's getting to where you are now. I know you can feel it too."

I already knew this, but the longer he talked, the longer I could rest. Even so, he was right about Graven. There was a growing energy inside him that only grew stronger as the seconds passed. He began hovering a meter or so off the ground and rotated to a standing position.

He opened his eyes and all three versions of his weapon appeared before him, only to come together and shrink down to one new sword. It was a black, tapered long sword with a purple blade and 'EXCALIBUR' in bold lettering etched down its center. He gripped his new sword, and his arms and legs began glowing. When the glow subsided, there were purple gauntlets across them. He stood with a newfound glow of authority.

"Now you two might be a real challenge," said Nail with a smile. "Come on, kill me." It sounded more like an expectation than a taunt.

"He has a death wish." Graven held his sword at the ready.

"I can tell," I said, readying my claw. "And it explains everything."

Nail launched a sword at us and we dodged it in separate directions.

Graven took flight and I stayed grounded. Nail kept his eyes on Graven while I circled around and rushed from the side.

Nail flung a scimitar flew my way.

I backhanded it away.

Directly behind the scimitar was a serrated sword hidden in the first sword's shadow. I didn't see it until the last second.

I caught and tossed it in my other hand without a second thought to find that both of my hands were now clawed. My right claw was now half the size it was and my new left one was comparable.

Nail made sure to keep Graven busy with projectiles. He must have learned his lesson from their last close-range encounter.

It wasn't long before I closed the distance.

As soon as Nail noticed me, he swerved around with a broadsword to meet me.

In response, I punched it and cast 'full send' to accelerate it into him. Next, I followed it up with a flurry of blows.

The sword bounced upward on impact. Nail caught it and traded blows with me.

Graven struck down with an 'anti-gravity blast'. He used my presence to mask the floating debris and punched a new hole in the ground.

In a blink, Nail jumped up and out of the way. Next, he cast a spell "***Blade rain.***" A myriad of bladed weapons appeared out of the flames hanging from the ceiling and fell at frightening speeds.

"***Implosion.***" Graven reached his hand into the air and a purple orb appeared above us that pulled in the surrounding weapons that fell continuously.

The gravity bubble split in half. Nail appeared from the other side of it as his blades hailed down.

On the ground, I was already casting a spell to hit him first. Ready to unleash it, I aimed my palms upward.

Nail vanished. He was completely gone. I couldn't come up with a logical explanation for his absence. If he teleported, I'd have felt it. If it was speed, there would have been a trail to follow. If he was invisible, it wouldn't be as if he was never there. If Graven did something to him, it would have been obvious. All I could sense was the feeling that death was tapping on my shoulder.

I looked behind me and all I could see was red. A torrent of fire, earth, and magma exploded into my face. My back gave out and I could only hope that my legs were still attached to the rest of me as it flung me into the wall.

Still unable to feel pain, I tried to move only to find myself unable to do so. The feeling of death grew ever closer until it swallowed me whole.

Concentrating my efforts, I forced my fingers and toes to move simultaneously. Once I was sure I could move, I cast 'shatter' to break away the lava rock that was now pinning me to the wall.

I looked around to see that Nail and Graven stopped fighting. They were both standing in place and looking as if the moon was coming down.

The feeling of death had not receded. Something big was happening. I didn't even want to think about what it might have been.

"The Shadow Master awakens," said Nail, "It looks like it'll take all of us. I honestly thought I'd be dead by now."

45-Black Soul

[Noah Black]

In every direction I looked, there was a new enemy to smite. Once they started moving, it was as if we were fighting against a living rainbow tidal wave. It was a struggle just to keep up with the sheer amount of slime-like creatures as they spilled over each other in a mad attempt to absorb any person that matched their color.

Catt and I were separated as she was swarmed by corpse shadows of every color. I was occupied with black and gray ones. Lights flared from different directions as wide-scale light spells wiped out tens of corpse shadows. More continued to rise. They spawned from the ground with increased frequency and swelled to overwhelming numbers.

Over time, they began merging into each other and became increasingly difficult to dispatch. As they merged, they became more durable and opaque. To make matters worse, my blade wouldn't stay in its light form. I had to keep concentration to keep it from changing color.

I was unaware of the toll this was taking on me until I cut into one and struggled to remove my blade. I knew I couldn't keep going like this, so I resorted to plan B.

"Catt, clear the area!" I called.

She responded, "Get ready to jump!" and punched the ground with a brilliant light following close after. "***Hallowed ground***." The outer edge of the radiating light took the shape of six torii gates that expanded outward, pushing away everything in a ten-meter radius.

I jumped. Instead of being pushed back, I was lifted higher and tossed into the air. "***Hell soul***." As soon as I cast the spell, my chest tightened, my vision blurred over, and my thoughts escaped me. I couldn't think straight, but I didn't need to. Landing, I reached into my pocket and retrieved the stones given to me by Sun and Snow. I was sure that now was the time to use them. I dropped the forever fire and plunged my black blade through it and into the ground. "***Twilight entropy***." A dark, slowly rotating orb formed from the tip of my sword and grew exponentially until it encompassed the entire battlefield. With the power boost given from a combination of 'hell soul' and the forever fire, this was achieved in under a minute instead of an hour. By the time the spell had completed casting, the forever fire had vanished.

As soon as the spell was in place, it became active. The harmless orb became a single large-scale attack as the ground began to tremble and everything in its radius was hit with enough force from all sides to crush an aircraft carrier. At least it would if it wasn't stretched far beyond capacity for such a thing. The worst anyone got was a gentile pressure across their entire body.

Despite the spell's lack of performance, it did what I wanted. The unique properties of my magic caused all the corpse shadows to be pulled straight toward me.

"Hurry up, the barrier won't last long." Catt was struggling to keep her spell up with both of her fists planted on the ground. Shadows were pressing against the barrier from all sides.

I pulled my sword from the ground, and the blade turned white. "Here we go," I said, unsure of the result of my next action. I reached my other hand out and summoned a porcelain sheath. In it, I dropped the pure essence and seated my blade. The two fused, supercharging my next spell. I assumed a stance. My sword and sheath began to glow even without my input. Gathering as much power as I could, I cast one more spell, "**Horizon's edge**." I unleashed my blade while turning in a full circle. The result was a thin, white circle that expanded outward and passed through everything as far as the eye could see. Anything that touched the outward edge would fall in half, but because of the nature of my magic, it passed harmlessly through every living thing and cut only my targets. The corpse shadows. "Did I do it?" I asked, not looking up from the ground.

"You definitely killed everything around here, but I don't know about everywhere else." Catt patted me on the back. "Good job, now rest. I know you're tired."

"I can't. A body in motion, you know?" I was restless. The effects of 'hell soul' were getting to me and there was a mounting pressure in my head. I couldn't dismiss the spell and I leaned in different directions uncontrollably, barely catching myself each time.

"Noah!" Catt held me to keep me from falling over. "Are you okay? There's this black aura coming from you and you're cold. What's wrong?"

Her voice was fuzzy and hard to follow. I looked at her and all I saw was a blob vaguely resembling her. "Oh, Catt." My mind went blank, and my feet left the ground.

I fell. I couldn't tell how long, and I didn't want to know either. It felt like I was falling forever, but forever wasn't long enough. I was surrounded by a pitch-blackness that I hoped was just the inside of my eyelids and that I'd come to when I landed. The conflict between natural versus supernatural both being held as preferred causes stirred within me.

Something brushed across my face and my eyes fluttered open to the sight of more darkness. The feeling of falling stopped and I sat up. To my right was the giant face of a snow-white tiger sitting next to me.

"Why am I here?" The rhetorical question escaped my mouth before anything else.

"The darkness has taken over." The gruff voice of the tiger tickled my ear.

"You mean the phantasm?" I said, looking around to find no sign of the creature.

"Yes. he has broken free and trapped you here with me." The tiger lifted his head and looked over at the gate.

Following his gaze, I saw the black stone-like interior of the gate was gone. In its place was a twisting wall of black ooze. I approached it with caution and placed my hand on the cool, formless surface.

"Somehow, I thought this might happen. I'm on a rampage right now, aren't I?"

"I can't tell. I am blind to the outside." He looked up wistfully into the darkness.

"It hasn't happened in so long that I hadn't even considered it until now." I slapped my hand against the goop, and it sank in slightly. "The darkness... Has it always been there?"

"Yes." The tiger responded unexpectedly. "And so have I."

"And he was restrained this whole time?"

"Yes."

"I see... I'd go on a rampage too, in that case. Well, I guess I am." I pushed my hand deeper.

"Don't. You'll be swallowed by darkness. Or is that what you want?"

"Dark doesn't mean bad. I've known that this whole time, but now, I understand. Color means nothing in the face of intention." The tiger only watched as I pushed deeper into the inky black.

The coldness seeped through my skin and into my bones. It was like wading through thick snow mixed with a hard gel that molded itself around my movements. I held my breath as I entered completely. Soon, my hand breached through the other side, followed by my foot and the rest of me in turn.

The other side was a white void as far as the eye could see. There was blank nothingness in every direction. Looking back at the gate, its coloring changed from pure white with pitch black goop inside to pitch black with pure white goop inside.

The stark whiteness of my surroundings was almost enough to hurt my eyes. There was a deep and longing silence like the aftermath of a battle, desperately attempting to regale one with a tale of past events.

I spotted something in the distance and tiptoed toward it as if to preserve the still nothingness. As I grew closer, I saw that lying in a heap on the ground was a large black and white striped rope. On top of it was a similarly sized black and white lock and what looked like pieces of shattered glass. Upon closer inspection, the glass was actually a seven-point seal. The rope was wrapped around something that was no longer there.

"**Pure spirit**," I said, hoping to no avail, that calling its name would summon the phantasm. "Even if you don't come when I call, you're still a part of me. I know you can hear me."

No answer.

I climbed the pile of rope and sat in the space in the center. "You're the side of me I was always afraid to let out, I'm sorry. When those people came and started hurting my family, you awakened. I know it was just to protect me, but it was too much for me to handle and I was scared... I still am and I probably always will be." I stood back up. "I don't remember much about what happened, but I know that, despite everything, whatever you're doing out there is for my sake. You want to protect me at all costs... Even if it means going against me, but I'm begging you, don't fight me on this."

"FOOL!" A deep rumble of a voice rose from the ground. "You are not ready for the weight of your actions!" The rope bound itself around me like a giant snake, squeezing as if to drain my life away.

"I don't need to be ready," I said, barely able to get my voice out, "I just need to accept it. And I will. All of it!"

"Then take it. The memories of what you've done. What you've discarded."

Through the emptiness of the void, colors formed, followed by many familiar scenes. None I ever wanted to see or experience again. I relived it again as well as everything else. The years of grief I didn't have and the well of tears I never shed. All of it came to me at once, as well as the guilt brought on by my own actions.

I was back home again. We lived in a large house out in the mountainside not far from a town in Roland. It was added on after my parents built it together for each child they had. There were ten of us now. The halls were often bustling with family members shuffling between different rooms. Today was a holiday. We had a couple of weeks away from everything and that made it even busier until things settled down in the afternoon.

Mom and Dad were able to convince Roger, Melonie, and Alison to come home for the holidays, the three oldest. They always avoided coming home if they could help it, but they all happened to not have any excuses this time. I could hear them arguing over what to build out of the fresh snow outside while I waited inside with Mary, Sean, and Frederick in front of the fire. We were the youngest, so we didn't really do all that much. Hariet, Mavis, and David were with Mom and Dad in the kitchen cooking.

I let Sean hold the fire poker and stoke the flames with it. He sat between my legs and the other two were beside me waiting their turn to poke the burning firewood. Christmas programs were on the TV, but we were under the TV where we couldn't see the screen while it hovered above us in an alcove above the fireplace. We could hear the TV, but we could hear our siblings even louder. Eventually, they'd stop arguing and just build something for everyone to enjoy.

When the arguing stopped, it was sudden. It was as if their attention was taken by something else. At the same time, my ears popped but I didn't think much of it.

"The fire got cold," said Sean, the first to notice.

"It did?" I put my hand close to the fire and noticed it was closer to room temperature if anything. "Weird." It was as if my eyes adjusted, and I could see through the fireplace. There was a wall of boxes instead of stone. The light from the flames was real, but that's the only thing that was. "I think it's an illusion."

I stood and my younger siblings stood with me. When we did, the ground started shaking. Trying not to panic, I searched around the room, walking through the illusion as it melded into the walls, only providing faint light as the details were overtaken by the surface they were pressed into. After a couple of minutes of looking around, we found the door and opened it. The gray marble of the hallway on the other side told me where we were. I closed the door.

"What is it?" asked Mary. She was right behind me.

"We're in the safe." The safe was a place deep under our home. It's where my older siblings trained in magic and where I was supposed to start in a few months.

"Did something happen?"

"I hope not. I think we should stay put just in case."

I went back to huddling with my siblings under a blanket. Over the next few minutes, the walls shook repeatedly. It was subtle at first but became noticeably less so as time went on. As it went on, the illusion around us grew faint until it vanished completely. By then, the automatic lights turned on and the room was well-lit.

I closed my eyes and listened. We were all deathly silent, trusting that whatever danger needed us to be in the safe would be gone soon. Not even a breath escaped any of us.

After a few seconds, I could feel something in my chest. It felt like it was trying to pierce me from the inside out. It was as if whatever I was feeling was both far away and uncomfortably close. The feeling only got stronger over time and I became increasingly nervous as the feeling began to spread and my chest began hurting.

A light flashed from across the room accompanied by a low rumble. In that light, I saw a person surrounded by an aura of purple energy. Behind them was a tunnel through the ground. Through this, my eyes were still closed and they snapped open to the same sight. It was a man in a purple suit with a long tailcoat and a broadsword in his hand. Close behind him were two others. One wore a blank white mask with no eye holes and a black cloak while the other wore a suit of brown leather armor.

There was no time to think as someone wearing a snowsuit appeared directly in front of me facing the pair. They nudged me backward. "Run." It was Roger. Beside him was Mom and Mavis.

I nodded and ran to the door, making sure Mary, Sean, and Frederick were behind me. As soon as we started moving, bright flashes of color and the sound of metal striking metal ensued in our wake. The sounds and color followed us down hallways and across corridors, increasing in amount and frequency the whole way.

In our panic, we had no idea where we were going but as long as there was somewhere to go, we kept running. Eventually, there was a dead end. I pivoted on my feet as soon as I saw the wall. When I turned around, I saw the battle wasn't far behind us. Melonie was holding up a silver shield with a white aura expanding around it, overtaking the hallway between us and the fight.

"Dead-end," I said.

Melonie looked around for a second as if in intense thought. She waved her hand towards our small group. "Get ready to run some more."

In a flash, we were back above ground. The snow was at our shins but it barely slowed us down. I made sure Mary, Sean, and Frederick were in front of me as we all sprinted through the snow and ice. Looking back, I saw Melonie covering our tracks with an opaque shield of snow. The concentrated flurry covered all of us from behind and kept us hidden while erasing our footprints through the forest.

Even though we were far enough that we couldn't even see our house in the distance, I felt like something was following us from much closer. My feeling was confirmed when the ground ahead of us grew into a wall. Just as quickly, it shattered as a beam of light pierced it. We kept running through the debris.

A couple of bangs behind us were followed by a sharp scream. I peeked behind me and saw Melonie scrambling up from the snow. Beside her was Dad, helping her up by her arm and tossing her in our direction.

Someone in a bright yellow cloak as well as the one in brown armor were closing in. One by ground and the other by air.

Between them, landed someone coated in a bright white light, forcing the two in opposite directions. I couldn't tell who it was. The light obscured their features.

The snow billowed upward and obscured my view as I continued sprinting. Melonie landed beside me but her run was more of a limp as she pressed her hand against my back while she pressed her other hand, glowing white on her abdomen.

The ground shook and a translucent white bubble surrounded me, Melonie, Mary, Sean, and Frederick individually as the ground sank beneath our feet. The ground reappeared as we were sent even further away. I could now see the town in the distance, but the sounds of battle were no further away.

A green flash and a bang nearby made my ears ring and we were flung forward. Not all of us landed on our feet and the red strewn across the ground beside me was unmistakable. Melonie was having a hard time getting to her feet while keeping her wound covered.

I went to her side to help her up when I heard the layered echo of powerful voices. "**Royal Guard**." Another bang with a green flash resounded but the most I felt was a breeze as two people cloaked in white, crackling like electricity stood behind us. Based on the spear and short sword in their hands, it was Alison and David. Alison looked at Melonie and nodded.

Melonie nodded back and pressed her bloodied hand into the snow. "***Safe room***." A white light accented in red surrounded us and the ground gave way again. This time, it encapsulated us with a floor, ceiling, and walls. The soft glow of the spell made sure there was some visibility. Melonie raised her hand and five white orbs of light appeared over her head. She gestured ahead of us and the lights went into the wall in that direction.

The rest of us crowded her, assessing her condition and assaulting her with questions about it.

She waved us away. "I'm fine." She seemed short of breath as she stood. "We should be hidden enough for now. I'll move us somewhere else while they chase those orbs. She staggered over to the wall and pressed her hand against it.

The ground shifted subtly and we were in motion. It felt like we were on a boat rocking in only one direction but not tipping over. The feeling was uncanny but I didn't have time to get used to it before I heard something shatter overhead. A shard of brown crystal struck nearby us and a hole was open to the surface.

Someone dropped in but I couldn't see who before a column of light followed and forced them further into the ground below us. Melonie placed both of her hands against the wall and the faint glow around us became stronger as the speed of the space around us became faster. The holes in the floor and ceiling vanished as we moved.

After only a few seconds, a deafening crash came from below and we were rocketed upward alongside rock shrapnel. I heard a hard thump as my body slammed against the ceiling. Immediately after, I saw the sky. Less than a second later, I felt a second thump as I landed in the snow.

I stood as fast as I could and a flash of color took my attention as two bladed weapons were stationary in front of my face. One was a sickle curved toward my throat and the other was a sword keeping the sickle at bay. They were both gone in another flash.

Quickly, I scanned my surroundings and saw Frederick was the only other one standing. Melonie was struggling to stand and Frederick was trying to help her up. Mary and Sean were closer to me. They both looked unconscious but when I shook them awake, only Mary stirred. She hopped onto her feet and fell back to the snow, holding her leg. She then scrambled back up. Sean, on the other hand, was completely unresponsive.

My heart sank. I shook him more and I wanted to call his name but I felt like that would put us in more danger. Mary helped me pick him up and put him on my back. I didn't feel his heartbeat against my back but I didn't know if it was just my adrenaline or my worst fears come to pass. Flashes of color and shockwaves of energy were still coming our way so I didn't have time to fully assess his condition.

Once we were all up, we ran to the best of our abilities. It didn't feel like we were going anywhere fast. Between Melonie and Mary's injuries slowing them down, and Sean's unresponsiveness, we moved in slow motion. Even so, I was sure we were getting somewhere. The town wasn't far and someone had to have noticed what was happening.

Something knocked me over. It hit Sean on my back and flipped over me as we fell. Not having time to worry about it, I scrambled back to my feet and picked up my little brother. When I did, I saw what hit us. David was splayed out in the snow, having collided with Mary as well. She was trying to pull him up and help him stand but she couldn't move his still body.

Unlike with Sean, I could tell at a glance. His motionlessness wasn't unconsciousness. There was no question. He wasn't getting up anymore. I didn't see any blood but I didn't need to.

Finding my strength, I snatched her away from his body and held her under my arm while I sprinted forward. Sean was under my other arm. Melonie was rushing toward David but we locked eyes for less than a glance and she stood her ground instead. Her body became shrouded in a white aura while she looked around with her sword and shield at the ready. She was looking for the certainly approaching danger.

I was sure that I didn't blink, but Melonie was now gone. The sound of clashing metal behind me told me where she went. Frederick didn't wait for us to catch up and turned to run as well.

A blue light swept over everything and a deafening boom followed from above. My gaze darted upward and I spotted a white laser pushing against the barrier.

I got a feeling of danger washing over me from behind. Even though I was already running for my life, this felt imminent. I whipped around to spot the danger and found Melonie lying at my feet. Her blank eyes were staring up at nothing. Even so, I got the impression she was still alive.

Staggering back, I narrowly avoided what looked like a blue line appearing in the air in front of me as someone in a blue cloak over glints of metal appeared before me. At the same time, the barrier around us shattered.

Someone coated in white landed between us and stood still. I tried to turn and run but something kept me rooted in place. That was when I noticed the glint of something just below my line of sight. The spot in my chest that felt uneasy was now pierced by what looked like a blue blade reaching through me. It went through the blinding white aura of the person trying to protect me.

I screamed. Not giving myself time to feel, I reached for the blade and pulled at it, unsure of when I dropped my siblings. It didn't move, but I now felt something else deep within me. It was as if it was coiling around the blade and spreading through my body. The pressure made my head hurt and a white light overtook my line of sight. Immediately after, everything went black.

Through the darkness, I could see the outline of the person in front of me as a white silhouette. I reached out and touched them and they melted into a mass of black goop on the ground. I could now see the person holding the other end of the sword running through me. They backed off but I lunged at them mindlessly. My fingers touched them and they vanished into white particles that scattered and coated the empty black ground at my feet.

More white silhouettes were darting around my field of view with splashes of white exchanged between them. Some were far away but I could still see them. I couldn't tell who was who, but something inside me assumed they were all hostile. With a wave of my hand, some of them fell into pieces mid-motion.

The remaining silhouettes started moving faster. Some of them vanished completely, but I still saw them as orbs of white moving rapidly in different directions.

One of the orbs moved toward me. I reached out and touched it. When I did, it compressed into a speck of white and fell to the ground. At the same time, a spray of black erupted from it, coating me and my surroundings.

The warm liquid reminded me of something and I shuddered. A morbid thought crossed my mind and the darkness closed in on me completely. The silhouettes vanished and all feeling was gone.

I blinked and my sight returned to normal. The eerie silence aided my confusion. I didn't know what I was looking at. The gruesome scene before me didn't even register in my mind. I just looked upon the sea of cold white stained a warm red in further confusion. Turning around, I looked at my siblings who wore shocked expressions. All of them had a strange glow in their eyes. The glow reminded me of when my older siblings awakened to their magic. I looked down at my hands and saw myself glowing. My attention was taken by Frederick as he began glowing brighter. His hands were outstretched and the glow was soon blinding.

Opening my mouth to say something, I saw that I was no longer on the snowy mountainside. I saw a rocky shoreline and waves crashing upon a beach. Snow was falling so lightly that I didn't notice it until I took a step and my foot sank into some loose sand. If this was an illusion, it was a powerful one. Regardless, I remembered the blade sticking through my chest and reached for it. There was nothing but a warm tingly feeling. The blade was gone, but something warm was leaking out of my chest. Before I had the chance to acknowledge it, everything went white.

The light faded and I was back, bound by a rope of entropy. cold tears rolled down my face. They were already, but now I could feel them. So much of what happened was out of my control.

I heard a faint scream in the distance. It sounded like someone calling for me. The blood-curdling voice of beauty stung like a pin to my heart. After all, who would call for someone like me so compassionately?

"I've done enough," I said, finding my eyes already closed. I felt cold again, and I only got colder as I fell ever deeper into the void. The voice became distorted until it mellowed out into static in the background, almost as if swallowed by nothingness.

A piercing shriek made me gasp as it choked my breath. It was someone else calling the same. This one was not fading in any capacity and only became stronger until I began shaking from the force of its pleas; ever so desperate. With it came the feeling of something warm pulsing through my being, but the feeling faded as quickly as it came.

Hearing the voice gave me the courage to let go completely and lose myself in the entropy. I could feel nothing, see nothing, and soon, hear nothing as the voice finally became more distant.

Content with my new purgatory, I let myself fall to oblivion.

Until the static returned.

Softly, the noise caressed my cheek, and a faint voice peaked through with sorrow and anguish. "Come back to me, please... This is a threat..." The words were followed by a warmth that permeated from my lips outward until it ran through my entire body.

I can't explain why, but this made me smile. It could have been the absurdity of the statement or the nostalgia of those words. Either way, I opened my eyes and said, "Ok, Catt."

The first thing to return was my sight. Catt was to my left with her fists up as if ready to strike. She looked like she just ran straight into a wall of blades with cuts and bruises dotting her face and arms. Her clothes were slightly tattered, and her stance was failing. To my right was Mary, holding up a shield large enough to cover all three of us. She was in better condition, but still beaten. I couldn't help but wonder if I caused that. On the ground beside me were shattered remains of the rest of the gems Sun and Snow gave me. I later found out that Catt used them to reach out to me and expended their energy in the process.

The next thing to return was feeling. The knuckles on my right hand hurt as if I punched a steel wall and my left arm was heavy and aching. Every heartbeat introduced another pain in a spot I didn't know was there and moving only stressed it.

I tasted the blood and dirt that seeped into my mouth over time, but it quickly faded.

The smell of sulfur wafted through the air, but it came with a hint of cold, as if it was watered down.

The last to return was hearing, as the sound of a battle resounded from the other side of the shield.

"Noah, are you back?" Catt placed her hand on my shoulder.

"Ow, yeah," I said, wobbling on my feet and nearly falling over. "How are you?"

"I've seen better days." She stretched her arms out and winced. "But this is nothing."

"Get ready," said Mary, seeming to struggle holding up the shield. "I can't hold this too much longer."

"Are there still any shadows left?" I looked at my sword to find it split evenly with white on one side and black on the other.

"You got all of them, now start moving." Mary ducked to the left, while Mary and I followed. The shield shattered, allowing a torrent of snow to pass through and freeze the ground on contact.

The origin of the blast was a woman in a cracked white fox mask and a C.H.E.S.S. uniform. She was holding a baton in one hand and a cane in the other; both as white as snow. She also looked like she had a run-in with a wild bear with barely healed cuts and gashes across her body. "Look who's back," said the woman.

An icy wind whipped up around us. Catt struck the ground with fire to counteract it and created a thick fog. I sent a black and a white blade wave in the woman's direction, resulting in an explosion that blew the fog away. Once it cleared, she was still standing there with the baton twirling before her.

"Noah, dolphin," commanded Catt, backing off.

"Are you sure?" I said, acknowledging the codeword.

"Go for it," said Mary.

"Dolphin it is." I sprinted toward the woman in white.

She responded by floating into the air.

Once I was under her, I stabbed my sword into the ground. "*Black pillar*."

She was hit by the spell and shot higher in a stream of energy.

I noticed a layer of frost appearing over my hands that was quickly trailing up my arms. Instead of backing off, I cast another spell. "*White pillar*." The black and white pillars mingled, causing an explosive reaction that left a hole in the ground.

There was a sound of clashing metal over my head, and I looked to see a morning star and an arrow flying away from each other; both white.

A white light accompanied by a sudden temperature drop shone in a circle under my feet.

I dodged out of it but the back of my shoe froze.

"*Avalanche*." The woman in white was still floating high in the air as a mountain of snow appeared overhead and fell unceremoniously.

It was clear that I couldn't dodge it and blocking would just trap me. "*Body of flames*." I jumped at it, surrounded by pure white flames.

The heat of my spell seemed to do little to protect me from frostbite and the cold put me in shock, but I recovered quickly enough to bash all the way through.

I emerged on the other side ready to cast another spell. "*Black bolt*." A compressed ball of darkness leaped from my palm toward the woman.

A bus-sized shard of ice came flying my way. The woman cast the spell before I penetrated the snow. My spell bounced harmlessly off it.

Instinctually, I cast 'corruption' and the ice shard became gray dust in an instant.

The woman responded by summoning two more. This seemed to take her a moment.

I took the opportunity to cast 'flash step', teleport behind her and pin her arms and legs with my own

She didn't seem to consider how long it took her to cast her spells. That's what I thought before I felt spikes pushing out at me from her back.

Before they could pierce my skin, I cast 'shadow binding' to keep her in place and 'shadow skin' to protect myself from both her and what was coming next. "Shark!" I called out the other code word.

Both Catt and Mary together blasted through the sheet of snow in a ball of fire. They were charging a light spell between their palms. "*Cosmic beacon*!" They cast it together and a brilliant, empty light bathed me and the lady in blinding light.

We were launched backward and apart. Despite my heavy resistance to light magic, it felt like what I'd imagine getting hit by a train would feel like. If there wasn't another person absorbing most of the blast, I'd have died.

A moment passed before I realized I already landed. My vision was bright white, and I couldn't see anything. Instinctively, I reached my hand out and someone helped me stand.

"Did we do it?" I asked.

"I'm still standing." The voice belonged to the woman in white.

I started casting 'Corruption'.

"*Silence*." Her spell canceled mine, and the word caught in my throat.

Still holding her hand, I attempted to fall backward and pull her with me, but she pulled back. Still blind, I continued pulling and jumped.

I felt something cylindrical whiz by my face.

I kicked toward where her head would approximately have been and made contact with something spiky instead.

Assuming it drew blood, I turned and wrapped my leg around it before extending my other one upward, making hard contact with something soft, resulting in a thump.

We both fell to the ground shortly. I heard her land beside me.

My vision cleared up momentarily, and I found that my body was covered in a thick layer of frost that was quickly melting away. I looked around to see everyone stopped in their place completely.

The woman in white was clearly distracted and staring at the distance. Half of her mask was gone and half her face was visible. There was a trickle of blood running from her mouth and the one crystal blue eye was open in shock. Catt and Mary were close by and doing the same.

People farther away who were fighting also stopped and looked. Nero was among them.

I stood with a mix of fear, panic, and dismay as a presence that I was unaware of was now barreling down on me from the same direction everyone else was looking. The C.E.H.E.S.S. base.

Whatever it was; it was a wielder, but what I saw wasn't a weapon. It was death.

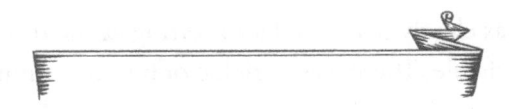

46-Of Magic and Legends

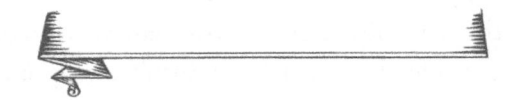

[Krow Hunt]

There was me, Doc, and Helen; the prince of Roland's personal guard, gaining speed down a labyrinth of corridors and hallways as we made our way down to the source of an immense negative energy. Twists and turns occurred randomly, and we backtracked more than once.

It seemed odd that Helen was there, but she didn't know where the prince was so she couldn't teleport to him. Instead, she went with us. She was sure wherever we were headed was where the prince was going as well.

Eventually, we met up with Carona, Ariel, Leuna, Caroline, and Sara. None of us were surprised to see each other. Graven wasn't far behind. When we made contact, Carona filled us in. It turned out that the walls were moving to direct us to each other. Graven added that if we hadn't met anyone else until that point, it was safe to assume that they were likely either already at the gate or dead. Graven's group was undoubtedly the last to reach the base.

Everyone had been fighting and nobody bothered to power down. The girls all looked like they were pushed far beyond their limits, having undergone various transformations and even transforming their weapons.

The way cleared of blocked passages and dead ends from there on. Graven received an emergency call and left with Carona. Doc's healing ability rivaled hers, so she was assured that we'd be fine if something happened as we continued without them.

We eventually met a long hall with bodies strewn across the ground. It looked like the fighting outside made it inside. There were Roland and C.H.E.S.S. soldiers alike in a stream of blood that didn't seem to stop.

All the blood led to a large metal door at the end of the hall. The energy was undoubtedly coming from the other side as well. The sounds of combat also radiated from there. The war wasn't over.

Doc reached his scythe toward the door and tapped it. The door fell and we all rushed in. Once we were inside, the door stood and magically replaced itself.

On the other side was a vast room with a giant gate in its center. One person was housed in six of the seven indentations on the surface of the gate. The seventh in its center was still empty. A woman in white hovered below the open space, hanging in the balance.

Near the base of the gate was where the battle was taking place. Leading all the way there was a wide trail of blood and bodies.

On the right side of the room, we spotted Prince Roland first. He was in golden armor with a light extending from a ring on his finger. Beside him was a group of soldiers. Surprisingly, both types of soldiers were fighting alongside him.

They were fighting a pale man in gray and black who fought bare-handed and a dragonoid with long and slender scales and thin wings, black all over.

Anyone the man got a solid hit on, fell as their body dissipated into black dust, leaving behind a puddle of blood.

The dragonoid struck fast with sharp claws and a breath of black smoke that melted armor and stone alike.

It wasn't hard to recognize a dragon I'd seen before. Keeping my focus on it made me realize its energy was the same as the man that Doc confronted back in New York. They were the same person. This led me to believe C.H.E.S.S. was behind the events that took place in the Vatican. However, I didn't have the time to deliberate on it.

On the left side were Rachel, Hiyaku, Naomi, and a woman I later learned was named Kirara. They were all struggling against Ferris Kaizer himself.

He seemed to use a mix of blood and time magic. He'd freeze any spell coming toward him in place. He'd then retaliate with a constant stream of blood he gained from the fallen bodies, forming it into shields and weapons. He was likely also using it as a catalyst for his time magic.

I was surprised to see Rachel, but if she was there, it meant she found her resolve. She had come to put an end to what was plaguing her.

Both sides were stalemated with neither giving an inch. That could change at a moment's notice.

After evaluating the situation, we each moved to where we thought we would be the most effective. Caroline and Sara went to the left while Doc and Helen went to the right. Leuna stayed in the middle and began charging a shot aimed at the gray man and Ariel followed me through the center. I went to retrieve the woman in white.

As I approached, I recognized the people already trapped in the gate. Four of them were part of the Seven Virtues, while one was Princess Roland, and the other was her Royal Guard. The woman in white was another Virtue, hanging in the balance.

The gray man and dragon both shot me a glance as if they were looking for me. A wall of darkness covered in purple lightning sprouted from the man's back and blocked my path. It was a thin, translucent draconic wing with a circular membrane-like pattern that the lightning arced across.

The dragon broke away from the battle and soared toward me with claws and fangs bared. Black smoke bellowed from its open maw.

Leuna sniped it out of the sky with a shot to its eye. It howled as it spiraled down in a green vortex of wind.

I struck the wing with my sword and I met heavy resistance. An electric shock carried through my entire body.

Ariel came close behind me. "***Diamond-blade: sandstorm.***" Her lance gained a crystalline sheen as she spiraled into the darkness. Her lance rotated, surrounded by a flurry of sand. She made contact and the sand dispersed the lightning.

A white laser struck right next to Ariel from the other side and she broke through.

"***Headwind.***" I boosted myself through behind her and reached the floating woman as fast as soon as I could.

I cradled her in my arms and looked her over. Traces of what looked like gold were splattered across her dress. She was visibly struggling despite being unable to move. The fatigue in her eyes showed she couldn't keep it up for long. Her fight against whatever force was trying to pull her into the gate was coming to an end. The light spell she just cast likely contributed to her declining condition.

"***Angel's descent.***" I cast the spell and white flames came to surround us. Despite my spell, we began rising. "***Dragon's ascent.***" It made no difference as a whirlwind replaced the flames. I wanted to rise past the indent she was being pulled toward but we didn't go up any faster.

"You're him." The elderly lady in my arms spoke barely above a whisper. She sounded as if she was on her deathbed. "The Legendary Corpse Hunter." Tear dots began forming in the corners of her eyes. "We made you do the impossible once, and I'm afraid you must do it again." Her eyes went blank, and her struggle ended.

I tried what I should've in the first place. "***Flicker.***" My feet met the ground but the lady was still hovering toward the gate. "Damn it." I teleported back, but it was too late.

When I reached out for her, I was hit by a shockwave that sent me flying in the opposite direction. Ariel, who was trying to break the gate from the bottom, was thrown as well. I hit the top of the door that led into the room and knocked it down. I then landed on the ground. Ariel slid across the floor and used her lance to stop her momentum.

Immediately after we were thrown away, an unnatural darkness filled the room, and a deep sense of foreboding spread from the same source. The darkness faded shortly, and the feeling worsened. It was like standing at the boundary of life and staring death in the mouth. I was going to be swallowed. However, this was something I've felt before.

Memories began flooding into my mind. Many of them were things I never thought I could forget. My birthday, my family, my first crush, my life, and my 'death'. I screamed, unable to take the sudden rush of information so terrestrial yet so alien to both my waking and unwaking mind. It all came back as he did.

It was always coming back. Because he was.

I looked up to see Rose squatting next to me, her hand stroking my back. Past her was a woman who looked similar to her, but she was in a tattered yellow C.H.E.S.S. uniform and she was covered in many wounds that were closing as she rested not far away.

An all-too-familiar figure stood in front of the gate. His skin was no longer gray, but closer to almond. His sunken features were now fully fleshed out. He was standing before the gate with restored power gushing out of him like a volcano of energy in all directions.

Everyone stood ready for whatever he was going to do as an echo of malevolence swept across everything. Figures resembling corpse shadows oozed from the walls. He absorbed them, adding to his power.

Ferris Kaizer used the momentary darkness to flee the room somehow. It didn't matter much since we had bigger things to worry about now.

Rose spoke. "Be real with me. Is this as bad as it feels?"

"Worse," I said, "But I'm gonna stop this before it gets to that." I stood. "Felix!"

The Shadow Master looked my way and smiled. "You can't stop me. Not this time."

Those words alone filled me with such rage that I couldn't see straight. My skin heated up hot enough to burn. Rose stood beside me with her shield summoned.

Before I could do anything, the object of my rage vanished in an orb of darkness and his gate disappeared along with the people in it. I felt his energy high above us. He was likely atop the base.

I concentrated on his energy and followed it in my mind. A hand formed a firm grip on my arm before I could teleport.

Doc held my arm. "What's left of the Seven Sins is up there. If they can't kill him, they'll at least stall him while we regroup."

"I remember what happened forever ago." My skin was now red and steaming. "I remember everything. If he uses that spell, everyone dies again."

"That's why we need to regroup. It took an army last time. This time is no different."

"It only took *one* move for him to take everything away from me. We stop him, now."

"I know. I was there, and I gave you my dragon for a reason."

I looked at him long and hard. "I thought I *knew* you but... Donte?"

"I never gave you this." He summoned a sword to his hand and handed it to me. "Now, it'll be complete."

The sword looked exactly as it used to, except it was missing the emerald tint it once had, replaced with pitch blackness.

I brushed my fingertips across its familiar blade hard enough to cut myself. "You know, it's funny how we came to be known as 'legendary corpse hunters'. Legendary anything, really. I guess now's the time to prove them right. **Black Flame**." I summoned my sword in my other hand and placed them together. They glowed with a mix of red and green, melding together in my hands until they became something else. A deeply serrated katana with an extended handle. A short chain linked the middle of the handle to the end. I pulled the handles apart and revealed another serrated blade hidden inside where the first one seemed hollow through its lower half.

"You'll achieve 'celestial' status in no time." My brother patted me on the back.

"What do I call you now?"

"I like Doc."

"But Donte is a cooler name. And it's your original name."

"I'm not the original me."

"Fair enough."

"And neither are you."

"I guess that's true, too."

Our conversation held the attention of everybody in the room. They crowded closer. Some nursing wounds, but all of them were beyond exhausted.

The prince was the first to say something. "Are you truly the ones who saved my people?" He sounded hopeful, almost to a fault.

"No," I said, "King Cerillo did that, though he wasn't king at the time. We just put down a monster."

"Then I ask, as Prince, and his son, that you do the same once more." The fire in his eyes was unmistakable. He was definitely his father's son.

"We will," said Doc.

"Or we'll die trying." I smiled.

"No. No dying today." Sara popped up between me and Doc, grabbing both of our arms.

"Guys, I was just talking to Mom." Ariel rushed over with a phone in her hand. "She's up top with Graven and the Sins. It looks like we did a little *too* good of a job weakening them. At least, I hope that's the case. There's no one to wait for and we need to get up there now."

"That's too far to teleport this many people." The prince was looking wistfully at the ceiling. "We need to all go simultaneously to be adequate. If we're separated, it could be a problem."

Sara responded, "You can leave that to me. I just won't be able to fight for a while after. Does that settle it?"

"How do you plan on doing that?" The prince was rightfully curious.

"I need everyone to grab on to me and we can all teleport together." Sara smiled smugly.

This time, Rachel spoke up. "I know what you're trying to do, but there are too many people for that. We can't all hold on to you."

Next was me. "I think I have a solution." I opened my grimoire and smiled. Everything in it was legible, and I flipped between two pages that were perfect for this. "*Crystal flame.*" A pure red flame sprouted from the ground with a small thud. It was crystalline and motionless aside for minute changes in its wave pattern across its many limbs as it stood. I bent down and shattered it with a flick of my finger before picking up the pieces. "For this to work, everyone needs one of these." I handed one to everyone. "*Crystal resonance.*" the center of all the crystal shards turned the same color as the magic, or color of arms, of the person holding it. "Okay Sara, send your mana through that and we should all be connected."

She concentrated on the crystal in her hands and it flashed pink and gold, followed by every other crystal doing the same. She looked at me and I nodded. "*Jump.*" She cast the spell and all the crystals began glowing again. The room began to vibrate violently, and the environment shifted from inside to outside.

We were standing in the remnants of the courtyard that housed the mural of Faramosa, the founder of C.H.E.S.S.

Sara reverted to her small form and sat down. "I did it. I knew I memorized this place for a reason." I helped her to a nearby bench. "I'll be fine here for a bit. You guys go."

The prince and his guard were already moving toward the sound of battle in the middle of the base. Everyone else followed aside for Leuna, who stayed behind to look after Sara. She couldn't do much with a broken weapon. The area before us was too dense of a mana field to teleport long distances, so we traveled as fast as we could. The fact that Sara could even teleport everyone within its boundary was insane.

I stayed close to Doc and said, "It turns out, M.A.G.E. is still alive."

"Is he really? I thought that technomancer was only using his body." He didn't seem particularly surprised.

"They have a summoning contract that keeps his soul bound to his body. At least, the girl said something like that when I talked to them. The guy himself only prompted her to speak."

"If he's alive, then we're just missing Senthia, Artemis, and Artime, but I know for a fact that they're dead. I saw them go when I came back."

"Damn, Artemis…"

"You'll have time to grieve later, but for now, focus, we're almost there." He was right. The stagnant energy was suffocating.

"We have so much to talk about later."

All the way there, we could see five figures swarming around a sixth. Bright flashes of color signified spells that rippled through the ground and sky, transforming the terrain into a wasteland of elemental energy.

Felix, the Shadow Master, was standing on the ground surrounded by a cloud of darkness. There were traces of other colors, but it all melded to a pitch black surrounding him. We got much closer until it was clear what was happening.

"He's absorbing massive amounts of energy," said Doc. "It's the corpse shadows. He's absorbing them. They're coming everywhere. Feels like even the ones across the world."

The closer we approached, the more pressure we were under from the condensed energy, and the fewer of us could continue. By the time we came within striking range, only Caroline, Doc, Rachel, the prince, and I were still flying along. Everyone else was either forced to stop and turn back or took to the ground to reduce the strain on themselves. On the way, we met Solo, Graven, and Carona. The two fighters were just healed by the healer who had someone's severed arm in her hands. They continued along with us as they were about to head back into the fray already.

In that time, the five remaining figures were reduced to none as the Sins fell from the sky one by one. Some still held signs of life as they were either healing new wounds or just rising from being felled any number of times.

I cast 'blink cyclone' to teleport behind Felix in a vortex of cutting winds. As soon as I arrived, his energy ejected me at rapid speeds. Someone caught me.

"Looks like you made it." Nail released me to my feet. "He crippled nearly all of us in an instant. I'm surprised you're still in one piece." He placed his left hand on his now missing right shoulder. "Did you guys come with a plan too, or did you come here to die like me?"

"Neither." I threw the wind side of my chained swords at Felix. The chain extended on at my will. "***Airblade, tailwind***." The combined spells allowed the blade to pierce the volatile aura of corruption and wrap around him. "***Chained explosion***." The chain broke where I was holding it, and the whole thing lit up like a giant firework snaking down to the blade I used as a catalyst. A flash lit up the darkness for only a split second, but the shockwave went farther than I expected.

In the center, Felix fell to one knee. Despite his overwhelming aura, he didn't see it coming. He stood and turned toward me. Nail summoned half of a broken sword to his hand, and three other fractured swords appeared, floating behind him. My blade regenerated in my hand.

The heavy miasma-like cloud of darkness hanging over the area vanished. All of it was concentrated energy and its sudden disappearance was more than a cause for concern. My heart sank as I realized the reason.

This happened before.

As quickly as I could, I grabbed Nail by his arm, turned, and threw him back in the direction I came. Next, I cast 'shout' and yelled, "Everyone, get away, you'll die! ***Horizon***!". The bubble of green, red, and white expanded outward and pushed everything away aside for me and Felix. I pushed the spell to its limits and nearly fainted from how much I exerted myself. At the time, I didn't know any other spell to that effect, and it left me the sole victim of the Shadow Master's most deadly spell.

"*Zero Life Radius*." As soon as I heard the words, the spell was already in effect. A bubble radiated outward from him before anyone even realized what was happening. His spell reached far but not as far as mine, though it would surpass it by far if he wanted it to. "This won't take long," he said, surrounding himself in darkness again.

My head went numb and with every heartbeat, I lost my sense of touch and felt as though I moved beyond myself. My soul was fighting against me. Strangely enough, there was no pain. Last time, there was nothing but agony and I couldn't stand. Now, it was as if there was barely any effect at all.

Small orbs of different colors began appearing around me. Some took the shape of people, and each one housed a small voice. Some of them were wailing and all of them were suffering. I wasn't sure if they were victims of the spell or just wayward souls.

At that moment, I realized something. "I survived it once." Righteous fury bubbled up to the surface. "I'm immune." My skin began to glow red-hot once again.

Fueled by this revelation, my feet ignited. I cast 'burning step' and raced toward Felix and struck at him with my sword. Despite being sure I made contact, I missed him.

Reorienting myself, I struck and missed again. By the third strike, I realized that I was hitting him. My attacks just had no effect.

There was no illusion. He was just on guard.

I didn't give up. I cast 'light speed' and went faster as my blade only slid harmlessly across his body.

I stopped for the shortest time to attack with a spell and found myself in a hole in the ground. It was as if my perspective shifted instead of a sudden momentum shift.

I couldn't tell how deep the hole was, but I could tell that I didn't see it happen. I didn't feel it either.

I jumped out of the hole as quickly as possible and continued my assault, not daring to slow down again. Even if my strikes didn't hurt him now, I thought they would eventually.

His arm twitched and then his hand was around my neck. He kept up with my speed. Maybe he simply tracked my patterns. Or simply guessed. Either way, he had me.

My blade slammed into the side of his neck and slid forward, making a sharp *screeching* sound.

"You're distracting me." My head jerked to the left with a deafening *snap*. "**Atomize**." He released me and I was sent flying backward to the sound of an earth-shattering *boom*.

I couldn't move or speak, and I was racing away at speeds too fast to even consider a landing any less than fatal.

I couldn't help but close my eyes and withdraw into myself.

Through the darkness of my mind stood a winged, feathered, green lizard with a look of raw intimidation the size of a building. Beside it was a bizarre amalgamate of perfectly sculpted yet twisted limbs and features bathed in white flames of similar size.

"Is this really my limit?" I looked each of them in the eye. "Do I die here?"

The heavy growl of the dragon reached my ears before its mouth opened. "Your limit, yes."

Next, a voice maybe more powerful yet melodious became resonant from the angel. "But not our limit." A bright white light shone from between a pair of feathery wings atop what would be its head and illuminated a gate that stood in the darkness behind me.

The lock and chains that once held tight were now loosely resting on the floor, and the eight-point seal lay shattered beneath them. There was no sign of the wind or flame that once guarded the structure, and the door was slightly ajar. I had opened it once myself, but I never saw inside. Now was my chance.

I took a brisk pace to the gate, but before I got there, a whirlwind backed by a vortex of flame obscured my path. The chains stood and snaked back around the gate, slamming it shut. The lock took its place at the center of the gate. The seal repaired itself and did the same.

"It's never that easy." I walked into the vortex. The wind whipped fiercely, and the flames licked at me, but I felt nothing. I thought there might at least be a tingle, but no, there was nothing. Next, the seal grew to cover the entire gate but shattered and fell as I touched it. The lock and chains fell all the same with a single yank and stayed immobile as I stepped over them. The door was now unguarded, and I stood before it.

I reached and laid my hand on its warm, smooth surface. When I pulled my hand back, the gate opened toward me. My palms became sweaty, and my breathing became deeper as my heart rate increased.

The inside of the gate was just as dark as the outside and there was no dragon or angel, but there was someone there.

A small child sat with a broken sword between his knees and chest in a fetal position. His messy hair and dingy clothes told well more than his hopeless demeanor ever could. He looked up at me with his dark eyes puffy from crying tears that had long run out. "What do you want?" he said, tiredly.

"I need you." I reached out my hand.

"You don't want me." He shifted so that the blade was more visible. "This is what you want, but I won't let you have it." He coveted it closely. "It's not *for* you."

I sighed. "Of course, it's not mine. It's yours." I stepped toward him with my arms out.

"No! Stay away from me!" He brandished the sword at me while slinking backward across the ground. "You can't have it!"

"I don't want it." As I reached for him, the sword stopped swinging as it cut into my arm. "Yep, it's still sharp." My blood flowed onto the blade, down the hilt, and onto the boy's hand.

"I can't fight... don't make me." Steam started rising from the blood on his hand, but not from the blood on the blade. "Why is this so hot?" His voice was panicked. "Why do you want me? Just take the sword and go already!" He let go of the sword and began a hasty retreat.

"I already told you; I don't want the sword." I pulled the blade out of my arm and threw it to the side. "I lost you once and it won't happen again." Tears were inexplicably forming in the corners of my eyes. "I can't lose myself again..." I wiped the now falling tears away. "I can't just fight for everyone else anymore. I have to fight for me, too. Because *I'm* the one fighting. I came here for everyone else. Now, here I am, fighting the big bad guy alone." I couldn't help but smile at the absurdity of the idea. "Only person I can fight for right now is me."

"But... But I'll get hurt if I fight-"

"Wrong!" I stamped my foot so hard it hurt. The ground shattered up at me and reformed back in a second. "You've seen just as well as I have that those who hurt the most are the ones who can't fight back, not the ones that do." I walked over to the sword and picked it up. Only now was when I dared to look directly at it.

The wide flat blade was seated in a dark red hilt with a hand guard that spiked upward, creating sword traps. In the center of the hilt was a triangular gem as red as blood, and its handle that I used to hold with two hands was now one-handed.

I tossed the sword toward the boy and walked away. "If you don't do it for anyone else, at least do it for me."

At that moment, I thought back to the kind of person I wanted to be when I grew up. I wanted to be someone who could do the impossible. The look of my back as I walked toward anything would be of inspiration. I'd have a long coat because my brother had one and I thought it was cool.

I clenched my sword and stood, following the powerful figure before me through the open gate. I reached for his hand, and he was gone.

"Oh yeah, that's me," I said, looking down at my little one-handed great sword. Looking back at the gate, all I saw was my younger self waving with a smile, proud of who I became.

I opened my eyes. I was still flying backward through the air. I could see the barrier I put up was still active. Normally, it'd be shattered by what just happened, but its properties changed with its size. It was now a different spell. I named it 'world horizon'.

The battlefield was getting farther and farther away but I couldn't stop myself. At some point, it vanished. I passed through the optical barrier around it and continued flying without even a trace of slowing down. It took so long that it felt like maybe a couple of minutes before I'd land, all the while wondering what would happen when I did.

Eventually, I noticed that I stopped moving when I could see dust falling slowly from my upper peripheral. I looked up and noticed that I could still move my neck. I jerked my head as hard as I could to the right and I heard a loud pop followed by excruciating pain. It was as if someone took a hot iron to the base of my skull. I thought maybe I accidentally killed myself until my hand jerked up to the back of my neck in response.

"*Pacific inferno*." I cast the most powerful healing spell I could and concentrated it to my neck. Flames erupted around me, and more popping noises ensued while the pain receded little by little.

I stood and noted that I was inside a hole created from my landing in a mountainside far inland. I examined myself to find that my skin was now much thicker and colored like a sunset, bright red with hints of silver. My skin was hard enough to sound like a turtle shell when I tapped my arm. My fingers were closer to claws on the surface but were still human-shaped.

I stood and my perspective shifted. I was looking down at myself from high up again. Atop my forehead stood two horns in a shape I could only describe as daggers. There was also a white ring of what looked like fire that sat stationary between them.

"A dragon and an angel together, huh? I probably look like a demon." I summoned my sword and with it came the other three floating behind me. "I guess this is 'celestial.'" My words brought me back to the ground. I leapt forward just shot through the air.

Expecting to land at some point, I put my feet out. Instead, I continued forward with no sign of descent. Looking over my shoulder, I spotted two sets of wings. One set was coated in green scales and the other in white feathers. I was gliding.

Readying my blade with the other swords behind me, I pierced each barrier including my own which shattered on my path going straight toward my target.

Everything below me seemed to be completely stationary. No one was reacting to anything, and the battlefield was at a complete standstill. Not even those still on the base were moving.

Felix looked like an ant in the distance. As I got closer, it was as if I was zooming in on him until I was right in front of his face. There was a shallow mark across his neck where my blade scraped against him.

I lashed at him and made contact.

My blade broke.

I let it go, grabbed one of the other ones, and did it again.

Each blade broke in turn and as they did, I replaced it with the next one and they regenerated in due time as they sat between my wings.

Every time I struck him, I did it with enough force to shatter my blades without having to do it on purpose.

I found myself both on and in the ground as well as high in the air and far away multiple times. Each time was preceded by an impact that sent ripples throughout my body. Each time, I altered my pattern. Not much, but just enough that he couldn't get a direct hit.

Felix was starting to react more appropriately to the situation. He moved and swayed, not to dodge, but more so to counter. He summoned something that hovered around his body. It was an axe, then it was a spear, then a great axe, then a halberd. He was a wielder.

At some point, my eyes and ears became irrelevant, and I only relied on feeling. I considered every minute motion. I was even starting to guess where I was going to be hit and dodging.

Neither of us cast a single spell for what felt like hours as I swarmed him with my attacks.

Eventually, it seemed like he had had enough and reacted with a full punch.

It was much slower than his other attacks, but I didn't expect it.

I skipped across the ground from the impact and a spurt of red followed me across the ground. My vision was blurry as I stood.

"I'm done with these shenanigans." Felix was no longer surrounded by an aura of darkness. "I have what I need to end this farce."

"Don't care..." I huffed and tossed my whole sword at him. He caught it before it exploded in his hand, followed by the millions of shards and shrapnel both on the ground and still falling through the air. "*Extreme breaker: dance of flames*..." The blast nearly carried me backward, but I was too far away. "I just came up with the name..."

The dust quickly cleared, and the Shadow Master was hovering over a hole in the ground that exposed some of the floors down. His entire body was coated in a black tar-like substance and covered in eyes that shifted across the surface. Each eye was a different color and some of them were blank. All of them were staring outward, unblinking, and ever-shifting. His hand was high above his head cradling a black ball the size of a house.

"*Anti-matter cannon*." What could only be described as a column of darkness both pitch-black and blindingly bright at the same time erupted from the ball and bound for me.

My legs wouldn't move. This was the worst time for fear to take me, but I'd never seen something so imminent. I thought I'd see my life flash before my eyes, but as the beam came, I was compelled forward.

Trusting, now more than ever, my inability to take even a step backward in the face of death, I pushed onward.

Instinctively, I reached into my pocket and pulled out the small, red crystal that I stored there. I held it toward death as if displaying my soul. "*Palm explosion*!" It burst into a bright white flame that was quickly surrounded by a vortex of emerald. It was the size of a baseball, but the power held within it sent shockwaves up my arm.

Once the two spells made contact, a flourish of colors bathed the world in light. There were even colors that I didn't know existed.

The thought crossed my mind that maybe I had died until something touched my still outstretched hand and began pushing back. My spell was expanding. I leaped and my wings carried me upward. I didn't get far enough before the explosion rocketed me higher.

I landed on my back with a soft thud and stood slowly. The explosion didn't hurt, but the landing knocked the wind out of me. Regaining my breath, I walked toward the floating debris. The feeling of dread that hung over everything had not yet subsided.

"**Gust**." I cast the spell and my wings flapped as if by command. The dust cleared as the wind carried it high into the air.

Felix was still in the same pose as before his attack, except the giant ball of energy was gone. "Why won't you die?" He growled.

"I could ask you the same thing," I said, almost struggling to speak.

"I must rid this world of humans. You and your trash must be ejected from this planet and the best way to do that is by sending you into the sun."

"Whoa, Whoa, Whoa..." I was more than surprised. "That's what this is all about? Humanity is the problem?" I laughed at the thought. "Of course, we are. So, your big plan this whole time was to gather enough power to cast a spell and send us all to the sun?"

"Not just humanity, but everything you've ever built. Including all of your waste."

"Now, the part about waste sounds... Wait a minute." My mind was drowned with thoughts, but one stuck out. "**Flash fire**." I snapped my fingers and the scene of Felix hovering before me seemed to burn away like a Polaroid photo bathed in white flames.

The man that was hovering in the air was now slumped on the ground. He was amidst a mad struggle to his feet. The eyes traveling around his body were now all completely red.

"Since we're at the end, there's no harm in telling you." He took a deep breath and coughed. "Far too many years ago, I was a philosopher searching for the answers to the universe. At some point, I got close. I found the olde gods and I learned. At first, I wasn't sure what I found, but I kept learning and once I realized what I was looking at, everything became clear." He raised his arms slightly and promptly dropped them. "The gods... They're within all of us. What you call a 'spirit animal' is really a god in the making. There's one within all of us. Each with their own domain and each born from the seeds of our own powers." He sat most of the way up and slouched back down unceremoniously. "But the ones we truly consider '*gods*' are beyond that. They live far beyond what we understand. I used what little I learned to enter their domain and commune with them directly. I don't know if they disliked a mortal entering their dominion or perhaps to punish this foolish mortal for having the audacity to try, but once they were aware of me, they made sure to take everything I had from me. They called it a *'reward'*. I didn't have much to start, but they poisoned every aspect of life until it became unlivable."

"How did they do that?" My curiosity forced me to speak.

"They made me immortal."

"I get it. Time passes for everyone but you and the next thing you know, everyone's gone. Now that I have my memory back, I realize I got something similar going on."

"No, you don't," he growled. "You don't understand. *I lived through everything*. Their domain only exists as long as we do and once everything 'human' is gone, everything 'god' will be too."

"I see where you're coming from, but you can't succeed with something like this. If I didn't stop you, someone else would."

"That's where you're wrong. **Soul restriction**." A series of ethereal spikes appeared, sticking from the ground around me. He stood as if he had no problem. "**Transmission purge**." He pointed his finger at me and I glowed red. "There's nothing you can do now. It would take a long time to send everything at once, but if it's just you... Enjoy deep space."

At that moment, I realized what he was doing the entire time. All the power he was gathering was going into charging the spell that would send all humans to the sun and all I was doing was slowing him down. I couldn't move despite my struggle. I couldn't nullify the spell and my joints popped from pushing against it.

"*Arcane transcendence*." Doc's voice sounded from inside my cloak, and a black vulture the size of a raven appeared from somewhere within. I stopped glowing, and it began. "Sorry Krow, looks like we can't have that talk." In a second, the vulture disappeared and there was a sudden lack of presence nearby.

My wings flared and the spikes shattered. In the same motion, I burst forward and stopped behind Felix. My blade broke on his body and the darkness coating him parted, exposing a multitude of freshly closed wounds like the one on his neck. I continued the assault until the darkness parted fully.

His clothes were falling to tatters, but he seemed relatively unfazed. I knew I hurt him. Now I had to make sure he couldn't heal himself as fast as I cut. That led me to one solution. Accepting the possibility of death, I stopped right in front of him.

The result was a spiked fist landing directly in the middle of my chest. His weapons were moving in from behind me as well.

There was a wash of colors ranging across the whole rainbow through my vision, and there were more than a few cracking sounds.

I caught his arm to prevent myself from flying backward and prepared a spell. I sacrificed my wings as the golden feathers became a concentrated flame in my palm and the emerald scales surrounded it in a vortex the size of a marble. The resulting shockwave sent the approaching weapons away.

"Just die already." The man sounded more tired than he had any right to be.

"I may fall… But you won't be here when I do." I touched him with the ball and it expanded, pushing me backward. Unlike before, it didn't stop expanding. It was like it was absorbing him and using his energy to fuel itself.

My eyes closed. Having used up all of my strength, I could use a rest. I was almost comfortable lying against the warm ball of energy, ready to pop and send me away.

"Wake up, dumbass!" My eyes fluttered open to see Rose next to me with her shield pressed against the bomb.

"When did you get here?" I asked, confused.

"What d'you mean? First, we all get flung back to the entrance wit' that spell a yers. A moment later, the guy you said was yer brother disappears and then there you are with a wall of unstable magic coming straight fer us."

"How long did that take?"

Another voice came from my right. "It took less than a minute." Graven was there, pushing back with his sword. I didn't notice before but there were tufts of fur sticking out between the cuts in his clothes.

Looking around, I could see everyone else was there as well. Most were flying, and some stayed grounded, but everyone was pushing either with magic or by hand with enchanted weapons. Even the Seven Sins were there. They were all glowing. Someone made sure everyone was powered up with a series of enchantments.

We were being pushed through piles of debris and buildings that were crumbling on top of us. Everything was bathed in a soft green hue from the ball of energy.

"Let's hope we can do this…" I slid down the dome to the base and began lifting. The ground beneath my feet splintered as I gained my footing. "We have to get this into the sky! When it stops growing, it'll blow!" I called out and everyone followed suit.

We cast spells and lifted the bomb continuously.

"What's this thing made of? It's not going anywhere." Whoever said it was right. It wasn't going anywhere and all of us were too powerless to stop it.

"I got an idea." Noah spoke louder and more confidently than ever. "Let's all cast spells that rise from the ground at the exact same time. The strongest spells we can."

Some were already on track and synchronized, but now everyone was on board. We all collectively took a step back and cast every spell we could that fit the criteria. The result was a spiral of color rising below a ball of red and green into the sky. It continued until it was the size of a grape when it popped.

I wasn't conscious for the rest of it, but I heard that the Shadow Master's gate reappeared with the people trapped in it before crumbling to dust. Most of them were fine with a lot of rest. Some of them didn't survive the strain of being subjected to those kinds of conditions. I mean, they basically drowned in pure malevolence on another plane of existence. Not many *could* survive that.

The Aftermath

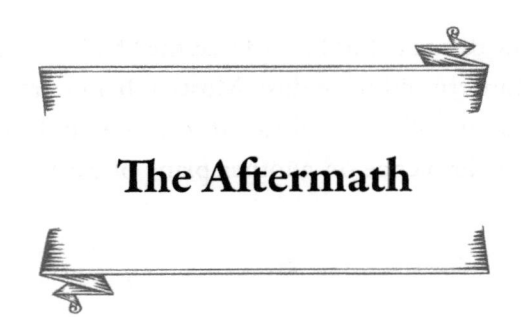

[Scribe]

Date: May 24—Day of the last interview with Krow Hunt (prefers to just be called Krow)

Location: Front office of 'Of Magic and Legends' in the Lower Arcane district of Chicago.

Interviewer - Would you tell us what happened when you finally awoke?

Krow - Yeah, I woke up in a white room. Had on a gown and everything. Thought I was dead, then, I heard the heart monitor. I called for Carona because I figured she'd be nearby. Turned out, she wasn't even in the building. First person I talked to was Vinessa. Rose was there, too. Apparently, they were with a group taking care of people affected by the whole 'war' thing. I was out for like, a year, I think. Carona got back eventually and I'll never forget the look on her face.

Interviewer - How did you feel after being in a coma for almost a year?

Krow - Hungry. Other than that, fine. Besides, I had two beautiful women looking after me. I mean, I don't think they were looking after *just* me, but, you know.

Interviewer - How do you feel about Docter and his absence? As his brother, how do you feel about it?

Krow - Yeah, he's my brother... You interviewed him already, right?

Interviewer - Yes.

Krow - Then you know he doesn't have much time left. He's been on borrowed time from the start. You'd think someone who survived in deep space for a month and rockets back down to earth just fine would live forever, but no. When he goes this time, he's gone for good. That's all... Until then, he'll travel around the world as he pleases. I don't think anybody will even know when he's gone. You're lucky you could even find him for an interview.

Interviewer - There are only a few more questions and we'll be out of your hair.

Krow - I don't have any problems with you guys being here. We never get too many commissions and you're the first guests I've had that didn't need my expertise on something and just wanted to talk. Hell, even interview me and my employees.

Noah - (From a distance) We're not your employees. We work for ourselves. It's in the contract.

Krow - (Responding) I know it's in the contract, I own the shop.

Cattherine - (Also from a distance) It's a guild base, not a shop.

Krow – (mumbling) Feels like one. (aloud) I still own the building... Kinda. Graven and I both own it, but you know how it be.

Interviewer - In the years following your awakening, how did you- (Interrupted by a loud thump)

(A large man in a suit enters through the front doors which close behind him. He spots us and moves briskly in our direction. His face is largely hidden under a wide hat.)

Krow - You might want to move over. It looks like we have another kind of visitor.

(Interviewer and Scribe make way for the man)

Krow - Welcome to Of Magic and-

(The man lifts his foot and puts his boot against Krow's chest. Krow is still seated.)

Man - Are you him?

Krow - Nice shoe. Give me a reason you should keep the leg it's on.

(The front doors open silently, and a woman walks in. Her identity is concealed under a face mask, but the aura she gives off makes her identity apparent.)

Woman - Please excuse my guard. He can be a little... forceful. Angelo, that's not how we ask for help.

(The man moves his boot to the floor and goes to stand silently next to the woman.)

Krow - So, you're the one who needs my help?

Woman - I am Bianka Roland; former princess of Roland and current head of C.H.E.S.S. I require your assistance on a matter pertaining to the Shadow Master.

Krow - I know who you are, and I already killed him. You tellin' me that ain't what happened?

Roland - This goes beyond him. We have found the whereabouts of Ferris Kaizer. He's still plotting.

Krow - (Stands) let's take this to the back.

This interviewer has decided to conclude this interview until further notice.

A Message From the Author

Hello, it's me, the author. I wasn't exactly sure where to put this, but I felt like the back of the book worked best. This was the first book I ever wrote. I put pencil to paper back in 2013 and never looked back. It took me ten years to write and numerous revisions but I'm sure it's still nowhere close to perfect. Keeping the core idea of the story while raising my standards for storytelling was a little difficult, but it means I can only get better from here.

This may have been my first book, but I wrote and published multiple books before this one was done. If I somehow finished this one sooner, I'd have finished even more. That being said, I'm glad I didn't finish it until now. The best things are always worth waiting for.

I'd like to use this next section to thank everyone who helped me on my writing journey over the past decade and inspired me to push my writing as far as I have and even further in the future. Not to mention inspiring a few characters. I'm not very good at showing gratitude, so I hope this page shows how much I appreciate them all.

Acknowledgments

I'd like to thank my family first and foremost. They've encouraged me down a path of my own creation and instilled in me the willingness to put my all into something I believe in. My mom, dad, sisters, brother, and all the rest. I couldn't have written this story without them.

Next, I'd like to thank my friends. They gave me so many life experiences and good times through my school days. Sadly, I lost contact with most of them over the years, but that's life.

Finally, I'd like to thank my teachers from middle through high school. Mostly because they allowed me to write this story through class, even after I transitioned from notebooks to my own personal laptop. Honestly, there's not much better encouragement than that.

There is, however, one teacher that showed her support in every way imaginable. Ms. Spears, who without, I probably wouldn't have gotten this far. She made me feel like I had legitimate standing in a field I hadn't even stepped into yet.

I feel like this section was a little short, but there aren't many more words I can use to express my gratitude. There are likely more people I could personally thank as well. I just can't remember them all. Well, there's at least the honorable mentions next.

Honorable Mentions

General Phishbac – This was a very on the nose reference to one of my personal influences in entertainment, but I like it. His, however, was the only referential character I ended up keeping since the rest of the references got lost in editing.

Various Anime References – I grew up with anime and I still watch it. Its influence can be felt from the beginning to the end of every single story I write. I can't even name enough anime to cover a quarter of the scope of what it influenced in this book alone.

Various Videogame References – If anime was on the list, videogames would soon follow. Everything from Final Fantasy to Metal Gear, to Devil May Cry, to well, you get it.

All in all, I've had a lot of influences in my writing, both direct and indirect. New influences show themselves every day and I'll continue to refine my writing to pay homage to what entertains and encourages me daily.

Oh, and let's not forget you, dear reader. You've helped me far more than you realize by just picking up this book and looking inside, even if you just opened it up to look at the back page. Thank you, from me.

-J.J.J.W

Also by J.J.J.W

Starry Eyes
My Eyes Are Stars
Starry Eyes: Blood Moon

Wielders of a Lost Paradigm
Wielders of a Lost Paradigm: Part 1

Standalone
I'll See You in Nirvana
The Horned Child of Reaver and Baroness
Records of a Magical Archive: Case 1
Coyote's Two Companions
Corpse Hunters

Milton Keynes UK
Ingram Content Group UK Ltd.
UKHW032152031124
450536UK00004B/7